THE PREQUEL TRILOGY

THE PREQUEL TRILOGY

THE PHANTOM MENACE™
TERRY BROOKS

BASED ON THE SCREENPLAY AND STORY
BY GEORGE LUCAS

ATTACK OF THE CLONES™
R. A. SALVATORE

BASED ON THE STORY BY GEORGE LUCAS
AND THE SCREENPLAY BY GEORGE LUCAS AND
JONATHAN HALES

REVENGE OF THE SITH™
MATTHEW STOVER

BASED ON THE STORY AND SCREENPLAY
BY GEORGE LUCAS

DEL REY
NEW YORK

A Del Rey Books Trade Paperback Original

Star Wars: Episode I *The Phantom Menace* copyright © 1999 by Lucasfilm Ltd. & ® or ™ where indicated.

Star Wars: Episode II *Attack of the Clones* copyright © 2002 by Lucasfilm Ltd. & ® or ™ where indicated.

Star Wars: Episode III *Revenge of the Sith* copyright © 2005 by Lucasfilm Ltd. & ® or ™ where indicated.

All Rights Reserved. Used under authorization.

Published in the United States by Del Rey Books, an imprint of
The Random House Publishing Group,
a division of Random House, Inc., New York.

Star Wars: Episode I *The Phantom Menace, Star Wars:* Episode II
Attack of the Clones, and *Star Wars:* Episode III *Revenge of the Sith*
were originally published separately by Del Rey Books,
an imprint of The Random House Publishing Group, a division of
Random House, Inc., in 1999, 2002, and 2005 respectively.

Del Rey is a registered trademark and the Del Rey colophon is a
trademark of Random House, Inc.

ISBN 978-0-345-49870-0

Printed in the United States of America

www.starwars.com
www.delreybooks.com

9 8 7 6 5

EPISODE I

THE PHANTOM MENACE™

TERRY BROOKS

BASED ON THE STORY AND SCREENPLAY
BY GEORGE LUCAS

To Lisa, Jill, Amanda, & Alex,
the kids who grew up with the story
&
to Hunter,
the first of the next generation

A LONG TIME AGO IN A GALAXY FAR, FAR AWAY....

Tatooine.

The suns burned down out of a cloudless blue sky, washing the vast desert wastes of the planet in brilliant white light. The resultant glare rose off the flat, sandy surface in a wet shimmer of blistering heat to fill the gaps between the massive cliff faces and solitary outcroppings of the mountains that were the planet's sole distinguishing feature. Sharply etched, the monoliths stood like sentinels keeping watch in a watery haze.

When the Podracers streaked past, engines roaring with ferocious hunger and relentless drive, the heat and the light seemed to shatter and the mountains themselves to tremble.

Anakin Skywalker leaned into the curve of the raceway that took him past the stone arch marking the entry into Beggar's Canyon on the first lap of the run, easing the thruster bars forward, giving the engines a little more juice. The wedge-shaped rockets exploded with power, the right a tad harder than the left, banking the Pod in which Anakin sat sharply left to clear the turn. Swiftly, he adjusted the steering to straighten the racer, boosted power further, and shot through the arch. Loose sand whiplashed in the wake of his passing, filling the air with a gritty sheen, whirling and dancing through the heat. He ripped into the canyon, fingers playing across the controls, hands steady on the steering.

It was all so quick, so instantaneous. One mistake, one misjudgment, and he would be out of the race and lucky if he weren't dead. That was the thrill of it. All that power, all that speed, just at his fingertips, and no margin for error. Two huge turbines dragged a fragile Pod over sandy flats, around jagged-edged mountains, down shadowed draws, and over heart-wrenching drops in a series of twisting, winding curves and jumps at the greatest speed a driver could manage. Control cables ran from the Pod to the engines, and energy binders locked the engines to each other. If any part of the three struck something solid, the whole of the assembly would collapse in a splintering of metal and a fiery wash of rocket fuel. If any part broke free, it was all over.

A grin split Anakin's young face as he injected a bit more power into the thrusters.

Ahead, the canyon narrowed and the shadows deepened. Anakin bore down on the slit of brightness that opened back onto the flats, keeping low to the ground where passage was widest. If he stayed high, he risked brushing the cliff faces on either side. That had happened to Regga in a race last month, and they were still looking for the pieces.

It would not happen to him.

He shoved the thruster bars forward and exploded through the gap onto the flats, engines screaming.

Sitting in the Pod with his hands on the controls, Anakin could feel the vibration of the engines travel up the control cables and fill him with their music. Wrapped in his rough-made jumpsuit, his racing helmet, his goggles, and his gloves, he was wedged so closely in his seat that he could feel the rush of the wind across the Pod's skin beneath him. When he raced like this, he was never simply the driver of a Podracer, never just an additional part. Rather, he was at one with the whole, and engines, Pod, and he were bound together in a way he could not entirely explain. Each shimmy, each small throb, each tug and twist of strut and tie were apparent to him, and he could sense at any given moment exactly what was happening throughout the length and breadth of his racer. It spoke to him in its own language, a mix of sounds and feelings, and though it did not use words, he could understand everything it said.

Sometimes, he thought dreamily, he could sense what it would say before it even spoke.

A flash of gleaming orange metal shot past him on his right, and he watched the distinctive split-X of Sebulba's engines flare out before him, taking away the lead he had seized through an unusually quick start. His brow wrinkled in disgust at himself for his momentary lapse of concentration and his dislike of the other racer. All gangly and crook-legged, Sebulba was as twisted inside as out, a dangerous adversary who won often and took delight in doing so at the expense of others. The Dug had caused more than a dozen crashes of other Podracers in the past year alone, and his eyes glinted with wicked pleasure when he recounted the tales to others on the dusty streets of Mos Espa. Anakin knew Sebulba well—and knew better than to take chances with him.

He rode the thruster bars forward, fed fresh power to the engines, and rocketed ahead.

It didn't help, he supposed as he watched the distance between them narrow, that he was human or, much worse, that he was the only human ever to drive in the Podraces. The ultimate test of skill and daring on Tatooine and the favorite spectator sport of the citizens of Mos Espa, it was supposed to be beyond the skill and capability of any human. Multiple arms and multi-hinged joints, stalk eyes, heads that swiveled 180 degrees, and bodies that twisted as if boneless gave advantages to other creatures that humans could not begin to overcome. The most famous racers, the best of a rare breed, were strangely shaped, complexly formed beings with a penchant for taking risks that bordered on insanity.

But Anakin Skywalker, while nothing like these, was so intuitive in his understanding of the skills required by his sport and so comfortable with its demands that his lack of these other attributes seemed to matter not at all. It was a source of some mystery to everyone, and a source of disgust and growing irritation to Sebulba in particular.

Last month, in another race, the wily Dug had tried to run Anakin into a cliff face. He had failed only because Anakin sensed him coming up from behind and underneath, an illegal razor saw extended to sever Anakin's right Steelton control cable, and Anakin lifted away to safety before the saw could do its damage. His escape cost him the race, but allowed him to keep his life. It was a trade he was still angry at having been forced to make.

The racers whipped through columns of ancient statuary and across the floor of the arena erected on the edge of Mos Espa. They swept under the winner's arch, past row upon row of seats crammed with spectators cheering them on, past pit droids, repair stations, and the boxes where the Hutts watched in isolated splendor above the commoners. From an overlook in a tower centered on the arch, the two-headed Troig who served as announcer would be shouting out their names and positions to the crowd. Anakin allowed himself a momentary glimpse of blurred figures that were left behind so fast they might have been nothing more than a mirage. His mother, Shmi, would be among them, worrying as she always did. She hated watching him drive in the Podraces, but she couldn't help herself. She never said so, but he thought she believed that simply by being there she could keep him from coming to harm. It had worked so far. He had crashed twice and failed to finish even once, but after more than half a dozen races he was unharmed. And he liked having her there. It gave him a strange sort of confidence in himself he didn't like to think about too closely.

Besides, what choice did they have in the matter? He raced because he was good at it, Watto knew he was good at it, and whatever Watto wanted of him he would do. That was the price you paid when you were a slave, and Anakin Skywalker had been a slave all his life.

Arch Canyon rose broad and deep before him, an expanse of rock leading into Jag Crag Gorge, a twisting channel the racers were required to navigate on their way to the high flats beyond. Sebulba was just ahead, rocketing low and tight across the ground, trying to put some distance between Anakin and himself. Behind Anakin, close now, were three other racers spread out against the horizon. A quick glance revealed Mawhonic, Gasgano, and Rimkar trailing in his strange bubble pod. All three were gaining. Anakin started to engage his thrusters, then drew back. They were too close to the gorge. Too much power there, and he would be in trouble. Response time in the channel was compacted down to almost nothing. It was better to wait.

Mawhonic and Gasgano seemed to agree, settling their Pods into place behind his as they approached the split in the rock. But Rimkar was not content to wait and roared past Anakin split seconds before they entered the cleft and disappeared into darkness.

Anakin leveled out his Pod, lifting slightly from the rock-strewn floor of the channel, letting his memory and his instincts take him down the winding cut. When he raced, everything around him slowed down rather than sped up. It was different than you'd expect. Rock and sand and shadows flew past in a wild mix of patterns and shapes, and still he could see so clearly. All the details seemed to jump out at him, as if illuminated by exactly what should make them so difficult to distinguish. He could almost close his eyes and drive, he thought. He was that much in tune with everything around him, that much aware of where he was.

He eased swiftly down the channel, catching glimpses of Rimkar's engine exhausts as they flashed crimson in the shadows. Far, far overhead, the sky was a brilliant blue streak down the center of the mountain, sending a frail streamer of light into the gap that lost brilliance with every meter it dropped so that by the time it reached Anakin and his fellow racers, it barely cut the dark. Yet Anakin was at peace, lost deep within himself as he drove his Pod, bonded with his engines, given over to the throb and hum of his racer and the soft, velvet dark that folded about.

When they emerged into the light once more, Anakin jammed the thruster bars forward and streaked after Sebulba. Mawhonic and Gasgano were right behind. Ahead, Rimkar had caught Sebulba and was trying to edge past. The lanky Dug lifted his split-X engines slightly to scrape against Rimkar's Pod. But Rimkar's rounded shell eased smoothly away, unaffected. Side by side the racers tore across the high flats, headed for Metta Drop. Anakin closed on them, drawing away from Mawhonic and Gasgano. People said what they wanted about Watto—and there was plenty to say that wasn't good—but he had an eye for Podracers. The big engines jumped obediently as Anakin fed fuel into the thrusters, and in seconds he was drawing alongside Sebulba's split-X.

They were even when they reached Metta Drop and rocketed over and tumbled straight down.

The trick with drops, as every racer knew, was to gather enough speed going down to gain time over your opponents, but not so much speed that the racer couldn't pull out of the drop and level out again before it nose-dived into the rocks below. So when Sebulba pulled out early, Anakin was momentarily surprised. Then he felt the backwash of the split-X engines hammer into his Pod. The treacherous Dug had only looked as if he would pull out and instead had lifted away and then deliberately fishtailed atop both Anakin and Rimkar, using his exhaust to slam them against the cliff face.

Rimkar, caught completely by surprise, jammed his thruster bars forward in an automatic response that took him right into the mountain. Metal fragments of Pod and engines careened away from the rock wall in a fiery shower, leaving a long black scar along the ravaged surface.

Anakin might have gone the same way but for his instincts. Almost before he knew what he was doing, at the same instant he felt the backwash of Sebulba's engines slam into him, he lifted out of his own descent and away from the mountain, almost colliding with a surprised Sebulba, who veered off wildly to save himself. Anakin's sudden wrenching of his Pod's steering took him spinning away into the midday, off course and out of control. He pulled back on the steering, eased off on the thrusters, cut the fuel supply to the big engines, and watched the ground rise up to meet him in a rush of sand and reflected light.

He struck the ground in a bone-wrenching skid that severed both control cables, the big engines flying off in two directions while the Pod careened first left, then right, and then began to roll. Anakin could only brace himself inside, spinning and twisting in a roil of sand and heat, praying that he didn't wind up against an outcropping of rock. Metal shrieked in protest and dust filled the Pod's interior. Somewhere off to his right, an engine exploded in a ground-shaking roar. Anakin's arms were stretched out to either side, keeping him squarely placed through the pummeling the Pod experienced as it continued to roll and then roll some more.

Finally, it stopped, tilted wildly to one side. Anakin waited a moment, then loosened his restraining belt and crawled out. The heat of the desert rose to meet him, and the blinding sunlight bore down through his goggles. Overhead, the last of the Pod-racers streaked away into the blue horizon, engines whining and booming. Silence followed, deep and profound.

Anakin glanced left and right at what remained of his engines, taking in the damage, assessing the work they would need to operate again. He looked finally at his Pod and grimaced. Watto would not be happy.

But then Watto seldom was.

Anakin Skywalker sat down with his back against the ruined Pod, gaining what small relief he could from its shadow in the glare of Tatooine's twin suns. A landspeeder would be along in a few minutes to pick him up. Watto would be there to chew him out. His mother would be there to give him a hug and take him home. He wasn't satisfied with how things had turned out, but

he wasn't discouraged either. He could have won the race if
Sebulba had played fair. He could have won easily.

He sighed and tipped back his helmet.

One day soon he would win a lot of races. Maybe even next
year, when he reached the age of ten.

Do you have any idea what this is going to cost me, boy? Do you have any idea at all? *Oba chee ka!*"

Watto hovered before him, launching into Huttese without even thinking about it, choosing a language that offered a vast array of insulting adjectives he could draw upon. Anakin stood stoically in place, his young face expressionless, his eyes fastened on the pudgy blue Toydarian hovering before him. Watto's wings were a blur of motion, beating with such ferocity it seemed as if they must surely fly off his lumpy little body. Anakin stifled an urge to laugh as he imagined this happening. It would not do to laugh just now.

When Watto paused for breath, Anakin said quietly, "It wasn't my fault. Sebulba flashed me with his port vents and nearly smashed me into Metta Drop. He cheated."

Watto's mouth worked as if chewing something, his snout wrinkling over his protruding teeth. "Of course he cheated, boy! He always cheats! That's how he wins! Maybe you should cheat just a little now and then! Maybe then you wouldn't crash your Pod time after time and cost me so much money!"

They were standing in Watto's shop in the merchants' district of Mos Espa, a dingy mud-and-sand hut fronting an enclosure packed with rocket and engine parts salvaged from scrapped and junked wrecks. It was cool and shadowy inside, the planet's heat shut out by the thick walls, but even here dust hung in the air in hazy streamers caught by the ambient light cast by glow lamps. The race had long since ended and the planet's twin suns had dropped toward the horizon with evening's slow approach. The wrecked Podracer and its engines had been transported by mechanic droids from the flats back to the shop. Anakin had been transported back as well, though with somewhat less enthusiasm.

"Rassa dwee cuppa, peedunkel!" Watto screamed, starting in again on Anakin in a fresh burst of Huttese.

The pudgy body lurched forward a few centimeters with each epithet, causing Anakin to step back in spite of his resolve. Watto's bony arms and legs gestured with the movements of his head and body, giving him a comical appearance. He was angry, but Anakin had seen him angry before and knew what to expect. He did not cringe or bow his head in submission; he stood his ground and took his scolding unflinchingly. He was a slave and Watto was his master. Scoldings were part of life. Besides, Watto would wind down shortly now, his anger released in a manner that would satisfy his need to cast blame in a direction other than his own, and things would go back to normal.

All three fingers of Watto's right hand pointed at the boy. "I shouldn't let you drive for me anymore! That's what I should do! I should find another driver!"

"I think that is a very good idea," Shmi agreed.

Anakin's mother had been standing to one side, not saying anything during the whole of Watto's diatribe, but now she was quick to take advantage of a suggestion she would have made herself, if asked.

Watto wheeled on her, spinning violently, wings whirring, and flew to confront her. But her calm, steady gaze brought him up short, pinning him in the air midway between mother and son.

"It's too dangerous in any case," she continued reasonably. "He's only a boy."

Watto was immediately defensive. "He's my boy, my property, and he'll do what I want him to do!"

"Exactly." Shmi's dark eyes stared out of her worn, lined face with resolution. "Which is why he won't race anymore if you don't want him to. Isn't that what you just said?"

Watto seemed confused by this. He worked his mouth and trunklike nose in a rooting manner, but no words would come out. Anakin watched his mother appreciatively. Her lank, dark hair was beginning to gray, and her once graceful movements had slowed. But he thought she was beautiful and brave. He thought she was perfect.

Watto advanced on her another few centimeters, then stopped once more. Shmi held herself erect in the same way that Anakin did, refusing to concede anything to her condition. Watto regarded her sourly for a moment more, then spun around and flew at the boy.

"You will fix everything you ruined, boy!" he snapped, shaking his finger at Anakin. "You will repair the engines and the Pod and make them as good as new! Better than new, in fact! And you'll start right now! Right this instant. Get out there and get to work!"

He spun back toward Shmi defiantly. "Still plenty of daylight for a boy to work! Time is money!" He gestured at first mother and then son. "Get on with it, the both of you! Back to work, back to work!"

Shmi gave Anakin a warm smile. "Go on, Anakin," she said softly. "Dinner will be waiting."

She turned and went out the door. Watto, after giving Anakin a final withering glance, followed after her. Anakin stood in the shadowed room for a moment, staring at nothing. He was thinking that he shouldn't have lost the race. Next time—and there would be a next time, if he knew Watto—he wouldn't.

Sighing in frustration, he turned and went out the back of the shop into the yard. He was a small boy, even at nine years of age, rather compactly built, with a mop of sandy hair, blue eyes, a pug nose, and an inquisitive stare. He was quick and strong for his age, and he was gifted in ways that constantly surprised those around him. He was already an accomplished driver in the Podraces, something no human of any age had ever been before. He was gifted with building skills that allowed him to put together almost anything. He was useful to Watto in both areas, and Watto was not one to waste a slave's talent.

But what no one knew about him except his mother was the way he sensed things. Frequently he sensed them before anyone even knew they would happen. It was like a stirring in the air, a whisper of warning or suggestion that no one else could feel. It had served him well in the Podraces, but it was also there at other times. He had an affinity for recognizing how things were or how they ought to be. He was only nine years old and he could already see the world in ways most adults never would.

For all the good it was doing him just at the moment.

He kicked at the sand in the yard as he crossed to the engines and Pod the droids had dumped there earlier. Already his mind was working on what it would take to make them operable again. The right engine was almost untouched, if he ignored the scrapes and tears in the metal skin. The left was a mess, though. And the Pod was battered and bent, the control panel a shambles.

"Fidget," he muttered softly. "Just fidget!"

Mechanic droids came out at his beckoning and set to work removing the damaged parts of the racer. He was only minutes into sorting through the scrap when he realized there were parts he needed that Watto did not have on hand, including thermal varistats and thruster relays. He would have to trade for them from one of the other shops before he could start on a reassembly. Watto would not like that. He hated asking for parts from other shops, insisting that anything worth having he already had, unless it came from off world. The fact that he was trading for what he needed didn't seem to take the edge off his rancor at having to deal with the locals. He'd rather win what he needed in a Podrace. Or simply steal it.

Anakin looked skyward, where the last of the day's light was beginning to fade. The first stars were coming out, small pin-pricks against the deepening black of the night sky. Worlds he had never seen and could only dream about waited out there, and one day he would visit them. He would not be here forever. Not him.

"Psst! Anakin!"

A voice whispered cautiously to him from the deep shadows at the back of the yard, and a pair of small forms slipped through the narrow gap at the fence corner where the wire had failed. It was Kitster, his best friend, creeping into view with Wald, another friend, following close behind. Kitster was small and dark, his hair cut in a close bowl about his head, his clothing loose and nondescript, designed to preserve moisture and deflect heat and sand. Wald, trailing uncertainly, was a Rodian, an off-worlder who had come to Tatooine only recently. He was several years younger than his friends, but bold enough that they let him hang around with them most of the time.

"Hey, Annie, what're you doing?" Kitster asked, glancing around doubtfully, keeping a wary eye out for Watto.

Anakin shrugged. "Watto says I have to fix the Pod up again, make it like new."

"Yeah, but not today," Kitster advised solemnly. "Today's almost over. C'mon. Tomorrow's soon enough for that. Let's go get a ruby bliel."

It was their favorite drink. Anakin felt his mouth water. "I can't. I have to stay and work on this until . . ."

He stopped. Until dark, he was going to say, but it was nearly dark already, so . . .

"What'll we buy them with?" he asked doubtfully.

Kitster motioned toward Wald. "He's got five druggats he says he found somewhere or other." He gave Wald a sharp look. "He says."

"Got 'em right here, I do." Wald's strange, scaly head nodded assurance, his protruding eyes blinking hard. He pulled on one green ear. "Don't you believe me?" Wald said in Huttese.

"Yeah, yeah, we believe you." Kitster winked at Anakin. "C'mon, let's go before old flapping wings gets back."

They went out through the gap in the fence and down the road behind, turned left, and hurried through the crowded plaza toward the food stores just ahead. The streets were still crowded, but the traffic was all headed homeward or to the Hutt pleasure dens. The boys zipped smoothly through knots of people and carts, past speeders hovering just off surface, down walks beneath awnings in the process of being drawn up, and along stacks of goods being set inside under lock and key.

In moments, they had reached the shop that sold ruby bliels and had worked their way up to the counter.

Wald was as good as his word, and he produced the requisite druggats in exchange for three drinks and handed one to each of his friends. They took them outside, sipping at the gooey mixture through straws, and made their way slowly back down the street, chatting among themselves about racers and speeders and mainline ships, about battle cruisers and starfighters and the pilots who captained them. They would all be pilots one day, they promised each other, a vow they sealed with spit and hand slaps.

They were right in the middle of a heated discussion over the merits of starfighters, when a voice close to them said, "Give me the choice, I'd take a Z-95 Headhunter every time."

The boys turned as one. An old spacer stood leaning on a speeder hitch, watching them. They knew what he was right away from his clothing, weapons, and the small, worn fighter corps insignia he wore stitched to his tunic. It was a Republic insignia. You didn't see many of those on Tatooine.

"Saw you race today," the old spacer said to Anakin. He was tall and lean and corded, his face weatherworn and sun-browned, his eyes an odd color of gray, his hair cut short so that it bristled from his scalp, his smile ironic and warm. "What's your name?"

"Anakin Skywalker," Anakin told him uncertainly. "These are my friends, Kitster and Wald."

The old spacer nodded wordlessly at the other two, keeping

his eyes fixed on Anakin. "You fly like your name, Anakin. You walk the sky like you own it. You show promise." He straightened and shifted his weight with practiced ease, glancing from one boy to the next. "You want to fly the big ships someday?"

All three boys nodded as one. The old spacer smiled. "There's nothing like it. Nothing. Flew all the big boys, once upon a time, when I was younger. Flew everything there was to fly, in and out of the corps. You recognize the insignia, boys?"

Again, they nodded, interested now, caught up in the wonder of coming face-to-face with a real pilot—not just of Podracers, but of fighters and cruisers and mainline ships.

"It was a long time ago," the spacer said, his voice suddenly distant. "I left the corps six years back. Too old. Time passes you by, leaves you to find something else to do with what's left of your life." He pursed his lips. "How're those ruby bliels? Still good? Haven't had one in years. Maybe now's a good time. You boys care to join me? Care to drink a ruby bliel with an old pilot of the Republic?"

He didn't have to ask twice. He took them back down the street to the shop they had just left and purchased a second drink for each of them and one for himself. They went back outside to a quiet spot off the plaza and stood sipping at the bliels and staring up at the sky. The light was gone, and stars were sprinkled all over the darkened firmament, a wash of silver specks nestled against the black.

"Flew all my life," the old spacer advised solemnly, eyes fixed on the sky. "Flew everywhere I could manage, and you know what? I couldn't get to a hundredth of what's out there. Couldn't get to a millionth. But it was fun trying. A whole lot of fun."

His gaze shifted to the boys again. "Flew a cruiser filled with Republic soldiers into Makem Te during its rebellion. That was a scary business. Flew Jedi Knights once upon a time, too."

"Jedi!" Kitster exhaled sharply. "Wow!"

"Really? You really flew Jedi?" Anakin pressed, eyes wide.

The spacer laughed at their wonder. "Cross my heart and call me bantha fodder if I'm lying. It was a long time ago, but I flew four of them to a place I'm not supposed to talk about even now. Told you. I've been everywhere a man can get to in one lifetime. Everywhere."

"I want to fly ships to those worlds one day," Anakin said softly.

Wald snorted doubtfully. "You're a slave, Annie. You can't go anywhere."

The old pilot looked down at Anakin. The boy couldn't look at him. "Well," he said softly, "in this life you're often born one thing and die another. You don't have to accept that what you're given when you come in is all you'll have when you leave."

He laughed suddenly. "Reminds me of something. I flew the Kessel Run once, long ago. Not many have done that and lived to tell about it. Lots told me I couldn't do it, told me not to bother trying, to give it up and go on to something else. But I wanted that experience, so I just went ahead and found a way to prove them wrong."

He looked down at Anakin. "Could be that's what you'll have to do, young Skywalker. I've seen how you handle a Podracer. You got the eyes for it, the feel. You're better than I was at twice your age." He nodded solemnly. "You want to fly the big ships, I think maybe you will."

He stared at the boy, and Anakin stared back. The old spacer smiled and nodded slowly. "Yep, Anakin Skywalker, I do think maybe one day you will."

He arrived home late for dinner and received his second scolding of the day. He might have tried making something up about having to stay late for Watto, but Anakin Skywalker didn't lie to his mother. Not about anything, not ever. He told her the truth, about stealing away with Kitster and Wald, about drinking ruby bliels, and about sharing stories with the old spacer. Shmi wasn't impressed. She didn't like her son spending time with people she didn't know, even though she understood how boys were and how capable Anakin was of looking after himself.

"If you feel the need to avoid the work you've been given by Watto, come see me about the work that needs doing here at home," she advised him sternly.

Anakin didn't argue with her, smart enough by now to realize that arguing in these situations seldom got him anywhere. He sat quietly, eating with his head down, nodding when nodding was called for, thinking that his mother loved him and was worried for him and that made her anger and frustration with him all right.

Afterward, they sat outside on stools in front of their home in the cool night air and looked up at the stars. Anakin liked sitting outside at night before bed. It wasn't so close and confined as it was inside. He could breathe out here. His home was small and shabby and packed tight against dozens of others, its thick walls comprised of a mixture of mud and sand. It was typical of quarters provided for slaves in this part of Mos Espa, a hut with a central room and one or two bumpouts for sleeping. But his mother kept it neat and clean, and Anakin had his own room, which was rather larger than most and where he kept his stuff. A large workbench and tools took up most of the available space. Right now he was engaged in building a protocol droid to help his mom. He was adding the needed parts a piece at a time, scavenging them from wherever he could, slowly restoring the whole. Already it could talk and move about and do a few things. He would have it up and running soon.

"Are you tired, Annie?" his mother asked after a long silence.

He shook his head. "Not really."

"Still thinking about the race?"

"Yes."

And he was, but mostly he was thinking about the old spacer and his tales of flying mainline ships to distant worlds, of going into battle for the Republic, and of rubbing shoulders with Jedi Knights.

"I don't want you racing Pods anymore, Annie," his mother said softly. "I don't want you to ask Watto to let you. Promise me you won't."

He nodded reluctantly. "I promise." He thought about it a moment. "But what if Watto tells me I have to, Mom? What am I supposed to do then? I have to do what he tells me. So if he asks, I have to race."

She reached over and put a hand on his arm, patting him gently. "I think maybe after today he won't ask again. He'll find someone else."

Anakin didn't say so, but he knew his mother was wrong. There wasn't anyone better than he was at Podracing. Not even Sebulba, if he couldn't cheat. Besides, Watto would never pay to have someone else drive when he could have Anakin do it for free. Watto would stay mad another day or two and then begin to think about winning again. Anakin would be back in the Podraces before the month was out.

He gazed skyward, his mother's hand resting lightly on his arm, and thought about what it would be like to be out there, flying battle cruisers and fighters, traveling to far worlds and strange places. He didn't care what Wald said, he wouldn't be a slave all his life. Just as he wouldn't always be a boy. He would find a way to leave Tatooine. He would find a way to take his mother with him. His dreams whirled through his head as he watched the stars, a kaleidoscope of bright images. He imagined how it would be. He saw it clearly in his mind, and it made him smile.

One day, he thought, seeing the old spacer's face in the darkness before him, the wry smile and strange gray eyes, I'll do everything you've done. Everything.

He took a deep breath and held it.

I'll even fly with Jedi Knights.

Slowly he exhaled, the promise sealed.

3

The small Republic space cruiser, its red color the symbol of ambassadorial neutrality, knifed through starry blackness toward the emerald bright planet of Naboo and the cluster of Trade Federation fleet ships that encircled it. The ships were huge, blocky fortresses, tubular in shape, split at one end and encircling an orb that sheltered the bridge, communications center, and hyperdrive. Armaments bristled from every port and bay, and Trade Federation fighters circled the big beasts like gnats. The more traditionally shaped Republic cruiser, with its tri-engines, flat body, and squared-off cockpit, looked insignificant in the shadow of the Trade Federation battleships, but it continued toward them, undeterred.

The cruiser's captain and copilot sat side by side at the forward console, hands moving swiftly over the controls as they steered closer to the ship with the Trade Federation viceroy insignia emblazoned on its bridge. There was a nervous energy to their movements that was unmistakable. From time to time, they would glance uneasily at each other—and over their shoulders at the figure who stood in the shadows behind.

On the viewscreen in front of them, captured from his position on the bridge of the battleship toward which they were headed, was Trade Federation Viceroy Nute Gunray, his reddish orange eyes staring out at them expectantly. The Neimoidian wore his perpetually sour expression, mouth downturned, bony brow emphasizing his discontent. His green-gray skin reflected the ambient lighting of the ship, all pale and cold in contrast to his dark robes, collar, and tricornered headdress.

"Captain."

The cruiser captain turned slightly in her seat to acknowledge the figure concealed in the shadows behind her. "Yes, sir?"

"Tell them we wish to board at once."

The voice was deep and smooth, but the measure of resolution it contained was unmistakable.

"Yes, sir," the captain said, giving the copilot a covert glance, which the copilot returned. The captain faced Nute Gunray on the screen. "With all due respect, Viceroy, the ambassadors for the supreme chancellor have requested that they be allowed to board immediately."

The Neimoidian nodded quickly. "Yes, yes, Captain, of course. We would be happy to receive the ambassadors at their convenience. Happy to, Captain."

The screen went dark. The captain hesitated, glancing back at the figure behind her. "Sir?"

"Proceed, Captain," Qui-Gon Jinn said.

The Jedi Master watched silently as the Trade Federation battleship loomed before them, filling the viewport with its gleaming bulk. Qui-Gon was a tall, powerfully built man with prominent, leonine features. His beard and mustache were close-cropped and his hair was worn long and tied back. Tunic, pants, and hooded robe were typically loose-fitting and comfortable, a sash binding them at his waist where his lightsaber hung just out of view, but within easy reach.

Qui-Gon's sharp blue eyes fixed on the battleship as if to see what waited within. The Republic's taxation of the trade routes between the star systems had been in dispute since its inception, but until now all the Trade Federation had done in response was to complain. The blockade of Naboo was the first act of outright defiance, and while the Federation was a powerful body, equipped with its own battle fleet and army of droids, its action here was atypical. The Neimoidians were entrepreneurs, not fighters. They lacked the backbone necessary to undertake a challenge to the Republic. Somehow they had found that backbone. It bothered Qui-Gon that he could not explain how.

He shifted his weight as the cruiser moved slowly into the gap in the Trade Federation flagship's outer wheel toward the hangar bay. Tractor beams took hold, guiding the cruiser inside where magnetic clamps locked the ship in place. The blockade had been in effect now for almost a month. The Republic Senate continued to debate the action, searching for an amicable way to resolve the dispute. But no progress had been made, and at last the supreme chancellor had secretly notified the Jedi Council that he had sent two Jedi directly to the ostensible initiators of the blockade, the Neimoidians, in an effort to resolve the matter more directly. It was a bold move. In theory, the Jedi Knights served the supreme chancellor, responding on his direction to life-threatening situations. But any interference in the internal politics of the Senate's member bodies, particularly where an armed conflict between worlds was involved, required Senate approval. The supreme chancellor was skirting the edges of his authority in this case. At best, this was a covert action and would spark heated debate in the Senate at a later date.

The Jedi Master sighed. While none of this was his concern, he could not ignore the implications of what it meant if he failed. The Jedi Knights were peacemakers; that was the nature of their order and the dictate of their creed. For thousands of years they had served the Republic, a constant source of stability and order in a changing universe. Founded as a theological and philosophical study group so far back that its origins were the stuff of myth, the Jedi had only gradually become aware of the presence of the Force. Years had been spent in its study, in contemplation of its meaning, in mastery of its power. Slowly the order had evolved, abandoning its practice of and belief in a life of isolated meditation in favor of a more outward-looking commitment to social responsibility. Understanding the Force sufficiently to master its power required more than private study. It required service to the greater community and implementation of a system of laws that would guarantee equal justice for all. That battle was not yet won. It probably never would be. But the Jedi Knights would not see it lost for lack of their trying.

In the time of Qui-Gon Jinn, ten thousand Jedi Knights in service to the Republic carried on the struggle each day of their lives in a hundred thousand different worlds spread across a galaxy so vast it could barely be comprehended.

He turned slightly as his companion in this present enterprise arrived on the bridge and came up to stand beside him. "Are we to board?" Obi-Wan Kenobi asked softly.

Qui-Gon nodded. "The viceroy will meet with us."

He glanced momentarily at his protégé, taking his measure. Obi-Wan, in his mid-twenties, was more than thirty years younger and still learning his craft. He was not yet a full Jedi, but he was close to being ready. Obi-Wan was shorter than Qui-Gon, but compact and very quick. His smooth, boyish face suggested an immaturity that had been long since shed. He wore the same type of clothes as Qui-Gon, but his hair was cut in the style of a Padawan learner, short and even, save for the tightly braided pigtail that hung over his right shoulder.

Qui-Gon was staring out the viewport at the interior of the Trade Federation battleship when he spoke again. "Why Naboo, do you think, my young apprentice? Why blockade this particular planet, when there are so many to choose from, most larger and more likely to feel the effects of such an action?"

Obi-Wan said nothing. Naboo was indeed an odd choice for an action of this sort, a planet at the edge of the galaxy, not particularly important in the scheme of things. Its ruler, Amidala, was something of an unknown. New to the throne, she had only been Queen a few months before the blockade had begun. She was young, but it was rumored she was prodigiously talented and extremely well trained. It was said she could hold her own with anyone in a political arena. It was said she could be circumspect or bold when necessary, and was wise beyond her years.

The Jedi had been shown a hologram of Amidala before they left Coruscant. The Queen favored theatrical paint and ornate dress, cloaking herself in trappings and makeup that disguised her true appearance while lending her an aura of both splendor and beauty. She was a chameleon of sorts, masking herself to the world at large and finding companionship almost exclusively with a cadre of handmaidens who were always with her.

Qui-Gon hesitated a moment longer, thinking the matter through, then said to Obi-Wan, "Come, let's be off."

They passed downward through the bowels of the ship to the main hatch, waited for the light to turn green, and released the locking bar so that the ramp could lower. Raising their hoods to help conceal their faces, they stepped out into the light.

A protocol droid named TC-14 was waiting to escort them to their meeting. The droid took them from the bay down a series of hallways to an empty conference room and motioned them inside.

"I hope your honored sirs will be comfortable here." The tinny voice reverberated inside the metal shell. "My master will be with you shortly."

The droid turned and went out, closing the door softly behind. Qui-Gon watched it go, glanced briefly at the exotic, birdlike creatures caged near the door, then moved to join Obi-Wan at a broad window that looked out through the maze of Federation battleships to where the lush green sphere of Naboo hung resplendent against the dark sky.

"I have a bad feeling about this," Obi-Wan said after a moment's contemplation of the planet.

Qui-Gon shook his head. "I don't sense anything."

Obi-Wan nodded. "It's not about here, Master. It's not about this mission. It's something . . . elsewhere. Something elusive . . ."

The older Jedi put his hand on the other's shoulder. "Don't center on your anxiety, Obi-Wan. Keep your concentration on the here and now, where it belongs."

"Master Yoda says I should be mindful of the future—"

"But not at the expense of the present." Qui-Gon waited until his young apprentice was looking at him. "Be mindful of the living Force, my young Padawan."

To his credit, Obi-Wan managed a small smile. "Yes, Master." He looked out the viewport again, eyes distant. "How do you think the viceroy will deal with the supreme chancellor's demands?"

Qui-Gon gave an easy shrug. "These people are cowards. They will not be hard to persuade. The negotiations will be short."

On the bridge of the Trade Federation battleship, Neimoidian Viceroy Nute Gunray and his lieutenant, Daultay Dofine, stood staring in shock at the protocol droid they had sent to look after the supreme chancellor's ambassadors.

"What did you say?" Gunray hissed furiously.

TC-14 was impervious to the look the Neimoidian gave it. "The ambassadors are Jedi Knights. One of them is a Jedi Master. I am quite certain of it."

Dofine, a flat-faced, restless sort, wheeled on his companion in dismay. "I knew it! They were sent to force a settlement! The game's up! Blind me, we're done for!"

Gunray made a placating gesture. "Stay calm! I'll wager the Senate is completely unaware of the supreme chancellor's moves in this matter. Go. Distract them while I contact Lord Sidious."

The other Neimoidian gaped at him. "Are you brain-dead? I'm not going in there with two Jedi Knights! Send the droid!"

He waved hurriedly at TC-14, who bowed, made a small squeaky sound in response, and went out.

When the protocol droid was gone, Dofine summoned Rune Haako, the third member of their delegation, drew both his compatriots to a closed, separate space on the bridge where they could be neither seen nor heard by anyone else, and triggered a holographic communication.

It took a few moments for the hologram to appear. As it did so, a stoop-shouldered, dark-robed shape appeared, cloaked and hooded so that nothing of its face could be seen.

"What is it?" an impatient voice demanded.

Nute Gunray found his throat so dry that for a moment he could not speak. "The Republic ambassadors are Jedi Knights."

"Jedi?" Darth Sidious breathed the word softly, almost reverently. There was a measure of calm about his acceptance of the news. "Are you sure?"

Nute Gunray found what little courage he had been able to muster for this moment quickly evaporating. He stared at the black form of the Sith Lord in mesmerized terror. "They have been identified, my lord."

As if unable to endure the silence that followed, Daultay Dofine charged into the gap, wild-eyed. "This scheme of yours has failed, Lord Sidious! The blockade is finished! We dare not go up against Jedi Knights!"

The dark figure in the hologram turned slightly. "Are you saying you would rather go up against me, Dofine? I am amused." The hood shifted toward Gunray. "Viceroy!"

Nute stepped forward quickly. "Yes, my lord?"

Darth Sidious's voice turned slow and sibilant. "I don't want this stunted piece of slime to pass within my sight again. Do you understand?"

Nute's hands were shaking, and he clasped them together to still them. "Yes, my lord."

He wheeled on Dofine, but the other was already making his way from the bridge, his face filled with terror, his robes trailing behind him like a shroud.

When he was gone, Darth Sidious said, "This turn of events is unfortunate, but not fatal. We must accelerate our plans, Viceroy. Begin landing your troops. At once."

Nute glanced quickly at Rune Haako, who was trying his best to disappear into the ether. "Ah, my lord, of course, but . . . is that action legal?"

"I will make it legal, Viceroy."

"Yes, of course." Nute took a quick breath. "And the Jedi?"

Darth Sidious seemed to grow darker within his robes, his

face lowering further into shadow. "The supreme chancellor should never have brought the Jedi into this. Kill them now. Immediately."

"Yes, my lord," Nute Gunray answered, but the hologram of the Sith Lord had already vanished. He stared at the space it had left behind for a moment, then turned to Haako. "Blow up their ship. I will send a squad of battle droids to finish them."

In the conference room in which they had been left, Qui-Gon and Obi-Wan stared at each other across a long table.

"Is it customary for Neimoidians to make their guests wait this long?" the younger Jedi asked.

Before Qui-Gon could respond, the door opened to admit the protocol droid bearing a tray of drinks and food. TC-14 crossed to their table, placed the tray before them, and handed each a drink. It stepped back then, waiting. Qui-Gon motioned to his young companion, and they lifted the drinks and tasted them.

Qui-Gon nodded at the droid, then looked at Obi-Wan. "I sense an unusual amount of maneuvering for something as trivial as this trade dispute. I sense fear as well."

Obi-Wan placed his drink back on the table. "Perhaps—"

An explosion rocked the room, spilling the drinks, sending the tray with its food skidding toward the edge. The Jedi leapt to their feet in response, lightsabers drawn and activated. The protocol droid backpedaled quickly, arms lifting, muttering its apologies, looking every which way at once.

"What's happened?" Obi-Wan asked quickly.

Qui-Gon hesitated, closed his eyes, and retreated deep within himself. His eyes snapped open. "They've destroyed our ship."

He glanced around swiftly. It took only a moment for him to detect a faint hissing sound from the vents near the doorway.

"Gas," he said to Obi-Wan in warning.

In the cage beside the door, the birdlike creatures began to drop like stones.

* * *

On the bridge, Nute Gunray and Rune Haako watched through a viewscreen as a squad of battle droids marched into the hallway just outside the conference room in which the Jedi were trapped. On crooked metal legs, they approached the doorway, blasters held at the ready, a hologram of Nute directing them from behind.

"They must be dead by now, but make certain," he directed the battle droids, and switched off the hologram.

The Neimoidians watched closely as the foremost of the battle droids opened the door and stepped back. A cloud of noxious green gas poured from the room, and a solitary figure stumbled into view, arms waving.

"Excuse me, sirs, I'm so sorry," TC-14 babbled as it maneuvered through the battle droids, holding aloft its tray of scattered food and spilled drinks.

In the next instant the Jedi appeared, charging from the room with lightsabers flashing. Qui-Gon's weapon sent a pair of the battle droids flying in a shower of sparks and metal parts that scattered everywhere. Obi-Wan's saber deflected blaster fire into several more. He raised his hand, palm outward, and another of the droids went crashing into the wall.

On the bridge viewscreen, smoke and lingering clouds of green gas obscured everything. Alarms began to sound throughout the battleship, reverberating off its metal skin.

"What in blazes is going on down there?" Nute Gunray demanded of his associate, eyes wide.

Rune Haako shook his head doubtfully. There was fear in his orange-red eyes. "You've never encountered Jedi Knights before, have you?"

"Well, no, not exactly, but I don't see . . ." The alarms continued to blare, and suddenly Nute Gunray was unabashedly afraid. "Seal off the bridge!" he shouted frantically.

Rune Haako backed away as the doors to the bridge began to close. His voice was small and went unheard as he whispered to himself, "That won't be enough."

In seconds, the Jedi were standing in the hallway outside the bridge, dispatching the last of the battle droids that stood in their way. An unstoppable force, the two men worked in unison against their adversaries, seemingly able to anticipate every form of attack. Lightsabers flashed and stabbed in brilliant bursts of color. Droids and blasters fell away in broken pieces.

"I want destroyer droids up here at once!" Nute Gunray screamed, watching as one of the Jedi began cutting through the bridge door with his lightsaber. He felt his throat tighten and his skin begin to crawl. "Close the blast doors! Now!"

One after another, the blast doors began to shut and seal with hissing sounds. The crew stood transfixed as on the viewscreen the Jedi continued their attack, lightsabers cutting at the massive doors, melting away the steelcrete like soft butter. Mutters of disbelief were heard, and Nute screamed at them to be silent. Sparks showered off the blast door under attack by the Jedi, and a red spot appeared at its center where the larger man plunged his lightsaber into the metal almost up to its hilt.

The viewscreen suddenly went blank. At the center of the door, the metal began to turn molten and drop away.

"They're still coming," Rune Haako whispered, gathering his robes as he backed away further.

Viceroy Nute Gunray said nothing in response. *Impossible!* he was thinking. *Impossible!*

Qui-Gon was hammering at the blast door with every ounce of strength he possessed, determined to break through to the treacherous Neimoidians, when his instincts warned him of danger from another quarter.

"Obi-Wan!" he shouted to his companion, who wheeled toward him at once. "Destroyer droids!"

The younger Jedi nodded, smiling. "Offhand, I'd say this mission is past the negotiation stage."

In the hallway just beyond the area in which the Jedi fought, ten destroyer droids rolled into view. They resembled gleaming metal wheels as they rounded a corner, smooth and silent in their approach. One by one they began to unfold, releasing tripods of spidery legs and stunted arms into which laser guns had been built. Crooked spines unlimbered, and the droids rose to a standing position, armored heads cocked forward. They were wicked-looking and deadly, and they were built for one purpose only.

Skittering around the final corner to the bridge entry, they triggered their laser guns, filling the open area with a deadly crossfire. When the lasers went still, the destroyer droids advanced, searching for their prey.

But the anteway was empty, and the Jedi Knights were gone.

On the bridge, Nute Gunray and Rune Haako watched the viewscreen flicker back to life. The destroyer droids were reverting to their wheeled forms, spinning away across the entry and down the hallway, clearly in pursuit of the Jedi.

"We have them on the run," Rune Haako breathed, scarcely able to believe their good fortune.

Nute Gunray said nothing, thinking that their escape had been entirely too close. It was ridiculous that they should be fighting Jedi Knights in any event. This was a matter of commerce, not of politics. The Trade Federation was fully justified in resisting the Republic Senate's foolish decision to impose a tax on trade routes when there was no basis in law for doing so. That the Neimoidians had found an ally to stand with them in this matter, to advise them on imposing a blockade and forcing a withdrawal of sanctions, was no cause for calling in the Jedi.

He hunched his shoulders and made a fuss over straightening his robes to disguise his shaking.

He was distracted suddenly by a call from the communications center behind him. "Sir, a transmission from the city of Theed on Naboo."

The viewscreen to the planet flickered to life, and a woman's face appeared. She was young, beautiful, and serene. An applied beauty mark of deepest crimson split her lower lip, and a golden headdress framed her powdery-white face. She stared out at the Neimoidians from the screen as if she were so far above and beyond them as to be unapproachable.

"It's Queen Amidala herself," Rune Haako whispered, just out of holocam view.

Nute Gunray nodded, moving closer. "At last we're getting results," he whispered back.

He moved to where he could be seen by the Queen. Cloaked in her ceremonial robes, Amidala sat on her throne, an ornate chair on a raised dais fronted by a low, flat-surfaced divider. The Queen was surrounded by five handmaidens, all of them cloaked and hooded in crimson. Her gaze was steady and direct as it took in the viceroy's leathery countenance.

"The Trade Federation is pleased you have chosen to come before us, Your Highness," he began smoothly.

"You will not be so pleased when you hear what I have to say, Viceroy," she said flatly, cutting him short. "Your trade boycott is ended."

Nute fought down his shock, regained his composure, and smirked at Rune. "Really, Your Highness? I was not aware—"

"I have word that the Senate is finally voting on the matter," she continued, ignoring him.

"I take it you know the outcome already, then." Nute felt a measure of uncertainty take hold. "I wonder why they bother to vote at all."

Amidala leaned forward slightly, and the Neimoidian could see the fire in her brown eyes. "I have had enough of pretense, Viceroy. I am aware that the supreme chancellor's ambassadors are with you now, and that you have been commanded to reach a settlement. What is it to be?"

Nute Gunray felt a deep hole open in his waning confidence. "I know nothing about any ambassadors. You must be mistaken."

There was a flicker of surprise on the Queen's face as she studied the viceroy carefully. "Beware, Viceroy," she said softly. "The Federation has gone too far this time."

Nute shook his head quickly, drawing himself up in a defensive posture. "Your Highness, we would never do anything in defiance of the Senate's will. You assume too much."

Amidala sat motionless, brown eyes fixed on him—as if she could see the truth he was trying to hide, as if he were made of glass. "We shall see," she said softly.

The viewscreen went blank. Nute Gunray drew a long breath and exhaled slowly, not caring much for how this woman made him feel.

"She's right," Rune Haako said at his elbow. "The Senate will never let—"

Nute lifted one hand to cut him short. "It's too late now. The invasion is under way."

Rune Haako was silent for a moment. "Do you think she suspects an attack?"

The viceroy wheeled away. "I don't know, but I don't want to take any chances. We must move quickly to disrupt all communications down there until we're finished!"

In the main hangar bay of the ship, Qui-Gon Jinn and Obi-Wan Kenobi crouched silently in the opening of a large circulation vent that overlooked six massive double-winged Federation landing ships surrounded by a vast array of transports. The transports were large boot-shaped vehicles with bulbous noses. The doors that formed those noses gaped open, racks were extended, and thousands of sleek silvery shapes were marching inside in perfect formation to be secured.

"Battle droids," Qui-Gon said softly. There was surprise and dismay in his deep voice.

"It's an invasion army," Obi-Wan said.

They continued to watch for a time, taking in the scene, counting transports and droids as they filled the half-dozen landing craft, taking measure of the size of the army.

"It's an odd play for the Federation," Qui-Gon observed. "We've got to warn the Naboo and contact Chancellor Valorum."

Obi-Wan nodded. "We'd best do it somewhere besides here."

His mentor glanced at him. "Maybe we can hitch a ride with our friends down there."

"It's the least they can do after the way they've treated us so far." Obi-Wan pursed his lips. "You were right about one thing, Master. The negotiations were short."

Qui-Gon Jinn smiled and beckoned him ahead.

A twilight that was misty and seemed perpetual lay in silvery gray layers over the green lushness of Naboo as the Federation landing ships descended out of the black infinity of space to settle slowly planetward. One set of three moved away from the others, dropping silently through clouds that hung still and endless across the world's emerald surface. Ghostlike as they passed through the haze, double wings shaped like a giant *I*, they materialized one by one near a vast, murky swamp. As they gently landed next to the dark waters and clumps of trees and grasses, their metal bodies parted to allow the bulbous-nosed transports to offload onto the surface and begin forming up.

Some distance away from the closest of the landing craft, Obi-Wan Kenobi's head broke the swamp's still waters. A quick breath, and he was gone again. He surfaced once more, farther away, and this time took a moment to look back at the invasion force. Dozens of transports filled with battle droids and tanks were moving into place in front of the landing craft. Some hovered above the swamp's waters. Some had found purchase on dry ground.

Far to his left, he caught sight of a shadowy form running through the mist and trees. Qui-Gon. Obi-Wan took another deep breath, submerged swiftly, and began to swim.

Qui-Gon Jinn slipped wraithlike through the swamp, listening to the sounds of heavy rustling and snapping branches behind him as the Trade Federation transports began to advance. Mixed with the deeper, heavier whine of the transport engines was the higher pitched buzzing of STAPs—single trooper aerial platforms—small, individually piloted mobile gun units used to transport battle droids as scouts for the main army. The STAPs whipped above the watery terrain of Naboo, fleeting shadows as they surged in front of the larger transports.

Animals of all shapes and sizes began to scatter from their places of concealment, racing past Qui-Gon in search of safety. Ikopi, fulumpasets, motts, peko pekos—the names recalled themselves instantly to the Jedi Master from his preparation for this journey. Dodging the frightened creatures stampeding around him, he cast about for Obi-Wan, then picked up his pace as the dark shadow of a transport appeared out of the mist directly behind him.

He was running out of firm ground and searching for a way past a large lake when he saw a strange froglike creature before him. It was squatting in the water, its rubbery body crouched over a shell it had just pried open, its long tongue licking out the insides with a quick whipping movement, its throat swallowing. Casting aside the empty shell, it rose to face Qui-Gon, its long, flat ears dangling from its amphibious head in broad flaps, its ducklike snout working thoughtfully around whatever delicacy it had removed from the shell. Eyes that protruded from the top of its head blinked in confusion, taking in Qui-Gon and the animals about him, then seeing clearly for the first time the massive shadow from which they fled.

"Oh, oh," the creature muttered, the syllables clouded, but recognizable.

Qui-Gon broke left past the strange creature, anxious to get out of the path of the approaching transport. The creature dropped the shell, eyes wide and frantic, and grabbed onto Qui-Gon's robes.

"Hep me, hep me!" it cried plaintively, rubbery face contorting in shock and desperation.

"Let go!" Qui-Gon snapped, trying in vain to break free.

The transport thundered toward them, skimming the surface of the swamp, flattening grasses and stirring up water spouts in the wake of its passing. It bore down on Qui-Gon as he fought to break free of the creature that clung to him, dragging it sideways in a futile effort to escape.

Finally, with the transport only meters away and looming over him like a building about to topple, the Jedi Master pushed the creature into the shallow water and sprawled facedown on top of it. The Trade Federation transport passed over them in a wash of sound and shocked air, the vibrations hammering into their prone forms, flattening them into the mire.

When it was safely past, Qui-Gon pulled himself out of the mud and took a deep, welcome breath. The strange creature rose with him, still clinging to his arm, cloudy water dripping from its flat-billed face. It gave a quick glance after the departing transport, then threw itself on Qui-Gon, hugging him ecstatically.

"Oh boi, oh boi!" it gasped with a high-pitched, warbled sound. "I love yous, love yous forever!"

The creature began kissing him.

"Let go!" Qui-Gon huffed. "Are you brainless? You almost got us killed!"

The creature looked offended. "Brainless? I speak!"

"The ability to speak does not make you intelligent!" Qui-Gon was having none of it. "Now let go of me and get out of here!"

He freed himself from the creature and began to move off, glancing around uneasily as the high-pitched buzz of STAPs sounded in the distance.

The creature hesitated, then began trailing after him. "No, no, me stay wit you! Me stay! Jar Jar be loyal, humble Gungan servant. Be yous friend, me."

The Jedi Master barely glanced at him, watching the shadows, searching now for Obi-Wan. "Thanks, but that won't be necessary. Better be off with you."

Jar Jar the Gungan splashed after him, billed mouth working, arms waving. "Oh, bot tis necessary! Tis demanded by da Guds. Tis life debt. Me know dis, sure as name be Jar Jar Binks!"

The swamp reverberated with the sound of STAP engines, and now two of the gun platforms burst from the mist, bearing down on a fleeing Obi-Wan Kenobi, battle droid drivers wheeling their speeders to the attack.

Qui-Gon pulled free his lightsaber, motioning Jar Jar away. "I have no time for this now—"

"But must take me wit yous, keep me—" Jar Jar stopped, hearing the STAPs, turning to see them bearing down, eyes going wide all over again. "Oh, oh, we gonna—"

Qui-Gon grabbed the Gungan and threw him facedown in the swamp water once more. "Stay put." He flicked on the lightsaber, bracing himself as Obi-Wan and the pursuing STAPs approached.

Jar Jar's head popped up. "We gonna die!" he screamed.

The battle droids opened fire with laser cannons from their gun platforms just as Obi-Wan reached his friend. Qui-Gon blocked the bolts with his lightsaber and deflected them back into the attack craft. The STAPs exploded in shards of hot metal and fell into the swamp.

An exhausted Obi-Wan wiped his muddied brow, gasping for breath. "Sorry, Master. The swamp fried my lightsaber."

He pulled out his weapon. The business end was blackened and burned. Qui-Gon took it from him and gave it a cursory inspection. Behind him, Jar Jar Binks pulled himself out of the muddy swamp water and blinked curiously at the newly arrived Jedi.

"You forgot to turn off your power again, didn't you, Obi-Wan?" his friend asked pointedly.

Obi-Wan nodded sheepishly. "It appears so, Master."

"It won't take long to recharge, but it will take some time to clean it up. I trust you have finally learned your lesson, my young Padawan."

"Yes, Master." Obi-Wan accepted the proffered lightsaber with a chagrined look.

Jar Jar pushed forward, amphibious feet flopping, ears flapping, long limbs looking as if they might take him in almost any direction. "Yous save me again, hey?" he asked Qui-Gon rhetorically.

Obi-Wan stared. "What's this?"

"A Gungan. One of the locals. His name's Jar Jar Binks." Qui-Gon's attention was directed out at the swamp. "Let's go, before more of those STAPs show up."

"More?" Jar Jar gasped worriedly. "Yous say more?"

Qui-Gon was already moving, shifting into a steady ,trot through the mire. Obi-Wan was only a step behind, and it took a moment for Jar Jar to catch up to them, his long legs working frantically, his eyes rolling.

"Exsqueeze me, but da most grand safest place is in Otoh Gunga," he gasped at them, trying to catch their attention. All about, lost somewhere in the mists, STAPs sounded their high-pitched whine. "Otoh Gunga," Jar Jar repeated. "Tis where I grew. Tis safe city!"

Qui-Gon brought them to a halt, staring fixedly now at the Gungan. "What did you say? A city?" Jar Jar nodded eagerly. "Can you take us there?"

The Gungan seemed suddenly distraught. "Ah, oh, oh . . . mebbe me not rilly take yous . . . not rilly, no."

Qui-Gon leaned close, his eyes dark. "No?"

Jar Jar looked as if he wished he could disappear into the swamp completely. His throat worked and his billed mouth opened and closed like a fish's. "Tis embarrassment, but . . . me afraid me be banished. Sent oot. Me forget Boss Nass do terrible hurt to me if go back dere. Terrible bad hurt."

A low, deep, pulsating sound penetrated the whine of the STAPs, rising up through mist and gloom, growing steadily louder. Jar Jar glanced around uneasily. "Oh, oh."

"You hear that?" Qui-Gon asked softly, placing a finger on the Gungan's skinny chest. Jar Jar nodded reluctantly. "There's a thousand terrible things heading this way, my Gungan friend . . ."

"And when they find you, they will crush you into dust, grind you into little pieces, and then blast you into oblivion," Obi-Wan added with more than a little glee.

Jar Jar rolled his eyes and gulped. "Oh, oh. Yous point very good one." He gestured frantically. "Dis way! Dis way! Hurry quick!"

In a rush, they raced away into the twilight mist.

Sometime later, the Jedi and the Gungan emerged from a deep stand of swamp grass and thick rushes at the edge of a lake so murky that it was impossible to see anything in the reflection of twilight off the surface. Jar Jar bent double, three-fingered hands resting on bony knees as he fought to catch his breath. His rubbery form twisted this way and that as he looked back in the direction from which they had come, long ears flapping with the movement. Obi-Wan shook his head at Qui-Gon Jinn in faint reproval. He was not happy with the Jedi Master's decision to link up with this foolish-looking creature.

Somewhere in the distance, they could hear the steady, deep thrum of Federation transport engines.

"How much farther?" Qui-Gon pressed their reluctant guide.

The Gungan pointed at the lake. "We go underwater, okeday?"

The Jedi looked at each other, then extracted small containers from their clothing, releasing portable breathing devices the size of the palms of their hands.

"Me warning yous." Jar Jar's eyes shifted from one to the other. "Gungans no like yous outlanders. Yous not gonna get warm welcome."

Obi-Wan shrugged. "Don't worry. This hasn't been our day for warm welcomes."

"Get going," Qui-Gon motioned, fitting the device between his teeth.

The Gungan shrugged, as if to disclaim all responsibility for what would follow, turned back to the lake, performed a wild double somersault, and disappeared into the gloom.

The Jedi waded after him.

Downward into the murkiness they swam, the Jedi following the slender form of the Gungan, who seemed far more at home in the water than on land. He swam smoothly and gracefully, long limbs extended, body undulating with practiced ease. They swam for a long time, angling steadily deeper, the light from the surface fading slowly away behind them. What light there was came from sources beneath the surface, not all of them visible. The minutes slipped away, and Obi-Wan began to have second thoughts about what they were doing.

Then suddenly there was a new light, this one a steady glow that came from ahead. Slowly Otoh Gunga came into view. The city was comprised of a cluster of bubbles that connected to one another like balloons and were anchored to several huge rock pillars. One by one, the bubbles grew more distinct, and it became possible to make out the particulars of the structures within and the features of the Gungans as they moved about their business.

Jar Jar swam directly toward one of the larger bubbles, the Jedi close on his heels. When he reached the bubble, he pushed at it with his hands and it gave way to him, accepting first his arms, then his head and body, and finally his legs, swallowing him whole and closing behind him without rupturing. Amazed, the Jedi followed, moving through the strange membrane, entering the bubble without resistance.

Once inside, they found themselves on a platform that led down to a square surrounded by buildings. Light emanated from the bubble's walls in a steady glow, brightening the space inside. The Jedi found the air breathable. As they descended to the square below, water dripping from their clothing, Gungans began to catch sight of them and to scatter with small cries of alarm.

In short order a squad of uniformed Gungan soldiers appeared, riding two-legged mounts with billed faces not entirely dissimilar to their own. Kaadu, Qui-Gon recalled—swamp runners with powerful legs, great endurance, and keen senses. The Gungans carried long, deadly-looking electropoles, which they used to motion back the distraught populace at the same time they advanced on the intruders.

"Heyday ho, Cap'n Tarpals," Jar Jar greeted the leader of the squad cheerfully. "Me back!"

"Notta gain, Jar Jar Binks!" the other snapped, clearly irritated. "Yous goen ta Boss Nass. See what he say. Yous mebbe in big trubble dis time."

Ignoring the Jedi, he gave Jar Jar a quick poke with his electropole, sending a shock through the hapless Gungan that lifted him a half meter off the ground. Jar Jar rubbed his backside ruefully, muttering.

The Gungan soldiers took them through the buildings of the city, down several connecting passages, and into what, Jar Jar whispered to his companions, was the High Tower Boardroom. The room was transparent on all sides, and small glowing fish swam about the outside of the membrane, tiny stars against a darker backdrop. A long, circular bench dominated one end of the room with one section set higher than the rest. All the seats were occupied by Gungan officials in their robes of office, and a way was quickly made for the newcomers through Gungans already present to conduct other business.

The Gungan occupying the highest seat was a heavyset, squat fellow so compressed by age and weight that it was impossible to imagine he had ever been as slender as Jar Jar Binks. Folds of skin draped from his body in loose layers, his neck was compressed into his shoulders, and his face bore such a sour look that even Jar Jar seemed more than a little cowed as they were motioned forward.

The Gungan officials stared, muttering among themselves as the Jedi approached. "What yous want, outlanders?" Boss Nass rumbled at them, after identifying himself.

Qui-Gon Jinn told him, relating what had brought the Jedi

to Naboo, warning of the invasion taking place above, asking the Gungans to give them help. The Gungan council listened patiently, saying nothing until Qui-Gon was finished.

Boss Nass shook his head, the flesh of his thick neck jiggling with the movement. "Yous can't be here. Dis army of maccaneks up dere tis not our problem."

Qui-Gon held his ground. "That army of battle droids is about to attack the Naboo. We must warn them."

"We no like da Naboo!" Boss Nass growled irritably. "And dey no like da Gungans. Da Naboo think dey more smart den us. Dey think dey brains so big. Dey have nutten ta do wit us cause we live in da swamp and dey live up dere. Long time no have nutten ta do wit each other. Dis not gonna change because of maccaneks."

"After that army takes control of the Naboo, they will come here and take control of you," Obi-Wan said quietly.

Boss Nass chuckled. "No, me think not. Me talk mebbe one, two times wit Naboo in whole life, and no talk ever wit maccaneks. Maccaneks no come here! Dey not even know Gungans exist!"

The remaining members of the council nodded in agreement, muttering their verbal approval of Boss Nass's wisdom.

"You and the Naboo are connected," Obi-Wan insisted, his youthful face intent, not ready to concede the matter. "What happens to one will affect the other. You must understand this."

Boss Nass dismissed him with a wave of one thick hand. "We know nutten of yous, outlander, and we no care about da Naboo."

Before Obi-Wan could continue his argument, Qui-Gon stepped forward. "Then speed us on our way," he demanded, bringing up one hand in a casual motion, passing it smoothly before the Gungan chief's eyes in a quick invocation of Jedi mind power.

Boss Nass stared at him, then nodded. "We speed yous far away."

Qui-Gon held his gaze. "We need transport to Theed."

"Okeday." Boss Nass nodded some more. "We give yous bongo. Da speedest way tada Naboo is goen through da core. Yous go now."

Qui-Gon stepped back. "Thank you for your help. We go in peace."

As the Jedi turned to leave, Obi-Wan whispered, "Master, what is a bongo?"

Qui-Gon glanced at him and cocked one eyebrow thoughtfully. "A ship of some sort, I hope."

They were moving away from Boss Nass and the other Gungan officials when they caught sight of Jar Jar Binks standing forlornly to one side, wearing wrist binders and awaiting his fate. Qui-Gon slowed and made eye contact with the unfortunate creature.

"Master," Obi-Wan said softly in warning. He knew Qui-Gon too well not to see what was coming.

The tall Jedi moved over to Jar Jar and stood looking at him.

"Dey setten yous up for bad fall!" the Gungan declared sullenly, glancing around to see if anyone else might be listening. "Goen through da core is bad danger."

Qui-Gon nodded. "Thank you, my friend."

Jar Jar Binks shrugged and looked sad. "Ahhh, tis okay." Then he gave the Jedi Master a slow, sheepish grin and a hopeful look. "Hey, any hep here would be hot."

Qui-Gon hesitated.

"We are short of time, Master," Obi-Wan advised quietly, moving to his side.

The Jedi Master turned to face his protégé, eyes distant. "Time spent here may help us later. Jar Jar might be of some use."

Obi-Wan shook his head in frustration. His mentor was too eager to involve himself when it was not necessary. He was too quick to adopt causes that were not his own. It had cost him time and time again with the Jedi Council. One day it would be his undoing.

He bent close. "I sense a loss of focus."

Qui-Gon's eyes fixed on him. "Be mindful, young Obi-Wan," he chastised gently. "Your sensitivity to the living Force is not your strength."

The younger Jedi held his gaze only a moment, then looked away, stung by the criticism. Qui-Gon turned from him and walked back to Boss Nass. "What is to become of Jar Jar Binks?" he asked.

Boss Nass, who was engaged in conversation with another of the Gungan officials, turned to him in annoyance, his heavy jowls puffing. "Binks breaks nocomeback law. Breaks exile. He be punished."

"Not too severely, I trust?" the Jedi Master pressed. "He has been of great help to us."

A slow laugh rumbled out of Boss Nass. "Pounded unto death, dis one."

Somewhere in the background, Jar Jar Binks moaned loudly. There were mutterings about the room. Even Obi-Wan, who was back at his Master's side, looked shocked.

Qui-Gon was thinking fast. "We need a navigator to get us through the core to Theed. I saved Jar Jar's life on the surface. He owes me for that. I claim a life debt on him."

Boss Nass stared at the Jedi in silence, a deep frown furrowing his brow and twisting his mouth. His head seemed to sink deeper into his shoulders, into the wattles of skin that obscured his neck.

Then his small eyes sought the unfortunate Jar Jar, and he gestured. "Binks?"

Jar Jar moved forward obediently to stand beside the Jedi.

"Yous haf life debt wit dis outlander?" Boss Nass demanded darkly.

Jar Jar nodded, head and ears hanging, but a flicker of hope springing into his eyes.

"Your gods demand he satisfy that debt," Qui-Gon insisted, passing his hand in front of Boss Nass's eyes, invoking his Jedi power once more. "His life belongs to me now."

The head Gungan considered the matter only a moment before nodding in agreement. "His life tis yous. Worthless, anywhat. Beggone wit him."

A guard came forward and removed Jar Jar's wrist binders.

"Come, Jar Jar," Qui-Gon Jinn advised, turning him away.

"Through da core?" Jar Jar gasped, realizing suddenly what had happened. "Count me outta dis! Better dead here den dead in da core! Me not go . . ."

But by then the Jedi were dragging him out of the room and all sight and sound of Boss Nass.

On the bridge of the Trade Federation's lead battleship, Nute Gunray and Rune Haako stood alone before a hologram of Darth Sidious. Neither of the Neimoidians was looking at the other, and both were hoping the Sith Lord could not sense what they were thinking.

"The invasion is on schedule, my lord," the viceroy was saying, robes and headdress hiding the occasional twitching of his limbs as he faced the cloaked and hooded form before him. "Our army nears Theed."

"Good. Very good." Darth Sidious spoke in a soft, calm voice. "I have the Senate bogged down in procedures. By the time this incident comes up for a vote, they will have no choice but to accept that your blockade has been successful."

Nute Gunray glanced quickly at his compatriot. "The Queen has great faith that the Senate will side with her."

"Queen Amidala is young and naive. You will find controlling her will not be difficult." The hologram shimmered. "You have done well, Viceroy."

"Thank you, my lord," the other acknowledged as the hologram faded away.

In the ensuing silence, the Neimoidians turned to each other with knowing looks. "You didn't tell him," Rune Haako said accusingly.

"Of the missing Jedi?" Nute Gunray made a dismissive gesture. "No need to tell him that. No need to tell him anything until we know for certain what has happened."

Rune Haako studied him a long time before turning away. "No, no need," he said softly, and walked from the room.

Obi-Wan Kenobi sat hunched over the controls of the bongo, familiarizing himself with their functions as Jar Jar Binks, positioned next to him, rambled on and on about nothing. Qui-Gon sat in the shadows behind them, silent and watchful.

"Dis is nutsen!" Jar Jar moaned as the bongo motored steadily away from the shimmering lighted bubbles of Otoh Gunga and deeper into the waters of Naboo.

The bongo was an ungainly little underwater craft that consisted mostly of an electrical power plant, guidance system, and passenger seating. It looked somewhat like a species of squid, having flat, swept-back fins and aft tentacles that rotated to propel the craft. Three bubble-canopied passenger compartments were arranged symmetrically, one on each wing and the third forward on the nose.

The Jedi and the Gungan occupied the nose compartment, where Obi-Wan had assumed command of the controls and Jar Jar had been instructed to start directing them through the core. It seemed that there were underwater passageways all through the planet, and if you were able to locate the right one, you could cut travel time considerably.

Or in the alternative, Obi-Wan thought darkly, you could cut your own throat.

"We doomed," Jar Jar muttered plaintively. His flat-billed face lifted away from the directional guidance system toward the Jedi, his long ears swaying like ridiculous flaps. "Heydey ho? Where we goen, Cap'n Quiggon?"

"You're the navigator," Qui-Gon observed.

Jar Jar shook his head. "Me? Yous dreaming. Don't know nutten 'bout dis, me."

Qui-Gon placed a hand on the Gungan's shoulder. "Just relax, my friend. The Force will guide us."

"Da Force? What tis da Force?" Jar Jar did not look impressed. "Maxibig thing, dis Force, yous betcha. Gonna save me, yous, all us, huh?"

Obi-Wan closed his eyes in dismay. This was a disaster waiting to happen. But it was Qui-Gon's disaster to manage. It was not his place to interfere. Qui-Gon had made the decision to bring Jar Jar Binks along, after all. Not because he was a skilled navigator or had displayed even the slightest evidence of talent in any other regard, but because he was another project that Qui-Gon, with his persistent disregard for the dictates of the Council, had determined had value and could be reclaimed.

It was a preoccupation that both mystified and frustrated Obi-Wan. His mentor was perhaps the greatest Jedi alive, a commanding presence at Council, a strong and brave warrior who refused to be intimidated by even the most daunting challenge, and a good and kind man. Maybe it was the latter that had gotten him into so much trouble. He repeatedly defied the Council in matters that Obi-Wan thought barely worthy of championing. He was possessed of his own peculiar vision of a Jedi's purpose, of the nature of his service, and of the causes he should undertake, and he followed that vision with unwavering single-mindedness.

Obi-Wan was young and impatient, headstrong and not yet at one with the Force in the way that Qui-Gon was, but he understood better, he thought, the dangers of overreaching, of taking on too many tasks. Qui-Gon would dare anything when he found a challenge that interested him, even if he risked himself in the undertaking.

So it was here. Jar Jar Binks was a risk of the greatest magnitude, and there was no reason to think that embracing such a risk would reap even the smallest reward.

The Gungan muttered some more, all the while casting about through the viewport as if seeking a road sign that would allow him to at least pretend he knew what he was doing. Obi-Wan gritted his teeth. Stay out of it, he told himself sternly. Stay out of it.

"Here, take over," he snapped at Jar Jar.

He moved out of his seat to kneel close to Qui-Gon. "Master," he said, unable to help himself, "why do you keep dragging these pathetic life-forms along with us when they are of so little use?"

Qui-Gon Jinn smiled faintly. "He seems that way now perhaps, but you must look deeper, Obi-Wan."

"I've looked deep enough, and there is nothing to see!" Obi-Wan flushed with irritation. "He is an unneeded distraction!"

"Maybe for the moment. But that may change with time." Obi-Wan started to say something more, but the Jedi Master cut him short. "Listen to me, my young Padawan. There are secrets hidden in the Force that are not easily discovered. The Force is vast and pervasive, and all living things are a part of it. It is not always apparent what their purpose is, however. Sometimes that purpose must be sensed first in order that it may be revealed later."

Obi-Wan's young face clouded. "Some secrets are best left concealed, Master." He shook his head. "Besides, why must you always be the one to do the uncovering? You know how the Council feels about these . . . detours. Perhaps, just once, the uncovering should be left to someone else."

Qui-Gon looked suddenly sad. "No, Obi-Wan. Secrets must be exposed when found. Detours must be taken when encountered. And if you are the one who stands at the crossroads or the place of concealment, you must never leave it to another to act in your place."

The last of the lights from Otoh Gunga disappeared in a wash of murkiness, and the waters closed around them in a dark cloud. Jar Jar Binks was taking the craft ahead at a slow, steady speed, no longer muttering or squirming, his hands fixed on the controls. He flipped on the lights as darkness closed about, and the broad yellow beams revealed vast stretches of multicolored coral weaving and twisting away through the black.

"I respect your judgment in this, Master," Obi Wan said finally. "But it doesn't stop me from worrying."

Like all of the Jedi Knights, Obi-Wan Kenobi had been identified and claimed early in his life from his birth parents. He no longer remembered anything of them now; the Jedi Knights had become his family. Of those, he was closest to Qui-Gon, his mentor for more than a dozen years, who had become his most trusted friend.

Qui-Gon understood his attachment and shared it. Obi-Wan was the son he would never have. He was the future he would leave behind when he died. His hopes for Obi-Wan were enormous, but he did not always share his student's beliefs.

"Be patient with me, Obi-Wan," he replied softly. "A little faith sometimes goes a long way."

The bongo navigated a coral tunnel, the bridge work revealed in deep fissures of crimson and mauve in the glow of the little craft's lights. All about, brightly colored fish swam in schools through the craggy rock.

"Are the Gungans and the Naboo at war with each other?" Qui-Gon asked Jar Jar thoughtfully.

The Gungan shook his head. "No war. Naboo and Gungans don't fight. Long time ago, mebbe. Now, Naboo keep outta swamp, Gungans keep outta plains. Dey don't even see each other."

"But they don't like each other?" the Jedi Master pressed.

Jar Jar snorted. "Da Naboo gotta big heads, alla time think dey so much better den da Gungans! Big nuttens!"

Obi-Wan bent over Jar Jar Binks, his eyes directed out the viewport. "Why were you banished, Jar Jar?" he asked.

The Gungan made a series of small smacking sounds with his billed lips. "Tis kinda long story, but keeping dis short, me . . . oh, oh, ahhh . . . kinda clumsy."

"You were banished because you're clumsy?" Obi-Wan exclaimed in disbelief.

The bongo turned down through an open stretch of water between two huge coral shelves. Neither the Jedi nor the Gungan saw the dark shape that detached itself from the larger outcropping and began to track them.

Jar Jar squirmed. "Me cause mebbe one or two little bitty axaudents. Boom da gasser, crash der Bosses' heyblibber. Den dey banish me."

Obi-Wan was not entirely sure what Jar Jar was telling him. But before he could ask for clarification, there was a loud thump as something struck the bongo, causing it to lurch sharply to one side. A huge crustacean with multiple legs and massive jaws ringed with teeth had hooked them with its long tongue and was drawing them steadily toward its widespread maw.

"Opee sea killer!" Jar Jar cried in dismay. "We doomed!"

"Full speed ahead, Jar Jar!" Qui-Gon ordered quickly, watching the jaws open behind them.

But instead of pushing the throttles forward, Jar Jar panicked and jammed them into reverse, causing the little ship to fly directly into the mouth of their attacker. The bongo slammed into the back of the monster's throat with a heavy thump that sent the Jedi reeling over the seats and into the walls. Rows of jagged teeth began to close about them as the lights on the control panel flickered uncertainly.

"Oh, oh," Jar Jar Binks said.

Obi-Wan leapt quickly back into the copilot's seat. "Here, give me the controls!"

He seized the throttles and steering apparatus and shoved everything into forward, full speed ahead. To his surprise, the opee sea killer's mouth opened with a spasmodic jerk, and they shot through its teeth as if from a laser cannon.

"We free! We free!" Jar Jar was jumping about in his seat, ecstatic over their good fortune.

But a quick glance back revealed that they were lucky for a different reason than they thought. The opee sea killer was caught in the jaws of a creature so huge that it dwarfed even the beast it was eating. A long, eel-like hunter with clawed forelegs, rear fins, and a wicked pair of jaws was crunching the sea killer into tiny bits and swallowing it down eagerly.

"Sando aqua monster, oh, oh!" Jar Jar Binks moaned, burying his face in his hands.

Obi-Wan increased power, trying to put more distance between themselves and this newest threat. The sando aqua monster disappeared behind them, but the lights of the bongo were flickering ominously. The little craft dived deeper, penetrating the planet's core. Suddenly something exploded inside a control panel behind them, showering the cabin with sparks. Seams split overhead, and water began leaking through the bongo's outer skin.

"Master," Obi-Wan said as the power-drive whine took a sudden dive, "we're losing power."

Qui-Gon was working over the troubled control panel, head lowered. "Stay calm. We're not in trouble yet."

"Not yet!" Jar Jar had lost all pretense of calm and was flailing about in his seat. "Monstairs out dere! Leakin in here. We sinkin with no power! Yous nuts! When yous think we in trubble?"

With that, the lights inside the bongo went completely black. Jar Jar Binks had his answer.

In the conference room of the lead battleship of the Trade Federation fleet, a hologram of Darth Sidious towered over Nute Gunray and Rune Haako. The Neimoidian viceroy and his lieutenant stood motionless before it, reddish orange eyes fixed and staring, reptilian faces betraying every bit of the fear that held them paralyzed.

The black-cloaked figure of Darth Sidious regarded them silently. There was no hint of expression on his shadowed countenance, which was mostly hidden within the folds of the cloak's hood. But the rigid posture of the Sith Lord's body spoke volumes.

"You disappoint me, Viceroy," he hissed at Nute Gunray.

"My lord, I am certain that all—" The subject of his anger tried futilely to explain.

"Worse, you defy me!"

The Neimoidian's face underwent a terrifying transformation. "No, my lord! Never! These Jedi are . . . resourceful, that's all. Not easily destroyed—"

"Alive, then, Viceroy?"

"No, no, I'm sure they're dead. They must be. We—we just haven't been able to confirm it . . . yet."

Darth Sidious ignored him. "If they are alive, they will show themselves. When they do, Viceroy, I want to know immediately. I will deal with them myself."

Nute Gunray looked as if he might collapse under the weight of the Sith Lord's penetrating stare. "Yes, my lord," he managed as the hologram vanished.

Inside the troubled bongo, Obi-Wan fought to keep control as the little craft began to drift aimlessly.

Abruptly the whine of the power drive came alive and the aft drive fins began to turn. "Power's back," Obi-Wan breathed gratefully.

The lights on the control panels blinked on, flickered, and steadied. The exterior directional lights followed, momentarily blinding them as they reflected off rock walls and jagged outcroppings. Then Jar Jar screamed. A new monster was sitting right in front of them, all spines and scales and teeth, crooked clawed forelegs raised defensively.

"Colo claw fish!" the Gungan shrieked. "Yous Jedi do something! Where da Force now, you think?"

"Relax," Qui-Gon Jinn said softly, placing his hand on Jar Jar's twitching shoulder. The Gungan jerked and promptly fainted.

"You overdid it," Obi-Wan observed, wheeling the bongo about and jetting away through the darkness.

Even without looking, he knew the colo claw fish was in pursuit. They were inside a tunnel that probably served as the creature's lair. They were lucky to have caught it by surprise. He angled the bongo toward the cave entrance and a series of overhangs that might provide them with a little protection on their way out. Something slammed into the bongo, held it fast momentarily, then released it. Obi-Wan increased power to the drive fins.

"Come on, come on!" he breathed softly.

They shot out of the cave directly into the jaws of the waiting sando aqua monster. The creature jerked back at the unexpected invasion, giving Obi-Wan just an instant to bank their craft hard to the right. The jaws of the aqua monster were still open as they sped between teeth the size of buildings.

Jar Jar's eyes flickered open. He caught sight of the teeth and promptly fainted again.

Out through a gap in the sando aqua monster's fangs they sped, the bongo shaking with the thrust of its power drive. But the colo claw fish, still in pursuit, did not veer aside quickly enough and flew right into the larger hunter's maw. The jaws came down, engulfing it.

Obi-Wan increased power to the drive fins as bits of the colo claw fish reemerged briefly through the sando aqua monster's grinding teeth, only to be sucked quickly from sight again.

"Let's hope that's all the snack he requires," the Jedi observed with a quick glance back.

Apparently it was, because it did not come after them. It took a while to revive Jar Jar and a good deal longer to complete their voyage through the core, but with the Gungan's somewhat questionable help, they finally emerged from the darkness of the deeper waters toward a blaze of sunlight. The bongo popped to the surface of an azure body of water, green hills and trees rising about them, clouds and blue sky overhead. Obi-Wan steered the little craft to the nearest shore, shut down the engines, and released the nose hatch. Qui-Gon rose and looked around.

"We safe now," Jar Jar observed with a grateful sigh, leaning back in his seat. "Tis okeday, hey?"

"That remains to be seen," the Jedi Master said. "Let's be off."

He climbed from the bongo onto the shore and started away. Obi-Wan glanced meaningfully at Jar Jar and followed.

The Gungan stared doubtfully after the departing Jedi. "Me comen, me comen," he muttered, and hurried after.

It was a little more than a week after the Podrace and the encounter with the old spacer that Watto summoned Anakin into the musty confines of the junk shop and told him he was to take a speeder out to the Dune Sea to do some trading with the Jawas. The Jawas, scavengers, were offering a number of droids for sale or trade, some of them mechanics, and while Watto wasn't about to part with usable currency, he didn't want to pass up a bargain if it could be had for a favorable barter. Anakin had traded on Watto's behalf before, and the Toydarian knew that the boy was good at this, too.

The blue face hovered close to Anakin's own, tiny wings beating madly. "Bring me what I need, boy! And don't mess up!"

Anakin was entrusted with a variety of difficult-to-obtain engine and guidance systems parts that the Jawas would covet and Watto could afford to give up for the right set of droids. The boy was to take the speeder out into the Dune Sea for a midday meeting with the Jawas, make his trade, and be back by sunset. No detours and no fooling around. Watto hadn't forgiven him yet for losing the Podrace and smashing his best racer, and he was letting the boy know it.

"March the droids back if you can't barter for a float sled." Watto flitted about, issuing orders, a blue blur. "If they can't walk this far, they aren't of any use to me. *Peedunkel!* Make sure you don't get taken! My reputation is at stake!"

Anakin listened attentively and nodded at all the right places, the way he had learned to do over the years. It was only a little past midmorning and there was plenty of time to do what was needed. He had traded with the Jawas many times, and he knew how to make certain they did not get the best of him.

There was a great deal Watto didn't know about Anakin Skywalker, the boy thought to himself as he went out the door to claim his speeder and begin his journey. One of the tricks to being a successful slave was to know things your master didn't know and to take advantage of that knowledge when it would do you some good. Anakin had a gift for Podracing and a gift for taking things apart and putting them back together and making them work better than they had before. But it was his strange ability to sense things, to gain insights through changes in temperament, reactions, and words, that served him best. He could tune in to other creatures, bond with them so closely he could sense what they were thinking and what they would do almost before they did. It had served him well in dealing with the Jawas, among others, and it gave him a distinct edge in bartering on Watto's behalf.

Anakin had a couple of important secrets he kept from Watto as well. The first was the protocol droid he was reconstructing in his bedroom work area. It was far enough along that even though it was missing its skin and an eye, it could stand and move around, and its intelligence and communications processors were up and running. Good enough to do the job he required of it, he concluded, which was to accompany him on his bartering mission. The droid could listen in on the Jawas in their own peculiar language, which Anakin did not understand or speak particularly well. By doing so, it could let Anakin know if they were trying to slip anything by him. Watto didn't know how far he had gotten with the droid, and there wasn't much danger Watto could find out while they were out in the Dune Sea.

The second and more important secret concerned the Pod-racer the boy was building. He had been working on it for almost two years, salvaging bits and pieces as he went, assembling it under cover of an old tarp in an area of the common refuse dump in back of the slave housing. His mother had indulged him, mindful of his interest in taking things apart and putting them back together. She didn't see the harm in allowing him to have this project to work on in his spare time, and Watto knew nothing of the Pod.

That was an inspired bit of subterfuge on Anakin's part. He knew, just as with the droid, that if it appeared to have any value at all, Watto would claim it. So he deliberately kept it looking as if it were a complete piece of junk, disguising its worth in a variety of clever ways. To all intents and purposes, it would never run. It was just another childish project. It was just a little boy's dream.

But for Anakin Skywalker, it was the first step in his life plan. He would build the fastest Podracer ever, and he would win every race in which it was entered. He would build a starfighter next, and he would pilot it off Tatooine to other worlds. He would take his mother with him, and they would find a new home. He would become the greatest pilot ever, flying all the ships of the mainline, and his mother would be so proud of him.

And one day, when he had done all this, they would be slaves no longer. They would be free.

He thought about this often, not because his mother encouraged him in any way or because he was given any reason to think it might happen, but simply because he believed, deep down inside where it mattered, that it must.

He thought about it now as he guided his speeder through the streets of Mos Espa, the protocol droid sitting in the rear passenger compartment, skeletal-like without its skin and motionless because he had deactivated it for the ride out. He thought about all the things he would do and places he would go, the adventures he would have and the successes he would enjoy, and the dreams he would see come true. He drove the speeder out from the city under Tatooine's suns, the heat rising off the desert sands in a shimmering wave, the light reflecting off the metal surface of the speeder like white fire.

He proceeded east for about two standard hours until he reached the edge of the Dune Sea. The meeting with the Jawas was already in place, arranged by Watto the day before by transmitter. The Jawas would be waiting by Mochot Steep, a singular rock formation about halfway across the sea. Goggles, gloves, and helmet firmly in place, the boy cranked up the power on the speeder and hastened ahead through the midday heat.

He found the Jawas waiting for him, their monstrous sandcrawler parked in the shadow of the Steep, the droids they wished to trade lined up at the end of the crawler's ramp. Anakin parked his speeder close to where the little robed figures waited, yellow eyes gleaming watchfully in the shadows of their hoods, and climbed out. He activated the protocol droid and ordered him to follow. With the droid trailing obediently, he walked slowly down the line of mechanicals, making a show of carefully studying each.

When he was finished, he drew his droid aside. "Which ones are best, See-Threepio?" he asked. He'd given it a number the night before, choosing *three* because the droid made the third member of his little family after his mother and himself.

"Oh, well, Master Anakin, I'm flattered that you would ask, but I would never presume to infringe on your expertise, my own being so meager, although I do have knowledge of some fifty-one hundred different varieties of droids and over five thousand different internal processors and ten times that many chips and—"

"Just tell me which ones are best!" Anakin hissed under his breath. He had forgotten that C-3PO was first and foremost a protocol droid and, while possessed of extensive knowledge, tended to defer to the humans he served. "Which ones, Threepio?" he repeated. "Left to right. Number them off to me."

C-3PO did so. "Do you wish me to enumerate their capabilities and design specialties, Master Anakin?" he asked solicitously, cocking his head.

Anakin silenced him with a wave of his hand as the head Jawa approached. They bartered back and forth for a time, Anakin getting a sense of how far the Jawas could be pushed, how much subterfuge was taking place with regard to their droids, and how badly they wanted the goods he was offering in exchange. He was able to determine that several of the best droids were still inside the crawler, a fact that C-3PO picked up from an unguarded comment made by a Jawa off to one side. The head Jawa squeaked at him furiously, of course, but the damage was done.

Three more droids were brought out, and again Anakin took a few moments to inspect them, C-3PO at his side. They were good models, and the Jawas were not particularly eager to part with them for anything less than a combination of currency and goods. Anakin and the head Jawa, who were of about the same height and weight, stood nose to nose arguing the matter for a long time.

When the bartering was completed, Anakin had traded a little more than half of what he had brought as barter for two mechanic droids in excellent condition, three more multipurpose droids that were serviceable, and a damaged hyperdrive converter that he could put back into service in no time. He could have traded for another two or three droids, but the quality of those that remained wasn't sufficiently high to part with any more of Watto's goods, and Watto would be quick to see that.

There was no float sled to be had, so Anakin lined up the newly purchased droids behind the speeder, placed C-3PO in the rear passenger compartment to keep an eye on them, and set off for Mos Espa. It was just after midday. The little procession was a curious sight, the speeder leading, hovering just off the sand, thrusters on dead slow, the droids trailing behind, jointed limbs working steadily to keep pace.

"That was an excellent trade, Master Anakin," C-3PO advised cheerfully, keeping his one good eye on their purchases.

"You are to be congratulated! I think those Jawas learned a hard lesson today! You really did show them a thing or two about hard bargaining! Why, that pit droid alone is worth much more than . . ."

The droid rattled on incessantly, but Anakin let him alone, ignoring most of what he said, content to let his mind wander for a bit now that the hard part was done. Even with the droids slowing them down, they should reach the edge of the Dune Sea before midafternoon and Mos Espa before dark. He would have time to sneak C-3PO back into his bedroom and deliver the purchased droids and the balance of the trade goods to Watto. Maybe that would get him back in the Toydarian's good graces. Certainly Watto would be pleased with the converter. They were hard to come by out here, and if it could be made to work—which Anakin was certain it could—it would be worth more than all the rest of the purchases combined.

They crossed the central flats and climbed the slow rise to Xelric Draw, a shallow, widemouthed canyon that split the Mospic High Range just inside the lip of the Dune Sea. The speeder eased inside the canyon, droids strung out in a gleaming mechanical line behind, passing out of sunlight into shadow. The temperature dropped a few degrees, and the silence changed pitch in the lee of the cliffs. Anakin glanced about warily, knowing the dangers of the desert as well as any who were from Mos Espa, although he was inclined to think from time to time that it was safer out here than in the city.

". . . a four-to-one ratio of Rodians to Hutts when the settlement began to take on the look and feel of a trading center, although even then it was clear the Hutts were the dominant species, and the Rodians might just as well have stayed home rather than chance a long and somewhat purposeless flight . . ."

C-3PO rambled on, changing subjects without urging, asking nothing in return for his nonstop narrative but to be allowed to continue. Anakin wondered if he was suffering some sort of sensory vocal deprivation from being deactivated for so long. These protocol droids were known to be temperamental.

His gaze shifted suddenly to the right, to something that seemed strange and out of place. At first it was just a shape and coloring amid the desert sand and rock, almost lost in the shadows. But as he stared harder, it took on fresh meaning. He banked the speeder sharply, bringing the line of droids around with him.

"Master Anakin, whatever are you doing?" C-3PO protested peevishly. His one eye fixed on Anakin. "Mos Espa is down the canyon draw, not through the side of the—Oh, my! Is that what I think it is? Master, there is every reason to turn right around—"

"I know." Anakin cut the droid short. "I just want a look."

C-3PO's arms fluttered anxiously. "I must protest, Master Anakin. This is most unwise. If I am correct, and I must tell you that I have calculated that degree of probability at ninety-nine point seven, then we are headed directly toward . . ."

But Anakin didn't need to be told what lay ahead, having already determined exactly what it was. A Tusken Raider lay crumpled on the ground, half-buried by a pile of rocks close against the cliff face. The look and garb of the Sand People were unmistakable, even at this distance. Loose, tan-colored clothing, heavy leather gloves and boots, bandolier and belt, cloth-wrapped head with goggles and breath mask, and a long, dual-handled blaster rifle lying a meter away from an outstretched arm. A fresh scar slicing down from the cliff face bore evidence of a slide. The Raider had probably been hiding above when the rock gave way beneath his feet and buried him in the fall.

Anakin stopped the speeder and climbed down.

"Master Anakin, I don't think this is a good idea at all!" C-3PO declared in a sharp tone of admonishment.

"I just want a look, that's all," the boy repeated.

He was wary and a little scared of doing this, but he had never seen a Tusken Raider up close, although he had heard stories about them all his life. The Tuskens were a reclusive, fierce, nomadic people who claimed the desert as their own and lived off those foolish enough to venture into their territory unprepared. On foot or astride the wild banthas they had claimed from the wastelands, they traveled where they chose, pillaging outlying homes and way stations, waylaying caravans, stealing goods and equipment, and terrorizing everyone in general. They had even gone after the Hutts on occasion. The residents of Mos Espa, themselves a less than respectable citizenry, hated the Sand People with a passion.

Anakin had not yet made up his mind about them. The stories were chilling, but he knew enough of life to know there were two sides to every story and mostly only one being told. He was intrigued by the wild, free nature of the Tuskens, of a life without responsibility or boundaries, of a community in which everyone was considered equal.

He left the speeder and walked toward the fallen Raider. Threepio continued to admonish him, to warn him he was making a mistake. In truth, he wasn't all that sure the droid was wrong. But his trepidation was overcome by his curiosity. What could it hurt to have just the briefest of looks? His boyish nature surfaced and took control. He would be able to tell his friends he had seen one of the Sand People close up. He would be able to tell them what one really looked like.

The Tusken Raider lay sprawled facedown, arms akimbo, head turned to one side. Rocks and debris buried most of the lower part of his body. One leg lay pinned beneath a massive boulder. Anakin edged closer to where the blaster rifle lay, then reached down and picked it up. It was heavy and unwieldy. A man would have to be strong and skilled to handle one, he thought. He noted the strange carvings on the stock—tribal markings perhaps. He had heard the Tuskens were a tribal people.

Suddenly the fallen Raider stirred, drawing back one arm, bracing himself, and lifting his wrapped head. Opaque goggles stared directly at Anakin. The boy backed away automatically. But the Tusken just stared at him for a moment, taking in who he was and what he was doing, then laid his head down again.

Anakin Skywalker waited, wondering what he should do. He knew what Watto would say. He knew what almost everyone would say. Get out of there! Now! He put the blaster rifle down again. This was no business of his. He took a step back, then another.

The Tusken Raider lifted his head once more and stared at him. Anakin stared back. He could sense the pain in the other's gaze. He could feel his desperation, trapped and helpless beneath that boulder, stripped of his weapon and his freedom both.

Anakin's brow furrowed. Would his mother tell him to get out of there, too? What would she say, if she were there?

"Threepio," he called back to the droid. "Bring everybody over here."

Protesting vehemently with every step, C-3PO gathered up the newly purchased droids and herded them to where the boy stood staring at the fallen Tusken. Anakin put the droids to work clearing away the smaller rocks and stones, then rigged a lever and used the speeder's weight to tilt the rock just enough that they could pull the pinned man free. The Tusken was awake briefly, but then lapsed back into unconsciousness. Anakin had the droids check for other weapons and kept the blaster rifle safely out of reach.

While the Tusken Raider was unconscious, the droids laid him on his back so he could be checked for injuries. The leg pinned by the boulder was smashed, the bones broken in several places. Anakin could see the damage through the torn cloth. But he wasn't familiar with Tusken physiology, and he didn't know exactly what to do to repair the damage. So he applied a quick-seal splint from the medical kit in the speeder to freeze the leg in place and left it alone.

He sat down then and thought about what he should do next. The light was beginning to fail. He had spent too much time freeing the Tusken to reach Mos Espa before nightfall. He could make the edge of the Dune Sea by dark, but only by leaving the Tusken behind, untended and alone. Anakin frowned. Given the things that roamed the desert when it got dark, he might as well bury the man and have done with it.

So he had the droids pull a small glow unit out of the landspeeder. When twilight descended, he powered up the glow unit and attached an extender fuel pack to assure it would burn all night. He broke out an old dried food pack and munched absently as he stared at the sleeping Tusken. His mother would be worried. Watto would be mad. But they knew him to be capable and reliable, and they would wait until daybreak to do anything about his absence. By then, he hoped, he would be well on his way home.

"Do you think he'll be all right?" he asked C-3PO.

He had placed the speeder and the other droids under the lee of a cliff face behind the glow unit, safely tucked from view, but had kept C-3PO with him for company. Boy and droid sat huddled close together on one side of the glow unit while the Tusken Raider continued to sleep on the other.

"I am afraid I lack the necessary medical training and information to make that determination, Master Anakin," C-3PO advised, cocking his head. "I certainly think you have done everything you possibly could."

The boy nodded thoughtfully.

"Master Anakin, we really shouldn't be out here at night," the droid observed after a moment. "This country is quite dangerous."

"But we couldn't leave him, could we?"

"Oh, well, that's a very difficult determination to make." C-3PO pondered the matter.

"We couldn't take him with us either."

"Certainly not!"

The boy sat in silence for a time, watching the Tusken sleep. He watched him for so long, in fact, that it came as something of a surprise when the Tusken finally stirred awake. It happened all at once, and it caught the boy off guard. The Tusken Raider shifted his weight with a lurching movement, exhaled sharply, propped himself up on one arm, looked at himself, then looked at the boy. The boy made no move or sound. The Tusken regarded him intently for a long minute, then slowly eased into a sitting position, his wounded leg stretched out in front of him.

"Uh, hello," Anakin said, trying out a smile.

The Tusken Raider made no response.

"Are you thirsty?" the boy asked.

No response.

"I don't think he likes us very much," C-3PO observed.

Anakin tried a dozen different approaches at conversation, but the Tusken Raider ignored them all. His gaze shifted only once, to where his blaster rifle lay propped against the rocks behind the boy.

"Say something to him in Tusken," he ordered C-3PO finally.

The droid did. He spoke at length to the Tusken in his own language, but the man refused to respond. He just kept staring at the boy. Finally, after C-3PO had gone on for some time, the Tusken glanced at him and barked a single word in response.

"Gracious!" the droid exclaimed.

"What did he say?" the boy asked, excited.

"Why he—he told me to shut up!"

That was pretty much the end of any attempt at conversation. The boy and the Tusken sat facing each other in silence, their faces caught by the glow of the fire, the desert's darkness all around. Anakin found himself wondering what he would do if the Tusken tried to attack him. It was unlikely, but the man was large and fierce and strong, and if he reached the boy, he could easily overpower him. He could take back his blaster rifle and do with the boy as he chose.

But somehow Anakin didn't sense that to be the Tusken's intent. The Tusken made no effort to move and gave no indication he had any intention of trying to do so. He just sat there, wrapped in his desert garb, faceless beneath his coverings, locked away with his own thoughts.

Finally he spoke again. The boy looked quickly at C-3PO. "He wants to know what you are going to do with him, Master Anakin," the droid translated.

Anakin looked back at the Tusken, confused. "Tell him I'm not going to do anything with him," he said. "I'm just trying to help him get well."

C-3PO spoke the words in Tusken. The man listened. He made no response. He did not say anything more.

Anakin realized suddenly that the Tusken was afraid. He could sense it in the way the other spoke, in the way he sat waiting. He was crippled and weaponless. He was at Anakin's mercy. The boy understood the Tusken's fear, but it surprised him anyway. It seemed out of character. The Sand People were supposed to be fearless. Besides, he wasn't afraid of the Tusken. Maybe he should have been, but he wasn't.

Anakin Skywalker wasn't afraid of anything.

Was he?

Staring into the opaque lenses of the goggles that hid the Tusken Raider's eyes, he contemplated the matter. Most times he thought there was nothing that could frighten him. Most times he thought he was brave enough that he would never be afraid.

But in that most secret part of himself where he hid the things he would reveal to no one, he knew he was cheating on the truth. He might not ever be afraid for himself, but he was sometimes very afraid for his mother.

What if something were to happen to her? What if something awful were to happen to her, something he could do nothing to prevent?

He felt a shiver go down his spine.

What if he were to lose her?

How brave would he be then, if the person he was closest to in the whole, endless universe was suddenly taken away from him? It would never happen, of course. It couldn't possibly happen.

But what if it did?

He stared at the Tusken Raider, and in the deep silence of the night he felt his confidence tremble like a leaf caught in the wind.

He fell asleep finally, and he dreamed of strange things. The dreams shifted and changed without warning and took on different story lines and meanings as they did so. He was several things in the course of his dreams. Once he was a Jedi Knight, fighting against things so dark and insubstantial he could not identify them. Once he was a pilot of a star cruiser, taking the ship into hyperspace, spanning whole star systems on his voyage. Once he was a great and feared commander of an army, and he came back to Tatooine with ships and troops at his command to free the planet's slaves. His mother was waiting for him, smiling, arms outstretched. But when he tried to embrace her, she vanished.

There were Sand People in his dreams, too. They appeared near the end, a handful of them, standing before him with their blaster rifles and long gaffi sticks lifted and held ready. They regarded him in silence, as if wondering what they should do with him.

He awoke then, jarred from his sleep by an unmistakable sense of danger. He jerked upright and stared about in confusion and fear. The glow unit had burned down to nothing. In the faint, silvery brightening of predawn, he found himself confronted by the dark, faceless shapes of the Sand People of his dreams.

Anakin swallowed hard. Motionless figures against the horizon's dim glow, the Tusken Raiders encircled him completely. The boy thought to break and run, but realized at once how foolish that would be. He was helpless. All he could do was wait and see what they intended.

A guttural muttering rose from their midst, and heads turned to look. Through a gap in the ranks, Anakin could just make out a figure being lifted and carried away. It was the Raider he had rescued, speaking to his people. The other Raiders hesitated, then slowly backed away.

In seconds, they were gone.

Sunlight began to crest the dark bulk of the Mospic, and C-3PO was speaking to him in a rush of words that tumbled over one another, the skeletal metal arms jerking this way and that.

"Master Anakin, they've gone! Oh, we're lucky to be alive! Thank goodness they didn't hurt you!"

Anakin climbed to his feet. There were Tusken Raider footprints everywhere. He glanced about quickly. The speeder and the droids obtained from the Jawas sat undisturbed beneath the overhang. The Tusken blaster rifle was gone.

"Master Anakin, what should we do?" C-3PO wailed in dismay.

Anakin looked around at the empty canyon floor, at the high ragged walls of the cliff face, and at the brightening sky where the stars were fading away. He listened to the deep silence and felt impossibly alone and vulnerable.

"We should go home," he whispered, and moved swiftly to make it happen.

Nute Gunray stood in silence at the center of the palace throne room in the Naboo capital city of Theed and listened patiently as Governor Sio Bibble protested the Trade Federation presence. Rune Haako stood at his side. Both wore their Federation robes of office and inscrutable expressions. Two dozen battle droids held the Naboo occupants of the room at gunpoint. The city had fallen shortly after sunrise. There had been little resistance; the Naboo were a peaceful people. The Trade Federation invasion had come as a surprise, and the droid army was inside the gates of the city before any substantial defense could be mounted. What few weapons there were had been confiscated and the Naboo removed to detention camps. Battle droids were combing the city even now to put an end to any lingering resistance.

Gunray resisted a smile. Apparently the Queen had believed right up to the end that negotiations would prevail and the Senate would provide the people of Naboo with protection.

"It is bad enough, Viceroy, that you dare to disrupt transmissions between the Queen and Senator Palpatine while he is attempting to argue our cause before the Republic Senate, bad enough that you pretend that this blockade is a lawful action, but landing an entire army on our planet and occupying our cities is too outrageous for words."

Sio Bibble was a tall, balding man with a sharply pointed beard and an even sharper tongue. He held the floor just at the moment, but Gunray was getting tired of listening to him.

He glanced at the other captives. Captain Panaka, the Queen's head of security, and four of the Queen's personal guards stood to one side, stripped of their weapons and helpless. Panaka was stone-faced and hard-eyed as he watched the Neimoidians. He was a big, powerfully built man with a dark, smooth face and quick eyes. The Neimoidian did not like the way those eyes were fixed on him.

The Queen sat upon her throne, surrounded by her hand-maidens. She was serene and aloof, detached from everything, as if what was taking place had no effect on her, could not touch her in any way. She wore black, her white-painted face in sharp contrast to the black feathered headdress that wrapped and framed it. A gold chain lay across her regal brow and the red beauty mark split her lower lip. She was considered beautiful, Gunray had been told, but he had no sense of human beauty and by Neimoidian standards she was simply colorless and small-featured.

What interested him was her youth. She was barely out of girlhood, certainly not a full-grown woman, and yet the people of Naboo had chosen her as their Queen. This wasn't one of those monarchies where blood determined right of rule and dynasties prevailed. The Naboo chose the wisest among them as their ruler by popular acclaim, and Queen Amidala governed at the sufferance of her people. Why they would choose someone so young and naive was a mystery to him. From his point of view it certainly hadn't served them well in this instance.

Governor Sio Bibble's voice echoed through the cavernous chamber, rising to the high, vaulted ceiling, bouncing off the smooth, sunlit walls. Theed was an opulent, prosperous city and the throne room reflected its history of success.

"Viceroy, I ask you point-blank." Sio Bibble was concluding

his oration. "How do you intend to explain this invasion to the Senate?"

The Neimoidian's flat, reptilian countenance managed a small flicker of humor. "The Naboo and the Trade Federation will forge a treaty that will legitimize our occupation of Theed. I have been assured that such a treaty, once produced, will be quickly ratified by the Senate."

"A treaty?" the governor exclaimed in astonishment. "In the face of this completely unlawful action?"

Amidala rose from her throne and stepped forward, surrounded by her cloaked and hooded handmaidens. Her eyes were sharp with anger. "I will not cooperate."

Nute Gunray exchanged a quick glance with Rune Haako. "Now, now, Your Highness," he purred. "Don't be too hasty with your pronouncements. You are not going to like what we have in store for your people. In time, their suffering will persuade you to see our point of view."

He turned away. "Enough talk." He beckoned. "Commander?" Battle droid OOM-9 stepped forward, narrow metal snout lowering slightly in response. "Process them," the viceroy ordered.

OOM-9 signaled for one of his sergeants to take over, metallic voice directing that the prisoners be taken to Camp Four. The battle droids herded the Queen, her handmaidens, Governor Bibble, Captain Panaka, and the Naboo guards from the room.

Nute Gunray's slit reddish orange eyes followed them out, then shifted back to Haako and the room. He felt a deep sense of satisfaction take hold. Everything was going exactly as it should.

The sergeant and a dozen battle droids moved the prisoners along the polished stone halls of the Theed palace and outside to where a series of terraced steps led downward through statuary and buttress work to a broad plaza. The plaza was filled with Federation tanks and battle droids and was empty of Naboo citizens. The tanks were squat, shovel-nosed vehicles with their main cannon mounted on a turret above and behind the cockpit and smaller blasters set low and to either side. They had the look of foraging beetles as they edged about the plaza's perimeter.

Beyond, the buildings of Theed stretched away toward the horizon, a vast sprawl of high stone walls, gilded domes, peaked towers, and sculpted archways. Sunlight bathed the gleaming edifices, their architecture in counterpoint to the lush greenness of the planet. The rush of waterfalls and bubble of fountains formed a soft, distant backdrop to the strange silence created by the absence of the populace.

The prisoners were taken across the plaza past the Trade Federation machines of war. No one spoke. Even Governor Bibble had gone silent, his gray-bearded head lowered in dark contemplation. They departed the plaza and turned down a broad avenue that led to the outskirts of the city and the newly constructed Trade Federation detention camps. STAPs hummed overhead, shadows flitting off the walls of the buildings, metal shells gleaming as they darted away.

The droids had just turned their prisoners down a quiet byway when their sergeant, who was leading the procession, brought them to an abrupt halt.

Two men stood directly in their way, both wearing loose robes over belted tunics, the taller with his hair worn long, the shorter with his cut to a thin braided pigtail. Their arms hung loosely at their sides, but they did not have the look of men who were unprepared.

For a moment, each group stared at the other in silence. Then the narrow face of a Gungan peeked out from behind the two robed figures, eyes wide and frightened.

Qui-Gon Jinn stepped forward. "Are you Queen Amidala of the Naboo?" he asked the young woman in the feathered headdress.

The Queen hesitated. "Who are you?"

"Ambassadors from the supreme chancellor." The Jedi Master inclined his head slightly. "We seek an audience with you, Your Highness."

The droid sergeant suddenly seemed to remember where he

was and what he was doing. He gestured to his soldiers. "Clear them away!"

Four of the battle droids moved to obey. They were just shifting their weapons into firing position when the Jedi activated their lightsabers and cut them apart. As the shattered droids collapsed, the Jedi moved quickly to dispatch the others. Laser bolts were blocked, weapons were knocked aside, and the remaining droids were reduced to scrap metal.

The sergeant turned to flee, but Qui-Gon brought up his hand, holding the droid fast with the power of the Force. In seconds, the sergeant lay in a ruined heap with his command.

Quickly, the Naboo soldiers moved to recover the fallen weapons. The Jedi Knights flicked off their lightsabers and motioned everyone out of the open street and into the shelter of an alley between two buildings. Jar Jar Binks followed, muttering in wonder at the cold efficiency with which the Jedi had dispatched their enemies.

Qui-Gon faced the Queen. "Your Highness, I am Qui-Gon Jinn and my companion is Obi-Wan Kenobi. We are Jedi Knights as well as ambassadors for the supreme chancellor."

"Your negotiations seem to have failed, Ambassador," Sio Bibble observed with a snort.

"The negotiations never took place." Qui-Gon kept his eyes directed toward the Queen. Her painted face showed nothing. "Your Highness," he continued, "we must make contact with the Republic."

"We can't," Captain Panaka volunteered, stepping forward. "They've knocked out all our communications."

An alarm was being given from somewhere close, and there was the sound of running. Qui-Gon glanced toward the street where the battle droids lay. "Do you have transports?"

The Naboo captain nodded, quick to see what the Jedi intended. "In the main hangar. This way."

He led the little group to the end of the alleyway, where they crossed to other passageways and backstreets, encountering no one. They moved quickly and silently through the growing sound of alarms and the wicked buzz of STAPs. To their credit, the Naboo did not resist Qui-Gon's leadership nor question his appearance. With Panaka and his men newly armed, the Naboo Queen and her companions had a sense of being in control of their own destiny once more and seemed more than ready to take a chance on their rescuers.

It did not take them long to reach their destination. A series of connected buildings dominated one end of a broad causeway, each one domed and cavernous, the central structures warded by arched entrances and low, flat-walled outbuildings. Battle droids were stationed everywhere, weapons held at the ready, but Captain Panaka was able to find an unguarded approach down a narrow corridor between adjoining buildings.

At a side door to the main hangar, Panaka brought the group to a halt. After a quick glance over his shoulder for droids, he unlocked and nudged open the hangar door. With Qui-Gon Jinn pressed close, he peered inside. A handful of Naboo ships were grouped at the center of the hangar, sleek gleaming transports, their noses pointed toward a wide opening in the far wall. Battle droids guarded each, positioned across the entire floor of the hangar to cut off any unseen approach.

Panaka pointed to a long, low ship on the far side of the hangar with swept-back wings and powerful Headon-5 engines. "The Queen's personal transport," he whispered to the Jedi Master.

Qui-Gon nodded. A J-type 327 Nubian. In the distance, the alarms continued to sound their steady wail. "That one will do," he said.

Panaka scanned the hangar interior. "The battle droids. There are too many of them."

The Jedi eased back from the door. "That won't be a problem." He faced the Queen. "Your Highness. Under the circumstances, I suggest you come to Coruscant with us."

The young woman shook her head, the feathers on her headdress rustling softly. Her white-painted face was calm and her gaze steady. "Thank you, Ambassador, but my place is here with my people."

"I don't think so," Qui-Gon responded, locking eyes. "The Trade Federation has other plans. They will kill you if you stay."

Sio Bibble pushed to the Queen's side. "They wouldn't dare!"

"They need her to sign a treaty to make this invasion of theirs legal!" Captain Panaka pointed out. "They can't afford to kill her!"

The Queen looked from face to face, the barest flicker of uncertainty showing in her eyes.

"The situation here is not what it seems," Qui-Gon pressed. "There is something else going on, Your Highness. There is no logic to the Federation's actions. My instincts tell me they will destroy you."

A shadow of real alarm crossed Sio Bibble's face as the Jedi Master finished. His strong features melted slightly. "Your Highness," he said slowly. "Perhaps you should reconsider. Our only hope is for the Senate to take our side in this matter. Senator Palpatine will need your help."

Captain Panaka was having none of it. "Getting past their blockade is impossible, Your Highness—even if we were to get off the planet! An escape attempt is too dangerous—"

"Your Highness, I will stay here and do what I can," Sio Bibble interrupted, shaking his head at Panaka. "They will have to retain the Council of Governors in order to maintain some semblance of order. But you must leave—"

Queen Amidala brought up her hand sharply to silence the debate. Turning from her governor and head of security and the Jedi as well, she looked suddenly to her handmaidens, who were pressed close about her. "Either choice presents great risk to all of us. . . ," she said softly, looking from face to face.

Qui-Gon watched the exchange, puzzled. What was the Queen seeking?

The handmaidens glanced at one another, faces barely visible within the confines of red and gold hooded robes. All were silent.

Finally, one spoke. "We are brave, Your Highness," Padmé said firmly.

Alarms continued to sound. "If you are to leave, Your Highness, it must be now," Qui-Gon urged.

Queen Amidala straightened and nodded. "So be it. I will plead our case before the Senate." She glanced at Sio Bibble. "Be careful, Governor."

She took the governor's hand briefly, then beckoned to three of her handmaidens. Those not chosen began to cry softly. Amidala embraced them and whispered words of encouragement. Captain Panaka selected two of the four guards to stay behind with the handmaidens and Sio Bibble.

The Jedi Knights moved through the side door and into the hangar, leading the way for Jar Jar and the Naboo. "Stay close," Qui-Gon admonished softly over his shoulder.

Captain Panaka moved next to him, dark face intense. "We need a pilot for the vessel." He pointed to where a group of Naboo were being held captive in a corner of the hangar by a squad of battle droids. The insignia on their uniforms indicated a mix of guards, mechanics, and pilots. "There."

"I'll take care of it," Obi-Wan declared, and veered toward the Naboo captives.

Qui-Gon and the rest continued on, striding boldly across the hangar floor, moving directly toward the Queen's vessel, ignoring the battle droids who moved to intercept them. Qui-Gon took note of the fact that the boarding ramp to the transport was lowered. More battle droids were closing on them, curious without yet being alarmed.

"Don't stop for anything," he said to the Queen, and he reached beneath his cloak for the lightsaber.

They were barely twenty meters from the Queen's transport when the nearest of the battle droids challenged them. "Where are you going?" it asked in its blank, metallic voice.

"Get out of the way," Qui-Gon ordered. "I am an ambassador for the supreme chancellor, and I am taking these people to Coruscant."

The droid brought up his weapon quickly, blocking the Jedi Master's passage. "You are under arrest!"

It was scrap metal within seconds, dissected by Qui-Gon's lightsaber. More of the battle droids rushed to stop the Jedi, who stood alone against them as his charges boarded the Nubian vessel. Captain Panaka and the Naboo guards formed a protective screen for the Queen and her handmaidens as they hurried up the ramp. Jar Jar Binks clambered after, holding on to his head with his long arms. Laser bolts lanced through the hangar from all directions, and new alarms blared wildly.

On the far side of the hangar, Obi-Wan Kenobi launched himself at the battle droids holding the Naboo pilots hostage, cutting into them with ferocious determination. Qui-Gon watched his progress, long hair flying out as he withstood yet another rush from the battle droids attempting to reclaim the Queen's transport, blocking their laser bolts as he fought to hold the boarding ramp. Obi-Wan was running toward him now, a handful of the Naboo in tow. Explosions rose all around them, deadly laser fire burning into metal and flesh. Several of the Naboo went down, but the battle droids were unable to slow the Jedi.

Qui-Gon called sharply to Obi-Wan as he went past, telling him to get the ship in the air. More battle droids were appearing at the hangar doors, weapons firing. Qui-Gon backed quickly up the loading ramp and into the transport's dimly lit interior. The ramp rose behind him and closed with a soft whoosh.

The Headon-5 engines were firing even before the Jedi Master reached the main cabin and flung himself into a chair. Laser fire hammered at the sides of the sleek craft, but it was already beginning to move forward. The pilot sat hunched forward over the controls, his weathered face intense, a sheen of sweat beading his forehead, hands steady on the controls. "Hold on," he said.

The Nubian shot through the hangar doors, ripping past battle droids and laser fire, lifting away from the city of Theed into the blue, sunlit sky. The planet of Naboo was left behind in seconds, the ship rising into the darkness of space, arcing toward a suddenly visible cluster of Trade Federation battleships blocking its way.

Qui-Gon left his seat and came forward to stand beside the pilot.

"Ric Olié," the other announced with a quick glance up at the Jedi. "Thanks for helping out back there."

Qui-Gon nodded. "Better save your thanks until we deal with what's up here."

The pilot gave him a rakish grin. "Copy that. What do we do about these big boys? Our communications are still jammed."

"We're past the point of talking. Just keep the ship on course." Qui-Gon turned to Obi-Wan. "Make sure everyone is settled safely in place." His eyes moved to where Jar Jar Binks was already up and poking about.

The younger Jedi moved quickly to take the Gungan in hand, propelling him forcibly through the main cabin door and into the anteway beyond. Ignoring Jar Jar's protests, he glanced about for somewhere to stash the bothersome creature. Catching sight of a low, cramped entry with the words ASTROMECH DROIDS lettered above, he released the retaining latch and shoved the Gungan inside.

"Stay here," he directed with a meaningful look. "And keep out of trouble."

Jar Jar Binks watched the door close behind him, then glanced around. A line of five R2 astromech droids stood against one wall, short, dome-topped, all-purpose mechanics painted different colors, their lights off, their engines quiet. Five identical units, each stout body positioned between two sturdy restraint arms, they gave no indication of being aware of him. The Gungan ambled along in front of them, waiting to be noticed. Maybe they weren't activated, he thought. Maybe they weren't even alive.

"Heydey ho, yous," he tried, hands gesturing. "Tis a long trip somewheres, hey?"

No response. Jar Jar tapped the closest R2 unit, a bright red droid, on the head. The tap made a hollow sound, and the head popped up a notch from the cylindrical body.

"Whoa!" Jar Jar said, surprised. He glanced around, wondering why the Jedi had put him down here when everyone else was up there. Nothing much to do down here, he thought disconsolately. Nothing much happening.

Curious, he gripped the red droid's head and lifted gently. "Dis opens?" he whispered. He lifted some more. Something caught. He yanked hard. "Dis . . . ooops!"

The head lifted right out of its seating. Springs and wires popped out in a tangled mess. Jar Jar quickly jammed the red droid's head back into place, easing his three-fingered hands away cautiously.

"Oh, oh, oh," he murmured, glancing about to make sure no one had seen, hugging himself worriedly.

He moved down the line of droids, still looking for something to occupy his time. He didn't want to be in this room, but he didn't think he should try to leave, either. The younger Jedi, the one who had stuck him in here, didn't like him much as it was. The Jedi would like him a whole lot less if he caught Jar Jar sneaking out of this room.

Explosions sounded close by the transport. Cannon fire. The ship rocked in response to a series of near misses. Jar Jar looked about wildly, suddenly not liking where he was at all. Then the running lights began to flicker, and the transport shook violently. Jar Jar moaned, and crouched down in a corner. More explosions sounded, and the craft was buffeted from side to side.

"We doomed," the frightened Gungan muttered. "Tis bad business, dis."

Abruptly the ship began to spin as if caught in a whirlpool. Jar Jar cried out, fastening his arms about a strut to keep from being thrown against the walls. The lights in the compartment all came on, and the droids were abruptly activated. One by one, they began to whir and beep. Released from their restraints, they rolled out of their racks toward an airlock at one end of the compartment—all but the red R2, who rolled directly into a wall and fell over, more parts tumbling out.

The R2 unit painted blue paused as it motored by its red counterpart, then charged past Jar Jar, giving out a loud screech that caused the Gungan to jerk away in fright.

One after another, the four R2 units entered the airlock lift and were sucked up toward the top of the ship.

Left behind in the storage compartment with the droid he had unwittingly sabotaged, Jar Jar Binks moaned in despair.

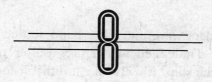

Obi-Wan Kenobi had just reentered the transport's cockpit when explosions began to buffet the ship. He could see a huge Trade Federation battleship looming ahead through the viewport, cannons firing. The Queen's transport was rocked so violently by the blasts that it was thrown from its trajectory. Ric Olié's gloved hands were locked onto the steering grips, fighting to bring the slender craft back into line.

"We should abort, sir!" the pilot shouted at Qui-Gon, who was braced at his side, eyes fixed on the battleship. "Our deflector shields can't withstand much more of this!"

"Stay on course," the Jedi Master ordered calmly. He glanced down at the controls. "Do you have a cloaking device?"

"This is not a warship!" Captain Panaka snapped, looking angry and betrayed. "We have no weapons, Ambassador! We're a nonviolent people, which is why the Trade Federation was brave enough to attack us in the first place!"

A series of explosions jarred the Nubian, and the lights on the control panel flickered weakly. An alarm sounded, shrill and angry. The transport shuddered, its power drive stalling momentarily in a high-pitched whine.

"No weapons," Qui-Gon Jinn breathed. Obi-Wan was next to him, feeling the weight of the other's gaze as it shifted to find him, steady and unwavering. One hand settled on Ric Olié's shoulder. "The Trade Federation uses pulser tracking for its weapons. Spin the ship. It will make it difficult for them to get a reading on us."

The pilot nodded, flipped a series of levers, and put the Nubian into a slow spin. Ahead, the battleship filled the viewport, then lost focus. The Queen's transport accelerated, racing toward the enemy craft, whipping past towers and gunports, bays and stabilizers, speeding down an alleyway of jagged metal protrusions and cannon fire. A laser bolt hammered into them, causing sparks and smoke to explode from one panel, sending the ship reeling. For a brief moment they were tumbling out of control. Then Ric Olié pulled back hard on the controls, and the hull of the battleship receded.

"Something's wrong," the pilot announced quietly, fighting the steering, feeling the ship shudder beneath. "Shields are down!"

They continued to spin, to hug the cavernous shell of the Trade Federation battleship, so close that the larger guns were rendered useless and only the smaller could chance firing at them. But without shields even a glancing hit could be disastrous.

"Sending out the repair crew!" Olié shouted, and flipped a lever.

On the viewscreen, an airlock snapped open, and one by one a series of astromech droids popped out of the hatch and onto the transport's hull. The transport straightened and leveled out, and the spinning stopped. The droids motored swiftly across the hull, seeking out the damage as Ric Olié hugged the battleship's shadow in an effort to protect them.

But now there was a new threat. Unable to bring the weapons of their warship to bear in an effective manner, the Trade Federation command dispatched a squad of starfighters. Small, sleek, robot attack ships, they consisted of twin compartments attached to a rounded, swept-back head. As they roared out of the battleship bays, their compartments opened into long slits that exposed their laser guns. Down the length of the mother ship they tore, seeking out the Queen's transport. Fast and maneuverable, they had no trouble working close to the battleship's hull. In seconds, they were on top of the transport, weapons firing. Ric Olié struggled to find cover and gain speed. Two of the R2 units were blown away, one on a direct hit, the second when its hold on the transport hull was shattered.

On the viewscreen, the blue R2 unit could be seen working furiously to connect a series of wires exposed by a damaged hull plate. Laser fire lanced all around it, but it continued its effort without stopping. The fourth droid, working close by, disappeared in a cloud of shattered metal and brilliant fire.

Now only the blue unit remained, still busy amid the onslaught of Trade Federation starfighters. Something changed on the cockpit display, and Ric Olié gave a shout of approval. "The shields are up! That little droid did it!" He jammed the thrusters all the way forward, and the transport rocketed away from both the battleship and the starfighters, leaving the Trade Federation blockade and the planet of Naboo behind.

The lone R2 unit turned and motored back into the airlock and disappeared from view.

When they were well away from any Trade Federation presence, Ric Olié made a thorough check of the controls, assessing their damage, trying to determine what was needed. Obi-Wan sat next to him in the copilot's seat, lending help. Qui-Gon and Captain Panaka stood behind them, awaiting their report. The Queen and the rest of the Naboo had been secured in other chambers.

Ric Olié shook his head doubtfully. "We can't go far. The hyperdrive is leaking."

Qui-Gon Jinn nodded. "We'll have to land somewhere to make repairs to the ship. What's out there?"

Ric Olié punched in a star chart, and they hunched over the monitor, studying it.

"Here, Master," Obi-Wan said, his sharp eyes picking out the only choice that made any sense. "Tatooine. It's small, poor, and out of the way. It attracts little attention. The Trade Federation has no presence there."

"How can you be sure?" Captain Panaka asked quickly.

Qui-Gon glanced at him. "It's controlled by the Hutts."

Panaka started in alarm. "The Hutts?"

"It's risky," Obi-Wan agreed, "but there's no reasonable alternative."

Captain Panaka was not convinced. "You can't take Her Royal Highness there! The Hutts are gangsters and slavers! If they discovered who she was—"

"It would be no different than if we landed on a planet in a system controlled by the Trade Federation," Qui-Gon interrupted, "except the Hutts aren't looking for the Queen, which gives us an advantage."

The Queen's head of security started to say something more, then thought better of it. He took a deep breath instead, frustration etched on his smooth, dark face, and turned away.

Qui-Gon Jinn tapped Ric Olié on the shoulder. "Set course for Tatooine."

In a remote conference room on the Trade Federation's flagship, Nute Gunray and Rune Haako sat side by side at a long table, staring nervously at a hologram of Darth Sidious positioned at the table's head. The hologram shimmered with the movements of the Sith Lord's dark cloak, a patchwork of small nuances that the Neimoidians found themselves unable to read.

The Sith Lord had not been summoned. The Neimoidians would have been happy if he had chosen not to communicate with them at all this day. But in keeping with the way he always seemed to sense when things were not going right, he had appeared on his own. Demanding a report on the progress of the invasion, he had settled back to listen to Nute Gunray's narrative and had said nothing since.

"We control all the cities in the northern and western part of the Naboo territory," the viceroy was relating, "and we are searching for any other settlements where resistance—"

"Yes, yes," Darth Sidious interrupted suddenly, his soft voice vaguely impatient. "You've done well. Now, then. Destroy all their high-ranking officials. Do so quietly, but be thorough." He paused. "What of Queen Amidala? Has she signed the treaty?"

Nute Gunray took a deep breath and let it out slowly. "She has disappeared, my lord. There was an escape—"

"An escape?" The Sith Lord spoke the words in a low hiss.

"One Naboo cruiser got past the blockade—"

"How did she escape, Viceroy?"

Nute Gunray looked at Rune Haako for help, but his counterpart was paralyzed with fear. "The Jedi, my lord. They found their way to her, overpowered her guards . . ."

Darth Sidious stirred within his robes like a big cat, shadows glimmering within the confines of his concealing hood. "Viceroy, find her! I want that treaty signed!"

"My lord, we have been unable to locate the ship she escaped on," the Neimoidian admitted, wishing he could sink into the floor right then and there.

"Viceroy!"

"Once it got by us, we tried to give pursuit, but it managed to elude us! Now it's out of our range—"

A wave of one robed arm cut him short. "Not for a Sith, it isn't," the other whispered.

Something shimmered in the background of the hologram, and a figure emerged from the darkness behind Darth Sidious. Nute Gunray froze. It was a second Sith Lord. But whereas Darth Sidious was a vague and shadowy presence, this new Sith was truly terrifying to look upon. His face was a mask of jagged red and black patterns, the design etched into his skin, and his skull was hairless and studded with a crown of short, hooked horns. Gleaming yellow eyes fixed on the Neimoidians, breaking past their defenses, stripping them bare and dismissing them as insignificant and foolish.

"Viceroy," Darth Sidious spoke softly in the sudden silence, "this is my apprentice, Lord Maul. He will find your lost ship."

Nute Gunray inclined his head slightly in acknowledgment, averting his eyes from the frightening presence. "Yes, my lord."

The hologram shimmered and disappeared, leaving the conference room empty of sound. The Neimoidians sat without moving, without even looking at each other, reptilian eyes fixed on the space the hologram had occupied.

"This is getting out of hand," Nute Gunray ventured finally, his voice high and tight, thinking that their plans for sabotaging the trade-routes tax did not contemplate risking their lives in the process.

Rune Haako managed a quick nod. "We should not have made this bargain. What will happen when the Jedi become aware that we are doing business with these Sith Lords?"

Nute Gunray, his hands clasped tightly before him, did not care to venture an answer.

Aboard the Queen's transport, the Jedi stood with Captain Panaka and the remaining R2 unit as the captain gave his report to the Queen on the events surrounding their escape through the Trade Federation blockade. Amidala sat surrounded by her three handmaidens, white face framed by the black headdress, dark eyes steady, listening as the captain concluded.

"We are lucky to have this one in our service, Your Highness." Panaka glanced down at the blue-domed astromech droid. "It is an extremely well put together little droid. Without a doubt, it saved the ship back there, not to mention our lives."

Amidala nodded, eyes shifting to the droid. "It is to be commended. What is its number?"

The little blue droid, lights blinking on and off as it processed the conversation, gave a series of small beeps and tweets. Captain Panaka reached down and scraped a large smudge off the droid's metal shell, then straightened.

"Artoo-Detoo, Your Highness."

Queen Amidala leaned forward, and a slender white hand came out to touch the droid's domed casing. "Thank you, Artoo-Detoo. You have proven both loyal and brave." She glanced over her shoulder. "Padmé."

One of her handmaidens came forward. Qui-Gon Jinn, listening to the exchange with half an ear as he considered the problems that lay ahead on Tatooine, noticed it was the young woman who had supported the Queen's decision to escape from Naboo. He frowned. Except, it hadn't been exactly like that . . .

"See to the cleaning up of this little droid." The Queen was speaking to the girl. "Artoo-Detoo deserves our gratitude." She turned back to Panaka. "Please continue with your report, Captain."

Panaka glanced uncomfortably at the Jedi Knights. "Your Highness, we are heading for a remote planet called Tatooine." He paused, unwilling to speak further on the matter.

"It is a system far beyond the reach of the Trade Federation." Qui-Gon stepped into the gap smoothly. "Once there, we will be able to make needed repairs to the ship, then to travel on to Coruscant and complete our journey."

"Your Highness," Captain Panaka said quickly, regaining his thoughts on the matter. "Tatooine is very dangerous. It's controlled by the Hutts. The Hutts are gangsters and slavers. I do not agree with the Jedi on their decision to land there."

The Queen looked at Qui-Gon. The Jedi did not waver. "You must trust my judgment, Your Highness."

"Must I?" Amidala asked quietly. She shifted her gaze to her handmaidens, ending with Padmé. The girl had not moved from the Queen's side, but seemed to remember suddenly she had been given a task to complete. She nodded briefly to the Queen, and moved to take R2-D2 in hand.

Amidala looked back at Qui-Gon Jinn. "We are in your hands," she advised, and the matter was settled.

Jar Jar Binks had been left in the droid storage hold until after the lone R2 unit returned through the airlock and the Naboo came to retrieve it. They didn't seem to have any orders regarding the Gungan, so they simply left him to his own devices. At first Jar Jar was reluctant to venture out, still thinking of the younger Jedi's admonishment to stay put and out of trouble. He'd managed one out of two, and he wasn't sure he wanted to tempt fate.

But in the end his curiosity and restlessness got the better of him. The transport had stopped spinning, the Trade Federation attack had ceased, and the warning alarms had been silenced. Everything was peaceful, and the Gungan saw no reason why he should have to stay shut away in this tiny room for one more minute.

So he cracked the door, stuck his billed face out for a look around, eyestalks swiveling guardedly, saw no one, and made his decision. He left the storage room and wandered along the ship's corridors—choosing a path that took him away from the cockpit, where the Jedi were likely to be found. He waited for someone to tell him to go back to where he had come from, but no one did, so he began to poke into things, careful what he touched, but unable to help himself sufficiently to forgo all investigation.

He was following a narrow corridor that led up from the lower levels of the transport to the main cabin when he poked his head through an airlock to find one of the Queen's handmaidens hard at work with an old cloth cleaning the R2 astromech droid.

"Heydey ho!" he called out.

The handmaiden and the R2 unit both started, the girl with a small cry and the droid with a loud beep. Jar Jar jumped in turn, then slowly eased himself through the opening, embarrassed that he had frightened them so badly.

"Me sorry," he apologized. "Me not mean to scare yous. Okeday?"

The girl smiled. "That's all right. Come over here."

Jar Jar came forward a few steps, studying the condition of the droid. "Me find oilcan back dere. Yous need it?"

The girl nodded. "It would help. This little guy is quite a mess."

Jar Jar scrambled back through the opening, groped about a

bit, found the oilcan he had remembered, and brought it to the girl. "This helps?"

"Thank you," she said, accepting the can. She flipped up the cap and poured some of the oil onto the cloth, then began rubbing the R2 unit's dome.

"Me Jar Jar Binks," Jar Jar said after a few moments, taking a chance on trying to continue the conversation. He liked this Naboo girl.

"I'm Padmé," the girl answered. "I attend Her Highness, Queen Amidala. This is Artoo-Detoo." She rubbed a black smudge from the droid's strut. "You're a Gungan, aren't you?" Jar Jar nodded, long ears flapping against his neck. "How did you end up here with us?"

Jar Jar thought about it a minute. "Me not know exactly. Da day start okeday wit da sunnup. Me munchen clams. Den, boom! Maccaneks every which way, dey flyen, dey scooten . . . Me get very scared. Den Jedi runnen, and me grab Quiggon, den maccaneks rollen over, den go down under da lake to Otoh Gunga ta da Boss Nass . . ."

He stopped, not knowing where else to go. Padmé was nodding encouragingly. R2-D2 beeped. "Tis 'bout it. Before me know what, pow! Me here!"

He sat back on his haunches and shrugged. "Get very, very scared."

He looked from the girl to the droid. Padmé smiled some more. R2-D2 beeped again. Jar Jar felt pretty good.

In the cockpit, Ric Olié was directing the transport toward a large yellowish planet that was steadily filling up the viewport as they approached its surface. The Jedi and Captain Panaka stood behind him, peering over his shoulder at the ground maps he had punched up on the monitors.

"Tatooine," Obi-Wan Kenobi confirmed, speaking to no one in particular.

Ric Olié pointed to one of the maps on the scopes. "There's

a settlement that should have what we need . . . a spaceport, it looks like. Mos Espa." He glanced up at the Jedi.

"Land near the city's outskirts," Qui-Gon Jinn ordered. "We don't want to attract attention."

The pilot nodded and began to guide the transport in. It took only moments to direct it down through the planet's atmosphere to a patch of desert just in sight of the city. The Nubian landed in a swirl of dust, settling comfortably in place atop its landing struts. In the distance, Mos Espa glimmered faintly through the shimmer of the midday heat.

Qui-Gon sent his protégé to uncouple the hyperdrive and Captain Panaka to advise the Queen of their landing. He was settled on going into the spaceport alone as he left the cockpit to find other clothing and came upon Jar Jar Binks, the Queen's handmaiden Padmé, and the little R2 unit.

He slowed, considering the possibility that going into the city alone would make him more noticeable. "Jar Jar," he said finally. "Get ready. You're going with me. The droid as well."

He continued on without looking back. The Gungan stared after him in disbelief, then in horror. By the time he regained his wits, the Jedi was out of view. Wailing in dismay, he chased after him and came upon Obi-Wan in the main cabin hoisting the hyperdrive out of the bowels of the ship.

"Obi-One, sire!" he gasped, throwing himself to his knees in front of the younger Jedi. "Pleeese, me no go wit Quiggon!"

Obi-Wan was inclined to agree, but knew better than to say so. "Sorry, but Qui-Gon is right. This is a multinational spaceport, a trading center. You'll make him appear less obvious by going along." His brow furrowed as he turned back to the hyperdrive. "I hope," he muttered to himself.

Jar Jar climbed to his feet and trudged disconsolately toward R2-D2, his mouth set in a grimace of forbearance. The astromech droid beeped in sympathy, then made a series of encouraging clicks.

Qui-Gon reappeared, dressed now as a farmer in tunic,

leggings, and a poncho. He walked past them to where Obi-Wan was studying the hyperdrive. "What have you found?"

Obi-Wan's young face clouded. "The generator is shot. We'll need a new one."

"I thought as much." The Jedi Master knelt next to his protégé. "Well, we can't risk a communication with Coruscant this far out on the edge of the galaxy. It might be intercepted and our position revealed. We'll have to get by on our own." He lowered his voice to a near whisper. "Don't let anyone send a transmission while I'm gone. Be wary, Obi-Wan. I sense a disturbance in the Force."

Obi-Wan's eyes lifted to find his. "I feel it also, Master. I will be careful."

Qui-Gon rose, gathered up Jar Jar and the R2 unit, and headed down the loading ramp to the planet's floor. An empty carpet of sand stretched away in all directions, broken only by massive rock formations and the distant skyline of Mos Espa. The suns that gave the planet life beat down with such ferocity that it seemed as if they were determined to steal that life back again. Heat rose off the sand in a shimmering wave, and the air was so dry it sucked the moisture from their throat and nose passages.

Jar Jar glanced skyward, eyestalks craning, billed amphibious face wrinkling in dismay. "Dis sun gonna do murder ta da skin of dis Gungan," he muttered.

At a signal from Qui-Gon, they began to walk—or, in the case of the R2 unit, to roll. A strange caravan of animals and riders, carts and sleds appeared against the distant skyline like a shadowy mirage, all misshapen and threatening to evaporate in the blink of an eye. Jar Jar muttered some more, but no one was paying attention.

They had not gotten far when a shout brought them around. Two figures were running toward them from the transport. As they neared, Qui-Gon was able to make out Captain Panaka and a girl dressed in rough peasant's garb. He stopped and waited until they caught up, a frown creasing his leonine features.

Panaka was sweating. "Her Highness commands you to take her handmaiden with you. She wishes for Padmé to give her own report of what you might—"

"No more commands from Her Highness today, Captain," Qui-Gon interrupted quickly, shaking his head in refusal. "Mos Espa is not going to be a pleasant place for—"

"The Queen wishes it," Panaka interrupted him right back, his face angry and set. "She is emphatic. She wishes to know more about this planet."

The girl took a step forward. Her dark eyes found Qui-Gon's. "I've been trained in self-defense. I speak a number of languages. I am not afraid. I can take care of myself."

Captain Panaka sighed, looking over his shoulder toward the ship. "Don't make me go back and tell her you refuse."

Qui-Gon hesitated, prepared to do exactly that. Then he looked at Padmé again, saw strength in her eyes, and changed his mind. She might be useful. Traveling with a girl, they might suggest a family in transit and present a less aggressive look.

He nodded. "I don't have time to argue the matter, Captain. I still think this is a bad idea, but she may come." He gave Padmé a look of warning. "Stay close to me."

He started away again, the others trailing. Captain Panaka stood watching with undisguised relief as the strange little procession of Jedi Master, handmaiden, Gungan, and astromech droid moved off into the sweltering landscape toward Mos Espa.

It was not yet midafternoon by the time the members of the little company under Qui-Gon Jinn's command reached Mos Espa and made their way toward the spaceport's center. Mos Espa was large and sprawling and had the look of a gnarled serpent hunkered down in the sand to escape the heat. The buildings were domed and thick-walled and curved to protect against the sun, and the stalls and shops were fronted by awnings and verandas that provided a measure of shade to their vendors. Streets were broad and packed with beings of every shape and size, most from off planet. Some rode the desert-seasoned eopies. Domesticated banthas, massive and horned, and lumbering dewbacks hauled carts, sleds, and wagons that ran on wheels and mechanical tracks by turn, a mishmash of commerce trafficking between Tatooine's smaller ports and the planets of star systems beyond.

Qui-Gon kept a close watch for trouble. There were Rodians and Dugs and others whose purpose was always suspect. Most of those they passed paid them no notice. One or two turned to glance at Jar Jar, but dismissed the Gungan almost out of hand once they got a good look at him. As a group, they blended in nicely. There were so many combinations of creatures of every species that the appearance of one more meant almost nothing.

"Tatooine is home to Jabba the Hutt, who controls the bulk of the trafficking in illegal goods, piracy, and slavery that generates most of the planet's wealth," Qui-Gon was explaining to Padmé. He had been on Tatooine before, though it had been some years ago. "Jabba controls the spaceports and settlements, all of the populated areas. The desert belongs to the Jawas, who scavenge whatever they can find to sell or trade, and to the Tuskens, who live a nomadic life and feel free to steal from everyone."

The Jedi kept his voice low and conversational. The girl walked silently at his elbow, her sharp eyes taking in everything. Speeders nosed by them, and droids of every size toiled in the service of desert-garbed aliens.

"There are a number of farms as well, outlying operations that take advantage of the climate—moisture farms for the most part, operated by off-worlders not a part of the indigenous tribes and scavengers, not connected directly to the Hutts." His eyes swept the street ahead. "This is a rough and dangerous place. Most avoid it. Its few spaceports have become havens for those who do not wish to be found."

Padmé glanced up at him. "Like us," she said.

A pair of domesticated banthas rumbled down the broad avenue, hairy bulks clearing a path for a sled train of quarry blocks and metal struts, horned heads nodding sleepily, padded feet stirring sand and dust in thick clouds with each lumbering step. Their driver dozed atop the foremost sled in the train, small and insignificant in their shadow.

Jar Jar Binks stayed as close as he could manage to the Jedi and the girl, his eyes darting left and right, head swiveling as if it might twist right off his shoulders. Nothing he saw was familiar or welcome. Hard looks followed after him. Sharp eyes measured him for things he would just as soon not think about. Stares were at best challenging and at worst unfriendly. He did not like this place. He wished he were almost anywhere else.

"Tis very bad, dis." He swallowed against a dryness in his throat that was caused by more than the heat. "Nutten good 'bout dis place!" He took a careless step and found himself ankle deep in a foul-smelling ooze. "Oh, oh. Tis icky!"

R2-D2 rolled cheerfully along at his side, beeping and chirping in a futile effort at reassuring the Gungan that all was well.

They traveled the main street of the spaceport to its far end and turned down a side street that led to a small plaza ringed with salvage dealers and junk shops. Qui-Gon glanced at the mounds of engine parts, control panels, and communication chips recovered from starships and speeders.

"We'll try one of these smaller dealers first," he advised, nodding toward one in which a vast pile of old transports and parts was heaped within an attached compound.

They walked through the shop's low entry and were greeted by a pudgy blue creature who flew into their faces like a crazed probe, tiny wings buzzing so fast they could barely be seen. *"Hi chubba da nago?"* it snapped in a frizzy, guttural voice, demanding to know their business.

A Toydarian, Qui-Gon thought. He knew enough to recognize one, but not much else. "I need parts for a J-type 327 Nubian," he advised the other.

The Toydarian fairly beamed with delight, his reticular snout curling over his toothy mouth and making odd smacking noises. "Ah, yes! Nubian! We have lots of that." The sharp, bulbous eyes flicked from one face to the other, ending with the Gungan. "What's this?"

Jar Jar shrank behind Qui-Gon fearfully. "Never mind that." The Jedi brushed the Toydarian's question aside. "Can you help us or not?"

"Can you pay me or not—that's the question!" The skinny blue arms crossed defiantly over the rounded torso as the Toydarian regarded them with disdain. "What kinda junk you after, farmer?"

"My droid has a readout of what I need," Qui-Gon advised the other with a glance down at the R2 unit.

Still hanging midair in front of Qui-Gon's nose, the Toydarian glanced over one shoulder. *"Peedunkel! Naba dee unko!"*

A small, disheveled boy raced in from the salvage yard, coming to an uncertain stop in front of them. His clothes were ragged and thick with grime, and he had the look of someone about to be given a beating. He flinched as the Toydarian wheeled back and lifted a hand in admonishment.

"What took you so long?"

"Mel tass cho-pas kee," the boy responded quickly, blue eyes taking in the newcomers with a quick glance. "I was cleaning out the bin like you—"

"Chut-chut!" The Toydarian threw up his hands angrily. "Never mind the bin! Watch the store! I've got some selling to do!"

He flitted back around to face his customers. "So, let me take you out back. You'll soon find what you need."

He darted toward the salvage yard, beckoning Qui-Gon eagerly. The Jedi followed, with R2-D2 trundling after. Jar Jar moved to a shelf and picked up an odd-looking bit of metal, intrigued by its shape, wondering what it was.

"Don't touch anything," Qui-Gon called over his shoulder, his tone of voice sharp.

Jar Jar put the item down and made a face at Qui-Gon's departing back, sticking out his long tongue in defiance. When the Jedi was out of sight, he picked up the part again.

Anakin Skywalker could not take his eyes off the girl. He noticed her the moment he entered Watto's shop, even before Watto said anything, and he hadn't been able to stop looking at her since. He barely heard what Watto said to him about watching the shop. He barely noticed the strange-looking creature that had come in with her and was poking around in the shelves and bins. Even after she noticed he was staring at her, he could not help himself.

He moved now to an open space on the counter, hoisted himself up, and sat watching her while pretending to clean a transmitter cell. She was looking back at him now, embarrassment turning to curiosity. She was small and slender with long, braided brown hair, brown eyes, and a face he found so beautiful that he had nothing to which he could compare it. She was dressed in rough peasant's clothing, but she seemed very self-possessed.

She gave him an amused smile, and he felt himself melting in confusion and wonder. He took a deep breath. "Are you an angel?" he asked quietly.

The girl stared. "What?"

"An angel." Anakin straightened a bit. "They live on the moons of Iego, I think. They are the most beautiful creatures in the universe. They are good and kind, and so pretty they make even the most hardened space pirates cry like small children."

She gave him a confused look. "I've never heard of angels," she said.

"You must be one of them," Anakin insisted. "Maybe you just don't know it."

"You're a funny little boy." The amused smile returned. "How do you know so much?"

Anakin smiled back and shrugged. "I listen to all the traders and pilots who come through here." He glanced toward the salvage yard. "I'm a pilot, you know. Someday, I'm going to fly away from this place."

The girl wandered to one end of the counter, looked away, then back again. "Have you been here long?"

"Since I was very little—three, I think. My mom and I were sold to Gardulla the Hutt, but she lost us to Watto, betting on the pod races. Watto's a lot better master, I think."

She stared at him in shock. "You're a slave?"

The way she said it made Anakin feel ashamed and angry. He glared at her defiantly. "I am a person!"

"I'm sorry," she said quickly, looking upset and embarrassed. "I don't fully understand, I guess. This is a strange world to me."

He studied her intently for a moment, thinking of other things, wanting to tell her of them. "You are a strange girl to me," he said instead. He swung his legs out from the counter. "My name is Anakin Skywalker."

She brushed at her hair. "Padmé Naberrie."

The strange creature she had come in with wandered back to the front of the shop and bent over a stout little droid body with a bulbous nose. Reaching up curiously, it pushed at the nose with one finger. Instantly armatures popped out from every direction, metal limbs swinging into place. The droid's motors whizzed and whirred, and it jerked to life and began moving forward. Padmé's odd companion went after it with a moan of dismay, grabbing on in an effort to slow it down, but the droid continued marching through the shop, knocking over everything it came in contact with.

"Hit the nose!" Anakin called out, unable to keep himself from laughing.

The creature did as it was told, pounding the droid's nose wildly. The droid stopped at once, the arms and legs retracted, the motors shut down, and the droid went still. Both Anakin and Padmé were laughing now, and their laughter increased as they saw the look on the unfortunate creature's long-billed face.

Anakin looked at Padmé and the girl at him. Their laughter died away. The girl reached up to touch her hair self-consciously, but she did not divert her gaze.

"I'm going to marry you," the boy said suddenly.

There was a moment of silence, and she began laughing again, a sweet musical sound he didn't mind at all. The creature who accompanied her rolled his eyes.

"I mean it," he insisted.

"You are an odd one," she said, her laughter dying away. "Why do you say that?"

He hesitated. "I guess because it's what I believe . . ."

Her smile was dazzling. "Well, I'm afraid I can't marry you . . ." She paused, searching her memory for his name.

"Anakin," he said.

"Anakin." She cocked her head. "You're just a little boy."

His gaze was intense as he faced her. "I won't always be," he said quietly.

* * *

In the salvage yard, Watto was studying the screen of a portable memory bank he held in one hand, tracing through his inventory record. Qui-Gon, arms folded into his farmer's poncho, stood waiting patiently, the R2 unit at his side.

"Ah, here it is. A T-14 hyperdrive generator!" The Toydarian's wings beat wildly as he hovered before the Jedi, his gnarled finger jabbing at the viewscreen. "You're in luck. I'm the only one hereabouts who has one. But you might as well buy a new ship. It would be cheaper. Speaking of which, how're you going to pay for all this, farmer?"

Qui-Gon considered. "I have twenty thousand Republic dataries to put toward—"

"Republic credits?" Watto exploded in disgust. "Republic credits are no good out here! I need something better than that, something of value . . ."

The Jedi Master shook his head. "I don't have anything else." One hand came up, passing casually in front of the Toydarian's face. "But credits will do fine."

"No, they won't!" Watto snapped, buzzing angrily.

Qui-Gon frowned, then passed his hand in front of the pudgy blue alien again, bringing the full force of his Jedi suggestive power to bear. "Credits will do fine," he repeated.

Watto sneered. "No, they won't!" he repeated. "What do you think you're doing, waving your hand around like that? You think you're some kinda Jedi? Hah! I'm a Toydarian! Mind tricks don't work on me—only money! No money, no parts, no deal! And no one else has a T-14 hyperdrive generator, I can promise you that!"

Chagrined, Qui-Gon wheeled back for the shop, the R2 unit following at his heels. The Toydarian shouted after them to come back when they had something worthwhile to trade, still scolding the Jedi Master for trying to foist Republic credits on him. Qui-Gon reentered the shop just as Jar Jar pulled a part from a large stack and sent the entire arrangement tumbling to the floor. His efforts at correcting the problem brought a second display crashing down as well.

The boy and the Queen's handmaiden were deep in discussion, paying no attention to the Gungan.

"We're leaving," Qui-Gon announced to the girl, moving toward the shop's entry, the R2 unit trundling along behind.

Jar Jar was quick to follow, anxious to escape his latest mess. Padmé gave the boy a warm smile. "I'm glad I met you, Anakin," she said, turning after them.

"I'm glad I met you, too," he called after, a reluctance evident in his voice.

Watto flew in from the salvage yard, shaking his head in disgust. "Outlanders! They think because we live so far from everything, we know nothing!"

Anakin was still staring longingly after Padmé, his gaze fixed on the empty doorway. "They seemed nice enough to me."

Watto snorted and flew into his face. "Clean up this mess, then you can go home!"

Anakin brightened, gave a small cheer, and went quickly to work.

Qui-Gon led his companions back through the little plaza of salvage shops toward the main avenue. At a place where two buildings divided to form a shadowed niche, the Jedi Master moved everyone from view and brought out his comlink from beneath his poncho. Padmé and the R2 unit stood waiting patiently, but Jar Jar prowled the space as if trapped, eyes fixed nervously on the busy street.

When Obi-Wan responded to the comlink's pulse, Qui-Gon quickly filled him in on the situation. "Are you sure there isn't anything of value left on board?" he concluded.

There was a pause at the other end. "A few containers of supplies, the Queen's wardrobe, some jewelry maybe. Not enough for you to barter with. Not in the amounts you're talking about."

"All right," Qui-Gon responded with a frown. "Another solution will present itself. I'll check back."

He tucked the comlink beneath his poncho and signaled to the others. He was moving toward the street again when Jar Jar grabbed his arm.

"Noah gain, sire," the Gungan pleaded. "Da beings here-abouts crazy nuts. We goen be robbed and crunched!"

"Not likely," Qui-Gon replied with a sigh, freeing himself. "We have nothing of value. That's our problem."

They started back down the street, Qui-Gon trying to think what to do next. Padmé and R2-D2 stayed close as they made their way through the crowds, but Jar Jar began to lag behind, distracted by all the strange sights and smells. They were passing an outdoor café, its tables occupied by a rough-looking bunch of aliens, among them a Dug who was holding forth on the merits of Podracing. Jar Jar hurried to catch up to his companions, but then caught sight of a string of frogs hanging from a wire in front of a nearby stall. The Gungan slowed, his mouth watering. He had not eaten in some time. He glanced around to see if anyone was looking, then unfurled his long tongue and snapped up one of the frogs. The frog disappeared into Jar Jar's mouth in the blink of an eye.

Unfortunately, the frog was still securely tied to the wire. Jar Jar stood there, the wire hanging out of his mouth, unable to move.

The vendor in charge of the stall rushed out. "Hey, that will be seven truguts!"

Jar Jar glanced frantically down the street for his compan-ions, but they were already out of sight. In desperation, he let go of the frog. The frog popped out of his mouth as if catapulted, winging away at the end of the taut wire. It ricocheted this way and that, breaking free at last to land directly in the Dug's soup, splashing gooey liquid all over him.

The gangly Dug leapt to his feet in fury, catching sight of the hapless Jar Jar as he tried to move away from the frog vendor. Springing across the table on all fours, he was on top of the Gun-gan in an instant, grabbing him by the throat.

"*Chubba!* You!" the Dug snarled through its corded snout. Feelers and mandibles writhed. "Is this yours?"

The Dug shoved the frog in the Gungan's face threateningly. Jar Jar could not get any words out, gasping for breath, fighting to break free. His eyes rolled wildly as he looked for help that wasn't there. Other creatures pushed forward to surround him, Rodians among them. The Dug threw Jar Jar to the ground, shouting at him, hovering over him in a crouch. Desperately, the Gungan tried to scramble to safety.

"No, no," he moaned plaintively as he sought an avenue of escape. "Why me always da one?"

"Because you're afraid," a voice answered calmly.

Anakin Skywalker pushed his way through the crowd, coming up to stand next to the Dug. The boy seemed unafraid of the creature, undeterred by the hard-eyed crowd, his bearing self-assured. He gave the Dug an appraising look. "*Chess ko*, Sebulba," he said. "Careful. This one's very well connected."

Sebulba turned to face the boy, cruel face twisting with disdain as he caught sight of the newcomer. "*Tooney rana dunko, shag?*" he snapped, demanding to know what the boy meant.

Anakin shrugged. "Connected—as in Hutt." The blue eyes fixed the Dug and saw a hint of fear in the other's face. "Big-time connected, this one, Sebulba. I'd hate to see you diced before we had a chance to race again."

The Dug spit in fury. "*Neek me chawa!* Next time we race, *wermo*, it will be the end of you!" He gestured violently. "*Uto notu wo shag!* If you weren't a slave, I'd squash you here and now!"

With a final glare at the cringing Jar Jar, Sebulba wheeled away, taking his companions with him, back to their tables and their food and drink. Anakin stared after the Dug. "Yeah, it'd be a pity if you had to pay for me," he said softly.

He was helping Jar Jar back to his feet when Qui-Gon, Padmé, and R2-D2, having finally missed the Gungan, reappeared hurriedly through the crowd.

"Hi!" he greeted cheerfully, happy to see Padmé again so soon. "Your buddy here was about to be turned into orange goo. He picked a fight with a Dug. An especially dangerous Dug."

"Nossir, nossir!" the chagrined Gungan insisted, brushing off dust and sand. "Me hate crunchen. Tis da last thing me want!"

Qui-Gon gave Jar Jar a careful once-over, glanced around at the crowd, and took the Gungan by the arm. "Nevertheless, the boy saved you from a beating. You have a penchant for finding trouble, Jar Jar." He gave Anakin a short nod. "Thank you, my young friend."

Padmé gave Anakin a warm smile as well, and the boy felt himself blush with pride.

"Me doen nutten!" Jar Jar insisted, still trying to defend himself, hands gesturing for emphasis.

"You were afraid," the boy told him, looking up at the long-billed face solemnly. "Fear attracts the fearful. Sebulba was trying to overcome his fear by squashing you." He cocked his head at the Gungan. "You can help yourself by being less afraid."

"And that works for you?" Padmé asked skeptically, giving him a wry look.

Anakin smiled and shrugged. "Well . . . up to a point."

Anxious to spend as much time as possible with the girl, he persuaded the group to follow him a short distance down the street to a fruit stand, a ramshackle affair formed by a makeshift ragged awning stretched over a framework of bent poles. Boxes of brightly colored fruit were arranged on a rack tilted toward the street for viewing. A weathered old lady, gray-haired and stooped, her simple clothing patched and worn, rose from a stool to greet them on their approach.

"How are you feeling today, Jira?" Anakin asked her, giving her a quick hug.

The old lady smiled. "The heat's never been kind to me, you know, Annie."

"Guess what?" the boy replied quickly, beaming. "I've found that cooling unit I've been searching for. It's pretty beat up, but I'll have it fixed up for you in no time, I promise. That should help."

Jira reached out to brush his pink cheek with her wrinkled hand, her smile broadening. "You're a fine boy, Annie."

Anakin shrugged off the compliment and began scanning the fruit display. "I'll take four pallies, Jira." He glanced at Padmé eagerly. "You'll like these."

He reached into his pocket for the truguts he had been saving, but when he brought them out to pay Jira, he dropped one. The farmer, standing next to him, bent to retrieve it. As he did, his poncho opened just far enough that the boy caught sight of the lightsaber hanging from the belt about his waist.

The boy's eyes went wide, but he masked his surprise by focusing on the coins. He only had three, he found. "Whoops, I thought I had more," he said quickly, not looking up. "Make that three pallies, Jira. I'm not that hungry anyway."

The old woman gave Qui-Gon, Padmé, and Jar Jar their pallies and took the coins from Anakin. A gust of wind whipped down the street, rattling the framework of poles and causing the awning to billow. A second gust sent dust swirling in all directions.

Jira rubbed her arms with her gnarled hands. "Gracious, my bones are aching. There's a storm coming, Annie. You'd better get home quick."

The wind gusted in a series of sharp blasts that sent sand and loose debris flying. Anakin glanced at the sky, then at Qui-Gon. "Do you have shelter?" he asked.

The Jedi Master nodded. "We'll head back to our ship. Thank you again, my young friend, for—"

"Is your ship far?" the boy interrupted hurriedly. All around them, shopkeepers and vendors were closing and shuttering windows and doors, carrying goods and wares inside, wrapping coverings over displays and boxes.

"It's on the city's outskirts," Padmé answered, turning away from the stinging gusts of sand.

Anakin took her hand quickly, tugging on it. "You'll never

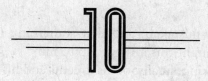

The sandstorm raged through the streets of Mos Espa in a blinding, choking whirlwind that tore at clothes and exposed skin with relentless force. Anakin held Padmé's hand so as not to lose her, the farmer, the amphibious creature, and the R2 unit trailing behind, fighting to reach his home in the city's slave quarters while there was still time. Other residents and visitors struggled past, engaged in a similar pursuit, heads lowered, faces covered, bodies bent over as if weighted by age. Somewhere in the distance, an eopie bawled in fright. The light turned an odd yellowish gray, obscured by sand and grit, and the buildings of the city disappeared in a deep, impenetrable haze.

Even as he fought his way through the storm, Anakin's thoughts were directed elsewhere. He was thinking of Padmé, of having the chance to take her home to meet his mother, of being able to show her his projects, of holding her hand some more. It sent a flush through him that was both warm and kind of scary. It made him feel good about himself. He was thinking of the farmer, too—if that's what he was, which Anakin was pretty sure he wasn't. He carried a lightsaber, and only Jedi carried lightsabers. It was almost too much to hope for, that a real Jedi might be going to his home, to visit him. But Anakin's instincts told him he was not mistaken, and that something mysterious and exciting had brought this little group to him.

He was thinking, finally, of his dreams and his hopes for himself and his mother, thinking that maybe something wonderful would come out of this unexpected encounter, something that would change his life forever.

They reached the slave quarters, a jumbled collection of hovels stacked one on top of the other so that they resembled anthills, each complex linked by common walls and switchback stairways, the plaza fronting them almost empty as the sandstorm chased everyone under cover. Anakin led his charges through the gritty gloom to his front door and pushed his way inside.

"Mom! Mom! I'm home!" he called excitedly.

Adobe walls, whitewashed and scrubbed, glimmered softly in a mix of storm-clouded sunlight admitted through small, arched windows and a diffuse electric glow from ceiling fixtures. They stood in the main room, a smallish space dominated by a table and chairs. A kitchen occupied one wall and a work space another. Openings led to smaller nooks and sleeping rooms.

Outside, the wind howled past the doors and windows, shaving a fresh layer of skin from the exterior of the walls.

Jar Jar Binks looked around with a mix of curiosity and relief. "Tis cozy," he murmured.

Anakin's mother entered from a work area off to one side, brushing her hands on her dress. She was a woman of forty, her long brown hair tied back from her worn face, her clothing rough and simple. She had been pretty once, and Anakin would say she was pretty still, but time and the demands of her life were catching up with her. Her smile was warm and youthful as she greeted her son, but it faded quickly as she caught sight of the people behind him.

"Oh, my!" she exclaimed softly, glancing uncertainly from face to face. "Annie, what's this?"

Anakin beamed. "These are my friends, Mom." He smiled at

Padmé. "This is Padmé Naberrie. And this is—" He stopped. "Gee, I guess I don't know any of your names," he admitted.

Qui-Gon stepped forward. "I'm Qui-Gon Jinn, and this is Jar Jar Binks." He indicated the Gungan, who made a sort of fluttering gesture with his hands.

The R2 unit made a small beep.

"And our droid, Artoo-Detoo," Padmé finished.

"I'm building a droid," Anakin announced quickly, anxious to show Padmé his project. "You wanna see?"

"Anakin!" His mother's voice stopped him in his tracks. Resolve tightened her features. "Anakin, why are they here?"

He looked at her, confused. "There's a sandstorm, Mom. Listen."

She glanced at the door, then out the windows. The wind howled past, a river of sand and grit.

"Your son was kind enough to offer us shelter," Qui-Gon explained. "We met at the shop where he works."

"Come on!" Anakin insisted, grabbing Padmé's hand once more. "Let me show you my droid."

He led Padmé toward his bedroom, already beginning a detailed explanation of what he was doing. The girl followed without arguing, listening attentively. R2-D2 went with them, beeping in response to the boy's words.

Jar Jar stayed where he was, still looking around, appearing to want someone to tell him what to do. Qui-Gon stood facing the boy's mother in awkward silence. Grains of sand beat against the thick glass of the windows with a rapid pocking sound.

"I'm Shmi Skywalker," she said, holding out her hand. "Anakin and I are pleased to have you as our guests."

Qui-Gon had already appraised the situation and determined what was needed. He reached under his poncho and pulled five small capsules from a pouch in his belt. "I know this is unexpected. Take these. There's enough food for a meal."

She accepted the capsules. "Thank you." Her eyes lifted and

lowered again. "Thank you very much. I'm sorry if I was abrupt. I'll never get used to Anakin's surprises, I guess."

"He's a very special boy," Qui-Gon offered.

Shmi's eyes lifted again, and the look she gave him suggested they shared an important secret.

"Yes," she said softly, "I know."

In his bedroom, Anakin was showing Padmé C-3PO. The droid lay on his workbench, deactivated at the moment because the boy was in the process of fabricating its metal skin. He had completed the internal wiring, but its torso, arms, and legs were still bare of any covering. One eye was out of its head as well, lying nearby where he had left it after tightening down the visual refractor the night before.

Padmé bent over his shoulder, studying the droid carefully.

"Isn't he great?" Anakin asked eagerly, anxious for her reaction. "He's not finished yet, but he will be soon."

"He's wonderful," the girl answered, genuinely impressed.

The boy flushed with pride. "You really like him? He's a protocol droid . . . to help Mom. Watch!"

He activated C-3PO with a flip of its power switch, and the droid sat up at once. Anakin rushed around hurriedly, searching, then snatched up the missing eye from his workbench and snapped it into its proper socket.

C-3PO looked at them. "How do you do? I am a protocol droid trained in and adept at cyborg relatives . . . customs and humans . . ."

"Ooops," Anakin said quickly. "He's a little confused."

He snatched up a long-handled tool with an electronic designator and fitted it carefully to a port in C-3PO's head, then ratcheted the handle several turns, studying the setting as he did so. When he had it where he wanted, he pushed a button on the handle. C-3PO jerked several times in response. When Anakin removed the designator, the droid stood up from the workbench and faced Padmé.

"How do you do? I am See-Threepio, human-cyborg relations. How may I serve you?"

Anakin shrugged. "I just named him the other day, but I forgot to enter the code in his memory banks so he could tell you himself."

Padmé grinned at Anakin, delighted. "He's perfect!"

R2-D2 sidled up to them and emitted a sharp flurry of beeps and whistles.

C-3PO glanced down curiously. "I beg your pardon . . . what do you mean, I'm naked?"

R2-D2 beeped some more.

"Goodness! How embarrassing!" C-3PO glanced quickly over his skeletal limbs. "My parts are showing? My goodness!"

Anakin pursed his lips. "Sort of. But don't worry, I'll fix that soon enough." He eased the droid back toward the workbench, glancing over his shoulder at Padmé. "When the storm is over, you can see my racer. I'm building a Podracer. But Watto doesn't know about it. It's a secret."

Padmé smiled. "That's okay. I'm very good at keeping secrets."

The storm continued throughout the remainder of the day, engulfing Mos Espa, sand blown in from the desert piling up against the shuttered buildings, forming ramps against doorways and walls, clouding the air, and shutting out the light. Shmi Skywalker used the food capsules Qui-Gon had given her to prepare dinner for them. As she worked on their meal and while Padmé was occupied with Anakin in the other room, Qui-Gon moved off alone into one corner and surreptitiously contacted Obi-Wan on the comlink. The connection was less than perfect, but they were able to communicate sufficiently for the Jedi Master to learn of the transmission from Naboo.

"You made the right choice, Obi-Wan," he assured his young protégé, keeping his voice low.

"The Queen is very upset," the other advised, his response crackling through the storm.

Qui-Gon glanced over to where Shmi was standing at the cook surface, her back turned. "That transmission was bait to establish a trace. I'm certain of it."

"But what if Governor Bibble is telling the truth and the Naboo are dying?"

Qui-Gon sighed. "Either way, we're running out of time," he advised quietly, and ended the transmission.

They sat down to eat Shmi's dinner a short while after, the storm still howling without, an eerie backdrop of sound against the silence within. Qui-Gon and Padmé occupied the ends of the table, while Anakin, Jar Jar, and Shmi sat at its sides. Anakin, in the way of small boys, began talking about life as a slave, in no way embarrassed to be doing so, thinking of it only as a fact of his life and anxious to share himself with his new friends. Shmi, more protective of her son's station, was making an effort to help their guests appreciate the severity of their situation.

"All slaves have transmitters placed inside their bodies," Shmi was explaining.

"I've been working on a scanner to try to locate them, but so far no luck," Anakin said solemnly.

Shmi smiled. "Any attempt at escape . . ."

". . . and they blow you up!" the boy finished. "Poof!"

Jar Jar had been slurping contentedly at his soup, listening with half an ear as he devoured the very tasty broth. He overdid it on hearing this, however, making such a loud noise that he stopped conversation altogether. All eyes turned on him momentarily. He lowered his head in embarrassment and pretended not to see.

Padmé looked back at Shmi. "I can't believe slavery is still permitted in the galaxy. The Republic's antislavery laws should—"

"The Republic doesn't exist out here," Shmi interrupted quickly, her voice hard. "We must survive on our own."

There was an awkward silence as Padmé looked away, not knowing what else to say.

"Have you ever seen a Podrace?" Anakin asked, trying to ease her discomfort.

Padmé shook her head no. She glanced at Shmi, noting the sudden concern on the woman's lined face. Jar Jar launched his tongue at a morsel of food nestled deep in a serving bowl at the far end of the table, deftly plucking it out, drawing it in, swallowing it, and smacking his lips in satisfaction. A disapproving look from Qui-Gon quickly silenced him.

"They have Podracing on Malastare," the Jedi Master observed. "Very fast, very dangerous."

Anakin grinned. "I'm the only human who can do it!" A sharp glance from his mother wiped the grin from his face. "Mom, what? I'm not bragging. It's true! Watto says he's never heard of a human doing it."

Qui-Gon studied him carefully. "You must have Jedi reflexes if you race Pods."

Anakin smiled broadly at the compliment. Jar Jar's tongue snaked toward the serving bowl in an effort to snare another morsel, but this time Qui-Gon was waiting. His hand moved swiftly, and in a heartbeat he had secured the Gungan's tongue between his thumb and forefinger. Jar Jar froze, his mouth open, his tongue held fast, his eyes wide.

"Don't do that again," Qui-Gon advised, an edge to his soft voice.

Jar Jar tried to say something, but it came out an unintelligible mumble. Qui-Gon released the Gungan's tongue, and it snapped back into place. Jar Jar massaged his billed mouth ruefully.

Anakin's young face lifted to the older man's, and his voice was hesitant. "I . . . I was wondering something."

Qui-Gon nodded for him to continue.

The boy cleared his throat, screwing up his courage. "You're a Jedi Knight, aren't you?"

There was a long moment of silence as the man and the boy stared at each other. "What makes you think that?" Qui-Gon asked finally.

Anakin swallowed. "I saw your lightsaber. Only Jedi Knights carry that kind of weapon."

Qui-Gon continued to stare at him, then leaned back slowly in his chair and smiled. "Perhaps I killed a Jedi and stole it from him."

Anakin shook his head quickly. "I don't think so. No one can kill a Jedi."

Qui-Gon's smile faded and there was a hint of sadness in his dark eyes. "I wish that were so . . ."

"I had a dream I was a Jedi," the boy said quickly, anxious to talk about it now. "I came back here and freed all the slaves. I dreamed it just the other night, when I was out in the desert." He paused, his young face expectant. "Have you come to free us?"

Qui-Gon Jinn shook his head. "No, I'm afraid not . . ." He trailed off, hesitating.

"I think you have," the boy insisted, defiance in his eyes. "Why else would you be here?"

Shmi was about to say something, to chastise her son for his impudence perhaps, but Qui-Gon spoke first, leaning forward conspiratorially. "I can see there's no fooling you, Anakin. But you mustn't let anyone know about us. We're on our way to Coruscant, the central system in the Republic, on a very important mission. It must be kept secret."

Anakin's eyes widened. "Coruscant? Wow! How did you end up out here in the Outer Rim?"

"Our ship was damaged," Padmé answered him. "We're stranded here until we can repair it."

"I can help!" the boy announced quickly, anxious to be of service to them. "I can fix anything!"

Qui-Gon smiled at his enthusiasm. "I believe you can, but our first task, as you know from our visit to Watto's shop, is to acquire the parts we need."

"Wit nutten ta trade," Jar Jar pointed out sourly.

Padmé was looking at Qui-Gon speculatively. "These junk dealers must have a weakness of some kind."

"Gambling," Shmi said at once. She rose and began clearing

the table of dishes. "Everything in Mos Espa revolves around betting on those awful Podraces."

Qui-Gon rose, walked to the window, and stared out through the thick, diffuse glass at the clouds of windblown sand. "Podracing," he mused. "Greed can be a powerful ally, if it's used properly."

Anakin leapt to his feet. "I've built a racer!" he declared triumphantly. His boy's face shone with pride. "It's the fastest ever! There's a big race day after tomorrow, on Boonta Eve. You could enter my Pod! It's all but finished—"

"Anakin, settle down!" his mother said sharply, cutting him short. Her eyes were bright with concern. "Watto won't let you race!"

"Watto doesn't have to know the racer is mine!" the boy replied quickly, his mind working through the problem. He turned back to Qui-Gon. "You could make him think it was yours! You could get him to let me pilot it for you!"

The Jedi Master had caught the look in Shmi's eyes. He met her gaze, silently acknowledged her consternation, and waited patiently for her response.

"I don't want you to race, Annie," his mother said quietly. She shook her head to emphasize her words, weariness and concern reflected in her eyes. "It's awful. I die every time Watto makes you do it. Every time."

Anakin bit his lip. "But, Mom, I love it!" He gestured at Qui-Gon. "And they need my help. They're in trouble. The prize money would more than pay for the parts they need."

Jar Jar Binks nodded in support. "We in kinda bad goo."

Qui-Gon walked over to Anakin and looked down at him. "Your mother's right. Let's drop the matter." He held the boy's gaze for a moment, then turned back to his mother. "Do you know of anyone friendly to the Republic who might be able to help us?"

Shmi stood silent and unmoving as she thought the matter through. She shook her head no.

"We have to help them, Mom," Anakin insisted, knowing he was right about this, that he was meant to help the Jedi and his companions. "Remember what you said? You said the biggest problem in the universe is that no one helps anyone."

Shmi sighed. "Anakin, don't—"

"But you said it, Mom." The boy refused to back down, his eyes locked on hers.

Shmi Skywalker made no response this time, her brow furrowed, her body still.

"I'm sure Qui-Gon doesn't want to put your son in danger," Padmé said suddenly, uncomfortable with the confrontation they had brought about between mother and son, trying to ease the tension. "We will find another way . . ."

Shmi looked over at the girl and shook her head slowly. "No, Annie's right. There is no other way. I may not like it, but he can help you." She paused. "Maybe he was meant to help you."

She said it as if coming to a conclusion that had eluded her until now, as if discovering a truth that, while painful, was obvious.

Anakin's face lit up. "Is that a yes?" He clapped his hands in glee. "That *is* a yes!"

Night blanketed the vast cityscape of Coruscant, cloaking the endless horizon of gleaming spires in deep velvet layers. Lights blazed from windows, bright pinpricks against the black. As far as the eye could see, as far as a being could travel, the city's buildings jutted from the planet's surface in needles of steel alloy and reflective glass. Long ago, the city had consumed the planet with its bulk, and now there was only the city, the center of the galaxy, the heartbeat of the Republic's rule.

A rule that some were intending to end once and for all. A rule that some despised.

Darth Sidious stood high on a balcony overlooking Coruscant, his concealing black robes making him appear as if he were a creature produced by the night. He stood facing the city, his eyes directed at its lights, at the faint movement of its air traffic, disinterested in his apprentice, Darth Maul, who waited to one side.

His thoughts were of the Sith and of the history of their order.

The Sith had come into being almost two thousand years ago. They were a cult given over to the dark side of the Force, embracing fully the concept that power denied was power wasted. A rogue Jedi Knight had founded the Sith, a singular dissident in an order of harmonious followers, a rebel who understood from the beginning that the real power of the Force lay not in the light, but in the dark. Failing to gain approval for his beliefs from the Council, he had broken with the order, departing with his knowledge and his skills, swearing in secret that he could bring down those who had dismissed him.

He was alone at first, but others from the Jedi order who believed as he did and who had followed him in his study of the dark side soon came over. Others were recruited, and soon the ranks of the Sith swelled to more than fifty in number. Disdaining the concepts of cooperation and consensus, relying on the belief that acquisition of power in any form lends strength and yields control, the Sith began to build their cult in opposition to the Jedi. Theirs was not an order created to serve; theirs was an order created to dominate.

Their war with the Jedi was vengeful and furious and ultimately doomed. The rogue Jedi who had founded the Sith order was its nominal leader, but his ambition excluded any sharing of power. His disciples began to conspire against him and each other almost from the beginning, so that the war they instigated was as much with each other as with the Jedi.

In the end, the Sith destroyed themselves. They destroyed their leader first, then each other. What few survived the initial bloodbath were quickly dispatched by watchful Jedi. In a matter of only weeks, all of them died.

All but one.

Darth Maul shifted impatiently. The younger Sith had not

yet learned his Master's patience; that would come with time and training. It was patience that had saved the Sith order in the end. It was patience that would give them their victory now over the Jedi.

The Sith who had survived when all of his fellows had died had understood that. He had adopted patience as a virtue when the others had forsaken it. He had adopted cunning, stealth, and subterfuge as the foundation of his way—old Jedi virtues the others had disdained. He stood aside while the Sith tore at each other like kriks and were destroyed. When the carnage was complete, he went into hiding, biding his time, waiting for his chance.

When it was believed all of the Sith were destroyed, he emerged from his concealment. At first he worked alone, but he was growing old and he was the last of his kind. Eventually, he went out in search of an apprentice. Finding one, he trained him to be a Master in his turn, then to find his own apprentice, and so to carry on their work. But there would only be two at any one time. There would be no repetition of the mistakes of the old order, no struggle between Siths warring for power within the cult. Their common enemy was the Jedi, not each other. It was for their war with the Jedi they must save themselves.

The Sith who reinvented the order called himself Darth Bane.

A thousand years had passed since the Sith were believed destroyed, and the time they had waited for had come at last.

"Tatooine is sparsely populated." His student's rough voice broke into his thoughts, and Darth Sidious lifted his eyes to the hologram. "The Hutts rule. The Republic has no presence. If the trace was correct, Master, I will find them quickly and without hindrance."

The yellow eyes glimmered with excitement and anticipation in the strange mosaic of Darth Maul's face as he waited impatiently for a response. Darth Sidious was pleased.

"Move against the Jedi first," he advised softly. "You will then have no difficulty taking the Queen back to Naboo, where she will sign the treaty."

Darth Maul exhaled sharply. Satisfaction permeated his voice. "At last we will reveal ourselves to the Jedi. At last we will have our revenge."

"You have been well trained, my young apprentice," Darth Sidious soothed. "The Jedi will be no match for you. It is too late for them to stop us now. Everything is going as planned. The Republic will soon be in my control."

In the silence that followed, the Sith Lord could feel a dark heat rise inside his chest and consume him with a furious pleasure.

In the home of Anakin Skywalker, Qui-Gon Jinn stood silently at the doorway of the boy's bedroom and watched him sleep. His mother and Padmé occupied the other bedroom, and Jar Jar Binks was curled up on the kitchen floor in a fetal position, snoring loudly.

But Qui-Gon could not sleep. It was this boy—this boy! There was something about him. The Jedi Master watched the soft rise and fall of his chest as he lay locked in slumber, unaware of Qui-Gon's presence. The boy was special, he had told Shmi Skywalker, and she had agreed. She knew it, too. She sensed it as he did. Anakin Skywalker was different.

Qui-Gon lifted his gaze to a darkened window. The storm had subsided, the wind abated. It was quiet without, the night soft and welcoming in its peace. The Jedi Master thought for a moment on his own life. He knew what they said about him at Council. He was willful, even reckless in his choices. He was strong, but he dissipated his strength on causes that did not merit his attention. But rules were not created solely to govern behavior. Rules were created to provide a road map to understanding the Force. Was it so wrong for him to bend those rules when his conscience whispered to him that he must?

The Jedi folded his arms over his broad chest. The Force was a complex and difficult concept. The Force was rooted in the balance of all things, and every movement within its flow risked an upsetting of that balance. A Jedi sought to keep the balance in place, to move in concert to its pace and will. But the Force existed on more than one plane, and achieving mastery of its multiple passages was a lifetime's work. Or more. He knew his own weakness. He was too close to the life Force when he should have been more attentive to the unifying Force. He found himself reaching out to the creatures of the present, to those living in the here and now. He had less regard for the past or the future, to the creatures that had or would occupy those times and spaces.

It was the life Force that bound him, that gave him heart and mind and spirit.

So it was he empathized with Anakin Skywalker in ways that other Jedi would discourage, finding in this boy a promise he could not ignore. Obi-Wan would see the boy and Jar Jar in the same light—useless burdens, pointless projects, unnecessary distractions. Obi-Wan was grounded in the need to focus on the larger picture, on the unifying Force. He lacked Qui-Gon's intuitive nature. He lacked his teacher's compassion for and interest in all living things. He did not see the same things Qui-Gon saw.

Qui-Gon sighed. This was not a criticism, only an observation. Who was to say that either of them was the better for how they interpreted the demands of the Force? But it placed them at odds sometimes, and more often than not it was Obi-Wan's position the Council supported, not Qui-Gon's. It would be that way again, he knew. Many times.

But this would not deter him from doing what he believed he must. He would know the truth about Anakin Skywalker. He would discover his place in the Force, both living and unifying. He would learn who this boy was meant to be.

Minutes later, he was stretched out on the floor, asleep.

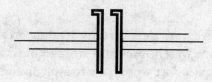

The new day dawned bright and clear, Tatooine's twin suns blazing down out of a clear blue sky. The sandstorm had moved on to other regions, sweeping the landscape clean of everything but the mountains and rocky outcroppings of the desert and the buildings of Mos Espa. Anakin was up and dressed before his guests stirred awake, eager to get to the shop and advise Watto of his plan for the upcoming Podrace. Qui-Gon warned him not to be too eager in making his suggestion to the Toydarian, but to stay calm and let Qui-Gon handle the bargaining. But Anakin was so excited he barely heard what the other was saying. The Jedi Master knew it would be up to him to employ whatever mix of cunning and diplomacy was required to achieve their ends.

Greed was the operative word in dealing with Watto, of course, the key that would open any door the Toydarian kept locked.

They walked from the slave quarters through the city to Watto's shop, Anakin leading the way, Qui-Gon and Padmé close at his heels, Jar Jar and R2-D2 bringing up the rear. The city was awake and bustling early, the shopkeepers and merchants shoveling and sweeping away drifts of sand, reassembling stalls and awnings, and righting carts and damaged fences. Eopies and rontos performed the heavy labor where sleds and droids lacked sufficient muscle. Wagons were already hauling fresh supplies and merchandise from warehouses and storage bins, and the receiving bays of the spaceport were back to welcoming ships from off planet.

Qui-Gon let Anakin go on ahead to the shop as they drew near, in order to give the boy a chance to approach Watto on the subject of the Podraces first. With the others in tow, the Jedi Master moved to a food stall across the way, persuaded a vendor to part with a handful of gooey dweezels, and bided his time. When the dweezels were consumed, he moved his group across the plaza to the front of Watto's shop. Jar Jar, already unsettled anew by all the activity, took up a position on a crate near the shop entry, his back to the wall, his eyes darting this way and that in anticipation of something awful befalling him. R2-D2 moved over beside him, beeping softly, trying to reassure him that everything was okay.

Qui-Gon told Padmé to keep a wary eye on the Gungan. He didn't want Jar Jar getting into any more trouble. He was starting into the shop when the girl put a hand on his arm.

"Are you sure about this?" she asked, doubt mirrored clearly in her brown eyes. "Trusting our fate to a boy we hardly know?" She wrinkled her smooth brow. "The Queen would not approve."

Qui-Gon met her gaze squarely. "The Queen does not need to know."

Her eyes blazed defiantly. "Well, I don't approve."

He gave her a questioning look, then turned away wordlessly.

Inside the salvage shop, he found Watto and Anakin engaged in a heated discussion, the Toydarian hovering centimeters from the boy's face, blue wings a blur of motion, snout curled inward as he gestured sharply and purposely with both hands.

"*Patta go bolla!*" he shouted in Huttese, chubby body jerking with the force of his words.

The boy blinked, but held his ground. "*No batta!*"

"*Peedunkel!*" Watto flitted backward and forward, up and down, everything moving at once.

"Banyo, banyo!" Anakin shouted.

Qui-Gon moved out of the shadowed entry and into the light where they could see him clearly. Watto turned away from Anakin at once, toothy mouth working, and flew into Qui-Gon's face in a frenzy of ill-concealed excitement.

"The boy tells me you want to sponsor him in the race tomorrow!" The words exploded out of him. "You can't afford parts! How can you afford to enter him in the race? Not on Republic credits, I think!"

He broke into raucous laughter, but Qui-Gon did not miss the hint of curiosity that gleamed in his slitted eyes.

"My ship will be the entry fee," the Jedi advised bluntly.

He reached beneath his poncho and brought out a tiny holoprojector. Clicking on the power source, he projected a hologram of the Queen's transport into the air in front of Watto. The Toydarian flitted closer, studying the projection carefully.

"Not bad. Not bad." The wrinkled blue proboscis bobbed. "A Nubian."

"It's in good order, except for the parts we need." Qui-Gon gave him another moment, then flicked off the holoprojector and tucked it back beneath his poncho.

"But what would the boy ride?" Watto demanded irritably. "He smashed up my Pod in the last race. It will take too long to fix it for the Boonta."

Qui-Gon glanced at Anakin, who was clearly embarrassed. "Aw, it wasn't my fault, really. Sebulba flashed me with his port vents. I actually saved the Podracer . . . mostly."

Watto laughed harshly. "That he did! The boy is good, no doubts there!" He shook his head. "But still . . ."

"I have acquired a Pod in a game of chance," Qui-Gon interrupted smoothly, drawing the other's attention back to him. "The fastest ever built."

He did not look at Anakin, but he imagined the expression on the boy's face.

"I hope you didn't kill anyone I know for it!" Watto

snapped. He burst into a new round of laughter before bringing himself under control again. "So, you supply the Podracer and the entry fee; I supply the boy. We split the winnings fifty-fifty, I think."

"Fifty-fifty?" Qui-Gon brushed the suggestion aside. "If it's going to be fifty-fifty, I suggest you front the cost of the entry. If we win, you keep all the winnings, minus the cost of the parts I need. If we lose, you keep my ship."

Watto was clearly caught by surprise. He thought the matter through, hand rubbing at his snout, wings beating the air with a buzzing sound. The offer was too good, and he was suspicious. Out of the corner of his eye, Qui-Gon saw Anakin glance over at him nervously.

"Either way, you win," Qui-Gon pointed out softly.

Watto pounded his fist into his open palm. "Deal!" He turned to the boy, chuckling. "Your friend makes a foolish bargain, boy! Better teach him what you know about how to deal for goods!"

He was still laughing as Qui-Gon left the shop.

The Jedi Master collected Padmé, Jar Jar, and R2-D2, and left word for Anakin to join them as soon as Watto would free him up to work on the Podracer. Since Watto was more interested in the upcoming race than in managing the shop, he dismissed the boy at once with instructions to make certain the racer he would be driving was a worthy contender and not some piece of space junk that would cause everyone to laugh at the Toydarian for his foolish decision to enter it in the first place.

As a result, Anakin was home almost before Qui-Gon and the others, eagerly leading them to where his project was concealed in the slave quarter bone yards. The Podracer was shaped like a narrow half cylinder with a rudder-skid attached to its flat bottom, a cockpit carved into its curved top, and steering arms attached at its sides. Sleek Radon-Ulzer fighter engines with scoop-air stabilizers towed the Pod at the end of Steelton cables. The effect was something like seeing a doop bug attached to a pair of banthas.

Working together, the company activated the antigrav lifts and guided the Pod and its enormous engines into the courtyard in back of Anakin's home. With Padmé, Jar Jar, and R2-D2 lending assistance and encouragement, the boy immediately went to work prepping the Pod for the upcoming race.

While Anakin and his helpers were thus engaged, Qui-Gon mounted the back porch of the Skywalker home, glanced around to make certain he was alone, and switched on the comlink to contact Obi-Wan. His protégé answered immediately, anxious for a report, and Qui-Gon filled him in on what was happening.

"If all goes well, we will have our hyperdrive generator by tomorrow afternoon and be on our way," he concluded.

Obi-Wan's silence was telling. "What if this plan fails, Master? We could be stuck here for a long time."

Qui-Gon Jinn looked out over the squalor of the slave quarters and the roofs of the buildings of Mos Espa beyond, the suns a bright glare overhead. "A ship without a power supply will not get us anywhere. We have no choice."

He switched off the comlink and tucked it away. "And there is something about this boy," he whispered to himself, leaving the thought unfinished.

Shmi Skywalker appeared through the back door and moved over to join him. Together they stood watching the activity in the courtyard below.

"You should be proud of your son," Qui-Gon said after a moment. "He gives without any thought of reward."

Shmi nodded, a smile flitting over her worn face. "He knows nothing of greed. Only of dreams. He has . . ."

"Special powers."

The woman glanced at him warily. "Yes."

"He can see things before they happen," the Jedi Master continued. "That's why he appears to have such quick reflexes. It is a Jedi trait."

Her eyes were fixed on him, and he did not miss the glimmer of hope that shone there. "He deserves better than a slave's life," she said quietly.

Qui-Gon kept his gaze directed out at the courtyard. "The Force is unusually strong with him, that much is clear. Who was his father?"

There was a long pause, long enough for the Jedi Master to realize he had asked a question she was not prepared to answer. He gave her time and space to deal with the matter, not pressing her, not making it seem as if it were necessary she answer at all.

"There is no father," she said finally. She shook her head slowly. "I carried him, I gave birth to him. I raised him. I can't tell you any more than that."

She touched his arm, drawing his eyes to meet hers. "Can you help him?"

Qui-Gon was silent for a long time, thinking. He felt an attachment to Anakin Skywalker he could not explain. In the back of his mind, he sensed he was meant to do something for this boy, that it was necessary he try. But all Jedi were identified within the first six months of birth and given over to their training. It was true for him, for Obi-Wan, for everyone he knew or had heard about. There were no exceptions.

Can you help him? He did not know how that was possible.

"I don't know," he told her, keeping his voice gentle, but firm. "I didn't come here to free slaves. Had he been born in the Republic, we would have identified him early, and he might have become a Jedi. He has the way. I'm not sure what I can do for him."

She nodded in resignation, but her face revealed, beneath the mask of her acceptance, a glimmer of hope.

As Anakin tightened the wiring on the thruster relays to the left engine, a group of his friends appeared. The older boys were Kitster and Seek, the younger girl was Amee, and the Rodian was Wald. Anakin broke off his efforts to complete the wiring long enough to introduce them to Padmé, Jar Jar, and R2-D2.

"Wow, a real astromech droid!" Kitster exclaimed, whistling softly. "How'd you get so lucky?"

Anakin shrugged. "That isn't the half of it," he declared, puffing up a bit. "I'm entered in the Boonta tomorrow."

Kitster made a face and pushed back his mop of dark hair. "What? With this?"

"That piece of junk has never even been off the ground," Wald said, nudging Amee. "This is such a joke, Annie."

"You've been working on that thing for years," Amee observed, her small, delicate features twisting in disapproval. She shook her blond head. "It's never going to run."

Anakin started to say something in defense of himself, then decided against it. Better to let them think whatever they wanted for now. He would show them.

"Come on, let's go play ball," Seek suggested, already turning away, a hint of boredom in his voice. "Keep it up, Annie, and you're gonna be bug squash."

Seek, Wald, and Amee hurried off, laughing back at him. But Kitster was his best friend and knew better than to doubt Anakin when he said he was going to do something. So Kitster stayed behind, ignoring the others. "What do they know?" he said quietly.

Anakin gave him a grin of appreciation. Then he noticed Jar Jar fiddling with the left engine's energy binder plate, the power source that locked the engines together and kept them in sync, and the grin disappeared.

"Hey! Jar Jar!" he shouted in warning. "Stay away from those energy binders!"

The Gungan, bent close to the protruding plate, looked up guiltily. "Who, me?"

Anakin put his hands on his hips. "If your hand gets caught in the beam, it will go numb for hours."

Jar Jar screwed up his face, then put his hands behind his back and stuck his billed face back down by the plate. Almost instantly an electric current arced from the plate to his mouth, causing him to yelp and jump back in shocked surprise. Both hands clamped over his mouth as he stood staring at the boy in disbelief.

"Ist numm! Ist numm!" Jar Jar mumbled, his long tongue hanging loosely. "My tongue is fat. Dats my bigo oucho." Anakin shook his head and went back to work on the wiring.

Kitster moved close to him, watching silently, his dark face intense. "You don't even know if this thing will run, Annie," he observed with a frown.

Anakin didn't look up. "It will."

Qui-Gon Jinn appeared at his shoulder. "I think it's about time we found out." He handed the boy a small, bulky cylinder. "Use this power pack. I picked it up earlier in the day. Watto has less need for it than you." One corner of his mouth twitched in a mix of embarrassment and amusement.

Anakin knew the value of a power pack. How the Jedi had managed to secure one from under Watto's nose, he had no idea and no interest in finding out. "Yes, sir!" he beamed.

He jumped into the cockpit, fitted the power pack into its sleeve in the control panel, and set the activator to the ON position. Then he pulled on his old, dented racing helmet and gloves. As he did so, Jar Jar, who had been fiddling around at the back of one of the engines, managed to get his hand caught in the afterburner. The Gungan began leaping up and down in terror, his mouth still numb from the shock he had received from the energy binders, his bill flapping to no discernible purpose. Padmé caught sight of him at the last minute—his arms windmilling frantically—and yanked him free an instant before the engines ignited.

Flame exploded from the afterburners, and a huge roar rose from the Radon-Ulzers, building steadily in pitch until Anakin eased off on the thrusters, then settling back into a throaty rumble. Cheers rose from the spectators, and Anakin waved his hand in response.

On the porch of their home, Shmi Skywalker watched wordlessly, her eyes distant and sad.

Twilight brought a blaze of gold and crimson in the wake of Tatooine's departing suns, a splash of color that filled the horizon in a long, graceful sweep. Night climbed after, darkening the sky, bringing out the stars like scattered shards of crystal. In the deepening black, the land was silent and watchful.

A gleam of bright metal caught the last of the fading suns' rays, and a small transport sped out of the Dune Sea toward Mos Espa. Shovel-nosed and knife-edged, its wings swept back and its vertical stabilizers crimped inward top to bottom, it hugged the landscape as it climbed promontories and descended valleys, searching. Dark and immutable, it had the look of a predator, of a hunter at work.

Beyond the Dune Sea, following the failing light, the craft settled swiftly on the broad plateau of a mesa that gave a long-range view of the land in all directions. Wild banthas scattered with its approach, tossing their hairy heads and massive horns, trumpeting their disapproval. The transport came to rest and its engines shut down. It sat there in silence, waiting.

Then the aft hatchway slid open, metal stairs lowered, and Darth Maul appeared. The Sith Lord had discarded his black robes and wore loose-fitting desert garb, a collared coat belted at the waist, his lightsaber hanging within easy reach. His stunted horns, fully exposed now with his hood removed, formed a wicked crown above his strange red-and-black-colored face. Ignoring the banthas, he walked to the edge of the mesa, produced a pair of low-light electrobinoculars, and began to scan the horizon in all directions.

Desert sand and rocks, he was thinking. Wasteland. But a city there, and another there. And there, a third.

He took the electrobinoculars from his eyes. The lights of the cities were clearly visible against the growing dark. If there were others, they were far on the other side of the Dune Sea where he had already been, or beyond the horizon much farther still where he would later be required to go.

But the Jedi, he believed, were here.

There was no expression on his mosaic face, but his yellow eyes gleamed expectantly. Soon now. Soon.

He lifted his arm to view the control panel strapped to his forearm, picked out the settings he wished to engage, and punched in the calculations required to identify the enemy he was looking for. Jedi Knights would manifest a particularly strong presence in the Force. It took only a minute. He turned back toward his ship. Spherical probe droids floated through the hatchway, one after another. When all were clear, they rocketed away toward the cities he had identified.

Darth Maul watched until they were out of view, the darkness closing quickly now. He smiled faintly. Soon.

Then he walked back to his ship to begin monitoring their response.

Darkness cloaked Mos Espa in deepening layers as night descended. Anakin sat quietly on the balcony rail of his back porch while Qui-Gon studied a deep cut in the boy's arm. Anakin had sustained the cut sometime during the afternoon's prep work on the Podracer, and in typical boy fashion, he hadn't even noticed it until now.

Anakin gave the injury a cursory glance as the Jedi prepared to clean it, then leaned back to look up at the blanket of stars in the sky.

"Sit still, Annie," Qui-Gon instructed.

The boy barely heard him. "There are so many! Do they all have a system of planets?"

"Most of them." Qui-Gon produced a clean piece of cloth.

"Has anyone been to all of them?"

Qui-Gon laughed. "Not likely."

Anakin nodded, still looking up. "I want to be the first one then, the first to see them all—ouch!"

Qui-Gon wiped a smear of blood from the boy's arm, then applied some antiseptic. "There, good as new."

"Annie! Bedtime!" Shmi called out from inside.

Qui-Gon produced a comlink chip and wiped a sample of Anakin's blood onto its surface. The boy leaned forward interestedly. "What are you doing?"

The Jedi barely looked up. "Checking your blood for infections."

Anakin frowned. "I've never seen—"

"Annie!" his mother called again, more insistent this time. "I'm not going to tell you again!"

"Go on," Qui-Gon urged, gesturing toward the doorway. "You have a big day tomorrow." He tucked the cloth into his tunic. "Good night."

Anakin hesitated, his eyes fixed on the Jedi Master, intense and questioning. Then he turned and darted off into his home. Qui-Gon waited a moment, making sure he was alone, then slipped the chip with the boy's blood sample into a relay slot in the comlink and called Obi-Wan aboard the Queen's transport.

"Yes, Master?" his protégé responded, alert in spite of the lateness of the hour.

"I'm transmitting a blood sample," Qui-Gon advised, glancing about guardedly as he spoke. "Run a midi-chlorian test on it."

He sent the blood readings through the comlink to Obi-Wan and stood waiting in the silence. He could feel the beating of his heart, quick and excited. If he was right about this . . .

"Master," Obi-Wan interrupted his musings. "There must be something wrong with the sample."

Qui-Gon took a slow, deep breath and exhaled softly. "What do the readings say, Obi-Wan?"

"They say the midi-chlorian count is twenty thousand." The younger Jedi's voice tightened. "No one has a count that high. Not even Master Yoda."

No one. Qui-Gon stood staring out into the night, staggered by the immensity of his discovery. Then he let his gaze wander back toward the hovel where the boy was sleeping, and stiffened.

Shmi Skywalker stood just inside the doorway, staring at him. Their eyes met, and for just an instant it felt to the Jedi Master as if the future had been revealed to him in its entirety. Then Shmi turned away, embarrassed, and disappeared back into her home.

Qui-Gon paused a moment, then remembered the open comlink. "Good night, Obi-Wan," he said softly, and clicked the transmitter off.

* * *

Midnight approached. Anakin Skywalker, unable to sleep, had slipped out of his bed and gone down into the backyard to complete a final check of the racer, of its controls, its wiring, its relays, its power source—everything he could think of. Now he stood staring at it, trying to determine what he might have missed, what he might have overlooked. He could afford no mistakes. He must make certain he had done all that he could.

So that he would win tomorrow's race.

Because he must.

He must.

He watched R2-D2 scuttle around the racer, applying paint in broad strokes to its polished metal body, aided by a light projecting from a receptacle mounted over his visual sensors and a steady stream of advice from C-3PO. The boy had activated the latter earlier on the advice of Padmé. Many hands make light work, she had intoned solemnly, then grinned. C-3PO wasn't much with his hands, but his vocoder was certainly tireless. In any case, R2-D2 seemed to like having him around, exchanging beeps and chirps with his protocol counterpart as he scuttled about the racer. The little astromech droid worked tirelessly, cheerfully, and willingly. Nothing perturbed him. Anakin envied him. Droids were either well put together or they weren't. Unlike humans, they didn't respond to weariness or disappointment or fear . . .

He chased the thought away quickly and looked up at the starry sky. After a moment, he sat down, his back against a crate of old parts, his goggles and racing helmet at his side. Idly, he fingered the japor carving in his pocket, the one he was working on for Padmé. His thoughts drifted. He couldn't explain it exactly, but he knew that tomorrow would change his life. That strange ability to see what others did not, that sometimes gave him insights into what would happen, told him so. His future was coming up on him in a rush, he sensed. It was closing fast, giving him no time to consider, ascending with the certainty of a sunrise.

What would it bring him? The question teased at the edges of his consciousness, refusing to show itself. Change, but in what form? Qui-Gon and his companions were the bringers of that change, but he did not think even the Jedi Knight knew for certain what the end result would be.

Maybe the freedom he had dreamed about for himself and his mother, he thought hopefully. Maybe an escape to a new life for both of them. Anything was possible if he won the Boonta. Anything at all.

That thought was still foremost in his cluttered, weary mind when his eyes closed and he fell asleep.

Anakin Skywalker dreamed that night, and in his dream he was of a different, but indeterminate age. He was young still, though not so young as now, but old, too. He was cut from stone, and his thoughts were emblazoned with a vision so frightening he could not bring himself to consider it fully, only to leave it just out of reach, simmering over a fire of ambition and hope. He was in a different place and time, in a world he did not recognize, in a landscape he had never seen. It was vague and shadowy in his dream, all flat and rugged at once, changing with the swiftness of a mirage born out of Tatooine's desert flats.

The dream shimmered, and voices reached out to him, soft and distant. He turned toward them, away from a wave of dark movement that suddenly appeared before him, away from the sleep that gave his dream life.

"I hope you're about finished," he heard Padmé say.

But Padmé was at the head of the dark wave of his dream, and the wave was an army, marching toward him . . .

R2-D2 whistled and beeped, and C-3PO chimed in with hasty assurances, saying everything was done, all was in readiness, and he stirred again.

A hand touched his cheek, brushing it softly, and the dream faded and was gone. Anakin blinked awake, rubbing at his eyes, yawning and turning over on his side. He was no longer stretched out by the parts crate where he had fallen asleep the night before, but was back in his own bed.

The hand lifted away from his cheek, and Anakin stared up at Padmé, at a face he found so beautiful it brought a tightness to his throat. Yet he stared at her in confusion, for she had been the central figure in his dream, different from now, older, sadder . . . and something more.

"You were in my dream," he said, swallowing hard to get the words out. "You were leading a huge army into battle."

The girl stared at him in wonder, then smiled. "I hope not. I hate fighting." Her voice was merry and light, dismissive in a way that bothered him. "Your mother wants you to get up now. We have to leave soon."

Anakin climbed to his feet, fully awake. He walked to the back door and stood looking out at the anthill complex of the slave quarters, at the bustle of slaves going about their daily work, at the clear, bright early morning sky that promised good weather for the Boonta Eve race. The Podracer hung level before him on its antigrav lifts, freshly painted and gleaming in the new day's sunlight. R2-D2 bustled about with a brush and can of paint, completing the final detailing of the craft. C-3PO, still missing most of his outer skin, his working parts clearly visible, followed along, pointing out missed patches, giving unsolicited opinions and bits of advice.

The sharp wheeze of an eopie brought him around to find Kitster riding toward them on the first of two of the beasts he had commandeered to help haul the Podracer to the arena. Kitster's dark face was aglow with expectation, and he waved eagerly at Anakin as he approached.

Anakin waved back, shouting, "Hook 'em up, Kitster!" He turned back to Padmé. "Where's Qui-Gon?"

The girl gestured. "He left with Jar Jar for the arena. They've gone to find Watto."

Anakin sprinted to his bedroom to wash and dress.

* * *

Qui-Gon Jinn strolled through the main hangar of the Mos Espa Podracer arena, glancing at the activity about him with seemingly casual interest. The hangar was a cavernous building that housed Podracers and equipment year round and served as a staging area for vehicles and crews on race days. A handful of racers were already in place on the service pads, dozens of aliens who had found their way to Tatooine from every corner of the galaxy crawling all over the Pods and engines as pit bosses and pilots shouted instructions. The clash and shriek of metal on metal echoed in an earsplitting din through the hangar's vast chamber, forcing conversations to be held at something approaching a shout.

Jar Jar hugged one shoulder of the Jedi Master while Watto buzzed close by the other. The former was his normal fretful, nervous self, eyes rolling on their stalks, head twisting this way and that with such frantic concern it seemed certain it must soon twist off altogether. Watto flew with blatant disregard for everything but his own conversation, which rambled on and on, covering the same points endlessly.

"So it must be understood clearly that our bargain is sealed, outlander," he repeated for at least the third time in the last ten minutes. His blue-snouted head bobbed with emphasis. "I'll want to see your spaceship the moment the race is over."

He made no bones about the fact that he believed that gaining lawful possession of the Naboo transport was only a matter of time. He had not once since Qui-Gon had found him at the betting booths suggested that things might work out otherwise.

The Jedi Master demurred with a shrug. "Patience, my blue friend. You'll have your winnings before the suns set, and my companions and I will be far away from here."

"Not if your ship belongs to me, I think!" Watto snorted, and gave a satisfied laugh. Just as quickly, his sharp eyes fixed on the Jedi. "I warn you, no funny business!"

Qui-Gon kept walking, his gaze directed elsewhere, carefully baiting the hook he had set for the Toydarian. "You don't think Anakin will win?"

Watto flew around in front of him and brought them all to a stop. Wings beating furiously, he motioned to a bright orange racer parked close at hand, its engines modified so that when the energy binders were activated and the engines joined, they formed a distinctive X-shape. Sitting to one side of the racer was the Dug who had attacked Jar Jar two days earlier, Sebulba, his wicked eyes fixed on them, his slender limbs drawn up in a vaguely menacing gesture. A pair of lithesome Twi'leks worked diligently massaging the Dug's neck and shoulders. The Twi'leks were humanoid aliens from the planet Ryloth; they had pointed teeth, smooth blue skin, and twin tentacles that draped gracefully from their hairless heads down their silken backs. Their red eyes lifted to Qui-Gon momentarily, interest flickering in their depths, then returned quickly to their master.

Watto snorted. "Don't get me wrong," he announced, shaking his head in an odd cocking motion. "I have great faith in the boy. He's a credit to your species." His snaggletoothed mouth tightened. "But Sebulba there is going to win, I think."

Qui-Gon pretended to study the Dug carefully. "Why?"

"Because he always wins!" The Toydarian broke into a fit of laughter, consumed by his own cleverness. "I'm betting heavily on Sebulba!"

"I'll take that bet," Qui-Gon said at once.

Watto stopped laughing instantly, jerking away as if scalded by hot oil. "What?" He shook his head in astonishment. "What do you mean?"

Qui-Gon advanced a step, backing the Toydarian away. "I'll wager my new racing Pod against . . ." He trailed off thoughtfully, letting Watto hang. "Against, say, the boy and his mother."

Watto was aghast. "A Pod for slaves! I don't think so!" The blue wings were a blur as he flitted this way and that, head cocked. "Well, perhaps. Just one. The mother, maybe. The boy isn't for sale."

Qui-Gon frowned. "The boy is small. He can't be worth much."

Watto shook his head decisively.

"For the fastest Pod ever built?"

Watto shook his head again.

"Both, or no bet."

They were standing near the front entry of the hangar, and the noise of the crew work had lessened. Beyond, the arena stands rose against the desert sky, a vast, curved complex complete with boxes for the Hutts, a race announcer's booth, course monitoring equipment, and food stands. Already the stands were beginning to fill, the population of Mos Espa turning out in full force for the event, shops and stalls closed, the city on holiday. Bright streamers and banners flew, and approaching racers flamed with the reflection of sunlight and polish.

Qui-Gon caught sight of Anakin appearing through the crowds, riding an eopie with Padmé up behind him, towing one of the massive Radon-Ulzer engines. His friend Kitster followed on a second eopie, towing the other engine. The eopies were gangly, long-snouted pack animals with tough, leathery skin and short fur particularly well-suited to resisting the Tatooine desert heat. R2-D2 and C-3PO trailed the little procession with the Pod and Shmi. The Jedi Master deliberately turned to watch their approach, drawing Watto's gaze after his own. The Toydarian's eyes glittered at the sight of the boy and the racer.

He looked back at Qui-Gon and gave an anxious snort. "No Pod's worth two slaves . . . not by a long shot! One slave or nothing!"

Qui-Gon folded his arms over his chest. "The boy, then."

Watto huffed and shook his head. He jerked with the tension his deliberation was generating inside his pudgy blue body. "No, no . . ."

Then abruptly he reached inside his pocket and produced a small cube, which he tossed from one hand to the other as if it were too hot to hold. "We'll let fate decide. Blue, it's the boy. Red, it's the mother."

Watto cast the cube to the hangar floor. As he did, Qui-Gon made a small, surreptitious gesture with one hand, calling on his Jedi power to produce a small inflection in the Force.

The cube bounced, rolled, settled, blue side facing up. Watto threw up his hands angrily, his eyes turning narrow and sharp.

"You won the toss, outlander!" he sneered in dismissal. "But you won't win the race, so it makes little difference, I think."

"We'll see," Qui-Gon replied calmly.

Anakin and the others reached them, entering the hangar with the Pod and engines. Watto wheeled away from Qui-Gon in a huff, pausing long enough to snap irritably at the boy.

"Better stop your friend's betting," he declared with an angry snort, "or I'll end up owning him, too!"

One of the eopies sniffed expectantly at him, and he swore at the beast in Huttese with such ferocity that it backed away. His wings beating madly, Watto gave Qui-Gon a withering glance and flew off into the hangar shadows.

"What did he mean by that?" Anakin asked as he slowed the eopie beside Qui-Gon, glancing after the retreating Toydarian.

Qui-Gon shrugged. "I'll tell you later."

Kitster pulled to a stop beside Anakin, his face alight with excitement as he looked around. "This is so wizard! I'm sure you'll do it this time, Annie!"

Padmé's gaze shifted from one to the other. "Do what?" she asked suspiciously.

Kitster beamed. "Finish the race, of course!"

The girl paled. Her eyes burned into Anakin. "You've never even *finished* a race?" she demanded incredulously.

The boy blushed. "Well . . . not exactly." His mouth tightened with determination. "But Kitster's right. I will this time."

Qui-Gon took the eopie's reins in his hand and patted the boy's leg. "Of course, you will," he agreed.

From atop the eopie, Padmé Naberrie just stared at him wordlessly.

* * *

In the center of Mos Espa the crowds were beginning to thin as the population gravitated in increasing numbers toward the Podracer arena at the edge of the spaceport. Most of the shops and stalls were already closed, and the rest were in the process of doing so. Owners and vendors were completing sales and glancing anxiously in the direction of the traffic's steady flow.

Amid the confusion and bustle, a Sith probe droid slowly floated along, mechanical eye traveling from shop to shop, from face to face, searching.

Over a hundred thousand beings had filled the Podracer arena by midmorning, jamming into the grandstand seats, crowding onto the broad viewing platforms, filling the available space. The arena became a vast sea of color and movement and sound in the emptiness of the surrounding desert. Flags and banners bearing the insignia of the racers and their sponsors waved over the assemblage, signifying favorites and creating impromptu cheering sections. Bands played in support of some racers, and isolated horns and drums beat in wild appreciation for all. Vendors walked the aisles, carrying food and drink from canopied stands below to sell to the crowd. Everywhere, excitement and anticipation was building.

Then a roar erupted as the racers began to emerge from the main hangar on the far side of the start line. One by one the Podracers hove into view, some towed by eopies, some by hand, some by repulsorsled, all part of a long procession of pilots, pit crews, and hangers-on. Standard bearers, each carrying a flag that identified the pilot and sponsor, marched along, forming a colorful line in front of the assembly of Podracers. Overhead, the twin suns of Tatooine shone down with a bright, hungry glare.

As the racers moved onto the track in front of the arena stands, a flurry of movement in the royal box signaled the arrival of Jabba the Hutt and Gardulla, his female friend. Slithering into the cooled interior of the box, the two Hutts oozed their way along the flooring to their designated places amid the bright silks that draped the rough stone. Jabba came foremost, proceeding directly to the arched overlook where he could be seen by the people of Mos Espa. Lifting his pudgy arm in greeting, he basked in the crowd's appreciative roar. Gardulla muttered her approval, nodding her neckless head on the end of a thick, shapeless body, slitted eyes glittering. A coterie of humans and aliens filed in behind the two Hutts, guests of Mos Espa's rulers on race day, a coveted designation. A line of slave girls of varying species came last, chained together, there for the amusement of those who had chosen freely to attend.

Below, the Podracer pilots formed a line facing the royal box and on command bowed deeply in recognition of and to pay homage to their benefactor.

"Chowbaso!" Jabba rumbled, his deep voice echoing through the sound enhancers and out across the flats. *"Tam ka chee Boonta rulee ya, kee madd ahdrudda du wundee!* Welcome!"

The crowd roared some more, arms and flags waving madly. Horns sounded as Jabba began his introduction of the racers.

"Kubba tee. Sebulba *tuta* Pixelito!"

The Dug, standing immediately next to Anakin, rose on his back legs and waved to the stands. A band played wildly in support, and Sebulba's fans and anxious bettors depending on the odds that favored the Dug cheered and shouted in response.

One by one, Jabba recognized the Podracer pilots. Gasgano. Boles Roor. Ben Quadinaros. Aldar Beedo. Ody Mandrell. Xelbree. Mars Guo. Clegg Holdfast. Bozzie Baranta. Wan Sandage. Anakin listened to the names, shifting anxiously, eager to begin. A glance over his shoulder revealed Kitster at work attaching the Radon-Ulzers to his Pod with the Steelton cables, checking the fastenings with sharp tugs.

". . . Mawhonic *tuta* Hok," Jabba boomed. "Teemto Pagalies *tuta* Moonus Mandel. Anakin Skywalker *tuta* Tatooine . . ."

Applause burst from the crowd, though it was not as enthusiastic as it had been for Sebulba or Gasgano or several of the others. Anakin waved in response, eyes traveling over the thousands gathered, his mind already out in the flats.

When he turned to walk to his racer, his mother was standing in front of him. Her worn face was calm and determined as she bent down to give him a hug and a kiss. Her eyes were steady as she backed him off, her hands gripping his shoulders, and she could not quite mask the worry reflected there.

"Be safe, Annie," she told him.

He nodded, swallowing. "I will, Mom. I promise."

She smiled, warm and reassuring, and moved away. Anakin continued on, watching Kitster and Jar Jar unhitch the eopies so that Kitster could lead them away. R2-D2 rolled up to Anakin and beeped with approval and reassurance. C-3PO solemnly warned against the dangers of driving too fast and wished his master well. All was ready.

Jar Jar patted the boy on the back, his billed face a mask of worry and consternation. "Tis very loony, Annie. May da Guds be kind, me friend."

Out of the corner of his eye Anakin saw Sebulba wander over from his own racer and begin examining the boy's. Hitching along on his spindly legs, he worked his way around the Radon-Ulzers with undisguised interest. Stopping finally at the left engine, he reached up suddenly and banged hard on a stabilizer, glancing around quickly to see if anyone had noticed.

Padmé appeared and bent down to kiss Anakin's cheek. Her dark eyes were intense. "You carry all our hopes," she said quietly.

Anakin's lower lip jutted out. "I won't let you down."

She gave him a long stare, then moved away. As she did so, Sebulba sidled up to him, his wizened, whiskery face angling close.

"You won't walk away from this one, slave scum," he wheezed softly, grinning. "You're bantha poodoo."

Anakin stood his ground, giving the Dug a stony look. "Don't count on it, slime face."

Qui-Gon was approaching, and Sebulba backed away toward his own racer, malevolence mirrored in his flat stare. Horns blared, and a new roar rose from the crowd. Jabba the Hutt oozed to the lip of the royal box, his thick arms lifting.

"Kaa bazza kundee da tam hdrudda!" he growled. "Let the challenge begin!"

The roar of the crowd began to build even further. Qui-Gon helped Anakin climb into his Pod. The boy settled himself in place in the seat, securing his straps, fitting his old, battered racing helmet over his head and bringing down his goggles.

"Are you all set, Annie?" the Jedi Master asked calmly. The boy nodded, eyes intense, steady. Qui-Gon held his gaze. "Remember, concentrate on the moment. Feel, don't think. Trust your instincts."

He put a hand on the boy's shoulder and smiled. "May the Force be with you, Annie."

Then he backed away, and Anakin Skywalker was alone.

Qui-Gon moved quickly through the crowd to the viewing platform where Shmi, Padmé, and Jar Jar waited. He glanced back only once at Anakin and found the boy calmly fitting his goggles in place. The Jedi Master nodded to himself. The boy would do all right.

He mounted the viewing platform with Jar Jar and the women just as it began to lift into position for the race. Shmi gave him a worried, questioning look.

"He's fine," Qui-Gon assured her, touching her shoulder.

Padmé shook her head doubtfully. "You Jedi are far too reckless," she said quietly. "The Queen—"

"The Queen trusts my judgment, young handmaiden," Qui-Gon interrupted smoothly, directing his words only to her. "Perhaps you should, too."

She glared at him. "You assume too much."

The viewing platform locked into place, and all eyes turned toward the racers. Energy binders were engaged, powerful electromagnetic currents arcing between coaxial plates, locking the twin engines of each Podracer together as a single unit. Now the engines themselves began to turn over, their booming coughs and rumbles mingling with and then overwhelming the roar of the crowd. Flag bearers and pit crews moved hastily aside, clearing the start line beneath the arch that marked the beginning and end of the race. Overhead, a red light held the racers in place. Anticipating the green, the pilots gunned their engines, the massive casings shaking with the force of the power they generated, the cables that bound them to the Pods and their drivers straining to break free.

Standing next to Qui-Gon, Jar Jar Binks covered his eyes in dismay. "Me no watch. Dis gonna be messy!"

Though he could not bring himself to say so, the Jedi Master was inclined to agree. *Steady, Anakin Skywalker,* he thought to himself. *Concentrate.*

Then the light over the starting line flashed bright green, and the race was under way.

When the starting light turned green, Anakin Skywalker jammed the twin thruster bars to the extreme forward position, sending maximum power to the Radon-Ulzers. The big rocket engines bucked, roared like a caged beast, and promptly died.

The boy froze. All around him, racers shot from the start in a cacophony of sound and a flashing of bright metal. Sand fountained in the wake of their passing, clouding the air in a whirlwind of grit. In seconds, the boy was alone, save for Ben Quadinaros's Quadra-Pod, which sat stalled at the starting line in mirror image of his own.

Anakin's mind raced desperately. He'd fed in too much fuel from a dead start. The reworked engines couldn't handle all that power at once if the racer wasn't already moving. He yanked back on the thruster bars, returning them to the neutral position. Ratcheting back the switches to the feeder dump, he cleared the lines, then sealed them anew. Taking a deep breath, he pressed the ignition buttons. The starters cranked over and caught, and the big Radon-Ulzers roared to life with a booming cough. He fed in fuel more cautiously this time, impatience flooding through him, then slid the thruster bars forward smoothly. The engines shot ahead, dragging the Pod and the boy after them, exploding out of the start.

Anakin gave chase with single-minded determination, not bothering with anything but the dots in the distance that marked the location of the other racers. He tore across the flats, the whine of the Pod's engines growing steadily sharper, the land beneath fading to a wash of heat and light. The course was flat and open in the beginning, and he pushed the thruster bars forward some more. He was accelerating so quickly that everything about him turned swiftly to a sun-drenched blur.

Ahead, the first set of rock formations rose up against the horizon. Anakin could see the other Podracers now, bright metal shapes whipping across the flats, engines throwing off fire and smoke. He closed on them quickly, the Radon-Ulzers screaming. In an open stretch, he knew, there were no other engines that could match them.

A flush of white-hot excitement burned through him as he caught the trailing Podracers.

He hauled back on the thruster bars as he came up on them, giving himself space to maneuver. He went by two as if they were standing still, angling his way left and then right, threading the needle of space they had left between them. When he was clear, he fed power to the engines anew, and the g-force slammed him back against his padded seat. He caught multilimbed Gasgano next. Easing up to the Troiken's snub-nosed Podracer, he got ready to pass. Arch Canyon loomed ahead, and he wanted to be clear of the others when he navigated through the ravine. Maneuvering cautiously, he prepared to overtake on the right. But Gasgano saw him, and quickly moved to cut him off. Anakin waited, then angled left for another try. Again, Gasgano cut him off. Back and forth they slid above the desert floor like a krayt dragon chasing a womp rat.

A cliff drop off a low mesa appeared as a ragged line on the horizon. Anakin slowed, giving Gasgano the impression he was preparing for a drop shift. The wiry pilot, glancing back quickly to make certain where the boy was, held his position until he reached the mesa edge, then took the drop first. The moment he did so, Anakin jammed the thruster bars all the way forward, and his racer accelerated with such speed that it rocketed right over the top of Gasgano before the other could do anything to prevent it.

The dark crease of the canyon loomed ahead, and Anakin threaded the eye of its needle opening with a seamstress's skill, racing into the cool shadows beyond. The Radon-Ulzers hummed anxiously, the energy binders keeping them in sync, the Steelton cables drawing on the racing Pod with just the right amount of give through the wicked turns. Anakin worked the thruster bars with small, precise movements, envisioning the course in his mind—each twist, each deviation, each rise and drop. Everything was clear and certain to him. Everything was revealed.

He shot through the canyon and back out onto the open flats. Ahead, beyond a dozen others, Mawhonic and Sebulba fought for the lead. The Dug's distinctive X-shaped engines lifted and rose, maneuvering for position. But Mawhonic's slender racer was slowly gliding away.

Then Sebulba accelerated and swung violently left, careening toward the other pilot. Mawhonic reacted instinctively, swinging left as well—and directly into a massive rock formation. Mawhonic disappeared in a huge ball of flame and black smoke.

Next it was Xelbree challenging, trying to sneak past Sebulba from above, much as Anakin had done with Gasgano. But the Dug sensed his presence and rose to block his passage. Xelbree slid left, drawing alongside, holding fast. Sebulba seemed to lose ground, to give way slightly. But when Xelbree was next to him, the Dug triggered a side vent in his left exhaust. Fire spewed laterally into Xelbree's engine, cutting apart the metal housing as if it were made of flimsiplast. Xelbree tried frantically to move away, but he was too slow. Fuel caught and ignited. The damaged engine exploded, and the remaining engine and its Pod flew off into a cliff face and shattered.

Without slowing, Sebulba sped away from the wreckage, alone at the head of the pack.

* * *

In the arena stands and from viewing platforms scattered throughout the course, the crowd watched the progress of the race on handheld viewscreens as pictures of the racers were transmitted from droid observation holocams. From a monitoring tower, a two-headed announcer who bantered incessantly with himself reported on the leaders. Qui-Gon studied a screen with Padmé and Shmi, but there was neither mention nor sight of Anakin. The announcer's twin voices rose and fell in measured cadence, filling the air with their inflection, building in pitch to stir the already frenzied crowd.

Qui-Gon stared out into the flats, searching for movement. On his right, Jar Jar bickered with a skinny, sour-faced alien named Fanta, trying to peer over his shoulder, besieging him with questions, trying to make friends in the mistaken belief that because they looked vaguely alike, the Poldt would reciprocate his overtures. It wasn't working out. Fanta wanted nothing to do with Jar Jar and kept his back turned to the Gungan, deliberately hiding the screen from view. Jar Jar was growing impatient.

Qui-Gon shifted his gaze. In the crew pits, R2-D2, C-3PO, and Kitster waited in solitary isolation.

In a private box somewhat in back of and lower than Jabba's, Watto laughed and joked with his friends. The Toydarian flitted this way and that, catching glimpses of the race on various viewscreens, rubbing his hands together anxiously. He caught sight of Qui-Gon and gestured rudely, his meaning clear.

Below, at the start line, Ben Quadinaros still struggled to ignite the engines of his Quadra-Pod.

Qui-Gon closed his eyes and blocked everything away, sounds and movements alike, becoming one with the Force, disappearing into its flow, searching for Anakin. He stayed lost within himself as the roar of the crowd lifted anew, and the sound of rocket engines rose out of the distance. At the edge of the horizon, a clump of dark specks hove into view.

On the starting line, Ben Quadinaros finally managed to start the engines of his racer, all four bulbous monsters roaring to life, vibrating wildly within their casings. Engines and Pod lurched as

Quadinaros locked in the thrusters. But in the next instant the energy binders collapsed under the strain, the connecting cables snapped, and the engines shot off in four separate directions, exploding against stone walls, rock formations, and low dune banks. The crowd gasped in shock, shielding eyes and covering ears as the Pod and Ben Quadinaros collapsed to the racetrack in a useless heap.

Almost simultaneously Sebulba's racer screamed past the arena, shooting under the finish arch, and rocketing off on the start of the second lap. Two other racers followed, their engines roaring loudly as they whipped past, their colorful metal bodies agleam in the midday suns.

There was no sign of Anakin.

Qui-Gon kept his eyes closed, searching within his consciousness. Beside him, Shmi and Padmé exchanged worried glances. Jar Jar still hung on Fanta, pounding him on the back now in excitement as the other grimaced and tried to move away.

Three more racers tore past, the sound of their engines dying into silence as they faded from view. A fourth, Ody Mandrell, turned into the pits, the engines of his Pod shaking and smoking as he screeched to a stop. Pit droids rushed to service the racer, swarming over the engines. Ody stood up in the cockpit, a big, squat, reptilian Er'Kit, arms gesturing. But when the engines ignited anew, DUM-4, a pit droid, was standing at the left intake, and the engine sucked it inside, chewed it up, and spit it out the exhaust in a mangled heap.

The crowd went back to their viewscreens, intent on the race.

Then R2-D2, standing with Kitster and C-3PO at the edge of their station, gave an excited beep.

Qui-Gon's eyes snapped open. "Here he comes!" he exclaimed quickly.

Anakin Skywalker exploded out of the midday glare, the big Radon-Ulzers howling in fury.

Amid the cheers and shouts of his companions and the crowd, Qui-Gon Jinn just smiled. Anakin had begun to overtake the pack.

* * *

At the beginning of the second lap, Anakin was in sixth place. As the race progressed, he was slowly disappearing into the workings of his racer, becoming one with its engines, feeling the strain and tug on each rivet and screw. Wind whipped by him in a screaming rush, locking him away in its white noise. There was only himself and the machine, all speed and response. It was the way racing affected him, melding his body with the Pod and engines until he was a part of both. Moment by moment, the symbiosis deepened, joining them, giving him insights and understandings that transcended his senses and knowledge, projecting him past the present and into a place others could not reach.

Approaching Arch Canyon, he bore down on the leaders, young face intense. Skimming the flats, he whipped past Aldar Beedo and sideslipped Clegg Holdfast. To one side, a fast-closing Ody Mandrell banked too hard over a sandy rise and caught his engine in the sand. Ody's racer cartwheeled in a spectacular twisting of engines and Pod and exploded apart.

Anakin was only four racers back from Sebulba and could see the Dug's craft clearly in the distance.

Everything happened quickly after that.

The racers whipped through Arch Canyon and out the other side in a ragged line, with Anakin narrowing the gap between himself and the others. Tusken Raiders, hiding in the rocks of the cliffs that formed the corner of Tusken Turn, got lucky and hit Teemto Pagalies. Teemto's racer simply exploded and was gone. Anakin flew through the vaporized wreckage in pursuit of the others. He passed Elan Mak and Habba Kee in a rush. Ahead, Mars Guo was closing on Sebulba, wary of the Dug, keeping down and away, trying to sneak past. Anakin drew nearer to both, leapfrogging sand dunes in a long depression, easing slowly up on Mars Guo.

Suddenly Sebulba reached out of his Pod's cockpit and released a ragged bit of metal directly into Mars Guo's left engine intake. Metal clashed violently against metal, and the damaged engine began to spew smoke and fire. Mars tried to hold the machine steady, but the failing engine bucked and lost power, causing the Pod to veer sharply into Anakin. The racers collided in a shriek of metal, and a leading edge of Mars Guo's vertical stabilizer snagged the Steelton line to Anakin's left engine and released the binding.

Instantly Anakin's Pod began to swing violently at the end of its single remaining line, whipsawing back and forth. The Radon-Ulzers continued to act in concert, locked together by the energy binders, but the racer was out of control. Anakin worked the stabilizer pedals with his feet, fighting to hold the Pod steady as it swung like a pendulum. The unhooked line snapped viciously in the wake of the engine's exhaust, threatening to tangle or snag on an outcropping and drag the racer down. Anakin groped along the floor of his cockpit, searching for the magnetic retriever. When he found it, he flicked on the power button and extended the retriever out to the left side, trying to make contact with the loose line. The effort forced him to pull back on the thruster bars to cut power, and he fell behind Sebulba once more. Elan Mak, Habba Kee, and now Obitoki as well swept by him, giving chase to the Dug.

Anakin glanced frantically over his shoulder. The bulk of the pack was closing on him once more.

After a dozen tries, he finally focused his concentration sufficiently to snag the loose engine line with the retriever and maneuver it back to its hook. Sweat and grit coated his face, and his jacket sleeve was ripped. Casting down the retriever, he jammed the thruster bars forward once more. Stabilized at the ends of the Steelton lines, the Pod held steady now as the Radon-Ulzers bucked, and the racer accelerated after the leaders.

Anakin caught Elan Mak first and slid around him easily. He was closing on Habba Kee when Obitoki tried to pass Sebulba. The Dug waited until his rival had pulled alongside, then used the same tactic he had employed against Xelbree. Opening a small side vent in the left exhaust, he sent a gush of fire into the housing of Obitoki's right engine. Fuel in the lines caught fire and exploded, and Obitoki's racer dived nose first into the desert, sending a wide spray of grit everywhere.

Habba Kee flew into it just ahead of Anakin, low and tight to the ground. Momentarily blinded, he swerved the wrong way and caught a piece of one of Obitoki's engines where it jutted from the sand. Engines and Pod tangled and crashed in a wild explosion. Anakin followed Habba Kee into the smoke and grit, blinded as well. A piece of steaming metal flew at him out of the haze, careening off his right engine housing and barely missing his head. But the boy was seeing with more than his eyes, sensing with his mind, calm and steady within himself. He could feel the danger waiting, and he worked the thruster bars smoothly, sliding past the wreckage.

Then he was in the clear again and bearing down on Sebulba.

He caught the Dug as they screamed past the arena and under the finish arch for the start of the third and final lap.

In his mind, Anakin could see Qui-Gon and Jar Jar watching him; Kitster, standing in the crew pits, his friend cheering wildly, and R2-D2 and C-3PO, the former beeping, the latter nattering back at him in response; Padmé, her beautiful face framed with worry; and his mother, her eyes filled with terror. He could see them all, as if he were standing among them, standing outside himself, watching the race . . .

He blocked their faces away, banished the images from his thoughts, and focused everything on Sebulba.

They were speeding out of Arch Canyon when Sebulba decided to put an end to Anakin once and for all. The Dug knew where all the droid observation cams were situated. He knew the angles of placement and how to avoid giving himself away. Swinging his racer close to Anakin's, he opened the side vent on his exhaust and tried to scorch the boy's engine housing as he had done with Xelbree and Obitoki. But Anakin had fallen victim to that particular trick once before and was looking for it this time. He shifted just above the cutting flame and out of reach. When Sebulba tried to follow, Anakin dropped down again—but too far, momentarily losing control. His racer veered from the course right into a line of warning signs, sending them flying in all directions. Desperate to recover, he lifted the nose of his craft skyward, jammed his thruster bars forward, and accelerated. The Radon-Ulzers boomed, his racer gave a frightening lurch, and he leapfrogged right over Sebulba to take the lead.

Down through the first set of caves and past Tusken Turn the racers tore, Anakin leading, Sebulba right on his tail. At speeds too great for maintaining proper control, the antagonists banked and angled as if safety were of no importance at all.

And finally burst into the clear once more.

Again, Sebulba tried to regain the lead, pushing for an opening. Anakin held him off, but then one of the horizontal stabilizers on the left engine began to shudder violently. A momentary vision of Sebulba hammering on his stabilizer just before the start of the race flashed through Anakin's mind. He eased off on the thruster bars, jettisoned the stabilizer, and switched to an auxiliary mount. In the process, he was forced to give way. Sebulba raced past him to take command of the lead once more.

Time and space were running out on Anakin Skywalker. He shoved the thruster bars forward and went after the Dug. Sebulba saw him coming and fishtailed his Pod back and forth in front of the boy to keep him from passing. Over the courseway they sped, jockeying for position. Anakin tried everything he knew, but Sebulba was a seasoned veteran and was able to counter each attempt. Metta Drop flew past as the racers roared out of the dune hills and onto the final stretch of flats.

Finally Anakin shifted left, then right. But this time when Sebulba moved to block him, Anakin faked a third shift, drawing the Dug left again. The instant Sebulba began his blocking move, Anakin jerked his racer hard to the right and nosed in beside the Dug.

Down the flat, open final stretch of the course the Podracers tore, side by side, the arena stands and warding statuary beginning to take shape ahead. Sebulba screamed in frustration and deliberately swerved his Pod into Anakin's. Infuriated by the boy's dogged persistence, he slammed into him, once, twice. But on the third strike, their steering rods caught, locking them together. Anakin fought with his controls, trying to break free, but the Pods were hooked fast. Sebulba laughed, jamming his racer against the boy's in an effort to force him into the ground. Anakin whipped the thruster bars forward and back, trying to disengage from the tangle. The Radon-Ulzers strained with the effort, and the steering rods groaned and bent.

Finally Anakin's rod broke completely, snapping off both the armature and the main horizontal stabilizer. The boy's Pod jerked and spun at the ends of the Steelton cables, shimmying with such force that Anakin would have been thrown from the Pod if he had not been strapped down.

But it was much worse for Sebulba. When Anakin's steering arm snapped, the Dug's Pod shot forward as if catapulted, collapsing the towlines, sending the engines screaming out of control. One engine slammed into a piece of the ancient statuary and disintegrated in flames. Then the second went, ramming into the sand and exploding in a massive fireball. The towing cables broke free, and the Dug's Pod was sent skidding through the flaming wreckage of the engines, twisting and bumping violently along the desert floor to a smoking stop. Sebulba extricated himself in a shrieking fit, throwing pieces of his ruined Pod in all directions only to discover that his pants were on fire.

Anakin Skywalker flew overhead, the exhausts from the big Radon-Ulzers sending sand and grit into the Dug's face in a stinging spray. Hanging on to maintain control as he crossed the finish line, he became, at nine years of age, the youngest winner ever of the Boonta Eve race.

As the viewing platform he occupied with Shmi, Padmé, and Jar Jar slowly lowered, Qui-Gon watched the crowd surge toward Anakin's racer. The boy had brought the Pod to a skidding halt in the center of the raceway, shut down the Radon-Ulzers, and climbed out. Kitster had already reached him and was hugging him tightly, and R2-D2 and C-3PO were scuttling around them both. When the crowd converged moments later, they hoisted Anakin aloft and carried him away, chanting and shouting his name.

Qui-Gon exchanged a warm smile with Shmi, nodding his approval of the boy's performance. Anakin Skywalker was special indeed.

The viewing platform settled in place smoothly, and its occupants off-loaded onto the raceway in a rush. Allowing his companions to join the celebration, the Jedi Master turned back toward the stands. Ascending the stairways swiftly, he reached Watto's private box in minutes. A knot of aliens departed just in front of him, laughing and joking in several languages, counting fistfuls of currency and credits. Watto was staring out at the chanting crowd, hovering at the edge of the viewport, a dejected look on his wrinkled blue face.

The moment he caught sight of Qui-Gon, his dejection transformed, and he flew at the Jedi Master in undisguised fury.

"You! You swindled me!" He bounced in the air in front of Qui-Gon, shaking with rage. "You knew the boy was going to win! Somehow you knew it! I lost everything!"

Qui-Gon smiled benignly. "Whenever you gamble, my friend, eventually you'll lose. Today wasn't your day." The smile dropped away. "Bring the hyperdrive parts to the main hangar right away. I'll come by your shop later so you can release the boy."

The Toydarian shoved his snout against Qui-Gon's nose. "You can't have him! It wasn't a fair bet!"

Qui-Gon looked him up and down with a chilly stare. "Would you like to discuss it with the Hutts? I'm sure they would be happy to settle the matter."

Watto jerked as if stung, his beady eyes filled with hate. "No, no! I want no more of your tricks." He gestured emphatically. "Take the boy! Be gone!"

He wheeled away and flew out of the box, body hunched beneath madly beating wings. Qui-Gon watched him depart, then started down the stairs for the racetrack, his mind already turning to other things.

Had he not been so preoccupied with his plans for what lay ahead, he might have caught sight of the Sith probe droid trailing after.

Within an hour, the arena had emptied, the racers had been stored or hauled away for repairs, and the main hangar left almost deserted. A few pit droids were still engaged in salvaging pieces of wreckage from the race, coming and going in steady pursuit of their work. Anakin alone of the Pod pilots remained, checking over his damaged racer. He was dirty and ragged, his hair spiky and his face streaked with sweat and grime. His jacket was torn in several places, and there was blood on his clothing where he had slashed his arm on a jagged piece of metal during the battle with Sebulba.

Qui-Gon watched him thoughtfully, standing to one side with Padmé and Shmi as the boy, Jar Jar, R2-D2, and C-3PO moved busily over the Pod and engines. Could it be? he was wondering for what must have been the hundredth time, pondering the way the boy handled a Podracer, the maturity he exhibited, and the instincts he possessed. Was it possible?

He shelved his questions for another time. It would be up to the Council to decide. Abruptly, he left the women, walking over to the boy and kneeling beside him.

"You're a bit worse for wear, Annie," he said softly, placing his hands on the boy's shoulders and looking him in the eyes, "but you did well." Smiling reassuringly, he wiped a patch of dirt off the boy's face. "There, good as new."

He ruffled the boy's unruly hair and helped bind his injured arm. Shmi and Padmé joined them and were moved to give Anakin fresh hugs and kisses, checking him over carefully, touching his cheeks and forehead.

"Ah, gee . . . enough of this," the boy mumbled in embarrassment.

His mother smiled, shaking her head. "It's so wonderful, Annie—what you've done here. Do you know? You've brought hope to those who have none. I'm so very proud of you."

"We owe you everything," Padmé added quickly, giving him an intense, warm look.

Anakin blushed scarlet. "Just feeling this good is worth anything," he declared, smiling back.

Qui-Gon walked over to where the hyperdrive parts were loaded on an antigrav repulsorsled harnessed to a pair of eopies. Watto had made delivery as promised, though not without considerable grumbling and a barrage of thinly veiled threats. Qui-Gon checked the container straps, glanced out into the midday heat, and walked back to the others.

"Padmé, Jar Jar, let's go," he ordered abruptly. "We've got to get these parts back to the ship."

The group moved over to the eopies, laughing and talking.

Padmé hugged and kissed Anakin again, then climbed onto one of the eopies behind Qui-Gon, taking hold of his waist. Jar Jar swung onto the second animal and promptly slid off the other side, collapsing in a heap. R2-D2 beeped encouragingly as the Gungan tried again, this time managing to keep his seat. Good-byes and thank-yous were exchanged, but it was an awkward moment for Anakin. He looked as if he wanted to say something to Padmé, moving up beside her momentarily, staring up at her expectantly. But all he could manage was a sad, confused look.

Slowly, the eopies began to move off, Anakin and his mother standing with C-3PO, waving after.

"I'll return the eopies by midday," Qui-Gon promised, calling over his shoulder.

Padmé did not look back at all.

Qui-Gon Jinn and company rode out of Mos Espa into the Tatooine desert, R2-D2 leading the way, rolling along in front of the eopies and sled at a steady pace. The suns were rising quickly to a midday position in the sky, and the heat rose off the sand in waves. But the journey back to the Queen's transport was accomplished swiftly and without incident.

Obi-Wan was waiting for them, appearing down the ramp-way as soon as they neared, his youthful face intense. "I was getting worried," he announced without preamble.

Qui-Gon dismounted, then helped Padmé down. "Start getting this hyperdrive generator installed," he ordered. "I'm going back. I have some unfinished business."

"Business?" his protégé echoed, arching one eyebrow.

"I won't be long."

Obi-Wan studied him a moment, then sighed. "Why do I sense we've picked up another stray?"

Qui-Gon took his arm and moved him away from the others. "It's the boy who's responsible for getting us these parts." He paused. "The boy whose blood sample you ran the midi-chlorian test on last night."

Obi-Wan gave him a hard, steady look, then turned away.

On a rise overlooking the spacecraft, hidden in the glare of the suns and the ripple of the dunes, the Sith probe droid hung motionless for a final transmission, then quickly sped away.

Anakin walked home with his mother and C-3PO, still wrapped in the euphoria of his victory, but wrestling as well with his sadness over the departure of Padmé. He hadn't thought about what would happen to her if he won the Boonta Eve, that it would mean Qui-Gon would secure the hyperdrive generator he needed to make their transport functional. So when she bent to kiss and hug him good-bye, it was the first time he had given the matter any serious thought since her arrival. He was stunned, caught in a mix of emotions, and all of a sudden he wanted to tell her to stay. But he couldn't bring himself to speak the words, knowing how foolish they would sound, realizing she couldn't do so in any case.

So he stood there like a droid without its vocoder, watching her ride away behind Qui-Gon, thinking it might well be the last time he would ever see her, and wondering how he was going to live with himself if it was.

Unable to sit still once he had walked his mother to their home, he placed C-3PO back in his bedroom, deactivated him, and went out again. Qui-Gon had told him he was relieved of any work today at Watto's, so he pretty much could do what he wanted until the Jedi returned. He gave no thought to what would happen then, wandering down toward Mos Espa Way, waving as his name was shouted out from every quarter on his journey, basking in the glow of his success. He still couldn't quite believe it, and yet it felt as if he had always known he would win this race. Kitster appeared, then Amee and Wald, and soon he was surrounded by a dozen others.

He was just approaching the connector to Mos Espa Way when a Rodian youngster, bigger than himself, blocked his way. Anakin had cheated, the Rodian sneered. He couldn't have won the Boonta Eve any other way. No slave could win anything.

Anakin was on top of him so fast the bigger being barely had time to put up his arms in defense before he was on the ground.

Anakin was hitting him as hard and fast as he could, not thinking about anything but how angry he was, not even aware that the source of his anger had nothing to do with his victim and everything to do with losing Padmé.

Then Qui-Gon, returned by now with the eopies, was looming over him. He pulled Anakin away, separating the two fighters, and demanded to know what this was all about. Somewhat sheepishly, but still angry, Anakin told him. Qui-Gon studied him carefully, disappointment registering on his broad features. He fixed the young Rodian with his gaze and asked him if he still believed Anakin had cheated. The youngster, glowering at Anakin, said he did.

Qui-Gon put his hand on Anakin's shoulder and steered him away from the crowd, not saying anything until they were out of hearing.

"You know, Annie," he said then, his deep voice thoughtful, "fighting didn't change his opinion. The opinions of others, whether you agree with them or not, are something you have to learn to tolerate."

He walked the boy back toward his home, counseling him quietly about the way life worked, hand resting on his shoulder in a way that made Anakin feel comforted. As they neared the boy's home, the Jedi reached beneath his poncho and produced a leather pouch filled with credits.

"These are yours," he announced. "I sold the Pod." He pursed his lips. "To a particularly surly and rather insistent Dug."

Anakin accepted the bag, grinning broadly, the fight and its cause forgotten.

He ran up the steps to his door and burst through, Qui-Gon following silently. "Mom, Mom!" he cried out as she appeared to greet him. "Guess what! Qui-Gon sold the Pod! Look at all the money we have!"

He produced the leather pouch and dropped it into her hands, enjoying the startled look on her face. "Oh, my goodness!" she breathed softly, staring down at the bulging pouch. "Annie, that's wonderful!"

Her eyes lifted quickly to meet Qui-Gon's. The Jedi stepped forward, holding her gaze.

"Annie has been freed," he said.

The boy's eyes went wide. "What?"

Qui-Gon glanced down at him. "You are no longer a slave."

Shmi Skywalker stared at the Jedi in disbelief, her worn face rigid, her eyes mirroring her shock and disbelief.

"Mom? Did you hear that, Mom?" Anakin let out a whoop and jumped as high as he could manage. It wasn't possible! But he knew it was true, knew that it really was!

He managed to collect himself. "Was that part of the prize, or what?" he asked, grinning.

Qui-Gon grinned back. "Let's just say Watto learned an important lesson about gambling."

Shmi Skywalker was shaking her head, still stunned by the news, still working it through. But the sight of Anakin's face made everything come clear for her in an instant. She reached out to him and pressed him to her.

"Now you can make your dreams come true, Annie," she whispered, her face radiant as she touched his cheek. "You're free."

She released him and turned to Qui-Gon, her eyes bright and expectant. "Will you take him with you? Is he to become a Jedi?"

Anakin beamed at the suggestion, wheeling quickly on Qui-Gon, waiting for his answer.

The Jedi Master hesitated. "Our meeting was not a coincidence. Nothing happens by accident. You are strong with the Force, Annie, but you may not be accepted by the Council."

Anakin heard what he wanted to hear, blocking away everything else, seeing the possibilities that had fueled his hopes and dreams for so long come alive in a single moment.

"A Jedi!" he gasped. "You mean I get to go with you in your starship and everything!"

And be with Padmé again! The thought struck him like a thunderbolt, wrapping him in such expectancy that it was all he could do to listen to what the Jedi Master said next.

Qui-Gon knelt before the boy, his face somber. "Anakin, training to be a Jedi will not be easy. It will be a challenge. And if you succeed, it will be a hard life."

Anakin shook his head quickly. "But it's what I want! It's what I've always dreamed about!" He looked quickly to his mother. "Can I go, Mom?"

But Qui-Gon drew him back with a touch. "This path has been placed before you, Annie. The choice to take it must be yours alone."

The man and the boy stared at each other. A mix of emotions roiled through Anakin, threatening to sweep him away, but at their forefront was the happiness he felt at finding the thing he wanted most in all the world within reach—to be a Jedi, to journey down the space lanes of the galaxy.

He glanced quickly at his mother, at her worn, accepting face, seeing in her eyes that in this, as in all things, she wanted what was best for him.

His gaze returned to Qui-Gon. "I want to go," he said.

"Then pack your things," the Jedi Master advised. "We haven't much time."

"Yippee!" the boy shouted, jumping up and down, anxious already to be on his way. He rushed to his mother and hugged her as hard as he could manage, then broke away for his bedroom.

He was almost to the doorway when he realized he had forgotten something. A chill swept through him as he wheeled back to Qui-Gon. "What about Mom?" he asked hurriedly, eyes darting from one to the other. "Is she free, too? You're coming, aren't you, Mom?"

Qui-Gon and his mother exchanged a worried glance, and he knew the answer before the Jedi spoke the words. "I tried to free your mother, Annie, but Watto wouldn't have it. Slaves give status and lend prestige to their owners here on Tatooine."

The boy felt his chest and throat tighten. "But the money from selling . . ."

Qui-Gon shook his head. "It's not nearly enough."

There was a hushed silence, and then Shmi Skywalker came

to her son and sat down in a chair next to him, taking both of his hands in hers and drawing him close. Her eyes were steady as she looked into his.

"Annie, my place is here," she said quietly. "My future is here. It is time for you to let go . . . to let go of me. I cannot go with you."

The boy swallowed hard. "I want to stay with you, then. I don't want things to change."

She gave him an encouraging smile, her brow knitting. "You can't stop change any more than you can stop the suns from setting. Listen to your feelings, Annie. You know what's right."

Anakin Skywalker took a long, slow breath and dropped his gaze, his head lowering. Everything was coming apart inside, all the happiness melting away, all the expectancy fading. But then he felt his mother's hands tighten over his own, and in her touch he found the strength he needed to do what he knew he must.

Nevertheless, his eyes were brimming as he lifted his gaze once more. "I'm going to miss you so much, Mom," he whispered.

His mother nodded. "I love you, Annie." She released his hands. "Now, hurry."

Anakin gave her a quick, hard hug, and raced from the room, tears streaking his face.

Once within his own room, Anakin stood staring about in sudden bewilderment. He was leaving, and he did not know when he would be coming back. He had never been anywhere but here, never known anyone but the people of Mos Espa and those who came to trade with them. He had dreamed about other worlds and other lives, about becoming a pilot of a mainline ship, and about becoming a Jedi. But the impact of what it actually meant to be standing at the threshold of an embarkation to the life he had so often wished for was overwhelming.

He found himself thinking of the old spacer, telling him that he wouldn't be surprised at all if Anakin Skywalker became something more than a slave. He had wanted that more than anything, had hoped with all his heart for it to happen.

But he had never, ever considered the possibility he would have to leave his mother behind.

He wiped the tears from his eyes, fighting back new ones, hearing his mother's and Qui-Gon's voices from the other room.

"Thank you," his mother was saying softly.

"I will watch after him. You have my word." The Jedi's deep voice was warm and reassuring. "Will you be all right?"

Anakin couldn't hear her reply. But then she said, "He was in my life for such a short time . . ."

She trailed off, distracted. Anakin forced himself to quit listening, and he began pulling clothes out and stuffing them into a backpack. He didn't have much, and it didn't take him long. He looked about for anything of importance he might have missed, and his eyes settled on C-3PO, sitting motionless on the workbench. He walked over to the protocol droid and switched him on. C-3PO cocked his head and looked at the boy blankly.

"Well, Threepio, I'm leaving," Anakin said solemnly. "I'm free. I'm going away, in a starship . . ."

He didn't know what else to say. The droid cocked his head. "Well, Master Anakin, you are my maker, and I wish you well. Although I'd like it better if I were a little less naked."

The boy sighed and nodded. "I'm sorry I wasn't able to finish you, Threepio—to give you coverings and all. I'm going to miss working on you. You've been a great pal. I'll make sure Mom doesn't sell you or anything. Bye!"

He snatched up his backpack and rushed from the room, hearing C-3PO call after him plaintively, "Sell me?"

He said good-bye to his mother, braver now, more determined, and walked out the door with Qui-Gon, his course of action settled. He had gotten barely a dozen meters from his home when Kitster, who had trailed them back from the fight, came rushing up to him.

"Where are you going, Annie?" his friend asked doubtfully.

Anakin took a deep breath. "I've been freed, Kitster. I'm going away with Qui-Gon. On a spaceship."

Kitster's eyes went wide, and his mouth opened in a silent exclamation. Anakin fished in his pockets and came out with a handful of credits, which he shoved at his friend. "Here. These are for you."

Kitster's dark face looked down at the credits, then back up at Anakin. "Do you have to go, Annie? Do you have to? Can't you stay? Annie, you're a hero!"

Anakin swallowed hard. "I . . ." He glanced past Kitster to his mother, still standing in the doorway looking after him, then down to where Qui-Gon was waiting. He shook his head. "I can't."

Kitster nodded. "Well."

"Well," Anakin repeated, looking at him.

"Thanks for everything, Annie," the other boy said. There were tears in his eyes as he accepted the credits. "You're my best friend."

Anakin bit his lip. "I won't forget."

He hugged Kitster impulsively, then broke away and raced toward Qui-Gon. But before he reached him, he glanced back one more time at his mother. Seeing her standing in the doorway brought him about. He stood there momentarily, undecided, conflicting emotions tearing at him. Then his already shaky resolve collapsed altogether, and he raced back to her. By the time he reached her, he was crying freely.

"I can't do it, Mom," he whispered, clinging to her. "I just can't!"

He was shaking, wracked with sobs, disintegrating inside so quickly that all he could think about was holding on to her. Shmi let him do so for a moment, comforting him with her warmth, then backed him away.

She knelt before him, her worn face solemn. "Annie, remember when you climbed that dune in order to chase the banthas away so they wouldn't be shot? You were only five. Remember how you collapsed several times in the heat, exhausted, thinking you couldn't do it, that it was too hard?"

Anakin nodded, his face streaked with tears.

Shmi held his gaze. "This is one of those times when you have to do something you don't think you can do. But I know how strong you are, Annie. I know you can do this."

The boy swallowed his tears, thinking she was wrong, he was not strong at all, but knowing, too, she had decided he must go, even if he found it hard, even if he resisted.

"Will I ever see you again?" he asked in desperation, giving voice to the worst of his fears.

"What does your heart tell you?" she asked quietly.

Anakin shook his head doubtfully. "I don't know. Yes, I guess."

His mother nodded. "Then it will happen, Annie."

Anakin took a deep breath to steady himself. He had stopped crying now, and he wiped the dampness of his tears from his face.

"I will become a Jedi," he declared in a small voice. "And I will come back and free you, Mom. I promise."

"No matter where you are, my love will be with you," Shmi told him, her kind face bent close to his. "Now be brave, and don't look back."

"I love you, Mom," Anakin said.

She hugged him one final time, then turned him around so he was facing away from her. "Don't look back, Annie," she whispered.

She gave him a small push, and he strode determinedly away, shouldering his pack, keeping his eyes fixed on a point well past where Qui-Gon stood waiting. He walked toward that point without slowing, marching right past the Jedi Master, fighting back the tears that threatened to come yet again. It took only a few minutes, and his mother and his home were behind him.

They went to Watto's shop first, where the Toydarian had completed the forms necessary to assure Anakin's freedom. The transmitter that bound Anakin to his life of slavery was deactivated permanently. It would be removed surgically at a later date.

Watto was still grumbling about the unfairness of things as they left him and went back out into the street.

From there, at Anakin's urging, they walked to Jira's fruit stand a short distance away. Anakin, much recovered from the trauma of leaving his mother, marched up to the old woman and put a handful of credits into her frail hands.

"I've been freed, Jira," he told her, a determined set to his jaw. "I'm going away. Use these for that cooling unit I promised you. Otherwise, I'll worry."

Jira looked at the credits in disbelief. She shook her white head. "Can I give you a hug?" she asked him softly. She reached out for him, drawing him against her thin body, her eyes closing as she held him. "I'll miss you, Annie," she said, releasing him. "There isn't a kinder boy in the galaxy. You be careful."

He left her in a rush, racing after Qui-Gon, who was already moving away, anxious to get going. They walked in silence down a series of side streets, the boy's eyes taking in familiar sights he would not soon see again, remembering his life here, saying good-bye.

He was lost in his own thoughts when Qui-Gon swung about with such swiftness it caught the boy completely by surprise. Down swept the Jedi's lightsaber in a brilliant arc, cutting through the shadows between two buildings, clashing momentarily with something made of metal that shattered in the wake of the weapon's passing.

Qui-Gon clicked off the lightsaber and knelt to inspect a cluster of metal parts still sparking and fizzing in the sand. The acrid smell of ozone and burning insulation hung in the dry air.

"What is it?" the boy asked, peering over his shoulder.

Qui-Gon rose. "Probe droid. Very unusual. Not like anything I've seen before." He glanced about worriedly, eyes sharp and bright as he cast up and down the street.

"Come on, Annie," he ordered, and they moved quickly away.

Qui-Gon Jinn took the boy out of Mos Espa swiftly, hurrying through the crowded streets to the less populated outskirts.
All the while, his eyes and mind were searching, the former the
landscape of Tatooine, the latter the landscape of the Force. His
instincts had alerted him to the presence of the probe droid
tracking them, and his Jedi training in the ways of the Force
warned him now of something far more dangerous. He could
feel a shifting in the balance of things that suggested an intrusion
on the harmony that the Force required, a dark weight descending like a massive stone.

Once out on the desert, in the open, he picked up the pace.
The Queen's transport came into view, a dark shape just ahead, a
haven of safety. He heard Anakin call out to him, the boy working hard to keep up, but beginning to fall behind.

Glancing over his shoulder to give his response and offer encouragement, he caught sight of the speeder and its dark-cloaked
rider bearing down on them.

"Drop, Anakin!" he shouted, wheeling about.

The boy threw himself facedown, flattening against the sand
as the speeder whipped overhead, barely missing him as it bore
down on Qui-Gon. The Jedi Master already had his lightsaber
out, the blade activated, the weapon held before him in two

hands. The speeder came at him, a saddle-shaped vehicle with no weapons in evidence, made to rely on quickness and maneuverability rather than firepower. It was like nothing the Jedi had ever seen, but vaguely reminiscent of something dead and gone.

Its rider rode out of the glare of the suns and was revealed. Bold markings of red and black covered a demonic face in strange, jagged patterns beneath a crown of stunted horns encircling its head. Man-shaped and humanoid, his slitted eyes and hooked teeth were nevertheless feral and predatory, and his howl was a hunter's challenge to his prey.

The primal scream had barely sounded before he was on top of Qui-Gon, wheeling the speeder aside deftly at the last moment, closing off its thruster, and leaping from the seat, all in one swift movement. He carried a lightsaber of another make, and the weapon was cutting at the Jedi Master even before the attacker's feet had touched the ground. Qui-Gon, surprised by the other's quickness and ferocity, barely blocked the blow with his own weapon, the blades sliding apart with a harsh rasp. The attacker spun away in a whirl of dark clothing, then attacked anew, lightsaber slashing at his intended prey, face alight with a killing frenzy that promised no quarter.

Anakin was back on his feet, staring at them, clearly unable to decide what he should do. Fighting to hold his ground, Qui-Gon caught sight of him out of the corner of his eye.

"Annie! Get out of here!" he cried out.

His attacker closed with him again, forcing him back, striking at him from every angle. Even without knowing anything else, Qui-Gon knew this man was trained in the fighting arts of a Jedi, a skilled and dangerous adversary. Worse, he was younger, quicker, and stronger than Qui-Gon, and he was gaining ground rapidly. The Jedi Master blocked him again and again, but could not find an opening that would provide any chance of escape.

"Annie!" he screamed again, seeing the boy immobilized. "Get to the ship! Tell them to take off! Go, go!"

Hammering at the demonic-faced attacker with renewed determination, Qui-Gon Jinn saw the boy at last begin to run.

In a rush of emotion dominated by fear and doubt, Anakin Skywalker raced past the combatants for the Naboo spacecraft. It sat not three hundred meters away, metal skin gleaming dully in the afternoon sunlight. Its loading ramp was down, but there was no sign of its occupants. Anakin ran faster, sweat streaking his body. He could feel his heart hammering in his chest as he reached the ramp and bounded onto the ship.

Just inside the hatchway, he found Padmé and a dark-skinned man in uniform coming toward him. When Padmé caught sight of him, her eyes went wide.

"Qui-Gon's in trouble!" the boy blurted out, gasping for breath. "He says to take off! Now!"

The man stared, eyes questioning and suspicious. "Who are you?" he demanded.

But Padmé was already moving, seizing Anakin by the arm, pulling him toward the front of the spacecraft. "He's a friend," she answered, leading the way forward. "Hurry, Captain."

They rushed down the hallway into the cockpit, Anakin trying to tell the girl what had happened, his words tumbling over one another, his face flushed and anxious. Padmé moved him along in a no-nonsense way, nodding her understanding, telling him to hurry, taking charge of everything.

When they reached the cockpit, they found two more men at work checking out the craft's control panel. They turned at the approach of Anakin and his companions. One wore a pilot's insignia on the breast of his jacket. The second, Anakin was quite certain from the cut of his hair and the look of his clothing, was another Jedi.

"Qui-Gon is in trouble," Padmé announced quickly.

"He says to take off," Anakin added in support.

The Jedi was on his feet at once. He was much younger than Qui-Gon, his face smooth, his eyes intense, his hair cut short save for a single braided pigtail that fell over his right shoulder. "Where is he?" he demanded. Then, without waiting for an answer, he wheeled back to the viewport and began scanning the empty flats.

"I don't see anything," the pilot said, peering over his shoulder.

"Over there!" The sharp eyes of the Jedi caught sight of movement just at the corner of the port. "Get us into the air and over there! Now! Fly low!"

The man called Ric threw himself into the pilot's seat, while the others, Anakin included, scrambled to find seats. The big repulsorlifts kicked in with a low growl, the rampway sealed, and the sleek transport rose and wheeled smoothly about.

"There," the Jedi breathed, pointing.

They could see Qui-Gon Jinn now, engaged in battle with the dark-garbed, demonic figure. The combatants surged back and forth across the flats, lightsabers flashing brightly with each blow struck, sand and grit swirling in all directions. Qui-Gon's long hair streamed out behind him in sharp contrast to the smooth horned head of his adversary. The pilot Ric took the spacecraft toward them quickly, skimming the ground barely higher than a speeder bike, coming in from behind the attacker. Anakin held his breath as they closed on the fighters. Ric's hand slid over the control that would lower the ramp, easing it forward carefully.

"Stand by," he ordered, freezing them all in place as he swung the ship about.

The combatants disappeared in a fresh swirl of sand and the glare of Tatooine's twin suns. All eyes shifted quickly to the viewscreens, searching desperately.

Then Qui-Gon appeared, leaping onto the lowered rampway of the transport, gaining purchase, one hand grasping a strut for support. Ric hissed in approval and fought to hold the spacecraft steady. But the horned attacker was already in pursuit, racing out of the haze and leaping onto the ramp as the ship began to rise. Balanced precariously against the sway of the ship, eyes flaring in rage, he fought to keep his footing.

Qui-Gon attacked at once, rushing the other man, closing with him at the edge of the ramp. They were twenty meters into the air by now, the pilot holding the spacecraft steady as he saw the combatants come to grips yet again, afraid to go higher while Qui-Gon was exposed. The Jedi Master and his adversary filled the viewscreen commanding the rampway entrance, faces tight with determination and streaked with sweat.

"Qui-Gon," Anakin heard the second Jedi say quietly, desperately, watching the battle for just a moment more, then tearing his eyes away from the viewscreen and racing down the open corridor.

On the screen, Anakin watched Qui-Gon Jinn step back, level his lightsaber, and swing a powerful, two-handed blow at his attacker. The horned man blocked it, but only barely, and in the process lost his balance completely. The blow's force swept him away, clear of the ramp and off into space. He dropped back toward the desert floor, landed in a crouch, and rose instantly to his feet. But the chase was over. He stood watching in frustration, yellow eyes aflame, as the ramp to the Queen's transport closed and the spacecraft rocketed away.

Qui-Gon had barely managed to scramble up the rampway and into the interior of the ship before the hatch sealed and the Nubian began to accelerate. He lay on the cool metal floor of the entry, his clothing dusty and damp with his sweat, his body bruised and battered. He breathed deeply, waiting for his pounding heart to quiet. He had barely escaped with his life, and the thought was worrisome. His opponent was strong and had tested him severely. He was getting old, he decided, and he did not like the feeling.

Obi-Wan and Anakin rushed down the hallway to help him to his feet, and it was hard to tell which of them looked the more worried. It made him smile in spite of himself.

The boy spoke first. "Are you all right?" he asked, his young face mirroring his concern.

Qui-Gon nodded, brushing himself off. "I think so. That was a surprise I won't soon forget."

"What sort of creature was it?" Obi-Wan pressed, brow furrowed darkly. *He wants to go back and pick up where I left off,* Qui-Gon thought.

The Jedi Master shook his head. "I'm not sure. Whoever or whatever he was, he was trained in the Jedi arts. My guess is he was after the Queen."

"Do you think he'll follow us?" Anakin asked quickly.

"We'll be safe enough once we're in hyperspace," Qui-Gon replied, sidestepping the question. "But I have no doubt he knows our destination. If he found us once, he can find us again."

The boy's brow furrowed. "What are we going to do about it?"

At this point, Obi-Wan turned to stare at the boy, giving him a look that demanded in no uncertain terms, *What do you mean, "we"?* The boy caught the look and stared back at him, expressionless.

"We will be patient," Qui-Gon advised, straightening himself, drawing their attention back to him. "Anakin Skywalker, meet Obi-Wan Kenobi."

The boy beamed. "Pleased to meet you. Wow! You're a Jedi Knight, too, aren't you?"

The younger Jedi looked from the boy to Qui-Gon and rolled his eyes in despair.

From the entry, they made their way back down the hall to the cockpit, where Ric Olié was at work preparing the ship for the jump to hyperspace. Qui-Gon introduced Anakin to each of those present, then moved to the console to stand next to Ric.

"Ready," the pilot announced over his shoulder, one eyebrow cocked expectantly.

Qui-Gon nodded. "Let's hope the hyperdrive works and Watto doesn't get the last laugh."

Standing in a group behind Ric, the company watched silently as he fitted his hands to the controls and engaged the hyperdrive. There was a quick, sharp whine, and the stars that filled the viewport turned from silver pinpricks to long streamers as the ship streaked smoothly into hyperspace, leaving Tatooine behind.

Night lay over the planet of Naboo, but the silence of Theed exceeded even that normally experienced by those anticipating sleep. In the ornately appointed throne room that had once been the sole province of Queen Amidala, a strange collection of creatures gathered to witness the sentencing of Governor Sio Bibble. Trade Federation Viceroy Nute Gunray had convened the assembled, which consisted of Rune Haako and several other Neimoidians, the governor and a handful of officials in the Queen's service, and a vast array of battle droids armed with blasters to keep the Naboo prisoners in line.

The Neimoidian was seated in a mechno-chair, a robotic walker that bore him from one part of the room to another, metal legs moving in response to a simple touch of his fingers. It carried him to Sio Bibble and the Naboo officials now, jointed armatures working in careful precision, allowing him to remain relaxed and comfortable as he took note of the fear in the eyes of the officials backing Bibble.

The governor was having none of it, however. Steadfast even now, he faced Gunray with anger and determination, his white head level, his eyes challenging. The Neimoidian glared at him; Sio Bibble was becoming a source of irritation.

"When are you going to give up this pointless strike?" he snapped at the governor, leaning forward slightly to emphasize his displeasure.

"I will give up the strike, Viceroy, when the Queen—"

"Your Queen is lost; your people are starving!"

Bibble stiffened. "The Naboo will not be intimidated, not even at the cost of innocent lives—"

"Perhaps you should worry more about yourself, Governor!" Gunray cut him off sharply. "The odds are good that you are going to die much sooner than your people!" He was shaking with rage, and all at once his patience was exhausted. "Enough of this!" he exploded. "Take him away!"

The battle droids moved quickly, surrounding Sio Bibble, separating him from his colleagues.

"This invasion will gain you nothing!" the governor called back over his shoulder as he was dragged out. "We are a democracy! The people have decided, Viceroy! They will not live in tyranny . . ."

The rest of what he said was lost as he disappeared through the doorway into the hall beyond. The Naboo officials filed out after him, silent and dejected.

The Neimoidian stared after them momentarily, then turned his attention to OOM-9 as the commander of his battle droids approached, metal face blank, voice devoid of inflection.

"My troops are in position to begin searching the swamps for the rumored underwater villages," OOM-9 reported. "They will not stay hidden for long."

Nute Gunray nodded and dismissed him with a wave of his hand. He thought nothing of these savages who occupied the swamps. They would be crushed in short order. For all intents and purposes, the planet was in his control.

He leaned back in the mechno-chair, a measure of calmness returning. All that remained was for the Sith Lords to bring him the Queen. Certainly they should have little difficulty in accomplishing that.

Nevertheless, he knew he wouldn't be happy until this business was over.

Aboard the Queen's transport, Anakin Skywalker sat shivering in a corner of the central chamber, trying to decide what he should do to get warm. Everyone else was asleep, and he had been asleep as well, but only for a short time, troubled by his dreams. He came awake to the silence and could not make himself move, paralyzed by more than simply the cold.

Jar Jar slept to one side, stretched out in a chair, head back, snoring loudly. Nothing kept the Gungan from sleeping. Or eating, for that matter. The boy smiled briefly. R2-D2 rested close by, upright and mostly silent, his lights blinking softly.

Anakin stared into the darkness, willing himself to move, to overcome his inertia. But his dreams haunted him still. He found himself thinking of his mother and home, and everything closed down inside. He missed her so much! He had thought it would get better once he was away, but it hadn't. Everything reminded him of her, and if he tried to close his eyes against those memories, he found her face waiting for him, suspended in the darkness of his thoughts, anxious and worn.

Tears came to his eyes, unbidden. Maybe he had made a mistake by coming. Maybe he should go home. Except he couldn't now. Maybe not ever again.

A slim figure entered the room, and Anakin watched the light of a viewscreen illuminate Padmé's soft face. Standing as if carved from stone, she clicked on a recording and stood watching the replay of Sio Bibble's plea to Queen Amidala to come home, to save her people from starvation, to help them in their time of need. She watched it all the way through, then shut it off again and stood staring at nothing, her head bent.

What was she doing?

Suddenly she seemed to sense him watching, and turned quickly toward where he crouched. Her beautiful face seemed tired and careworn as she approached and knelt beside him. He stiffened, trying desperately to stop from crying, but he couldn't hide either the tears or his shivering, and was left huddled before her, revealed.

"Are you all right, Annie?" she asked him softly.

"It's very cold," he managed to whisper.

She smiled and removed her heavy overjacket, wrapping it around his shoulders and tucking it about him. "You're from a warm planet, Annie. Space is cold."

Anakin nodded, pulling the jacket tighter. He brushed at his eyes. "You seem sad," he said.

If she saw the irony in his observation, she did not say so. "The Queen is worried. Her people are suffering, dying. She must convince the Senate to intervene, or else . . ." She trailed off, unwilling to speak the words. "I'm not sure what will happen," she finished, her voice distant, her eyes sliding away from his to fix on something else.

"I'm not sure what's going to happen to me, either," he admitted worriedly. "I don't know if I'll ever see—"

He stopped, his throat tightening, the words fading away into silence. He took a deep breath, furrowed his brow, and reached into his pocket.

"Here," he said, "I made this for you. So you'd remember me. I carved it out of a japor snippet. Take it. It will bring you good fortune."

He handed her an intricately carved wooden pendant. She studied it a moment, face lowered in shadow, then slipped it around her neck.

"It's beautiful. But I don't need this to remember you." Her face lifted to his with a smile. "How could I forget my future husband?" She looked down at the pendant, fingering it thoughtfully. "Many things will change when we reach Coruscant, Annie. My caring for you will not be one of them."

The boy nodded, swallowing. "I know. And I won't stop caring for you, either. Only, I miss—"

His voice broke, and the tears sprang into his eyes once more.

"You miss your mother," the girl finished quietly.

Anakin nodded, wiping at his face, unable to speak a word as Padmé Naberrie drew him against her and held him close.

Even before an off-world traveler was close enough to understand why, he could tell that Coruscant was different from other planets. Seasoned veterans were always amazed at how strange the planet looked from space, casting not the softer blue and white shades of planets still verdant and unspoiled, but an odd silvery glow that suggested the reflection of sunlight off metal.

The impression was not misleading. The days in which Coruscant could be viewed in any sort of natural state were dead and gone. The capital city had expanded over the centuries, building by building, until it wrapped the entire planet. Forests, mountains, bodies of water, and natural formations had been covered over. The atmosphere was filtered through oxygen regulators and purified by scrubbers, and water was gathered and stored in massive artificial aquifers. Native animals, birds, plants, and fish could be found in the museums or the climate-controlled indoor preserves. As Anakin Skywalker could clearly see from the viewport of Queen Amidala's slowly descending transport, Coruscant had become a planet of skyscrapers, their gleaming metal towers stretching skyward in a forest of spear points, an army of frozen giants blanketing the horizon in every direction.

The boy stared at the city-planet in awe, searching for a break in the endless forest of buildings, finding none. He glanced at Ric Olié in the pilot's seat, and Ric smiled.

"Coruscant, capital of the Republic, an entire planet evolved into one city." He winked. "A nice place to visit, but I wouldn't want to live there."

"It's so huge!" the boy breathed softly.

They dropped into a landfall traffic lane and cruised slowly through the maze of buildings, sliding along the magnetic guidance lines that directed airborne vehicles. Ric explained how it worked to Anakin, who listened with half an ear, his attention still held captive by the vastness of the cityscape. In the background, the Jedi moved silently. Jar Jar crouched to one side, peering over the console through the viewport, clearly terrified by what he was seeing. Anakin knew the Gungan must long for the familiarity of his swamp home, just as the boy was thinking how much better he liked the desert.

The Queen's transport slowed now, edging its way out of the traffic lane, onto a landing dock that floated near a cluster of huge buildings. Anakin peered down doubtfully. They were several hundred stories up, hundreds and hundreds of meters in the air. He tore his gaze away, swallowing hard.

The ship docked with a soft bump on the landing platform, its antigrav clamps locking in place. The Queen was waiting in the main corridor with her retinue of handmaidens, guards, and Captain Panaka. She nodded at Qui-Gon, indicating that he should lead the way. Giving Padmé a quick smile, Anakin followed close on the heels of the Jedi Master as he moved to the hatchway.

The hatch slid open, the loading ramp lowered, and the Jedi Knights, Anakin Skywalker, and Jar Jar Binks exited into the sunlight of Coruscant. The boy spent the first few minutes concentrating on not being overwhelmed, which became even more difficult once he was outside the ship. He kept his eyes on the rampway and Qui-Gon, not allowing himself to look around at first for fear he might walk right off into space.

Two men clothed in robes of office of the Republic Senate stood at the end of the ramp, flanked by a contingent of Republic guards. The Jedi approached the pair and bowed formally in greeting. Anakin and Jar Jar were quick to do the same, though only Anakin knew who they were bowing to and why.

Now Queen Amidala appeared, dressed in her black and gold robes with the feathered headpiece lending height and flow to her movements as she descended the ramp. Her handmaidens surrounded her, wrapped in their cloaks of crimson, faces barely visible in the shadows of their drawn hoods. Captain Panaka and his complement of Naboo guards escorted them.

Amidala stopped before the two men who waited, eyes shifting to the man with the kindly face and anxious eyes. Senator Palpatine, the Queen's emissary to the Republic Senate, bowed in welcome, hands clasped in the folds of his blue-green robes.

"It is a great relief to see you alive and well, Your Majesty," he offered with a smile, straightening once more. "May I present Supreme Chancellor Valorum."

Valorum was a tall, silver-haired man of indeterminate age, neither young nor old in appearance, but something of each, his bearing and voice strong, but his face and startling blue eyes tired and worried.

"Welcome, Your Highness," he said, a faint smile working its way onto his stern features. "It is an honor to finally meet you in person. I must relay to you how distressed everyone is over the current situation on Naboo. I have called for a special session of the Senate so that you may present your request for relief."

The Queen held his gaze without moving even a fraction of a centimeter, tall and regal in her robes of office, white-painted face as still and cool as ice. "I am grateful for your concern, Chancellor," she said quietly.

Out of the corner of his eye, Anakin recognized Padmé staring out at him from beneath her concealing hood. When he turned toward her, she gave him a wink, and he felt himself blush.

Palpatine had moved to the Queen's side and was indicating

an air shuttle that was awaiting them. "There is a question of procedure, but I feel confident we can overcome it," he was saying, guiding her along the rampway, her handmaidens, Captain Panaka, and the Naboo guards in tow.

Anakin started to follow, Jar Jar at his side, then stopped as he saw that the Jedi were still standing with Supreme Chancellor Valorum. Anakin glanced back questioningly at Qui-Gon, not certain where he was supposed to go. The Queen and her retinue slowed in response, and Amidala motioned for Anakin and the Gungan to join them. Anakin looked again at Qui-Gon, who nodded wordlessly.

Moving into the air shuttle with the Queen, Anakin and Jar Jar settled quietly into place in the very back seat. Senator Palpatine glanced over his shoulder at them from the front, a look of skepticism crossing his face before he turned away again.

"Me not feelen too good 'bout being here, Annie," the Gungan whispered doubtfully.

Anakin nodded and tightened his mouth determinedly.

They flew only a short distance to another cluster of buildings and another loading dock, this one clearly meant for shuttle-craft. There, they disembarked and were escorted by Palpatine to his quarters, a portion of which had been made ready for the Queen and her entourage. Anakin and Jar Jar were given a room and a chance to clean up and were left alone. After a time, they were collected by one of the handmaidens—not Padmé, Anakin noted with disappointment—and escorted to a waiting room situated outside what appeared to be Palpatine's office.

"Wait here," the handmaiden instructed, and disappeared back down the hallway.

The doors to the senator's office were open, and the boy and the Gungan could see inside clearly. The Queen was present, dressed now in a gown of purple velvet, which was wrapped about her slim form in layers, the sleeves long and full, hanging gracefully from her slender arms. A fan-shaped crown with ornate beadwork and tassels rested upon her head. She was sitting in a chair, listening as Palpatine spoke to her. Her handmaidens stood to one side, crimson robes and hoods drawn close about them. Anakin did not think either was Padmé. He wondered if he should try to find her instead of waiting here, but he did not know where to look.

The conversation within seemed decidedly one-sided, Senator Palpatine gesturing animatedly as he stalked the room, the Queen as still as stone. Anakin wished he could hear what was being said. He glanced at Jar Jar, and he could tell from the Gungan's restless eyes he was thinking the same thing.

When Captain Panaka walked past them and entered the room beyond, screening them from view for just a moment, Anakin rose impulsively. Motioning for Jar Jar to stay where he was, putting a finger to his lips in warning, he moved to one side of the doorway, pressing close. Through the crack between the open door and the jamb, he could just make out the voices of Palpatine and the Queen, muffled and indistinct.

Palpatine had stopped moving and was standing before the Queen, shaking his head. "The Republic is not what it once was. The Senate is full of greedy, squabbling delegates who are only looking out for themselves and their home systems. There is no interest in the common good—no civility, only politics." He sighed wearily. "It's disgusting. I must be frank, Your Majesty. There is little chance the Senate will act on the invasion."

Amidala was silent a moment. "Chancellor Valorum seems to think there is hope."

"If I may say so, Your Majesty," the senator replied, his voice kind, but sad, "the chancellor has little real power. He is mired in baseless accusations of corruption. A manufactured scandal surrounds him. The bureaucrats are in charge now."

The Queen rose, standing tall and fixed before him. "What options do we have, Senator?"

Palpatine seemed to think on the matter for a moment. "Our best choice would be to push for the election of a stronger supreme chancellor—one who could take control of the bureaucrats, enforce the laws, and give us justice." He brushed back his thick hair, worrying his forehead with steepled fingers. "You could call for a vote of no confidence in Chancellor Valorum."

. Amidala did not seem convinced. "Valorum has been our strongest supporter. Is there no other way?"

Palpatine stood before her. "Our only other choice would be to submit the matter to the courts—"

"There is no time for that," the Queen interrupted quickly, a hint of anger in her voice. "The courts take even longer to decide things than the Senate." She shifted purposefully, an edge sharpening her words further. "Our people are dying—more and more each day. We must do something quickly. We must stop the Trade Federation before this gets any worse."

Palpatine gave Amidala a stern look. "To be realistic about the matter, Your Highness, I believe we are going to have to accept Trade Federation control as an accomplished fact—for the time being, at least."

The Queen shook her head slowly. "That is something I cannot do, Senator."

They faced each other in the silence that followed, eyes locked, and Anakin Skywalker, hiding behind the door without, found himself wondering suddenly what had become of Qui-Gon Jinn.

Unlike other buildings in the vast sprawl of Coruscant, the Jedi Temple stood alone. A colossal pyramid with multiple spires rising skyward from its flat top, it sat apart from everything at the end of a broad promenade linking it with bulkier, sharper-edged towers in which solitude and mediation were less likely to be found. Within the Temple were housed the Jedi Knights and their students, the whole of the order engaged in contemplation and study of the Force, in codification of its dictates and mastery of its disciplines, and in training to serve the greater good it embodied.

The Jedi Council room dominated a central portion of the complex. The Council itself was in session, its doors closed, its proceedings hidden from the eyes and ears of all but four-teen people. Twelve of them—some human, some nonhuman—comprised the Council, a diverse and seasoned group who had gravitated to the order from both ends of the galaxy. The final two Jedi, who were guests of the Council this afternoon, were Qui-Gon Jinn and Obi-Wan Kenobi.

The seats of the twelve Council members formed a circle facing inward to where Qui-Gon and Obi-Wan stood, the former relating the events of the past few weeks, the latter a step behind his Master, listening attentively. The room was circular and domed, supported by graceful pillars spaced between broad windows open to the city and the light. The shape of the room and the Council seating reflected the Jedi belief in the equality of and interconnection between all things. In the world of the Jedi, the balance of life within the Force was the pathway to understanding and peace.

Qui-Gon studied the faces of his listeners as he spoke, each of them familiar to him. Most were Jedi Masters like himself, among them Yoda and Mace Windu, seniors in rank among those seated. They were more compliant in the ways of the Jedi order than he had ever been or would probably ever be.

He stood apart in the mosaic circle that formed a speaker's platform for those who addressed the Council, his tall, broad form and deep voice commanding the attention of those gathered, his blue eyes fixing them each in turn, constantly searching for a reaction to his words. They watched him carefully—stately Ki-Adi-Mundi, young and beautiful Adi Gallia, slender Depa Billaba, crested and marble-faced Even Piell, and all the others, each different and unique in appearance, each with something vital to offer as a representative of the Council.

Qui-Gon brought his eyes back to Mace Windu and Yoda, the ones he must convince, the ones most respected and powerful of those who sat in judgment.

"My conclusion," he finished quietly, his story completed, "is that the one who attacked me on Tatooine is a Sith Lord."

The silence that followed was palpable. Then there was a stirring of brown robes, a shifting of bodies and limbs. Glances were exchanged and murmurs of disbelief quickly voiced.

"A Sith Lord?" Mace Windu repeated with a growl, leaning forward. He was a strong, dark-skinned man with a shaved head and penetrating eyes, smooth-faced despite his years.

"Impossible!" Ki-Adi-Mundi snapped irritably, not bothering to hide his dismay at the suggestion. "The Sith have been gone for a millennium!"

Yoda shifted only slightly in his chair, a small and wizened presence in the company of much larger beings, his eyes gone to slits like a contented sand panther's, his whiskery wrinkled face turned toward Qui-Gon's thoughtfully.

"Threatened, the Republic is, if the Sith are involved," he observed in his soft, gravelly voice.

The others began to mutter anew among themselves. Qui-Gon said nothing, waiting them out. They had believed the Sith destroyed. They had believed them consumed by their own lust for power. He could feel Obi-Wan shift uncomfortably at his shoulder, having trouble maintaining his silence.

Mace Windu leaned back heavily, his strong brow furrowing. "This is difficult to accept, Qui-Gon. I do not understand how the Sith could have returned without us knowing."

"Hard to see, the dark side is," Yoda said with a small snort. "Discover who this assassin is, we must."

"Perhaps he will reveal himself again," Ki-Adi-Mundi suggested with a nod to Qui-Gon.

"Yes," Mace Windu agreed. "This attack was with purpose, that much is clear. The Queen is his target. Since he failed once, he may try again."

Yoda lifted one skinny arm, pointing at Qui-Gon. "With this Naboo Queen, you must stay, Qui-Gon. Protect her, you must."

The others murmured their approval, evidencing the confidence they felt in the Jedi Master's abilities. Still Qui-Gon said nothing.

"We shall use all our resources to unravel this mystery and

discover the identity of your attacker," Mace Windu advised. One hand lifted in dismissal. "May the Force be with you, Qui-Gon Jinn."

"May the Force be with you," Yoda echoed.

Obi-Wan turned to leave. He stopped when Qui-Gon did not follow, but instead remained standing before the Council. Obi-Wan held his breath, knowing what was coming.

Yoda cocked his head questioningly. "More to say, have you, Qui-Gon Jinn?"

"With your permission, my Master," the Jedi replied, gaze steady. "I have encountered a vergence in the Force."

Yoda's eyes widened slightly. "A vergence, you say?"

"Located around a person?" Mace Windu asked quickly.

Qui-Gon nodded. "A boy. His cells have the highest concentration of midi-chlorians I have ever seen in a life-form." He paused. "It is possible he was conceived by midi-chlorians."

There was a shocked silence this time. Qui-Gon Jinn was suggesting the impossible, that the boy was conceived not by human contact, but by the essence of all life, by the connectors to the Force itself, the midi-chlorians. Comprising collective consciousness and intelligence, the midi-chlorians formed the link between everything living and the Force.

But there was more that troubled the Jedi Council. There was a prophecy, so old its origins had long since been lost, that a chosen one would appear, imbued with an abundance of midi-chlorians, a being strong with the Force and destined to alter it forever.

It was Mace Windu who gave voice to the Council's thoughts. "You refer to the prophecy," he said quietly. "Of the one who will bring balance to the Force. You believe it is this boy."

Qui-Gon hesitated. "I don't presume—"

"But you do!" Yoda snapped challengingly. "Revealed, your opinion is, Qui-Gon!"

The Jedi Master took a deep breath. "I request the boy be tested."

Again, there was silence as the members of the Council exchanged glances, communicating without words.

Eyes shifted back to Qui-Gon. "To be trained as a Jedi, you request for him?" Yoda asked softly.

"Finding him was the will of the Force." Qui-Gon pressed ahead recklessly. "I have no doubt of it. There is too much happening here for it to be anything else."

Mace Windu held up one hand, bringing the debate to a close. "Bring him before us, then."

Yoda nodded somberly, eyes closing. "Tested, he will be."

"It is time to be going, Your Majesty," Senator Palpatine advised, moving to gather up a pile of data cards from his desk.

Queen Amidala rose, and Anakin hurried back to his seat beside Jar Jar, giving the Gungan another warning glance for good measure. Jar Jar looked hurt.

"Me not gonna tell dem," he protested.

A moment later Palpatine ushered the Queen and her handmaidens from his office and into the antechamber where the boy and the Gungan sat waiting. The senator went by them without a glance and was out the door immediately.

Queen Amidala slowed just a fraction as she passed Anakin.

"Why don't you come with us," the handmaiden Rabé said without looking at him, her voice a whisper. "This time you won't have to listen from behind a door."

Anakin and Jar Jar exchanged a startled, chagrined look, then rose and followed after.

While the others waited without, Queen Amidala, accompanied by her handmaidens, retreated to her chambers long enough to change into yet another ensemble, this one clearly meant to emphasize her status as leader of the Naboo. She emerged wearing a broad-shouldered cloak of crimson velvet trimmed with gold lace and a crown of woven cloth horns and tassels with a center plate of hammered gold. The gown and headdress lent both size and majesty, and she walked past a wondering Anakin and Jar Jar as if come down out of the clouds to mix with mortals, all cool grace and extraordinary beauty, aloof and untouchable.

Eirtaé and Rabé, the handmaidens who had accompanied her earlier, were present again, and they trailed the Queen in a silent glide, wrapped in their crimson hooded robes. Again Anakin looked for Padmé and did not find her.

"Please lead the way," Amidala requested of Palpatine, beckoning the boy, the Gungan, and Captain Panaka to accompany them.

They walked from Palpatine's quarters down a series of corridors that connected to other chambers and, eventually, to other buildings. The halls were empty of almost everyone, save for a scattering of Republic guards, and the company proceeded unchallenged. Anakin glanced around in awe at the tall ceilings and high windows, at the forest of buildings visible without, imagining what it would be like to live in a place like Coruscant.

When they reached the Senate chamber, he had cause to wonder anew.

The chamber had the look of an arena, circular and massive, with doors opening off exterior rampways at various levels above the main floor. At the center of the chamber a tall, slender column supported the supreme chancellor's platform, a broad, semienclosed area that allowed Valorum, who was already present, to sit or stand as he chose in the company of his vice chair and staff. All around the smooth interior walls of the arena, Senate boxes jutted from hangar bays off entry doors, some fixed in place while their senators conferred with staff and visitors, others floating just off their moorings. When a senator requested permission to speak and was recognized by the chair, his box would float to the center of the arena, close to the supreme chancellor's podium, where it remained until the speech was concluded.

Anakin picked up on all this in a matter of seconds, trailing the Queen and Palpatine to the entry doors opening onto the Naboo Senate box, which sat waiting at its docking. Banners and curtains hung from the rounded ceiling in brilliant streamers, and indirect lighting glowed softly from every corner, brightening the rotunda's cavernous interior. Droids bustled along the exterior rampways, carrying messages from one delegation to the next, the movement of their metal bodies giving the chamber the look of a complex piece of machinery.

"If the Federation moves to defer the motion, Your Majesty," Senator Palpatine was saying to the Queen, his head bent close, his voice low and insistent, "I beg of you to ask for a resolution to end this session and call for the election of a new supreme chancellor."

Amidala did not look at him, continuing to advance toward the Naboo box. "I wish I had your confidence in this proposal, Senator," she replied quietly.

"You must force a new election for supreme chancellor," Palpatine pressed. "I promise you there are many who will support us. It is our best chance." He glanced toward the podium and Valorum. "Our only chance."

A murmur had risen from the assembled as they caught sight of Amidala standing at the entry to the Naboo box, robes of office flowing out behind her, head erect, face calm. If she heard the change in tenor of the level of conversation around her, she gave no sign. Her eyes shifted momentarily to Palpatine.

"You truly believe Chancellor Valorum will not bring our motion to a vote?" she asked quietly.

Palpatine shook his head, his high brow furrowing. "He is distracted. He is afraid. He will be of no help."

Rabé handed a small metal viewscreen to Anakin and Jar Jar and motioned for them to wait where they were. Stepping into the Senate box with Palpatine, Amidala was joined by her hand-maidens and Panaka. Anakin was disappointed at not being included, but grateful when he discovered that the viewscreen Rabé had provided allowed him to see and hear what was happening in the Naboo box.

"She's going to ask the Senate for help, Jar Jar," he whispered, leaning over excitedly. "What do you think?"

The Gungan wrinkled up his billed mouth and shook his floppy-eared head. "Me think dis bombad, Annie. Too many peoples to be agreeing on da one thing."

The Naboo box detached from its docking and floated a short distance toward the supreme chancellor's podium, waiting for permission to advance all the way. Palpatine, Amidala, and the rest of the occupants were seated now, facing forward.

Valorum nodded his short-cropped white head in the direction of Palpatine. "The chair recognizes the senator from the sovereign system of Naboo."

The Naboo box glided to the center of the arena, and Palpatine rose to his feet, taking in the assemblage with a slow sweeping gaze that drew all eyes toward his.

"Supreme Chancellor, delegates of the Senate," his voice

boomed, quieting the chamber. "A tragedy has occurred on my homeworld of Naboo. We have become caught up in a dispute, one of which you are all well aware. It began with a taxation of trade routes and has evolved into an oppressive and lawless occupation of a peaceful world. The Trade Federation bears responsibility for this injustice and must be made to answer . . ."

A second box was rushing forward by now, this one bearing the markings of the Trade Federation and occupied by the Federation's senator, Lott Dod, and a handful of trade barons in attendance.

"This is outrageous!" the Trade Federation senator thundered, gesturing toward the podium and Valorum. A lean, wizened Neimoidian, he loomed out of the low-railed box like a willowy tree. "I object to Senator Palpatine's ridiculous assertions and ask that he be silenced at once!"

Valorum's white head swiveled briefly in Lott Dod's direction and one hand lifted. "The chair does not recognize the senator from the Trade Federation at this time." The supreme chancellor's voice was soft, but steady. "Return to your station."

Lott Dod looked as if he might say something more, but then he lowered himself back into his seat as his box slowly retreated.

"To state our allegations in full," Palpatine continued, "I present Queen Amidala, the recently elected ruler of the Naboo, to speak on our behalf."

He stepped aside, and Amidala rose to a light scattering of applause. Moving to the front of the box, she faced Valorum. "Honorable representatives of the Republic, distinguished delegates, and Supreme Chancellor Valorum. I come to you under the gravest of circumstances. In repudiation and violation of the laws of the Republic, the Naboo have been invaded and subjugated by force by droid armies of the Trade Federation—"

Lott Dod was on his feet again, voice raised angrily. "I object! This is nonsense! Where is the proof?" He did not wait for recognition as he turned to the chamber at large. "I recommend a commission be sent to Naboo to ascertain the truth of these allegations."

Valorum shook his head. "Overruled."

Lott Dod sighed heavily and threw up his hands as if with that single word his life had become hopeless. "Your Honor, you cannot allow us to be condemned without granting our request for an impartial observation. It is against all the rules of procedure!"

He scanned the chamber for help, and there was a murmur of agreement from the delegates. A third box glided forward to join those of Naboo and the Trade Federation. The chair recognized Aks Moe, the senator from the planet of Malastare.

Stocky and slow moving, his three eyestalks waving gently, Aks Moe put the thick, heavy pads of his hands on his hips. "The senator from Malastare concurs with the honorable delegate from the Trade Federation." His voice was thick and gnarly. "A commission, once requested, must be appointed, where there is a dispute of the sort we have encountered here. It is the law."

Valorum hesitated. "The point is . . ."

He trailed off uncertainly, left the sentence unfinished, and turned to confer with his vice chair, identified on the printed register as Mas Amedda. Amedda was of a species Anakin had never encountered, human in form, but with a head swollen by a pillow of cushioning tissue narrowing into a pair of tentacles that drooped over either shoulder and feelers that jutted from above the forehead. Together with their aides, the chair and vice chair engaged in a hurried discussion. Anakin and Jar Jar exchanged worried glances as Palpatine's voice reached them through the handheld viewscreen's tiny speaker.

"Enter the bureaucrats, the true rulers of the Republic, and on the payroll of the Trade Federation, I might add," he was whispering to the Queen. Anakin could see their heads bent close. Palpatine's tone was heavy. "This is where Chancellor Valorum's strength will disappear."

Valorum had moved back to the podium, a worn look on his

face. "The point is conceded. Section 523A takes precedence here." He nodded in the direction of the Naboo box. "Queen Amidala of the Naboo, will you defer your motion in order to allow a Senate commission to explore the validity of your accusations?"

Anakin could see the Queen stiffen in surprise, and when she spoke, her voice was edged with anger and determination.

"I will not defer," she declared, eyes locked on Valorum. "I have come before you to resolve this attack on Naboo sovereignty now. I was not elected Queen to watch my people suffer and die while you discuss this invasion in committee. If the chancellor is not capable of action, I suggest new leadership is needed." She paused. "I move for a vote of no confidence in the supreme chancellor."

Voices rose immediately in response, some in support, some in protest. Senators and spectators alike came to their feet, loud mutterings quickly building to shouts that echoed through the cavernous chamber. Valorum stood speechless at the podium, stunned and disbelieving. He stared at Amidala, his face etched in sudden shock as the impact of her words registered. Amidala faced him boldly, waiting.

Mas Amedda moved in front of Valorum, taking charge of the podium. "Order!" he bellowed, his strange head swelling. "We shall have order!"

The assembly quieted then, and the delegates reseated themselves, responding to Amedda's command. Anakin noted that the Trade Federation box had maneuvered into position close beside the Naboo box. Lott Dod exchanged a quick glance with Palpatine, but neither spoke.

A new box floated to the center of the chamber, and the vice chair recognized Edcel Bar Gan, the senator from Roona.

"Roona seconds the motion for a vote of no confidence in Chancellor Valorum," Bar Gan intoned in a sibilant voice.

Mas Amedda did not look pleased. "The motion has been seconded."

He turned now to Valorum, speaking quickly to him, keeping his voice low and his words hidden behind his hand. Valorum looked at him uncomprehendingly, eyes distant and lost.

"There must be no delays," Aks Moe of Malastare declared in a loud voice, drawing Mas Amedda's attention back to him. "The motion is on the floor and must be voted on at once."

Lott Dod was back on his feet. "I move the motion be sent to the procedures committee for further study—"

The Republic Senate erupted anew, chanting loudly, "Vote now! Vote now!" Mas Amedda was deep in discussion with Supreme Chancellor Valorum, hands on his shoulders as if to bring him back from wherever he'd gone by sheer force of determination.

"You see, Your Majesty, the tide is with us," Anakin heard Palpatine announce quietly to the Queen. The boy's eyes dropped to the viewscreen. "Valorum will be voted out, I assure you, and they will elect a new chancellor, a strong chancellor, one who will not let our tragedy be ignored . . ."

Mas Amedda was back at the podium, addressing the chamber. "The supreme chancellor requests a recess."

Shouts rose from the delegates, echoing across the chamber in waves as Valorum stared at Senator Palpatine and Queen Amidala, and even from where he stood watching now at the entry doors to the Naboo box, Anakin Skywalker could discern the look of betrayal registered on the supreme chancellor's anguished face.

Less than an hour later, Anakin burst through the open doors of the Queen's antechamber in search of Padmé and found himself face-to-face with Amidala instead. The Queen was standing alone in the center of the room, her eyes directed toward him, her robed form radiant and solitary.

"Excuse me," Anakin said quickly. "Your Majesty."

She nodded silently, white face smooth and perfect.

"I was looking for Padmé," he continued, standing rooted in place just inside the doorway, undecided on whether to stay or go. He glanced around doubtfully. "Qui-Gon says he will take me before the Jedi Council. I wanted Padmé to know."

A small smile flitted across the Queen's painted lips. "Padmé isn't here, Anakin. I sent her on an errand."

"Oh," he said quietly.

"But I will give her your message."

The boy grinned. "Maybe I will become a Jedi Knight!" he exclaimed, unable to contain his excitement.

Amidala nodded. "Maybe you will."

"I think Padmé would like that."

"I think she would, too."

Anakin backed away. "I didn't mean to . . ." He searched for the word and couldn't find it.

"Good luck, Anakin," the Queen said softly. "Do well."

He wheeled away with a broad smile and was out the door.

The day passed quickly for Qui-Gon Jinn and Obi-Wan Kenobi, and sunset found them standing together on a balcony outside the Jedi Temple overlooking Coruscant. Neither had said anything to the other for some time. They had collected Anakin Skywalker from Senator Palpatine's quarters following his return from the Republic Senate and brought him before the Council for examination. Now they were awaiting a decision.

As far as Obi-Wan was concerned, it was a foregone conclusion. The young Jedi was frustrated and embarrassed for his Master, who had clearly overstepped his bounds once again. Qui-Gon had been right in his suspicion that the boy was possessed of an inordinately high midi-chlorian count. Obi-Wan had run the test himself. But that alone was not enough to demonstrate Anakin was the chosen one. If there even was such a one, which Obi-Wan seriously doubted. There were hundreds of these old prophecies and legends, handed down through the centuries as a part of Jedi lore. In any case, Qui-Gon was relying on instinct once again, and instinct was useful only if born of the Force and not of emotion. Qui-Gon was insistent on championing the causes of underdogs, of empathizing with creatures he found in some peculiar, inscrutable way he alone could comprehend significant in the scheme of things.

Obi-Wan studied his mentor surreptitiously. Why did he insist on pursuing these hopeless causes? The Council might find the boy possessed of more midi-chlorians than normal, but they would never accept him for Jedi training. The rules were clear and established, and the reasons supporting them were proven and unassailable. Training for the order after more than a year of life was doomed to fail. At nine years of age, Anakin Skywalker was simply too old.

But Qui-Gon would not let it go. He would brace the Council once again, and the result would be the same as it had been on so many other occasions: Qui-Gon would be denied and his stature as a Jedi Master would fall a little further.

Obi-Wan moved to where the older Jedi stood staring out at the endless horizon of skyscrapers. He stood close to him, silent for a moment longer before speaking.

"The boy will not pass the Council's tests, Master," he said softly, "and you know it. He is far too old."

Qui-Gon kept his gaze directed toward the sunset. "Anakin will become a Jedi, I promise you."

Obi-Wan sighed wearily. "Don't defy the Council, Master. Not again."

The older man seemed to go very still, perhaps even to stop breathing, before he turned to his protégé. "I will do what I must, Obi-Wan. Would you have me be any other way?"

"Master, you could be sitting on the Council by now if you would just follow the code. You deserve to be sitting on the Council." Obi-Wan's frustration surfaced in a burst of momentary anger. His eyes sought the other's and held them. "They will not go along with you this time."

Qui-Gon Jinn studied him a moment, then smiled. "You still have much to learn, my young Padawan."

Obi-Wan bit off his reply and looked away, thinking to himself that Qui-Gon was right, but that maybe this time he should consider taking his own advice.

* * *

Inside, Anakin Skywalker faced the Jedi Council, standing in the same place Qui-Gon Jinn had stood some hours earlier. He was nervous at first, brought into the chamber by Qui-Gon, then left alone with the twelve members of the Council. Standing in the mosaic circle and ringed by the silent assemblage, awestruck and uncertain of what was expected of him, he felt vulnerable and exposed. The eyes of the Jedi were distant as they viewed him, but he sensed they were looking not past him, but inside.

They began to question him then, without preliminary introductions or explanations, without expending any effort at all to make him feel comfortable or welcome. He knew some of them by name, for Qui-Gon had described a few, and he was quick to put faces to names. They questioned him at great length, testing memory and knowledge, seeking insights at which he could only guess. They knew of his existence as a slave. They knew of his background on Tatooine, of his mother and his friends, of his Podracing, of Watto, of everything factual and past, of the order of his life.

Now Mace Windu was looking at a screen the boy could not see, and Anakin was giving names to images that flashed across its liquid surface. Images appeared in Anakin's mind with such speed he was reminded of the strange blur of desert and mountains whipping past his cockpit during a Podrace.

"A bantha. A hyperdrive. A proton blaster." The images whizzed through his mind as he named them off. "A Republic cruiser. A Rodian cup. A Hutt speeder."

The screen went blank, and Mace looked up at the boy.

"Good, good, young one," the wizened alien called Yoda praised. The sleepy eyes fixed on him, intent behind their lids. "How feel you?"

"Cold, sir," Anakin confessed.

"Afraid, are you?"

The boy shook his head. "No, sir."

"Afraid to give up your life?" the dark one called Mace Windu asked, leaning forward slightly.

"I don't think so," he answered, then hesitated. Something about the answer didn't feel right.

Yoda blinked and his long ears cocked forward. "See through you, we can," he said quietly.

"Be mindful of your feelings," Mace Windu said.

The old one called Ki-Adi-Mundi stroked his beard. "Your thoughts dwell on your mother."

Anakin felt his stomach lurch at the mention of her. He bit his lip. "I miss her."

Yoda exchanged glances with several others on the Council. "Afraid to lose her, I think."

Anakin flushed. "What's that got to do with anything?" he asked defensively.

Yoda's sleepy eyes fixed on him. "Everything. To the dark side, fear leads. To anger and to hate. To suffering."

"I am not afraid!" the boy snapped irritably, anxious to leave this discussion and move on.

Yoda did not seem to hear him. "The deepest commitment, a Jedi must have. The most serious mind. Much fear in you, I sense, young one."

Anakin took a deep breath and let it out slowly. When he spoke, his voice was calm again. "I am not afraid."

Yoda studied him a moment. "Then continue, we will," he said softly, and the examination resumed.

Jar Jar Binks of the Gungans and Queen Amidala of the Naboo stood together at a window that ran floor to ceiling in the Queen's chambers, looking out at the gleaming spires of Coruscant. An odd pairing at best, the Queen regal and composed, the Gungan awkward and jittery, they kept company in silence and watched the sunset color the sky a brilliant gold that reflected here and there off the flat metal and glass surfaces of the city in sudden, blinding explosions of light.

They had returned from the Republic Senate some hours ago, Jar Jar, Anakin, the Queen, and her handmaidens. They had come back principally because there seemed to be nothing else they could do to change the course of events regarding the future of Naboo. Senator Palpatine had stayed behind to politick with his colleagues over the selection of a new supreme chancellor, and Captain Panaka had remained with him, asked by the Queen to bring her news when there was any to offer. None had been forthcoming as yet. Now Anakin was gone as well, taken by Qui-Gon to the Jedi Temple where he was to meet with the Council, and no one had seen Padmé in some time.

So Jar Jar had rattled around in Palpatine's quarters rather like a stray kaadu until Amidala had taken pity on him and invited him to sit with her. She had gone into seclusion on her return, changing out of her Senate robes into a less imposing gold-trimmed black gown that emphasized how slender and small she really was. She wore an inverted, crescent-shaped crown with a beaded gold medallion arced down over her smooth fore-head, but even so she stood several centimeters shorter than the Gungan.

She was clearly in pain, her eyes so sad and distant that it made Jar Jar want to comfort her. If it had been Annie or Padmé, he might have reached over and patted her on the head, but he was not about to try that with the Queen. There were no guards, but her handmaidens, Eirtaé and Rabé, cloaked in their crimson hooded robes and forever watchful, stood in waiting near the door, and he was certain there were guards somewhere close as well. He was careless of many things, oblivious to others, and in general given over to enjoying life in a haphazard way, but he was no fool.

Finally, though, he could ignore the situation no longer. He shuffled his feet and cleared his throat, drawing the Queen's at-tention. She turned, her white-painted face with red dots on each cheek and a red slash in the center of her lower lip doll-like and expressionless.

"Me wonder sometimes why da Guds invent pain," he of-fered sympathetically.

Amidala's cool gaze was steady and clear. "To motivate us, I imagine."

"Yous think yous people gonna die?" he asked, working his billed mouth around the bitter words as if he could taste them.

The Queen considered the question and shook her head slowly. "I don't know, Jar Jar."

"Gungans gonna get pasted, too, eh?"

"I hope not."

Jar Jar straightened, and a fierce pride brightened his eyes. "Gungans no die without a fight. We warriors! We gotta grand army!"

"An army?" she repeated, a hint of surprise in her soft voice.

"A grand army! Lotta Gungans. Dey come from all over. Dat why no swamp beings give us trubble. Too many Gungans. Gotta big energy shields, too. Nutten get through. Gotta energy balls, fly outta slings and splat electricity and goo. Bombad stuff. Gungans no ever give up to maccaneks or anyone!"

He paused, shrugged uncomfortably. "Dat why Naboo no like us, mebbe."

She was studying him closely now, her detached gaze replaced by something more intense, as if she were turning an unexpected thought over in her mind. She was preparing to speak to that thought, he believed, when Senator Palpatine and Captain Panaka strode through the doorway in a rush.

"Your Highness," Captain Panaka greeted, barely able to contain his excitement as both men bowed quickly and straightened. "Senator Palpatine has been nominated to succeed Valorum as supreme chancellor!"

Palpatine's smile was contained and deferential, and his voice carefully modulated as he spoke. "A surprise, to be sure, but a welcome one. I promise, Your Majesty, if I am elected, I will restore democracy to the Republic. I will put an end to the corruption that has plagued the Senate. The Trade Federation will lose its influence over the bureaucrats, and our people will be freed from the tyranny of this unlawful and onerous invasion—"

"Who else has been nominated?" Amidala asked abruptly, cutting him short.

"Bail Antilles of Alderaan and Aks Moe of Malastare," Panaka told her, avoiding Palpatine's eyes.

The senator was quick to recover from the unexpected interruption of his speech. "Your Majesty, I feel confident that our situation will generate strong support for us when the voting takes place tomorrow." He paused meaningfully. "I will be chancellor, I promise you."

The Queen did not look impressed. She moved past Jar Jar to the window and stared out at the lights of the city as they brightened with the fading of the sunset. "I fear by the time you have taken control of the bureaucrats, Senator, there will be nothing left of our cities, our people, or our way of life to salvage."

Palpatine looked taken aback. "I understand your concern, Your Majesty. Unfortunately, the Federation has seized possession of our planet. It will be nearly impossible to immediately dislodge them."

"Perhaps." Amidala turned from the window to face him. Her eyes were bright with anger and determination. "With the Senate in transition, there is nothing more I can do here." She walked to where he stood with Panaka. "Senator, this is your arena. I must return now to mine. I have decided to go back to Naboo. My place is with my people."

"Go back!" Palpatine was aghast, his pale face stricken. Panaka looked quickly from one to the other. "But, Your Majesty, be realistic! You will be in great danger! They will force you to sign the treaty!"

The Queen was calm and composed. "I will sign no treaty. My fate will be no different from that of my people." She turned to Panaka. "Captain!"

Panaka snapped to attention. "Yes, Your Highness?"

"Ready my ship."

Palpatine stepped forward quickly to intercept her. "Please, Your Majesty. Stay here, where it is safe."

Amidala's voice was edged with iron. "No place is safe, if the Senate doesn't condemn this invasion. It is clear to me now that the Republic no longer functions." Her eyes locked on his. "If you win the election, Senator, I know you will do everything possible to stop the Federation. I pray you will find a way to restore sanity and compassion to the Republic."

She moved past him in a smooth, gliding motion and was out the door, her handmaidens and Panaka at her heels. Jar Jar Binks followed, shuffling after as unobtrusively as he could manage, glancing just once at Palpatine in passing.

He was surprised to catch the barest glimpse of a smile on the senator's shrewd face.

* * *

In the Temple of the Jedi, Qui-Gon Jinn, Obi-Wan Kenobi, and Anakin Skywalker stood before the Council of twelve. Clustered together at the center of the speaker's platform, they faced the circle of chairs in which the members of the Council were seated, and awaited their decision on the boy. Outside, the light was pale and wan as twilight replaced sunset, and night began its slow descent across the city.

"Finished, we are, with our examination of the boy," Yoda advised in his guttural, whispery voice. His eyes were lidded and sleepy, his pointed ears pricked forward. "Correct, you were, Qui-Gon."

Mace Windu nodded his concurrence, his dark, smooth face expressionless in the dim light. "His cells contain a very high concentration of midi-chlorians." There was emphasis on the word *very* as he spoke.

"The Force is strong in him," Ki-Adi-Mundi agreed.

Qui-Gon felt a rush of satisfaction on hearing the words, a vindication of his insistence on freeing the boy from his life on Tatooine and bringing him here. "He is to be trained, then," he declared in triumph.

There was an uncomfortable silence as the Council members looked from one to the other.

"No," Mace Windu said quietly. "He will not be trained."

Anakin's face crumpled, and there were tears in his eyes as he glanced quickly at Qui-Gon.

"No?" the Jedi Master repeated in disbelief, shocked almost speechless. He tried hard to ignore the I-told-you-so look on Obi-Wan's young face.

Mace Windu nodded, dark eyes steady. "He is too old. There is already too much anger in him."

Qui-Gon was incensed, but he held himself in check. This decision made no sense. It could not be allowed to stand. "He *is* the chosen one," he insisted vehemently. "You must see it!"

Yoda cocked his round head contemplatively. "Clouded, this boy's future is. Masked by his youth."

Qui-Gon searched the faces of the other members of the Jedi

Council, but found no help. He straightened and nodded his acceptance of their decision. "Very well. I will train him then. I take Anakin Skywalker as my Padawan apprentice."

Out of the corner of his eye, he saw Obi-Wan stiffen in shock. He saw, as well, the sudden flicker of hope that crossed Anakin's face. He did not respond to either, keeping his gaze directed toward the Council.

"An apprentice, you already have, Qui-Gon," Yoda pointed out sharply. "Impossible, to take on a second."

"We forbid it," Mace Windu advised darkly.

"Obi-Wan is ready," Qui-Gon declared.

"I am!" his protégé agreed heatedly, trying unsuccessfully to mask his surprise and disappointment in his mentor's unexpected decision. "I am ready to face the trials!"

Yoda's sleepy eyes shifted. "Ready so early, are you? What know you of ready?"

Qui-Gon and Obi-Wan exchanged quick, hard looks, and the measure of their newfound antagonism was palpable. The breach in their relationship was widening so quickly it could no longer be mapped.

Qui-Gon took a deep breath and turned back to the Council. "Obi-Wan is headstrong, and he has much to learn still about the living Force, but he is capable. There is little more he will learn from me."

Yoda shook his wizened face. "Our own counsel we will keep on who is ready, Qui-Gon. More to learn, he has."

"Now is not the time for this," Mace Windu stated with finality. "The Senate will vote tomorrow for a new supreme chancellor. Queen Amidala returns home, we are advised, which will put pressure on the Federation and could widen the confrontation. Those responsible will be quick to act on these new events."

"Drawn out of hiding, her attackers will be," Yoda whispered.

"Events are moving too fast for distractions such as this," Ki-Adi-Mundi added.

Mace Windu took a quick look about at the others sitting on the Council, then turned once more to Qui-Gon. "Go with the Queen to Naboo and discover the identity of this dark warrior who attacked you, be it Sith or otherwise. That is the clue we need to unravel this mystery."

Yoda's nod was slow and brooked no argument. "Decided later, young Skywalker's fate will be."

Qui-Gon took a deep breath, filled with frustration and disappointment at the unexpected turn of events. Anakin would not be trained, even though he had offered to take the boy as his Padawan. Worse, he had offended Obi-Wan, not intentionally perhaps, but deeply nevertheless. The rift was not permanent, but it would take time for the younger man's pride to heal—time they could not afford.

He bowed his acquiescence to the Council. "I brought Anakin here; he must stay in my charge. He has nowhere else to go."

Mace Windu nodded. "He is your ward, Qui-Gon. We do not dispute that."

"But train him not!" Yoda admonished sharply. "Take him with you, but train him not!"

The words stung, the force behind them unmistakable. Qui-Gon flinched inwardly, but said nothing.

"Protect the Queen," Mace Windu added. "But do not intercede if it comes to war until we have the Senate's approval."

There was a long silence as the members of the Council regarded Qui-Gon Jinn gravely. He stood there, trying to think of something more to say, some other argument to offer. Outside, the last of the twilight faded into darkness, and the lights of the city began to blink on like watchful eyes.

"May the Force be with you," Yoda said finally, signaling to the Jedi Master that the audience was over.

The Jedi and the boy, having been made aware of Amidala's imminent departure for Naboo, went directly to the landing platform where the Queen's transport was anchored to await her arrival. The shuttle ride over was marked by a strained silence between the Jedi and a discomfort in the boy he could not dispel. He looked down at his feet most of the time, wishing he could think of a way to stop Qui-Gon and Obi-Wan from being angry at each other.

When they disembarked from the shuttle at the landing platform, R2-D2 was already bustling about. The little droid beeped at Anakin cheerfully, then wandered over to the edge of the rampway to look down at the traffic. In doing so, he leaned out too far and tumbled over. Anakin gasped, but a second later the astromech droid reappeared, boosted back onto the rampway by his onboard jets. On hearing R2-D2's ensuing flurry of chirps and whistles, the boy smiled in spite of himself.

At the head of the loading ramp, Qui-Gon Jinn and Obi-Wan Kenobi were engaged in a heated discussion. Wind whipped down the canyons of the city's towering buildings, hiding their words from the boy. Carefully, he edged closer so that he could listen in.

"It is not disrespect, Master!" Obi-Wan was saying vehemently. "It is the truth!"

"From your point of view, perhaps." Qui-Gon's face was hard and tight with anger.

The younger Jedi's voice dropped a notch. "The boy is dangerous. They all sense it. Why can't you?"

"His fate is uncertain, but he is not dangerous," Qui-Gon corrected sharply. "The Council will decide Anakin's future. That should be enough for you." He turned away dismissively. "Now get on board!"

Obi-Wan wheeled away and stalked up the ramp into the ship. R2-D2 followed, still whistling happily. Qui-Gon turned to Anakin, and the boy walked up to him.

"Master Qui-Gon," he said uncomfortably, riddled with doubt and guilt over what was happening, "I don't want to be a problem."

Qui-Gon placed a reassuring hand on his shoulder. "You won't be, Annie." He glanced toward the ship, then knelt before the boy. "I'm not allowed to train you, so I want you to watch me instead and be mindful of what you see. Always remember, your focus determines your reality." He paused, eyes locked on Anakin. "Stay close to me, and you will be safe."

The boy nodded his understanding. "Can I ask you something?" The Jedi Master nodded. "What are midi-chlorians?"

Wind whipped at Qui-Gon's long hair, blowing strands of it across his strong face. "Midi-chlorians are microscopic life-forms that reside within the cells of all living things and communicate with the Force."

"They live inside of me?" the boy asked.

"In your cells." Qui-Gon paused. "We are symbionts with the midi-chlorians."

"Symbi-what?"

"Symbionts. Life-forms living together for mutual advantage. Without the midi-chlorians, life could not exist, and we would have no knowledge of the Force. Our midi-chlorians continually speak to us, Annie, telling us the will of the Force."

"They do?"

Qui-Gon cocked one eyebrow. "When you learn to quiet your mind, you will hear them speaking to you."

Anakin thought about it a moment, then frowned. "I don't understand."

Qui-Gon smiled, and his eyes were warm and secretive. "With time and training, Annie, you will."

A pair of shuttles eased up to the loading dock, and Queen Amidala, her handmaidens, Captain Panaka, and an escort of officers and guards disembarked. Last off the second shuttle was Jar Jar Binks. Amidala was wearing a purple velvet travel cloak that draped her body in soft folds and a gold-rimmed cowl that framed her smooth white face like a cameo portrait.

Qui-Gon rose and stood waiting beside Anakin as the Queen and her handmaidens approached.

"Your Highness," Qui-Gon greeted with a deferential inclination of his head. "It will be our pleasure to continue to serve and protect you."

Amidala nodded. "I welcome your help. Senator Palpatine fears the Federation means to destroy me."

"I promise you, we will not let that happen," the Jedi Master advised solemnly.

The Queen turned and with her handmaidens followed Panaka and the Naboo guards and officers into the transport.

Jar Jar hurried over and enveloped Anakin in a huge hug. "Weesa goen home, Annie!" he exclaimed with a grin, and Anakin Skywalker hugged him back.

Moments later they were all aboard, and the sleek transport had lifted off, leaving Coruscant behind.

It was night in the Naboo capital city of Theed, the streets empty and silent save for the occasional passing of battle-droid patrols and the whisper of the wind. In the Queen's throne room, Nute Gunray and Rune Haako stood attentively before a hologram of Darth Sidious. The hologram filled the space at one end of the room, rising up before them menacingly.

The dark-cloaked figure at its center gestured. "The Queen is on her way to you," the Sith Lord intoned softly. "When she arrives, force her to sign the treaty."

There was a momentary pause as the Neimoidians exchanged worried looks. "Yes, my lord," Nute Gunray agreed reluctantly.

"Viceroy, is the planet secure?" The dark figure in the hologram shimmered with movement.

"Yes, my lord." Gunray was on firmer ground here. "We have taken the last pockets of resistance, consisting of mostly primitive life-forms. We are now in complete control."

The faceless speaker nodded. "Good. I will see to it that in the Senate things stay as they are. I am sending Darth Maul to join you. He will deal with the Jedi."

"Yes, my lord." The words were a litany.

The hologram and Darth Sidious faded away. The Neimoidians stood where they were, frozen in place.

"A Sith Lord, here with us?" Rune Haako whispered in disbelief, and this time Nute Gunray had nothing to say at all.

Aboard the Queen's transport, coming out of hyperspace and approaching the Naboo star system, Qui-Gon Jinn paused on his way to a meeting with the Queen to study Anakin Skywalker.

The boy stood at the pilot's console next to Ric Olié. The Naboo pilot was bent forward over the controls, pointing each one out in turn and explaining its function. Anakin was absorbing the information with astonishing quickness, brow furrowed, eyes intense, concentration total.

"And that one?" The boy pointed.

"The forward stabilizer." Ric Olié glanced up at him expectantly, waiting.

"And those control the pitch?" Anakin indicated a bank of levers by the pilot's right hand.

Ric Olié's weathered face broke into a grin. "You catch on pretty quick."

As quick as anyone he had ever encountered, Qui-Gon Jinn thought. That was the reason Anakin was so special. It gave evidence of his high midi-chlorian count. It suggested anew that he was the chosen one.

The Jedi Master sighed. Why could the Council not accept

that this was so? Why were they so afraid of taking a chance on the boy, when the signs were so clear?

Qui-Gon found himself frustrated all over again. He understood their thinking. It was bad that Anakin was so old, but not fatal to his chances. What troubled them was not his age, but the conflict they sensed within him. Anakin was wrestling with his parentage, with his separation from his mother, his friends, and his home. Especially his mother. He was old enough to appreciate what might happen, and the result was an uncertainty that worked within him like a caged animal seeking to break free. The Jedi Council knew that it could not tame that uncertainty from without, that it could be mastered only from within. They believed Anakin Skywalker too old for this, his thinking and his beliefs too settled to be safely reshaped. He was vulnerable to his inner conflict, and the dark side would be quick to take advantage of this.

Qui-Gon shook his head, staring over at the boy from the back of the cockpit. Yes, there were risks in accepting him as an apprentice. But few things of worth were accomplished in life without risk. The Jedi order was founded on strict adherence to established procedures in the raising and educating of young Jedi, but there were exceptions to all things, even this. That the Jedi Council was refusing even to consider that this was an instance in which an exception should be made was intolerable.

Still, he must keep faith, he knew. He must believe. The decision not to train Anakin would be reconsidered on their return and reversed. If the Council did not embrace the boy's training as a Jedi voluntarily, then it would be up to Qui-Gon to find a way to make it do so.

He turned away then and walked from the cabin to the passageways beyond and descended one level to the Queen's chambers. The others she had called together for this meeting were already present when he arrived. Obi-Wan gave him a brief, neutral nod of recognition, standing next to a glowering Captain Panaka. Jar Jar Binks hugged the wall to one side, apparently trying to disappear into it. Amidala sat on her shipboard throne on a raised dais set against one wall, two of her handmaidens, Rabé and Eirtaé, flanking her. Her white-painted face was composed and her gaze cool as it met his own, but there was fire in the words she spoke next.

"When we land on Naboo," she advised the Jedi Master after he had bowed and taken up a position next to Panaka, "it is my intention to act on this invasion at once. My people have suffered enough."

Panaka could barely contain himself, his dark face tight with anger. "When we *land*, Your Highness, the Trade Federation will arrest you and force you to sign their treaty!"

Qui-Gon nodded thoughtfully, curious as to the Queen's thinking. "I agree. I'm not sure what you hope to accomplish by this."

Amidala might have been carved from stone. "The Naboo are going to take back what is ours."

"There are only twelve of us!" Panaka snapped, unable to keep silent. "Your Highness," he added belatedly. "We have no army!"

Her eyes shifted to Qui-Gon. "The Jedi cannot fight a war for you, Your Highness," he advised. "We can only protect you."

She let her gaze drift from them to settle on Jar Jar. The Gungan was studying his toes. "Jar Jar Binks!" she called.

Jar Jar, clearly caught off guard, stiffened. "Me, Your Highness?"

"Yes," Amidala of the Naboo affirmed. "I have need of your help."

Deep in the Naboo swamps, at the edge of the lake that bored downward to the Gungan capital city of Otoh Gunga, the fugitives from the Queen's transport were grouped at the water's edge, waiting for the return of Jar Jar Binks. Amidala and her handmaidens, the Jedi Knights, Captain Panaka, Anakin, R2-D2, Ric Olié and several other pilots, and a handful of Naboo guards clustered uneasily in the misty silence. It was safe to say that even now no one but the Queen knew exactly what it was she was attempting to do. All she had been willing to reveal to those in a position to inquire was that she wished to make contact with the Gungan people and Jar Jar would be her emissary. She had insisted on landing in the swamp, even after both Panaka and the Jedi had advised against it.

A single battleship orbited the planet, all that remained of the Trade Federation blockade. Housed within was the control station responsible for directing the droid army that occupied Naboo. When Panaka wondered aloud at the absence of the other battleships, Qui-Gon pointed out rather dryly that you don't need a blockade once you control the port.

Anakin, standing apart from the others with R2-D2, studied the group surreptitiously. Jar Jar had been gone a long time, and everyone but the Queen was growing restless. She stood wrapped in her soft robes, silent and implacable in the midst of her handmaidens. Padmé, Eirtaé, and Rabé had changed from their crimson hooded cloaks into more functional trousers, tunics, boots, and long-waisted overcoats, and there were blasters strapped to their waists. The boy had never seen Padmé like this, and he found himself wondering how good a fighter she was.

As if realizing he was thinking of her, Padmé broke away from the others and came over to him.

"How are you, Annie?" she asked quietly, her kind eyes locking on his.

He shrugged. "Okay. I've missed you."

"It's good to see you again. I'm sorry I haven't had a chance to talk with you before, but I've been very busy."

They hadn't spoken more than a few words to each other since leaving Tatooine, and Anakin hadn't even seen Padmé since their departure from Coruscant. It had bothered him, but he'd kept it to himself.

"I didn't—I—" he stuttered, looking down at his boots. "They decided not to make me a Jedi."

He recounted the story for her, detailing the events surrounding his appearance before the Jedi Council. Padmé listened intently, then touched his cheek with her cool fingers. "They can change their minds, Annie. Don't give up hope."

She bent close then. "I have something to tell you. The Queen has made a painful, difficult decision—a decision that will change everything for the Naboo. We are a peaceful people, and we do not believe in war. But sometimes there is no choice. Either you adapt or you die. The Queen understands this. She has decided to take an aggressive posture with the Trade Federation army. The Naboo are going to fight to regain their freedom."

"Will there be a battle?" he asked quickly, trying unsuccessfully to hide his excitement.

She nodded. "I'm afraid so."

"Will you be involved?" he pressed.

She smiled sadly. "Annie, I don't have a choice."

Qui-Gon and Obi-Wan stood together some distance away. The Jedi still weren't speaking to each other, or only barely so. Their words on the journey out from Coruscant had been reserved almost exclusively for others. The hard feelings caused by Qui-Gon's bid to train Anakin did not soften. The boy had tried to talk to Obi-Wan once aboard the Queen's ship, just to say he was sorry this had happened, but the younger Jedi had brushed him off.

Now, though, Obi-Wan was beginning to feel uncomfortable with the situation. He had been close with Qui-Gon for too long to let a momentary disagreement put an end to twenty-odd years of friendship. Qui-Gon was like a father to him, the only father he knew. He was angry that the Jedi Master would dismiss him so abruptly in favor of the boy, but he realized, too, the depth of Qui-Gon's passion when he believed in something. Training this boy to be a Jedi was a cause Qui-Gon championed as he had championed no other in Obi-Wan's memory. He did not do so to slight his protégé. He did so because he believed in the boy's destiny.

Obi-Wan understood. Who could say? Perhaps this time

Qui-Gon was right. Perhaps Anakin Skywalker's training was a cause worth fighting for.

"I've been thinking," Qui-Gon announced suddenly, keeping his voice low, his eyes directed toward the others. "We are treading on dangerous ground. If the Queen intends to fight a war, we cannot become involved. Not even in her efforts to persuade the Gungans to join with the Naboo against the Federation, if that is what she intends by coming here. The Jedi have no authority to take sides."

"But we do have authority to protect the Queen," Obi-Wan pointed out.

Qui-Gon's eyes shifted to find his. "It is a fine line we walk, then."

"Master," Obi-Wan said, facing him now. "I behaved badly on Coruscant, and I am embarrassed. I meant no disrespect to you. I do not wish to be difficult in the matter of the boy."

"Nor have you been," the older Jedi replied, a faint smile appearing. "You have been honest with me. Honesty is never wrong. I did not lie when I told the Council you were ready. You are. I have taught you all I can. You will be a great Jedi, my young Padawan. You will make me proud."

They gripped hands impulsively, and as quickly as that the breach that had opened between them was closed.

Moments later, a dark shape broke the surface of the water with a splash, and Jar Jar Binks climbed from the lake, shaking water from his amphibious skin onto the assembled. Long ears dripping, billed mouth shedding water like a duck's, he shook his head worriedly.

"Tis nobody dere! Deys all gone!" His eyestalks swiveled. "Some kinda fight, deys have. Maccaneks, mebbe. Very bombad. Otoh Gunga empty. All Gungans gone. All gone."

"Do you think they have been taken to the camps?" Panaka asked quickly, glancing around at the group.

"More likely they were wiped out," Obi-Wan offered in disgust.

But Jar Jar shook his head. "Me no think so. Gungans too smart. Go into hiding. When dey in trubble, go to sacred place. Maccaneks no find dem dere."

Qui-Gon stepped forward. "Sacred place?" he repeated. "Can you take us there, Jar Jar?"

The Gungan sighed heavily, as if to say "Here we go again," and beckoned for them to follow.

They traversed the swamp for some time, first skirting the lake, then plunging deep into a forest of massive trees and tall grasses, following a water-screened pathway that connected a series of knolls. Somewhere in the distance, Trade Federation STAPs buzzed and whined as a search for the transport fugitives commenced in earnest. Jar Jar glanced about apprehensively as he picked his way through the mire, but did not slow.

Finally, they emerged in a clearing of marshy grasses and stands of trees with roots tangled so thickly they formed what appeared to be an impassable hedge. Jar Jar stopped, sniffed the air speculatively, and nodded. "Dissen it."

He lifted his head and made a strange chittering noise though his billed mouth, the sound echoing eerily in the silence. The group waited, eyes searching the misty gloom.

Suddenly Captain Tarpals and a scouting party of Gungans riding kaadu emerged from the haze, electropoles and energy spears held at the ready.

"Heydey ho, Cap'n Tarpals," Jar Jar greeted cheerfully.

"Binks!" the Gungan leader exclaimed in disbelief. "Notta gain!"

Jar Jar shrugged nonchalantly. "We come ta see da Boss!"

Tarpals rolled his eyes. "Ouch time, Binks. Ouch time for alla yous, mebbe."

Herding them together, Gungans on kaadu providing a perimeter escort on all sides, Tarpals led them deeper into the swamp. The canopy formed by the limbs of the trees became so thick that the sky and the sun almost disappeared. Bits and pieces of statuary began to surface, crumbling stone facades and plinths sinking in the mire. Vines snaked their way across the broken remains, dropping down from limbs that twisted and wound to-gether in vast wooden nets.

Pushing through a high stand of saw grass, they arrived in a clearing filled with Gungan refugees—men, women, and chil-dren of all ages and descriptions, huddled together on a broad, dry rise, many with their possessions gathered around them. Tarpals led the company past the refugees to where the ruins of what had once been a grand temple were being slowly reclaimed by the swamp. Platforms and stairs were all that remained intact, the columns and ceilings having long ago collapsed and broken apart. The massive heads and limbs of stone statues poked out of the mire, fingers clutching weapons and eyes staring sightlessly into space.

At the far end of the ruins, Boss Nass appeared, lumbering out of shadows with several more of the Gungan council to stand atop a stone head partially submerged in the water. Amidala and her retinue approached to within hailing distance over a network of causeways and islands.

"Jar Jar Binks, whadda yous doen back?" Boss Nass rumbled angrily. "Yous suppose ta take dese outlanders and no come back! Yous pay good dis time!" The fleshy head swiveled. "Who yous bring here ta da Gungan sacred place?"

The Queen stepped forward at once, white face lifting. "I am Amidala, Queen of the Naboo."

"Naboo!" Boss Nass thundered. "No like da Naboo! Yous bring da maccaneks! Dey bust up our homes! Dey drive us all out!" A heavy arm lifted, pointing at the Queen. "Yous all bom-bad! Yous all die, mebbe!"

Anakin noticed suddenly that they were completely sur-rounded by Gungans, some on kaadu, some on foot, all with electropoles, energy spears, and some sort of throwing device. Captain Panaka and the Naboo guards were looking around ner-vously, hands straying toward their blasters. The Jedi flanked the Queen and her handmaidens, but their arms hung loose at their sides.

"We wish to form an alliance with you," Amidala tried again.

"We no form nutten wit da Naboo!" Boss Nass roared angrily.

Abruptly Padmé detached herself from the others and stepped in front of the Queen. "You did well, Sabé. But I will have to do this myself," she said quietly, and turned to face Boss Nass.

"Who dis?" the head Gungan snapped.

Standing next to Anakin, R2-D2 beeped softly in recognition. The droid had figured it out first.

Padmé straightened. "I am Queen Amidala," she announced in a loud, clear voice. "Sabé serves from time to time as my decoy, my loyal bodyguard. I am sorry for my deception, but given the circumstances, I am sure you can understand." She turned to the Jedi, her eyes shifting momentarily to find Anakin. "Gentlemen, I apologize for misleading you."

Her eyes returned quickly to Boss Nass, who was frowning suspiciously, clearly not understanding any of what was happening. "Although our people do not always agree, Your Honor," she continued, her voice softening, "we have always lived in peace. Until now. The Trade Federation, with its tanks and its 'maccaneks,' has destroyed all that we have worked so hard to build. The Gungans are in hiding, and the Naboo have been imprisoned in camps. If we do not act quickly, all that we value will be lost forever."

She stretched out her hands. "I ask you to help us, Your Honor." She paused. "No, I beg you to help us."

She dropped abruptly to one knee in front of the astonished leader of the Gungans. There was an audible gasp of surprise from the Naboo. "We are your humble servants, Your Honor," Padmé said so that all could hear. "Our fate is in your hands. Please help us."

She motioned, and one by one, her handmaidens, Panaka, and the Naboo pilots and guards dropped to their knees beside her. Anakin and the Jedi were the last to join them. Out of the corner of his eye, Anakin saw Jar Jar standing virtually alone in their midst, staring around in wonderment and shock.

For a moment, no one said anything. Then a slow, deep rumble of laughter rose out of the throat of Boss Nass. "Ho, ho, ho! Me like dis! Dis good! Yous no think yous greater den da Gungans!"

The head Gungan came forward, reaching out with one hand. "Yous stand, Queen Amidoll. Yous talk wit me, okay? Mebbe we gonna be friends after all!"

The senior Sith Lord appeared in a shimmer of robes and shadows as his protégé and the Neimoidians walked slowly down the corridor leading from the throne room back to the plaza.

"We have sent out patrols," Nute Gunray said, concluding his report to the ominous figure in the projection. "We have already located their starship in the swamp. It won't be long until we have them in hand, my lord."

Darth Sidious was silent. For a moment Nute Gunray was afraid he hadn't been heard. "This is an unexpected move for the Queen," the Sith Lord said at last, his voice so low it could barely be heard. "It is too aggressive. Lord Maul, be mindful."

"Yes, Master," the other Sith growled softly, yellow eyes gleaming.

"Be patient," Darth Sidious purred, head lowered in cowled shadows, hands folded into black robes. "Let them make the first move."

In silence, Darth Maul and the Neimoidians continued on as the hologram slowly faded away.

Boss Nass was as mercurial as he was large, and his change of attitude toward the Naboo was dramatic. Once he decided that the Queen did not consider herself his superior, that she was in fact quite sincere in her plea for Gungan help, he was quick to come around. The fact that his dislike of the battle droids was every bit as strong as hers didn't hurt matters, of course. Perhaps he had been hasty in his belief that the "maccaneks" wouldn't find the Gungans in the swamps. Otoh Gunga had been attacked at daybreak two days earlier and its inhabitants driven from their homes. Boss Nass was not about to sit still for that. If a plan could be put together to drive the invaders out, the Gungan army would do its part to help.

He took Amidala and her companions out of the swamp to the edge of the grass plains that ran south to the Naboo capital city of Theed. Any attack would be mounted from here, and the Queen had come to the Gungans with a very specific plan of attack in mind.

The first step in that plan involved sending Captain Panaka on a reconnaissance of the city.

As they stood looking out from the misty confines of the swamp toward the open grasslands, waiting for Panaka's return, Boss Nass trundled up to Jar Jar.

"Yous doen grand, Jar Jar Binks!" he rumbled, wrapping a meaty arm around the slender Gungan's shoulders. "Yous bring da Naboo and da Gungan together! Tis very brave thing."

Jar Jar shuffled his feet and looked embarrassed. "Ah, yous no go sayen dat. Tis nutten."

"No, yous grand warrior!" Boss Nass declared, squeezing the air out of his compatriot with a massive hug.

"No, no, no," the other persisted bashfully.

"So," Boss Nass concluded brightly, "we make yous bombad general in da Gungan army!"

"What?" Jar Jar exclaimed in dismay. "General? Me? No, no, no!" he gasped, and his eyes rolled up, his tongue fell out, and he fainted dead away.

Padmé was in conference with the Jedi and the Gungan generals, to whose number Jar Jar Binks had just been added, so Anakin, at loose ends, had wandered over to keep company with the Gungan sentries who were keeping lookout for Panaka. The Gungans patrolled the swamp perimeter on kaadu and kept watch through macrobinoculars from treetops and the remains of ancient statuary, making certain Federation scouting parties didn't come up on them unexpectedly. Anakin stood at the base of a temple column, still trying to come to terms with Padmé's revelation. Everyone had been surprised, of course, but no one more than he. He wasn't sure how he felt about her now, knowing she wasn't just a girl, but a Queen. He had declared he would marry her someday, believing it so, but how could someone who had been a slave all his life marry a Queen? He wanted to talk to her, but there wasn't any opportunity for that here.

He supposed things wouldn't be the same after this, but he wished they could. He liked her as much now as he had before, and to tell the truth he didn't care if she was a Queen or not.

He glanced over at the girl and the Jedi Knights and thought how different things were here than they had been on Tatooine. Nothing had worked out the way he had hoped for any of them, and it remained to be seen if leaving his mother and home to come with them was a good idea after all.

The Gungan lookout standing atop a piece of statuary above him gave a grunt. "Dey comen," he called down, peering out into the grasslands through his macrobinoculars.

Anakin gave a yell in response and raced over to Padmé, the Jedi, and the Gungan generals. "They're back!" he shouted.

Everyone turned to watch a squad of four speeders skim over the flats and pull to a stop in the concealing shadow of the swamp. Captain Panaka and several dozen Naboo soldiers, officers, and starfighter pilots jumped down. Panaka made his way directly to the Queen.

"I think we got through without being detected, Your Highness," he advised quickly, brushing the dust from his clothing.

"What is the situation?" she asked as the others crowded close to them.

Panaka shook his head. "Most of our people are in the detention camps. A few hundred officers and guards have formed an underground movement to resist the invasion. I've brought as many of the leaders as I could find."

"Good." Padmé nodded appreciatively toward Boss Nass. "The Gungans have a larger army than we imagined."

"Very, very bombad!" the Gungan chief rumbled.

Panaka exhaled wearily. "You'll need it. The Federation army is much larger than we thought, too. And stronger." He gave the Queen a considering look. "In my opinion, this isn't a battle we can win, Your Highness."

Standing at the edge of the circle, Jar Jar Binks looked down at Anakin and rolled his eyes despairingly.

But Padmé was undeterred. "I don't intend to win it, Captain. The battle is a diversion. We need the Gungans to draw the droid army away from Theed, so we can infiltrate the palace and capture the Neimoidian viceroy. The Trade Federation cannot function without its head. Neimoidians don't think for themselves. Without the viceroy to command them, they will cease to be a threat."

She waited for them to consider her plan, eyes fixing automatically on Qui-Gon Jinn. "What do you think, Master Jedi?" she asked.

"It is a well-conceived plan," Qui-Gon acknowledged. "It appears to be your best possible move, Your Highness, although there is great risk. Even with the droid army in the field, the viceroy will be well guarded. And many of the Gungans may be killed."

Boss Nass snorted derisively. "They bombad guns no get through our shields! We ready to fight!"

Jar Jar gave Anakin another eye roll, but this time Boss Nass saw him do so and gave his new general a hard warning look.

Padmé was thinking. "We could reduce the Gungan casualties by securing the main hangar and sending our pilots to knock out their orbiting control ship. Without the control ship to signal them, the droid army can't function at all."

Everyone nodded in agreement. "But if the viceroy should escape, Your Highness," Obi-Wan pointed out darkly, "he will return with another droid army, and you'll be no better off than you are now. Whatever else happens, you must capture him."

"Indeed, we must," Padmé agreed. "Everything depends on it. Cut off the head, and the serpent dies. Without the viceroy, the Trade Federation collapses."

They moved on to other matters then, beginning a detailed discussion of battle tactics and command responsibilities. Anakin stood listening for a moment, then eased his way close to Qui-Gon and tugged on his sleeve.

"What about me?" he asked quietly.

The Jedi Master put a hand on the boy's head and smiled. "You stay close to me, Annie, do as I say, and you'll be safe."

Keeping safe wasn't quite what the boy had in mind, but he let the matter drop, satisfied that as long as he was close to Qui-Gon, he wouldn't be far from the action.

In the Theed palace throne room, Darth Sidious loomed in hologram form before Darth Maul, Battle Droid Commander OOM-9, and the Neimoidians. Smooth and silky, his voice oozed through the shadowy ether.

"Our young Queen surprises me," he whispered thoughtfully, hidden within his dark robes. "She is more foolish than I thought."

"We are sending all available troops to meet this army of hers," Nute Gunray offered quickly. "It appears to be assembling at the edge of the swamp. Primitives, my lord—nothing better. We do not expect much resistance."

"I am increasing security at all Naboo detention camps," OOM-9 intoned.

Darth Maul glared at nothing, then shook his horned head. "I feel there is more to this than what we know, my Master. The two Jedi may be using the Queen for their own purposes."

"The Jedi cannot become involved," Darth Sidious soothed, hands spreading in a placating motion. "They can only protect the Queen. Even Qui-Gon Jinn cannot break that covenant. This will work to our advantage."

Darth Maul snorted, anxious to get on with it.

"I have your approval to proceed, then, my lord?" Nute Gunray asked hesitantly, avoiding the younger Sith's mad eyes.

"Proceed," Darth Sidious ordered softly. "Wipe them out, Viceroy. All of them."

By midday, with the sun overhead in a cloudless sky and the wind died away to nothing, the grasslands lying south of Theed between the Naboo capital city and the Gungan swamp lay empty and still. Heat rose off the grasslands in a soft shimmer, and it was so quiet that from a hundred meters away the chirp of birds and the buzz of insects could be heard as if they were settled close by.

Then the Trade Federation army's bubble-nosed transports and armor-wrapped tanks roared onto the rolling meadows, skimming the tall grasses in gleaming waves of bright metal.

It was quiet in the swamps as well, the perpetual twilight hushed and expectant beneath the vast canopy of limbs and vines, the surface of the mire as smooth and unbroken as glass, the reeds and rushes motionless in the windless air. Here and there a water bug jumped soundlessly from place to place, stirring puddles to life in the wake of its passing, bending blades of grass like springboards. Birds swooped and banked in bright flashes of color, darting from limb to limb. Small animals crept from cover to drink and feed, eyes bright, noses twitching, senses alert.

Then the Gungan army surfaced in a rippling of murky water

and a stream of bubbles, lop-eared heads popping up like corks, first one, then another, and finally hundreds and eventually thousands.

Both on the plain and in the swamp, the small animals raced back into hiding, the birds took wing, and the insects went to ground.

Astride their kaadu, the Gungans rode from their concealment with armor strapped to their amphibious bodies and weapons held at the ready. They carried long-hafted energy spears and metal-handled ball slings for long-distance fighting and energy shields for close combat. The kaadu shook themselves as they reached dry ground, shedding the swamp water from their smooth skins, eyes picking out the solid patches of ground as their riders urged them on. Numbers swelling as they reached the fringes of the swamp, the Gungans began to form up in ranks of riders that stretched away as far as the eye could see.

As the first wave rode clear, the swamp boiled anew with the appearance of fambaa—huge, four-legged lizards with long necks and tails and massive, scaly bodies. The fambaa bore shield generators atop their broad backs, machines that when linked would activate a force field to protect the Gungan soldiers against Trade Federation weaponry. The fambaa lumbered heavily beneath their loads, necks craning from side to side as their drivers prodded them impatiently.

Jar Jar Binks rode with them at the head of his new command, wondering what it was he was supposed to do. Mostly, he believed, he was supposed to stay out of the way. Certainly the other generals and even his own subordinate officers had made it clear that this was what they preferred. Boss Nass might think it clever to make him a general in the Gungan army, but the career officers found it less amusing. General Ceel, who was commander-in-chief, grunted sourly at Jar Jar, on being informed of his new position, and told him to set a good example for his people and die well.

Jar Jar had responded to all this by keeping a low profile until the march out of the swamp began, and then he had assumed his required position at the head of his command. He had gotten barely a hundred meters after emerging from concealment when he had fallen off his kaadu. No one had bothered to stop to help him climb back on, and so now he was riding somewhere in the middle of his troops.

"Tis very bombad," he kept whispering to himself as he rode with the others through the marshy haze.

Slowly, steadily, the Gungan army cleared the tangle of the swamps and moved out onto the open grasslands where the Trade Federation army was already waiting.

Anakin Skywalker hunkered down in the shadows of a building directly across from the main hangar of the Naboo starfleet in the city of Theed. It was quiet here as well, the bulk of the battle droids dispatched to the field to deal with the Gungan army, the remainder scattered throughout the city in patrols and on perimeter watch. Nevertheless, tanks crowded the plaza fronting the hangar complex, and a strong contingent of battle droids warded the Naboo fleet. Seizing control of the starfighters was not going to be easy.

Anakin glanced over at those with him. Padmé, dressed as a handmaiden, crouched with Eirtaé beside the Jedi, waiting for Captain Panaka's command to get into position on the other side of the square. Sabé, the decoy Queen, and her handmaidens wore battle dress, loose-fitting and durable, with blasters strapped to their sides. R2-D2 blinked silently from behind them in the company of twenty-odd Naboo officers, guards, and pilots, all armed and ready. It seemed to the boy like a pathetically small number of fighters to carry the day, but it was all they had.

At least Qui-Gon and Obi-Wan were talking again. They had begun doing so on the journey in from the swamps, a few words here, a few there, exchanging comments guardedly, testing the waters. Anakin had listened carefully, more attuned to the nuances of their conversation than others could be, hearing in the inflection of their voices more than simply the words spoken. After a time, when the words had healed enough of the breach that they felt comfortable again, there were smiles, brief and almost sad, but clear in their purpose. The Jedi were old friends and their relationship that of father and son. They did not want to toss it all away over a single disagreement. Anakin was thankful for that—especially since the disagreement in question was over him.

Padmé had spoken to him as well, joining him for a few moments as they approached the city through the forests east, her smile banishing all his doubts and fears in a moment's time.

"I'm sorry I couldn't tell you sooner," she said, apologizing for hiding her identity. "I know it was a surprise."

"It's okay," he said, shrugging bravely.

"I guess knowing I'm a Queen makes you feel differently about me, doesn't it?" she asked.

"I guess, but that's okay. Just so you still like me. Because I still like you." He looked over at her hopefully.

"Of course, Annie. Telling you who I really am doesn't mean my feelings for you have changed. I was the same person before, whether you knew the truth about me or not."

He thought about it a moment. "I suppose." He brightened. "So I guess my feelings for you shouldn't be any different now either."

She moved away, smiling broadly back at him, and just at that moment he felt ten meters tall.

So now he was at peace with himself about the Jedi and Padmé, but was beset with new concerns. What if something happened to them during the fight ahead? What if they were hurt or even . . . He couldn't bring himself to finish the thought. Nothing bad would happen to them, that was all. He wouldn't let it. He glanced at them, kneeling in silence at the edge of the plaza, and promised himself he would keep them safe no matter what. That would be his job. His mouth tightened with determination as he made his pledge.

"Once we get inside, Annie, you find a safe place to hide until this is over," Qui-Gon advised suddenly, bending close, almost as if he could read the boy's mind.

"Sure," Anakin promised.

"And stay there," the Jedi Master added firmly.

Across the way, Panaka and his contingent of fighters were in position now, placing the tanks and battle droids in a crossfire with Padmé's group. Padmé produced a small glow rod and flashed a coded signal to Panaka across the square.

All around Anakin, weapons slid free of holsters and fastenings, and safeties were released.

Then Panaka's fighters opened up on the battle droids, blasters shattering their metal bodies in a hail of laser fire. Other droids wheeled about in response and began exchanging fire, drawn toward the source of the conflict and away from Padmé's group.

Qui-Gon came to his feet. "Stay close," Qui-Gon whispered to him.

A moment later, the boy was running with the Jedi, Padmé, Eirtaé, R2-D2, and their Naboo contingent of soldiers and pilots toward the open door of the hangar.

Jar Jar sat tall astride his kaadu, having regained his composure and resumed his position at the head of his troop. The Gungan army was spread out all along the grasslands on either side of where he rode for as far as the eye could see. Birdlike, the kaadu picked their way through the tall grasses, heads dipping, Gungan riders swaying with the motion. The Gungans wore leather and metal headgear and body armor, with small, circular shields strapped at their hips and tri-plate energy packs for abetting the force field jutting like metal feathers from their saddle backs. The fambaa, bearing the shield generators, were spaced evenly down their lines to achieve maximum protection once the generators were activated. Like tanks, the massive lizards lumbered amidst the more nimble kaadu, and the grasslands shook with the weight of their passing.

At the head of the army rode General Ceel and his command unit, the flags of Otoh Gunga and the other Gungan cities borne in their wake at the end of long poles.

The army crested a rise, a great, rolling wave of dark bodies, and on a hand signal from General Ceel, drew to a halt.

Across a long, shallow depression, its position secure on the next ridge over, the Trade Federation army waited. Lines of STAPs and tanks formed the first rank, spread out over a distance of more than a kilometer, armor plating and weapons gleaming in the midday sun. Buttressing the smaller vehicles were the huge Federation transports, massive bodies hovering just off the ground, bulbous-nose gates closed and pointed forward toward the Gungans. Battle droids controlled tanks and STAPs, faceless and empty metal shells impervious to pain, devoid of emotion, and programmed to fight until destroyed.

Jar Jar Binks stared at the droid army in awe. There was not a living creature in sight, not one made of flesh and blood, not one that would react to the terrible roil of battle as the Gungans would. It made his skin crawl to think of what that meant.

The fambaa were in place now, and General Ceel activated the shield generators. The big turbines hummed to life, and a pulse of red light arced from a generator atop one fambaa to a dish atop the next, the beam widening and broadening as it grew in size to encompass the whole of the Gungan army until each soldier and kaadu was safely enfolded. The coloring of the protective light changed from red to gold, shimmering like a mirage on a desert. The effect was to make it appear as if the Gungan army was underwater, as if it had been swallowed in a bright, clear sea.

The Federation was quick to test the shield's effectiveness. On a signal from Droid Commander OOM-9, who in turn was responding to a command from the deep-space control center, the tanks opened fire, their laser cannons sending round after round into the covering. Searing beams hammered into the shield and shattered ineffectively against the liquid energy surface, unable to penetrate.

Within their protective covering, the Gungans waited patiently, weapons ready, trusting the strength of their shield. Astride his kaadu, Jar Jar Binks flinched and squirmed fearfully, muttering various prayers to ward off the destruction he was certain would find him otherwise. Relentlessly, the Trade Federation cannons continued their attack, streamers of energy lancing from their barrel mounts, pounding at the covering. The flash and burn and explosion were blinding and deafening, but the Gungans held their ground.

Finally, the Trade Federation guns went still. Try as they might, they could not break through the Gungan energy shield. Within their protective canopy, the Gungans cheered and brandished their weapons triumphantly.

But now the tanks and STAPs withdrew, and the massive transports advanced to the fore. The rounded-nose doors opened, widening to reveal a cluster of racks mounted within. The racks rolled forward on long rails, revealing row after row of battle droids neatly folded up and suspended on hooks. When the racks were fully extended, they began to lower and separate outward, filling the open space in front of the transports with thousands of droids.

Positioned at the forefront of their army, General Ceel and his Gungan commanders exchanged worried looks.

Now the racks began to release the battle droids, who unfolded in unison into standing positions, arms and legs extended, bodies straight. Metal hands reached back over shoulders to pull free the blaster rifles with which each unit was equipped.

On command from OOM-9, the entire array of battle droids began to march toward the Gungan army, bright metal ranks filling the grasslands from horizon to horizon.

The Gungan shield wall was designed to deflect large, slow-moving objects of density and mass such as artillery vehicles and small, fast-moving objects generating extreme heat such as projectiles from weapons fire. But it would not deflect small, slow-moving droids—even massed together in such numbers as they were here. Jar Jar Binks began to wish he were somewhere else, thinking that as mighty as the Gungan army was, it was dwarfed by the metal machine that marched against it now.

But the Gungans had come prepared for battle, and they were not so deterred by the number of their enemies that they were ready to quit. All up and down their lines, Gungans activated their energy spears and straight-handled slings, arming them for the attack. At the foot of the rise on which they waited, the front ranks of the battle droids reached the perimeter of the energy field and began to pass through. The shield had no effect on them. Lifting their blasters to their shoulders, they began to fire.

Amid a wail of great, curved battle horns, the Gungans retaliated. A shower of spears rained down on the advancing droids, shafts and points exploding on impact, ripping metal limbs and torsos apart. Energy balls flung from the slings followed, inflicting further damage. Mortars dumped their loads in the center of the droid ranks, opening huge gaps in the attack. The battle droids reeled and slowed, then regained momentum and came on, hundreds more taking the place of those who had fallen, marching mindlessly through the protective shield and into the range of the Gungan weapons.

At the center of his command unit, General Ceel urged his warriors on, tightening his defensive lines in front of the fambaa and the shield generators to protect them from harm, knowing that if the force field came down, the Trade Federation's tanks would strike the Gungans as well.

Battle-droid ranks, metal parts reflecting sun and fire, and Gungan lines, orange-skinned and supple, closed to do battle.

Resisting the temptation to shut his eyes against what he knew was coming, Jar Jar Binks kicked his heels into the flanks of his kaadu and charged ahead with the rest of his command.

In the relative seclusion of the Theed palace throne room, in a place they had believed safely removed from any real danger, Nute Gunray and Rune Haako stared at a giant viewscreen and its rapidly changing images of the battle taking place in the main hangar. The Jedi Knights were inside the complex, accompanied by Naboo soldiers and pilots, their lightsabers wreaking havoc on the battle droids who tried to stop them.

"How did they get into the city?" Rune Haako whispered in dismay.

Nute Gunray shook his head. "I don't know. I thought the battle was going to take place far from here." His eyes were wide and staring. "This is too close!"

They turned as one when Darth Maul stalked into the room, bearing a long-handled lightsaber. Yellow eyes gleamed out of the Sith's red and black tattooed face, and his dark cloak billowed out behind him.

Nute Gunray and Rune Haako backed away instinctively, neither of them wanting to get in the way. "Lord Maul," Gunray greeted, inclining his head briefly.

Darth Maul glanced at him disdainfully. "I told you there was more to this than was apparent!" His eyes had a wild, manic look to them. "The Jedi have come to Theed for a reason, Viceroy. They have a plan of their own for defeating us."

"A plan?" the Neimoidian asked worriedly.

"One that will fail, I assure you." The striped face glinted wickedly in the light. "I have waited a long time for this. I have trained for it endlessly. The Jedi will regret their decision to return here."

There was an edge to his rough voice that was frightening. The Sith was anxious for this confrontation, his body coiled and ready, his hands flexing about his weapon. The Neimoidians did not envy those he sought.

"Wait here until I return," he ordered abruptly, and swept past them.

"Where are you going?" Nute Gunray demanded frantically as the Sith Lord crossed toward the speeder docks.

"Where do you think I'm going, Viceroy?" the other sneered. "I'm going to the main hangar to rid you of the Jedi once and for all."

Anakin Skywalker rushed through the open doors of the main hangar after the Jedi and Padmé, with R2-D2 and the rest of the Naboo freedom fighters on their heels. Battle droids turned to confront them, but lightsabers and blasters cut apart the foremost before the others even knew what was happening. The droids rallied in response, summoning help from without, but Panaka and his men had those in the plaza already occupied, and for a moment the Jedi and the Naboo were in control.

Mindful of Qui-Gon's admonition, Anakin ducked beneath the fuselage of the closest starfighter, laser bolts searing the air around him in brilliant bursts of fire.

"Get to your ships!" Padmé shouted at her pilots, leading the contingent of Naboo soldiers under her command in pursuit of the retreating battle droids.

Ducking and crouching, she fired her blaster with quick, precise moves, bringing down droid after droid, her charges finding their targets with unerring accuracy. The Jedi fought just ahead of her, blocking droid laser fire with their lightsabers, striking down those unfortunate enough to cross their path. But it was Padmé on whom Anakin's eyes were riveted, for not only had he never seen this side of her, he hadn't even known it existed. She moved with the skill and training of a seasoned fighter, no longer seeming in any way a young girl, becoming instead a deadly combatant.

He thought suddenly of his dream of Padmé leading an army in another time and place, and suddenly the dream didn't seem so impossible.

Pilots from the attacking force and R2 units freed from storage in the hangar lockers moved quickly to board the Naboo fighters, scattering swiftly through the hail of blaster fire. Clambering aboard their starships, pilots in the cockpits, R2 units in their sockets, they switched on their control panels and ignited their engines. A roar of power filled the massive hangar, drowning out the sound of laser fire, building to an ear-shattering crescendo. One by one, the fighters began to levitate and shift into position for takeoff.

A Naboo pilot rushed past Anakin and climbed into the fighter he was crouched behind. "Better get out of here, kid!" she called down from the cockpit. "Find yourself a new hiding place! You're about to lose this one!"

Anakin darted away in a low crouch, droid blaster fire crisscrossing the air above him, centering on the departing ships. The fighter he had abandoned began to lift off, wheeling toward the open hangar doors. Other ships were already speeding away into the blue, engines booming.

As the Jedi and the Naboo fighters continued to push the droid hangar watch steadily back, Anakin searched hastily for a new hiding place. Then he heard R2-D2 whistle at him from another fighter close at hand, the little droid already ensconced in his socket, domed head rotating, control lights flashing. The boy raced across the hangar floor littered with the shattered bodies of battle droids, laser fire whizzing all about him, and jumped into the cockpit with a gasp of relief.

Peering out from the safety of his bolt-hole, he watched the last pair of Naboo fighters rocket out of the hangar. The first got free, but the second was hit by tank fire and knocked sideways so that it pinwheeled into the ground and exploded in a ball of flame. Anakin winced and crouched lower.

Now Panaka, Sabé, and the Naboo soldiers who had been engaged in combat outside the hangar burst through the doors as well, firing as they came. Caught in a crossfire, the remaining battle droids were quickly overwhelmed and destroyed. There was a hurried conference between the Jedi, Padmé, and Panaka, and then the entire Naboo fighting force began to move toward an exit in the hangar that took them directly past Anakin's hiding place.

"Hey, where are you going?" the boy asked, popping his head out of the cockpit as they passed.

"Annie, you stay there!" Qui-Gon ordered, motioning him back down. His long hair was wild and his face intense. "Stay right where you are!"

The boy ignored him, standing up instead. "No, I want to go with you and Padmé!"

"Stay in that cockpit!" Qui-Gon snapped in a tone of voice that brooked no argument.

Anakin froze, undecided, as the contingent hurried past him toward the exit door, weapons at the ready. He did not want to be left behind. He had no intention of letting Qui-Gon and Padmé go on without him, especially since he could do nothing to help them if he was stuck here in this empty hangar.

He was still wrestling with the matter when the entire group slowed in front of the exit door. A dark-cloaked figure stepped through the opening to confront them. Anakin's breath caught in his throat. It was the Sith Lord who had attacked them on the Tatooine desert, a dangerous adversary, Qui-Gon had advised the boy later, an enemy of the Jedi Knights. He stepped out of the shadows like a large sand panther, his red and black tattooed face a terrifying mask, his yellow eyes bright with anticipation and rage.

Blocking the way out, he stood waiting for the Jedi and their charges, a long-handled lightsaber held before him. Captain Panaka and his fighters backed away at once. Then, on command from Qui-Gon, Padmé and her handmaidens gave ground as well, though less quickly and with more obvious reluctance.

Qui-Gon Jinn and Obi-Wan Kenobi stood alone in the Sith Lord's path. Together, they removed their capes and ignited their lightsabers. Their horned antagonist stripped away his cloak as well, then lifted the long-handled lightsaber he bore as if offering it for inspection. Gleaming blade fire jutted from both ends of the handle, revealing a deadly, dual-blade weapon. A smile crossed the bearer's feral face as he swung the weapon before him in an idle, casual gesture, beckoning the Jedi ahead.

Spreading out to either side, Qui-Gon and Obi-Wan slowly advanced to meet him.

On the plains south of Theed, the battle between the Trade Federation and the Gungan armies was fully joined. Gungans and battle droids were locked in close combat, a tangle of amphibious bodies and metal shells. The shield generators still held the Trade Federation tanks at bay. Only the droids had broken through, but there were many more of them than there were of the Gungans, and General Ceel had committed all his reserves to the struggle.

Jar Jar Binks fought at the center of the maelstrom, wielding a broken energy spear as a club, wheeling and stumbling this way and that, careening wildly. Caught up in the wiring of a battle droid he had decapitated, he could not manage to free himself from the debris, and so was dragging the headless torso after him. The droid, still operating on autopilot despite the loss of its head, was firing its blaster continuously as Jar Jar whipped it this way and that, finding droid targets more often than Gungans, cutting a swath through their faltering ranks.

"Tis bombad! Tis bombad!" The Gungan shouted out the refrain over and over as he swung his shattered spear and fought to get free of his headless companion.

When at last he broke away and was able to smash the remains of the droid into the ground, he was left standing in a wide open space that everyone on both sides was trying desperately to avoid. For a terrifying moment, Jar Jar literally did not know which way to turn.

Then a cry went up from the Gungans closest. "Jar Jar Binks! Jar Jar Binks!"

"Who, me?" the befuddled Gungan gasped.

Inspired troops rallied around him and pressed ahead once more, sweeping him along in a wild and unexpected counterattack.

But the Trade Federation, unlike the Gungans, had other weapons left to call upon. OOM-9, responding to orders from the orbiting battleship command station, unleashed a battalion of destroyer droids from the transports. Down long rampways they wheeled, across the grasslands, over the bodies of shattered battle droids, and through the Gungan energy shield. Transforming into battle mode, they began to advance through the carnage, twin blasters firing in steady cadence. Gungans and kaadu went down in broken heaps, but other Gungans moved quickly to fill the gaps in their lines, slowing the destroyer droids, fighting to hold their ground.

Back and forth the battle raged, the outcome undecided.

Anakin Skywalker had made a promise to himself that he would protect Qui-Gon Jinn and Padmé Naberrie from harm, that he would see to it somehow that nothing bad happened to them. He knew when he made the promise how hard it was going to be to keep. Somewhere in the back of his mind where he would admit such things privately, he knew how foolish it was even to make such a commitment. But he was young and brave at heart, and he had lived his life pretty much on his own terms because to live it any other way would have broken him long ago. It hadn't been easy doing so, especially as a slave. He had survived mostly because he had been able to find small victories in difficult situations and because he had always believed that one day he would find a way to overcome the circumstances of his birth.

His belief in himself had been rewarded. His life had been changed forever by his victory just days earlier in the Boonta Eve Podrace on Tatooine.

It was not so strange then that he should decide he could

somehow affect the lives of a Jedi Knight and a Naboo Queen as well, even if he did not know precisely how. He was not afraid to accept such responsibility. He was not daunted by the challenge his decision presented.

But now his resolve was put to the test.

Qui-Gon and Obi-Wan closed with the Sith Lord in a clash of lightsabers that produced the shriek of diamond-edged saw blades cutting through metal. Wheeling across the center of the hangar, the combatants lunged and parried, attack and counter-attack carried out in a fierce, no-holds-barred, no-quarter-given struggle. The Sith Lord was supple and quick, and he worked his way between the Jedi with confidence and ease, whipping his two-ended lightsaber back and forth between them, more than holding his own against their efforts to bring him down. He was skilled, Anakin saw—more skilled, perhaps, than the men he faced. And he was confident in a way that was disturbing. He would not be overcome easily.

But Padmé and the Naboo faced a more dangerous situation still. At the far end of the hangar, from off the plaza, a cluster of three destroyer droids wheeled through the doorway and began to unfold, assuming battle stance. R2-D2 saw them first and beeped a warning to the boy. Anakin tore his gaze away from the Jedi and the Sith Lord. The destroyer droids had transformed and were already moving forward, laser guns firing into the Naboo. Several soldiers went down, and Sabé was stung by a glancing blow that knocked her backward into the arms of Panaka. Padmé and her companions resisted determinedly, but already they were falling back to find cover.

"We've got to help, Artoo," the boy declared, standing up in the cockpit with the intention of doing something, anything, casting about futilely for a weapon.

But R2-D2 was way ahead of him. The little droid had plugged himself into the starfighter's computer system, lights blinking across his control panel as he triggered the big engines. Everything roared to life at once, startling Anakin, who fell back in the pilot's seat in surprise.

Slowly, the ship began to levitate, wheeling out of its mooring space.

"Great work, Artoo!" Anakin shouted excitedly, reaching at once for the steering bars. "Now, let's see . . ."

He wheeled the fighter about so that it was facing toward the combatants. His eyes scanned the control panel desperately, searching for the weapons systems. He knew something of fighters from salvaging wrecks, but nothing of Naboo fighters in particular or of weapons systems in general. Most of what he knew was about guidance systems and engines, and most of that about Pods, speeders, and aging transports.

"Which one, which one?" he muttered, his fingers passing over buttons and levers and switches, undecided.

He lifted his eyes momentarily. One of the Naboo soldiers went down in a crumpled heap, his helmet and blaster flying away in a clatter of metal. Laser charges burned the metal girders and walls about the defenders as the destroyer droids continued their relentless attack on Padmé's dwindling force.

In desperation, Anakin threw a bank of switches set into a red panel. The fighter began to shake violently, a reaction to a shift in the stabilizers.

"Uh-oh, wrong ones," the boy breathed, throwing the switches back into place. His gaze roamed to a bank of four dark buttons recessed deep into finger holes and circled in green. "Maybe these . . ."

He pressed down on the buttons. Instantly, the nose lasers fired, their charges ripping into the battle droids. Three went down, charred and smoking scrap.

"Yeah! Droid blasters!" he shouted gleefully, and behind him, R2-D2 beeped his approval.

The remaining destroyer droids wheeled toward him, spreading out across the hangar floor to present a more difficult target. Behind them, Padmé, her handmaidens, Panaka, and the remainder of the Naboo soldiers were racing for the door that led back toward the palace. Anakin watched over the rim of the cockpit as they disappeared safely out the door. "Good luck," he whispered.

The destroyer droids were advancing on him now, their blasters firing, charges exploding all around him, shaking the fighter's slim frame. Anakin had a momentary glimpse of the Sith Lord driving the Jedi across the hangar and through an opening into a room beyond, pressing them backward relentlessly, pursuing them with a fury that was terrifying.

Then they disappeared from view as well, and the boy was alone with his attackers.

A laser blast struck the nose of his craft and knocked the ship sideways. The boy tightened his grip on the steering. He fired his own lasers in retaliation, but the destroyer droids had moved too far to either side to be affected, and his charges missed everything but the hangar walls.

He dropped below the rim of the cockpit once more, eyes searching the control panel anew. "Shields up," he hissed, forcing himself to concentrate as laser blasts streaked all around. "Always on the right side! Shields are always on the right!"

He flipped several likely switches, and the afterburner ignited with a rumble. He pushed another, then one more. The steering handle fought itself free of his grip, and the fighter wheeled about and streaked out through the hangar doors, lifting swiftly away.

The cockpit hood slid smoothly into place, locking about the boy. "Artoo, what's happening?" he screamed. R2-D2's nervous beeps and whistles sounded through the intercom speakers. "Yes, I know I pushed something!" the boy answered. "No, I'm not doing anything!" He caught his breath as the beeps continued, and read R2's words on his cockpit display. "It's on automatic pilot? Well, try to override it!"

The sleek yellow fighter had left the Naboo atmosphere and was entering deep space, leaving the planet behind, a green and blue jewel receding into the black.

Ahead, a series of small, silver dots appeared, growing steadily larger. Other ships.

"Artoo, where are we going?" Anakin gasped, still trying to decipher the control panel.

The comm system squawked, and suddenly he was hearing

the voices of Ric Olié and the Naboo pilots who had taken off ahead of him.

"This is Bravo Leader." Ric's leathery voice broke through the static. "Bravo Two, intercept enemy fighters. Bravo Three, make your run on the transmitter station."

"Copy, Bravo Leader," the response came back.

Anakin could see them now, the silver dots taking on recognizable shape, transforming into Naboo starfighters, spread out against the blackness, approaching the larger, blockier form of the Federation battleship.

"Enemy fighters straight ahead," Ric Olié warned suddenly on the comm.

At the same moment, R2-D2 beeped hurriedly at Anakin. The boy felt his stomach lurch as he read the display. "What do you mean, the autopilot is searching for the other ships? What other ships?" His eyes shifted to the Naboo fighters ahead. "Not those?"

R2-D2 whistled a quick confirmation. Anakin collapsed in his seat. "The autopilot is taking us up there, with them? Into battle?" His mind raced. "Well, get us off autopilot, Artoo!"

The astromech droid beeped and whistled some more. "There is no manual override!" Anakin shouted in despair. "Or at least not any I can find! You'll have to rewire or something! Artoo, hurry!"

He stared helplessly through the cockpit glass as his fighter streaked directly toward the heart of the Trade Federation swarm, wondering what in the world he was going to do to save himself now.

Qui-Gon Jinn was one of the most able swordsmen in the
Jedi order. The Jedi Master he had trained under had considered
him one of the best the Master had taught in his more than four
hundred years in the order. Qui-Gon had fought in conflicts all
across the galaxy in the span of his life and against odds so great
that many others would not have stood a chance. He had survived battles that had tested his skill and resolve in every conceivable way.

But on this day, he had met his match. The Sith Lord he
battled with Obi-Wan was more than his equal in weapons training, and he had the advantage of being younger and stronger.
Qui-Gon was nearing sixty; his youth was behind him and his
strength was beginning to diminish. His edge now, to the extent
that he had one, came from his long experience and intuitive
grasp of how an adversary might employ a lightsaber against him.

Obi-Wan brought youth and stamina to the combat, but he
had fought in only a few contests and was not battle hardened.
Together, they were able to hold their own against the Sith Lord,
but their efforts at attack, at assuming the offensive against this
dangerous adversary, were woefully inadequate.

Darth Maul was a warrior in his prime, never to be any better, his powers at their apex. In addition, he was driven by his

messianic hatred for and disdain of the Jedi Knights, the enemies of the Sith for millennia. He had worked and trained all his life for this moment, for a chance to meet a Jedi Knight in combat. It was an added bonus that he was able to engage two. He had no fear for himself, no doubt that he would win. He was focused in a way that Qui-Gon recognized at once—a Jedi's focus, mindful of the present, locked in on what was needed in the here and now. Qui-Gon saw it in his mad eyes and in the set of his red and black tattooed features. The Sith Lord was a living example of what the Jedi Master was always telling Obi-Wan about how best to hear the will of the Force.

The three combatants fought their way across the hangar floor, lightsabers flashing, bringing to bear every skill they had acquired over the years. The Jedi Knights tried continually to press the attack, and indeed, the Sith Lord was moving away from the Naboo and the starfighters and back toward the hangar's far wall. But Qui-Gon recognized that while it might seem as if the Jedi were driving him before them, it was the Sith Lord who was controlling the struggle. Wheeling and spinning, leaping and somersaulting with astonishing ease, their enemy was taking them with him, drawing them on to a place of his own choosing. His agility and dexterity allowed him to keep them both at bay, constantly attacking while at the same time effectively blunting their counterattacks, relentlessly searching for an opening in their defense.

Qui-Gon pressed hard in the beginning, sensing how dangerous this man was, wanting to put an end to the combat quickly. Long hair flying out behind him, he attacked with ferocity and determination. Obi-Wan came with him, following his lead. They had fought together before, and they knew each other's moves. Qui-Gon had trained Obi-Wan, and while the younger Jedi was not yet his equal, he believed that one day Obi-Wan would be better than he had ever been.

So they challenged the Sith Lord quickly, and just as quickly discovered that their best efforts were not good enough to achieve an early resolution. They settled into a pattern then, working as a team against their enemy, waiting for an opening. But the Sith Lord was too smart to give them one, and so the battle had gone on.

They fought their way out of the main hangar through an entry that led into a power station. Catwalks and overhangs crisscrossed a pit in which a tandem of generators that served the starship complex was housed. The room was cavernous and filled with the noise of heavy machinery. Ambient light filtered away in clouds of steam and layers of shadows. The Jedi and the Sith Lord battled onto one of the catwalks suspended above the generators, and the metal frame rang with the thudding of their boots and the clash of their lightsabers.

Alone in the power station, hidden from the rest of Theed and its occupants, they intensified their struggle.

The Sith Lord leapt from the bridge on which they fought to the one above, strange face shining with the heat of the battle and his own peculiar joy. The Jedi followed, one coming up in front of him, one behind, so that they had him pinned between them. Down the length of the catwalk they fought, lightsabers flashing, sparks flying from the metal railing of the walk as they smashed against it.

Then Darth Maul caught Obi-Wan off balance and with a powerful kick knocked the Jedi completely over the railing. Taking advantage of the Sith Lord's assault on Obi-Wan, Qui-Gon forced Darth Maul over the railing as well. Down the Sith Lord tumbled, landing hard on a catwalk several levels below Obi-Wan. The force of the fall or perhaps the unexpectedness of it left him visibly stunned, and Qui-Gon leapt down after him, sensing a chance to put an end to things. But the Sith Lord struggled back to his feet quickly and raced away, taking the battle in a new direction.

By the time Obi-Wan had recovered, Qui-Gon was in pursuit of Darth Maul, following him down the catwalk toward a small door at the far end of the power station. The Jedi Master went swiftly, legs and arms pumping, lightsaber flashing. He was worn and battered by now, close to exhaustion, but the Sith Lord was

·on the defensive at last, and he did not want to give him a chance to regroup.

"Qui-Gon!" Obi-Wan called after him, trying to catch up, but the Jedi Master did not slow.

One after the other, the three antagonists passed through the small door into a corridor beyond. They were moving quickly in their frenzied chase and were into the corridor before they realized what it was. Lasers ricocheted off buffer struts, pulsing in long bursts of crisscrossing brilliance that segmented the corridor at five points. The lasers had just begun to kick in when the Sith Lord and the Jedi Knights rushed through the entry. Darth Maul, in the lead, got farthest down the corridor and found himself trapped between walls four and five. Qui-Gon, in close pursuit, was caught only one wall away. Obi-Wan, who was farthest away in the chase, did not get past even the first wall.

Shocked into immobility by the buzz and flash of the lasers, the antagonists froze where they were, casting about for an escape, finding none. Qui-Gon took a quick measure of their location. They were in the service corridor for the melting pit, the disposal unit of the power station's residue. The service corridor was armed with lasers against unauthorized intrusion. There would be a shutoff switch somewhere at both ends of the passage, but it was too late to look for it now.

The Jedi Knights stared down the laser-riddled corridor at the Sith Lord, who gave them a wicked grin. Don't worry, they could read in his dark countenance, you won't have long to wait for me.

Qui-Gon exchanged a meaningful glance with Obi-Wan, then dropped into a guarded crouch to meditate and wait.

Padmé Naberrie, Queen of the Naboo, along with her handmaidens and Captain Panaka and his soldiers, followed the passageways that led out of the main hangar through the city and back to the palace. It was a running battle fought building by building, corridor by corridor, against the battle droids who had been left behind to garrison Theed. They encountered the droids both singly and in entire squads, and there was nothing for it each time but to fight their way clear without becoming entangled in a full-fledged engagement.

As a consequence, they avoided a direct route in favor of one less likely to necessitate contact with the droids. At first they had no choice but to make straight for the palace, fleeing the battle in the main hangar, hoping that speed and surprise would carry them through. When that failed, Panaka began to take a more cautious approach. They used underground tunnels, hidden passageways, and connecting skywalks that avoided the patrols scouring the streets and plazas. When they were discovered, they fought their way clear as quickly as possible and went to ground, all the while continuing steadily on.

In the end, they reached the palace much more quickly than Padmé had dared to hope, entering from a skywalk bridging to a watchtower, then making their way along the palace halls toward the throne room.

They were in the midst of this endeavor when an entire patrol of battle droids rounded a corner of the passage ahead of them and opened fire. Padmé and her followers pressed back into the alcoves and doorways of the hall, firing their own weapons in response, searching for a way out. More battle droids were appearing, and alarms were sounding throughout the palace.

"Captain!" Padmé shouted at Panaka above the din of weapons fire. "We don't have time for this!"

Panaka's sweat-streaked face glanced about hurriedly. "Let's try outside!" he shouted back.

Turning his blaster on a tall window, he blew out the frame and transparisteel. While her handmaidens and the bulk of the Naboo soldiers provided covering fire, the Queen and Panaka, together with half a dozen guards, broke from cover and climbed swiftly out the shattered window.

But now Padmé and her defenders found themselves trapped on a broad ledge six stories above a thundering waterfall and catchment that fed into a series of connecting ponds dotting the palace grounds. Pressed against the stone wall, the Queen cast about furiously for an escape route. Panaka shouted at his men to use their ascension guns, motioning toward a ledge four stories farther up on the building. The Naboo pulled the grapple-line units from their belts, fitted them to the barrels of their blasters, pointed them skyward, and fired. Slender cables uncoiled like striking snakes, the steel-clawed ends embedding themselves in the stone.

Swiftly Padmé and the other Naboo activated the ascension mechanism and were towed up the wall.

From behind, in the hallway where her handmaidens and the rest of the Naboo soldiers still held the battle droids at bay, the firing grew more intense. Padmé ignored the sounds, forcing herself to continue ahead.

When they were on the ledge above, they cast away the cables, and Panaka used his blaster on a window to open a way back into the building. Transparisteel and permacrete shards lay everywhere as they climbed through once more, finding themselves in yet another hallway. They were close to the throne room now; it lay only another story up and several corridors back. Padmé felt a fierce exultation. She would have the Neimoidian viceroy as her prisoner yet!

But the thought was no sooner completed than a pair of destroyer droids wheeled around one end of the hallway, swiftly transforming into battle mode. Mere seconds later, a second pair appeared at the other end, weapons held at the ready.

In a hollow, mechanical monotone, the foremost of the droids ordered them to throw down their weapons.

Padmé hesitated. There was no possibility for an escape unless they went back out the window, and if they did that, they would be trapped on the ledge and rendered helpless. They could try to fight their way free, but while they stood a reasonable chance against battle droids, they were seriously overmatched by their more powerful cousins.

In the wake of this chilling assessment, an inspired thought occurred to her, a solution that might give them the victory they sought in spite of their situation. She straightened, held out her arms in surrender, and tossed aside her blaster.

"Throw down your weapons," she ordered Captain Panaka and his soldiers. "They win this round."

Panaka blanched. "But, Your Majesty, we can't—"

"Captain," Padmé interrupted, her eyes locking with his. "I said to throw down your weapons."

Panaka gave her a look that suggested he clearly thought she had lost her mind. Then he dropped his blaster to the floor and motioned for his men to do the same.

The destroyer droids skittered forward to take them prisoner. But before they reached the Naboo, Padmé was able to complete a quick transmission on her comlink.

"Have faith, Captain," she urged a bewildered Panaka, her voice cool and collected as she slipped the comlink out of sight again.

Things were not going well for the Gungan army. Like the Naboo, the Gungans were no match for the destroyer droids. Slowly, but surely, they were being pushed back, unable to stand against the relentless Trade Federation attack. Here and there along their beleaguered lines, cracks were beginning to appear in their defense.

Jar Jar Binks was at the heart of one of those points.

For a time, his had been one of the strongest positions, his soldiers rallied by what they mistakenly believed to be his unrivaled bravery, turning a rout into a counterattack. But the counterattack had extended itself too far, and with the appearance of the destroyer droids, it collapsed completely. Now Jar Jar and his comrades were in flight, falling back to where the rest of the army crouched in the shadow of the failing generator shield, desperately trying to find a way to regroup.

Jar Jar, his kaadu long since lost, was running for his life. Desperate to increase the distance between himself and the pursuing destroyer droids, he caught up with a fleeing wagon filled with dozens of the energy balls used by the Gungan catapults. Grabbing hold of the wagon gate, he tried to haul himself into the bed, the wagon jouncing and creaking over the uneven ground. But in his effort to save himself, he unwittingly released the latch on the gate, causing it to flop open. Energy balls released out the back in a wild tumble, bouncing and rolling backward in a swarm. Jar Jar danced out of the way, scrambling to avoid being struck. He was successful in this, but the less nimble destroyer droids on his heels were not. Energy balls smashed into them, exploding on contact, and droid after droid went up in a rain of fire and shattered metal.

"Tis good!" Jar Jar howled in glee, watching the Federation droids wheeling this way and that in an effort to escape the carpet of energy balls rolling into them.

Elsewhere, however, the battle was taking a turn for the worse. Destroyer droids had broken through the Gungan lines fronting the shield generators, and were firing their weapons into the machines over and over. The fambaa on which the generators rode shuddered and dropped to their knees, the generators smoking and sparking. Abruptly, the force field began to waver and fade. OOM-9, watching it all through electrobinoculars, was quick to report back to the Neimoidian command. Federation tanks were ordered forward at once, their guns firing anew.

When General Ceel saw the shield generators lose power, he realized the battle was lost. The Gungans had done all they could for the Queen of the Naboo. Turning to his staff, he signaled for a retreat. The battle horns sounded the call, wailing out across the grasslands, and the entire Gungan army began to fall back.

Jar Jar had gained control of a new mount and was riding madly for the safety of the swamp. Fleeing in the midst of pursuing droids and tanks, he had his kaadu blown out from under him and was thrown sideways onto the back of a nearby tank's gun turret. Hanging on for dear life, he rode the enemy vehicle across the plains as the battle raged on all about him. The droids inside the tank quickly became aware of his presence, and the driver tried to throw him off by swiveling the turret gun from side to side. But Jar Jar had a death grip on the barrel, hugging it tightly to him, and refused to be dislodged.

"Hep me! Hep me!" he screamed out.

Captain Tarpals astride a kaadu worked his way alongside the tank, yelling at Jar Jar to jump. Laser fire ricocheted off the tank, barely missing Jar Jar as he struggled to overcome his fear and break free of his precarious perch. Hatches were beginning to open and droid heads to appear. His eyes widened as he saw weapons being lifted and brought to bear.

He jumped then, flinging himself clear of the tank, landing awkwardly behind the Gungan who had stayed to save him. The kaadu, burdened by two riders, lurched wildly, then righted itself and swerved quickly away.

Explosions mushroomed all around them, sending gouts of dirt skyward, and Jar Jar Binks, arms wrapped around the other rider, eyes closed in terror against the chaos taking place all around him, was pretty sure that this was the end.

Anakin Skywalker, meanwhile, was caught up in the midst of a dogfight between Naboo and Federation starfighters. Still struggling to get off autopilot, he had avoided engagement with the enemy mostly because his craft was flying in an erratic, evasive manner that took it out of combat range every time it got too close for comfort. Fighters were exploding all around him, some so close he could see the pieces as they flew past his canopy.

"Whoo, boy, this is tense!" he breathed as he tried switch after switch on the control panel, the fighter dipping and yawing in response to his unwelcome interference with its operation.

But he was learning the control panel, too, his trial-and-error exploration yielding knowledge of what various switches, buttons, and levers did. The downside to all this was that the firing triggers to the laser guns had locked, and try as he might, he could not find a way to break them free.

He glanced up from his search at a loud beep from R2-D2 to find a pair of Federation fighters approaching him head-on.

"Artoo, Artoo, get us off—!"

The astromech droid overrode the rest of what he was going to say with a series of frantic whistles.

"I've got control?" Anakin exclaimed in shock.

He seized the steering, flipped on the power feeds, and jammed the thruster bars left. To his surprise and everlasting gratitude, the fighter banked sharply in response, and they shot past the fighters and rode into a new swarm of combatants.

"Yes! I've got control!" Anakin was ecstatic. "You did it, Artoo!"

The astromech droid beeped at him through the intercom, a short, abrupt exchange.

Anakin's eyebrows shot up as he read the display. "Go back to Naboo? Forget it! Qui-Gon told me to stay in this cockpit, and that's what I'm gonna do! Now, hang on!"

His enthusiasm overrode his good sense, and he whipped his fighter toward the center of the battle. All of his flying instincts kicked in, and he was back in the Podraces on Tatooine, a part of his ship, locked in on the intoxicating challenge of winning. Forgotten was his promise to look after Qui-Gon and Padmé; they were too far away for him to think about them now. All that mattered was that he had found his way into space, taken command of a starfighter, and been given a chance to live his dream.

An enemy fighter drifted into his sights ahead. "Sit tight, Artoo," he warned. "I'm gonna blast this guy."

He brought his ship into firing position behind the Trade Federation craft, remembering belatedly that the triggers to his laser guns were locked. Frantically, he searched for the release.

"Which one, Artoo?" he shouted into his helmet. "How do I fire this thing?"

R2-D2 beeped wildly.

"Which one? This one?"

He punched the button the astromech droid had indicated, but instead of releasing the firing mechanism, it accelerated the fighter right past the enemy ship.

"Whoa!" Anakin gasped in dismay.

Now the Trade Federation fighter was on his tail, maneuver-

'ing into firing position against him. Anakin yanked hard on the steering, shooting past the massive Federation battleship, screaming out into the void in a series of evasive actions.

"That wasn't the release!" the boy screamed into his intercom. "That was the overdrive!"

R2-D2 whistled a sheepish reply. The enemy fighter was behind them again and closing. Anakin banked his ship hard to the right and brought it back toward the blockade and the swarming fighters. Wrenching the stabilizers in opposite directions, he began to spin his fighter like a top. R2-D2 shrieked in despair.

"I know we're in trouble!" Anakin shrieked back. "Just hang on! The way out of this mess is the way we got into it!"

He streaked toward the control station, taking the enemy fighter with him. Laser blasts ripped past him, barely missing. He waited a second longer, until he was so close to the battleship that the emblem of the Trade Federation painted on the bridge work loomed like a wall, then engaged the reverse thrusters and banked right again.

His fighter nearly stalled, dropping away like a stone for a heart-wrenching moment before stabilizing. The enemy fighter, on the other hand, had no time to respond to the maneuver and rocketed past him into the side of the battleship, exploding in a shower of fire and metal parts.

Reengaging the forward thrusters, Anakin wheeled the ship about, searching for new enemies. Through his canopy, he could see a handful of Naboo starfighters engaged in attacking the Trade Federation flagship.

Ric Olié's voice came over the intercom. "Bravo Three! Go for the central bridge!"

"Copy, Bravo Leader," came the response.

A squad of four fighters plummeted toward the battleship, lasers firing, but the big ship's deflector shields turned the attack aside effortlessly. Two of the fighters were hit by cannon fire and exploded into ash. The remaining two broke off the attack.

"Their shields are too strong!" one of the surviving pilots shouted angrily. "We'll never get through!"

Anakin, in the meantime, was under attack once more. Another Federation fighter had found him and was giving chase. The boy jammed the thruster bars forward and sped down the hull of the flagship, twisting and turning through its channels and around its tangle of protrusions, laser fire ricocheting past in a constant stream.

"I know this isn't Podracing!" Anakin snapped at R2-D2, as the astromech droid beeped reprovingly at him.

But in his heart, it felt as if it were. A fierce glee rushed through him as he whipped the Naboo fighter along the length of the battleship. The speed and the quickness of the battle fed into him in a rush of adrenaline. He would not have been anywhere else for the world!

But this time his luck ran out. As he neared the ship's tail, a laser blast struck his fighter a solid blow, knocking it into a stomach-lurching spin. R2-D2 screamed anew, and Anakin fought desperately to regain control.

"Great gobs of bantha poodoo!" the boy hissed, fighting to stabilize his stricken craft.

He was hurtling directly toward the hull, and he pulled back on the thruster bars, cutting power and drifting into a long slide. He regained control too late to turn back, and pointed the ship toward a giant opening at the battleship's center. Cannon fire whipped all about him as the droids controlling the flagship's guns tried to bring him down, but he was past them in a microsecond, rocketing into the battleship's cavernous main hangar. Reverse thrusters on full power, dodging transports, tanks, fighters, and stacks of supplies, he struggled to keep his fighter airborne as he looked for a place to land.

R2-D2 was beeping wildly. "I'm trying to stop!" Anakin shouted in reply. "Whoa! Whoa! I'm trying!"

The Naboo fighter struck the decking and bounced, reverse thrusters powering up in an effort to brake the craft. A bulkhead loomed ahead, blocking the way. Anakin brought the fighter down on the decking with a bone-jarring thud and held it there, skidding down the rampway in a screech of metal. The fighter slowed and did a half turn and came to an unsteady halt. The power drive stalled and then failed completely.

R2-D2 whistled in relief.

"All right, all right!" Anakin gasped, nodding to himself. "We're down. Let's get the engines started again and get out of here!"

He ducked down to adjust the feeders to the fuel lines, checking the control panel indicators worriedly. "Lights are all red, Artoo. Everything's overheated."

He was working on the coolants when R2-D2 beeped suddenly in warning. The boy popped his head over the edge of the cockpit and looked out into the hangar. "Oh, oh," he muttered softly.

Dozens of battle droids were approaching across the hangar floor, weapons raised menacingly. Their only escape route was blocked.

Obi-Wan Kenobi prowled the front end of the service corridor to the melting pit like a caged animal. He was furious at
himself for getting trapped so far from Qui-Gon and furious with
Qui-Gon for letting this happen by rushing ahead instead of
waiting for him. But he was worried, too. He could admit it to
himself, privately, if only just. They should have won this battle
long ago. Against any other opponent, they would have. But the
Sith Lord was battle trained and seasoned well beyond anyone
they had ever encountered before. He had matched them blow
for blow, and they weren't any closer to winning this fight now
than they had been in the beginning.

Obi-Wan stared down the length of the corridor, measuring
the distance he would have to travel to reach Qui-Gon and his
antagonist when the lasers paused. He had caught a glimpse of
them deactivating while rushing to catch up with Qui-Gon, then
of reactivating again in a matter of seconds. He would have to be
quick. Very quick. He did not want the Master facing this tattooed madman alone.

Down the way, pinned between two walls of laser beams,
Qui-Gon Jinn knelt in meditation, facing toward the Sith Lord
and the melting pit, his head lowered over his lightsaber. He was
gathering himself for a final assault, bringing himself in tune with

the Force. Obi-Wan did not like the weariness he saw in the slump of the older man's shoulders, in the bow of his back. He was the best swordsman Obi-Wan had ever seen, but he was growing old.

Beyond, the Sith Lord worked at binding up his wounds, a series of burns and slashes marked by charred tears in his dark clothing. He was backed to the edge of the chamber beyond, keeping a close watch on Qui-Gon, his red and black face intense, his yellow eyes glinting in the half light. His lightsaber rested on the floor before him. He saw Obi-Wan staring and smiled in open derision.

At that instant, the laser beams warding the service corridor went off.

Obi-Wan sprinted ahead, launching himself down the narrow passageway, lightsaber raised. Qui-Gon was on his feet as well, his own weapon flashing. He catapulted through the opening that led into the melting pit and closed with the Sith Lord, forcing him back, out of the passageway completely. Obi-Wan put on a new burst of speed, howling out at the antagonists ahead, as if by the sound of his voice he could bring them back to him.

Then he heard the buzz of the capacitors kicking in once more, cycling to reactivate the lasers. He threw himself ahead, still too far from the corridor's end. He cleared all the gates but the last, and the lasers crisscrossed before him in a deadly wall, bringing him to an abrupt stop just short of where he needed to be.

Lightsaber clutched in both hands, he stood watching helplessly as Qui-Gon Jinn and Darth Maul battled on the narrow ledge that encircled the melting pit. A stream of electrons was all that separated him from the combatants, but it might as well have been a wall of permacrete three meters thick. Desperately he cast about for a triggering device that might shut the system down, but he had no better luck here than he'd had at the other end. He could only watch and wait and pray that Qui-Gon could hold on.

It appeared that the Jedi Master would. He had found a fresh reserve of strength during his meditation, and now he was attacking with a ferocity that seemed to have the Sith Lord stymied. With quick, hard strokes of his lightsaber, he bored into his adversary, deliberately engaging in close-quarters combat, refusing to let the other bring his double-bladed weapon to bear. He drove Darth Maul backward about the rim of the overhang, keeping the Sith Lord constantly on the defensive, pressing in on him steadily. Qui-Gon Jinn might no longer be young, but he was still powerful. Darth Maul's ragged face took on a frenzied look, and the glitter of his strange eyes brightened with uncertainty.

Good, Master, Obi-Wan thought, urging him on voicelessly, anticipating Qui-Gon's sword strokes as if they were his own.

Then Darth Maul back-flipped across the melting pit, giving himself some space in which to recover, gaining just enough time to assume a new battle stance. Qui-Gon was on him in an instant, covering the distance separating them in a rush, hammering into the Sith Lord anew. But he was beginning to weary now from carrying the battle alone. His strokes were not so vigorous as before, his face bathed with sweat and taut with fatigue.

Slowly, Darth Maul began to edge his way back into the fight, becoming the aggressor once more.

Hurry! Obi-Wan hissed soundlessly, willing the lasers to pause and the gates to come down.

Stroke for stroke, Qui-Gon and Darth Maul battled about the rim of the melting pit, locked in a combat that seemed endless and forever and could be won by neither.

Then the Sith Lord parried a downstroke, whirled swiftly to the right, and with his back to the Jedi Master, made a blind, reverse lunge. Too late, Qui-Gon recognized the danger. The blade of the Sith Lord's lightsaber caught him directly in the midsection, its brilliant length burning through clothing and flesh and bone.

Obi-Wan thought he heard the Jedi Master scream, then

realized it was himself, calling his friend's name in despair. Qui-Gon made no sound as the blade entered him, stiffening with the impact, then taking a small step back as it was withdrawn. He stood motionless for an instant, fighting against the shock of the killing blow. Then his eyes clouded, his arms lowered, and a great weariness settled over his proud features. He dropped to his knees, and his lightsaber clattered to the stone floor.

He was slumped forward and motionless when the lasers abruptly went off again, and Obi-Wan Kenobi, seething with rage, rushed to his rescue.

Nute Gunray stood with Rune Haako and four members of the Trade Federation Occupation Council as Captain Panaka, one of the Queen's handmaidens, and the six Naboo soldiers who had fought to protect them were marched into the Theed palace throne room by a squad of ten battle droids. The viceroy recognized Panaka at once, but he was unclear as to the identity of the handmaiden who accompanied him. He was looking for the Queen, and while this handmaiden bore a certain resemblance to her . . .

He caught himself in surprise. It *was* the Queen, without her makeup and ornate robes, stripped of her symbols of office. She looked even younger than she had in ceremonial garb, but her eyes and that cool gaze were unmistakable.

He glanced at Rune Haako and saw the same confusion mirrored in his associate's face.

"Your Highness," he greeted as she was led up to him.

"Viceroy," she replied, confirming his conclusion as to her identity.

That settled, he swiftly assumed the pose of a captor confronting his captive. "Your little insurrection is at an end, Your Highness. The rabble army you sent against us south of the city has been crushed. The Jedi are being dealt with elsewhere. And you are my captive."

"Am I?" she asked quietly.

The way she spoke the words was unnerving. There was

something challenging in the way she said them, as if she were daring him to disagree. Even Panaka turned to look at her.

"Yes, you are." He pressed ahead, wondering suddenly if he had missed something. His face lifted. "It is time for you to put an end to the pointless debate you instigated in the Republic Senate. Sign the treaty now."

There was a commotion outside the doorway leading into the throne room, the sound of blasters and the shattering of metal, and all at once Queen Amidala was standing in the anteway beyond, a clutch of battle droids collapsed on the floor and a handful of Naboo soldiers warding their Queen against the appearance of more.

"I will not be signing any treaty, Viceroy!" she called out to him, already beginning to move away. "You've lost!"

For a moment Nute Gunray was so stunned he could not make himself move. A second Queen? But this was the real one, dressed in her robes of office, wearing her white face paint, speaking to him in that imperious voice he had come to recognize so well.

He wheeled toward the battle droids holding Panaka and the false Queen at bay. "You six! After her!" He gestured in the direction of the disappearing Amidala. "Bring her to me! The real one, this time—not some decoy!"

The droids he had indicated rushed from the room in pursuit of the Queen and her guards, leaving the Neimoidians and the four remaining droids with their Naboo captives.

Gunray wheeled on the handmaiden. "Your Queen will not get away with this!" he snapped, enraged at having been deceived.

The handmaiden seemed to lose all her bravado, turning away from him with her head lowered in defeat, moving slowly toward the Queen's throne and slumping dejectedly into it. Nute Gunray dismissed her almost at once, turning his attention to the other Naboo, anxious to have them taken away to the camps.

But in the next instant the handmaiden was back on her feet, any sign of dejection or weariness banished, a blaster in either hand, pulled from a hidden compartment in the arm of the throne. Tossing one of the blasters to Captain Panaka, she began firing the second into the depleted squad of battle droids. The droids were caught completely by surprise, their attention fixed on the Naboo guards, and the handmaiden and Panaka dispatched them in a flurry of shots that left the throne room ringing with the sound of weapons fire.

Shouting instructions to the Naboo, the handmaiden—if that's who she really was, because by now Nute Gunray was beginning to think otherwise—moved to the throne room doors, triggering the locks. The doors swung shut, the bolts engaged, and the girl smashed the locking mechanism with the butt of her weapon.

She turned then to the Neimoidians, who were huddled together in confusion at the center of the room, eyes darting this way and that in a futile search for help. All the battle droids lay shattered on the floor, and the Naboo had seized their blasters.

The handmaiden walked up to Gunray. "Let's start again, Viceroy," she said coolly.

"Your Highness," he replied, tight-lipped, realizing the truth too late.

She nodded. "This is the end of your occupation."

He stood his ground. "Don't be absurd. There are too few of you. It won't be long before hundreds of destroyer droids break in here to rescue us."

Even before he finished, there was the sound of heavy wheels in the anteway, then of metal bodies unfolding. The viceroy permitted himself a satisfied smile. "You see, Your Highness? Rescue is already at hand."

The Queen gave him a hard look. "Before they make it through that door, we will have negotiated a new treaty, Viceroy. And you will have signed it."

Free at last of the laser wall, Obi-Wan Kenobi charged out of the service tunnel and into the chamber that housed the melting pit. Abandoning any pretense of observing even the slightest caution, he barreled into Darth Maul with such fury that he almost knocked both of them off the ledge and into the abyss. He struck at the Sith Lord with his lightsaber as if his own safety meant nothing, lost in a red haze of rage and frustration, consumed by his grief for Qui-Gon and his failure to prevent his friend's fall.

The Sith Lord was borne backward by the Jedi Knight's initial rush, caught off guard by the other's wild assault, and pressed all the way back to the far wall of the melting pit. There he struggled to keep the young Jedi at bay, trying to open enough space between them to defend himself. Lightsabers scraped and grated against each other, and the chamber echoed with their fury. Lunging and twisting, Darth Maul regained the offensive and counterattacked, using both ends of his lightsaber in an effort to cut Obi-Wan's legs out from under him. But Obi-Wan, while not so experienced as Qui-Gon, was quicker. Anticipating each blow, he was able to elude his antagonist's efforts to bring him down.

The struggle took them around the edge of the melting pit and into the nooks and alcoves beyond, into shadowed recesses and around smoky pillars and pipe housings. Twice, Obi-Wan went down, losing his footing on the smooth flooring of the melting pit's rim. Once, Darth Maul hammered at him with such determination that he scorched the young Jedi's tunic, shoulder to waist, and it was only by countering with an upthrust counterstrike to the other's midsection and by rolling quickly away and back to his feet that Obi-Wan was able to escape.

They fought their way back toward the laser-riddled service passage, past Qui-Gon's still form, and into a tangle of vent tubes and circuit housings. Steam burst from ruptured pipes, and the air was filled with the acrid smell of scorched wiring. Darth Maul began to use his command of the Force to fling heavy objects at Obi-Wan, trying to throw him off balance, to disable him, to disrupt the flow of his attack. Obi-Wan responded in kind, and the air was filled with deadly missiles. Lightsabers flicked right and left to ward off the objects, and the clash of errant metal careening off stone walls formed an eerie shriek in the gloom.

The battle wore on, and for a time it was fought evenly. But Darth Maul was the stronger of the two and was driven by a frenzy that surpassed even the frantic determination that fueled Obi-Wan. Eventually, the Sith Lord began to wear the young Jedi down. Bit by bit, he pressed him back, carrying the attack to him, looking to catch him off guard. Obi-Wan could sense his body weakening, and his fear of what it would mean if he, too, were to fall, began to grow.

Never! he swore furiously.

Qui-Gon's words came back to him. *Don't center on your fears. Concentrate on the here and now.* He struggled to do so, to contain the emotions warring within and bearing him down. *Be mindful of the living Force, my young Padawan. Be strong.*

Sensing his opportunity slipping away from him and his strength waning, Obi-Wan mounted a final assault. He rushed the Sith Lord with a series of side blows designed to bring the two-bladed lightsaber horizontal. Then he feinted an attack to his enemy's left and brought his own lightsaber over and down with such force that he severed the other's weapon.

Crying out in fury, he cut triumphantly at the Sith Lord's horned head, a killing blow.

And missed completely.

Darth Maul, anticipating the maneuver, had stepped smoothly away. Discarding the lesser half of his severed weapon, he counterattacked swiftly, striking at Obi-Wan with enough force that he knocked the young Jedi sideways and off balance. Quickly he struck him again, harder still, and this time Obi-Wan lost his footing completely and tumbled over the edge of the pit, his lightsaber flying from his hand. For an instant, he was falling, tumbling away into the dark. He reached out in desperation and caught hold of a metal rung just below the lip of the pit.

There he hung, helpless, staring up at a triumphant Darth Maul.

* * *

When Anakin Skywalker got a look at the number of battle droids surrounding his starfighter, he ducked back out of sight again at once. If it had been at all possible, he would have vanished into the ship's fuselage and willed them both right through the hangar floor to a safer haven.

"This is not good," he told himself softly.

Sweat beaded on his forehead as he tried to decide what to do. He was just a boy, but he had experience with being in tight places and a cool head when it came to dealing with trouble. Find a way out of this! he admonished himself.

A quick glance at the main and sublevel control panels revealed that all the indicator lights were still red. No help there.

"Artoo," he whispered. "The systems are still overheated. Can you do something?"

Footsteps approached, and a metallic droid voice demanded, "Where is your pilot?"

R2-D2 beeped bravely in reply.

"You are the pilot?"

The astromech droid whistled affirmatively.

There was a confused pause. "Show me your identification," the battle droid commanded, reverting to rote.

Anakin could hear the sound of switches clicking and circuits kicking in. R2-D2 was still trying to save them. Good old Artoo. The astromech droid beeped softly at Anakin, and the boy saw the systems lights change abruptly from red to green.

"Yes, Artoo!" he hissed in relief. "We're up and running!"

He threw the ignition switches, and the fighter's engines roared to life. Swiftly, he leapt from hiding and took his place in the pilot's seat, hands reaching for the steering.

The droid commander saw him now and brought up his weapon. "Leave the cockpit immediately or we will disable your craft!"

"Not if I can help it!" the boy threw back, reaching for the deflectors. "Shields up!"

Hauling back on the steering, he released the antigrav lifts.

The starfighter rose from the hangar floor, throwing off the droid commander, sending him sprawling in a crumpled heap. The droids under his command began firing their blasters, the laser beams ricocheting off the fighter's deflectors, angling away in a tangle of bright streamers.

R2-D2 beeped wildly. "The gun locks are off!" Anakin exclaimed with a joyful shout. "Now we'll show them!"

He punched in the firing buttons and held them down, rotating the fighter clockwise above the hangar floor. Laser beams rocketed in a pinwheel pattern, scything into the unprotected battle droids, disabling them before they could even think to flee. Anakin was howling with glee, caught up in the exhilaration of finding himself back in control. Lasers firing, he swept the hangar floor clean of droids, watching those still distant rush for cover, watching ships and supplies fly apart as the deadly beams cut through them.

Then something moved at the end of a long corridor, no more than a shadow, and deep inside, his instincts kicked into high gear, shrieking at him in a frenzy of need. He didn't know if what he was seeing was a weapon or a machine or something else, and it didn't matter. He was back in the Podraces, locked in battle with Sebulba, and he could see what no one else could, what was hidden from all others. He reacted without thinking, responding to a voice that spoke to him alone, that whispered always of the future while warding him in the present.

Acting of its own accord, faster than thought, his hand left the laser firing buttons and threw a double-hinged switch to the right. Instantly, a pair of torpedoes sped down the corridor in the direction of the shadow. The torpedoes whipped past the battle droids, supply stacks, transports, and everything else, and disappeared through a broad vent.

The boy groaned. "Darn! Missed everything!"

Giving the matter no further thought, he swung the fighter about swiftly and threw the thruster bars forward. The power drive kicked in with a ferocious roar, and the starfighter shot across the hangar deck, scattered droids in every direction, and catapulted back out into space, cannon fire from the battleship chasing after it in a stream of deadly white fire.

Darth Maul walked slowly to the edge of the melting pit, tattooed face bathed in sweat, eyes wild and bright with joy. The battle was finished. The last Jedi was about to be dispatched. He smiled and shifted the remnant of his shattered lightsaber from one hand to the other, savoring the moment.

Eyes fixed on the Sith Lord, Obi-Wan Kenobi went deep inside himself, connecting with the Force he had worked so hard to understand. Calming himself, stilling the trembling of his heart, and banishing his anger and fear, he called upon the last of his reserves. With clarity of purpose and strength of heart, he launched himself away from the side of the pit and catapulted back toward its lip. Imbued with the power of the Force, he cleared the rim easily, somersaulting behind the Sith Lord in a single smooth, powerful motion. Even as he landed, he was drawing Qui-Gon Jinn's fallen lightsaber to his outstretched hand.

Darth Maul whirled to confront him, shock and rage twisting his red and black face. But before he could act to save himself, Qui-Gon's lightsaber slashed through his chest, burning him with killing fire. The stricken Sith Lord howled in pain and disbelief.

Then Obi-Wan turned, thumbed his saber off, and watched his dying enemy tumble away into the pit.

"Whoa, this is way better than Podracing!" Anakin Skywalker shouted at R2-D2, grinning broadly as he zigzagged his Naboo fighter back and forth to throw the gunners off.

The astromech droid was beeping and chirping as if he had fried all his circuits, but the boy refused to listen, rolling and banking the starfighter wildly, angling back toward Naboo and away from the control station.

Then a shocked voice came over the intercom from another of the fighters. "Bravo Leader, what's happening to the control ship?"

In the next instant, a flash of pulsing light swept past him. He glanced over his shoulder and saw the battleship he had escaped wracked by a series of explosions. Huge chunks tore away from the core, hurtling into space.

"It's blowing up from the inside!" the voice on the intercom exclaimed.

"Wasn't us, Bravo Two," Ric Olié replied quickly. "We never hit it."

The battleship continued to break apart, the explosions tearing through it, shattering it, engulfing it, and finally consuming it altogether in a brilliant ball of light.

Debris flew past the canopy of Anakin's fighter, and the light of the explosions faded to black.

"Look!" Bravo Two broke the sudden silence anew. "That's one of ours! Outta the main hold! Must've been him!"

Anakin cringed. He had hoped he might get back to the planet unseen, avoid having to explain to Qui-Gon what he was doing up here. There was no chance of that now.

R2-D2 beeped reprovingly at him. "I know, I know," he muttered wearily, and wondered just how much trouble he had gotten himself into this time.

Blaster shots hammered into the door of the throne room in the palace at Theed. Captain Panaka and the Naboo soldiers spread out to either side in a defensive stance, preparing a crossfire for the droids. Nute Gunray wanted to move out of range, but the Queen was still facing him, her blaster leveled at his midsection, and he did not care to risk provoking her into a hasty action. So he stood there with the others of the Trade Council, frozen in place.

Then abruptly, everything went still. All sound of weapons fire and droid movement beyond the battered throne room doors ceased.

Captain Panaka looked at the Queen, his dark face uncertain. "What's going on?" he asked worriedly.

Amidala, her weapon pointed at Nute Gunray, shook her head. "Try communications. Activate the viewscreens."

Her head of security moved quickly to do so. All eyes were on him as he slowly brought the outer screens into focus.

On the Naboo grasslands, the Gungan army had been over-run. Some of the Gungans had escaped back into the swamp on their kaadu, and some had fled into the hills west. All were being chased by battle droids on STAPs and by Trade Federation tanks. There was not much hope that they would remain free for long.

Most of the Gungans had already been taken prisoner, Jar Jar Binks among them. He stood now in a group of Gungan officers that included General Ceel. All around them, their fellow Gun-gans were being herded away by Trade Federation droids.

"Dis very bombad," Jar Jar ventured disconsolately.

General Ceel nodded, equally forlorn. "Me hope dis worken for da Queen."

Jar Jar sighed. And Annie, Quiggon, Obi-One, Artoo, and all the rest. He wondered what had happened to them. Had they been captured, too? He thought suddenly of Boss Nass. Da Boss wasn't gonna like this one bit. Jar Jar hoped he wasn't going to get the blame, but he couldn't quite rule out the possibility.

Suddenly, all the droids started shaking violently. Some be-gan to run around in circles, others to dip and sway as if their gears had snapped and their circuits shorted out. Tanks skidded to a halt and STAPs crashed. All activity came to a complete stop.

Jar Jar and General Ceel exchanged a confused look. The droid army had locked up. For as far as the eye could see, it stood frozen in place.

Gungan prisoners stared at the motionless droids. Finally, at General Ceel's urging, Jar Jar edged out of the containment circle and touched one of his metal captors. The droid tipped over and lay lifeless on the grass.

"Dis loony," Jar Jar whispered, and wondered what in the world was going on.

* * *

Obi-Wan did not pause to consider what it had cost him to win his victory over Darth Maul, but rushed immediately to Qui-Gon. Kneeling at the Jedi Master's side, he lifted his head and shoulders and cradled him gently in his arms.

"Master!" he breathed in a whisper.

Qui-Gon's eyes opened. "Too late, my young Padawan."

"No!" Obi-Wan shook his head violently in denial.

"Now you must be ready, whether the Council thinks you so or not. You must be the teacher." The strong face twisted in pain, but the dark eyes were steady. "Obi-Wan. Promise me you will train the boy."

Obi-Wan nodded instantly, agreeing without thinking, willing to say or do anything that would ease the other's pain, desperate to save him. "Yes, Master."

Qui-Gon's breathing quickened. "He is the chosen one, Obi-Wan. He will bring balance to the Force. Train him well."

His eyes locked on Obi-Wan's and lost focus. His breathing stopped. The strength and the life went out of him.

"Master," Obi-Wan Kenobi repeated softly, still holding him, bringing him closer now, hugging the lifeless body against his chest, and crying softly. "Master."

Three days later, Obi-Wan Kenobi stood in a small room of the Theed temple in which the deaths of heroes were mourned and their lives celebrated. Qui-Gon Jinn's body lay in state on a bier in the plaza just outside, awaiting cremation. Already the citizenry and officials of the Naboo and the Gungan peoples were gathering to honor the Jedi Master.

Much had changed in the lives of those who had fought in the struggle for Naboo sovereignty. With the collapse of the droid army, the Trade Federation's control over Naboo had been broken. All of the ground transports, tanks, STAPs, and weapons and supplies were in the hands of the Republic. Viceroy Nute Gunray, his lieutenant, Rune Haako, and the remainder of the Neimoidian occupation council had been shipped as prisoners to Coruscant to await trial. Senator Palpatine had been elected as supreme chancellor of the Republic, and he had promised swift action in the dispensing of justice to the captives.

Queen Amidala had outfoxed the Neimoidians one final time by pretending to surrender so she could gain safe access to the viceroy before he had time to flee. She had communicated to Sabé to break away from the struggle taking place several floors below and to use the service passages to reach the Queen's chambers and then make her appearance before the viceroy. It was a calculated risk, and Sabé might not have been able to get there in time. Had she not, Amidala would have triggered the secret compartment release and fought for her freedom in any case. She was young, but she was not without courage or daring. She had shown intelligence and insight from the beginning of the time the Jedi had come to assist her. Obi-Wan thought she would make a very good Queen.

But it was a nine-year-old boy who had saved them all. Even without knowing exactly what he was doing, Anakin Skywalker had flown a starfighter into the teeth of the Federation defense, penetrated their shields, landed in the belly of the Neimoidian flagship, torpedoed the ship's reactor, and set off a chain reaction of explosions that destroyed the control station. It was the destruction of the central transmitter that had caused the droid army to freeze in place, their communications effectively short-circuited. Anakin claimed not to have attacked with any sort of plan in mind or fired his starfighter's torpedoes with any expectation of hitting the reactor. But after hearing the boy's tale and questioning him thoroughly, Obi-Wan believed Anakin was guided by something more than the thinking of ordinary men. That extraordinarily high midi-chlorian count gave the boy a connection to the Force that even Jedi Masters on the order of Yoda might never achieve. Qui-Gon, he now believed, had been right. Anakin Skywalker was the chosen one.

He paced the room, dressed in fresh clothing for the funeral, soft, loose-fitting, sand-colored Jedi Knight garb, Qui-Gon's lightsaber, now his own, hanging from his belt. The Jedi Council had come to Naboo for the funeral and to speak again with Anakin. They were doing so now, close by, making a final assessment based on what had transpired since their last session with the boy. Obi-Wan thought the outcome of their deliberations must be a foregone conclusion. He could not imagine now that it wouldn't be.

He stopped his pacing and stared momentarily at nothing,

thinking of Qui-Gon Jinn, his Master, his teacher, his friend. He had failed Qui-Gon in life. But he would carry on his work now, honoring him in death by fulfilling his promise to train the boy, no matter what.

Listen to me, he thought, smiling ruefully. I sound like him.

The door opened, and Yoda appeared. He entered the room in a slow shuffle, leaning on his walking stick, his wizened face sleepy-eyed and contemplative.

"Master Yoda," Obi-Wan greeted, hurrying forward to meet him, bowing deferentially.

The Jedi Master nodded. "Confer on you the level of Jedi Knight, the Council does. Decided about the boy, the Council is, Obi-Wan," he advised solemnly.

"He is to be trained?"

The big ears cocked forward, and the lids to those sleepy eyes widened. "So impatient, you are. So sure of what has been decided?"

Obi-Wan bit his tongue and kept his silence, waiting dutifully on the other. Yoda studied him carefully. "A great warrior, was Qui-Gon Jinn," he gargled softly, his strange voice sad. "But so much more he could have been, if not so fast he had run. More slowly, you must proceed, Obi-Wan."

Obi-Wan stood his ground. "He understood what the rest of us did not about the boy."

But Yoda shook his head. "Be not so quick to judge. Not everything, is understanding. Not all at once, is it revealed. Years, it takes, to become a Jedi Knight. Years more, to become one with the Force."

He moved over to a place where the fading light shone in through a window, soft and golden. Sunset approached, the appointed time for their farewell to Qui-Gon.

Yoda's gaze was distant when he spoke. "Decided, the Council is," he repeated. "Trained, the boy shall be."

Obi-Wan felt a surge of relief and joy flood through him, and a grateful smile escaped him.

Yoda saw the smile. "Pleased, you are? So certain this is right?" The wrinkled face tightened. "Clouded, this boy's future remains, Obi-Wan. A mistake to train him, it is."

"But the Council—"

"Yes, decided." The sleepy eyes lifted. "Disagree with that decision, I must."

There was a long silence as the two faced each other, listening to the sounds of the funeral preparations taking place without. Obi-Wan did not know what to say. Clearly the Council had decided against the advice of Yoda. That in itself was unusual. That the Jedi Master chose to make a point of it here emphasized the extent of his concerns about Anakin Skywalker.

Obi-Wan spoke carefully. "I will take this boy as my Padawan, Master. I will train him in the best way I can. But I will bear in mind what you have told me here. I will go carefully. I will heed your warnings. I will keep close watch over his progress."

Yoda studied him a moment, then nodded. "Your promise, then, remember well, young Jedi," he said softly. "Sufficient, it is, if you do."

Obi-Wan bowed in acknowledgment. "I will remember."

Together, they went out into a blaze of light.

The funeral pyre was lit, the fire building steadily around the body of Qui-Gon Jinn, the flames slowly beginning to envelop and consume him. Those who had been chosen to honor him encircled the pyre. Queen Amidala stood with her handmaidens, Supreme Chancellor Palpatine, Governor Sio Bibble, Captain Panaka, and an honor guard of one hundred Naboo soldiers. Boss Nass, Jar Jar Binks, and twenty Gungan warriors stood across from them. Linking them together were the members of the Jedi Council, including Yoda and Mace Windu. Another clutch of Jedi Knights, those who had known Qui-Gon longest and best, completed the circle.

Anakin Skywalker stood with Obi-Wan, his young face intense as he fought to hold back his tears.

A long, sustained drum roll traced the passage of the flames as they reduced Qui-Gon to spirit and ash. When the fire had taken him away, a flight of snowy doves was released into a crimson sunset. The birds rose in a flutter of wings and a splash of pale brilliance, winging swiftly away.

Obi-Wan found himself remembering. For his entire life, he had studied under the Jedi, and Qui-Gon Jinn, in particular. Now Qui-Gon was gone, and Obi-Wan had passed out of an old life and into a new. Now he was a Jedi Knight, not a Padawan. Everything that had gone before was behind a door that had closed on him forever. It was hard to accept, and at the same time, it gave him an odd sense of release.

He looked down at Anakin. The boy was staring at the ashes of the funeral bier, crying softly.

He put his hand on one slim shoulder. "He is one with the Force, Anakin. You must let him go."

The boy shook his head. "I miss him."

Obi-Wan nodded. "I miss him, too. And I will remember him always. But he is gone."

Anakin wiped the tears from his face. "What will happen to me now?"

The hand tightened on the boy's shoulder. "I will train you, just as Qui-Gon would have done," Obi-Wan Kenobi said softly. "I am your new Master, Anakin. You will study with me, and you will become a Jedi Knight, I promise you."

The boy straightened, a barely perceptible act. Obi-Wan nodded to himself. Somewhere, he thought, Qui-Gon Jinn would be smiling.

Across the way, Mace Windu stood with Yoda, his strong dark face contemplative as he watched Obi-Wan put his hand on Anakin Skywalker's shoulder.

"One life ends and a new one begins in the Jedi order," he murmured, almost to himself.

Yoda hunched forward, leaning on his gnarled staff, and shook his head. "Not so sure of this one as of Qui-Gon, do I feel. Troubled, he is. Wrapped in shadows and difficult choices."

Mace Windu nodded. He knew Yoda's feelings on the matter, but the Council had made its decision. "Obi-Wan will do a good job with him," he said, shifting the subject. "Qui-Gon was right. He is ready."

They knew of what the young Padawan had done to save himself from the Sith Lord in the melting pit after Qui-Gon had been struck down. It took an act of extraordinary courage and strength of will. Only a Jedi Knight fully in tune with the Force could have saved himself against such an adversary. Obi-Wan Kenobi had proved himself beyond everyone's expectations that day.

"Ready this time, he was," Yoda acknowledged grudgingly. "Ready to train the boy, he may not be."

"Defeating a Sith Lord in combat is a strong test of his readiness for anything," the Council leader pressed. His eyes stayed with Obi-Wan and Anakin. "There is no doubt. The one who tested him was a Sith."

Yoda's sleepy eyes blinked. "Always two there are. No more, no less. A master and an apprentice."

Mace Windu nodded. "Then which one was destroyed, do you think—the master or the apprentice?"

They looked at each other now, but neither could provide an answer to the question.

That night Darth Sidious stood alone on a balcony overlooking the city, a shadowy figure amid the multitude of twinkling lights, his visage dark and angry as he contemplated the loss of his apprentice. Years of training had gone into the preparation of Darth Maul as a Sith Lord. He had been more than the equal of the Jedi Knights he had faced and should have been able to defeat them easily. It was bad luck and chance that had led to his death, a combination that even the power of the dark side could not always overcome.

Not in the short run, at least.

His brow furrowed. It would be necessary to replace Darth Maul. He would need to train another apprentice. Such a one would not be easy to find.

Darth Sidious walked to the railing and put his hands on the cool metal. One thing was certain. Those responsible for killing Darth Maul would be held accountable. Those who had opposed him would not be forgotten. All would be made to pay.

His eyes glittered. Still, he had gotten what he wanted most from this business. Even the loss of Darth Maul was worth that. He would bide his time. He would wait for his chance. He would lay the groundwork for what was needed.

A smile played across his thin lips. A day of reckoning would come about soon enough.

There was a grand parade the following day to publicly recognize the newfound alliance of the Naboo and Gungan peoples, to celebrate their hard-fought victory over the Trade Federation invaders, and to honor those who had fought to secure the planet's freedom. Crowds lined the streets of Theed as columns of Gungan warriors astride kaadu and Naboo soldiers aboard speeders rode through the city to the sounds of cheering and singing. Fambaa lumbered down the avenues, draped in rich silks and embroidered harnesses, heads weaving from side to side on long necks. Here and there, a captured Federation tank hovered amidst the marchers, Naboo and Gungan flags flying from cannons and hatchways. Jar Jar Binks and General Ceel led the Gungans, both riding their kaadu, Jar Jar managing to stay aboard this time for the entire parade, though he looked to those in attendance to be having a bit of trouble doing so.

Captain Panaka and the Queen's own guards stood at the top of the stone steps in the central plaza, watching the parade approach. Panaka's uniform was creased, metal insignia on his epaulets gleaming, proud and strong.

Anakin Skywalker stood with Obi-Wan Kenobi near the Queen. He was feeling out of place and embarrassed. He thought the parade wonderful, and he appreciated being honored with the others, but his mind was elsewhere.

It was with Qui-Gon, gone back into the Force.

It was with Padmé, who had barely spoken to him since he had been accepted for training by the Jedi Council.

It was with his home, to which he might never return.

It was with his mother, whom he wished could see him now.

He wore the clothing of a Jedi Padawan, his hair cut short in the Padawan style, a student in training to become a Knight of the order. He had achieved all that he had hoped in coming with Qui-Gon to Coruscant and beyond. He should have been happy and satisfied, and he was. But his happiness and satisfaction were clouded by the sadness he could not banish at losing Qui-Gon and his mother both. They were lost to him in different ways, to be sure, but they were gone out of his life. Qui-Gon had provided the stability he required to leave his mother behind. With the Jedi Master's death, Anakin was left adrift. There was no one who could give him the grounding that Qui-Gon had provided—not Obi-Wan, not even Padmé. One day, perhaps. One day, each of them would play a part in his life that would change him forever. He could sense that. But for now, when it mattered most, he felt all alone.

So he smiled, but he was sick in spirit and lost in his heart.

Perhaps sensing his discomfort, Obi-Wan reached over to put a reassuring hand on his shoulder. "It's the beginning of a new life for you, Anakin," he ventured.

The boy smiled back dutifully, but said nothing.

Obi-Wan looked off at the crowds in front of them. "Qui-Gon always disdained celebrations. But he understood the need for them, as well. I wonder what he would have made of this one."

Anakin shrugged.

The Jedi smiled. "He would have been proud to see you a part of it."

The boy looked at him. "Do you think so?"

"I do. Your mother would be proud of you as well."

Anakin's mouth tightened, and he looked away. "I wish she was here. I miss her."

The Jedi's hand tightened on his shoulder. "One day you will see her again. But when you do, you will be a Jedi Knight."

The parade wound through the central plaza to where the Queen and her guests viewed the procession. She stood with her handmaidens, Governor Sio Bibble, Supreme Chancellor Palpatine, Boss Nass of the Gungans, and the twelve members of the Jedi Council. R2-D2 occupied a space just below the handmaidens and next to Anakin and Obi-Wan, domed head swiveling from side to side, lights blinking as his sensors took everything in.

R2 beeped at the boy, and Anakin touched the little droid's shell gently.

Boss Nass stepped forward and held the Globe of Peace high over his head. "Dis grand party!" an exuberant Jar Jar shouted above the noise of cheering and clapping. "Gungans and Naboo, dey be friends forever, hey?"

His enthusiasm made Anakin smile in spite of himself. The Gungan was dancing up and down, long ears flapping, gangly limbs twisting this way and that as he mounted the steps. Jar Jar would never let the bad things in life get him down, the boy thought. Maybe there was a lesson to be learned in that.

"We bombad heroes, Annie!" Jar Jar laughed, lifting his arms over his head and showing all his teeth.

The boy laughed. He guessed maybe they were.

On the broad avenue below, in a long, colorful ribbon of life, the parade that had carried them to this place and time continued on.

EPISODE II

ATTACK OF THE CLONES™

R. A. SALVATORE

BASED ON THE STORY BY
GEORGE LUCAS

AND THE SCREENPLAY BY
GEORGE LUCAS
AND
JONATHAN HALES

His mind absorbed the scene before him, so quiet and calm and . . . normal.

It was the life he had always wanted, a gathering of family and friends—he knew that they were just that, though the only one he recognized was his dear mother.

This was the way it was supposed to be. The warmth and the love, the laughter and the quiet times. This was how he had always dreamed it would be, how he had always prayed it would be. The warm, inviting smiles. The pleasant conversation. The gentle pats on shoulders.

But most of all there was the smile of his beloved mother, so happy now, no more a slave. When she looked at him, he saw all of that and more, saw how proud she was of him, how joyful her life had become.

She moved before him, her face beaming, her hand reaching out for him to gently stroke his face. Her smile brightened, then widened some more.

Too much more.

For a moment, he thought the exaggeration a product of love beyond normal bounds, but the smile continued to grow, his mother's face stretching and contorting weirdly.

She seemed to be moving in slow motion then. They all did, slowing as if their limbs had become heavy.

No, not heavy, he realized, his warm feelings turning suddenly hot. It was as if these friends and his mother were becoming rigid and stiff, as if they were becoming something less than living and breathing humans. He stared back at that caricature of a smile, the twisted face, and recognized the pain behind it, a crystalline agony.

He tried to call out to her, to ask her what she needed him to do, ask her how he could help.

Her face twisted even more, blood running from her eyes. Her skin crystalized, becoming almost translucent, almost like glass.

Glass! She was glass! The light glistened off her crystalline highlights, the blood ran fast over her smooth surface. And her expression, a look of resignation and apology, a look that said she had failed him and that he had failed her, drove a sharp point straight into the helpless onlooker's heart.

He tried to reach out for her, tried to save her.

Cracks began to appear in the glass. He heard the crunching sounds as they elongated.

He cried out repeatedly, reached for her desperately. Then he thought of the Force, and sent his thoughts there with all his willpower, reaching for her with all his energy.

But then, she shattered.

The Jedi Padawan jumped to a sitting position in his cot on the starship, his eyes popping open wide, sweat on his forehead and his breath coming in gasps.

A dream. It was all a dream.

He told himself that repeatedly as he tried to settle back down on the cot. It was all a dream.

Or was it?

He could see things, after all, before they happened.

"Ansion!" came a call from the front of the ship, the familiar voice of his Master.

He knew that he had to shake the dream away, had to focus

on the events at hand, the latest assignment beside his Master, but that was easier said than done.

For he saw her again, his mother, her body going rigid, crystallizing, then exploding into a million shattered shards.

He looked up ahead, envisioning his Master at the controls, wondering if he should tell all to the Jedi, wondering if the Jedi would be able to help him. But that thought washed away as soon as it had crossed his mind. His Master, Obi-Wan Kenobi, would not be able to help. They were too involved in other things, in his training, in minor assignments like the border dispute that had brought them so far out from Coruscant.

The Padawan wanted to get back to Coruscant, as soon as possible. He needed guidance now, but not the kind he was getting from Obi-Wan.

He needed to speak with Chancellor Palpatine again, to hear the man's reassuring words. Palpatine had taken a great interest in him over the last ten years, making sure that he always got a chance to speak with him whenever he and Obi-Wan were on Coruscant.

The Padawan took great comfort in that now, with the terrible dream so vivid in his thoughts. For the Chancellor, the wise leader of all the Republic, had promised him that his powers would soar to previously unknown heights, that he would become a power even among the powerful Jedi.

Perhaps that was the answer. Perhaps the mightiest of the Jedi, the mightiest of the mighty, could strengthen the fragile glass.

"Ansion," came the call again from the front. "Anakin, get up here!"

Shmi Skywalker Lars stood on the edge of the sand berm
marking the perimeter of the moisture farm, one leg up higher,
to the very top of the ridge, knee bent. With one hand on that
knee for support, the middle-aged woman, her dark hair slightly
graying, her face worn and tired, stared up at the many bright
dots of starlight on this crisp Tatooine night. No sharp edges
broke the landscape about her, just the smooth and rounded
forms of windblown sand dunes on this planet of seemingly endless sands. Somewhere out in the distance a creature groaned, a
plaintive sound that resonated deeply within Shmi this night.

This special night.

Her son Anakin, her dearest little Annie, turned twenty this
night, a birthday Shmi observed each year, though she hadn't
seen her beloved child in a decade. How different he must be!
How grown, how strong, how wise in the ways of the Jedi by
now! Shmi, who had lived all of her life in a small area of drab
Tatooine, knew that she could hardly imagine the wonders her
boy might have found out there among the stars, on planets so
different from this, with colors more vivid and water that filled
entire valleys.

A wistful smile widened on her still-pretty face as she remembered those days long ago, when she and her son had been

slaves of the wretch Watto. Annie, with his mischief and his dreams, with his independent attitude and unsurpassed courage, used to so infuriate the Toydarian junk dealer. Despite the hardships of life as a slave, there had been good times, too, back then. Despite their meager food, their meager possessions, despite the constant complaining and ordering about by Watto, she had been with Annie, her beloved son.

"You should come in," came a quiet voice behind her.

Shmi's smile only widened, and she turned to see her stepson, Owen Lars, walking over to join her. He was a stocky and strong boy about Anakin's age, with short brown hair, a few bristles, and a wide face that could not hide anything that was within his heart.

Shmi tousled Owen's hair when he moved beside her, and he responded by draping an arm across her shoulders and kissing her on the cheek.

"No starship tonight, Mom?" Owen asked good-naturedly. He knew why Shmi had come out here, why she came out here so very often in the quiet night.

Shmi turned her hand over and gently stroked it down Owen's face, smiling. She loved this young man as she loved her own son, and he had been so good to her, so understanding of the hole that remained within her heart. Without jealousy, without judgment, Owen had accepted Shmi's pain and had always given her a shoulder to lean on.

"No starship this night," she replied, and she looked back up at the starry canopy. "Anakin must be busy saving the galaxy or chasing smugglers and other outlaws. He has to do those things now, you know."

"Then I shall sleep more soundly from this night forward," Owen replied with a grin.

Though she was kidding, of course, Shmi did realize a bit of truth in her presumption about Anakin. He was a special child, something beyond the norm—even for a Jedi, she believed. Anakin had always stood taller than anyone else. Not physically—physically, as Shmi remembered him, he was just a smiling little boy, with curious eyes and sandy-blond hair. But Annie could do things, and so very well. Even though he was only a child at the time, he had raced Pods, defeating some of the very best racers on all of Tatooine. He was the first human ever to win one of the Podraces, and that when he was only nine years old! And in a racer that, Shmi remembered with an even wider smile, had been built with spare parts taken from Watto's junkyard.

But that was Anakin's way, because he was not like the other children, or even like other adults. Anakin could "see" things before they happened, as if he was so tuned to the world about him that he understood innately the logical conclusion to any course of events. He could often sense problems with his Podracer, for example, long before those problems manifested themselves in a catastrophic way. He had once told her that he could feel the upcoming obstacles in any course before he actually saw them. It was his special way, and that was why the Jedi who had come to Tatooine had recognized the unique nature of the boy and had freed him from Watto and taken him into their care and instruction.

"I had to let him go," Shmi said quietly. "I could not keep him with me, if that meant living the life of a slave."

"I know," Owen assured her.

"I could not have kept him with me even if we were not slaves," she went on, and she looked at Owen, as if her own words had surprised her. "Annie has so much to give to the galaxy. His gifts could not be contained by Tatooine. He belongs out there, flying across the stars, saving planets. He was born to be a Jedi, born to give so much more to so many more."

"That is why I sleep better at night," Owen reiterated, and when Shmi looked at him, she saw that his grin was wider than ever.

"Oh, you're teasing me!" she said, reaching out to swat her stepson on the shoulder. Owen merely shrugged.

Shmi's face went serious again. "Annie wanted to go," she went on, the same speech she had given Owen before, the same speech that she had silently repeated to herself every night for the last ten years. "His dream was to fly about the stars, to see every world in the whole galaxy, to do grand things. He was born a slave, but he was not born *to be* a slave. No, not my Annie.

"Not my Annie."

Owen squeezed her shoulder. "You did the right thing. If I was Anakin, I would be grateful to you. I'd understand that you did what was best for me. There is no greater love than that, Mom."

Shmi stroked his face again and even managed a wistful smile.

"Come on in, Mom," Owen said, taking her hand. "It's dangerous out here."

Shmi nodded and didn't resist at first as Owen started to pull her along. She stopped suddenly, though, and stared hard at her stepson as he turned back to regard her. "It's more dangerous out there," she said, sucking in her breath, her voice breaking. Alarm evident in her expression, she looked back up at the wide and open sky. "What if he is hurt, Owen? Or dead?"

"It's better to die in pursuit of your dreams than to live a life without hope," Owen said, rather unconvincingly.

Shmi looked back at him, her smile returning. Owen, like his father, was about as grounded in simple pragmatism as any man could be. She understood that he had said that only for her benefit, and that made it all the more special.

She didn't resist anymore as Owen began to lead her along again, back to the humble abode of Cliegg Lars, her husband, Owen's father.

She had done the right thing concerning her son, Shmi told herself with every step. They had been slaves, with no prospects of finding their freedom other than the offer of the Jedi. How could she have kept Anakin here on Tatooine, when Jedi Knights were promising him all of his dreams?

Of course, at that time, Shmi had not known that she would meet Cliegg Lars that fateful day in Mos Espa, and that the moisture farmer would fall in love with her, buy her from Watto, and free her, and only then, once she was a free woman, ask her to marry him. Would she have let Anakin go if she had known the changes that would come into her life so soon after his departure?

Wouldn't her life be better now, more complete by far, if Anakin were beside her?

Shmi smiled as she thought about it. No, she realized, she would still have wanted Annie to go, even if she had foreseen the dramatic changes that would soon come into her life. Not for herself, but for Anakin. His place was out there. She knew that.

Shmi shook her head, overwhelmed by the enormity of it all, by the many winding turns in her life's path, in Anakin's path. Even in hindsight, she could not be sure that this present situation was not the best possible outcome, for both of them.

But still, there remained a deep and empty hole in her heart.

"I can help with that," Beru said politely, moving to join Shmi, who was cooking dinner. Cliegg and Owen were out closing down the perimeter of the compound, securing the farm from the oncoming night—a night that promised a dust storm.

Smiling warmly, and glad that this young woman was soon to be a member of their family, Shmi handed a knife over to Beru. Owen hadn't said anything yet about marrying Beru, but Shmi could tell from the way the two looked at each other. It was only a matter of time, and not much time at that, if she knew her stepson. Owen was not an adventurous type, was as solid as the ground beneath them, but when he knew what he wanted, he went after it with single-minded purpose.

Beru was exactly that, and she obviously loved Owen as deeply as he loved her. She was well suited to be the wife of a moisture farmer, Shmi thought, watching her methodically go about her duties in the kitchen. She never shied from work, was very capable and diligent.

And she doesn't expect much, or need much to make her happy, Shmi thought, for that, in truth, was the crux of it. Their existence here was simple and plain. There were few adventures, and none at all that were welcomed, for excitement out here usually meant that Tusken Raiders had been seen in the region, or that a gigantic sandstorm or some other potentially devastating weather phenomenon was blowing up.

The Lars family had only the simple things, mostly the company of each other, to keep them amused and content. For Cliegg, this had been the only way of life he had ever known, a lifestyle that went back several generations in the Lars family. Same thing for Owen. And while Beru had grown up in Mos Eisley, she seemed to fit right in.

Yes, Owen would marry her, Shmi knew, and what a happy day that would be!

The two men returned soon after, along with C-3PO, the protocol droid Anakin had built back in the days when he had Watto's junkyard to rummage through.

"Two more tangaroots for you, Mistress Shmi," the thin droid said, handing Shmi a pair of orange-and-green freshly picked vegetables. "I would have brought more, but I was told, and not in any civil way, that I must hurry."

Shmi looked to Cliegg, and he gave her a grin and a shrug. "Could've left him out there to get sandblasted clean, I suppose," he said. "Of course, some of the bigger rocks that are sure to be flying about might've taken out a circuit or two."

"Your pardon, Master Cliegg," C-3PO said. "I only meant—"

"We know what you meant, Threepio," Shmi assured the droid. She placed a comforting hand on his shoulder, then quickly pulled it away, thinking that a perfectly silly gesture to offer to a walking box of wires. Of course, C-3PO was much more than a box of wires to Shmi. Anakin had built the droid . . . almost. When Anakin had left with the Jedi, 3PO had been perfectly functional, but uncovered, his wires exposed. Shmi had left him that way for a long time, fantasizing that Anakin would return to complete the job. Just before marrying Cliegg had Shmi finished the droid herself, adding the dull metal coverings. It had been quite a touching moment for Shmi, an admission of sorts that she was where she belonged and Anakin was where he belonged. The protocol droid could be quite annoying at times, but to Shmi, C-3PO remained a reminder of her son.

"Course, if there are Tuskens about, they'd likely have gotten him under wraps before the storm," Cliegg went on, obviously taking great pleasure in teasing the poor droid. "You're not afraid of Tusken Raiders, are you, Threepio?"

"There is nothing in my program to suggest such fear," 3PO replied, though he would have sounded more convincing if he hadn't been shaking as he spoke, and if his voice hadn't come out all squeaky and uneven.

"Enough," Shmi demanded of Cliegg. "Oh, poor Threepio," she said, patting the droid's shoulder again. "Go ahead, now. I've got more than enough help this evening." As she finished, she waved the droid away.

"You're just terrible to that poor droid," she remarked, moving beside her husband and playfully patting him across his broad shoulder.

"Well, if I can't have fun with him, I'll have to set my sights on someone else," the rarely mischievous Cliegg replied, narrowing his eyes and scanning the room. He finally settled a threatening gaze on Beru.

"Cliegg," Shmi was quick to warn.

"What?" he protested dramatically. "If she's thinking to come out and live here, then she had better learn to defend herself!"

"Dad!" Owen cried.

"Oh, don't fret about old Cliegg," Beru piped in, emphasizing the word *old*. "A fine wife I would make if I couldn't outduel that one in a war of words!"

"Aha! A challenge!" Cliegg roared.

"Not so much of one from where I'm sitting," Beru dryly returned, and she and Cliegg began exchanging some goodnatured insults, with Owen chiming in every now and again.

Shmi hardly listened, too engaged in merely watching Beru. Yes, she would certainly fit in, and well, about the moisture farm. Her temperament was perfect. Solid, but playful when the situation allowed. Gruff Cliegg could verbally spar with the best of them, but Beru had to be counted among that elite lot. Shmi went back to her dinner preparations, her smile growing wider every time Beru hit Cliegg with a particularly nasty retort.

Intent on her work, Shmi never saw the missile coming, and when the overripe vegetable hit her on the side of the face, she let out a shriek.

Of course, that only made the other three in the room howl with laughter.

Shmi turned to see them sitting there, staring at her. From the embarrassed expression on Beru's face, and from the angle, with Beru sitting directly behind Cliegg, it seemed obvious to Shmi that Beru had launched the missile, aiming for Cliegg, but throwing a bit high.

"The girl listens when you tell her to stop," Cliegg Lars said, his sarcastic tone shattered by a burst of laughter that came right from his belly.

He stopped when Shmi smacked him with a piece of juicy fruit, splattering it across his shoulders.

A food fight began—measured, of course, and with more threats hurled than actual missiles.

When it ended, Shmi began the cleanup, the other three helping for a bit. "You two go and spend some time together without your troublemaking father," Shmi told Owen and Beru. "Cliegg started it, so Cliegg will help clean it up. Go on, now. I'll call you back when dinner's on the table."

Cliegg gave a little laugh.

"And if you mess up the next one, you're going to be hungry," Shmi told him, threateningly waving a spoon his way. "And lonely!"

"Whoa! Never that!" Cliegg said, holding his hands up in a sign of surrender.

With a wave of the spoon, Shmi further dismissed Owen and Beru, and the two went off happily.

"She'll make him a fine wife," Shmi said to Cliegg.

He walked up beside her and grabbed her about the waist, pulling her tight. "We Lars men fall in love with the best women."

Shmi looked back to see his warm and sincere smile, and she returned it in kind. This was the way it was supposed to be. Good honest work, a sense of true accomplishment, and enough free time for some fun, at least. This was the life Shmi had always wanted. This was perfect, almost.

A wistful look came over her face.

"Thinking of your boy again," Cliegg Lars stated, instead of asked.

Shmi looked at him, her expression a mixture of joy and sadness, a single dark cloud crossing a sunny blue sky. "Yes, but it's okay this time," she said. "He's safe, I know, and doing great things."

"But when we have such fun, you wish he could be here."

Shmi smiled again. "I do, and in all other times, as well. I wish Anakin had been here from the beginning, since you and I first met."

"Five years ago," Cliegg remarked.

"He would love you as I do, and he and Owen . . ." Her voice weakened and trailed away.

"You think that Anakin and Owen would be friends?" Cliegg asked. "Bah! Of course they would!"

"You've never even met my Annie!" Shmi scolded.

"They'd be the best of friends," Cliegg assured her, tightening his hug once again. "How could they not be, with you as that one's mother?"

Shmi accepted the compliment gracefully, looked back and gave Cliegg a deep and appreciative kiss. She was thinking of Owen, of the young man's flowering romance with the lovely Beru. How Shmi loved them both!

But that thought brought with it some level of discomfort. Shmi had often wondered if Owen had been part of the reason she had so readily agreed to marry Cliegg. She looked back at her husband, rubbing her hand over his broad shoulder. Yes, she loved him, and deeply, and she certainly couldn't deny her joy at finally being relieved of her slave bonds. But despite all of that, what part had the presence of Owen played in her decisions? It had been a question that had stayed with her all these years. Had there been a need in her heart that Owen had filled? A mother's need to cover the hole left by Anakin's departure?

In truth, the two boys were very different in temperament. Owen was solid and staid, the rock who would gladly take over the farm from Cliegg when the time came, as this moisture farm had been passed down in the Lars family from generation to generation. Owen was ready, and even thrilled, to be the logical and rightful heir to the place, more than able to accept the often difficult lifestyle in exchange for the pride and sense of honest accomplishment that came with running the place correctly.

But Annie . . .

Shmi nearly laughed aloud as she considered her impetuous and wanderlust-filled son put in a similar situation. She had no doubts that Anakin would give Cliegg the same fits he had always given Watto. Anakin's adventurous spirit would not be tamed by any sense of generational responsibility, Shmi knew. His need to leap out for adventure, to race the Pods, to fly among the stars, would not have been diminished, and it surely would have driven Cliegg crazy.

Now Shmi did giggle, picturing Cliegg turning red-faced with exasperation when Anakin had let his duties slide once again.

Cliegg hugged her all the tighter at the sound, obviously having no clue of the mental images fluttering through her brain.

Shmi melted into that hug, knowing that she was where she belonged, and taking comfort in the hope that Anakin, too, was where he truly belonged.

She wasn't wearing one of the grand gowns that had marked the station of her life for the last decade and more. Her hair was not done up in wondrous fashion, with some glittering accessory woven into the thick brown strands. And in that plainness, Padmé Amidala only appeared more beautiful and more shining.

The woman sitting beside her on the bench swing, so obviously a relation, was a bit older, a bit more matronly, perhaps, with clothes even more plain than Padmé's and with her hair a bit more out of place. But she was no less beautiful, shining with an inner glow equally strong.

"Did you finish your meetings with Queen Jamillia?" Sola asked. It was obvious from her tone that the meetings to which she had referred were not high on her personal wish list.

Padmé looked over at her, then looked back to the playhouse where Sola's daughters, Ryoo and Pooja, were in the midst of a wild game of tag.

"It was one meeting," Padmé explained. "The Queen had some information to pass along."

"About the Military Creation Act," Sola stated.

Padmé didn't bother to confirm the obvious. The Military Creation Act now before the Senate was the most important piece of business in many years, one that held implications for the Republic even beyond those during the dark time when Padmé had been Queen and the Trade Federation had tried to conquer Naboo.

"The Republic is all in a tumult, but not to fear, for Senator Amidala will put it all aright," Sola said.

Padmé turned to her, somewhat surprised by the level of sarcasm in Sola's tone.

"That's what you do, right?" Sola innocently asked.

"It's what I try to do."

"It's *all* you try to do."

"What is that supposed to mean?" Padmé asked, her face twisting with puzzlement. "I am a Senator, after all."

"A Senator after a Queen, and probably with many more offices ahead of her," Sola said. She looked back at the playhouse and called for Ryoo and Pooja to ease up.

"You speak as if it's a bad thing," Padmé remarked.

Sola looked at her earnestly. "It's a great thing," she said. "If you're doing it all for the right reasons."

"And what is that supposed to mean?"

Sola shrugged, as if she wasn't quite sure. "I think you've convinced yourself that you're indispensable to the Republic," she said. "That they couldn't get along at all without you."

"Sis!"

"It's true," Sola insisted. "You give and give and give and give. Don't you ever want to take, just a little?"

Padmé's smile showed that Sola's words had caught her off guard. "Take what?"

Sola looked back to Ryoo and Pooja. "Look at them. I see the sparkle in your eyes when you watch my children. I know how much you love them."

"Of course I do!"

"Wouldn't you like to have children of your own?" Sola asked. "A family of your own?"

Padmé sat up straight, her eyes going wide. "I . . ." she started, and stopped, several times. "I'm working right now for something I deeply believe in. For something that's important."

"And after this is settled, after the Military Creation Act is far behind you, you'll find something else to deeply believe in, something else that's really important. Something that concerns the Republic and the government more than it really concerns you."

"How can you say that?"

"Because it's true, and you know it's true. When are you going to do something just for yourself?"

"I am."

"You know what I mean."

Padmé gave a little laugh and a shake of her head, and turned back to Ryoo and Pooja. "Is everyone to be defined by their children?" she asked.

"Of course not," Sola replied. "It's not that at all. Or not just that. I'm talking about something bigger, Sis. You spend all of your time worrying about the problems of other people, of this planet's dispute with that planet, or whether this trade guild is acting fairly toward that system. All of your energy is being thrown out there to try to make the lives of everyone else better."

"What's wrong with that?"

"What about *your* life?" Sola asked in all seriousness. "What about Padmé Amidala? Have you even thought about what might make your life better? Most people who have been in public service as long as you have would have retired by now. I know you get satisfaction in helping other people. That's pretty obvious. But what about something deeper for you? What about love, Sis? And yes, what about having kids? Have you even thought about it? Have you even wondered what it might be like for you to settle down and concern yourself with those things that will make your own life fuller?"

Padmé wanted to retort that her life didn't need to be any fuller, but she found herself holding back the words. Somehow they seemed hollow to her at that particular moment, watching her nieces romping about the backyard of the house, now jumping all about poor R2-D2, Padmé's astromech droid.

For the first time in many days, Padmé's thoughts roamed free of her responsibilities, free of the important vote she would have to cast in the Senate in less than a month. Somehow, the words *Military Creation Act* couldn't filter through the whimsical song that Ryoo and Pooja were then making up about R2-D2.

"Too close," Owen remarked gravely to Cliegg, the two of them walking the perimeter of the moisture farm, checking the security. The call of a bantha, the large and shaggy beasts often ridden by Tuskens, had interrupted their conversation.

They both knew it was unlikely that a bantha would be roaming wild about this region, for there was little grazing area anywhere near the desolate moisture farm. But they had heard the call, and could identify it without doubt, and they suspected that potential enemies were near.

"What is driving them so close to the farms?" Owen asked.

"It's been too long since we've organized anything against them," Cliegg replied gruffly. "We let the beasts run free, and they're forgetting the lessons we taught them in the past." He looked hard at Owen's skeptical expression. "You have to go out there and teach the Tuskens their manners every now and again."

Owen just stood there, having no response.

"See how long it's been?" Cliegg said with a snort. "You don't even remember the last time we went out and chased off the Tuskens! There's the problem, right there!"

The bantha lowed again.

Cliegg gave a growl in the general direction of the sound, waved his hand, and walked off toward the house. "You keep Beru close for a bit," he instructed. "The both of you stay within the perimeter, and keep a blaster at your side."

Owen nodded and dutifully followed as Cliegg stalked into the house. Right before the pair reached the door, the bantha lowed again.

It didn't seem so far away.

"What's the matter?" Shmi asked the moment Cliegg entered the house.

Her husband stopped, and managed to paste on a bit of a comforting smile. "Just the sand," he said. "Covered some sensors, and I'm getting tired of digging them out." He smiled even wider and walked to the side of the room, heading for the refresher.

"Cliegg . . ." Shmi called suspiciously, stopping him.

Owen came through the door then, and Beru looked at him. "What is it?" she asked, unconsciously echoing Shmi.

"Nothing, nothing at all," Owen replied, but as he crossed the room, Beru stepped before him and took him by the arms, forcing him to look at her directly, into an expression too serious to be dismissed.

"Just signs of a sandstorm," Cliegg lied. "Far off, and probably nothing."

"But already enough to bury some sensors on the perimeter?" Shmi asked.

Owen looked at her curiously, then heard Cliegg clear his throat. He looked to his father, who nodded slightly, then turned back to Shmi and agreed. "The first winds, but I don't think it will be as strong as Dad believes."

"Are you both going to stand there lying to us?" Beru snapped suddenly, stealing the words from Shmi's mouth.

"What did you see, Cliegg?" Shmi demanded.

"Nothing," he answered with conviction.

"Then what did you hear?" Shmi pressed, recognizing her husband's semantic dodge clearly enough.

"I heard a bantha, nothing more," Cliegg admitted.

"And you think it was a Tusken mount," Shmi stated. "How far?"

"Who can tell, in the night, and with the wind shifting? Could've been kilometers."

"Or?"

Cliegg walked back across the room to stand right before his wife. "What do you want from me, love?" he asked, taking her in a firm hug. "I heard a bantha. I don't know if there was a Tusken attached."

"But there have been more signs of the Raiders about," Owen admitted. "The Dorrs found a pile of bantha poodoo half covering one of their perimeter sensors."

"It may be just that there's a few banthas running loose in the area, probably half starved and looking for some food," Cliegg offered.

"Or it might be that the Tuskens are growing bolder, are coming right down to the edges of the farms, and are even beginning to test the security," Shmi said. Almost prophetically, just as she finished, the alarms went off, indicating a breach about the perimeter sensor line.

Owen and Cliegg grabbed their blaster rifles and rushed out of the house, Shmi and Beru close behind.

"You stay here!" Cliegg instructed the two women. "Or go get a weapon, at least!" He glanced about, indicated a vantage point to Owen, and motioned for his son to take up a defensive position and cover him.

Then he rushed across the compound, blaster rifle in hand, zigzagging his way, staying low and scanning for any movement, knowing that if he saw a form that resembled either Tusken or bantha, he'd shoot first and investigate after.

But it didn't come to that. Cliegg and Owen searched the whole of the perimeter, scanned the area and rechecked the alarms, and found no sign of intruders.

All four stayed on edge the remainder of that night, though, each of them keeping a weapon close at hand, and sleeping only in shifts.

The next day, out by the eastern rim, Owen found the source of the alarm: a footprint along a patch of sturdier ground near the edge of the farm. It wasn't the large round depression a bantha would make, but the indentation one might expect from a foot wrapped in soft material, much like a Tusken would wear.

"We should speak with the Dorrs and all the others," Cliegg said when Owen showed the print to him. "Get a group together and chase the animals back into the open desert."

"The banthas?"

"Them, too," Cliegg snarled. He spat upon the ground, as steely-eyed and angry as Owen had ever seen him.

Senator Padmé Amidala felt strangely uneasy in her office, in the same complex as, but unattached to, the royal palace of Queen Jamillia. Her desk was covered in holodisks and all the other usual clutter of her station. At the front of it, a holo played through the numbers, a soldier on one scale, a flag of truce on the other, tallying the predicted votes for the meeting on Coruscant. The hologram depiction of those scales seemed almost perfectly balanced.

Padmé knew that the vote would be close, with the Senate almost evenly divided over whether the Republic should create a formal army. It galled her to think that so many of her colleagues would be voting based on personal gain—everything from potential contracts to supply the army for their home systems to direct payoffs from some of the commerce guilds—rather than on what was best for the Republic.

In her heart, Padmé remained steadfast that she had to work to defeat the creation of this army. The Republic was built on tolerance. It was a vast network of tens of thousands of systems, and even more species, each with a distinct perspective. The only element they shared was tolerance—tolerance of one another. The creation of an army might prove unsettling, even threatening, to so many of those systems and species, beings far removed from the great city-planet of Coruscant.

A commotion outside drew Padmé to the window, and she looked down upon the complex courtyard to see a group of men jostling and fighting as the Naboo security forces rushed in to control the situation.

There came a sharp rap on the door to her office, and as she turned back that way, the portal slid open and Captain Panaka strode in.

"Just checking, Senator," said the man who had served as her personal bodyguard when she was Queen. Tall and dark-skinned, he had a steely gaze and an athletic physique only accentuated by the cut of his brown leather jerkin, blue shirt, and pants, and the mere sight of Panaka filled Padmé with comfort. He was in his forties now, but still looked as if he could outfight any man on Naboo.

"Shouldn't you be seeing to the security of Queen Jamillia?" Padmé asked.

Panaka nodded. "She is well protected, I assure you."

"From?" Padmé prompted, nodding toward the window and the continuing disturbance beyond.

"Spice miners," Panaka explained. "Contract issues. Nothing

to concern you, Senator. Actually, I was on my way here to speak with you about security for your return trip to Coruscant."

"That is weeks away."

Panaka looked to the window. "Which gives us more time to properly prepare."

Padmé knew better than to argue with the stubborn man. Since she would be flying an official starship of the Naboo fleet, Panaka had the right, if not the responsibility, to get involved. And in truth, his concern pleased her, although she'd never admit it to him.

A shout outside and renewed fighting drew her attention briefly, making her wince. Another problem. There was always a problem, somewhere. Padmé had to wonder if that was just the nature of people, to create some excitement when all seemed well. Given that unsettling thought, Sola's words came back to her, along with images of Ryoo and Pooja. How she loved those two carefree little sprites!

"Senator?" Panaka said, drawing her out of her private contemplations.

"Yes?"

"We should discuss the security procedures."

It pained Padmé to let go of the images of her nieces at that moment, but she nodded and forced herself back into her responsible mode. Captain Panaka had said that they had to discuss security, and so Padmé Amidala had to discuss security.

The Lars family was being serenaded through yet another night by the lowing of many banthas. None of the four had any doubt that Tuskens were out there, not far from the farm, perhaps even then watching its lights.

"They're wild beasts, and we should have gotten the Mos Eisley authorities to exterminate them like the vermin they are. Them and the stinking Jawas!"

Shmi sighed and put her hand on her husband's tense forearm. "The Jawas have helped us," she reminded him gently.

"Then not the Jawas!" Cliegg roared back, and Shmi jumped. Taking note of Shmi's horrified expression, Cliegg calmed at once. "I'm sorry. Not the Jawas, then. But the Tuskens. They kill and steal whenever and wherever they can. No good comes of them!"

"If they try to come in here, there'll be less of them to chase back out into the desert," Owen offered, and Cliegg gave him an appreciative nod.

They tried to finish their dinner, but every time a bantha sounded, they all tensed, hands shifting from utensils to readied blasters.

"Listen," Shmi said suddenly, and they all went perfectly quiet, straining their ears. All was quiet outside; no banthas were lowing.

"Perhaps they were just moving by," Shmi offered when she was certain the others had caught on. "Heading back out into the open desert where they belong."

"We'll go out to the Dorrs' in the morning," Cliegg said to Owen. "We'll get all the farmers organized, and maybe get a call in to Mos Eisley, as well." He looked to Shmi and nodded. "Just to make sure."

"In the morning," Owen agreed.

At dawn the next day, Owen and Cliegg started out from the compound before they had even eaten a good breakfast, for Shmi had gone out ahead of them, as she did most mornings, to pick some mushrooms at the vaporators.

They expected to pass her on their way out to the Dorrs' farm but instead found her footprints, surrounded by the imprints of many others, the soft boots of the Tuskens.

Cliegg Lars, as strong and tough a man as the region had ever known, fell to his knees and wept.

"We have to go after her, Dad," came a suddenly solid and unwavering voice.

Cliegg looked up and back to see Owen standing there, a man indeed and no more a boy, his expression grim and determined.

"She is alive and we cannot leave her to them," Owen said with a strange, almost supernatural calm.

Cliegg wiped away the last of his tears and stared hard at his son, then nodded grimly. "Spread the word to the neighboring farms."

There they are!" Sholh Dorr cried, pointing straight ahead, while keeping his speeder bike at full throttle.

The twenty-nine others saw the target, the rising dust of a line of walking banthas. With a communal roar, the outraged farmers pressed on, determined to exact revenge, determined to rescue Shmi, if she was still alive among this band of Tusken Raiders.

Amidst the roar of engines and cries of revenge, they swept down the descending wash, closing fast on the banthas, eager for battle.

Cliegg pumped his head, growling all the while, as if pleading with his speederbike to accelerate even more. He swerved in from the left flank, cutting into the center of the formation, then lowered his head and opened the speederbike up, trying to catch the lead riders. All he wanted was to be in the thick of it, to get his strong arms about a Tusken throat.

The banthas were clearly in sight, then, along with their robed riders.

Another cry went up, one of revenge.

One that fast turned to horror.

The leading edge of the farmer army plowed headlong into a

wire cleverly strung across the field, at neck height to a man riding a speeder bike.

Cliegg's own cry also became one of horror as he watched the decapitation of several of his friends and neighbors, as he watched others thrown to the ground. Purely on instinct, knowing he couldn't stop his speeder in time, Cliegg leapt up, planting one foot on the seat, then leapt again.

Then he felt a flash of pain, and he was spinning head over heels. He landed hard on the rocky ground, skidding briefly.

All the world about him became a blur, a frenzy of sudden activity. He saw the boots of his fellow farmers, heard Owen crying out to him, though it seemed as if his son's voice was far, far away.

He saw the wrapped leather of a Tusken boot, the sand-colored robes, and with a rage that could not be denied by his disorientation, Cliegg grabbed the leg as the Tusken ran past.

He looked up and raised his arms to block as the Tusken brought its staff slamming down at him. Accepting the pain, not even feeling it through his rage, Cliegg shoved forward and wrapped both his arms around the Tusken's legs, tugging the creature down to the ground before him. He crawled over it, his strong hands battering it, then finding the hold he wanted.

Cries of pain, from farmers and Tuskens alike, were all about him, but Cliegg hardly heard them. His hands remained firmly about the Tusken's throat. He choked with all his considerable strength; he lifted the Tusken's head up and bashed it back down, over and over again, and continued to choke and to batter long after the Tusken stopped resisting.

"Dad!"

That cry alone brought Cliegg from his rage. He dropped the Tusken Raider back to the ground and turned about, to see Owen in close battle with another of the Raiders.

Cliegg spun about and started to rise, putting one leg under him, coming up fast . . .

. . . And then he fell hard, his balance inexplicably gone.

Confused, he looked down expecting that another Tusken had tripped him up. But then he saw that it was his own body that had failed him.

Only then did Cliegg Lars realize that he had lost his leg.

Blood pooled all about the ground, pouring from the severed limb. Eyes wide with horror, Cliegg grabbed at his leg.

He called for Owen. He called desperately for Shmi.

A speeder bike whipped past him, a farmer fleeing the massacre, but the man did not slow.

Cliegg tried to call out, but there was no voice to be found past the lump in his throat, the realization that he had failed and that all was lost.

Then a second speeder came by him, this one stopping fast. Reflexively, Cliegg grabbed at it, and before he could even begin to pull himself up at all, it sped away, dragging him along.

"Hold on, Dad!" Owen, the driver, cried to him.

Cliegg did. With the same stubbornness that had sustained him through all the difficult times at the moisture farm, the same gritty determination that had allowed him to conquer the harsh wild land of Tatooine, Cliegg Lars held on. For all his life, and with Tuskens in fast pursuit, Cliegg Lars held on.

And for Shmi, for the only chance she had of any rescue, Cliegg Lars held on.

Back up the slope, Owen stopped the speeder and leapt off, grabbing at his father's torn leg. He tied it off as well as he could with the few moments he had, then helped Cliegg, who was fast slipping from consciousness, to lie over the back of the speeder.

Then Owen sped away, throttle flat out. He knew that he had to get his father home, and quickly. The vicious wound had to be cleaned and sealed.

It occurred to Owen that only a single pair of speeders were to be seen fleeing the massacre ahead of him, and that through all the commotion behind, he didn't hear the hum of a single speeder engine.

Forcing despair away, finding the same grounded determination that sustained Cliegg, Owen didn't think of the many lost friends, didn't think of his father's plight, didn't think of anything except the course to his necessary destination.

"This is not good news," Captain Panaka remarked, after delivering the blow to Senator Amidala.

"We've suspected all along that Count Dooku and his separatists would court the Trade Federation and the various commercial guilds," Padmé replied, trying to put a good face on it all. Panaka had just come in with Captain Typho, his nephew, with the report that the Trade Federation had thrown in with the separatist movement that now threatened to tear the Republic apart.

"Viceroy Gunray is an opportunist," she continued. "He will do anything that he believes will benefit him financially. His loyalties end at his purse. Count Dooku must be offering him favorable trade agreements, free run to produce goods without regard to the conditions of the workers or the effect on the environment. Viceroy Gunray has left more than one planet as a barren dead ball, floating in space. Or perhaps Count Dooku is offering the Trade Federation absolute control of lucrative markets, without competition."

"I'm more concerned with the implications to you, Senator," Panaka remarked, drawing a curious stare from Padmé.

"The separatists have shown themselves not to be above violence," he explained. "There have been assassination attempts across the Republic."

"But wouldn't Count Dooku and the separatists consider Senator Amidala almost an ally at this time?" Captain Typho interjected, and both Panaka and Padmé looked at the usually quiet man in surprise.

Padmé's look quickly turned into a stare; there was an angry edge to her fair features. "I am no friend to any who would dissolve the Republic, Captain," she insisted, her tone leaving no room for debate—and of course, there would be no debating that point. In the few years she had been a Senator, Amidala had shown herself to be among the most loyal and powerful supporters of the Republic, a legislator determined to improve the system, but to do so within the framework of the Republic's constitution. Senator Amidala fervently believed that the real beauty of the governing system was its built-in abilities, even demands, for self-improvement.

"Agreed, Senator," Typho said with a bow. He was shorter than his uncle but powerfully built, muscles filling the blue sleeves of his uniform, his chest solid under the brown leather tunic. He wore a black leather patch over his left eye, which he had lost in the battle with that same Trade Federation a decade before. Typho had been just a teenager then, but had shown himself well, and made his uncle Panaka proud. "And no offense meant. But on this issue concerning the creation of an army of the Republic, you have remained firmly in the court of negotiation over force. Would not the separatists agree with your vote?"

When Padmé put her initial outrage aside and considered the point, she had to agree.

"Count Dooku has thrown in with Nute Gunray, say the reports," Panaka cut in, his tone flat and determined. "That mere fact demands that we tighten security about Senator Amidala."

"Please do not speak about me as though I am not here," she scolded, but Panaka didn't blink.

"In matters of security, Senator, you *are* not here," he replied. "At least, your voice is not. My nephew reports to me, and his responsibilities on this matter cannot be undermined. Take all precautions."

With that, he bowed curtly and walked away, and Padmé suppressed her immediate desire to rebuke him. He was right, and she was better off because he dared to point it out. She looked back at Captain Typho.

"We will be vigilant, Senator."

"I have my duty, and that duty demands that I soon return to Coruscant," she said.

"And I have my duty," Typho assured her, and like Panaka, he offered a bow and walked away.

Padmé Amidala watched him go, then gave a great sigh, remembering Sola's words to her and wondering honestly if she would ever find the opportunity to follow her sister's advice—advice that she was finding strangely tempting at that particular moment. She realized then that she hadn't seen Sola, or the kids, or her parents, in nearly two weeks, not since that afternoon in the backyard with Ryoo and Pooja.

Time did seem to be slipping past her.

"It won't move fast enough to catch up to the Tuskens!" Cliegg Lars bellowed in protest as his son and future daughter-in-law helped him into a hoverchair that Owen had fashioned. He seemed oblivious to the pain of his wound, where his right leg had been sheared off at midthigh.

"The Tuskens are long gone, Dad," Owen Lars said quietly, and he put his hand on Cliegg's broad shoulder, trying to calm him. "If you won't use a mechno-leg, this powerchair will have to do."

"You'll not be making me into a half-droid, that's for sure," Cliegg retorted. "This little buggy will do fine."

"We'll get more men together," he said, his voice rising frantically, his hand instinctively moving down to the stump of his leg. "You get to Mos Eisley and see what support they'll offer. Send Beru to the farms."

"They've no more to offer," Owen replied honestly. He moved close to the chair and bent low, looking Cliegg square in the face. "All the farms will be years in recovering from the ambush. So many families have been shattered from the attack, and even more from the rescue attempt."

"How can you talk like that with your mother out there?" Cliegg Lars roared, his frustration boiling over—and all the more so because in his heart, he knew that Owen was speaking truthfully.

Owen took a deep breath, but did not back down from that imposing look. "We have to be realistic, Dad. It's been two weeks since they took her," he said grimly, leaving the implications unspoken. Implications that Cliegg Lars, who knew the dreaded Tuskens well, surely understood.

All of a sudden, Cliegg's broad shoulders slumped in defeat, and his fiery gaze softened as his eyes turned toward the ground. "She's gone," the wounded man whispered. "Really gone."

Behind him, Beru Whitesun started to cry.

Beside him, Owen fought back his own tears and stood calm and tall, the firm foundation determined above all to hold them together during this devastating time.

The four starships skimmed past the great skyscrapers of Coruscant, weaving in and out of the huge amber structures, artificial stalagmites rising higher and higher over the years, and now obscuring the natural formations of the planet unlike anywhere else in the known galaxy. Sunlight reflected off the many mirrorlike windows of those massive structures, and gleamed brilliantly off the chrome of the sleek ships. The larger starship, which resembled a flying silver boomerang, almost glowed, smooth and flowing with huge and powerful engines set on each of its arms, a third of the way to the wingtip. Alongside it soared several Naboo starfighters, their graceful engines set out on wings from the main hulls with their distinctive elongated tails.

One of the starfighters led the procession, veering around and about nearly every passing tower, running point for the second ship, the Naboo Royal Cruiser. Behind that larger craft came two more fighters, running swift and close to the Royal Cruiser, shielding her, pilots ready to instantly intercept any threat.

The lead fighter avoided the more heavily trafficked routes of the great city, where potential enemies might be flying within the cover of thousands of ordinary vehicles. Many knew that Senator

Amidala of Naboo was returning to the Senate to cast her vote against the creation of an army to assist the overwhelmed Jedi in their dealings with the increasingly antagonistic separatist movement, and there were many factions that did not want such a vote to be cast. Amidala had made many enemies during her reign as Naboo's Queen, powerful enemies with great resources at their disposal, and with, perhaps, enough hatred for the beautiful young Senator to put some of those resources to work to her detriment.

In the lead fighter, Corporal Dolphe, who had distinguished himself greatly in the Naboo war against the Trade Federation, breathed a sigh of relief as the appointed landing platform came into sight, appearing secure and clear. Dolphe, a tough warrior who revered his Senator greatly, flew past the landing platform to the left, then cut a tight turn back to the right, encircling the great structure, the Senatorial Apartment Building, adjacent to the landing platform. He kept his fighter up and about as the other two fighters put down side by side on one end of the platform, the Royal Cruiser hovering nearby for just a moment, then gently landing.

Dolphe did another circuit, then, seeing no traffic at all in the vicinity, settled his fighter across the way from his companion craft. He didn't put it down all the way just yet, though, but remained ready to swivel about and strike hard at any attackers, if need be.

Opposite him, the other two fighter pilots threw back their respective canopies and climbed from their cockpits. One, Captain Typho, recently appointed as Amidala's chief security officer by his uncle Panaka, pulled off his flight helmet and shook his head, running a hand over his short, woolly black hair and adjusting the black leather patch he wore over his left eye.

"We made it," Typho said as his fellow fighter pilot leapt down from a wing to stand beside him. "I guess I was wrong. There was no danger at all."

"There's always danger, Captain," the other responded in a distinctly female voice. "Sometimes we're just lucky enough to avoid it."

Typho started to respond, but paused and looked back toward the cruiser, where the ramp was already lowering to the platform. The plan had been to get the contingent off the exposed platform and into a transport vehicle as quickly as possible. Two Naboo guards appeared, alert and ready, their blaster rifles presented before them. Typho nodded grimly, glad to see that his soldiers were taking nothing for granted, that they understood the gravity of the situation and their responsibility here in protecting the Senator.

Next came Amidala, in her typical splendor, with her paradoxical beauty, both simple and involved. With her large brown eyes and soft features, Amidala could outshine anyone about her, even if she was dressed in simple peasant's clothing, but in her Senatorial attire, this time a fabulous weave of black and white, and with her hair tied up and exaggerated by a black headdress, she outshone the stars themselves. Her mixture of intelligence and beauty, of innocence and allure, of courage and integrity and yet with a good measure of a child's mischievousness, floored Typho every time he looked upon her.

The captain turned from the descending entourage back to Dolphe across the way, offering a satisfied nod in acknowledgment of the man's point-running work.

And then, suddenly, Typho was lying facedown on the permacrete, thrown to the ground by a tremendous concussion, blinded for a moment by a brilliant flash as an explosion roared behind him. He looked up as his vision returned to see Dolphe sprawled on the ground.

Everything seemed to move in slow motion for Typho at that terrible moment. He heard himself yelling "No!" as he scrambled to his knees and turned about.

Pieces of burning metal spread through the Coruscant sky like fireworks, fanning high and wide from the wreckage. The remaining hulk of the Royal Cruiser burned brightly, and seven figures lay on the ground before it, one wearing the decorated raiments that Typho knew so very well.

Disoriented from the blast, the captain stumbled as he tried to rise. A great lump welled in his throat, for he knew what had happened.

Typho was a veteran warrior, had seen battle, had seen people die violently, and in looking at those bodies, in looking at Amidala's beautiful robes, at their placement about the very still form, he instinctively knew.

The woman's wounds were surely mortal. She was fast dying, if not already dead.

"You reset the coordinates!" Obi-Wan Kenobi said to his young Padawan. Obi-Wan's wheat-colored hair was longer now, hanging loosely about his shoulders, and a beard, somewhat unkempt, adorned his still-young-looking face. His light brown Jedi traveling clothes, loose fitting and comfortable, seemed to settle on him well. For Obi-Wan had become comfortable, had grown into the skin of Jedi Knight. No longer was he the intense and impulsive Jedi Padawan learner under the training of Qui-Gon Jinn.

His companion at this time, however, appeared quite the opposite. Anakin Skywalker looked as if his tall, thin frame simply could not contain his overabundance of energy. He was dressed similarly to Obi-Wan, but his clothing seemed tighter, crisper, and his muscles under it always seemed taut with readiness. His sandy-blond hair was cropped short now, except for the thin braid indicative of his status as a Jedi Padawan. His blue eyes flashed repeatedly, as if bursts of energy were escaping.

"Just to lengthen our time in hyperspace a bit," he explained. "We'll come out closer to the planet."

Obi-Wan gave a great and resigned sigh and sat down at the console, noting the coordinates Anakin had input. There was little the Jedi could do about it now, of course, for a hyperspace leap couldn't be reset once the jump to lightspeed had already been made. "We cannot exit hyperspace too close to Coruscant's approach lanes. There's too much congestion for a safe flight. I've already explained this to you."

"But—"

"Anakin," Obi-Wan said pointedly, as if he were scolding a pet perootu cat, and he tightened his wide jaw and stared hard at his Padawan.

"Yes, Master," Anakin said, obediently looking down.

Obi-Wan held the glare for just a moment longer. "I know that you're anxious to get there," he conceded. "We have been too long away from home."

Anakin didn't look up, but Obi-Wan could see the edges of his lips curl up in a bit of a smile.

"Never do this again," Obi-Wan warned, and he turned and walked out of the shuttle's bridge.

Anakin flopped down into the pilot's chair, his chin falling into his hand, his eyes set on the control panels. The order had been about as direct as one could get, of course, and so Anakin silently told himself that he would adhere to it. Still, as he considered their current destination, and who awaited them there, he thought the scolding worth it, even if his resetting of the coordinates had bought him only a few extra hours on Coruscant. He was indeed anxious to get there, though not for the reason Obi-Wan had stated. It wasn't the Jedi Temple that beckoned to the Padawan, but rather a rumor he had heard over the comm chatter that a certain Senator, formerly the Queen of Naboo, was on her way to address the Senate.

Padmé Amidala.

The name resonated in young Anakin's heart and soul. He hadn't seen her in a decade, not since he, along with Obi-Wan and Qui-Gon, had helped her in her struggle against the Trade Federation on Naboo. He had only been ten years old at that time, but from the moment he had first laid eyes on Padmé, young Anakin had known that she was the woman he would marry.

Never mind that Padmé was several years older than he was. Never mind that he was just a boy when he had known her, when she had known him. Never mind that Jedi were not allowed to marry.

Anakin had simply known, without question, and the image of beautiful Padmé Amidala had stayed with him, had been burned into his every dream and fantasy, every day since he had left Naboo with Obi-Wan a decade ago. He could still smell the freshness of her hair, could still see the sparkle of intelligence and passion in her wondrous brown eyes, could still hear the melody that was Padmé's voice.

Hardly registering the movement, Anakin let his hands return to the controls of the nav computer. Perhaps he could find a little-used lane through the Coruscant traffic congestion to get them home faster.

Klaxons blared and myriad alarms rent the air all about the area, screaming loudly, drowning out the cries from the astonished onlookers and the wails of the injured.

Typho's companion pilot raced past him, and the captain scrambled to regain his footing and follow. Across the way, Dolphe was up and similarly running toward the fallen form of the Senator.

The female fighter pilot arrived first, dropping to one knee beside the fallen woman. She pulled the helmet from her head and quickly shook her brown tresses free.

"Senator!" Typho yelled. It was indeed Padmé Amidala kneeling beside the dying woman, her decoy. "Come, the danger has not passed!"

But Padmé waved the captain back furiously, then bent low to her fallen friend.

"Cordé," she said quietly, her voice breaking. Cordé was one of her beloved bodyguards, a woman who had been with her, serving her and serving Naboo, for many years. Padmé gathered Cordé up in her arms, hugging her gently.

Cordé opened her eyes, rich brown orbs so similar to Padmé's own. "I'm sorry, m'Lady," she gasped, struggling for breath with every word. "I'm . . . not sure I . . ." She paused and lay there, staring at Padmé. "I've failed you."

"No!" Padmé insisted, arguing the bodyguard's reasoning, arguing against all of this insanity. "No, no, no!"

Cordé continued to stare at her, or stare past her, it seemed to the grief-stricken young Senator. Looking past her and past everything, Cordé's eyes stared into a far different place.

Padmé felt her relax suddenly, as if her spirit simply leapt from her corporeal form.

"Cordé!" the Senator cried, and she hugged her friend close, rocking back and forth, denying this awful reality.

"M'Lady, you are still in danger!" Typho declared, trying to sound sympathetic, but with a clear sense of urgency in his voice.

Padmé lifted her head from the side of Cordé's face, and took a deep and steadying breath. Looking upon her dead friend, remembering all at once the many times they had spent together, she gently lowered Cordé to the ground. "I shouldn't have come back," she said as she stood up beside the wary Typho, tears streaking her cheeks.

Captain Typho came up out of his ready stance long enough to lock stares with his Senator. "This vote is very important," he reminded her, his tone uncompromising, the voice of a man sworn to duty above all else. So much like his uncle. "You did your duty, Senator, and Cordé did hers. Now come."

He started away, grabbing Padmé's arm, but she shrugged off his grasp and stood there, staring down at her lost friend.

"Senator Amidala! Please!"

Padmé looked over at the man.

"Would you so diminish Cordé's death as to stand here and risk your own life?" Typho bluntly stated. "What good will her sacrifice be if—"

"Enough, Captain," Padmé interrupted.

Typho motioned for Dolphe to run a defensive perimeter behind them, then he led the stricken Padmé away.

Back over at Padmé's Naboo fighter, R2-D2 beeped and squealed and fell into line behind them.

The Senate Building on Coruscant wasn't one of the tallest buildings in the city. Dome-shaped and relatively low, it did not soar up to the clouds, catching the afternoon sun as the others did in a brilliant display of shining amber. And yet the magnificent structure was not dwarfed by those towering skyscrapers about it, including the various Senate apartment complexes. Centrally located in the complex, and with a design very different from the typical squared skyscraper, the bluish smooth dome provided a welcome relief to the eye of the beholder, a piece of art within a community of simple efficiency.

The interior of the building was no less vast and impressive, its gigantic rotunda encircled, row upon row, by the floating platforms of the many Senators of the Republic, representing the great majority of the galaxy's inhabitable worlds. A significant number of those platforms stood empty now, because of the separatist movement. Several thousand systems had joined in with Count Dooku over the last couple of years to secede from a Republic that had, in their eyes, grown too ponderous to be effective, a claim that even the staunchest supporters of the Republic could not completely dispute.

Still, with this most important vote scheduled, the walls of

the circular room echoed, hundreds and hun<del>ds of voices chat-</del>
tering all at once, expressing emotions from<del>er to regret to</del>
determination.

In the middle of the main floor, standing<del>stationary</del>
dais, the one unmoving speaking platform in th<del>building,</del>
Supreme Chancellor Palpatine watched and list<del>aking in</del>
the tumult and wearing an expression that showed<del>oncern.</del>
He was past middle age now, with silver hair and <del>ceased</del>
by deep lines of experience. His term limit had <del>eral</del>
years ago, but a series of crises had allowed him to s<del>ice</del>
well beyond the legal limit. From a distance, one <del>dot</del>
thought him frail, but up close there could be no do<del>t</del>
strength and fortitude of this accomplished man.

"They are afraid, Supreme Chancellor," Palpatine's
Gizen, remarked to him. "Many have heard reports
demonstrations, even violent activity near this very bu
The separatists—"

Palpatine held up his hand to quiet the nervous aide. "
are a troublesome group," he replied. "It would seem that Co
Dooku has whipped them into murderous frenzy. Or perhaps,
he said with apparent reflection, "their frustrations are mounting
despite the effort of that estimable former Jedi to calm them. Either way, the separatists must be taken seriously."

Uv Gizen started to respond again, but Palpatine put a finger to pursed lips to silence him, then nodded to the main podium, where his majordomo, Mas Amedda, was calling for order.

"Order! We shall have order!" the majordomo cried, his bluish skin brightening with agitation. His lethorn head tentacles, protruding from the back side of his skull and wrapping down over his collar to frame his head like a cowl, twitched anxiously, their brownish-tipped horns bobbing on his chest. And as he turned side to side, his primary horns, standing straight for almost half a meter above his head, rotated like antennae gathering information on the crowd. Mas Amedda was an imposing

figure in the S^ce, but the chatter, the thousand private conversations, c^ued.
"Senat^lease!" Mas Amedda called loudly. "Indeed, we
have mu^discuss. Many important issues. But the motion
before ^his time, to commission an army to protect the Re-
publi^at precedence. That is what we will vote on at this
tim^at alone! Other business must defer."
     ^s complaints came back at Mas Amedda, and a few con-
     ^llor seemed to gather momentum, but then Supreme
     ^thering Palpatine stepped up to the podium, staring out over
     ^ference, and the great hall went silent. Mas Amedda bowed
     ^oulders to the great man and stepped aside.
Palpatine placed his hands on the rim of the podium, his
noticeably sagging, his head bowed. The curious pos-
ure only heightened the tension, making the cavernous room
seem even more silent, if that was possible.

"My esteemed colleagues," he began slowly and deliberately,
but even with that effort, his voice wavered and seemed as if it
would break apart. Curiosity sent murmurs rumbling throughout the nervous gathering once more. It wasn't often that
Supreme Chancellor Palpatine appeared rattled.

"Excuse me," Palpatine said quietly. Then, a moment later,
he straightened and inhaled deeply, seeming to gather inner
strength, which was amply reflected in his solid voice as he repeated, "My esteemed colleagues. I have just received some
tragic and disturbing news. Senator Amidala of the Naboo system . . . has been assassinated!"

A shock wave of silence rolled about the crowd; eyes
went wide; mouths, for those who had mouths, hung open in
disbelief.

"This grievous blow is especially personal to me," Palpatine
explained. "Before I became Chancellor, I was a Senator, serving Amidala when she was Queen of Naboo. She was a great
leader who fought for justice. So beloved was she among her
people that she could have been elected Queen for life!" He

dala. His expression was one of blatant shock, for just a moment, but then he shook himself out of it and a smile widened upon his face.

"My noble colleagues," Amidala said loudly, and the sound of her most familiar voice quieted many of the Senators, who turned to regard her. "I concur with the Supreme Chancellor. At all costs, we do not want war!"

Gradually at first, but then more quickly, the Senate Hall went quiet, and then came a thunderous outburst of cheering and applause.

"It is with great surprise and joy that the chair recognizes the Senator from Naboo, Padmé Amidala," Palpatine declared.

Amidala waited for the cheering and clapping to subside, then began slowly and deliberately. "Less than an hour ago, an assassination attempt was made upon my life. One of my bodyguards and six others were ruthlessly and senselessly murdered. I was the target, but, more important, I believe this security measure before you was the target. I have led the opposition to building an army, but there is someone who will stop at nothing to assure its passage."

Cheers became boos from many areas of the gallery as those surprising words registered, and many others shook their heads in confusion. Had Amidala just accused someone in the Senate of trying to assassinate her?

As she stood there, her gaze moving about the vast, circular room, Amidala knew that her words, on the surface, could be seen as an insult to many. In truth, though, she wasn't thinking along those lines concerning the source of the assassination. She had a definite hunch, one that went against the obvious logic. The people who would most logically want her silenced were indeed those in favor of the formation of an army of the Republic, but for some reason she could not put her finger on—some subconscious clues, perhaps, or just a gut feeling—Amidala believed that the source of the attempt was exactly those who would not logically, on the surface, at least, want her silenced. She remembered Panaka's warning about the Trade Federation reportedly joining hands with the separatists.

She took a deep breath, steeling herself against the growing rancor in the audience, and steadfastly went on. "I warn you, if you vote to create this army, war will follow. I have experienced the misery of war firsthand; I do not wish to do so again."

The cheering began to outweigh the booing.

"This is insanity, I say!" Orn Free Taa yelled above it all. "I move that we defer this vote, immediately!" But that suggestion only led to more yelling.

Amidala looked at the Twi'lek Senator, understanding his sudden desire to defer a vote that her mere presence had cast into doubt.

"Wake up, Senators—you must wake up!" she went on, shouting him down. "If we offer the separatists violence, they can only show us violence in return! Many will lose their lives, and all will lose their freedom. This decision could well destroy the very foundation of our great Republic! I pray you do not let fear push you into a disastrous decision. Vote down this security measure, which is nothing less than a declaration of war! Does anyone here want that? I cannot believe they do!"

Ask Aak, Orn Free Taa, and Darsana, on their floating platforms down by the podium, exchanged nervous glances as the cheers and boos echoed about the great hall. The fact that Amidala had just survived an assassination attempt and yet was here begging the Senate to put off raising an army against the likely perpetrators only added strength to her argument, only elevated Amidala higher in the eyes of many—and the former Queen of Naboo, having stood firm against the Trade Federation a decade before, was already held in high esteem by many.

At Ask Aak's nod, Orn Free Taa demanded the floor, and was given it promptly by Palpatine.

"By precedence of order, my motion to defer the vote must be dealt with first," Orn Free Taa demanded. "That is the rule of law!"

Amidala glared at the Twi'lek, her expression both angry and frustrated by the obvious delaying tactic. She turned plaintively to Palpatine, but the Supreme Chancellor, though his responding expression seemed to be sympathetic to her plight, could only shrug. He moved to the podium and held up his hands for order, and when the room was quiet enough, announced, "In view of the lateness of the hour and the seriousness of this motion, we will take up these matters tomorrow. Until then, the Senate stands adjourned."

Traffic clogged the Coruscant sky, flowing slowly about the meandering smoggy haze. The sun was up, giving the sprawling city an amber glow, but many lights were still on, shining behind the windows of the great skyscrapers.

The massive towers of the Republic Executive Building loomed above it all, seeming as if they would reach the very heavens. And that seemed fitting indeed, for inside, even at this early hour, the events and participants took on godlike stature to the trillions of common folk of the Republic.

Supreme Chancellor Palpatine sat behind his desk in his spacious and tasteful office, staring across at his four Jedi Master visitors. Across the room, a pair of red-clad guards flanked the door, imposing, powerful figures, with their great curving helmets and wide, floor-length capes.

"I fear this vote," Palpatine remarked.

"It is unavoidable," replied Mace Windu, a tall and muscular human, bald, and with penetrating eyes, standing next to the even taller Ki-Adi-Mundi.

"And it could unravel the remainder of the Republic," Palpatine said. "Never have I seen the Senators so at odds over any issue."

"Few issues would carry the import of creating a Republic

army," Jedi Master Plo Koon remarked. He was a tall, sturdy Kel Dor, his head ridged and ruffled at the sides like the curly hair of a young girl, and with dark, shadowed eyes and a black mask over the lower portion of his face. "The Senators are anxious and afraid, and believe that no vote will ever be more important than this one now before them."

"And this way or that, much mending must you do," said Master Yoda, the smallest in physical stature, but a Jedi Master who stood tall against anyone in the galaxy. Yoda's huge eyes blinked slowly and his tremendous ears swiveled subtly, showing, for those who knew him, that he was deep in thought, giving this situation his utmost attention. "Unseen is much that is here," he said, and he closed his eyes in contemplation.

"I don't know how much longer I can hold off the vote, my friends," Palpatine explained. "And I fear that delay on this definitive issue might well erode the Republic through attrition. More and more star systems are joining the separatists."

Mace Windu, a pillar of strength even among the Jedi, nodded his understanding of the dilemma. "And yet, when the vote is done, if the losers do break away—"

"I will not let this Republic that has stood for a thousand years be split in two!" Palpatine declared, slamming a fist determinedly on his desk. "My negotiations will not fail!"

Mace Windu held his calm, keeping his rich voice even and controlled. "But if they do, you must realize there aren't enough Jedi to protect the Republic. We are keepers of the peace, not soldiers."

Palpatine took a few steadying breaths, trying to digest it all. "Master Yoda," he said, and he waited for the greenish-skinned Jedi to regard him. "Do you really think it will come to war?"

Again Yoda closed his eyes. "Worse than war, I fear," he said. "Much worse."

"What?" an alarmed Palpatine asked.

"Master Yoda, what do you sense?" Mace Windu prompted.

"Impossible to see, the future is," the small Jedi Master replied, his great orbs still looking inward. "The dark side clouds everything. But this I am sure of . . ." He popped open his eyes and stared hard at Palpatine. "Do their duty, the Jedi will."

A brief look of confusion came over the Supreme Chancellor, but before he could begin to respond to Yoda, a hologram appeared on his desk, the image of Dar Wac, one of his aides. "The loyalist committee has arrived, my Lord," said Dar Wac, in Huttese.

"Send them in."

The hologram disappeared and Palpatine rose, along with the seated Jedi, to properly greet the distinguished visitors. They came in two groups, Senator Padmé Amidala walking with Captain Typho, Jar Jar Binks, her handmaiden Dormé, and majordomo Mas Amedda, followed by two other Senators, Bail Organa of Alderaan and Horox Ryyder.

Everyone moved to exchange pleasant greetings, and Yoda pointedly tapped Padmé with his small cane.

"With you, the Force is strong, young Senator," the Jedi Master told her. "Your tragedy on the landing platform, terrible. To see you alive brings warm feelings to my heart."

"Thank you, Master Yoda," she replied. "Do you have any idea who was behind this attack?"

Her question had everyone in the room turning to regard her and Yoda directly.

Mace Windu cleared his throat and stepped forward. "Senator, we have nothing definitive, but our intelligence points to disgruntled spice miners on the moons of Naboo."

Padmé looked to Captain Typho, who shook his head, having no answers. They had both witnessed the frustration of those spice miners back on Naboo, but those demonstrations seemed a long way from the tragedy that had occurred on the landing platform here on Coruscant. Releasing Typho from her gaze, she stared hard at Mace Windu, wondering if it would be wise to voice her hunch at this time. She knew the controversy she might stir, knew the blatant illogical ring to her claim, but still . . .

"I do not wish to disagree," she said, "but I think that Count Dooku was behind it."

A stir of surprise rippled about the room, and the four Jedi Masters exchanged looks that ranged from astonishment to disapproval.

"You know, M'Lady," Mace said in his resonant and calm voice, "Count Dooku was once a Jedi. He wouldn't assassinate anyone. It's not in his character."

"He is a political idealist," Ki-Adi-Mundi, the fourth of the Jedi contingent, added. "Not a murderer." With his great domed head, the Cerean Jedi Master stood taller than anyone in the room, and the ridged flaps at the side of his pensive face added a measure of introspection to his imposing physical form.

Master Yoda tapped his cane, drawing attention to himself, and that alone exerted a calming influence over the increasingly tense mood. "In dark times, nothing is what it appears to be," the diminutive figure remarked. "But the fact remains, Senator, in grave danger you are."

Supreme Chancellor Palpatine gave a dramatic sigh and walked over to the window, staring out at the Coruscant dawn. "Master Jedi," he said, "may I suggest that the Senator be placed under the protection of your graces?"

"Do you think that a wise use of our limited resources at this stressful time?" Senator Bail Organa was quick to interject, stroking his well-trimmed black goatee. "Thousands of systems have gone over fully to the separatists, and many more may soon join them. The Jedi are our—"

"Chancellor," Padmé interrupted, "if I may comment. I do not believe the—"

"Situation is that serious," Palpatine finished for her. "No, but I do, Senator."

"Chancellor, please!" she pleaded. "I do not want any more guards!"

Palpatine stared at her as would an overprotective father, a look that Padmé might have viewed as condescending from any other man. "I realize all too well that additional security might be disruptive for you," he began, and he paused, and then a look came over him as if he had just struck upon a logical and acceptable compromise. "But perhaps someone you are familiar with, an old friend." Smiling cleverly, Palpatine looked to Mace Windu and Yoda. "Master Kenobi?" he finished with a nod, and his smile only widened when Mace Windu nodded back.

"That's possible," the Jedi confirmed. "He has just returned from a border dispute on Ansion."

"You must remember him, M'Lady," Palpatine said, grinning as if it was a done deal. "He watched over you during the blockade conflict."

"This is not necessary, Chancellor," Padmé said determinedly, but Palpatine didn't relinquish his grin in the least, showing clearly that he knew well how to defeat the independent Senator's argument.

"Do it for me, M'Lady. Please. I will rest easier. We had a big scare today. The thought of losing you is unbearable."

Several times, Amidala started to respond, but how could she possibly say anything to deny the Supreme Chancellor's expressed concern? She gave a great defeated sigh, and the Jedi rose and turned to leave.

"I will have Obi-Wan report to you immediately, M'Lady," Mace Windu informed her.

As he passed, Yoda leaned in close to Padmé and whispered so that only she could hear, "Too little about yourself you worry, Senator, and too much about politics. Be mindful of your danger, Padmé. Accept our help."

They all left the room, and Padmé Amidala stared at the door and the flanking guards for a long while.

Behind her, at the back of his office, Chancellor Palpatine watched them all.

"It troubles me to hear Count Dooku's name mentioned in such a manner, Master," Mace said to Yoda as the Jedi made their way back to their Council chamber. "And from one as esteemed as Senator Amidala. Any mistrust of Jedi, or even former Jedi, in times such as these can be disastrous."

"Deny Dooku's involvement in the separatist movement, we cannot," Yoda reminded him.

"Nor can we deny that he began in that movement because of ideals," Mace argued. "He was once our friend—that we must not forget—and to hear him slandered and named as an assassin—"

"Not named," Yoda said. "But darkness there is, about us all, and in that darkness, nothing is what it seems."

"But it makes little sense to me that Count Dooku would make an attempt on the life of Senator Amidala, when she is the one most adamantly opposed to the creation of an army. Would the separatists not wish Amidala well in her endeavors? Would they not believe that she is, however unintentionally, an ally to their cause? Or are we really to believe that they want war with the Republic?"

Yoda leaned heavily on his cane, seeming very weary, and his huge eyes slowly closed. "More is here than we can know," he said very quietly. "Clouded is the Force. Troubling it is."

Mace dismissed his forthcoming reflexive response, a further defense of his old friend Dooku. Count Dooku had been among the most accomplished of the Jedi Masters, respected among the Council, a student of the older and, some would say, more profound Jedi philosophies and styles, including an arcane lightsaber fighting style that was more front and back, thrust and riposte, than the typical circular movements currently employed by most of the Jedi. What a blow it had been to the Jedi Order, and to Mace Windu, when Dooku had walked away from them, and for many of the same reasons the separatists were now trying to walk away: the perception that the Republic had grown too ponderous and unresponsive to the needs of the individual, even of individual systems.

It was no less troubling to Mace Windu concerning Dooku, as it was, no doubt, to Amidala and Palpatine concerning the separatists, that some of the arguments against the Republic were not without merit.

As the lights of Coruscant dimmed, gradually replaced by the natural lights of the few twinkling stars that could get through the nearly continual glare, the great and towering city took on a vastly different appearance. Under the dark evening sky, the skyscrapers seemed to become gigantic natural mono- liths, and all the supersized structures that so dominated the city, that so marked Coruscant as a monument to the ingenuity of the reasoning species, seemed somehow the mark of folly, of futile pride striving against the vastness and majesty beyond the grasp of any mortal. Even the wind at the higher levels of the structures sounded mournful, almost as a herald to what would eventually, inevitably, become of the great city and the great civilization.

As Obi-Wan Kenobi and Anakin Skywalker stood in the turbolift of the Senate apartment complex, the Jedi Master was indeed pondering such profound universal truths as the subtle change of day to night. Beside him, though, his young Padawan certainly was not. Anakin was about to see Padmé again, the woman who had captured his heart and soul when he was but ten years old and had never let it go.

"You seem a little on edge, Anakin," Obi-Wan noted as the lift continued its climb.

ATTACK OF THE CLONES

"Not at all," came the unconvincing reply.

"I haven't seen you this nervous since we fell into that nest of gundarks."

"You fell into that nightmare, Master, and I rescued you. Remember?"

Obi-Wan's little distraction seemed to have the desired effect, and the pair shared a much-needed laugh. Coming out of it, though, Anakin remained obviously on edge.

"You're sweating," Obi-Wan noted. "Take a deep breath. Relax."

"I haven't seen her in ten years."

"Anakin, relax," Obi-Wan reiterated. "She's not the Queen anymore."

The lift door slid open and Obi-Wan started away, while Anakin, behind him, muttered under his breath, "That's not why I'm nervous."

As the pair stepped into the corridor, a door across the way slid open and a well-dressed Gungan, wearing fine red and black robes, stepped into the corridor opposite them. The three regarded each other for just a moment, and then the Gungan diplomat, losing all sense of reserve and propriety, began hopping around like a child.

"Obi! Obi! Obi!" Jar Jar Binks cried, tongue and ears flapping. "Mesa so smilen to see'en yousa! Wahoooo!"

Obi-Wan smiled politely, though his glance at Anakin did show that he was a bit embarrassed, and he patted his hands gently in the air, trying to calm the excitable fellow. "It's good to see you, too, Jar Jar."

Jar Jar continued to hop about for just a moment, then suddenly, and with obvious great effort, calmed down. "And this, mesa guessen, issen yousa apprentice," he went on, and the Gungan seemed to have much more control of himself. For a moment, at least, until he took a good look at the young Padawan, and all pretense melted away. "Noooooooo!" he shrieked, clapping his hands together. "Annie? Nooooooooo! Little bitty Annie?" Jar Jar grabbed the Padawan and pulled him forcefully to arm's length, studying him head to toe. "Noooooooo! Yousa so biggen! Yiyiyiyi! Annie! Mesa no believen!"

Now it was Anakin's turn to wear the embarrassed smile. Politely, he offered no resistance as the overexcited Gungan slammed him into a crushing hug, childish hops shaking him violently.

"Hi, Jar Jar," Anakin managed to say, and Jar Jar just continued on, hopping and crying out his name, and issuing a series of strange *yiyi* sounds. It seemed as if it would go on forever, but then Obi-Wan gently but firmly grabbed Jar Jar by the arm. "We have come to speak with Senator Amidala. Could you show us to her?"

Jar Jar stopped bouncing and looked at Obi-Wan intently, his duck-billed face taking on a more serious expression. "Shesa expecting yousa. Annie! Mesa no believen!" His head bobbed a bit more, then he grabbed Anakin by the hand and pulled him along.

The apartment inside was tastefully decorated, with cushiony chairs and a divan set in a circular pattern in the center, and a few, well-placed artworks set about the walls. Dormé and Typho were in the room, standing beside the divan, the captain wearing his typical military garb, blue uniform under a brown leather tunic, with black leather gloves and a stiff cap, its brim and band of black leather. Beside him stood Dormé in one of the elegant, yet understated dresses typical of Padmé's handmaidens.

Anakin, though, didn't see either of them. He focused on the third person in the room, Padmé, and on her alone, and if he had ever held any moments of doubt that she was as beautiful as he remembered her, they were washed away, then and there. His eyes roamed the Senator's small and shapely frame in her black and deep purple robes, taking in every detail. He saw her thick brown hair, drawn up high and far at the back of her head in a basketlike accessory, and wanted to lose himself in it. He saw her eyes and wanted to stare into them for eternity. He saw her lips, and wanted to . . .

Anakin closed his eyes for just a moment and inhaled deeply, and he could smell her again, the scent that had been burned into him as Padmé's.

It took every ounce of willpower he could muster to walk in slowly and respectfully behind Obi-Wan, and not merely rush in and crush Padmé in a hug . . . and yet, paradoxically, it took every bit of his willpower to move his legs, which were suddenly seeming so very weak, and take that first step into the room, that first step toward her.

"Mesa here. Lookie! Lookie!" screeched Jar Jar, hardly the announcement Obi-Wan would have preferred, but one that he knew he had to expect from the emotionally volatile Gungan. "Desa Jedi arriven."

"It's a pleasure to see you again, M'Lady," Obi-Wan said, moving to stand before the beautiful young Senator.

Standing behind his Master, Anakin continued to stare at the woman, to note her every move. She did glance at him once, though very briefly, and he detected no recognition in her eyes.

Padmé took Obi-Wan's hand in her own. "It has been far too long, Master Kenobi. I'm so glad our paths have crossed again. But I must warn you that I think your presence here is unnecessary."

"I am sure that the members of the Jedi Council have their reasons," Obi-Wan replied.

Padmé wore a resigned, accepting expression at that answer, but a look of curiosity replaced it as she glanced again behind the Jedi Knight, to the young Padawan standing patiently. She took a step to the side, so that she was directly in front of Anakin.

"Annie?" she asked, her expression purely incredulous. Her smile and the flash in her eyes showed that she needed no answer.

For just a flicker, Anakin felt her spirit leap.

"Annie," Padmé said again. "Can it be? My goodness how you've grown!" She looked down and then followed the line of his lean body, tilting her head back to emphasize his height, and he realized that he now towered over her.

That did little to bolster Anakin's confidence, though, so lost was he in the beauty of Padmé. Her smile widened, a clear sign that she was glad to see him, but he missed it, or the implications of it, at least. "So have you," he answered awkwardly, as if he had to force each word from his mouth. "Grown more beautiful, I mean." He cleared his throat and stood taller. "And much shorter," he teased, trying unsuccessfully to sound in control. "For a Senator, I mean."

Anakin noted Obi-Wan's disapproving scowl, but Padmé laughed any tension away and shook her head.

"Oh, Annie, you'll always be that little boy I knew on Tatooine," she said, and if she had taken the lightsaber from his belt and sliced his legs out from under him, she would not have shortened Anakin Skywalker any more.

He looked down, his embarrassment only heightened by the looks he knew that both Obi-Wan and Captain Typho were throwing his way.

"Our presence will be invisible, M'Lady," he heard Obi-Wan assure Padmé.

"I'm very grateful that you're here, Master Kenobi," Captain Typho put in. "The situation is more dangerous than the Senator will admit."

"I don't need any more security," Padmé said, addressing Typho initially, but turning to regard Obi-Wan as she continued. "I need answers. I want to know who is trying to kill me. I believe that there might lie an issue of the utmost importance to the Senate. There is something more here . . ." She stopped as a frown crossed Obi-Wan Kenobi's face.

"We're here to protect you, Senator, not to start an investigation," he said in calm and deliberate tones, but even as he finished, Anakin contradicted him.

"We will find out who's trying to kill you, Padmé," the Padawan insisted. "I promise you."

As soon as he finished, Anakin recognized his error, one that clearly showed on the scowl that Obi-Wan flashed his way. He had been fashioning a response to Padmé in his thoughts, and had hardly even registered his Master's explanation before he had blurted out the obviously errant words. Now he could only bite his lip and lower his gaze.

"We are not going to exceed our mandate, my young Padawan learner!" Obi-Wan said sharply, and Anakin was stung to be so dressed down publicly—especially in front of this particular audience.

"I meant, in the interest of protecting her, Master, of course."

His justification sounded inane even to Anakin.

"We are not going through this exercise again, Anakin," Obi-Wan continued. "You will pay attention to my lead."

Anakin could hardly believe that Obi-Wan was continuing to do this in front of Padmé. "Why?" he asked, turning the question and the debate, trying desperately to regain some footing and credibility.

"What?" Obi-Wan exclaimed, as taken aback as Anakin had ever seen him, and the young Padawan knew that he was pushing too far and too fast.

"Why else do you think we were assigned to her, if not to find the killer?" he asked, trying to bring a measure of calm back to the situation. "Protection is a job for local security, not for Jedi. It's overkill, Master, and so an investigation is implied in our mandate."

"We will do as the Council has instructed," Obi-Wan countered. "And you will learn your place, young one."

"Perhaps with merely your presence about me, the mysteries surrounding this threat will be revealed," offered Padmé, ever the diplomat. She smiled alternately at Anakin and at Obi-Wan, an invitation for civility, and when both leaned back, shoulders visibly relaxing, she added, "Now, if you will excuse me, I will retire."

They all bowed as Padmé and Dormé exited the room, and then Obi-Wan stared hard at his young Padawan again, neither seeming overly pleased with the other.

"Well, I know that I'm glad to have you here," Captain Typho offered, moving closer to the pair. "I don't know what's going on here, but the Senator can't have too much security right now. Your friends on the Jedi Council seem to think that miners have something to do with this, but I can't really agree with that."

"What have you learned?" Anakin asked.

Obi-Wan threw him a look of warning.

"We'll be better prepared to protect the Senator if we have some idea of what we're up against," Anakin explained to his Master, logic he knew that Obi-Wan had to accept as reasonable.

"Not much," Typho admitted. "Senator Amidala leads the opposition to the creation of a Republic army. She's very determined to deal with the separatists through negotiation and not force, but the attempts on her life, even though they've failed, have only strengthened the opposition to her viewpoint in the Senate."

"And since the separatists would not logically wish to see a Republic army formed . . ." Obi-Wan reasoned.

"We're left without a clue," Typho said. "In any such incident, the first questioning eyes turn toward Count Dooku and the separatists." A frown crossed Obi-Wan's face, and Typho quickly added, "Or to some of those loyal to his movement, at least. But why they'd go after Senator Amidala is anyone's guess."

"And we are not here to guess, but merely to protect," Obi-Wan said, in tones that showed he was finished with this particular line of discussion.

Typho bowed, hearing him clearly. "I'll have an officer on every floor, and I'll be at the command center downstairs."

Typho left, then, and Obi-Wan began a search of the room and adjoining chambers, trying to get a feel for the place. Anakin started to do likewise, but he stopped when he walked by Jar Jar Binks.

"Mesa bustin wit happiness seein yousa again, Annie."

"She didn't even recognize me," Anakin said, staring at the door through which Padmé had departed. He shook his head despondently and turned to the Gungan. "I've thought about her every day since we parted, and she's forgotten me completely."

"Why yousa sayen that?" Jar Jar asked.

"You saw her," Anakin replied.

"Shesa happy," the Gungan assured him. "Happier than mesa see'en her in a longo time. These are bad times, Annie. Bombad times!"

Anakin shook his head and started to repeat his distress, but he noted Obi-Wan moving toward him and wisely held his tongue.

Except that his observant Master had already discerned the conversation.

"You're focusing on·the negative again," he said to Anakin. "Be mindful of your thoughts. She was pleased to see us—leave it at that. Now, let's check the security here. We have much to do."

Anakin bowed. "Yes, Master."

He could say the compliant words because he had to, but the young Padawan could not dismiss that which was in his heart and in his thoughts.

Padmé sat at her vanity, brushing her thick brown hair, staring into the mirror but not really seeing anything there. Her thoughts were replaying again and again the image of Anakin, the look he had given her. She heard his words again, ". . . grown more beautiful," and though Padmé was undeniably that, those were not words she was used to hearing. Since she had been a young girl, Padmé had been involved in politics, quickly rising to powerful and influential positions. Most of the men she had come into contact with had been more concerned with what she could bring to them in practical terms than with her beauty, or, for that matter, with any true personal feelings for her. As Queen of Naboo and now as Senator, Padmé was well aware that she was attractive to men in ways deeper than physical attraction, in ways deeper than any emotional bond.

Or perhaps not deeper than the latter, she told herself, for she could not deny the intensity in Anakin's eyes as he had looked at her.

But what did it mean?

She saw him again, in her thoughts. And clearly. Her mental eye roamed over his lean and strong frame, over his face, tight with the intensity that she had always admired, and yet with eyes sparkling with joy, with mischief, with . . .

With longing?

That thought stopped the Senator. Her hands slipped down to her sides, and she sat there, staring at herself, judging her own appearance as Anakin might.

After a few long moments, Padmé shook her head, telling herself that it was crazy. Anakin was a Jedi now. That was their dedication and their oath, and those things, above all else, were things Padmé Amidala admired.

How could he even look at her in such a manner?

So it was all her imagination.

Or was it her fantasy?

Laughing at herself, Padmé lifted her brush to her hair again, but she paused before she had even begun. She was wearing a silky white nightgown, and there were, after all, security cams in her room. Those cams had never really bothered her, since she had always looked at them clinically. Security cams, with guards watching her every move, were a fact of her existence, and so she had learned to go about her daily routines, even the private ones, without a second thought to the intrusive eyes.

But now she realized that a certain young Jedi might be on the other end of those lenses.

Clad in gray armor that was somewhat outdated, burned from countless blaster shots, but still undeniably effective, the bounty hunter stood easily on the ledge, a hundred stories and more up from the Coruscant street. His helmet, too, was gray, except for a blue ridge crossing his eyes and running down from brow to chin. His perch seemed somewhat precarious, considering the wind at this height, but to one as agile and skilled as Jango, and with a penchant for getting himself into and out of difficult places, this was nothing out of the ordinary.

Right on time, a speeder pulled up near the ledge and hovered there. Jango's associate, Zam Wesell, nodded to him and climbed out, stepping lithely onto the ledge in front of a couple of bright advertisement windows. She wore a red veil over the bottom half of her face. This was not a statement of modesty or fashion. Like everything else she wore, from her blaster to her armor to her other concealed and equally deadly weapons, Zam's veil was a practical implement, used to hide her Clawdite features.

Clawdites were not a trusted species, for obvious reasons.

"You know that we failed?" Jango asked, getting right to the point.

"You told me to kill those in the Naboo starship," Zam said.

"I hit the ship, but they used a decoy. Those who were aboard are all dead."

Jango fixed her with a smirk, and didn't bother to call her words a dodge. "We'll have to try something more subtle this time. My client is getting impatient. There can be no more mistakes." As he finished, he handed Zam a hollow, transparent tube containing a pair of whitish centipedelike creatures as long as his forearm.

"Kouhuns," he explained. "Very poisonous."

Zam Wesell lifted the tube to examine the marvelous little murderers more closely, her black eyes sparkling with excitement, and her cheekbones lifting as her mouth widened beneath the veil. She looked back at Jango and nodded.

Certain that she understood, Jango nodded and started around the corner toward his waiting speeder. He paused before stepping in, and looked back at his hired assassin.

"There can be no mistakes this time," he said.

The Clawdite saluted, tapping the tube containing the deadly kouhuns to her forehead.

"Tidy yourself up," Jango instructed, and he headed away.

Zam Wesell turned back to her own waiting speeder and pulled off her veil. Even as she lifted the cloth, her features began to morph, her mouth tightening, her black eyes sinking back into shapely sockets, and the ridges on her forehead smoothing. In the time it took her to unhook her veil, she had already assumed a shapely and attractive female human form, with dark and sensuous features. Even her clothing seemed to fit her differently, flowing down gracefully from her face.

Off to the side, Jango nodded approvingly and sped away. As a Clawdite, a changeling, Zam Wesell did bring some advantages to the trade, he had to admit.

The vast Jedi Temple sat on a flat plain. Unlike so many of Coruscant's buildings, monuments of efficiency and spare design, this building itself was a work of art, with many ornate columns and soft, rounded lines that drew in the eye and held it.

Bas-reliefs and statues showed in many areas, with lights set at varying angles to distort the shadows into designs of mystery.

Inside, the Temple was no different. This was a place of contemplation, a place whose design invited the mind to wander and to explore, a place whose lines themselves asked for interpretation. Art was as much a part of what it was to be a Jedi Knight as was warrior training. Many of the Jedi, past and present, considered art to be a conscious link to the mysteries of the Force, and so the sculptures and portraits that lined every hall were more than mere replicas—they were artistic interpretations of the great Jedi they represented, saying in form alone what the depicted Masters might speak in words.

Mace Windu and Yoda walked slowly down one polished and decorated corridor, the lights low, but with a brightly illuminated room in the distance before them.

"Why couldn't we see this attack on the Senator?" Mace pondered, shaking his head. "This should have been no surprise to the wary, and easy for us to predict."

"Masking the future is this disturbance in the Force," Yoda replied. The diminutive Jedi seemed tired.

Mace understood well the source of that weariness. "The prophecy is coming true. The dark side is growing."

"And only those who have turned to the dark side can sense the possibilities of the future," Yoda said. "Only by probing the dark side can we see."

Mace spent a moment digesting that remark, for what Yoda referred to was no small thing. Not at all. Journeys to the edges of the dark side were not to be taken lightly. Even more dire, the fact that Master Yoda believed that the disturbance all the Jedi had sensed in the Force was so entrenched in the dark side was truly foreboding.

"It's been ten years and the Sith still have not shown themselves," Mace remarked, daring to say it aloud. The Jedi didn't like to even mention the Sith, their direst of enemies. Many times in the past, the Jedi had dared hope that the Sith had been eradicated, their foul stench cleansed from the galaxy, and so they all would have liked to deny the existence of the mysterious dark Force-users.

But they could not. There could be no doubt and no denying that the being who had slain Qui-Gon Jinn those ten years before on Naboo was a Sith Lord.

"Do you think the Sith are behind this present disturbance?" Mace dared to ask.

"Out there, they are," Yoda said with resignation. "A certainty that is."

Yoda was referring to the prophecy, of course, that the dark side would rise and that one would be born who would bring balance to the Force and to the galaxy. Such a potential chosen one was now known among them, and that, too, brought more than a little trepidation to these hallowed halls.

"Do you think Obi-Wan's learner will be able to bring balance to the Force?" Mace asked.

Yoda stopped walking and slowly turned to regard the other Master, his expression showing a range of emotions that reminded Mace that they didn't know what bringing balance to the Force might truly mean. "Only if he chooses to follow his destiny," Yoda replied, and as with Mace's question, the answer hung in the air between them, a spoken belief that could only lead to more uncertainty.

Both Yoda and Mace Windu understood the places that some of the Jedi, at least, might have to travel to find the true answers, and those places, emotional stops and not physical, could well test all of them to the very limits of their abilities and sensibilities.

They resumed their walk, the only sound the patter of their footsteps. In their ears, though, both Mace and Yoda heard the ominous echo of the diminutive Jedi Master's dire words.

"Only by probing the dark side can we see."

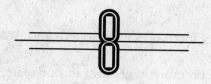

The door chime was not unexpected; somehow, Padmé had known that Anakin would come to speak with her as soon as the opportunity presented itself. She started for the door, but paused, and moved instead to retrieve her robe, aware suddenly that her nightgown was somewhat revealing.

Her movements again struck her as curious, though, for never before had Padmé Amidala harbored any feelings of modesty.

Still, she pulled the robe up tight as she opened the door, finding, predictably, Anakin Skywalker standing before her.

"Hello," he said, and it seemed as if he could hardly draw his breath.

"Is everything all right?"

Anakin stuttered over a response. "Oh yes," he finally managed to say. "Yes, my Master has gone to the lower levels to check on Captain Typho's security measures, but all seems quiet."

"You sound disappointed."

Anakin gave an embarrassed laugh.

"You don't enjoy this," Padmé remarked.

"There is nowhere else in all the galaxy I'd rather be," Anakin blurted, and it was Padmé's turn to give an embarrassed little laugh.

"But this . . . inertia," she reasoned, and Anakin nodded as he caught on.

"We should be more aggressive in our search for the assassin," he insisted. "To sit back and wait is to invite disaster."

"Master Kenobi does not agree."

"Master Kenobi is bound by the letter of the orders," Anakin explained. "He won't take a chance on doing anything that isn't explicitly asked of him by the Jedi Council."

Padmé tilted her head and considered this impetuous young man more carefully. Was not discipline a primary lesson of the Jedi Knights? Were they not bound, strictly so, within the structure of the Order and their Code?

"Master Kenobi is not like his own Master," Anakin said. "Master Qui-Gon understood the need for independent thinking and initiative—otherwise, he would have left me on Tatooine."

"And you are more like Master Qui-Gon?" Padmé asked.

"I accept the duties I am given, but demand the leeway I need to see them to a proper conclusion."

"Demand?"

Anakin smiled and shrugged. "Well, I ask, at least."

"And presume, when you can't get the answers you desire," Padmé said with a knowing grin, though in her heart she was only half teasing.

"I do the best I can with every problem I am given," was the strongest admission Anakin would offer.

"And so sitting around guarding me is not your idea of fun."

"We could be doing better and more exciting things," Anakin said, and there was a double edge to his voice, one that intrigued Padmé and made her pull her robe up even tighter.

"If we catch the assassin, we might find the root of these attempts," the Padawan explained, quickly putting the discussion back on a professional level. "Either way, you will be safer, and our duties will be made far easier."

Padmé's mind whirled as she tried to sort out Anakin's thoughts, and his motivations. He was surprising her with every word, considering that he was a Jedi Padawan, and yet, given the fire that she clearly saw burning behind his blue eyes, he was not surprising her. She saw trouble brewing there, in those simmering and too-passionate eyes, but even more than that, she saw excitement and the promise of thrills.

And, perhaps, the promise of finding out who it was that was trying to kill her.

Obi-Wan Kenobi stepped off the turbolift tentatively, warily, glancing left and right. He noted the two posted guards, alert and ready, and he nodded his approval to them. Every corridor had been like this throughout the massive apartment complex, and in this particular area, above, below, and near Amidala's room, the place was locked down tight.

Captain Typho had been given many soldiers at his disposal, and he had situated them well, overseeing as fine a defensive perimeter as Obi-Wan had ever witnessed. The Jedi Master took great comfort in that, of course, and knew that Typho was making his job easier.

But Obi-Wan could not relax. He had heard about the attack on the Naboo cruiser in great detail from Typho, and considering the many precautions that had been taken to protect the vessel—everything from broadcasting false entry lanes to the appointed landing pad to the many shielding fighters, the three accompanying the ship directly, and many more, both Naboo and Republic, covering every conceivable attack lane—these assassins could not be underestimated. They were good and they were well connected, to be sure.

And, likely, they were stubborn.

To get at Senator Amidala through the halls of this building, though, would take an army.

Obi-Wan nodded to the guards and walked a circuit of this lower floor then, satisfied, headed back to the turbolift.

Padmé took a deep breath, her thoughts lost in the last images of Anakin as he had left her room. Images of her sister Sola flitted about her, almost as if she could hear Sola teasing her already.

The Senator shook all of the thoughts, of Sola and particularly of Anakin, away and motioned to R2-D2, the little droid standing impassively against the wall beside the door. "Implement the shutdown," she instructed.

R2-D2 replied with a fearful *"oooo."*

"Go ahead, Artoo. It's all right. We have protection here."

The droid gave another worried call, but extended a probe out to the security panel on the wall beside him.

Padmé looked back to the door, recalling again the last images of Anakin, her tall and lean Jedi protector. She could see his shining blue eyes as surely as if he was standing before her, full of intensity, watching over her more carefully than any security cam ever could.

Anakin stood in the living room of Padmé's apartment, absorbing the silence around him, using the lack of physical noise to bolster his mental connection to that more subtle realm of the Force, feeling the life about him as clearly as if his five physical senses were all attuned to it.

His eyes were closed, but he could see the region about him clearly enough, could sense any disturbance in the Force.

Anakin's eyes popped open wide, his gaze darting about the room, and he pulled his lightsaber from his belt.

Or almost did, stopping fast when the door slid open and Master Kenobi walked into the room.

Obi-Wan looked about curiously, his gaze settling on Anakin. "Captain Typho has more than enough men downstairs," he said. "No assassin will try that way. Any activity up here?"

"Quiet as a tomb," Anakin replied. "I don't like just waiting here for something to happen."

Obi-Wan gave a little shake of his head, a movement showing his resignation concerning Anakin's predictability, and took a view scanner from his belt, checking his screen. His expression, shifting from curious to confused to concerned, spoke volumes to Anakin: He knew that Obi-Wan could see only part of Padmé's bedroom—the door area and R2-D2 standing by the wall, but nothing more.

The Jedi Knight's expression asked the question before he even spoke the words.

"Padmé . . . Senator Amidala, covered the cam," the Padawan explained. "I don't think she liked me watching her."

Obi-Wan's face tensed and he let out a little growl. "What is she thinking? Her security is paramount, and is compromised—"

"She programmed Artoo to warn us if there's an intruder," Anakin explained, trying to calm Obi-Wan before his concern could gain any real momentum.

"It's not an intruder I'm worried about," Obi-Wan countered. "Or not merely an intruder. There are many ways to kill a Senator."

"I know, but we also want to catch this assassin," Anakin said, his tone determined, stubborn even. "Don't we, Master?"

"You're using her as bait?" Obi-Wan asked incredulously, his eyes widening with shock and disbelief.

"It was her idea," Anakin protested, but his sharp tone showed clearly that he agreed with the plan. "Don't worry. No harm will come to her. I can sense everything going on in that room. Trust me."

"It's too risky," Obi-Wan scolded. "Besides, your senses aren't that attuned, my young apprentice."

Anakin parsed his words and his tone carefully, trying to sound not defensive, but rather suggestive. "And yours are?"

Obi-Wan could not deny the look of intrigue that crossed his face. "Possibly," he admitted.

Anakin smiled and nodded, and closed his eyes again, falling into the sensations of the Force, following them to Padmé, who was sleeping quietly. He wished that he could see her, could watch the quiet rise and fall of her belly, could hear her soft breathing, could smell the freshness of her hair, could feel the smoothness of her skin, could kiss her and taste the sweetness of her lips.

He had to settle for this, for feeling her life energy in the Force.

A place of warmth, it was.

In a different way, Padmé was thinking of Anakin, as well. He was there beside her, in her dreams.

She saw the fighting match that she knew would soon ensue in the Senate, the screaming and fist waving, the threats and the loud objections. How badly it drained her.

Anakin was there.

Her dream became a nightmare, some unseen assassin chasing her, blaster bolts whipping past her, and her feet seemed as if they were stuck in deep mud.

But Anakin rushed past, his lightsaber ignited and waving, deflecting the blaster bolts aside.

Padmé shifted a bit and gave a little groan, on many levels as uncomfortable with the identity of her rescuer as she was with the presence of the assassin. She didn't truly awaken, though, just thrashed a bit and raised her head, opening her eyes only briefly before burying her face in her pillow.

She didn't see the small round droid hovering behind the blinds outside her window. She didn't see the appendages come out of it, attaching to the window, or the sparks arcing about those arms as the droid shut down the security system. She didn't see the larger arm deploy, cutting a hole in the glass, nor did she hear the slight, faint sound as the glass was removed.

Over by the door in Padme's room, R2-D2's lights went on. The droid's domed head swiveled about, scanning the room, and he gave a soft *"wooo"* sound.

But then, apparently detecting nothing amiss, the droid shut back down.

Outside, a small tube came forth from the probe droid, moving to the hole in the window, and crawling through it, into Padmé's room, came a pair of kouhuns, like bloated white maggots with lines of black legs along their sides and nasty mandibles. Dangerous as those mandibles looked, though, the true danger of the kouhuns lay at the other end, the tail stinger, dripping of venom. The vicious kouhuns crawled in through the blinds and started immediately toward the bed and the sleeping woman.

"You look tired," Obi-Wan said to Anakin in the adjoining room.

The Padawan, still standing, opened his eyes and came out of his meditative trance. He took a moment to register the words, and then gave a little shrug, not disagreeing. "I don't sleep well anymore."

That was hardly news to Obi-Wan. "Because of your mother?" he asked.

"I don't know why I keep dreaming about her now," Anakin answered, frustration coming through in his voice. "I haven't seen her since I was little."

"Your love for her was, and remains, deep," Obi-Wan said. "That is hardly reason for despair."

"But these are more than . . ." Anakin started to say, but he stopped and sighed and shook his head. "Are they dreams, or are they visions? Are they images of what has been, or do they tell of something that is yet to be?"

"Or are they just dreams?" Obi-Wan said, his gentle smile showing through his scraggly beard. "Not every dream is a premonition, some vision or some mystical connection. Some dreams are just . . . dreams, and even Jedi have dreams, young Padawan."

Anakin didn't seem very satisfied with that. He just shook his head again.

"Dreams pass in time," Obi-Wan told him.

"I'd rather dream of Padmé," Anakin replied with a sly smile. "Just being around her again is . . . intoxicating."

Obi-Wan's sudden frown erased both his and Anakin's smiles. "Mind your thoughts, Anakin," he scolded in no uncertain tone. "They betray you. You've made a commitment to the Jedi Order, a commitment not easily broken, and the Jedi stand on such relationships is uncompromising. Attachment is forbidden." He gave a little derisive snort and looked toward the sleeping Senator's room. "And don't forget that she's a politician. They're not to be trusted."

"She's not like the others in the Senate, Master," Anakin protested strongly.

Obi-Wan eyed him carefully. "It's been my experience that Senators focus only on pleasing those who fund their campaigns, and they are more than willing to forget the niceties of democracy to get those funds."

"Not another lecture, Master," Anakin said with a profound sigh. He had heard this particular diatribe repeatedly. "At least not on the economics of politics."

Obi-Wan was no fan of the politics of the Republic. He started speaking again, or tried to, but Anakin abruptly interrupted.

"Please, Master," Anakin said emphatically. "Besides, you're generalizing. I know that Padmé—"

"Senator Amidala," Obi-Wan sternly corrected.

"—isn't like that," Anakin finished. "And the Chancellor doesn't seem to be corrupt."

"Palpatine's a politician. I've observed that he is very clever at following the passions and prejudices of the Senators."

"I think he is a good man," Anakin stated. "My instincts are very positive about . . ."

The young Padawan trailed off, his eyes widening, his expression becoming one of shock.

"I sense it, too," Obi-Wan said breathlessly, and the two Jedi exploded into motion.

Inside the bedroom, the kouhuns crawled slowly and deliberately toward the sleeping Padmé's exposed neck and face, their mandibles clicking excitedly.

"Wee oooo!" R2-D2 shrieked, catching on to the threat. The droid tootled a series of alarms and focused a light on the bed, highlighting the centipede invaders perfectly as Obi-Wan and Anakin burst into the room.

Padmé awoke, her eyes going wide, sucking in her breath in terror as the wicked little creatures stood up and hissed, and came at her.

Or would have, except that Anakin was there, his blue lightsaber blade slashing across, just above the bedcovers, once and again, slicing both creatures in half.

"Droid!" Obi-Wan cried, and Anakin and Padmé turned to see him rushing for the window. There, hovering outside, was the remote assassin, its appendages retracting fast.

Obi-Wan leapt into the blinds, taking them with him right through the window, shattering the glass. He reached into the Force as he leapt, using it to extend his jump, to send him far through the air to catch hold of the retreating droid assassin. With his added weight, the floating droid sank considerably, but it compensated and stabilized quickly, leaving the Jedi hanging on to it a hundred stories up.

Off flew the droid, taking Obi-Wan with it.

"Anakin?" Padmé asked, turning to him. When she saw him return the look, and saw the sudden flicker of intensity in his blue eyes, she pulled her nightdress higher about her shoulders.

"Stay here!" Anakin instructed. "Watch her, Artoo!" He rushed for the door, only to stop abruptly as Captain Typho and a pair of guards, along with the handmaiden Dormé, charged in.

"See to her!" was all that Anakin explained as he scrambled past them, running full out for the turbolift.

Not without defensive systems, the probe droid repeatedly sent electrical shocks arcing over its surface, stinging Obi-Wan's hands.

The Jedi Knight gritted through the pain, having no alternative but to hold on. He knew he shouldn't look down, but he did so anyway, to see the city teeming far, far below.

Another shock nearly sent him plummeting toward that distant bustle.

Reflexively, and hardly considering all the implications, the Jedi fumbled with one hand, found a power wire, and pulled it free, ceasing the electrical shocks.

But ending, too, the power that kept the probe droid aloft.

Down they went, falling like stones, the lights of the various floors flashing past them like strobes as they dropped.

"Not good, not good!" Obi-Wan said over and over as he worked frantically to reconnect the wire. Finally, he got it. The probe droid's lights blinked back on, and off the remote soared, with Obi-Wan hanging on desperately. The droid wasted no time in reigniting the series of electrical shocks, stinging the Jedi, but not shaking the stubborn man free.

Anakin was in no mood to wait for a turbolift. Out came his lightsaber, and with a single well-placed thrust the Padawan had the doors open, though the turbolift car was nowhere near his floor. Anakin didn't even pause long enough to discern if it was above him or below, he just leapt into the shaft, catching hold of one of the supporting poles with one arm, propping the side of his foot tight against it, and spinning downward. His mind whirled, trying to remember the layout of the building, and which levels held the various docking bays.

Suddenly that sixth sense, feeling through the Force, alerted him to danger.

"Yikes!" he yelled as he looked down to see the turbolift racing up at him.

Grabbing on tighter to the pole, he held his open palm downward, then sent a tremendous Force push below, not to stop the lift, but to propel himself back up the shaft, keeping him ahead of the lift with sufficient speed for him to reorient himself and land, sprawled, atop the speeding car.

Again, whipping out his lightsaber, he stabbed it through the catch on the lift's top hatch. Ignoring the shrieks from the car's occupants below, Anakin pulled open the hatch, grabbed the edge as he shut off his blade, then somersaulted into the car.

"Docking bay level?" he asked the pair of stunned Senators, a Sullustan and a human.

"Forty-seven!" the human responded at once.

"Too late," the Sullustan added, noting the rolling floor numbers. The diminutive Senator started to add, "Next is sixty-something," but Anakin slammed the brake button, and when that didn't work fast enough for him, he reached into the Force again and grabbed at the braking mechanisms, forcing them even more tightly into place.

All three went off the floor with the sudden stop, the Sullustan landing hard.

Anakin banged on the door, yelling for it to open. A hand on his shoulder slowed him, and he turned to see the human Senator step by, one finger held up in a gesture bidding the eager young Jedi to wait.

The Senator pushed a button, clearly marked on the panel, and the turbolift door slid open.

With a shrug and a sheepish smile, Anakin had to fall to his belly and squeeze through the opening to drop to the hallway below. He ran frantically, left and then right, finally spotting a balcony adjacent to the parking garage. Out he ran, then vaulted over a rail, dropping to a line of parked speeders. One yellow, snub-nosed speeder was open, so he jumped in, firing it up and zooming away, off the platform and then up, up, heading for the line of traffic flowing high above.

He tried to get his bearings as he rose. What side of the building was he now on? And which side had Obi-Wan flown away from? And what angle had the fleeing probe droid taken?

As he tried to sort it all out, Anakin realized that only one of two things could possibly put him on Obi-Wan's trail, dumb luck or . . .

The Padawan fell into the Force yet again, searching for the sensation that he could identify as his Jedi Master.

* * *

Zam Wesell leaned against the side of her speeder, impatiently tapping her gloved fingers on the roof of the old vehicle. She wore an oversized purple helmet, front-wedged and solid save a small rectangle cut out about her eyes, but while that hid her assumed beauty, her formfitting grav-suit showed every feminine curve.

Zam didn't think much about it at that time, though, for with this particular mission it was more important that she merely blend in. Often she had taken assignments where her assumed feminine wiles had helped her tremendously, where she had played upon the obvious weakness of a male to get close.

Those wiles weren't going to help her with this assignment, though, and Zam knew it. This time, she was out to kill a woman, a Senator, and one who was very well guarded by beings absolutely devoted to her, as protective of her as a parent might be to a child. Zam wondered what this woman might have done to so invoke the wrath of her employers.

Or at least, she started to wonder, as she had started to wonder several times since Jango had hired her to kill the Senator. The professional assassin never truly let her thoughts travel down that path. It wasn't her business. She was not a moral gauge for anyone, not one to decide the value of her assignment or the justice or injustice involved—she was just a tool, in many ways, a machine. She was the extension of her employers and nothing more.

Jango had bade her to kill Amidala, and so she would kill Amidala, fly back and collect her due, and go on to the next assignment. It was clean and it was simple.

Zam could hardly believe that the explosive charge she had managed to hide on the landing platform had not done the job, but she had taken that lesson to heart, had come to understand that the weaknesses of Senator Amidala were not easily discerned and exploited.

The changeling banged her fist on the roof of the speeder.

She hated that she had been forced to go outside for help, to procure a probe droid to do the task that she so relished handling personally.

But now there were Jedi about Amidala, by all the rumors, and Zam had little desire to do battle with one of those troublesome fanatics.

She glanced into the speeder, to the timepiece on the console, and nodded grimly. The job should be completed by now. The poisonous kouhuns had been delivered, likely, and one scratch of a venomous stinger should be more than enough.

Zam stood up straight, sensing something, some sudden feeling of uneasiness.

She heard a cry, of surprise or of fear, and she glanced all about, and then her eyes, within the cut-out rectangle of the helmet, went wide indeed. She watched in blank amazement as the probe droid, her programmed assassin, wove through the towering buildings of Coruscant, with a man, dressed like a Jedi, hanging on to it! Zam's fear lessened and her smile widened, though, as she watched the droid go into defensive action, for this one was well programmed. It smacked against the side of a building, nearly dislodging the Jedi, and when that didn't work, the clever droid dived back into the traffic lane, soaring behind a speeder, just above the vehicle's exhaust.

The Jedi squirmed and tucked and somehow managed to keep himself out of that fiery exhaust, and so the droid swooped off to the side, taking a different tack. It flew in low over the top of one building.

Zam's eyes widened as she watched the spectacle. She was impressed at the way the Jedi did not allow himself to be slammed off, but rather tucked his legs enough to run along the rooftop as the droid skimmed across it. Oh, he was good!

This was truly entertaining to the confident bounty hunter, but enough was enough.

Zam reached into the speeder and pulled out a long blaster rifle, casually lifting and leveling. She fired off a series of shots, and explosions ignited all about the Jedi and the droid.

Zam looked up from her sights, stunned to see that the crafty man had somehow avoided those shots, had dodged, or had, she mused, used his Jedi powers to deflect them.

"Block this," the bounty hunter said, raising the rifle again. Taking aim at the Jedi's chest, she lifted the barrel just a bit and squeezed the trigger.

The probe droid exploded.

The Jedi plummeted from sight.

Zam sighed and shrugged, telling herself that the cost of the probe droid was worth the show. And hopefully the victory. If Senator Amidala lay dead in her room, then that cost would be a minor thing indeed, for this bounty exceeded anything Zam had ever hoped to collect.

The bounty hunter slipped her rifle back into her speeder, then bent low and squeezed in, soaring off into the Coruscant traffic lanes.

Obi-Wan screamed as he dropped . . . ten stories . . . twenty. There was nothing in his Jedi repertoire to save him this time. He looked all about frantically, but there was nothing—no handholds, no platform, no awning of thick and padded cloth.

Nothing. Just another five hundred stories to the ground!

He tried to find his sense of calm, tried to fall into the Force and accept this unwelcomed end.

And then a speeder swooped beside him and he saw that cocky smile of his unruly Padawan, and never in his life had Obi-Wan Kenobi been happier to see anything.

"Hitchhikers usually stand on the platforms," Anakin informed him, and he swooped the speeder near enough for Obi-Wan to grab on. "A novel approach, though. Gets the attention of passing traffic."

Obi-Wan was too busy clawing his way into the passenger seat to offer a retort. He finally settled in next to Anakin.

"I almost lost you there," the Padawan remarked.

"No kidding. What took you so long?"

Anakin eased back in his seat, putting his left arm up on the door of the open speeder and assuming a casual posture. "Oh, you know, Master," he said flippantly. "I couldn't find a speeder I really liked. One with an open cockpit, of course, and with the right speed capabilities to catch your droid scooter. And then, you know, I had to hold out for just the right color—"

"There!" Obi-Wan shouted, pointing up to a closed-in speeder, recognizing it as the one behind the assassin who had been shooting at him. It soared above them, and Anakin cut hard on the wheel and the stick, angling in fast pursuit.

Almost immediately, an arm came out of the lead speeder's open window, holding a blaster pistol, and the bounty hunter squeezed off a series of shots.

"If you'd spend as much time working on your lightsaber skills as you do on your wit, young Padawan, you would rival Master Yoda!" Obi-Wan said, and he ducked, getting jostled about, as Anakin cut a series of evasive turns.

"I thought I already did."

"Only in your mind, my very young Padawan," Obi-Wan retorted. He gave a little cry and ducked reflexively as Anakin dived in and out of traffic, narrowly missing several vehicles. "Careful! Hey, easy! You know I don't like it when you do that!"

"Sorry, I forgot you don't like flying, Master!" Anakin said, his voice rising at the end as he took the speeder down suddenly to avoid another blaster bolt from the stubborn bounty hunter.

"I don't mind flying," Obi-Wan insisted. "But what you're doing is suicide!" His words nearly caught in his throat, along with his stomach, as Anakin cut hard to the right, then dropped suddenly, punched the throttle, pulled back to the left, and lifted the nose, zipping the speeder up through the traffic lane and back in sight of the bounty hunter—only to see another line of blaster bolts coming at them.

Then the bounty hunter dived to the side suddenly, and both

Jedi opened their eyes and their mouths wide, their screams drowned out by a commuter train crossing right in front of them.

Obi-Wan tasted bile again, but somehow, Anakin managed to avoid the train, coming out the other side. Obi-Wan looked over to his Padawan, to see him assuming a casual, in-control posture.

"Master, you know I've been flying since before I could walk," Anakin said with a sly grin. "I'm very good at this."

"Just slow down," Obi-Wan instructed, in a voice that suggested the dignified Jedi Knight was about to throw up.

Anakin ignored him, taking the speeder in fast pursuit of the assassin, right into a line of giant trucks. Around and around they went, cutting fast corners through the traffic, over the traffic, under the traffic, and around the buildings, always keeping the assassin's speeder in sight. Anakin took his craft right up on edge, skimming the side of one building.

"He can't lose me," the Padawan boasted. "He's getting desperate."

"Great," Obi-Wan answered dryly.

"Oh wait," Obi-Wan added when the speeder in front dived into a tram tunnel. "Don't go in there!"

But Anakin zoomed right in, and then zoomed right back out, a huge rushing train chasing him, Obi-Wan screaming about as loudly as the train was blowing its horn. "You know I don't like it when you do that!"

"Sorry, Master," Anakin answered unconvincingly. "Don't worry. This guy's gonna kill himself any minute now."

"Well, let him do that alone!" Obi-Wan insisted.

They watched as the assassin zoomed right into traffic, soaring the wrong way down a congested lane.

Anakin went in right behind.

Both speeders zigged and zagged wildly, frantically, the occasional blaster bolt shooting back from the lead one. And then, suddenly, the assassin cut fast, straight up, a tight loop that brought Zam behind the two Jedi.

"Great move," Anakin congratulated. "I got one, too." He slammed on his brakes, reversing thrust, and the assassin's speeder flashed up right beside them.

And there was the assassin, firing point blank at Obi-Wan.

"What are you doing?" Obi-Wan demanded. "He's going to blast me!"

"Right," Anakin agreed, working frantically to maneuver away. "This isn't working."

"Nice of you to notice." Obi-Wan dodged, then lurched as the speeder dropped suddenly, Anakin taking it right under the assassin's.

"He can't shoot us down here," the Padawan congratulated himself, but his smile lasted only the split second it took for their opponent's new tactic to register. The assassin swerved out of the traffic lane and shot straight for a building, coming in at an angle to just skim the rooftop.

Obi-Wan started to shout out Anakin's name, but the word came out as *"Ananananana."* The Padawan was in control, though, and he slowed and lifted his speeder's nose just up over the edge of the rooftop.

Another obstacle showed itself almost immediately, a large craft coming in low and slow.

"It's landing!" Obi-Wan shouted, and when Anakin didn't immediately respond, he added desperately, "On us!"

It came out, *"On uuuuuuuuuuuuus!"* as Anakin brought the speeder up on edge and zipped around a corner, clipping a flagpole and taking its cloth contents free.

"Clear that," the seemingly unshakable Padawan said, nodding down to the torn flag, which had caught itself on one of the speeder's front air scoops.

"What?"

"Clear the flag! We're losing power! Hurry!"

Complaining under his breath with every movement, Obi-Wan crawled out of the cockpit and gingerly onto the front engine. He bent low and tugged the flag free, and the speeder lurched forward, nearly dislodging him.

"Don't do that!" he screamed. "I don't like it when you do that!"

"So sorry, Master."

"He's heading for the power refinery," Obi-Wan said. "But take it easy. It's dangerous near those power couplings."

Anakin zoomed right past one of the couplings, and a huge electrical bolt had the air crackling all about them.

"Slow down!" Obi-Wan ordered. "Slow down! Don't go through there!"

But Anakin did just that, banking left, right, left.

"What are you doing?"

"Sorry, Master!"

More bolts crackled all about them. Right, left, right again, up and over, down and around, and somehow, incredibly, out the other side.

"Oh, that was good," Obi-Wan admitted.

"That was crazy," the rattled Anakin corrected. The older Jedi snapped a glare at him, recognized the greenish color that had suddenly come to the Padawan's face, and then just put his head in his hands and groaned.

"Got him now!" Anakin announced. The assassin was sliding his speeder sidelong around a corner between two buildings up ahead.

Anakin went right around behind, only to find the lead speeder stopped and blocking the alleyway, the assassin leaning out the door, blaster pistol leveled.

"Ah, blast," the Padawan remarked.

"Stop!" Obi-Wan told him, and both ducked as a line of bolts came at them.

"No, we can make it!" Anakin insisted, punching the throttle.

He dived his speeder under the assassin's, barely missing it, then went up on edge, slipping through a small gap in the building. But there were pipes there, and no level of flying could put the speeder safely through them. They bounced sidelong, then flipped end over end, narrowly missing a giant crane and clipping some struts. The damage brought forth a giant fiery gas ball, nearly immolating them, and in the uncontrolled spin that followed, they bounced off yet another building and the speeder stalled out.

Anakin winced, expected a line of curses to come at him, but when he finally looked at Obi-Wan, he saw the Jedi staring straight ahead, eyes wide and unblinking, and saying, "I'm crazy, I'm crazy, I'm crazy . . ." over and over again.

"But it worked," Anakin dared to say. "We made it."

"It didn't work!" Obi-Wan yelled at him. "We've stalled! And you almost got us killed!"

Anakin looked down at his hands and body, and waggled his fingers. "I think we're still alive!" He grinned, trying to disarm his fuming Master, but Obi-Wan seemed as if he was about to explode.

"It was stupid!" Obi-Wan roared.

Anakin worked wildly, trying to restart the speeder. "I could have made it," he protested sheepishly. His confident expression strengthened as the speeder roared back to life.

"But you didn't! And now we've lost him!"

Even as Obi-Wan finished, a barrage of laser bolts rained down around them, setting off explosions that rocked them back and forth. The pair looked up, to see the assassin zooming away.

"No, we didn't," a smiling Anakin said. He took the speeder up, the sudden thrust violently throwing them both back in their seats. They came through the area of smoke and carnage with several small fires burning on their speeder. Obi-Wan slapped at flames on the control panel.

Again they chased the assassin into the main travel lanes, dodging and turning fast about incoming traffic. Up ahead, the assassin cut fast to the left, between two buildings, and Anakin responded, going right and up.

"Where are you going?" a perplexed Obi-Wan asked. "He went down there, the other way."

"This is a shortcut. I think."

"What do you mean, *you think*? What kind of shortcut? He went completely the other way! You've lost him!"

"Master, if we keep this chase going, that creep's gonna end up deep-fried," Anakin tried to explain. "Personally, I'd very much like to find out who he is, and who he's working for."

"Oh," Obi-Wan replied, his voice dripping with sarcasm. "So that's why we're going in the wrong direction."

Anakin took them up and around, finally settling into a hover some fifty stories up from the street.

"Well, you lost him," Obi-Wan said.

"I'm deeply sorry, Master," Anakin replied. Again, he seemed hardly convincing, as if he was saying just what he had to say to keep Obi-Wan from scolding him further. The Jedi Knight looked at him hard, ready to call him on it, when he noticed that Anakin, seemingly deep in concentration, was counting softly.

"Excuse me for a moment," the Padawan said. He stood up and, to Obi-Wan's complete shock, stepped out of the speeder.

Obi-Wan lurched over to the edge and stared down, watching Anakin drop—about five stories, before landing atop the roof of a familiar speeder that was zooming beneath them.

"I hate it when he does that," Obi-Wan muttered incredulously, shaking his head.

Zam Wesell skimmed close to the buildings, staying to the side of the main traffic lanes. She didn't know whether the probe droid had successfully completed its mission, but she was feeling pretty good at that moment, having outwitted a pair of Jedi.

Suddenly her speeder shook hard. At first she thought she had been hit by a blaster bolt, but then, surveying for damage, she came to know the truth of the missile, and to know that it—that he—had somehow landed on her speeder.

Zam backed off on the throttle, then slammed it out full, lurching the craft ahead. The force of the sudden acceleration nearly dislodged Anakin, sending him sliding back to the tail, but he hung on stubbornly and, to Zam's dismay, even began crawling back toward the cockpit.

With a sneer, Zam hit the brakes, hard, and Anakin went sliding and bouncing past her.

But the stubborn young Jedi caught one of the twin front forks of the speeder and hung on yet again.

Zam accelerated and reached out her blaster pistol, letting fly a series of bolts in Anakin's general direction. The angle was wrong, though, and she couldn't score any hits. And there he was, crawling back stubbornly toward the roof despite all of Zam's evasive maneuvers. Her Clawdite form came back, suddenly and briefly, as she lost concentration, but she recovered quickly.

The bounty hunter cursed under her breath and swooped back into traffic, trying to formulate some plan for ridding herself of the troublesome Jedi. She went back into her evasive, traffic-dodging maneuvers yet again, entertaining the thought of moving in close to some of the heavier traffic and letting the exhaust plume smoke the fool atop her craft.

She had almost convinced herself to do just that when suddenly a glowing blue blade of energy sheared through the top of her speeder and plunged down beside her. She looked up to see the stubborn young Jedi cutting through the roof.

Swerving all about, she fired off a shot at him, then another. Finally, to her relief, a shot took the lightsaber from his hand, though whether she had taken the hand, as well, or just the weapon, she could not tell.

Obi-Wan had finally caught sight of Zam's speeder, with Anakin scrambling atop it, when the lightsaber tumbled from the Padawan's grasp. Obi-Wan gave a shake of his head and dived his speeder toward the street, angling for an interception.

* * *

Anakin's hand plunged through the hole in the roof, and
Zam lifted her blaster pistol in his direction. He didn't reach for
her, just held his hand there outstretched, and before she could
fire, some unseen force yanked the pistol from her hand, throwing it right into the Jedi's grasp. "No!" the bounty hunter yelled,
gasping in astonishment. She lurched in her seat, letting go of
her speeder's controls to grab the pistol desperately with both
hands. The pair struggled over the weapon, the speeder dipping
right and left, and then the pistol went off, hitting neither opponent, but blowing a hole in the flooring of Zam's speeder, cutting some control pipes in the process.

The speeder careened out of control, and Zam fell back over
the controls, desperately but futilely.

They dived and spun, sidelong and head over. Screaming, both hung on for dear life as they spiraled toward the
street.

Finally, at the last possible second, Zam gained some control, enough to turn the impending crash into a spark-throwing
skid along the broken permacrete of this seedy section of Coruscant's belly.

The speeder bounced up on edge and slammed to a halt,
and Anakin went flying, tumbling along the street for a long,
long way. When he finally got control, he saw the assassin leaping from the speeder and running down the street, so he
climbed back to his feet and started to follow.

The splash as he stepped in one dirty puddle woke Anakin to
the harsh realities about him. This was the underbelly of Coruscant, the smelly and dirty streets. He slowed—the assassin was
out of sight anyway—and looked about curiously, noting the
many lowlifes, mostly nonhumans of quite a variety of species.
Many beings were panhandling up and down the street.

He shook it all away quickly, though, reminding himself of
the real reason he was here, and of Padmé and her need for security. Spurred by images of the beautiful Senator from Naboo,

the young Jedi sprinted along the broken sidewalk, catching sight of the assassin moving through a crowd of ruffians. Anakin charged right in behind, pushing and shoving, but making little headway against the press.

He spotted the assassin at the last second, before the helmeted killer disappeared through a doorway.

Anakin shoved through, finally, and glanced up to see the glare of the gambling sign above the establishment. Undaunted, he started again for the door, and then stopped as he heard Obi-Wan calling.

A familiar yellow speeder dropped to a resting place on the side of the street.

"Anakin!" Obi-Wan walked toward the young Jedi, pointedly holding Anakin's dropped lightsaber in his hand.

"She went into that club, Master!"

Obi-Wan patted his hand in the air to calm the Padawan, not even registering Anakin's surprising use of the feminine pronoun. "Patience," he said. "Use the Force, Anakin. Think."

"Sorry, Master."

"He went in there to hide, not run," Obi-Wan reasoned.

"Yes, Master."

Obi-Wan held the lightsaber out toward his student. "Next time try not to lose it."

"Sorry, Master."

Obi-Wan pulled the precious weapon back as Anakin reached for it, and held the young Padawan's gaze with his own stern look. "A Jedi's lightsaber is his most precious possession."

"Yes, Master." Again, Anakin reached for the lightsaber, and again Obi-Wan pulled it back, never letting Anakin go from his scrutinizing stare.

"He must keep it with him at all times."

"I know, Master," Anakin replied, a bit of exasperation creeping into his tone.

"This weapon is your life."

"I've heard this lesson before."

Obi-Wan held it out again, finally relinquishing that awful stare, and Anakin took the weapon and replaced it on his belt.

"But you haven't learned anything, Anakin," the Jedi Knight said, turning away.

"I try, Master."

There was sincerity in his tone, Obi-Wan clearly recognized, and a bit of regret, perhaps, and that reminded Obi-Wan of the difficult circumstances under which Anakin had entered the Order. He had been far too old, nearly ten years of age, and Master Qui-Gon had taken him in without permission, without the blessing of the Jedi Council. Master Yoda had seen potential danger in young Anakin Skywalker. No one they had ever encountered had been stronger with the Force, in terms of sheer potential. But the Jedi Order normally required training from the earliest possible age. The Force was too powerful a tool—no, not a tool, and that was the problem. An unwise Jedi might consider the Force a tool, a means to his own ends. But a true Jedi understood that the Force was a partner on a concurrent course, a common pathway to true harmony and understanding.

After Qui-Gon's death at the hands of a Sith Lord, the Jedi Council had rethought their decision about young Anakin, and had allowed his training to go forward, with Obi-Wan fulfilling his promise to Qui-Gon that he would take the talented young boy under his tutelage. The Council had been hesitant, though, and obviously not happy about it. Yoda had seemed almost resigned, as if this path was one that they could not deny, rather than one they would willingly and eagerly walk. For the whispers spoke of Anakin as the chosen one, the one who would bring balance to the Force.

Obi-Wan wasn't sure what that meant, and he was more than a little fearful. He looked up at Anakin, who was standing patiently, properly subdued after the tongue-lashing, and he took comfort in that image, in this incredibly likable, somewhat stubborn, and obviously brash young man.

He hid his smile only because it would not do for Anakin to understand himself forgiven so easily for his rash actions and the loss of his weapon.

Obi-Wan had to disguise a chuckle as a cough. After all, hadn't he been the one who had leapt out through a window a hundred stories above the streets of Coruscant?

The Jedi Knight led the way into the gambling club. Humans and nonhumans mingled about in the smoky air, sipping drinks of every color and puffing on exotic pipes full of exotic plants. Many robes showed bulges reminiscent of weapons, and in looking around, both Jedi understood that everyone was a potential threat.

"Why do I think that you're going to be the death of me?" Obi-Wan commented above the clamor.

"Don't say that, Master," Anakin replied seriously, and the intensity of his tone surprised Obi-Wan. "You're the closest thing I have to a father. I love you, and I don't want to cause you pain."

"Then why don't you listen to me?"

"I will," Anakin said eagerly. "I'll do better. I promise."

Obi-Wan nodded and glanced all around. "Do you see him?"

"I think he's a she."

"Then be extra careful," Obi-Wan said, and he gave a snort.

"And I think she's a changeling," Anakin added.

Obi-Wan nodded to the crowd ahead of them. "Go and find her." He started the opposite way.

"Where are you going, Master?"

"To get a drink," came the short response.

Anakin blinked in surprise to see his Master heading for the bar. He almost started after, to inquire further, but he recalled the scolding he had just received and his promise to do better, to obey his Master. He turned and started away, milling through the crowd, trying to hold his calm against the wave of faces staring at him, most with obvious suspicion, some even openly hostile.

Over at the bar, Obi-Wan watched him for a bit, out of the corner of his eye. He signaled to the bartender, then watched as a glass was placed in front of him and amber liquid poured in.

"Wanna buy some death sticks?" came a guttural voice from the side.

Obi-Wan didn't even turn to fully regard the speaker, who wore a wild mane of dark hair, with two antennae twirled up from his hair like curly horns.

"Nobody's got better death sticks than Elan Sleazebaggano," the ruffian added with a perfectly evil smile.

"You don't want to sell me death sticks," the Jedi coolly said, waggling his fingers slightly, bringing the weight of the Force into his voice.

"I don't want to sell you death sticks," Elan Sleazebaggano obediently repeated.

Again the Jedi waggled his fingers. "You want to go home and rethink your life."

"I want to go home and rethink my life," Elan readily agreed, and he turned and walked away.

Obi-Wan tossed back his drink and motioned for the bartender to fill it up.

A short distance away, walking among the crowd, Anakin continued his scan. Something didn't seem quite right to him— but of course, how could he expect it to be in this seedy place? Still, some sensation nagged at him, some mounting evil that seemed above the level expected even in here.

He didn't actually see the blaster pistol coming out of the holster, didn't see it rising up toward the apparently unsuspecting Obi-Wan's back.

But he felt . . .

Anakin spun as Obi-Wan spun, to see his Master coming around, lightsaber igniting, in a beautiful and graceful turn with perfect balance. It seemed almost as if in slow motion to Anakin, though of course Obi-Wan was moving with deadly speed and precision, as his blade, blue like Anakin's, cut a short vertical loop and then a second, reaching farther out toward his foe. The would-be assassin—and he could see clearly now that it was a woman, since she had taken off her helmet—shrieked in agony as her arm, still clutching the blaster, fell free to the floor, sheared off above the elbow.

The room exploded into motion, with Anakin rushing to Obi-Wan's side, club patrons leaping up all about them, bristling with nervous energy.

"Easy!" Anakin said loudly, patting his hands in the air, imbuing his voice with the strength of the Force. "Official business. Go back to your drinks."

Gradually, very gradually, the club resumed its previous atmosphere, with conversations beginning again. Seeming hardly concerned, Obi-Wan motioned for Anakin to help him, and together they helped the assassin out to the street.

They lowered her gently to the ground, and she started awake as soon as Obi-Wan began to attend her wounded arm.

She growled ferally and winced in agony, all the while staring up hatefully at the two Jedi.

"Do you know who it was you were trying to kill?" Obi-Wan asked her.

"The Senator from Naboo," Zam Wesell said matter-of-factly, as if it hardly mattered.

"Who hired you?"

Her answer was a glare. "It was just a job."

"Tell us!" Anakin demanded, coming forward threateningly.

The tough bounty hunter didn't even flinch. "The Senator's going to die soon anyway," she said. "It won't end with me. For the price they're offering, there'll be bounty hunters lining up to take the hit. And the next one won't make the same mistake I did."

Tough as she was, she ended with a grunt and a groan.

"This wound's going to need more treatment than I can give it here," an obviously concerned Obi-Wan explained to Anakin, but if the younger man even cared, he didn't show it. His expression angry, he came forward.

"Who hired you?" he asked again, and then he continued, throwing the full weight of the Force into his demand, a strength that surprised Obi-Wan, that came from something more than prudence or dedication to his current job. "Tell us. Tell us now!"

The bounty hunter continued to glare at him, but, lips twitching, she started to answer. "It was a bounty hunter called—"

They heard a puff from above and the bounty hunter twitched and gasped, and simply expired, her human female features twisting grotesquely back into the lumpy form of her true Clawdite nature.

Anakin and Obi-Wan tore their eyes away from the spectacle to look up, and heard the roar as they watched an armored rocket-man lift away into the Coruscant night, disappearing into the sky.

Obi-Wan looked back to the dead creature and pulled a small item from her neck, holding it up for Anakin to see. "Toxic dart."

Anakin sighed and looked away. So they had foiled this attempt and killed one assassin.

But it was clear to him that Senator Amidala—Padmé—remained in grave danger.

Anakin stood quietly in the Jedi Council chamber, encircled by the Masters of the Order. Beside him stood Obi-Wan, his Master, but not one of *the* Masters. Obi-Wan, like the majority of the ten thousand Jedi, was a Knight, but these select few sitting around the edges of this room were Masters, the highest-ranking members of this Order. Anakin had never been comfortable in this esteemed company. He knew that more than half of the Jedi Masters sitting here had expressed grave doubts about allowing him into the Order at the advanced age of ten. He knew that even after Yoda had swayed the vote to allow him to begin studying under Obi-Wan, a few continued to hold those doubts.

"Track down this bounty hunter, you must, Obi-Wan," Master Yoda said as the others passed the toxic dart about.

"Most importantly, find out who he's working for," Mace Windu added.

"What about Senator Amidala?" Obi-Wan asked. "She will still need protecting."

Anakin, anticipating what might be coming, straightened as Yoda turned his gaze his way.

"Handle that, your Padawan will."

Anakin felt his heart soar at Yoda's declaration, both because of the confidence obviously being shown in him, and also because this was one assignment he knew that he would truly enjoy.

"Anakin, escort the Senator back to her home planet of Naboo," Mace added. "She'll be safer there. And don't use registered transport. Travel as refugees."

Anakin nodded as the assignment was explained, but he knew immediately that there would be a few obstacles to such a course. "As the leader of the opposition to the Military Creation Act, it will be very difficult to get Senator Amidala to leave the capital."

"Until caught this killer is, our judgment she must respect," Yoda replied.

Anakin nodded. "But I know how deeply she cares about this upcoming vote, Master," he replied. "She is more concerned with defeating the act than with—"

"Anakin," Mace interrupted, "go to the Senate and ask Chancellor Palpatine to speak with her." The tone of his voice made it clear that they had spent enough time on these issues. The Jedi Knight and his Padawan had their assignments, and Yoda dismissed them with a nod.

Anakin started to say something further, but Obi-Wan had his arm almost immediately, guiding him out of the room.

"I was only going to explain Padmé's passion about this vote," Anakin said when he and Obi-Wan were out in the hall.

"You made Senator Amidala's feelings quite clear," Obi-Wan replied. "That is why Master Windu bade you to have the Chancellor intervene." The two started walking down the corridor, Anakin biting back any responses that came to him.

"The Jedi Council understands, Anakin," Obi-Wan remarked.

"Yes, Master."

"You must trust in them, Anakin."

"Yes, Master." Anakin's response was automatic. He had already gone past this issue in his thoughts. He knew that Padmé wouldn't be easily convinced to leave the planet before the vote, but in truth, it hardly mattered to him. The important thing was that he would be with her, guarding her. With Obi-Wan off chasing the bounty hunter, Padmé would be his sole responsibility, and that was no small thing to Anakin.

No small thing at all.

Anakin was not nervous in the office of Chancellor Palpatine. Certainly he understood the man's power, and certainly he respected the office itself, but the young Padawan felt very comfortable here, felt as if he was with a friend. He hadn't spent much time with Palpatine, but on those few occasions when he had spoken with the man privately, he had always felt as if the Supreme Chancellor was taking an honest interest in him. In some ways, Anakin felt as if Palpatine was an additional mentor—not as directly as Obi-Wan, of course, but offering solid and important advice.

More than that, though, Anakin always felt as if he was welcome here.

"I will talk to her," Palpatine agreed, upon hearing Anakin's request that he speak with Padmé about leaving Coruscant for the relative safety of Naboo. "Senator Amidala will not refuse an executive order. I know her well enough to assure you of that."

"Thank you, Your Excellency."

"And so, my young Padawan, they have finally given you an assignment," the Chancellor said with a wide and warm smile, the way a father might talk to a son. "Your patience has paid off."

"Your guidance more than my patience," Anakin replied. "I doubt my patience would have held, had it not been for your assurances that my Jedi Masters were watching me, and that they would trust me with some important duties before too long."

Palpatine nodded and smiled. "You don't need guidance, Anakin," he said. "In time you will learn to trust your feelings. Then you will be invincible. I have said it many times, you are the most gifted Jedi I have ever met."

"Thank you, Your Excellency," Anakin replied coolly, though in truth, he had to consciously stop himself from trembling. Hearing such a compliment from one who did not understand—

like from his mother—was much different than hearing it from Palpatine, the Supreme Chancellor of the Republic. This was an accomplished man, more accomplished, perhaps, than anyone else in all the galaxy. He was not an underling of Yoda or Mace Windu. Anakin understood that a man like Palpatine would not throw out such compliments if he did not believe them.

"I see you becoming the greatest of all the Jedi, Anakin," Palpatine went on. "Even more powerful than Master Yoda."

Anakin hoped his legs wouldn't simply buckle beneath him. He could hardly believe the words, and yet a part of him did believe them. There was a strength within him, a power beyond the limits the Jedi seemed to place upon him, and upon themselves. Anakin sensed that clearly. He knew that Obi-Wan didn't understand, and that was his biggest frustration with his Master. To Anakin's thinking, Obi-Wan's leash was far too short.

He had no idea of how he might answer Palpatine's continuing compliments, so he just stood in the center of the room and smiled for a bit, while the Chancellor stood by the window, looking out at the endless streams of Coruscant traffic.

After many moments had passed, Anakin worked up the courage to move around the desk and join him following the Supreme Chancellor's gaze up at the traffic lanes.

"I am concerned for my Padawan," Obi-Wan Kenobi said to Yoda and Mace Windu as the three walked along the corridors of the Jedi Temple. "He is not ready to be given this assignment on his own."

"The Council is confident in this decision, Obi-Wan," Yoda said.

"The boy has exceptional skills," Mace agreed.

"But he still has much to learn, Master," Obi-Wan explained. "His skills have made him . . . well, arrogant."

"Yes, yes," Yoda agreed. "It's a flaw more and more common among Jedi. Too sure of themselves, they are. Even the older, more experienced Jedi."

Obi-Wan considered the words with an assenting nod. They certainly rang true, and the current conditions among the Jedi in this time of mounting tension were a bit unsettling, with many off on their own far from Coruscant. And had not arrogance played a major role in Count Dooku's decision to depart the Order, and the Republic?

"Remember, Obi-Wan," Mace remarked, "if the prophecy is true, your apprentice is the only one who can bring the Force into balance."

How could Obi-Wan ever forget that little fact? Qui-Gon had been the first to see it, the first to predict that Anakin would be the one to fulfill the prophecy. What Qui-Gon, or anyone else for that matter, had failed to explain, was exactly what bringing balance to the Force might mean.

"If he follows the right path," the Jedi Knight said to the two Masters, and neither of them corrected him.

"Attend to your own duties, you must," Yoda reminded, drawing Obi-Wan from his distracting contemplation as surely as if he was reading the Jedi's mind. "When solved is this mystery of the assassin, other riddles might be answered."

"Yes, Master," Obi-Wan replied, and he held the small dart he had taken from the dead Clawdite up before his eyes.

With gentle hands, Shmi Skywalker Lars lifted the dull bronze chest piece up to the wiry droid, setting it in place. She smiled at C-3PO, and, though his face could not similarly twist, she could tell that he, too, in that curious droidlike way, was pleased. How often he had complained about the sand blowing into his wiring, chipping away at the silicon coverings, even breaking through and causing jarring jolts on a couple of occasions. And now Shmi was taking care of that problem, was finishing what Anakin had started in building the droid.

"Now?" she managed to ask aloud, through lips caked with dried blood. No, she realized, it was not now. She had covered C-3PO all those days ago—or was it weeks ago, or even years ago?—when Cliegg had taken her to the moisture farm. Yes, there were spare coverings to fit the protocol droid in the garage area, against the wall, under an old workbench.

She remembered that, so clearly, but she had no idea of when it had been.

And now . . . now she was . . . somewhere.

She couldn't open her eyes to look around; she didn't have the strength at that moment, and the blood on them had dried, making any flutter of her eyelids painful.

She thought it curious that her eyelids were the only place where she actually felt any real pain at that moment. She thought she was injured.

She thought. . .

Shmi heard something behind her. Shuffling footsteps? Then some mumbling. Yes, they were always mumbling.

Her thoughts went back to C-3PO, poor 3PO, who still needed his battered wiry arms covered. *Gently, she lifted the covering . . .*

She heard a sharp sound—or she knew it was a sharp sound, though she heard it only distantly—then felt a brush across her back.

There were no nerves left there to register the bite of the whip any more clearly than that.

Anakin Skywalker and Jar Jar Binks stood at the door separating Padmé's bedroom from the anteroom where Anakin and Obi-Wan had kept watch the night before. Looking through the room to the broken window, the pair watched the Coruscant skyline, the endless lines of traffic.

Padmé and her handmaiden Dormé rushed about the bedroom, throwing the luggage together, and from her sharp movements, both Anakin and Jar Jar knew that they would do well to keep a fair distance from the upset and angry young Senator. As the Jedi had requested, Chancellor Palpatine had intervened to bid Padmé to return to Naboo. She was complying, but that did not mean that she was happy about it.

With a profound sigh, Padmé stood straight, one hand on her lower back, which ached from all the bending. She sighed again and moved before the two observers.

"I'm taking an extended leave of absence," she said to Jar Jar, her voice thick and somber, as if she was hoping to inject some of that gravity into the goofy Gungan. "It will be your responsibility to take my place in the Senate. Representative Binks, I know I can count on you."

"Mesa honored . . ." Jar Jar blurted in reply, standing at attention, except that his head was wagging, and his ears were flopping. One could dress a Gungan up like a dignitary, but such a creature's nature was not so easily changed.

"What?" Padmé's voice was stern and showed more than a little exasperation. She was entrusting something important to Jar Jar, and was obviously not thrilled to hear him acting like his old, goofy self.

Obviously embarrassed, Jar Jar cleared his throat and stood a bit straighter. "Mesa honored to be taken on dissa heavy burden. Mesa accept this with muy . . . muy humility andda—"

"Jar Jar, I don't wish to hold you up," Padmé interrupted. "I'm sure you have a great deal to do."

"Of course, M'Lady." With a great bow, as if trying to use pretense to cover up the fact that he was blushing like a Darellian fire crab, the Gungan turned and left, flashing a bright smile Anakin's way as he passed.

Anakin's eyes followed the retreating Gungan, but any levity or sense of calm he felt from that last exchange was washed away a moment later, when Padmé addressed him in a tone that reminded him that she was not in the best of moods.

"I do not like this idea of hiding," she said emphatically.

"Don't worry. Now that the Council has ordered an investigation, it won't take Master Obi-Wan long to find out who hired that bounty hunter. We should have done that from the beginning. It is better to take the offensive against such a threat, to find out the source rather than try to react to the situation." He meant to go on, to claim credit for asking for such an investigation from the very beginning, to let Padmé know that he had been right all along and that it had taken the Council long enough to come around to his way of thinking. He could see, though, that her eyes were already beginning to glaze over, so he quieted and let her speak.

"And while your Master investigates, I have to hide away."

"That would be most prudent, yes."

Padmé gave a little sigh of frustration. "I haven't worked for a year to defeat the Military Creation Act not to be here when its fate is decided!"

"Sometimes we have to let go of our pride and do what is requested of us," Anakin replied—a rather unconvincing statement, coming from him—and he knew as soon as he spoke the words that he probably shouldn't have phrased things quite like that.

"Pride!" came the roaring response. "Annie, you're young, and you don't have a very firm grip on politics. I suggest you reserve your opinions for some other time."

"Sorry, M'Lady, I was only trying to—"

"Annie! No!"

"Please don't call me that."

"What?"

"Annie. Please don't call me 'Annie.' "

"I've always called you that. It is your name, isn't it?"

"My name is Anakin," the young Jedi said calmly, his jaw firm, his eyes strong. "When you say Annie, it's like I'm still a little boy. And I'm not."

Padmé paused and looked him over, head to toe, nodding as she took the sight of him in completely. He could see sincerity on her face as she nodded her agreement, and her tone, too, became one of more respect. "I'm sorry, Anakin. It's impossible to deny you've . . . that you've grown up."

There was something in the way she said that, Anakin sensed, some suggestion, some recognition from Padmé that he was indeed a man now, and perhaps a handsome one at that. That, combined with the little smile she flashed him, had him a bit flushed and put him back up on his heels. He found an ornament sitting on a shelf to the side, then, and using the Force, picked it up, letting it hover above his fingers, needing the distraction.

Still, he had to clear his throat to cover his embarrassment, for he was afraid that his voice would break apart as he admitted, "Master Obi-Wan manages not to see it. He criticizes my every move, as if I was still a child. He didn't listen to me when I insisted that we go in search of the source of the assassination—"

"Mentors have a way of seeing more of our faults than we would like," Padmé agreed. "It's the only way we grow."

With a thought, Anakin used the Force to lift the little globe ornament higher into the air, manipulating it all about. "Don't get me wrong," he remarked. "Obi-Wan is a great mentor, as wise as Master Yoda and as powerful as Master Windu. I am truly thankful to be his learner. Only . . ." He paused and shook his head, looking for the words. "Only, although I'm a Padawan learner, in some ways—in a lot of ways—I'm ahead of him. I'm ready for the trials. I know I am! He knows it, too. He feels I'm too unpredictable—other Jedi my age have gone through the trials and made it. I know I started my training late, but he won't let me move on."

Padmé's expression grew curious, and Anakin could well understand her puzzlement, for he, too, was surprised at how openly he was speaking, critically, of Obi-Wan. He thought that he should stop right there, and silently berated himself.

But then Padmé said, with all sympathy, "That must be frustrating."

"It's worse!" Anakin cried in response, willingly diving into that warm place. "He's overly critical! He never listens! He just doesn't understand! It's not fair!"

He would have gone on and on, but Padmé began to laugh, and that stopped Anakin as surely as a slap across the face.

"I'm sorry," she said through her giggles. "You sounded exactly like that little boy I once knew, when he didn't get his way."

"I'm not whining! I'm not."

Across the room, Dormé, too, began to chuckle.

"I didn't say it to hurt you," Padmé explained.

Anakin took a deep breath, then blew it all out of him, his shoulders visibly relaxing. "I know."

He seemed so pitiable then, not pitiful, but just like a lost little soul. Padmé couldn't resist. She walked over to him and lifted her hand to gently stroke his cheek. "Anakin."

For the first time since they had been reunited, Padmé truly looked into the blue eyes of the young Padawan, locked stares with him so that they each could see beneath the surface, so that they each could view the other's heart. It was a fleeting moment, made so by Padmé's common sense. She quickly altered the mood with a sincere but lighthearted request. "Don't try to grow up too fast."

"I am grown up," Anakin replied. "You said it yourself." He finished by making his reply into something suggestive, as he looked deeply into Padmé's beautiful brown eyes again, this time even more intensely, more passionately.

"Please don't look at me like that," she said, turning away.

"Why not?"

"Because I can see what you're thinking."

Anakin broke the tension, or tried to, with a laugh. "Oh, so you have Jedi powers, too?"

Padmé looked past the young Padawan for a moment, glimpsing Dormé, who was watching with obvious concern and not even trying to hide her interest anymore. And Padmé understood that concern, given the strange and unexpected road this conversation had taken. She looked squarely at Anakin again and said, with no room for debate, "It makes me feel uncomfortable."

Anakin relented and looked away. "Sorry, M'Lady," he said professionally, and he stepped back, allowing her to resume her packing.

Just the bodyguard again.

But he wasn't, Padmé knew, no matter how much she wished it were true.

On a water-washed, wind-lashed world, far to the most remote edges of the Outer Rim, a father and his son sat on a skirt of shining black metal, watching carefully in the few somewhat calm pools created by the currents swirling about the gigantic caryatid that climbed out of the turbulent ocean. The rain had let up a bit, a rare occasion in this watery place, allowing for some calm surface area, at least, and the pair stared hard, searching for the meter-long dark silhouettes of rollerfish.

They were on the lowest skirt of one of the great pillars that supported Tipoca City, the greatest city on all of Kamino, a place of sleek structures, all rounded to deflect the continual wind, rather than flat-faced to battle against it. Kamino had been designed, or upgraded at least, by many of the best architects the galaxy could offer, who understood well that the best way to battle planetary elements was to subtly dodge them. Towering transparisteel windows looked out from every portal—the father, Jango, often wondered why the Kaminoans, tall and thin, pasty white creatures with huge almond-shaped eyes set in oblong heads on necks as long as his arm, wanted so many windows. What was there to see on this violent world other than rolling waters and nearly constant downpours?

Still, even Kamino had its better moments. It was all relative, Jango supposed. Thus, when he saw that it was not raining very hard, he had taken his boy outside.

Jango tapped his son on the shoulder and nodded toward one of the quiet eddies, and the younger one, his face showing all the exuberance of a ten-year-old boy, lifted his pocker, an ion-burst-powered atlatl, and took deadly aim. He didn't use the laser sighting unit, which automatically adjusted for watery refraction. No, this kill was to be a test of his skill alone.

He exhaled deeply, as his father had taught him, using the technique to go perfectly steady, and then, as the prey turned sidelong, he snapped his arm forward, throwing the missile. Barely a meter from the boy's extended hand, the back of the missile glowed briefly, a sudden and short burst of power that shot it off like a blaster bolt, knifing through the water and taking the fish in the side, its barbed head driving through.

With a shout of joy, the boy twisted the atlatl handle, locking the nearly invisible but tremendously strong line, and then, when the fish squirmed away enough to pull the line taut, the boy slowly and deliberately turned the handle, reeling in his catch.

"Well done," Jango congratulated. "But if you had hit it a centimeter forward, you would have skewered the primary muscle just below the gill and rendered it completely helpless."

The boy nodded, unperturbed that his father, his mentor, could always find fault, even in success. The boy knew that his beloved father did so only because it forced him to strive for perfection. And in a dangerous galaxy, perfection allowed for survival.

The boy loved his father even more for caring enough to criticize.

Jango went tense suddenly, sensing a movement nearby, a footfall, perhaps, or just a smell, something to tell the finely attuned bounty hunter that he and his boy were not alone. There weren't many enemies to be found on Kamino, except far out in the watery wastes, where giant tentacled creatures roamed. Here there was little life above the water, other than the Kaminoans themselves, and so Jango wasn't surprised when he saw that the newcomer was one of them: Taun We, his usual contact with the Kaminoans.

"Greetings, Jango," the tall, lithe creature said, holding up a slim arm and hand in a gesture of peace and friendship.

Jango nodded but didn't smile. Why had Taun We come out here—the Kaminoans were hardly ever out of their city of globes—and why would she interrupt Jango when he was with his son?

"You have been scarce within the sector of late," Taun We remarked.

"Better things to do."

"With your child?"

In response, Jango looked over at the boy, who was lining up another rollerfish. Or at least, he was appearing to, Jango recognized, and the insight brought a knowing nod of satisfaction to the crusty bounty hunter. He had taught his son well the art of deception and deflection, of appearing to do one thing while, in reality, doing something quite different. Like listening in on the conversation, measuring Taun We's every word.

"The tenth anniversary approaches," the Kaminoan explained.

Jango turned back to her with a sour expression. "You think I don't know Boba's birthday?"

If Taun We was fazed at all by the sharp retort, the delicately featured Kaminoan didn't show it. "We are ready to begin again."

Jango looked back at Boba, one of his thousands of children, but the only one who was a perfect clone, an exact replica with no genetic manipulation to make him more obedient. And the only one who hadn't been artificially aged. The group that had been created beside Boba had all reached maturity now, were adult warriors, in perfect health.

Jango had thought that policy of accelerating the aging process a mistake—wasn't experience as much a part of attaining warrior skill as genetics?—but he hadn't complained openly to the Kaminoans about it. He had been hired to do a job, to serve as the source, and questioning the process wasn't in his job description.

Taun We cocked her head a bit to the side, eyes blinking slowly.

Jango recognized her expression as curiosity, and it nearly brought a chuckle bubbling to his lips. The Kaminoans were much more alike than were humans, especially humans from different planets. Perhaps their singular concept, their commonness within their own species, was a part of their typical reproductive process, which now included a fair amount of genetic manipulation, if not outright cloning. As a society, they were practically of one mind and one heart. Taun We seemed genuinely perplexed, and so she was, to see a human with so little apparent regard for other humans, clones or not.

Of course, hadn't the Kaminoans just created an army for the Republic? There wouldn't be wars without some disagreement, now, would there?

But that, too, held little interest for Jango. He was a solitary bounty hunter, a recluse—or he would have been if not for Boba. Jango didn't care a whit about politics or war or this army of his clones. If every one of them was slaughtered, then so be it. He had no attachment to any.

He looked to the side as he considered that. To any except for Boba, of course.

Other than that, though, this was just a job, well paying and easy enough. Financially, he couldn't have asked for more, but more important, only the Kaminoans could have given him Boba—not just a son, but an exact replica. Boba would give Jango the pleasure of seeing all that he might have become had he grown up with a loving and caring father, a mentor who cared enough to criticize, to force him to perfection. He was as good as it got concerning bounty hunters, concerning warriors, but he had no doubt that Boba, bred and trained for perfection, would far outshine him to become one of the greatest warriors the galaxy had ever known.

This, then, was Jango Fett's greatest reward, right here, sitting with his son, his young replica, sharing quiet moments.

Quiet moments within the tumult that had been Jango Fett's entire life, surviving the trials of the Outer Rim alone practically from the day he learned to walk. Each trial had made him stronger, had made him more perfect, had honed the skills that he would now pass along to Boba. There was no one better in all the galaxy to teach his son. When Jango Fett wanted you caught, you were caught. When Jango Fett wanted you dead, you were dead.

No, not when Jango "wanted" those things. This was never personal. The hunting, the killing, it was all a job, and among the most valuable of lessons Jango had learned early on was how to become dispassionate. Completely so. That was his greatest weapon.

He looked at Taun We, then turned to grin at his son. Jango could be dispassionate, except for those times when he could spend time alone with Boba. With Boba, there was pride and there was love, and Jango had to work constantly to keep both of those potential weaknesses at a minimum. While he loved his son dearly—*because* he loved his son dearly—Jango had been

teaching him those same attributes of dispassion, even callousness, from his earliest days.

"We will commence the process again as soon as you
are ready," Taun We remarked, bringing Jango back from his
contemplations.

"Don't you have enough of the material to do it without me?"

"Well, since you are here anyway, we would like you to be
involved," Taun We said. "The original host is always the best
choice."

Jango rolled his eyes at the thought—of the needles and the
probing—but he did nod his agreement; this was really an easy
job, considering the rewards.

"Whenever you are ready." Taun We bowed and turned and
walked away.

If you wait for that, you'll be waiting forever, Jango thought,
but he kept quiet, and again he turned to Boba, motioning for
the boy to put his atlatl back to work. *Because now I have all that
I wanted,* Jango mused, watching Boba's fluid motions, his eyes
darting about, searching for the next rollerfish.

The industrial sector of Coruscant held perhaps the greatest
freight docks in all the galaxy, with a line of bulky transports
coming in continually, huge floating cranes ready to meet them
and unload the millions of tons of supplies necessary to keep
alive the city-planet, which long ago had become too populous
to support itself through its own resources. The efficiency of
these docks was nothing short of amazing, and yet the place was
still tumultuous, and sometimes gridlocked by the sheer number
of docking ships and floating cranes.

This was also a place for living passengers, the peasantry of
Coruscant, catching cheap rides on freighters outbound, thousands and thousands of people looking to escape the sheer
frenzy that had become the world.

Blended into that throng, Anakin and Padmé walked along,
dressed in simple brown tunics and breeches, the garb of Out-

land refugees. They walked side by side to the shuttle exit as they approached the dock and walkway that would take them to one of the gigantic transports. Captain Typho, Dormé, and Obi-Wan stood waiting for them at that exit door.

"Be safe, M'Lady," Captain Typho said with genuine concern. It was clear that he was not thrilled with allowing Padmé out of his sight and control. He handed a pair of small luggage bags over to Anakin and gave a nod of confidence to the young Jedi.

"Thank you, Captain," Padmé replied, her voice thick with gratitude. "Take good care of Dormé. The threat will be on you two now."

"He'll be safe with me!" Dormé put in quickly.

Padmé smiled, appreciating the small attempt at levity. Then she embraced her handmaiden in a great and tight hug, squeezing all the tighter when she heard Dormé start to weep.

"You'll be fine," Padmé whispered into the other woman's ear.

"It's not me, M'Lady. I worry about you. What if they realize you've left the capital?"

Padmé moved back to arm's length and managed a smile as she looked over to Anakin. "Then my Jedi protector will have to prove how good he is."

Dormé gave a nervous chuckle and wiped a tear from her eye as she smiled and nodded.

Off to the side, Anakin held his smile within, deciding consciously to wear a posture that exuded confidence and control. But inside he was thrilled to hear Padmé's compliments coming his way.

Obi-Wan shattered that warmth, pulling the young Padawan off to the side.

"You stay on Naboo," Obi-Wan said. "Don't attract attention. Do absolutely nothing without checking in with me or the Council."

"Yes, Master," Anakin answered obediently, but inside, he was churning, wanting to lash out at Obi-Wan. Do nothing, absolutely nothing, without checking in, without asking for permission? Hadn't he earned a bit more respect than that? Hadn't he proven himself a bit more resourceful, a Padawan to be trusted?

"I will get to the bottom of this plot quickly, M'Lady," he heard Obi-Wan say to Padmé. Anakin seethed inwardly. Hadn't that been exactly the course he had suggested to his Master when they had first been assigned to watch over the Senator?

"You'll be back here in no time," Obi-Wan assured her.

"I will be most grateful for your speed, Master Jedi."

Anakin didn't appreciate hearing Padmé speak of any gratitude at all toward Obi-Wan. At least, he didn't want Padmé to elevate Obi-Wan's importance in all of this above his own. "Time to go," he said, striding forward.

"I know," Padmé answered him, but she didn't seem pleased.

Anakin reminded himself not to take it personally. Padmé felt that her duty was here. She wasn't thrilled with running offplanet—and she wasn't thrilled with having another of her dear handmaidens stepping into the line of fire in her stead, especially with images of dead Cordé so fresh in her mind.

Padmé and Dormé shared another hug. Anakin took up the luggage and led the way off the speeder bus, onto a landing where R2-D2 waited.

"May the Force be with you," Obi-Wan said.

"May the Force be with you, Master." Anakin meant every word of it. He wanted Obi-Wan to find out who was behind the assassination attempts, to make the galaxy safe for Padmé once again. But he had to admit that he hoped it wouldn't happen too quickly. His duty now put him right beside the woman he loved, and he wouldn't be happy if this assignment proved a short one, if duty pulled him away from her yet again.

"Suddenly I'm afraid," Padmé said to him as they walked away, heading toward the giant star freighter that would take them to Naboo. Behind the pair, R2-D2 rolled along, tootling cheerily.

"This is my first assignment on my own. I am, too." Anakin turned about, taking Padmé's gaze with his own, and grinned widely. "But don't worry. We've got Artoo with us!"

Again, the levity was much needed.

Back at the bus, waiting for it to take them back to the main city, the three left behind watched Anakin, Padmé, and R2-D2 blend into the throng of the vast spaceport.

"I hope he doesn't try anything foolish," Obi-Wan said. The mere fact that he would speak so openly concerning his student showed Captain Typho how much the Jedi Knight had come to trust him.

"I'd be more concerned about *her* doing something than him," Typho replied. He shook his head, his expression serious. "She's not one to follow orders."

"Like-minded traveling companions," Dormé observed.

Obi-Wan and Typho turned to regard her, and Typho shook his head helplessly again. Obi-Wan didn't disagree with Dormé's assessment, however innocently she meant it. Padmé Amidala was a stubborn one indeed, one of strong and independent thinking and more than willing to trust her own judgment above that of others, whatever their position and experience.

But of the pair who had just left the speeder bus, she wasn't the most headstrong.

It was not a comforting thought.

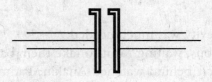

The great Jedi Temple was a place of reflection and of hard training, and it was also a place of information. The Jedi were traditionally the keepers of the peace, and also of knowledge. Beneath their high ceilings, off the main corridor of the Temple, stood the glass cubicles, the analysis rooms, filled with droids of various shapes and sizes, and various purposes.

Obi-Wan Kenobi was thinking of Anakin and Padmé as he made his way through the Temple. He wondered, not for the first time and certainly not for the last, about the wisdom of sending Anakin off with the Senator. The eagerness with which the Padawan had embraced his new duty set off warning bells in Obi-Wan's head, but he had allowed the mission to go forth anyway, mostly because he knew that he'd be too busy following the leads he hoped he could garner here, uncovering the source of Amidala's troubles.

The analysis cubicles were busy this day, as they were nearly every day, with students and Masters alike hard at their studies. Obi-Wan found one open cubicle with an SP-4 analysis droid, the type he needed. He sat down in front of the console and the droid responded immediately, sliding open a tray.

"Place the subject for analysis on the sensor tray, please," the droid's metallic voice said. Obi-Wan was already moving, pulling forth the toxic dart that had killed the subcontracting bounty hunter.

As soon as the tray receded, the screen before Obi-Wan lit up and began scrolling through a series of diagrams and streams of data.

"It's a toxic dart," the Jedi explained to the SP-4. "I need to know where it came from and who made it."

"One moment, please." More diagrams rolled by, more reams of data scrolling, and then the screen paused, showing a somewhat similar dart. But it wasn't a match and the scrolling started again. Images of the dart flashed up before Obi-Wan, superimposed with diagrams of similar objects. Nothing matched.

The screen went blank. The tray slid back out.

"As you can see on your screen, subject weapon does not exist in any known culture," SP-4 explained. "Markings cannot be identified. Probably self-made by a warrior not associated with any known culture. Stand away from the sensor tray, please."

"Excuse me? Could you try again please?" There was no hiding the frustration in Obi-Wan's voice.

"Master Jedi, our records are very thorough. They cover eighty percent of the galaxy. If I can't tell you where it came from, nobody can."

Obi-Wan picked up the dart, looked at the droid, and sighed, not so sure that he agreed with that particular assessment. "Thanks for your assistance," he said. He wondered if SP-4s were equipped to understand the inflections of sarcasm. "You may not be able to figure this out, but I think I know someone who might."

"The odds do not suggest such a possibility," SP-4 started to reply, and began rolling along with a dissertation about the completeness of its data banks, of its unequaled search capabilities, of . . .

It didn't matter, for Obi-Wan was long gone, walking briskly along the great corridor and out of the Jedi Temple.

He left without a word to anyone, his thoughts turned inward, trying to find some focus. He needed answers, and quickly. He knew that instinctively, but he had a nagging feeling that it wasn't necessarily about Senator Amidala's safety. He sensed that something more might be at stake here, though what it was, he could only guess. Anakin's mind-set? A greater plot against the Republic?

Or perhaps he was just being jumpy because the normally reliable SP-4 droid hadn't been able to help him at all. He needed answers, and conventional methods of attaining them wouldn't suffice, apparently. But Obi-Wan Kenobi was not a conventional Jedi, in many ways. Although he tended to be reserved, especially when dealing with his Padawan, his former Master, Qui-Gon Jinn, had left a mark on Obi-Wan.

He knew where to get his answers.

He took a speeder to the business section of Coco town, far from where he and Anakin had caught the would-be assassin.

Obi-Wan stopped his vehicle and exited to the street. He moved to one small building, its windows foggy, its walls metallic and brightly painted. Lettering above the door named the place, and though he could not read that particular script, Obi-Wan knew well what it said: DEX'S DINER.

He smiled. He hadn't seen Dex in a long time. Far too long, he mused as he entered.

The inside of the diner was fairly typical of the establishments along the lower level, with booths set against the walls and many small freestanding circular tables surrounded by tall stools. There was a counter area, as well, partly lined with stools and partly open, a variety of beings standing and leaning against it, mostly freighter drivers and dockworkers, people who still used their muscles in a galaxy grown soft through technology.

The Jedi moved to one small table, sliding onto its stool as a waitress droid wiped the table down with a rag.

"Can I help ya?" the droid asked.

"I'm looking for Dexter."

The waitress droid made a rather unpleasant sound.

Obi-Wan just smiled. "I do need to speak with Dexter."

"Waddya want him for?"

"He's not in trouble," the Jedi assured her. "It's personal."

The droid stared at him for a short while, sizing him up, then, with a shake of her head, she moved to the open serving hatch behind the counter. "Someone to see ya, honey," she said. "A Jedi, by the looks of him."

A huge head poked through the open hatchway almost immediately, accompanied by a line of grayish steam. A wide smile—on a mouth wide enough to swallow Obi-Wan's head whole—with huge block teeth grew on the immense face as he set his gaze on the visitor. "Obi-Wan!"

"Hey, Dex," Obi-Wan replied, standing and moving to the counter.

"Take a seat, old buddy! Be right with ya!"

Obi-Wan glanced around. The waitress droid had gone about her business, tending to other customers. He moved to a booth just to the side of the counter.

"You want a cup of ardees?" the droid asked, her demeanor much more accommodating.

"Thank you."

She moved off toward the counter, slipping aside as the infamous Dexter Jettster moved through the counter door, walking with a stiff gait. He was an impressive sort, a neckless mound of flesh, dwarfing most of the toughies who frequented his establishment. His great belly poked out beneath his grimy shirt and breeches. He was bald and sweaty, and though he had seen many years and did not move fluidly any longer, with too many old injuries slowing him, Dexter Jettster was obviously not a creature anyone wanted to fight—especially since he was possessed of four huge arms, each with a massive fist that could fully bust a man's face. Obi-Wan noted the many respectful glances that went his way as he moved to the booth.

"Hey, ol' buddy!"

"Hey, Dex. Long time."

With great effort, Dexter managed to squeeze himself into

the seat opposite Obi-Wan. The waitress droid was back by then, setting two steaming mugs of ardees in front of the old friends.

"So, my friend, what can I do for ya?" Dexter asked, and it was obvious to Obi-Wan that Dex genuinely wanted to help. Obi-Wan was hardly surprised. He didn't always approve of Dexter's antics, of the seedy diner and the many fights, but he knew Dex to be among the most loyal of friends that anyone could ever ask for. Dex would crush the life out of an enemy, but would give his own life for someone he cared about. That was the code among the star wanderers, and one that Obi-Wan could truly appreciate. In many, many ways, being here with Dex appealed to the Jedi Knight much more than the time he had to spend among the ruling elite.

"You can tell me what this is," Obi-Wan answered. He put the dart on the table, watching Dex all the time, noting how the being quickly placed his mug back down, his eyes widening as he regarded the curious and distinctive item.

"Well, waddya know," Dex said quietly, as if he could hardly draw breath. He picked up the dart delicately, almost reverently, the weapon nearly disappearing within the folds of his fat fingers. "I ain't seen one of these since I was prospecting on Subterrel beyond the Outer Rim."

"Do you know where it came from?"

Dexter placed the dart down before Obi-Wan. "This baby belongs to them cloners. What you got here is a Kamino saberdart."

"Kamino saberdart?" Obi-Wan echoed. "I wonder why it didn't show up in our analysis archive."

Dex poked down at the dart with a stubby finger. "It's these funny little cuts on the side that give it away," he explained. "Those analysis droids you've got over there only focus on symbols, you know. I should think you Jedi have more respect for the difference between knowledge and wisdom."

"Well, Dex, if droids could think, there'd be none of us here, would there?" Obi-Wan answered with a laugh.

The Jedi Knight sobered quickly, though, remembering the

gravity of his mission. "Kamino . . . doesn't sound familiar. Is it part of the Republic?"

"No, it's beyond the Outer Rim. I'd say about twelve parsecs outside the Rishi Maze, toward the south. It should be easy to find, even for those droids in your archive. These Kaminoans keep to themselves, mostly. They're cloners. Good ones, too."

Obi-Wan picked up the dart again, holding it between them, his elbow resting on the table. "Cloners?" he asked. "Are they friendly?"

"It depends."

"On what?" The Jedi looked past the dart as he asked, and the grin on Dexter's face gave him his answer before it was spoken aloud.

"On how good your manners are and how big your pocketbook is."

Obi-Wan looked back at the saberdart, hardly surprised.

Senator Padmé Amidala, formerly Queen Amidala of Naboo, certainly wasn't used to traveling in this manner. The freighter held one class, steerage, and in truth, it was nothing more than a cargo ship, with several great open holds more suitable to inanimate cargo than to living beings. The lighting was terrible and the smell was worse, though whether the odor came from the ship itself or the hordes of emigrants, beings of many, many species, Padmé did not know. Nor did she care. In some ways, Padmé was truly enjoying this voyage. She knew that she should be back on Coruscant, fighting the efforts to create a Republic army, but somehow, she felt relaxed here, felt free.

Free of responsibility. Free to just be Padmé for a while, instead of Senator Amidala. Moments such as these were rare for her, and had been since she was a child. All of her life, it seemed, had been spent in public service; all of her focus had always been for the greater, the public, good, with hardly any time ever being given just to Padmé, to her needs and her desires.

The Senator didn't regret that reality of her life. She was proud of her accomplishments, but more than that, even, she felt a profound sense of warmth, of community, of belonging to something greater than herself.

Still, these moments when the responsibility was lifted were undeniably enjoyable.

She looked over at Anakin, who was sleeping somewhat restlessly. She could see him now, not as a Jedi Padawan and her protector, but just as a young man. A handsome young man, and one whose actions repeatedly professed his love for her. A dangerous young man, to be sure, a Jedi who was thinking about things he should not. A man who was inevitably following the call of his heart above that of pragmatism and propriety. And all for her. Padmé couldn't deny the attractiveness of that. She and Anakin were on similar roads of public service, she as a Senator, he as a Jedi Padawan, but he was showing rebellion against the present course, or at least, against the Master who was leading him along the present course, as Padmé never had.

But hadn't she wanted to? Hadn't Padmé Amidala wanted to be just Padmé? Once in a while, at least?

She smiled widely and pointedly turned away from Anakin, scanning the gloomy room for signs of her other companion. She finally spotted R2-D2 in a food line, where he stuck out among the throng of living creatures. Just before the droid, servers ladled out bowls of bland-looking mush, and each being who took one inevitably gave out a low groan of disapproval.

Padmé watched with amusement as one of the servers began yelling and waving his hand at R2-D2, motioning for the droid to move along. "No droids in the food line!" the server yelled. "Get out of here!"

R2-D2 started past the counter, but stopped suddenly, and a hollow tube came forth from his utilitarian body, hovering over the buffet and sucking up some of the mush and placing it in a storage container for transport to his companions.

"Hey, no droids!" the server yelled again.

R2-D2 took another fast gulp of the mush, reached out with a claw arm to grab a piece of bread, then turned and tootled and rushed away, the server shaking his fist and shouting behind him.

The droid came fast across the wide floor, veering to avoid the many sleeping emigrants, making as straight a line as possible toward the beaming Padmé.

"No, no," came a call beside her. It was Anakin. "Mom, no!"

Padmé turned about quickly, to see that her companion was still asleep, but sweating and thrashing, obviously in the throes of some nightmare.

"Anakin?" She gave him a little shake.

"No, Mom!" he cried, pulling away from her, and she looked down to see his feet kicking, as if he was running away from something.

"Anakin," Padmé said again, more forcefully. She shook him again, harder.

His blue eyes blinked open and he looked about curiously before focusing on Padmé. "What?"

"You seemed to be having a nightmare."

Anakin continued to stare at her, his expression ranging from curiosity to concern.

Padmé took a bowl of mush and a piece of bread from R2-D2. "Are you hungry?"

Anakin took the food as he sat up, rubbing a hand through his hair and shaking his head.

"We went to hyperspace a while ago," she explained.

"How long was I asleep?"

Padmé smiled at him, trying to comfort him. "You had a good nap," she answered.

Anakin smoothed the front of his tunic and straightened himself, looking all around, trying to get his bearings. "I look forward to seeing Naboo again," he remarked and he shifted, trying to orient himself. His expression soured as he looked down at the off-white mush, and he crinkled his nose, bending low to sniff it. "Naboo," he said again, looking back to Padmé. "I've thought about it every day since I left. It's by far the most beautiful place I've ever seen."

As he spoke, his eyes bored into her, taking her in deeply,

and she blinked and averted her own gaze, unnerved. "It may not be as you remember it. Time changes perception."

"Sometimes it does," Anakin agreed, and when Padmé looked up to see that he was continuing to scrutinize her, she knew what he was talking about. "Sometimes for the better."

"It must be difficult having sworn your life to the Jedi," she said, taking a different tack to pull his gaze off her. "Not being able to visit the places you like. Or do the things you like."

"Or be with the people I love?" Anakin could easily see where she was leading him.

"Are you allowed to love?" Padmé asked bluntly. "I thought it was forbidden for a Jedi."

"Attachment is forbidden," Anakin began, his voice dispassionate, as if he was reciting. "Possession is forbidden. Compassion, which I would define as unconditional love, is central to a Jedi's life, so you might say we're encouraged to love."

"You have changed so much," Padmé heard herself saying, and in a tone that seemed inappropriate to her, seemed to invite. . .

She blinked as Anakin turned her words back on her. "You haven't changed a bit. You're exactly the way I remember you in my dreams. I doubt if Naboo has changed much either."

"It hasn't. . ." Padmé's voice was breathless. They were too close together. She knew that. She knew that she was in dangerous territory here, both for herself and for Anakin. He was a Padawan learner, a Jedi, and Jedi were not allowed . . .

And what about her? What about all that she had worked so hard for all her adult life? What about the Senate, and the all-important vote against the creation of an army? If Padmé got involved with a Jedi, the implications concerning her vote would become huge! The army, if one was created, would be made to stand beside the Jedi and their duties, and yet Padmé would stand against that army, and so . . .

And so?

It was all so complicated, but even more important than that, it was all so dangerous. She thought of her sister then, and their last conversation before Padmé had flown back to Coruscant. She thought of Ryoo and Pooja.

"You were dreaming about your mother earlier," she remarked, needing to change the subject. She sat back, putting some distance between her and Anakin, gaining some margin of safety between them. "Weren't you?"

Anakin leaned back and looked away, nodding slowly. "I left Tatooine so long ago. My memory of her is fading." He snapped his intense gaze back over Padmé. "I don't want to lose that memory. I don't want to stop seeing her face."

She started to say, "I know," and started to lift her hand to stroke his cheek, but she held back and let him continue.

"I've been seeing her in my dreams. Vivid dreams. Scary dreams. I worry about her."

"I'd be disappointed in you if you didn't," Padmé answered him, her voice soft and full of sympathy. "You didn't leave her in the best of circumstances."

Anakin winced, as if those words had hurt him.

"But it was right that you left," Padmé reminded him, taking his arm. She held his gaze with her own. "Your leaving was what your mother wanted for you. What she needed for you. The opportunity that Qui-Gon offered you gave her hope. That's what a parent needs for her child, to know that he, that you, had been given a chance at a better life."

"But the dreams—"

"You can't help but feel a little guilty about leaving, I suppose," Padmé answered, and Anakin was shaking his head, as if she was missing the point. But she didn't believe that to be the case, so she continued. "It's only natural that you'd want your mother off Tatooine, out here with you, perhaps. Or on Naboo, or Coruscant, or someplace that you feel is safer, and more beautiful. Trust me, Anakin," she said softly but intently, and she put her hand on his forearm again. "You did the right thing in going. For yourself, but more importantly, for your mother."

Her expression, so full of compassion, so full of caring, was not one that Anakin Skywalker could argue against.

The great port city of Theed was in many ways akin to Coruscant, with freighters and shuttles coming down from the skies in lines. Unlike Coruscant, though, this city on Naboo was soft in appearance, with few towering, imposing skyscrapers of hard metal and shining transparisteel. The buildings here were of stone and many other materials, with rounded rooflines and delicate colors. Vines of all sorts were everywhere, crawling up the sides of the buildings, adding vibrancy and scents. Adding comfort.

Anakin and Padmé lugged their bags across a familiar square, a place where they had seen battle a decade before against the droids of the Trade Federation. R2-D2 came behind them, rolling along easily, whistling a happy song, as if he were an extension of the comfortable aura of Theed.

Padmé kept covertly glancing at Anakin, noting the serenity on his face, the widening grin.

"If I grew up here, I don't think I'd ever leave," Anakin remarked.

Padmé laughed. "I doubt that."

"No, really. When I started my training, I was very homesick and very lonely. This city and my mom were the only pleasant things I had to think about."

Padmé's expression turned to one of curiosity and confusion. Anakin's time here had been spent, mostly, in deadly battle! Had he so obsessed about her, about Naboo, that even the bad memories paled against his warm feelings?

"The problem was," Anakin went on, "the more I thought about my mom, the worse I felt. But I would feel better if I thought about Naboo and the palace."

He didn't say it outright, but Padmé knew that what

he really meant was that he felt better when he thought about her, or at least that he would include her in those pleasant thoughts.

"The way the palace shimmers in the sunlight, the way the air always smells of flowers."

"And the soft sound of the distant waterfalls," Padmé added. She could not deny the sincerity in Anakin's voice and in his words, and she found herself agreeing and embracing that truth of Naboo, despite her resolve to stay away from those feelings. "The first time I saw the capital, I was very young. I'd never seen a waterfall before. I thought they were so beautiful. I never thought that one day I'd live in the palace."

"Well, tell me, did you dream of power and politics when you were a little girl?"

Again Padmé had to laugh aloud. "No, that was the last thing I thought of." She could feel the wistfulness creeping into her, the memories of those long-ago days before her innocence had been shattered by war, and even more so, by the constant deceptions and conniving of politics. She could hardly believe that she was opening up to Anakin like this. "My dream was to work in the Refugee Relief Movement. I never thought of running for elected office. But the more history I studied, the more I realized how much good politicians could do. So when I was eight, I joined the Apprentice Legislators, which is like making a formal announcement that you're entering public service here on Naboo. From there, I went on to become a Senatorial Adviser, and attacked my duties with such a passion that before I knew it, I was elected Queen."

Padmé looked at Anakin and shrugged, trying not to throw all humility away. "Partly because I scored so high on my education certificate," she explained. "But for the most part, my ascent was because of my conviction that reform was possible. The people of Naboo embraced that dream wholeheartedly, so much so that my age was hardly an issue in the campaign. I wasn't the youngest Queen ever elected, but now that I think back on it,

I'm not sure I was old enough." She paused and locked stares with Anakin. "I'm not sure I was ready."

"The people you served thought you did a good job," Anakin reminded her. "I heard they tried to amend the constitution so that you could stay in office."

"Popular rule is not democracy, Anakin. It gives the people what they want, not what they need. And truthfully, I was relieved when my two terms were up." Padmé chuckled as she continued, adding emphasis. "So were my parents! They worried about me during the blockade and couldn't wait for it all to be over. Actually, I was hoping to have a family by now. . . ."

She turned away a bit, feeling her face flushing. How could she be so open to him, and so quickly? He was not a longtime friend, she reminded herself, but the warning sounded hollow in her thoughts. She looked back at Anakin, and she felt so at ease, so comfortable with him, almost as if they had been friends for all their lives. "My sister has the most amazing, wonderful kids." Her eyes were sparkling, she knew, but she blinked the emotion away, as Padmé had often blinked away her personal desires for the sake of what she perceived to be the greater good. "But when the Queen asked me to serve as Senator, I couldn't refuse her," she explained.

"I agree!" Anakin replied. "I think the Republic needs you. I'm glad you chose to serve—I feel things are going to happen in our generation that will change the galaxy in profound ways."

"A Jedi premonition?" Padmé kidded.

Anakin laughed. "A feeling," he explained, or tried to explain, for it was obvious that he wasn't quite sure what he was trying to say. "It just seems to me as if it's all grown stale, as if something has to happen—"

"I think so, too," Padmé put in sincerely.

They had arrived at the great doors of the palace, and paused to take in the beautiful scene. Unlike most of Coruscant's buildings, which seemed to have been designed with utter efficiency in mind, this structure was more akin to the Jedi Temple, an understanding that aesthetics were important, that form went hand in hand with purpose.

Padmé knew her way about the place, obviously, and she was well known by almost all of the people within, and so the two walked along easily to the throne room, where they were announced at once.

Smiling faces greeted them. Sio Bibble, Padmé's dear friend and her trusted adviser when she was Queen, stood by the throne, flanking Queen Jamillia as he had so often flanked Padmé. He hadn't aged much over the last years, his white hair and beard still distinguished and perfectly coiffed, his eyes still full of that intensity that Padmé so loved.

Beside him, Jamillia looked every bit the part of Queen. She wore a great headdress and flowing embroidered robes, the same type of outfit Padmé had worn for so very long, and the Senator thought that Jamillia looked at least as regal in them as she had.

Handmaidens, advisers, and guards were all about, and Padmé reflected that one of the side effects of being Queen, and not a pleasant one, was that one was never allowed to be alone.

Queen Jamillia, standing perfectly straight so that her headdress did not topple, rose and walked over to take Padmé's hand. "We've been worried about you. I'm so glad you're here, Padmé," she said, her voice rich and with a southeastern accent that made her enunciate the consonants powerfully.

"Thank you, Your Highness. I only wish I could have served you better by staying on Coruscant for the vote."

"Supreme Chancellor Palpatine has explained it all," Sio Bibble interjected. "Returning home was the only real choice you could have made."

Padmé gave him a resigned nod. Still, being sent home to Naboo bothered her; she had worked so very hard against the creation of a Republic army.

"How many systems have joined Count Dooku and the separatists?" Queen Jamillia asked bluntly. She had never been one for small talk.

"Thousands," Padmé answered. "And more are leaving the Republic every day. If the Senate votes to create an army, I'm sure it's going to push us into civil war."

Sio Bibble punched his fist into his open hand. "It's unthinkable!" he said, gnashing his teeth with every word. "There hasn't been a full-scale war since the formation of the Republic."

"Do you see any way, through negotiations, to bring the separatists back into the Republic?" Jamillia asked, staying calm despite Sio Bibble's obvious agitation.

"Not if they feel threatened." It amazed Padmé to realize how secure she was in these estimations. She felt as if she was beginning to fully understand the nuances of her position, as if she could trust her instincts implicitly. And all of her talents would be needed, she knew. "The separatists don't have an army, but if they are provoked, they will move to defend themselves. I'm sure of that. And with no time or money to build an army, my guess is they will turn to the Commerce Guild or the Trade Federation for help."

"The armies of commerce!" Queen Jamillia echoed with anger and distaste. All on Naboo knew well the problems associated with such free-ranging groups. The Trade Federation had nearly brought Naboo to its knees, and would have had it not been for the heroics of Amidala, a pair of Jedi, a young Anakin, and the brave flying of the dedicated Naboo pilots. Even that would not have been enough, had not Queen Amidala forged an unexpected alliance with the heroic Gungans. "Why has nothing been done in the Senate to restrain them?"

"I'm afraid that, despite the Chancellor's best efforts, there are still many bureaucrats, judges, and even Senators on the pay-rolls of the guilds," Padmé admitted.

"Then it is true that the guilds have moved closer to the separatists, as we suspected," Queen Jamillia reasoned.

Sio Bibble punched his open palm again, drawing their attention. "It's outrageous!" he said. "It's outrageous that after all those hearings and four trials in the Supreme Court, Nute

Gunray is still the viceroy of the Trade Federation. Do those money-mongers control everything?"

"Remember, Counselor, the courts were able to reduce the Trade Federation's armies," Jamillia reminded, again holding her calm and controlled voice. "That's a move in the right direction."

Padmé winced, knowing that she had to report honestly. "There are rumors, Your Highness, that the Federation's army was not reduced as they were ordered."

Clearing his throat, Anakin Skywalker stepped forward. "The Jedi have not been allowed to investigate," he explained. "It would be too dangerous for the economy, we were told."

Queen Jamillia looked to him and nodded, looked back to Padmé, then squared her shoulders and firmed her jawline, looking regal in the ornate raiments—very much the planetary ruler obedient to the Republic. "We must keep our faith in the Republic," she declared. "The day we stop believing democracy can work is the day we lose it."

"Let's pray that day never comes," Padmé quietly answered.

"In the meantime, we must consider your own safety," Queen Jamillia said, and she looked to Sio Bibble, who motioned to the attendants. All of them, advisers, attendants, and handmaidens, bowed and quickly left the room. Sio Bibble moved near to Anakin, the appointed protector, then paused, waiting for all of the others to be gone. At last he spoke. "What is your suggestion, Master Jedi?"

"Anakin's not a Jedi yet, Counselor," Padmé interrupted. "He's still a Padawan learner. I was thinking—"

"Hey, hold on a minute!" Anakin cut her short, his eyes narrowed, brow furrowed, obviously agitated and put off by her dismissal.

"Excuse me!" Padmé shot right back, not backing down from Anakin's imposing glare. "I was thinking I would stay in the Lake Country. There are some places up there that are very isolated."

"Excuse me!" Anakin said, giving it right back to her, in words and in tone. "I am in charge of security here, M'Lady."

Padmé started to fight back, but she noted then the exchange of suspicious looks between Sio Bibble and Queen Jamillia. She and Anakin should not be fighting in this manner in public, she realized, not without making others believe that something might be going on between them. She calmed down and softened her expression and her voice. "Anakin, my life is at risk and this is my home. I know it very well—that is why we're here. I think it would be wise for you to take advantage of my knowledge in this instance."

Anakin looked around at the two onlookers, and then back at Padmé, and the hardness melted from his expression. "Sorry, M'Lady."

"She is right," an obviously amused Sio Bibble said, taking Anakin's arm. "The Lake Country is the most remote part of Naboo. Not many people up there, and a clear view of the surrounding terrain. It would be an excellent choice, a place where you would have a much easier time protecting Senator Amidala."

"Perfect!" Queen Jamillia agreed. "It's settled then."

Padmé could tell from the way Anakin was looking at her that he wasn't overly pleased. She offered an innocent shrug in response.

"Padmé," Queen Jamillia went on, "I had an audience with your father yesterday. I told him what was happening. He hopes you will visit your mother before you leave. Your family's very worried about you."

How could they not be? Padmé thought, and it pained her to consider that the dangers her strong positions were bringing to her were affecting other people whom she loved. *How could they not?* It was a perfect reminder of why family and public service didn't usually mix. Padmé Amidala had made a conscious and definitive choice: public service or family. Some on Naboo juggled the two, but Padmé had always known that such a dual role as wife, perhaps even mother, and Senator would not do well for family or state.

She hadn't been worried about her own safety at all through these trials, willing to make whatever sacrifices were necessary. But now, suddenly, she had to remember that her choices and positions could affect others on a very personal level, as well.

She wore no smile as she walked with Anakin, Sio Bibble, and Queen Jamillia out of the throne room and down the palace's main staircase.

The largest room in the vast Jedi Temple on Coruscant was the hall of the Archives. Lighted computer panels stretched out in long, long lines of bluish dots along the walls, running so far that a person viewing them from one end of the room would see them converging at the other end. Throughout were the images of Jedi past and present, groups of sculpted busts done in bronze by many of the finest artisans of Coruscant.

Obi-Wan Kenobi stood at one of these busts, studying it, touching it, as if examining the facial features of the person depicted would give him some insight to the man's motivations. There weren't many visitors in the Archives today—there rarely were more than a few—and so the Jedi expected that his call to Madame Jocasta Nu, the Jedi Archivist, would be answered shortly.

He stood patiently, studying the strong features on the bust, the high and proud cheekbones, the meticulous hairstyle, the eyes, wide and alert. Obi-Wan hadn't known this man, this legend, Count Dooku, very well, but he had seen him on occasion and he knew that this bust captured the essence of Dooku perfectly. There was an intensity about the man as palpable as that which had sometimes surrounded Master Qui-Gon, especially when Qui-Gon had found a particularly important cause. Qui-

Gon would go against the Jedi Council when he felt that he was right, as he had done with Anakin some ten years earlier, before the Council had agreed to recognize that the boy's special circumstances, the incredible Force potential and the promise that he might be the one spoken of in prophecy.

Yes, Obi-Wan had seen this kind of intensity in Qui-Gon on occasion, but what he knew of Dooku was that, unlike Qui-Gon, the man had never been able to shut it off, had always been stomping around, chewing over an issue. The lights in his eyes were ever-burning fires.

But Dooku had taken it to extremes, and dangerous ones, Obi-Wan realized. He had left the Jedi Order, had walked out on his calling and on his peers. Whatever problems Dooku must have seen, he should have recognized that he could better repair them by remaining within the Jedi family.

"Did you call for assistance?" came a stern voice behind Obi-Wan, drawing him from his thoughts. He turned to see Madame Jocasta Nu standing beside him, her hands folded together before her, practically disappearing within the folds of her Jedi robes. She was a frail-looking creature, quite elderly, and noting that brought a smile to Obi-Wan's face. How many younger and less experienced Jedi had looked upon that facade, the thin and wrinkled face and neck, the white hair tied tight, thinking that they could push the woman around, getting her to do their studying for them, only to encounter the truth that was Jocasta Nu? She was a firebrand, that weak facade hiding her true strength and determination. Jocasta Nu had been the Archivist for many, many years, and this was her place, her domain, her kingdom. Any Jedi coming in here, even the most exalted of Jedi Masters, would play by the rules of Jocasta Nu, or they would surely face her wrath.

"Yes, yes I did," Obi-Wan finally managed to respond, realizing that Jocasta Nu was staring at him inquisitively, awaiting an answer.

The old woman smiled and walked past him to regard the bust of Count Dooku. "He has a powerful face, doesn't he?"

she commented, her quiet tone taking the tension out of the meeting. "He was one of the most brilliant Jedi I have had the privilege of knowing."

"I never understood why he quit," Obi-Wan said, following Jocasta Nu's look to the bust. "Only twenty Jedi have ever left the Order."

"The Lost Twenty," Jocasta Nu said with a profound sigh. "And Count Dooku was the most recent and the most painful. No one likes to talk about it. His leaving was a great loss to the Order."

"What happened?"

"Well, one might say he was a bit out of step with the decisions of the Council," the Archivist replied. "Much like your old Master, Qui-Gon."

Even though Obi-Wan had just been thinking the same thing, somewhat, to hear Jocasta Nu speak the words so definitively caught him off guard, and painted Qui-Gon in a more rebellious light than he had ever considered. He knew that his former Master had his moments, of course, the greatest of those being the confrontations concerning Anakin, but he had never thought of Qui-Gon as that much of a rebel. Apparently, Jocasta Nu, who had her finger as squarely as anyone on the pulse of the Jedi Temple, did.

"Really?" Obi-Wan prompted, wanting the information about Dooku, of course, but also hoping to garner some insight into his old and beloved Master.

"Oh, yes, they were alike in many ways. Very individual thinkers. Idealists." She stared at the bust intently, and it seemed to Obi-Wan as if she had suddenly gone far, far away. "He was always striving to become a more powerful Jedi. He wanted to be the best. With a lightsaber, in the old style of fencing, he had no match. His knowledge of the Force was . . . unique. In the end, I think he left because he lost faith in the Republic. He believed that politics were corrupt . . ."

Jocasta Nu paused for a moment and looked at Obi-Wan, a

very revealing expression that showed she did not think Dooku as out of step as many of the others apparently did.

"And he felt that the Jedi betrayed themselves by serving the politicians," the Archivist stated.

Obi-Wan blinked, soaking in the words. He knew that many, Qui-Gon included—even himself included, at times—often felt the same way.

"He always had very high expectations of government," Jocasta Nu went on. "He disappeared for nine or ten years, then just showed up recently as the head of the separatist movement."

"Interesting," Obi-Wan remarked, looking from the bust to the Archivist. "I'm still not sure I understand."

"None of us does," Jocasta Nu replied, her serious expression melting into a warm smile. "Well, I'm sure you didn't call me over here for a history lesson. Are you having a problem, Master Kenobi?"

"Yes, I'm trying to find a planet system called Kamino. It doesn't seem to show up on any of the archive charts."

"Kamino?" Jocasta Nu looked around, as if she was searching for the system right then and there. "It's not a system I'm familiar with. Let me see."

A few steps brought them to the computer screen where Obi-Wan had been searching. She bent low, and pressed a couple of commands. "Are you sure you have the right coordinates?"

"According to my information, it should be in this quadrant somewhere," said Obi-Wan "Just south of the Rishi Maze."

A few more taps of the keyboard brought nothing more than a frown to Jocasta Nu's old and weathered face. "But what are the exact coordinates?"

"I only know the quadrant," Obi-Wan admitted, and Jocasta Nu turned up to regard him.

"No coordinates? It sounds like the sort of directions you'd get from a street tout—some old miner or furbog trader."

"All three, actually," Obi-Wan admitted with a grin.

"Are you sure it exists?"

"Absolutely."

Jocasta Nu sat back and rubbed a hand pensively over her chin. "Let me do a gravitational scan," she said, as much to herself as to Obi-Wan.

The star map hologram of the target quadrant went into motion after a few more keystrokes, and the pair studied the movements. "There are some inconsistencies here," the sharp Archivist noted. "Maybe the planet you're seeking was destroyed."

"Wouldn't that be on record?"

"It ought to be, unless it was very recent," Jocasta Nu replied, but she was shaking her head even as she spoke the words, not even convincing herself. "I hate to say it, but it looks like the system you're searching for doesn't exist."

"That's impossible—perhaps the Archives are incomplete."

"The Archives are comprehensive and totally secure, my young Jedi," came the imposing response, the Archivist stepping back from her familiarity with Obi-Wan and assuming again the demeanor of archive kingdom ruler. "One thing you may be absolutely sure of: If an item does not appear in our records, it does not exist."

The two stared at each other for a long moment, Obi-Wan taking note that there wasn't the slightest tremor of doubt in Jocasta Nu's declaration.

He looked back to the map, perplexed, caught within a seemingly unanswerable question. He knew that no one in the galaxy was more reliable for information that Dexter Jettster, unless that person was Jocasta Nu, and yet the two were obviously at odds here concerning their information. Dexter had seemed every bit as certain of the origins of the saberdart as Jocasta Nu was now. Both couldn't be right.

The puzzle of finding Senator Amidala's would-be assassin would not be easily solved, it seemed, and that troubled Obi-Wan Kenobi for many, many reasons. With Jocasta Nu's permission, the Jedi punched a few buttons on the keyboard, downloading the archive information on that region of the quadrant to a small hologlobe. Then, the item in hand, he left the area.

But not without one long, last look at the imposing bust of Count Dooku.

Later on that day, Obi-Wan turned away from the Archives and the analysis droids and turned within, to his own insights, instead. He found a small, comfortable room along the Temple's grand balcony, one of many such rooms designed for quiet moments of Jedi reflection. A small fountain bubbled off to the side of him as he settled on a soft but firm mat and crossed his legs. The water trickled down to a bed of polished stones, making a delicate sound, a background noise natural in its beauty and in the simplicity of its song.

Before Obi-Wan, a painting of reds, shifting and darkening to a deep crimson and then to black, a liberal representation of a cooling lava field, hung on the wall, inviting him not to look into it, but to surround himself with it, both its image and the soft warmth and hissing sound helping him to fall far away from his corporeal surroundings.

There, in his trance, Obi-Wan Kenobi sought his answers. He focused on the mystery of Kamino first, expecting that Dexter's analysis was correct. But why hadn't the system shown up in the Archives?

Another image invaded Obi-Wan's meditations as he tried to sort through that puzzle, an image of Anakin and Padmé together on Naboo.

The Jedi Knight started, suddenly afraid that this was a premonition, and that some danger would visit his Padawan and the young Senator . . .

But no, he realized, settling back. No danger was about; the two were relaxed and at play.

Obi-Wan's relief lasted only as long as it took him to realize that the continuing scene in his mind might be the most dangerous thing of all. He dismissed it, though, unsure if this was a premonition, an image of reality, or just his own fears playing out before him. Obi-Wan pointedly reminded himself that the sooner he solved the mystery of Kamino, the mystery of who so desperately wanted Amidala dead, the sooner he could return to Anakin and offer the proper guidance.

The Jedi Knight focused again on the bust of Count Dooku, searching for insights, but for some reason, the image of Anakin kept becoming interposed with that of the renegade Count . . .

Soon after, a frustrated and thoroughly bewildered Obi-Wan walked out of the small meditation chamber, shaking his head and no more certain of anything than he had been when he had entered the place.

His patience exhausted into frustration, the Jedi Knight decided to seek a higher authority, one wiser and more experienced. His short trip took him out of the Temple proper and onto the veranda, and there he paused and watched, and in the innocent scene before him found some relief from the frustration.

Master Yoda was leading twenty of the youngest Jedi recruits, children only four or five years old, through their morning training exercises, battling floating training droids with miniature lightsabers.

Obi-Wan recalled his own training. He couldn't see the eyes of the youngsters, for they wore protective full-face helmets, but he could well imagine the range of emotions playing out on their innocent faces. There would be intensity, and then great joy whenever an energy bolt from a training droid was blocked, and that elation would inevitably dissipate in the next instant, when the joy brought distraction and distraction allowed the next energy bolt to slip past and bring a sudden, jolting sting.

And those little bolts did sting, Obi-Wan remembered, as much physically as in pride. There was nothing worse than getting zapped, particularly in the backside. It always caused one to do a little hopping and twisting dance, which naturally made the embarrassment all the worse. Obi-Wan recalled that feeling vividly, recalled thinking that everyone in the courtyard was staring at him.

The training could be humiliating.

But it was also energizing, because with the failures would come the successes, each one building confidence, each one lending insights into the flowing beauty that was the Force, heightening the connection that separated a Jedi from the rest of the galaxy.

To see Yoda leading the training this day, looking exactly as he had when he had led Obi-Wan's training a quarter century before, brought a flush of warmth to the Jedi Knight.

"Don't think . . . feel," Yoda instructed the group. "Be as one with the Force."

Obi-Wan, smiling, mouthed the exact words as Yoda finished, "Help you, it will."

How many times he had heard that!

He was still grinning widely when Yoda turned to him. "Younglings, enough!" the great Jedi Master commanded. "A visitor we have. Welcome him."

Twenty little lightsabers clicked off and the students came to attention together, removing their helmets and tucking them properly under their left arms.

"Master Obi-Wan Kenobi," Yoda said, keeping enough gravity in his voice so that the younglings wouldn't feel mocked.

"Welcome, Master Obi-Wan!" the twenty called out together.

"I am sorry to disturb you, Master," Obi-Wan said with a slight bow.

"What help to you, can I be?"

Obi-Wan considered the question for a moment. He had specifically come out here looking for Yoda, but now, in seeing the diminutive Master at his important work, he wondered if he had let his patience fall away too quickly. Was it his place to ask Yoda to help him with a mission that was his own responsibility? It didn't take long for Obi-Wan to dismiss the question. He was a Jedi Knight, Yoda, a Master, and his responsibilities and Yoda's were ultimately one and the same. He didn't expect that Yoda could help him with this particular problem, but then again,

Yoda had always been full of surprises, full of going far beyond any expectations.

"I'm looking for a planet described to me by an old friend," he explained, and he knew that Yoda was absorbing every word. "I trust him and the information he provided, but the system doesn't show up on the archive maps." As he finished, he showed Yoda that he had a hologlobe with him.

"An interesting puzzle," Yoda answered. "Lost a planet, Master Obi-Wan has. How embarrassing . . . how embarrassing. An interesting puzzle. Gather, younglings, around the map reader. Clear your minds and find Obi-Wan's wayward planet, we will try."

They went into a room to the side of the veranda. A narrow shaft was set in the middle, with a hollow depression at the top. Off to the side, Obi-Wan took up the hologlobe, then moved and placed it in the hollow of the shaft. The shades closed as soon as he put it there, darkening the room, and a star map hologram appeared, glittering distinctly.

Obi-Wan paused a moment before presenting his dilemma, allowing the younglings to get past the initial excitement. He watched with amusement as some reached up and tried to touch the projected starlights. Then, when all quieted, he walked into the middle of the projection. "This is where it ought to be," he explained. "Gravity is pulling all the stars in this area inward to this spot. There should be a star here, but there isn't."

"Most interesting," Yoda said. "Gravity's silhouette remains, but the star and all its planets have disappeared. How can this be? Now, younglings, in your mind, what is the first thing you see? An answer? A thought? Anyone?"

Obi-Wan took Yoda's quiet cue and paused then, watching the Jedi Master look over his gathering.

A hand went up, and while Obi-Wan felt the urge to chuckle at the idea of a youngling solving a riddle that had befuddled a trio of accomplished Jedi, including Yoda and Madame Jocasta Nu, he noted that Yoda was quite focused and serious.

Yoda nodded to the student, who answered at once. "Because someone erased it from the archive memory."

"That's right!" another of the children agreed at once. "That's what happened! Someone erased it!"

"If the planet blew up, the gravity would go away," another one of the children called out.

Obi-Wan stared blankly at the excited group, stunned, but Yoda only chuckled.

"Truly wonderful, the mind of a child is," he explained. "Uncluttered. The data must have been erased."

Yoda started out of the room and Obi-Wan moved to follow, flicking his hand as he passed the reader shaft, Force-pulling the hologlobe back to his grasp and instantly dismissing the starry scene.

"To the center of the pull of gravity go, and find your planet you will," Yoda advised him.

"But Master Yoda, who could have erased information from the Archives? That's impossible, isn't it?"

"Dangerous and disturbing this puzzle is," Yoda replied with a frown. "Only a Jedi could have erased those files. But who and why, harder to answer. Meditate on this, I will. May the Force be with you."

A thousand questions filtered through Obi-Wan's mind, but he understood that Yoda had just dismissed him. They each had their riddles, it seemed, but at least now Obi-Wan's path seemed much clearer before him. He gave a deferential bow, but Yoda, already back to his work with the children, didn't seem to notice. Obi-Wan walked away.

Soon after, not wanting to waste a moment, Obi-Wan was out on the landing platform standing beside his readied starfighter, a long and sleek delta-wing fighter, of a triangular design, with the cockpit set far aft. Mace Windu was there beside him, the tall and strong-featured Master regarding Obi-Wan with his typically calm and controlled demeanor. There was something reassuring about Mace Windu, a sense of power and, even more than that, of destiny. Mace Windu had a way of silently assuring all those around him that things would work out as they were supposed to.

"Be wary," he said to Obi-Wan, tilting his head back just a bit as he spoke, a posture that made him seem all the more impressive. "This disturbance in the Force is growing stronger."

Obi-Wan nodded, though in truth, his concerns were more focused and tangible at that moment. "I'm concerned for my Padawan. He is not ready to be on his own."

Mace gave a nod, as if to remind Obi-Wan that they had covered this already. "He has exceptional skills," the Master replied. "The Council is confident in its decision, Obi-Wan. Not all of the questions about him have been answered, of course, but his talents cannot be dismissed, and we are not disappointed in the progress he has made under your tutelage."

Obi-Wan considered the words carefully and nodded again, knowing that he was walking a fine line here. If he overstated his concerns about Anakin's temperament, he might be doing a great disservice to the Jedi and to the galaxy. And yet, if he let the magnitude of his assignment in training Anakin Skywalker bring him to silence on legitimate questions, then was he doing great harm?

"If the prophecy is true, Anakin will be the one to bring balance to the Force," Mace finished.

"But he still has much to learn. His skills have made him . . . well—" Obi-Wan paused, trying to walk that delicate line. "—arrogant. I realize now what you and Master Yoda knew from the beginning. The boy was too old to start the training, and . . ."

The frown spreading on Mace Windu's face signaled Obi-Wan that he might be pushing a bit too hard.

"There's something else," Mace observed.

Obi-Wan took a deep and steadying breath. "Master, Anakin and I should not have been given this assignment. I'm afraid Anakin won't be able to protect the Senator."

"Why?"

"He has a . . . an emotional connection with her. It's been there since he was a boy. Now he's confused, and distracted." As he spoke, Obi-Wan started toward his starfighter. He climbed up the cockpit ladder and into his seat.

"So you have already stated," Mace reminded. "And your concerns were weighed properly, and did not change the decision of the Council. Obi-Wan, you must have faith that Anakin will take the right path."

It made sense, of course. If Anakin was to become a great leader, a creature of prophecy, then surely his character tests must be passed. Anakin was waging one of those tests right now, Obi-Wan knew, off in seclusion on a distant planet with a woman whom he loved too deeply. He had to be strong enough to pass that test; Obi-Wan just hoped that Anakin recognized the trial for what it was.

"Has Master Yoda gained any insight as to whether or not this war will come about?" he asked, somewhat changing the subject, though he felt that it was all very connected. Finding the assassin, making peace with the separatists—all of these things would allow him to focus more closely on Anakin's training and would keep things at a more even keel around the troubled Padawan.

"Probing the dark side is a dangerous process," Mace stated. "I know not when he will choose to begin, but when he does, it is quite possible that he will remain in seclusion for days."

Obi-Wan nodded his agreement and Mace gave him a smile and a wave. "May the Force be with you."

"Set the course to the hyperspace ring, Arfour," Obi-Wan instructed his astromech droid, an R4-P unit that was hardwired into the left wing of the sleek starfighter. Silently, the Jedi Knight added to himself, *Let's get this thing moving*.

It was a scene of simplicity, of children playing and adults sitting quietly under the warm sun, or gossiping across neatly trimmed hedgerows. It was a scene of absolute normalcy for Naboo, but it was nothing like Anakin Skywalker had ever witnessed. On Tatooine, the houses were singular, out in the desert, or they were clustered tightly in cities like Mos Eisley, with its hustle and bustle and bright colors and brighter characters. On Coruscant, there were no streets like this one any longer. There were no hedgerows and trees lining the ground, just permacrete and old buildings and the gray foundations of the towering skyscrapers. People did not gossip, with children running carefree about them, in either place.

To Anakin, it was a scene of simple beauty.

He was back to wearing his Jedi robes, the peasant garb discarded. Padmé walked alongside him in a simple blue dress that only seemed to enhance her beauty. Anakin kept glancing her way, stealing images of her to burn into his mind, to hold forever in a special place. She could be wearing anything, he realized, and still be beautiful.

Anakin smiled as he recalled the ornate outfits Padmé had often worn as Queen of Naboo, huge gowns with intricate embroidery and studded with gemstones, tremendous headpieces of plumes and swirls and curves and twists.

He liked her better like this, he decided. All of the decorations of her Queenly outfits had been beautifully designed, but still could only detract from the more beautifully designed Padmé. Wearing a great headpiece only hid her silken brown hair. Painting her face in whites and bright red only hid her beautiful skin. The embroidery on the great gowns only blurred the perfection of her form.

This was the way Anakin wanted to see her, where her clothing was just a finishing touch.

"There's my house!" Padmé cried suddenly, startling Anakin from his pleasant daydreams.

He followed her gaze to see a simple but tasteful structure, surrounded, like everything on Naboo, by flowers and vines and hedges. Padmé started off immediately for the door, but Anakin didn't follow right away. He studied the house, every line, every detail, trying to see in it the environment that had produced her. She had told him many stories of her childhood in this house during their trip from Coruscant, and he was replaying those tales, seeing them in context now that the yard was in view.

"What?" Padmé asked him from some distance ahead, when she noticed that he was not following. "Don't tell me you're shy!"

"No, but I—" the distracted Anakin started to answer, but he was interrupted by the squeals of two little girls, running out from the yard toward his companion.

"Aunt Padmé! Aunt Padmé!"

Padmé's smile went as wide as Anakin had ever seen it and she rushed ahead, bending low to scoop the pair, who looked to be no more than a few years old, one a bit taller than the other, into her arms. One had hair short and blond and curly, the other, the older of the two, had hair that resembled Padmé's.

"Ryoo! Pooja!" Padmé cried, hugging them and twirling

them about. "I'm so happy to see you!" She kissed them both and set them down, then took them by the hand and led them toward Anakin.

"This is Anakin. Anakin, this is Ryoo and Pooja!"

The blush on the pair as they shyly said hello brought a burst of laughter from Padmé and a smile to Anakin's face, though he was equally ill at ease as the two children.

The girls' shyness lasted only as long as it took for them to notice the little droid rolling behind Anakin, trying to catch up.

"Artoo!" they shouted in unison. Breaking away from Padmé, they rushed to the droid, leaping upon him, hugging him cheek to dome.

And R2-D2 seemed equally thrilled, beeping and whistling as happily as Anakin had ever heard.

Anakin couldn't help but be touched by the scene, a view of innocence that he had never known.

Well, not never, he had to admit. There were times when Shmi had found some way to produce such moments of joy amid the drudgery that was life as a slave on Tatooine. In their own way, in that dusty, dirty, hot, and smelly place, Anakin and his mother had carved out a few instants of innocent beauty.

Here, though, such moments seemed so much more the norm than the memorable exception.

Anakin turned back to Padmé, to see that she was no longer looking his way, but had turned toward the house, where another woman, who looked very much like Padmé, was approaching.

Not exactly like Padmé, Anakin noted. She was a little older, a little heavier, and a little more . . . *worn*, was the only word he could think of. But not in a bad way. Yes, he could see it now, he thought, watching as she and Padmé hugged tightly. This was whom Padmé could become—more settled, more content, perhaps. Considering the amazing resemblance, Anakin was hardly surprised when Padmé introduced the woman as her sister, Sola.

"Mom and Dad will be so happy to see you," Sola said to Padmé. "It's been a difficult few weeks."

Padmé frowned. She knew that word of the attempts on her life would have reached her parents' ears, and that was possibly the most disturbing thing of all to her.

Anakin saw it all on her face, and he understood it well, and he loved her all the more for that generosity. Padmé wasn't really afraid of anything—she could handle the reality of her current situation, the reality of the fact that someone was trying to kill her, with determination and courage. But the one thing about it all that troubled her, aside from the political ramifications of such distractions, the ways they might weaken her position in the Senate, was the effect of such danger upon those she loved. He knew that she didn't want to bring pain to her family.

Anakin, who had left his mother as a slave on Tatooine, could appreciate that.

"Mom's making dinner," Sola explained, noting Padmé's discomfort and generously changing the subject. "As usual, your timing is perfect." She started toward the house. Padmé waited for Anakin to move beside her, then took his hand, looked up, smiled at him, and led him toward the door. R2-D2 rolled along right behind, with Ryoo and Pooja bouncing all about him.

The interior of the house was just as simply wonderful and just as full of life and soft color as was the yard. There were no glaring lights, no beeping consoles or flickering computer screens. The furniture was plush and comfortable; the floors were made of cool stone or covered in soft carpeting.

This was not a building as Anakin had known on Coruscant, and not a hovel, as he had known all too well on Tatooine. No, seeing this place, this street, this yard, this home, made the young Padawan even more convinced of what he had declared to Padmé not so long before: that if he had grown up on Naboo, he would never leave.

The next introductions were a bit more uncomfortable, but only for a moment, as Padmé showed Anakin to Ruwee, her father, a strong-shouldered man with a face that was plain and strong and compassionate all at once. He wore his brown hair short, but still it was a bit out of place, a bit . . . comfortable.

Padmé introduced Jobal next, and Anakin knew that the woman was her mother without being told. The moment he met her, he understood where Padmé had gotten her innocent and sincere smile, a look that could disarm a mob of bloodthirsty Gamorrean raiders. Jobal's face had that same comforting quality, that same obvious generosity.

Soon after, Anakin, Padmé, and Ruwee were sitting at the dinner table, comfortably quiet and listening to the bustle in the next room, which included the clanking of stoneware plates and mugs, and Sola repeatedly saying, "Too much, Mom." And every time she said that, Ruwee and Padmé smiled knowingly.

"I doubt they've been starving all the way from Coruscant," an exasperated Sola said as she exited the kitchen, glancing back over her shoulder as she spoke. She returned carrying a bowl full of food.

"Enough to feed the town?" Padmé asked Sola quietly as her older sister put the bowl on the table.

"You know Mom," came the answer, and the tone told Anakin that this was not an isolated incident, that Jobal was quite the hostess. Despite the fact that he had eaten recently, the bowl of food looked and smelled temptingly good.

"No one has ever left this house hungry," Sola explained.

"Well, one person did once," Padmé corrected. "But Mom chased him down and dragged him back in."

"To feed him or cook him?" the quick-witted Padawan retorted, and the other three stared at him for just a moment before catching on and bursting out in laughter.

They were still chuckling when Jobal entered the room, holding an even larger bowl of steaming food, which of course only made them laugh all the louder. But then Jobal fixed an imposing stare over her family and the chuckling quieted.

"They arrived just in time for dinner," Jobal said. "I know what that means." She set the plate down near Anakin and put her hand on his shoulder. "I hope you're hungry, Anakin."

"A little." He looked up and gave her a warm smile.

The look of gratitude was not lost on Padmé. She tossed a

little wink his way when he looked back at her. "He's being polite, Mom," she said. "We're starving."

Jobal grinned widely and nodded, offering superior glances
at Sola and Ruwee, who just laughed again. It was all so comfortable to Anakin, so natural and so . . . so much like what he
had always been wanting in his life, though perhaps he had not
known it. This would be perfect, absolutely perfect, except that
his mother wasn't there.

A brief cloud passed over his face as he thought of his mother
on Tatooine, and considered the disturbing dreams that had
been finding their way into his sleep of late. He pushed the
thoughts away quickly and glanced around, glad that no one
seemed to have noticed.

"If you're starving, then you came to the right place at the
right time," Ruwee said, looking at Anakin as he finished. "Eat
up, son!"

Jobal and Sola took their seats and began passing the food
bowls all around. Anakin took a good helping of several different dishes. The food was all unfamiliar, but the smells told him
that he wouldn't be disappointed. He sat quietly as he ate, listening with half an ear to the chatter all about him. He was
thinking of his mom again, of how he wished he could bring her
here, a free woman, to live the life she so deserved.

Some time passed before Anakin tuned back in, cued by the
sudden seriousness in Jobal's voice as she said to Padmé, "Honey,
it's so good to see you safe. We were so worried."

Anakin looked up just in time to see the intense, disapproving glare that Padmé answered with. Ruwee, obviously trying to
dispel the tension before it could really begin, put his hand on
Jobal's arm and quietly said, "Dear—"

"I know, I know!" said the suddenly animated Jobal. "But I
had to say it. Now it's done."

Sola cleared her throat. "Well, this is exciting," she said, and
everyone looked at her. "Do you know, Anakin, you're the first
boyfriend my sister ever brought home?"

"Sola!" Padmé exclaimed. She rolled her eyes. "He isn't my boyfriend! He's a Jedi assigned by the Senate to protect me."

"A bodyguard?" Jobal asked with great concern. "Oh, Padmé, they didn't tell us it was that serious!"

Padmé's sigh was intermixed with a groan. "It's not, Mom," she said. "I promise. Anyway, Anakin's a friend. I've known him for years. Remember that little boy who was with the Jedi during the blockade crisis?"

A couple of "ahs" of recognition came back in response, along with nodding heads. Then Padmé smiled at Anakin and said, with just enough weight to make him recognize that her previous claims about his place here weren't entirely true, "He's grown up."

Anakin glanced at Sola and saw that she was staring at him, scrutinizing him. He shifted uncomfortably in his seat.

"Honey, when are you going to settle down?" Jobal went on. "Haven't you had enough of that life? I certainly have!"

"Mom, I'm not in any danger," Padmé insisted, taking Anakin's hand in her own.

"Is she?" Ruwee asked Anakin.

The Padawan stared hard at Padmé's father, recognizing the honest concern. This man, who obviously loved his daughter so much, deserved to know the truth. "Yes, I'm afraid she is."

Even as the words left his mouth, Anakin felt Padmé's grip tighten. "But not much," she added quickly, and she turned to Anakin, smiling, but in a *you'll-pay-for-that-later* kind of way. "Anakin," she said quietly, her teeth gritted, locked into that threatening smile.

"The Senate thought it prudent to give her some time away, and under the protection of the Jedi," he said, his tone casual, showing no reflections of the pain he was feeling as Padmé's fingernails dug into his hand. "My Master, Obi-Wan, is even now seeing to the matter. All should be well soon enough."

His breath came easier as Padmé loosened her grip, and

Ruwee, and even Jobal, seemed to relax. Anakin knew that he had done well, but he was surprised to see that Sola was still staring at him, still smiling as if she knew a secret.

He gave her a quizzical look, but she only smiled all the wider.

"Sometimes I wish I'd traveled more," Ruwee admitted to Anakin as the two walked in the garden after dinner. "But I must say, I'm happy here."

"Padmé tells me you teach at the university."

"Yes, and before that I was a builder," Ruwee answered with a nod. "I also worked for the Refugee Relief Movement, when I was very young."

Anakin looked at him curiously, not really surprised. "You seem quite interested in public service," he remarked.

"Naboo is generous," Ruwee explained. "The planet itself, I mean. We have all that we want, all that we could want. Food is plentiful, the climate is comfortable, the surroundings are—"

"Beautiful," Anakin put in.

"Quite so," said Ruwee. "We are a very fortunate people, and we know it. That good fortune should not be taken for granted, and so we try to share and try to help. It is our way of saying that we welcome the friendship of those less fortunate, that we do not think ourselves entitled to that which we have, but rather, that we feel blessed beyond what we deserve. And so we share, and so we work, and in doing so, we become something larger than ourselves, and more fulfilled than one can become from idly enjoying good fortune!"

Anakin considered Ruwee's words for a few moments. "It is the same with the Jedi, I suppose," he said. "We have been given great gifts, and we train hard to make the most of those. And then we use our given powers to try to help the galaxy, to try to make everything a little bit better."

"And to make the things we love a little bit safer?"

Anakin looked at him, catching the meaning, and he smiled and nodded. He saw respect in Ruwee's eyes, and gratitude, and he was glad for both. He could not deny the way Padmé looked at her family, the love that seemed to flow from her whenever any of them entered the room, and he knew that if Ruwee or Jobal or Sola didn't like him, his relationship with Padmé would be hurt.

He was glad, then, that he had come to this place, not only as Padmé's companion, but also as her protector.

Back in the house, Padmé, Sola, and Jobal were working together to clear the dishes and the remaining food. Padmé noted the tension in her mother's movements, and she knew that these latest events—the assassination attempts, the fights in the Senate over an issue that could well lead to war—were weighing heavily on her.

She looked to Sola, too, to see if she might find some clue as to how to help alleviate the tension, but all she found there was an obvious curiosity that set her off her balance more than had her mother's concerned expression.

"Why haven't you told us about him?" Sola asked with a sly grin.

"What's there to talk about?" Padmé replied as casually as she could. "He's just a boy."

"A boy?" Sola repeated with a laugh. "Have you seen the way he looks at you?"

"Sola! Stop it!"

"It's obvious he has feelings for you," Sola went on. "Are you saying, little baby sister, that you haven't noticed?"

"I'm not your baby sister, Sola," Padmé said flatly, her tone turning to true consternation. "Anakin and I are friends. Our relationship is strictly professional."

Sola grinned again.

"Mom, would you tell her to stop it?" Padmé burst out in embarrassed frustration.

Now Sola began laughing out loud. "Well, maybe you *haven't* noticed the way he looks at you. I think you're afraid to."

"Cut it out!"

Jobal stepped between the two and gave Sola a stern look. Then she turned back to Padmé. "Sola's just concerned, dear," she said. But her words sounded to Padmé like condescension, as if her mother was still trying to protect a helpless little girl.

"Oh, Mom, you're impossible," she said with a sigh of surrender. "What I'm doing is important."

"You've done your service, Padmé," Jobal answered. "It's time you had a life of your own. You're missing so much!"

Padmé tilted her head back and closed her eyes, trying to accept the words in the spirit with which they were offered. For a moment, she regretted coming back here, to see the same old sights and hear the same old advice.

For just a moment, though. Truthfully, when she considered it all, Padmé had to admit she was glad to have people who loved her and cared about her so much.

She offered her mother an appeasing smile, and Jobal nodded and gently tapped Padmé's arm. She turned to Sola next, and saw her sister still grinning.

What did Sola see?

"Now tell me, son, how serious is this thing?" Ruwee asked bluntly as the two neared the door that would take them back into the house. "How much danger is my daughter really in?"

Anakin didn't hesitate, realizing, as he had at dinner, that Padmé's father deserved nothing but honesty from him. "There have been two attempts on her life. Chances are, there'll be more. But I wasn't lying to you and wasn't trying to minimize anything. My Master is tracking down the assassins. I'm sure he'll find out who they are and take care of them. This situation won't last long."

"I don't want anything to happen to her," Ruwee said, with the gravity of a parent concerned over a beloved child.

"I don't either," Anakin assured him, with almost equal weight.

* * *

Padmé stared at her older sister until, at last, Sola broke down and asked, "What?"

The two of them were alone together, while Jobal and Ruwee entertained Anakin out in the sitting room.

"Why do you keep saying such things about me and Anakin?"

"Because it's obvious," Sola replied. "You see it—you can't deny it to yourself."

Padmé sighed and sat down on the bed, her posture and expression giving all the confirmation that Sola needed.

"I thought Jedi weren't supposed to think such things," Sola remarked.

"They're not."

"But Anakin does." Sola's words brought Padmé's gaze up to meet hers. "You know I'm right."

Padmé shook her head helplessly, and Sola laughed.

"You think more like a Jedi than he does," she said. "And you shouldn't."

"What do you mean?" Padmé didn't know whether to take offense, having no idea of where her sister was heading with this.

"You're so tied up in your responsibilities that you don't give any weight to your desires," Sola explained. "Even with your own feelings toward Anakin."

"You don't know how I feel about Anakin."

"You probably don't either," Sola said. "Because you won't allow yourself to even think about it. Being a Senator and being a girlfriend aren't mutually exclusive, you know."

"My work is important!"

"Who said it wasn't?" Sola asked, holding her hands up in a gesture of peace. "It's funny, Padmé, because you act as if you're prohibited, and you're not, while Anakin acts as if he's under no such prohibitions, and he is!"

"You're way ahead of everything here," Padmé said. "Anakin and I have only been together for a few days—before that, I hadn't seen him in a decade!"

Sola shrugged. Her look went from that sly grin she had been sporting since dinner to one of more genuine concern for her sister. She sat down on the bed beside Padmé and draped an arm across her shoulders. "I don't know any of the details, and you're right, I don't know how you feel—about any of this. But I know how he feels, and so do you."

Padmé didn't disagree. She just sat there, comfortable in Sola's hug, gazing down at the floor, trying not to think.

"It frightens you," Sola remarked. Surprised, Padmé looked back up.

"What are you afraid of, Sis?" Sola asked sincerely. "Are you afraid of Anakin's feelings and the responsibilities that he cannot dismiss? Or are you afraid of your own feelings?"

She lifted Padmé's chin, so that they were looking at each other directly, their faces only a breath apart. "I don't know how you feel," she admitted again. "But I suspect that it's something new to you. Something scary, but something wonderful."

Padmé said nothing, but she knew that disagreement would not be honest.

"They're a lot to digest, all at once," Padmé said to Anakin later on, when the two were alone in her room. She had barely unpacked her things, and was now throwing clothes into her bag once more. Different clothes this time, though. Less formal than the outfits she had to wear as a representative of Naboo.

"Your mother is a fine cook," Anakin replied, drawing a curious stare from Padmé, until she realized that he was joking and had understood her point perfectly well.

"You're lucky to have such a wonderful family," Anakin said more seriously, and then, with a teasing grin, he added, "Maybe you should give your sister some of your clothes."

Padmé smirked right back at him, but then looked about at the mess and couldn't really disagree. "Don't worry," she assured him. "This won't take long."

"I just want to get there before dark. Wherever *there* is, I mean." Anakin continued to scan the room, surprised at the number of closets, all of them full. "You still live at home," he said, shaking his head. "I didn't expect that."

"I move around so much," Padmé replied. "I've never had the time to even begin to find a place of my own, and I'm not sure I want to. Official residences have no warmth. Not like here. I feel good here. I feel at home."

The simple beauty of her statement gave Anakin pause. "I've never had a real home," he said, speaking more to himself than to Padmé. "Home was always where my mom was." He looked up at her then, and took comfort in her sympathetic smile.

Padmé went back to her packing. "The Lake Country is beautiful," she started to explain, but she stopped when she glanced back at Anakin, to see him holding a holograph and grinning.

"Is this you?" he asked, pointing to the young girl, seven or eight at the most, in the holo, surrounded by dozens of little green smiling creatures, and holding one in her arms.

Padmé laughed, and seemed embarrassed. "That was when I went with a relief group to Shadda-Bi-Boran. Their sun was imploding and the planet was dying. I was helping to relocate the children." She walked over to stand beside Anakin and placed one hand on his shoulder, pointing to the holograph with the other. "See that little one I'm holding? His name was N'a-kee-tula, which means 'sweetheart.' He was so full of life—all those kids were."

"Were?"

"They were never able to adapt," she explained somberly. "They were never able to live off their native planet."

Anakin winced, then quickly picked up another holograph, this one showing Padmé a couple of years later, wearing official robes and standing between two older and similarly robed Legislators. He looked back at the first holo, then to this one, noting that Padmé's expression seemed much more severe here.

"My first day as an Apprentice Legislator," Padmé explained. Then, as if she was reading his mind, she added, "See the difference?"

Anakin studied the holograph a moment longer, then looked

up and laughed, seeing Padmé wearing that same long and stern expression. She laughed as well, then squeezed his shoulder and went back to her packing.

Anakin put the holographs down side by side and looked at them for a long, long time. Two sides of the woman he loved.

The water speeder zoomed above the lake, the downthrusters churning only a slight, almost indistinguishable, wake. Every so often, a wave clipped in, and a fine spray broke over the bow. Anakin and Padmé reveled in the cool water and the wind, eyes half closed, Padme's rich brown hair flying out behind her.

Beside them at the wheel, Paddy Accu gave a laugh at every spray, his graying hair spreading out widely. "Always better over the water!" he shouted in his gruff voice, against the wind and the noise of the speeder. "Are you liking it?"

Padmé turned a sincere smile upon him, and the grizzled man leaned in close and backed off the accelerator. "She's even more fun if I put her down," he explained. "You think you'll like that, Senator?"

Both Padmé and Anakin looked at him curiously, neither quite understanding.

"We were going out to the island," Anakin remarked, a note of concern in his voice.

"Oh, I'll get you there!" Paddy Accu said with a wheezing laugh. He pushed forward a lever—and the speeder dropped into the water.

"Paddy?" Padmé asked.

The man laughed all the harder. "Don't tell me you've forgotten!" he roared, kicking in the accelerator. The speeder jetted off across the water, no longer smooth in flight, but bouncing across the rippling surface.

"Oh, yes!" Padmé said to him. "I do remember!"

After a moment of initial shock, looking from Padmé to Paddy, wondering if the man was up to some dark deception, Anakin caught on, and was also swept away by the bouncing ride.

The spray was nearly continuous, thrown up by the prow and washing over them.

"It's wonderful!" Padmé exclaimed.

Anakin couldn't disagree. "We spend so much time in control," he replied. His mind went back to his younger days, on Tatooine, Podracing along wild courses, skirting disaster. This was somewhat like that, especially when Paddy, in no apparent hurry to reach the island dock, flipped the speeder up and down from one edge to the other, zigzagging his way. It amazed Anakin how this little adjustment, dropping into the water instead of smoothly skimming above it, had changed the perspective of this journey. It was true, he knew, that technology had tamed the galaxy, and while that seemed a good thing in terms of efficiency and comfort, he had to believe that something, too, had been lost: the excitement of living on the edge of disaster. Or the simple tactile feeling of a ride like this, bouncing across the waves, feeling the wind and the cold spray.

At one point, Paddy put the speeder so far up on edge that both Anakin and Padmé thought they would tip over. Anakin almost reached into the Force to secure the craft, but stopped himself in order to enjoy the thrill.

They didn't tip. Paddy was an expert driver who knew how to take his speeder to the very limits without crashing over. It was some time later that he slowed the craft and allowed it to drift in against the island dock.

Padmé grabbed the older man's hand and leaned in to kiss his cheek. "Thank you!"

Anakin was surprised that he could see Paddy's blush through the man's ruddy skin. "It was . . . fun," he admitted.

"If it isn't, then what's the point?" the gruff-looking man replied with a great belly laugh.

While Paddy secured the speeder, Anakin hopped onto the dock. He reached back to take Padmé's hand, helping her stay balanced while she debarked with her suitcase in her other hand.

"I'll bring the bags up for you," Paddy offered, and Padmé looked back and smiled. "You go and see what you can see— don't want to be wasting your time on the little chores!"

"Wasting time," Padmé echoed. There was an unmistakable wistfulness in her voice.

The young couple walked up a long flight of wooden stairs, past flower beds and hanging vines. They came onto a terrace overlooking a beautiful garden, and beyond that, the shimmering lake and the mountains rising behind it, all blue and purple.

Padmé leaned her crossed forearms on the balustrade and stared out at the wondrous view.

"You can see the mountains in the water," Anakin remarked, shaking his head and grinning. The water was still, the light just right, so that the mountains in the lake seemed almost perfect replicas.

"Of course," she agreed without moving.

He gazed at her until she turned to look back at him.

"It seems an obvious thing to you," he said, "but where I grew up, there weren't any lakes. Whenever I see this much water, every detail of it . . ." He ended by shaking his head, obviously overwhelmed.

"Amazes you?"

"And pleases me," he said with a warm smile.

Padmé turned back to the lake. "I guess it's hard to hold on to appreciation for some things," she admitted. "But after all these years, I still see the beauty of the mountains reflected in the water. I could stare at them all day, every day."

Anakin stepped up to the balustrade beside her, leaning in very close. He closed his eyes and inhaled the sweet scent of Padmé, felt the warmth of her skin.

"When I was in Level Three, we used to come here for

school retreat," she said. She pointed out across the way, to another island. "See that island? We used to swim there every day.
I love the water."

"I do, too. I guess it comes from growing up on a desert
planet." He was staring at her again, his eyes soaking in her
beauty. He could tell that Padmé sensed his stare, but she pointedly continued to look out over the water.

"We used to lie on the sand and let the sun dry us . . . and
try to guess the names of the birds singing."

"I don't like the sand. It's coarse and rough and irritating.
And it gets everywhere."

Padmé turned to look back at him

"Not here," Anakin went on. "It's like that on Tatooine—
everything's like that on Tatooine. But here, everything's soft,
and smooth." As he finished, hardly even aware of the motion,
he reached out and stroked Padmé's arm.

He nearly pulled back when he realized what he was doing,
but since Padmé didn't object, he let himself stay close to her. She
seemed a bit tentative, a bit scared, but she wasn't pulling away.

"There was a very old man who lived on the island," she
said. Her brown eyes seemed to be looking far away, across the
years. "He used to make glass out of sand—and vases and neck-
laces out of the glass. They were magical."

Anakin moved a bit closer, staring at her intensely until she
turned to face him. "Everything here is magical," he said.

"You could look into the glass and see the water. The way it
ripples and moves. It looked so real, but it wasn't."

"Sometimes, when you believe something to be real, it becomes real." It seemed to Anakin as if she wanted to look away.
But she didn't. Instead, she was falling deeper into his eyes, and
he into hers.

"I used to think if you looked too deeply into the glass, you
would lose yourself," she said, her voice barely a whisper.

"I think it's true . . ." He moved forward as he spoke,
brushing his lips against hers, and for a moment, she didn't
resist, closing her eyes, losing herself. Anakin pressed in closer,

a real and deep kiss, sliding his lips across hers slowly. He could lose himself here, could kiss her for hours, forever . . .

But then Padmé pulled back, suddenly, as if waking from a dream. "No, I shouldn't have done that."

"I'm sorry," Anakin said. "When I'm around you, my mind is no longer my own."

He stared at her hard again, beginning that descent into the glass, losing himself in her beauty.

But the moment had passed, and Padmé gathered her arms in close and leaned again on the balustrade, looking out over the water.

As soon as the starlight shrank back from its speed-shift elongation, Obi-Wan Kenobi saw the "missing" planet, exactly where the gravity flux had predicted it would be.

"There it is, Arfour, right where it should be," he said to his astromech droid, who tootled in response from the left wing of the fighter. "Our missing planet, Kamino. Those files *were* altered."

R4 beeped curiously.

"I have no idea who might have done it," Obi-Wan replied. "Maybe we'll find some answers down there."

He ordered R4 to disengage the hyperspace ring, a band encircling the center area of the starfighter, with a pair of powerful hyperdrive engines, one on either side. Then he took the Delta-7 away, gliding in casually, registering information on his various scanners.

As he neared the planet, he saw that it was an ocean world, with no visible landmasses showing behind the nearly solid cloud cover. He checked his sensors, searching for any other ships that might be in the area, not really sure of what he should expect. His computer registered a transmission directed his way, asking for identification, and he flipped his signal beacon on, transferring all the information. A moment later, to his relief, there came a second transmission from Kamino, this one containing approach coordinates to a place called Tipoca City.

"Well, here we go, Arfour. Time to find some answers."

The droid beeped and set the coordinates into the nav computer, and the fighter swooped down at the planet, breaking atmosphere and soaring along over rain-lashed, whitecapped seas. The trip across the stormy sky was rougher than the atmospheric entry, but the fighter held its course perfectly, and soon after, Obi-Wan got his first look at Tipoca City. It was all gleaming domes and angled, gracefully curving walls, built on gigantic stilts rising out of the lashing sea.

Obi-Wan spotted the appropriate landing pad, but did a flyby first, crossing the city and circling about, wanting to observe this spectacular place from all angles. It seemed as much a work of art as a practical and magnificent piece of engineering, the whole of the city reminding him more of the Senate Building and the Jedi Temple on Coruscant. It was brightly lit at all the right places to highlight the domes and curving walls.

"There's so much to see, Arfour," the Jedi lamented. He had visited hundreds of worlds in his life, but viewing a place as strange and beautiful as Tipoca City only reminded him that there were thousands and thousands more yet to see, too many for any one person to visit even if he did nothing else for the entirety of his life.

At last Obi-Wan put his fighter down on the designated landing pad. He pulled his hood up tight over him, then slid back his canopy and scrambled out against the wind and the rain, rushing across the permacrete to a tower across the way. A door slid open before him, spilling out brilliant light, and he went through, crossing into a brightly lit white room.

"Master Jedi, so good to see you," came a melodic voice.

Obi-Wan pushed back his hood, which had offered little protection from the driving rain, and brushed the water from his hair. Wiping his face, he turned to face the speaker, and then he paused, caught by the image of the Kaminoan.

"I am Taun We," she introduced herself.

She was taller than Obi-Wan, pasty white and amazingly

slender, with gracefully curving lines, but there was nothing insubstantial about her. Thin, yes, but packed with a solid and powerful presence. Her eyes, huge, almond-shaped, and dark, were sparkling clear, like those of an inquisitive child. Her nose was no more than a pair of vertical slits, connected by a horizontal one, sitting on the bridge above her upper lip. She reached out gracefully toward him with an arm that moved as smoothly as any dancer might.

"The Prime Minister expects you."

The words finally distracted Obi-Wan from his bemused perusal of her strangely beautiful physique. "I'm expected?" he asked, doing little to hide his incredulity. How in the galaxy could these beings possibly have been expecting him?

"Of course." Taun We replied. "Lama Su is anxious to see you. After all these years, we were beginning to think you weren't coming. Now please, this way."

Obi-Wan nodded and tried to play it cool, hiding the million questions buzzing about in his thoughts. *After all these years? They were thinking that I wasn't coming?*

The corridor was nearly as brightly lit as the room, but as his eyes adjusted, Obi-Wan found the light strangely comfortable. They passed many windows, and Obi-Wan could see other Kaminoans busy in side rooms, males—distinguished by a crest atop their heads—and females working about furniture that was highlighted at every edge by shining light, as if that light supported and defined it. He was struck by how clean this place was, everything polished and shining and smooth. He kept his questions to himself, though, as anxious to see this Prime Minister, Lama Su, as Taun We seemed to be in getting him there, judging from the swift pace.

The Kaminoan stopped at one side door and sent it sliding open with a wave of her hand, then motioned for Obi-Wan to enter first.

Another Kaminoan, a bit taller and with the distinctive male crest, greeted them. He looked down at Obi-Wan, blinked his huge eyes, and smiled warmly. With a wave of his hand, he brought an egg-shaped chair gracefully spiraling down from the ceiling.

"May I present Lama Su, Prime Minister of Kamino," Taun We said, then to Lama Su, she added, "This is Master Jedi—"

"Obi-Wan Kenobi," the Jedi finished, nodding his head deferentially.

The Prime Minister indicated the chair, then sat back in his own, but Obi-Wan remained standing, soaking in the scene before him.

"I trust you are going to enjoy your stay," the Prime Minister said. "We are most happy you have arrived at the best part of the season."

"You make me feel most welcome." Obi-Wan didn't add that if the deluge outside was "the best part of the season," he'd hate to see the worst.

"Please . . ." Lama Su indicated the chair once more. When Obi-Wan finally sat down, the Kaminoan continued. "And now to business. You will be delighted to hear we are on schedule. Two hundred thousand units are ready, with another million well on the way."

Obi-Wan's tongue suddenly seemed fat in his mouth, but he fought past the stutter and tucked his questions away, and improvised, "That is good news."

"We thought you would be pleased."

"Of course."

"Please tell your Master Sifo-Dyas that we have every confidence his order will be met, on time and in full. He is well, I hope."

"I'm sorry," the overwhelmed Jedi replied. "Master? . . ."

"Jedi Master Sifo-Dyas. He is still a leading member of the Jedi Council, is he not?"

The name, known to Obi-Wan as that of a former Jedi Master, elicited yet another surge of questions, but again, he put them out of mind and focused on keeping Lama Su talking and giving out potentially valuable information. "I'm afraid to say that Master Sifo-Dyas was killed almost ten years ago."

Lama Su blinked his huge eyes again. "Oh, I'm so sorry to hear that. But I'm sure he would have been proud of the army we've built for him."

"The army?" Obi-Wan asked before he could even think the direction through.

"The army of clones. And I must say, one of the finest we've ever created."

Obi-Wan didn't know how far he could press this. If it was indeed Sifo-Dyas who had commissioned an army of clones, then why hadn't Master Yoda or any of the others said anything about it? Sifo-Dyas had been a powerful Jedi before his untimely death, but would he have acted alone on an issue as important as this? The Jedi studied his two companions, even reaching into the Force to gain a feeling about them. Everything seemed straightforward here, and open, and so he followed his instincts and kept the conversation rolling along. "Tell me, Prime Minister, when my Master first contacted you about the army, did he say who it was for?"

"Of course he did," the Kaminoan offered unsuspiciously. "The army is for the Republic."

Obi-Wan almost blurted out, *The Republic!* but his discipline allowed him to keep his surprise well buried, along with the tumult in his thoughts, a mounting storm as furious as the one that raged outside. What in the galaxy was going on here? An army of clones for the Republic? Commissioned by a Jedi Master? Did the Senate know of this? Did Yoda, or Master Windu?

"You understand the responsibility you incur in creating such an army for the Republic?" he asked, trying to cover his confusion. "We expect, and must have, the very best."

"Of course, Master Kenobi," Lama Su said, seeming supremely confident. "You must be anxious to inspect the units for yourself."

"That's why I'm here," Obi-Wan answered. Taking Lama

Su's cue, he rose and followed the Prime Minister and Taun We out of the room.

Lush grasses sprinkled with flowers of all colors and shapes graced the hilly meadow. Beyond its borders, shining waterfalls spilled into the lake, and from this spot, many other lakes could be seen about the distant hills, all the way to the horizon.

Puffballs floated by on the warm breeze, and puffy clouds drifted across the shining blue sky above. It was a place full of life and full of love, full of warmth and full of softness.

To Anakin Skywalker, it was a place perfectly reflective of Padmé Amidala.

A herd of benevolent creatures called shaaks grazed contentedly nearby, seemingly oblivious to the couple. They were curious-looking four-legged beasts, with huge, bloated bodies. Insects buzzed about in the air, too busy with the flowers to take any time to bother either Anakin or Padmé.

Padmé sat on the grass, absently picking flowers, bringing them up to deeply inhale their scents. Every so often, she glanced over at Anakin, but only briefly, almost afraid to let him notice. She loved the way he was reacting to this place, to all of Naboo, his simple joys forcing her to see things as she had when she was younger, before the real world had pushed her to a place of responsibility. It surprised her that a Jedi Padawan would be so . . .

She couldn't think of the word. *Carefree? Joyous? Spirited?* Some combination of the three?

"Well?" Anakin prompted, forcing Padmé to consider again the question he had just asked her.

"I don't know," she said dismissively, purposely exaggerating her frustration.

"Sure you do! You just don't want to tell me!"

Padmé gave a helpless little laugh. "Are you going to use one of your Jedi mind tricks on me?"

"They only work on the weak-minded," Anakin explained. "You are anything but weak-minded." He ended with an innocent, wide-eyed look that Padmé simply could not resist.

"All right," she surrendered. "I was twelve. His name was Palo. We were both in the Legislative Youth Program. He was a few years older than I . . ." She narrowed her eyes as she finished, teasing Anakin with sudden intensity. "Very cute," she said, her voice taking on a purposeful, suggestive tone. "Dark curly hair . . . dreamy eyes . . ."

"All right, I get the picture!" the Jedi cried, waving his hands in exasperation. He calmed a moment later, though, and settled back more seriously. "Whatever happened to him?"

"I went into public service. He went on to become an artist."

"Maybe he was the smart one."

"You really don't like politicians, do you?" Padmé asked, a bit of anger creeping in despite the warm wind and the idyllic setting.

"I like two or three," Anakin replied. "But I'm not really sure about one of them." His smile was perfectly disarming and Padmé had to work hard to keep any semblance of a frown against it.

"I don't think the system works," Anakin finished, matter-of-factly.

"Really?" she replied sarcastically. "Well, how would you have it work?"

Anakin stood up, suddenly intense. "We need a system where the politicians sit down and discuss the problem, agree what's in the best interests of the people, and then do it," he said, as if it was perfectly simple and logical.

"Which is exactly what we do," came Padmé's unhesitating reply.

Anakin looked at her doubtfully.

"The trouble is that people don't always agree," she explained. "In fact, they hardly ever do."

"Then they should be made to."

That statement caught Padmé a bit off guard. Was he so convinced that he had the answers that he . . . No, she put that unsettling thought out of her mind. "By whom?" she asked. "Who is going to make them?"

"I don't know," he answered, waving his hands again in obvious frustration. "Someone."

"You?"

"Of course not me!"

"But someone."

"Someone wise."

"That sounds an awful lot like a dictatorship," Padmé said, winning the debate. She watched Anakin as a mischievous little grin began to spread across his face.

"Well," he said calmly, "if it works . . ."

Padmé tried to hide her shock. What was he talking about? How could he believe that? She stared at him, and he returned the severe look—but he couldn't hold it, and burst out laughing.

"You're making fun of me!"

"Oh no," Anakin said, backing away and falling to sit on the soft grass, hands out defensively before him. "I'd be much too frightened to tease a Senator."

"You're so bad!" She reached over, picked up a piece of fruit, and threw it at him, and when he caught it, she threw another, and then another.

"You're always so serious," Anakin scolded, and he began juggling the fruit.

"I'm so serious?" Her incredulity was feigned, because Padmé agreed with the assessment to a great extent. For all her life, she had watched people like Palo go off and follow their hearts, while she had followed the path of duty. She had known great triumph and great joy, to be sure, but all of it had been wrapped up in the extravagant outfits of Naboo's Queen, and now in the endless responsibilities of a Galactic Senator. Maybe she just wanted to take off all those trappings, all those clothes, and dive into the sparkling water, for no better reason than to feel its cool comfort, for no better reason than to laugh.

She grabbed up another piece of fruit and threw it at Anakin, and he caught it and seamlessly put it up with the others. Then another, and another, until too many went his way and he lost control, then tried futilely to duck away from the dropping fruit.

Padmé had to clutch at her belly, she was laughing so hard. Caught up in the whirlwind of the moment, Anakin sprang to his feet and ran off to the side, cutting in front of a shaak and frightening it with his sheer jubilance.

The normally passive grazers gave a snort and took up the chase, with Anakin running in circles and then off over the hill.

Padmé sat back and considered this moment, this day, and her companion. What was happening here? She couldn't dismiss the pangs of guilt that she was out here playing without purpose, while others worked hard to carry on the fight against the Military Creation Act, or while Obi-Wan Kenobi scoured the galaxy in search of those who would see her dead.

She should be out there, somewhere, doing something . . .

Her thoughts fell away in another burst of incredulous laughter as Anakin and the shaak came by once more, this time with the Jedi riding the beast, one hand clenched on a fold of its flesh, the other high and waving behind him for balance. What made it all the more ridiculous was that Anakin was riding backward, facing the shaak's tail!

"Anakin!" she cried in amazement. A bit of trepidation crept into her voice as she repeated the call, for the shaak had broken into a full gallop, and Anakin was trying to stand up on its back.

He almost made it, but then the lumbering creature bucked and he flew away, tumbling to the ground.

Padmé howled with laughter, clutching her stomach.

But Anakin lay very still.

She stopped and stared at him, suddenly frightened. She scrambled up, thinking her whole world had just crashed down around her, and rushed to his side. "Annie! Annie! Are you all right?"

Gently, Padmé turned him over. He seemed serene and still.

And then his face twisted into a perfectly stupid expression and he burst out laughing.

"Oh!" Padmé cried, and she punched out at him. He caught her hand and pulled her in close, and she willingly crashed onto him, wrestling with fury.

Anakin finally managed to roll her over and pin her, and Padmé stopped struggling, suddenly aware of the closeness. She looked into his eyes and felt the press of his body upon hers.

Anakin blushed and let go, rolling away, but then he stood up and very seriously reached his hand out to her.

All self-consciousness was gone now from Padmé. She looked hard into Anakin's blue eyes, finally and silently admitting the truth. She took his hand and followed him to the shaak, which was grazing contentedly once more.

Anakin climbed onto its back and pulled Padmé up behind him, and they rode off across the meadow, with Padmé's arms about his waist, her body pressed up against his, a swirl of emotions and questions spinning about in her mind.

Padmé jumped at the sound of the knock on the door. She knew who it was, and knew she was safe—from everything but her own feelings.

The afternoon at the meadow replayed in her thoughts, particularly the ride on the shaak, when Anakin had taken her back to the lodge. For the minutes of that ride, Padmé had not hidden behind a mask of denial, or behind anything else. Sitting behind Anakin, her arms about his waist, her head resting on the back of his shoulder, she had felt safe and secure, perfectly content and . . .

She had to take a deep breath to keep her hand from trembling as she reached up for the doorknob.

She pulled the door back, and could see nothing but the tall and lean silhouette, backlit by the setting sun.

Anakin shifted just a bit, blocking the rosy glow enough so that Padmé could see his smile. He started to move in, but she held her ground. It wasn't a conscious decision; she was simply entranced, for it seemed to her as if the sun was setting behind Anakin's shoulders and not behind the horizon, as if he was big enough to dismiss the day. Orange flames danced about his silhouette, dulling the distinction between Anakin and eternity.

Padmé had to consciously remember to breathe. She stepped back and Anakin sauntered in, apparently oblivious to the wondrous moment she had just experienced. He was grinning mischievously, and for some reason she felt embarrassed. She wondered for a moment if she should have chosen a different outfit, for the evening dress she was wearing was black and off the shoulder, showing quite a bit of flesh. She wore a black choker, as well, with a line of sheer fabric running down over the front of the dress, barely concealing her cleavage.

She moved to close the door, but paused and looked back over the lake, at the rose-colored tint filtering across the shimmering water.

When she turned back, Anakin was already standing by the table, looking over the bowl of fruit and the settings Padmé had put out. She watched him glance up at one of the floating light globes, its glow growing as the sunlight began to diminish outside. He playfully poked at it, seemingly oblivious that she, or anyone else, was watching him, and his smile nearly reached his ears as the globe bounced away from his touch, elongating the soft sphere of light.

The next few moments of just watching Anakin were quite pleasant for Padmé, but the next few after that, when he started looking back at her, his expression alternately playful and intense, proved more than a bit uncomfortable.

Soon enough, though, the pair had settled in at the table, seated across from each other. Two of the resort waitresses, Nandi and Teckla, served them their meal, while Anakin began recounting some of the adventures he had known over the last ten years, training and flying with Obi-Wan.

Padmé listened attentively, captivated by Anakin's flair for storytelling. She wanted to do more, though. She wanted to talk about what had happened out at the meadow, to try to make some sense of it with Anakin, to share with him the solution as they had shared the out-of-bounds emotions and moments. But she could not begin, and so she just allowed him to ramble on, contenting herself with enjoying his tales.

Dessert was Padmé's favorite, yellow-and-cream-colored shuura fruit, juicy and sweet. She grinned as Nandi put a bowl before her.

"And when I went to them, we went into . . ." Anakin paused, drawing Padmé's full attention, a wry smile on his face. "Aggressive negotiations," he finished, and then he thanked Teckla as she placed some dessert fruit before him.

"Aggressive negotiations? What's that?"

"Uh, well, negotiations with a lightsaber," the Padawan said, still grinning wryly.

"Oh," Padmé said with a laugh, and she eagerly went for her dessert, stabbing with her fork.

The shuura moved and her fork hit the plate. A bit confused, Padmé stabbed at it again.

It moved.

She looked up at Anakin, a bit confused and embarrassed, but then she saw that he was fighting hard not to laugh, staring down at his own plate a bit too innocently.

"You did that!"

He looked up, his expression wide-eyed. "What?"

Padmé scowled, pointing her fork at him and waving it threateningly. Then, suddenly, she went for the shuura again.

But Anakin was quicker. The fruit slipped out of the way, and she stabbed the plate. Then, before she could scowl at him again, the shuura rose into the air to hover before her.

"That!" Padmé answered. "Now stop it!" She couldn't hold her feigned anger, though, and laughed aloud as she finished. Anakin started laughing, too. Half looking at him, Padmé snapped her hand at the floating fruit.

He waggled his fingers and the fruit looped about her hand.

"Anakin!"

"If Master Obi-Wan was here, he'd be very grumpy," the Padawan admitted. He pulled back his hand, and the shuura flew across the table to his waiting grasp. "But he's not here," he added, cutting the fruit into several slices. Reaching for the Force, he made one piece float upward and slide toward Padmé. She bit it right out of the air.

Padmé laughed and so did Anakin. They finished their dessert with many fleeting glances, and then, as Teckla and Nandi returned to clean up the plates, the couple retreated to the sitting area, with its comfortable chairs and sofa, and a huge warm fire blazing in the hearth.

Nandi and Teckla finished and bade the couple good-bye, and then they were alone, completely alone, and the tension returned almost immediately.

She wanted him to kiss her, so desperately, and it was precisely that out-of-control sensation that had stopped her cold. This was not right—she knew that in her head, despite what her heart might be telling her. They each had bigger responsibilities for the time being; she had to deal with the continuing split of the Republic, and he had to continue his Jedi training.

Anakin settled back into the sofa. "From the moment I met you, all those years ago, a day hasn't gone by when I haven't thought of you." His voice was husky, intense, and the sparkle in his eyes bored right through her. "And now that I'm with you again, I'm in agony. The closer I get to you, the worse it gets. The thought of not being with you makes my stomach turn over, my mouth go dry. I feel dizzy! I can't breathe! I'm haunted by the kiss you never should have given me. My heart is beating, hoping that kiss will not become a scar."

Padmé's hand slowly dropped to her side and she sat listening in amazement at how honestly he was opening up before her, baring his heart though he knew she might tear it asunder with a single word. She was honored by the thought, and truly touched. And afraid.

"You are in my very soul, tormenting me," Anakin went on, not a bit of falseness in his tone. This was no ploy to garner any physical favors; this was honest and straightforward, refreshingly so to the woman who had spent most of her life being attended by handmaidens whose job it was to please and entertaining dignitaries whose agendas were never quite what they seemed.

"What can I do?" he asked softly. "I will do anything you ask."

Padmé looked away, overwhelmed, finding security in the distracting dance of the flames in the hearth. Several moments of silence slipped by uncomfortably.

"If you are suffering as much as I am, tell me," Anakin prompted.

Padmé turned on him, her own frustrations bubbling over. "I can't!" She sat back and struggled to collect herself. "We can't," she said as calmly as she could. "It's just not possible."

"Anything's possible," Anakin replied, leaning forward. "Padmé, please listen—"

"*You* listen," she scolded. Somehow, hearing her own denial brought some strength to her—much-needed strength. "We live in a real world. Come back to it, Anakin. You're studying to become a Jedi Knight. I'm a Senator. If you follow your thoughts through to conclusion, they will take us to a place we cannot go . . . regardless of the way we feel about each other."

"Then you do feel something!"

Padmé swallowed hard. "Jedi aren't allowed to marry," she pointed out, needing to deflect attention away from her feelings at that debilitating moment. "You'd be expelled from the Order. I will not let you give up your future for me."

"You're asking me to be rational," Anakin replied without the slightest hesitation, and his confidence and boldness here caught Padmé a bit by surprise. There was no longer anything of the child in the man before her. She felt her control slip a notch.

"That is something I know I cannot do," he went on. "Believe me, I wish I could wish my feelings away. But I can't."

"I am not going to give in to this," she said with all the conviction she could muster. She finished with her jaw clenched very tightly, knowing that she had to be the strong one here, for

Anakin's sake more than for her own. "I have more important things to do than fall in love."

He turned away, looking wounded, and she winced. He stared into the fire, his face twisting this way and that as he tried to sort through it all. She knew he was trying to find a way around her resolve.

"It wouldn't have to be that way," he said at length. "We could keep it a secret."

"Then we'd be living a lie—one we couldn't keep up even if we wanted to. My sister saw it, so did my mother. I couldn't do that. Could you, Anakin? Could you live like that?"

He stared at her intensely for a moment, then looked back to the fire, seeming defeated.

"No, you're right," he finally admitted. "It would destroy us."

Padmé looked from Anakin to the fire. Which would destroy her—destroy *them*—she had to wonder. The action or the thought?

Wow!" Boba Fett exclaimed, rushing across the landing pad to view the sleek starfighter up close.

"Beautiful ship," Jango agreed, strolling to catch up to his son, studying the craft with every stride. He noted the markings and design, the extra firepower, and, particularly, the astromech droid hardwired into the left wing, tootling happily.

"This is a Delta-Seven," the excited Boba announced, pointing out the rear-cockpit position. Jango nodded, glad that his son had been taking his lessons seriously. These were new ships—so new that they hadn't yet been fitted with hyperdrive engines, Jango realized, and he inadvertently glanced up at the cloudy sky, wondering if parent ships were up there. He shook the thought away, turning back to Boba.

"And what of the droid?" he asked. "Can you identify the unit?"

Boba climbed up the side of the fighter and studied the markings for a moment, then turned back to his father, finger to pursed lips, an intense expression on his face. "It's an Arfour-Pea," he said.

"And is that a common droid for this type of starfighter?"

"No," Boba answered without hesitation. "A Delta-Seven pilot would usually use an Arthree-Dee. It's better at keeping the guns targeted, and the fighter is so maneuverable that handling the laser cannons is tricky. I read that some pilots wind up shooting their own nose cones off in this fighter! They do a snap-roll, coming out over and around, but they haven't compensated the manual swivel . . ." As he spoke, he moved his arms over each other and about, tangling them up in front of him.

Jango was hardly listening to the details, though he was thrilled that Boba had taken to his lessons with such energy. "Suppose the pilot didn't need the extra gunnery skills of an Arthree-Dee?" he asked.

Boba looked at him curiously, as if he didn't understand.

"Would the Arfour-Pea then be a better choice?"

"Yes," came the halting response.

"And what pilot wouldn't need the extra droid gunnery skills?"

Boba stared blankly, but then a smile spread on his face. "You!" he blurted, seeming quite pleased with himself.

Jango took the compliment with an appreciative smile—and it was true enough. Jango could wheel any fighter, and if he ever had the opportunity to fly in a Delta-7, he'd likely choose an R4-P over the R3-D. But that wasn't what he had in mind right now, for he knew of one other type of pilot, pilots with heightened senses, who would similarly choose the better nav, but less weapon-oriented droid.

Jango Fett looked back up at the sky, wondering if a host of Jedi were about to descend upon Tipoca City.

Great racks holding glass spheres stretched across the immense room to the end of Obi-Wan's vision. Each sphere contained an embryo, suspended in fluid, and when the Jedi reached into the Force, he sensed strong waves of life energy.

"The hatchery," he stated more than asked.

"The first phase, obviously," Lama Su replied.

"Very impressive."

"I hoped you would be pleased, Master Jedi," the Prime Minister said. "Clones can think creatively. You'll find that they are immensely superior to droids, and that ours are the best in all the galaxy. Our methods have been perfected over many centuries."

"How many are there?" Obi-Wan asked. "In here, I mean."

"We have several hatcheries throughout the city. This, of course, is the most crucial phase, though with our techniques, we expect a survival rate of over ninety percent. Every so often, an entire batch will develop a . . . an issue, but we expect the clone production to remain steady, and with our accelerated growth methods, these before you will be fully matured and ready for battle in just over a decade."

Two hundred thousand units are ready, with another million well on the way. Lama Su's previous boast echoed ominously in Obi-Wan's thoughts. A production center, supremely efficient, producing a steady stream of superbly trained and conditioned warriors. The implications were staggering.

Obi-Wan stared at the closest embryo, floating contentedly in its fluid, curled and with its little thumb stuck into its mouth. In ten short years, that tiny creature, that tiny man, would be a soldier, killing and, likely, soon enough killed.

He shuddered and looked to his Kaminoan guide.

"Come," Lama Su bade him, walking along the corridor.

Next on the tour was a huge classroom, with desks in neat, orderly rows and with students in neat, orderly rows. They all looked to be about ten years of age. All dressed the same, all with the same haircut, all with exactly the same features and posture and expressions. Obi-Wan reflexively looked at the shining white walls of the huge room, almost expecting to see mirrors there, playing a trick on his eyes to make one boy seem to be many.

The students went about their studies without paying any more heed to the visitors than a quick glance.

Disciplined, Obi-Wan thought. *Much more so than any normal children.*

Another thought grabbed him. "You mentioned growth acceleration—"

"Oh yes, it's essential," the Prime Minister replied. "Otherwise a mature clone would take a lifetime to grow. Now we can do it in half the time. The units you will soon see on the parade ground we started ten years ago, when Sifo-Dyas first placed the order, and they're already mature and quite ready for duty."

"And these were started about five years ago?" the Jedi reasoned, and Lama Su nodded.

"Would you care to inspect the final product now?" the Prime Minister asked, and Obi-Wan could hear excitement in his voice. Clearly he was proud of this accomplishment. "I would like your approval before you take delivery."

The callousness of it all struck Obi-Wan profoundly. *Units. Final product.* These were living beings they were talking about. Living, breathing, and thinking. To create clones for such a singular purpose, under such control, even stealing half their childhood for efficiency, assaulted his sense of right and wrong, and the fact that a Jedi Master had begun all of this was almost too much to digest.

The tour took him through the commissary next, where hundreds of adult clones—all young men Anakin's age—sat in neat rows, all dressed in red, all eating the same food in the same manner.

"You'll find that they are totally obedient," Lama Su was saying, seemingly oblivious to the Jedi's discomfort. "We modified their genetic structure to make them less independent than the original, of course."

"Who was the original?"

"A bounty hunter named Jango Fett," Lama Su offered without any hesitation. "We felt that a Jedi would be the perfect choice, but Sifo-Dyas handpicked Jango himself."

The notion that a Jedi might have been used nearly floored Obi-Wan. An army of clones strong in the Force?

"Where is this bounty hunter now?" he asked.

"He lives here," Lama Su replied. "But he's free to come and go as he pleases." He kept walking as he spoke, leading Obi-Wan along a long corridor filled with narrow transparent tubes.

The Jedi watched with amazement as clones climbed up into

those tubes and settled in place, closing their eyes and going to sleep.

"Very disciplined," he remarked.

"That is the key," Lama Su replied. "Disciplined, and yet with the ability to think creatively. It is a mighty combination. Sifo-Dyas explained to us the Jedi aversion to leading droids. He told us Jedi could only command an army of life-forms."

And you wanted a Jedi as host? Obi-Wan thought, but he did not say it aloud. He took a deep breath, wondering how Master Sifo-Dyas, how any Jedi, could have so willingly and unilaterally crossed the line to create *any* army of clones. Obi-Wan realized that he had to suppress his need for a direct answer to that right now, and simply listen and observe, gather as much information as he could so that he and the Jedi Council might sort it out.

"So Jango Fett willingly remains on Kamino?"

"The choice is his alone. Apart from his pay, which is considerable, I assure you, Fett demanded only one thing—an unaltered clone for himself. Curious, isn't it?"

"Unaltered?"

"Pure genetic replication," the Prime Minister explained. "No tampering with the structure to make it more docile. And no growth acceleration."

"I would very much like to meet this Jango Fett," Obi-Wan said, as much to himself as to Lama Su. He was intrigued. Who was this man selected by Sifo-Dyas as the perfect source for a clone army?

Lama Su looked to Taun We, who nodded and said, "I would be most happy to arrange it for you."

She left them, then, as the tour continued, with Lama Su taking Obi-Wan along the areas that showed him pretty much the entire routine of the clones at every level of their development. The culmination came later on, when Taun We rejoined the pair on a balcony, sheltered from the brutal wind and rain and overlooking a huge parade ground. Below them, thousands and thousands of clone troopers, dressed in white armor and wearing full-face helmets, marched and drilled with all the precision of programmed droids. Entire formations, each made up of hundreds of soldiers, moved as one.

"Magnificent, aren't they?" Lama Su said.

Obi-Wan looked up at the Kaminoan, to see his eyes glowing with pride as he looked out upon his creation. There were no ethical dilemmas as far as Lama Su was concerned, Obi-Wan knew immediately. Perhaps that was why the Kaminoans were so good at cloning: their consciences never got in the way.

Lama Su looked down at him, smiling widely, prompting a response, and Obi-Wan offered a silent nod.

Yes, they were magnificent, and the Jedi could only imagine the brutal efficiency this group would exhibit in battle, in the arena for which they were grown.

Once again, a shudder coursed down Obi-Wan Kenobi's spine. For the first time, he appreciated Senator Amidala's crusade to stop the creation of an Army of the Republic, and the inevitable consequence: war!

A Jedi Knight here on Kamino. The thought was more than a little unsettling to Jango Fett.

The bounty hunter fell back in his seat and tightened his face in frustration—such were the problems with working for the Trade Federation. They were masters at weaving deception within deception, and they were up to so much right now that there was no single focus Jango could determine.

He looked across the room at Boba, who was hard at work poring over the schematics and capabilities of a Delta-7 starfighter, and matching them up against the known strengths and weaknesses of an R4-P unit.

Life was so simple for the boy, Jango thought with a touch of envy. For Boba, there was the love of and for his father, and his studies. Other than those two givens, the only real challenge before the boy was in finding enjoyable things to do at those times when Jango was away or busy with the Kaminoans.

At that moment, looking at his son, Jango Fett felt vulnerable, so very vulnerable, and it was not an emotion with which he was the least bit comfortable. He almost told Boba to go and pack, then and there, so they could blast away from Kamino, but he recognized the danger of that course. He would be leaving without learning anything about his potential enemy, this Jedi Knight who had arrived unexpectedly. His boss would want that information.

And Jango would need that information. If he took off now, after receiving a note from Taun We telling him that he would be receiving a visitor later that same day, it would be fairly obvious that he was fleeing.

Then he'd have a Jedi Knight on his tail, and one about whom he knew practically nothing.

Jango continued to stare at Boba, at the only thing that really mattered.

"Play it cool," he whispered to himself. "You're nothing more than a clone source, well paid enough to want to know nothing about why you're being cloned."

That was his litany, that was his plan. And it had to work.

For Boba's sake.

A wave of Taun We's hand brought forth the chime of an unseen bell, reminding Obi-Wan yet again of how foreign this world of Kamino, this city of Tipoca, really was. He didn't give it much thought, though, for he was focused on the locking mechanism on the door before him, an elaborate electronic clasp and bolt. Quite a bit of security, it seemed to him, given the supposedly genteel nature of Jango Fett's relationship with the Kaminoans, and the obvious control the cloners held over their city. Was the locking mechanism designed to keep people out, or to keep Jango in?

Likely the former, he reasoned. Jango was a bounty hunter, after all. Perhaps he had made more than a few dangerous enemies.

He was still studying the device when the door suddenly

opened, revealing a young boy, an exact replica of those Obi-Wan had been viewing all day.

The identical one that Jango had demanded, only this one was *actually* ten years old.

"Boba," Taun We said with great familiarity, "is your father home?"

Boba Fett stood staring at the human visitor for a long moment. "Yep."

"May we see him?"

"Sure," Boba answered. He stepped back, but his eyes never left Obi-Wan as the Jedi and Taun We stepped across the threshold.

"Dad!" Boba yelled.

The title struck Obi-Wan as curious, given that this was a clone and not a natural son. Was there a connection here? A real one? Had Jango wanted the exact replica not for any professional gain but simply because he had wanted a son?

"Dad!" the boy shouted again. "Taun We's here!"

Jango Fett walked in, dressed in simple shirt and trousers. Obi-Wan recognized him immediately, though he was many years older than the oldest clone, his face scarred and pitted, and unshaven. His body had thickened with age, but he was still physically imposing, much like many of the old gutter dwellers Obi-Wan encountered in far-flung places. A few extra pounds, sure, but those covered muscles hardened by years of tough living. Tattoos crossed both of Jango's muscular forearms, of a strange design that Obi-Wan did not recognize.

As he glanced up, he recognized the clear suspicion with which Jango was eyeing him. The man was on edge here, dangerously so, Obi-Wan understood.

"Welcome back, Jango," Taun We remarked. "Was your trip productive?"

Obi-Wan studied the bounty hunter intensely. Back from where? But Jango was a professional, and his expression revealed not the slightest tic or wince.

"Fairly," the man casually offered. He continued to size up Obi-Wan as he spoke, his eyes narrowing in an almost open threat.

"This is Jedi Master Obi-Wan Kenobi," Taun We said, her tone lighter, obviously an attempt to relieve some of the palpable tension. "He's come to check on our progress."

"That right?" If Jango cared, his tone didn't show it.

"Your clones are very impressive," Obi-Wan said. "You must be very proud."

"I'm just a simple man trying to make my way in the universe, Master Jedi."

"Aren't we all?" Obi-Wan finally broke eye contact with Jango as he spoke, scanning the room, looking for clues. He focused on the half-open door through which Jango had appeared, and thought he saw pieces of body armor in there, battered and stained, much like that worn by a rocket-man after delivering a toxic dart into the changeling Zam Wesell. And he saw a curving bluish line, like the goggle and breather area of the helmet he had seen back on Coruscant. Before he could scrutinize the sight any more closely, though, Jango walked in front of him, pointedly blocking his view.

"Ever make your way as far into the interior as Coruscant?" Obi-Wan asked, rather bluntly.

"Once or twice."

"Recently?"

Again the bounty hunter's gaze became obviously suspicious. "Possibly . . ."

"Then you must know Master Sifo-Dyas," Obi-Wan remarked, not out of any logical follow-up reasoning, but simply to gauge the man's reaction.

There was none, nor did Jango Fett move a centimeter out of Obi-Wan's line of sight, and when the Jedi tried to subtly alter his angle to gain a view, Jango said, in a coded language, "Boba, close the door."

Not until that bedroom door shut did Jango Fett move to

the side, and then it seemed to Obi-Wan as if the man was stalking him. "Master who?" Jango asked.

"Sifo-Dyas. Isn't he the one who hired you for this job?"

"Never heard of him," Jango replied, and if there was a lie in his words, Obi-Wan could not detect it.

"Really?"

"I was recruited by a man called Tyranus on one of the moons of Bogden," Jango explained, and again it seemed to Obi-Wan as if he was speaking truthfully.

"Curious . . ." Obi-Wan muttered. He glanced down, surprised and at a loss as to what all of this might mean.

"Do you like your army?" Jango Fett asked him.

"I look forward to seeing them in action," the Jedi replied.

Jango continued to stare at him, to try to see the intent behind his words, Obi-Wan knew. And then, as if it hardly mattered, the bounty hunter gave a toothy smile. "They'll do their job well. I'll guarantee that."

"Like their source?"

Jango Fett continued to smile.

"Thanks for your time, Jango," Obi-Wan said against that uncompromising stare. Then he turned to Taun We and started for the door.

"Always a pleasure to meet a Jedi," came the reply. It was heavy with double meaning, almost like a veiled threat.

But Obi-Wan wasn't about to call him on it. Jango Fett was clearly a dangerous man, streetwise and cunning, and likely better than most with any weapon handy. Before he pushed things any further, Obi-Wan realized that he should relay all that he had learned thus far back to Coruscant and the Jedi Council. This discovery of a clone army was nothing short of amazing, and more than a little unsettling, and none of it made much sense.

And *was* Jango the rocket-man Obi-Wan had seen in Coruscant that night when Padmé Amidala had been attacked?

Obi-Wan's gut told him that Jango was, but how did that

jibe with the man also being the host for a clone army supposedly commissioned by a former Jedi Master?

With Taun We beside him, the Jedi left the apartment, and
the door slid closed behind him. Obi-Wan paused and focused
his senses back, even reaching out with the Force.

The door lock quietly secured.

"It was his starfighter, wasn't it, Dad?" Boba Fett asked.
"He's a Jedi Knight, so he can use the Arfour-Pea."

Jango gave his son an absent nod.

"I knew it!" Boba squealed, but then Jango abruptly stole
the moment.

Jango fixed Boba with a no-nonsense look that the young
boy had learned well not to ignore.

"What is it, Dad?"

"Pack your things. We're leaving."

Boba started to reply, but—

"Now," the bounty hunter said, and Boba practically tripped
over himself, scrambling for his bedroom.

Jango Fett shook his head. He didn't need this aggrava-
tion. Not at this time. Not for the first time, the bounty hunter
questioned his decision to take the contract against Padmé Amidala. He had been surprised when the Trade Federation had
approached him with the offer. They had been adamant, explaining only that the death of the Senator was critical to securing necessary allies, and they had made an offer too lucrative for
Jango to refuse, one that would set him and Boba up forever on
a planet of their choosing.

Little had Jango known, though, that taking the contract on
Senator Amidala would put him in the crosshairs of the Jedi
Knights.

He looked across the way to Boba.

That was not a place he wanted to be at this time. Not at all.

Padmé awoke suddenly, her senses immediately tuning in to her surroundings. Something was wrong, she knew instinctively, and she jumped up, scrambling about out of fear that another of those centipede creatures was upon her.

But her room was quiet, with nothing out of place.

Something had awakened her, but not something in here.

"No!" came a cry from the adjoining bedroom, where Anakin was sleeping. "No! Mom! No, don't!"

Padmé slipped out of bed and ran to the door, not even bothering to grab a robe, not even caring or noticing that she was wearing a revealing silken shift. At the door, she paused and listened. Hearing cries from within, followed by more jumbled yelling, she realized that there was no immediate danger, that this was another of Anakin's nightmares, like the one that had gripped him on the shuttle ride to Naboo. She opened the door and looked in on him.

He was thrashing about on the bed, yelling "Mom!" repeatedly. Unsure, Padmé started in.

But then Anakin calmed and rolled back over, the dream, the vision, apparently past.

Then Padmé did become aware of her revealing dress. She moved back through the door, shutting it gently, then waited

for a long while. When she heard no further screaming or tossing, she went back to her bed.

She lay awake in the dark for a long, long while, thinking of
Anakin, thinking that she wanted to be in there beside him,
holding him, helping him through his troubled dreams. She
tried to dismiss the notion—they had already covered this dangerous ground and had come to an understanding of what must
be. And that agreement did not include her climbing into bed
beside Anakin.

The next morning, she found him on the east balcony of the
lodge, overlooking the lake and the budding sunrise. He was
standing by the balustrade, so deep in thought that he did not
notice her approach.

She moved up slowly, not wanting to disturb him, for as she
neared, she realized that he was doing more than thinking here,
that he was actually deep in meditation. Recognizing this as a
private time for Anakin, she turned and started away, as quietly
as she could.

"Don't go," Anakin said to her.

"I don't want to disturb you," she told him, surprised.

"Your presence is soothing."

Padmé considered those words for a bit, taking pleasure
in hearing them, then scolding herself for taking that pleasure.
But still, as she stood there looking upon him, his face now
serene, she couldn't deny the attraction. He seemed to her like
a young hero, a budding Jedi—and she had no doubt that he
would be among the greatest that great Order had ever known.
And at the same time, he seemed to her to be the same little
kid she had known during the war with the Trade Federation, inquisitive and impetuous, aggravating and charming all
at once.

"You had a nightmare again last night," she said quietly,
when Anakin at last opened his blue eyes.

"Jedi don't have nightmares," came the defiant reply.

"I heard you," Padmé was quick to answer.

Anakin turned to regard her. There was no compromise in

her expression—she knew perfectly well that his claim was ludicrous, and she let him know that she knew it.

"I saw my mother," he admitted, lowering his gaze. "I saw her as clearly as I see you now. She is suffering, Padmé. They're killing her! She is in pain!"

"Who?" Padmé asked, moving toward him, putting a hand on his shoulder. When she looked at him more closely, she noted a determination so solid that it took her by surprise.

"I know I'm disobeying my mandate to protect you," Anakin tried to explain. "I know I will be punished and possibly thrown out of the Jedi Order, but I have to go."

"Go?"

"I have to help her! I'm sorry, Padmé," he said. She saw from his expression that he meant it, that leaving her was the last thing he ever wanted to do. "I don't have a choice."

"Of course you don't. Not if your mother is in trouble."

Anakin gave her an appreciative nod.

"I'll go with you," she decided.

Anakin's eyes widened. He started to reply, ready to argue, but Padmé's smile held his words in check.

"That way, you can continue to protect me," she reasoned. Somehow she made it sound perfectly logical. "And you won't be disobeying your mandate."

"I don't think this is what the Jedi Council had in mind. I fear that I'm walking into danger, and to take you with me—"

"Walking into danger," Padmé echoed, and she laughed aloud. "A place I've never been before."

Anakin stared at her, hardly believing what he was hearing. He couldn't resist, though, and his smile, too, began to widen. For some reason he did not quite understand, the Padawan found a good measure of justification in his abandoning the letter of his orders now that Padmé was in on, and agreeing with, the plan.

Neither Padmé nor Anakin could miss the stark contrast when they took her sleek starship out of hyperspace and saw the brown planet of Tatooine looming before them. How different it was from Naboo, a place of green grasses and deep blue water, with cloud patterns swirling all across it. Tatooine was just a ball of brown hanging in space, as barren as Naboo was alive.

"Home again, home again, to go to rest," Anakin recited, a common children's rhyme.

"By hearth and heart, house and nest," Padmé added.

Anakin looked over at her, pleasantly surprised. "You know it?"

"Doesn't everyone?"

"I don't know," Anakin said. "I mean, I wasn't sure if anyone else . . . I thought it was a rhyme my mother made up for me."

"Oh, I'm sorry," Padmé said. "Maybe she did—maybe hers was different than the one my mother used to tell me."

Anakin shook his head doubtfully, but he wasn't bothered by the possibility. In a strange way, he was glad that Padmé knew the rhyme, glad that it was a common gift from mothers to their children.

And glad, especially, that he and Padmé had yet another thing in common.

"They haven't signaled any coordinates yet," she noted.

"They probably won't, unless we ask," Anakin replied. "Things aren't very strict here, usually. Just find a place and park it, then hope no one steals it while you go about your business."

"As lovely as I remember it."

Anakin looked at her and nodded. How different things were now than that decade before when Padmé had been forced to land on Tatooine with Obi-Wan and Qui-Gon in order to effect repairs on their ship. He tried to manage a smile, but the edge of his nervousness kept it from appearing genuine. Too many disturbing thoughts assaulted him. Was his mother all right? Was his dream a premonition of what was to come, or a replay of something that had already happened?

He brought the ship down fast, breaking through the

atmosphere and soaring across the sky. "Mos Espa," he explained when the skyscape of the city came into sight against the horizon.

He went in hard, and some protests did squeal over the comlink. But Anakin knew his way around this place as surely as if he had never left. He did a flyby over the edge of the city, then put the starship down in a large landing bay amid a jumble of vessels of all merchant and mercenary classes.

"Yous can't just drop in uninvited!" barked the dock officer, a stout creature with a piggish face and spikes running down the length of his back and tail.

"It's a good thing you invited us, then," Anakin said calmly, with a slight wave of his hand.

"Yes, it's a good thing I invited you then!" the officer happily replied, and Anakin and Padmé walked past.

"Anakin, you're bad," Padmé said as they exited onto the dusty street.

"It's not like there are dozens of ships lined up to fill the bay," Anakin replied, feeling pretty good about himself and the ease with which he had Force-convinced the piggish officer. He waved down a floating rickshaw pulled by an ES-PSA droid, a short and thin creature with a wheel where its legs should have been.

Anakin gave it the address and off it went, pulling them behind in the floating rickshaw, charging along the streets of Mos Espa, expertly zigging and zagging to avoid the heavy traffic, and blasting forth a shrill sound whenever someone didn't get out of the way.

"Do you think he was involved?" Padmé asked Anakin.

"Watto?"

"Yes, that was his name, right? Your former master?"

"If Watto has hurt my mother in any way, I will pluck his wings from his back," he promised, meaning every word. He wasn't sure how he would feel about seeing the slaver, even if Watto had nothing to do with bringing any harm to Shmi. Watto had treated him better than most in Mos Espa treated their slaves, and hadn't beaten him too often, but still, it hung in Anakin's thoughts that Watto had not let Shmi go with him when Obi-Wan and Qui-Gon had bought out his slave debt. Anakin understood that he was probably just deflecting some of his own guilt about leaving his mother with Watto, who was a businessman, after all.

"Here, Espasa," Anakin said to the droid, and the rickshaw glided to a stop in front of a shop all too familiar to Anakin Sky-walker. There, sitting on a stool near the door, fiddling with an electronic driver on a broken piece of equipment that looked like a droid component, was a rounded, winged Toydarian with a long snout. A black round hat adorned his head, and a small vest was pulled as far as it would go about his girth. Anakin recognized him immediately.

He paused for so long in just staring at Watto that Padmé got out before him and held her hand to help him.

"Wait here," she instructed the droid. "Please."

"No chuba da wanga, da wanga!" Watto yelled at the broken component, and at a trio of pit droids who were scrambling all about, trying to help.

"Huttese," Anakin explained to Padmé.

"No, not that one—that one!" she replied, and at Anakin's expression of surprise that she knew the strange language, she added, "You think it's easy being the Queen?"

Anakin shook his head and looked back to Watto, then glanced at Padmé once or twice as they neared. *"Chut chut, Watto,"* he greeted.

"Ke booda?" came the surprised response.

"Di nova, chut chut," Anakin reiterated, his words barely audible above the clamoring pit droids.

"Go ana bopa!" Watto yelled at the trio, and on his command, they immediately shut down and snapped back into their storage position.

"Ding mi chasa hopa," Anakin offered, taking the piece of the broken droid from Watto, and manipulating it expertly.

Watto watched him for a moment, his buglike eyes growing even larger in surprise.

"*Ke booda?*" he asked. "*Yo baan pee hota. No wega mi con-dorta. Kin chasa du Jedi. No bata tu tu.*"

"He doesn't know you," Padmé whispered to Anakin, try-ing to hold back her laughter at Watto's last statement, which translated to "Whatever it is, I didn't do it."

"*Mi boska di Shmi Skywalker,*" Anakin bluntly stated.

Watto's eyes narrowed suspiciously. Who would be looking for his old slave? The Toydarian's gaze went from Anakin to Padmé, then back to Anakin.

"Annie?" he asked in Basic. "Little Annie? Naaah!"

Anakin's answer came with a deft twist of his hands, and the sound of the little piece of equipment whirring to life. Smiling widely, he handed it back to Watto.

There weren't many around who could work such magic on broken droid parts.

"You *are* Annie!" the Toydarian cried. "It *is* you!" His wings started beating furiously, lifting him from the stool to hover in the air. "Ya sure sprouted!"

"Hello, Watto."

"Weehoo!" the Toydarian cried. "A Jedi! Waddya know? Hey, maybe you couldda help wit some deadbeats who owe me a lot of money—"

"My mother—" Anakin prompted.

"Oh yeah, Shmi. She's not mine no more. I sold her."

"Sold her?" Anakin felt Padmé squeeze his forearm.

"Years ago," Watto explained. "Sorry, Annie, but you know, business is business. Sold her to a moisture farmer named Lars. Least I think it was Lars. Believe it or not, I heard he freed her and married her. Can ya beat that?"

Anakin just shook his head, trying hard to digest it all. "Do you know where they are?"

"Long way from here. Someplace over on the other side of Mos Eisley, I think."

"Could you narrow it down?"

Watto thought about it for a moment, then just shrugged.

"I'd like to know," Anakin said, his tone and expression grim and determined, even threatening. The way Watto's features seemed to tighten showed that he got the hint that Anakin wasn't fooling around.

"Yeah, sure," he said. "Absolutely. Let's go look at my records."

The three went into the shop, and seeing the place brought memories swirling back to Anakin. How many hours, years, he had toiled in here, fixing everything Watto threw his way. And out back, where he had put all the spare parts he could find, so that he could build a Podracer. Not all of the memories were bad, he had to admit, but the good ones did not overcome the reality that he had been a slave. Watto's slave.

Fortunately for Watto, his records gave a location for the moisture farm of one Cliegg Lars.

"Stay a while, Annie," the Toydarian offered after sharing the information on Shmi's new owner—or was it her husband?

Without a word, Anakin turned about and walked away. This was the last time he would look at Watto and the shop, he decided. Unless of course, he found out that Watto was lying to him about Shmi's fate, or that Watto had somehow hurt his mother.

"Back to the lot, Espasa," he said to the droid as he and Padmé rushed back to the rickshaw. "Fast."

"Ya sure I can't get ya something to drink?" Watto called to them from the door of his shop, but they were already rushing away, kicking up dust in their wake.

"*Annie du Jedi,*" Watto remarked, and he waved both his hands dismissively at the departing rickshaw. "Waddya know."

Anakin took the starship out even more furiously than he had brought it in, blasting away from the lot and nearly colliding with a small freighter as it maneuvered to put down. Calls of protest came into him from Mos Espa control, but he just switched off the comm and zoomed off across the city. Soon after, they passed over the race grounds where the younger Anakin had often raced in his Pods, but he barely glanced at it as he put the ship out straight over the desert, heading for Mos Eisley. When that port came into view, he veered to the north and crossed past it, moving higher in the sky.

They spotted one moisture farm, and then another, and then the third, almost in a direct line from the city.

"That one," Padmé said. Anakin nodded grimly, and brought the ship down on a bluff overlooking the homestead.

"I'm really going to see her again," he breathed, shutting down the engines.

Padmé squeezed his arm and offered him a comforting smile.

"You don't know what it's like, to leave your mother like that," he said.

"I leave my family all the time," she replied. "But you're right. It's not the same. I can't imagine what it's like to be a slave, Anakin."

"It's worse to know that your mother is one."

Padmé nodded, conceding the point. "Stay with the ship, Artoo," she instructed the droid, who beeped in reply.

The first form that came into view as they walked toward the homestead was that of a very thin droid, dull gray in color, with weatherbeaten metal coverings. Obviously in need of a good oil bath, he bent stiffly and worked on some sort of fence sensor. Then he rose with a jerky motion, seeing their approach. "Oh, hello," he greeted. "How might I be of service? I am See—"

"Threepio?" Anakin said breathlessly, hardly believing his eyes.

"Oh my!" the droid exclaimed, and he began to shake violently. "Oh, my maker! Master Anakin! I knew you would return! I knew you would! And this must be Miss Padmé!"

"Hello, Threepio," Padmé said.

"Oh, my circuits! I'm so pleased to see you both!"

"I've come to see my mother," Anakin explained. The droid turned sharply up toward him, then seemed to shrink back.

"I think . . . I think," C-3PO stuttered. "Perhaps we'd better go indoors." He turned toward the homestead, motioning with his hand for the couple to follow.

Anakin and Padmé exchanged nervous glances. Anakin could not shake the feeling of doom that lingered long after the imagery of his nightmares had faded . . .

By the time they caught up to the droid, he was in the courtyard, shouting, "Master Cliegg! Master Owen! Might I present two important visitors?"

A young man and woman came rushing out of the house almost immediately, but slowed at the site of Padmé and Anakin.

"I'm Anakin Skywalker," Anakin said at once.

"Anakin?" the man echoed, his eyes going wide. "Anakin!"

The woman at his side brought her hand up to cover her mouth. "Anakin the Jedi," she whispered breathlessly.

"You know of me? Shmi Skywalker is my mother."

"Mine, too," said the man. "Not my real mom," he added at Anakin's obviously puzzled look, "but as real a mom as I've ever known." He extended his hand. "Owen Lars. This is my girlfriend, Beru Whitesun."

Beru nodded and said, "Hello."

Padmé, after giving up on Anakin ever remembering to introduce her, came forward. "I'm Padmé."

"I guess I'm your stepbrother," Owen said, his eyes never leaving the young Jedi of whom he had heard so very much. "I had a feeling you might show up."

"Is my mother here?"

"No, she's not," came a gruff answer from behind Owen and Beru, from the shadows of the house door. All four turned to see a heavyset man glide out on a hoverchair. One of his legs was heavily bandaged, the other, missing, and Anakin knew at once that these were fairly recent wounds. His heart seemed to leap into his throat.

"Cliegg Lars," the man said, moving in close and extending

his hand. "Shmi is my wife. We should go inside. We have a lot to talk about."

Anakin followed as if in a dream, a very horrible dream.

"It was just before dawn," Cliegg was saying, gliding toward the table in the homestead kitchen with Owen beside him, while Beru peeled off to gather some food and drinks for the guests.

"They came out of nowhere," Owen added.

"A band of Tusken Raiders," Cliegg explained.

A sinking feeling nearly buckled Anakin's knees and he slumped into a seat across from Owen. He'd had some experience with Tusken Raiders, but on a very limited basis. Once he had tended the wound of one gravely injured Raider, and when the Tusken's friends showed up, they had let him go— something unheard of among the more civilized species of Tatooine. But still, despite that one anomaly, Anakin didn't like hearing the name of Shmi spoken in the same breath as the grim words, *Tusken Raiders.*

"Your mother had gone out early, like she always did, to pick mushrooms that grow on the vaporators," Cliegg explained. "From the tracks, she was about halfway home when they took her. Those Tuskens walk like men, but they're vicious, mindless monsters."

"We'd seen many signs that they were about," Owen piped in. "She shouldn't have gone out!"

"We can't live huddled in fear!" Cliegg scolded, but he calmed at once and turned back to Anakin. "All signs were that we'd chased the Tuskens away. We didn't know how strong this raiding band was—stronger than anything any of us have ever seen. Thirty of us went out after Shmi. Four of us came back."

He grimaced and rubbed his leg, and Anakin felt the man's pain clearly.

"I'd still be out there, only . . . after I lost my leg . . . " Cliegg nearly broke down, and it struck Anakin how much the man loved Shmi.

"I just can't ride anymore," Cliegg went on. "Until I heal."

The proud man drew in a deep breath and forcibly steadied himself, squaring his broad shoulders. "This isn't the way I wanted to meet you, son," he said. "This isn't how your mother and I planned it. I don't want to give up on her, but she's been gone a month. There's little hope she's lasted this long."

The words hit Anakin like a stinging slap, and he retreated from them, back into himself, back into the Force. He reached out, using his bond with his mother to try to somehow feel her presence in the Force.

Then he shot to his feet.

"Where are you going?" Owen asked.

"To find my mother," came the grim reply.

"No, Anakin!" Padmé cried out, rising to grab his forearm.

"Your mother's dead, Son," the resigned Cliegg added. "Accept it."

Anakin glowered at him, at them all. "I can feel her pain," he said, his jaw clenched, teeth gritted. "Continuing pain. And I will find her."

A moment of silence ensued, and then Owen offered, "Take my speeder bike." He jumped up from his seat and strode by Anakin.

"I know she's alive," Anakin said, turning to face Padmé. "I *know* it."

Padmé winced but said nothing, and she let go of Anakin's arm as he moved to follow Owen.

"I wish he'd have come a bit earlier," Cliegg lamented.

Padmé looked over at him, and at Beru, who was standing over the tearful man, hugging him.

Then, having no words to offer, Padmé turned and rushed out to join Anakin and Owen. By the time she caught up, Owen was heading back for the house and Anakin was standing near the speeder, staring out over the empty desert.

"You're going to have to stay here," Anakin said to her as she hurried to his side. "These are good people. You'll be safe."

"Anakin . . . "

"I know she's alive," he said, still staring out at the dunes.

Padmé hugged him tightly. "Find her," she whispered.

"I won't be long," he promised. He straddled the speeder bike, kicked it to life, and rocketed away across the dunes.

When the call beamed into the Jedi Temple on Coruscant, using scramble code 5 and in care of "the old folks home," Mace Windu and Yoda knew that it was important. Extremely important.

They took the call in Yoda's apartment, after Mace checked the corridor both ways, then pointedly closed the door.

The hologram of Obi-Wan Kenobi appeared before them. The man was obviously on edge, glancing repeatedly over his shoulder.

"Masters, I have successfully made contact with Lama Su, the Prime Minister of Kamino."

"Ah, good it is that your planet you have found," Yoda said.

"Right where your students predicted," Obi-Wan replied. "These Kaminoans are cloners—best in the galaxy I've been told, and from what I've seen, I don't doubt the claims."

Both Jedi Masters frowned.

"They are using a bounty hunter named Jango Fett to create a clone army."

"An army?" Mace repeated.

"For the Republic," came Obi-Wan's startling answer. "What's more, I have a strong feeling that this bounty hunter is behind the plot to assassinate Senator Amidala."

"Do you think these cloners are involved in that, as well?"

"No, Master, there appears to be no motive."

"Do not assume anything, Obi-Wan," Yoda advised. "Clear, your mind must be if you are to discover the real villain behind this plot."

"Yes, Master," Obi-Wan said. "Prime Minister Lama Su has informed me that the first battalion of clone troopers are ready for delivery. He also wanted me to remind you that if we require more—and they've another million well on the way to completion—it will take more time to grow them."

"A million clone warriors?" Mace Windu asked in disbelief.

"Yes, Master. They say Master Sifo-Dyas placed the order for the clone army almost ten years ago. I was under the impression he was killed before that. Did the Council ever authorize the creation of a clone army?"

"No," Mace answered without hesitation, and without even looking to Yoda for confirmation. "Whoever placed that order did not have the authorization of the Jedi Council."

"Then how? And why?"

"The mystery deepens," Mace said. "And it is one that needs unraveling, for more reasons than the safety of Senator Amidala."

"The clones are impressive, Master," Obi-Wan explained. "They have been created and trained for one purpose alone."

"Into custody, take this Jango Fett," Yoda instructed. "Bring him here. Question him, we will."

"Yes, Master. I will report back when I have him." Obi-Wan glanced over his shoulder again and abruptly instructed R4 to cut the transmission.

"A clone army," Mace remarked, alone with Yoda once again, the hologram gone. "Why would Sifo-Dyas—"

"When placed, this order was, may provide insight," Yoda said, and Mace nodded. If the timing of the order was correct, then Sifo-Dyas must have placed it right before he died.

"If this Jango Fett was involved in trying to kill the Senator, and just happened to be chosen as the source for a clone army, created for the Republic . . . " Mace Windu stopped and shook his head. The coincidence was too great for those two items to be simple chance. But how could one tie in with the other? Was it possible that whoever decided to create the clone army was afraid that Senator Amidala would be a strong enough voice to prevent that army from being used?

The Jedi Master rubbed a hand over his forehead and looked to Yoda, who sat with his eyes closed. Probably contemplating the same riddles as he was, Mace knew. And equally troubled, if not more so.

"Blind we are, if the development of this clone army we could not see," Yoda remarked.

"I think it is time to inform the Senate that our ability to use the Force has diminished."

"Only the Dark Lords of the Sith know of our weakness," Yoda replied. "If informed the Senate is, multiply our adversaries will."

For the two Jedi Masters, this surprising development was troubling on several different levels.

Obi-Wan moved along the corridor carefully. He knew nothing of Jango Fett's accomplishments, but he figured they must be considerable, given the selection of the man as the prototype for a clone army. Pausing, he closed his eyes and reached out to the Force, searching for hidden enemies. A moment later, convinced that Jango wasn't in the immediate area, he approached the door. Gently, he ran his fingers along the frame, sensing for potential traps, then finally touched the locking mechanism. Holding one hand there, he tried the door.

It didn't budge.

Obi-Wan reached for his lightsaber thinking to shear through the portal, but he changed his mind, preferring subtlety. He closed his eyes and sent his strength through his outstretched hand and into the lock, manipulating the mechanism easily. Then, one hand going to his lightsaber, he tried the door again, and it slid open.

As soon as he viewed the room inside, he knew that he

wouldn't be needing his weapon. The apartment was in complete disorder. The drawers of every cabinet hung open, some lay on the floor, and the chairs were knocked all askew.

To the side, the bedroom door was open, and it, too, was a wreck. All the signs within pointed to a hurried departure.

Obi-Wan glanced all about, looking for some clue, and his gaze finally settled on a thin computer screen set on a counter in the main living area. Rushing to it, he turned it on and recognized it at once as a security network, tied in to various cams set about the immediate area. Obi-Wan scrolled from view to view, noting the corridor he had just traversed and various angles of the apartment itself. An outside view of the area showed the apartment's rain-lashed roof—and he could see himself through the transparisteel window.

He continued his scroll, widening the lens and zooming in on anything suspicious.

Then he got a shot of a nearby landing pad and an odd-looking ship with a wide, flat base, narrowed to a point on the closest end and thinning as it climbed to a small compartment, perhaps large enough for two or three men.

Rushing about the parked craft was a familiar figure, either Boba Fett or another clone.

Obi-Wan nodded and smiled knowingly as he followed the boy's movements, recognizing from the fluidity and randomness of some small actions that this was indeed Boba and not a perfectly controlled and conditioned clone.

Obi-Wan's grin didn't hold, though, as another familiar figure came into view. It was Jango, dressed in the armor and rocket pack the Jedi had seen before, on the streets of Coruscant. If Obi-Wan had had any doubts that Jango was the man who had hired Zam Wesell, those doubts were now gone. He bolted from the apartment and ran down the corridor, looking for a way out.

"Yeah, I'll let you fly it," Jango said to Boba.

Boba punched a fist into the air in triumph, thrilled that his father was going to let him get behind the controls of *Slave I*. It had been a long time, months, since Boba had been allowed to sit behind the controls.

"Not to take her out, through," Jango added, somewhat dimming the boy's jubilance. "We're going out hot, son, but we'll take her back out of lightspeed early so you can get some time working her about."

"Can I put her down?"

"We'll see."

Boba knew that his father really meant "no," but he didn't press the point. He understood that something big and dangerous was going on around him, and so he decided to take whatever his dad offered, and be happy with that. He hoisted another bag and climbed up the ramp to the small storage hold. He looked back at Jango as he did so, then looked past Jango, to a human form rushing out of the tower's turbolift and toward them through the driving rain.

"Dad! Look!"

As Jango swung about, Boba's eyes went wider still. The running figure was their Jedi visitor—and he was drawing his lightsaber and igniting a blue blade that hissed in the downpour.

"Get on board!" Jango called to him, but Boba hesitated, watching his father pull out his blaster and fire off a bolt at the charging Jedi. With amazing reflexes, Obi-Wan snapped his lightsaber about, deflecting the bolt harmlessly wide.

"Boba!" Jango yelled, and the boy came out of his trance and scrambled up the ramp and into *Slave I*.

Obi-Wan launched himself through the air at the bounty hunter. Another blaster shot followed, then another, and the Jedi easily picked them both off, deflecting one and turning the other back at Jango. But as the bolt ricocheted toward him, the bounty hunter leapt away, his rocket pack flaring to life, sending him up to the top of the nearby tower.

Obi-Wan tumbled headlong, turning while he rolled to come around as Jango fired again. Without even thinking of the movement, letting the Force guide his hand, the Jedi brought his lightsaber to the left and down, knocking the energy bolt aside.

"You're coming with me, Jango," he called.

The man answered with a series of shots, a line of bolts coming at the Jedi. The lightsaber went alternately left then right, picking off each one, and when Jango altered the pattern, left, right, left, right, then right again, the Force guided Obi-Wan's hand true.

"Jango!" he started to call out. But then he realized that the bounty hunter's latest shot was not a bolt but an explosive pack, and the next moment he was diving, enhancing his leap with the Force.

All of *Slave I* recoiled from the explosion outside, and the jolt sent Boba tumbling to the side. "Dad!" he cried. He scrambled to the viewscreen, flicking it on and orienting the cam on the scene below.

He saw his father immediately, and burst out in tears of relief. He calmed himself quickly, though, scanning the area for the enemy Jedi, and saw Obi-Wan coming over from a roll, back to his feet—and blocking another series of bolts with seeming ease.

Boba scanned the panel, trying to remember all his lessons about *Slave I,* glad that he had been so diligent in his studies. With a wicked grin that would have made his father proud, Boba fired up the energy packs and clicked off the locking mechanism of the main laser.

"Block this, Jedi," he whispered. He took a bead on Obi-Wan and pulled the trigger.

"You have a lot to answer!" Obi-Wan called to Jango, his voice sounding thin in the thunderous downpour and lashing wind. "It'll go easier on you, and on your son, if—"

He stopped suddenly, registering the report of a heavy laser somewhere in his subconscious. The Force had him moving instinctively before he even understood what was happening, leaping and flying across the air in a double somersault.

He landed to find the ground shaking violently under his feet, quaking from the thunder of *Slave I*'s heavy laser cannon, which swung around to follow him.

Obi-Wan had to dive again, but this time the bouncing report sent him sprawling to the ground, his lightsaber skidding from his grasp across the rain-slickened surface.

Fortunately, *Slave I*'s cannon went quiet, the energy pack depleted for the moment, and Obi-Wan wasted no time leaping to his feet and charging at Jango Fett, who was coming hard his way.

A blaster bolt led the bounty hunter in, but Obi-Wan leapt above the streaking line of energy, flying forward and spinning around to snap-kick the weapon from Jango's hand.

The bounty hunter didn't flinch. He charged right into the Jedi as Obi-Wan landed, looping his arms over Obi-Wan's and bearing him backward.

He tried to wrestle Obi-Wan to the ground, but the Jedi's feet were too quick for that, setting him in perfect balance almost immediately. He slid one leg between the bounty hunter's feet and started to twist to the side, weakening Jango's hold on his arms.

Jango smiled wickedly and snapped his forehead into Obi-Wan's face, dazing him for a moment. The bounty hunter pulled a hand free and launched a heavy punch, but realized his mistake immediately as the Jedi ducked the blow and did a tight, stationary somersault right under the swinging arm, double-kicking out as he came over, his feet slamming Jango in the chest and throwing him backward.

Now Obi-Wan had gained the initiative and he used it with a fierce charge, slamming into the stumbling bounty hunter, thinking to bring him down to the ground beneath him, where the encumbering armor the man wore would work against him.

But Jango showed the Jedi why he had been chosen as the basis for the clones. He went with the flow of the tackle for a moment, then suddenly reversed his footing and his momentum, stopping Obi-Wan's progress cold.

Jango launched a left hook. Obi-Wan ducked and snapped out a straight right in response. Jango slipped his head to the side so that the blow barely grazed him. A short rocket burst had him in the air and spinning a circle kick out at Obi-Wan, who dropped to his knees and ducked it, then came up high in a leap, over the second kick as Jango came around again.

Now Obi-Wan snapped off a kick of his own, but Jango accepted the blow against his lowered hip and snapped his left arm down across the Jedi's shin, locking the leg long enough for him to drive a right cross into Obi-Wan's inner thigh.

The Jedi threw his head and torso back, lying flat out and lifting his left leg as he did, kicking Jango under the side of his ribs. A sudden scissor-twist, right leg going down and across, left leg shooting across the other way above it, had Jango and Obi-Wan spinning sidelong. Obi-Wan caught himself with extended arms as he turned facedown, broke his feet from their hold on Jango, and mule-kicked the falling man backward. Then, going down to the platform to launch himself right back up to his feet, he turned about and rushed forward, gaining an advantage on the off-balance and struggling Jango.

A right cross smashed the bounty hunter across the face, followed by a looping left hook that should have laid the man low. But again, with brilliant reflexes, Jango ducked the brunt of that blow and caught the surprised Obi-Wan with a sudden and short, but heavy, left and right in the gut.

The Jedi's right hand waved across between his face and Jango's, and he used a quick Force shove to throw the man back a step until he could straighten and find a defensive posture once more.

Jango came right back in, fiercely, wildly, kicking and punching with abandon.

Obi-Wan's hands worked vertically before him, hardly moving, amazingly precise, turning blow after blow harmlessly aside. He turned one hand in and down suddenly, taking the momentum from a heavy kick, then came right back up to lift Jango's jabbing fist up high. Then he snapped his hand straight out, his stiffened fingers smashing against a seam in the bounty hunter's armor. Jango winced and fell back. Obi-Wan launched himself forward, diving onto the man, going for the victory.

But Jango had an answer, firing his rockets and lifting both himself and the grappling Jedi up into the air. A burst of a side-thruster sent the pair out past the landing pad proper to the sloping skirt of the structure.

Jango's hands worked almost imperceptibly, twisting in and about the Jedi's arms and hands, expertly loosening Obi-Wan's grip. Then he fired his thrusters, left and right, causing a sudden and repeated jerk that broke him free of Obi-Wan's grasp.

Obi-Wan hit the deck hard and slid perilously close to the edge—close enough to hear the great waves breaking against the platform's stilts below him. He caught a hold and reached into the Force, using it to grab his lightsaber, recognizing that he was suddenly vulnerable.

He heard a shot from the side, not the screech of a blaster bolt, but a *pfizzt* sound, and rolled as far as he could.

But not far enough. He lost his concentration, along with his grasp on his lightsaber, as a thin wire slid under his wrists, then wrapped about them, securing him tightly.

And then he was sliding, back up the sloping skirt and across the platform, towed by the rocket-man. With reflexes honed by years of intensive training, and with the Force-strength of a Jedi Master, Obi-Wan snap-rolled his body forward, back up over his outstretched arms, tumbling to his feet, then leaping out to the side as the towline again went taut, jerking him along. He rolled about a pylon and came back to his feet again, now having the leverage of the metal pole helping to hold him there.

Reaching deeply in the Force once more, he grounded himself, becoming, for an instant, almost as one with the platform.

Immovable.

The wire snapped tightly, but Obi-Wan didn't budge.

He felt the angle of the pull change dramatically as the rocket-man plunged to the deck, his pack breaking away.

Obi-Wan started around the pole, but stopped and shielded his eyes as Jango Fett's rocket pack exploded with a burst of light and a tremendous concussion.

"Dad!" Boba Fett cried as the rocket pack blew apart, his face coming right to the viewscreen. But then he saw Jango, off to the side and apparently unharmed, though tugging frantically against the pull of the wire—that was now being controlled by the Jedi.

Boba slapped one hand helplessly against the screen, mouthing "Dad" again, and then he winced as the Jedi slammed into his father, kicking and butting him, and both of them, locked together, went rolling off the back edge of the landing pad, sliding fast down the skirt and toward the raging ocean.

Obi-Wan kicked and tried to find his way back to the Force, but Jango punched him repeatedly. He could hardly believe that the bounty hunter would waste the effort, with certain death awaiting them both at the end of the slide and fall. He managed to pull back somewhat and saw Jango lift one forearm, a strange smile on his face. The bounty hunter clenched his fist, and a line of claws popped forth from the armor.

Obi-Wan instinctively recoiled as Jango lifted that arm higher, but then the bounty hunter slammed it down, not on Obi-Wan, but on the platform skirt. At the same time, Jango worked his other hand, releasing the locking mechanism of the wire-launching bracelet, and it slid free of his arm.

He screeched to a halt, and Obi-Wan slid past him.

"Catch a rollerfish for me," the Jedi heard Jango say, and then he was falling, over the lip and down toward the raging whitecaps.

"Dad! Oh, Dad!" Boba Fett cried in relief as he spotted his father clambering back over the skirt lip and onto the platform.

Jango climbed to his feet and stumbled toward *Slave I*, and Boba rushed to the hatch, sliding it open and reaching down to help his father aboard.

"Get us out of here," the dazed and battered Jango said, and Boba grinned and rushed to the control panel, firing up the engines.

"I'll put her right to lightspeed!"

"Just break atmosphere and take her straight out!" Jango ordered, and his words came out with a growl of pain as he held his bruised side. Then he noticed his son's wounded look. "Get the nav computer on line and have it set the coordinates for the jump," he conceded.

Boba's smile beamed brighter than ever. "Liftoff!" he shouted.

Obi-Wan used the Force to grab the trailing, loose end of the wire that still held him by the wrists, and he threw that end out, looping it over a crossbeam in the platform structure. His descent stopped with a sudden jerk.

He glanced around, then began to swing, back and forth, gaining momentum until he was far enough out to pull himself free of the bond and drop lightly onto a small service platform, barely above the lashing waves.

He took only a moment to catch his breath, and then opened the door of the service turbolift with a wave of his hand. Even before the door opened at the landing platform, he heard the engines of the bounty hunter's ship roar to life.

He came over the lip, spotting his lightsaber immediately and calling it in to him with the Force.

But he was too late. The ship was already shuddering, ready to blast away.

Obi-Wan pulled a small transmitter from his belt and threw it out long and far at *Slave I*. The magnetic lock of the tracking device grasped on to the ship's hull just in time.

Rain and steam pouring all about him, Obi-Wan Kenobi stood there for a long while until *Slave I* disappeared from view.

He looked around at the platform, replaying the battle in his head, his respect for this bounty hunter, Jango Fett, growing considerably. He understood now why Jango had been selected by Sifo-Dyas, or Tyranus, or whoever it was that selected him. The man was good, full of tricks and full of skill.

He had taken Obi-Wan Kenobi, a Jedi Knight, the man who had defeated the Sith Lord Darth Maul, to the very precipice of disaster.

But Obi-Wan was still pleased at the way it had played out. He would track Jango now. Perhaps at the end of the coming journey, he would finally get some answers instead of even more riddles.

Boba sat quietly, sensing the tension, as *Slave I* blasted away from Kamino. He wanted to talk about his shot with the laser cannon, about how he had knocked the Jedi down and sent his lightsaber flying away. But this wasn't the time, he knew, for Jango wore an intense expression that Boba recognized all too well, one that told him clearly that now was not the time for him to speak.

The boy rested back against the wall farthest from his father as Jango worked the controls, setting the coordinates for the jump to hyperspace. "Come on, come on," Jango said repeatedly, rocking back and forth as if urging the ship on, and glancing over at the sensors every few seconds as if he expected a fleet of starships to be chasing them away.

Then he gave a shout of victory and punched the hyperdrive, and Boba went back against the wall, watching the stars elongate.

Jango Fett slumped back in his seat and breathed a sigh of relief, his expression softening almost immediately. "Well, that was a bit too close," he said with a laugh.

"You smashed him good," Boba replied, his excitement beginning to bubble up again. "He never had a chance against you, Dad!"

Jango smiled and nodded. "To tell the truth, Son, he had me in real trouble there," he admitted. "After he dodged that explosive pack, I'd about run out of tricks."

Boba frowned at first, wanting to argue against anyone ever getting the upper hand on his father, but then, as he considered the moment Jango had mentioned, his frown became a wide smile. "I got him good with the laser cannon!"

"You did great," Jango replied. "You fired at just the right time, and were right there, ready to help me in when it was time for us to go. You're learning well, Boba. Better than I ever believed possible."

"That's because I'm a little you," the boy reasoned, but Jango was shaking his head.

"You're better than I was at your age, and by a long way. And if you keep working hard, you'll be the best bounty hunter this galaxy's ever seen."

"Which was your plan from the beginning with the Kaminoans, right, Dad? That's why you wanted me!"

Jango Fett moved over and lifted one hand to tousle Boba's hair. "That and a lot of other reasons," he said quietly, reverently. "And in every regard, in every hope and dream, you've done better than I ever expected."

There was nothing that anyone in all the galaxy could ever have said to young Boba Fett to make him feel better than those words from his father.

Jango took *Slave I* out of hyperspace a bit early, so that Boba could have some time piloting the ship on the approach to Geonosis. For Boba, sitting in the chair beside his father, working the controls deftly, even showing off a bit, there could be no greater moment, and the boy was saddened by the sight of the red planet, Geonosis, and the asteroid belts that ringed it.

"Security's tight here," Jango explained, taking the helm. "It'll be better if I put her down."

Boba sat back in the chair without complaint. He knew his father was right, and even if he had disagreed, he wouldn't have done so openly.

He turned his attention to the scan screens, showing the composition of the asteroid field nearby, and some distant traffic around the other side of the planet.

He noted one blip in particular, disengaging from the asteroid belt and moving out behind *Slave I*. He didn't think too much of it at first, until a second blip appeared, right behind *Slave I*, though nothing substantial enough to be a separate ship.

"Nearly there, Son," Jango remarked.

"Dad, I think we're being tracked," Boba told him. "Look at the scan screen. Isn't that a cloaking shadow of our own ship?"

Jango looked at him doubtfully, then turned that skeptical expression upon the scan screen. Boba watched with mounting excitement as his father's gaze turned intense and he slowly began to nod.

"That Jedi must have put a tracking device on our hull before we left Kamino," he agreed. "But how? I thought he was dead."

"Someone's following us," Boba observed.

"We'll fix that," Jango assured him. "Hang on, son! Watch me put us into that asteroid field—he won't be able to follow us there." He looked over at Boba and winked. "And if he does, we'll leave him a couple of surprises."

Jango opened a side panel and pulled a lever, releasing an electric charge along his hull that was designed to destroy just such tracking devices. A quick look at the scan screen showed that the cloaking shadow had disappeared.

"Here we go," Jango said, and he dived *Slave I* into the asteroid field, pulling a fast circuit over and around a nearby rock, then diving out fast to the side, rolling about a spinning boulder, and cutting fast between another pair. In and around he wove, with no apparent pattern, and a few moments later, Boba, who was still studying the scanner, announced, "He's gone."

"Maybe he's smarter than I thought and headed on toward the planet surface," Jango said with a grin and another wink.

Even as he finished, though, the scanner beeped.

"Look, Dad!" Boba cried, pointing out the blip, now inside the asteroid field, as well. "He's back!"

"Hang on!" Jango said, and he put *Slave I* through a wild series of dips, climbs, and turns, then finished with a straight-out run, while uncapping a firing trigger and squeezing the plunger. "Seismic charge," he explained to Boba, who grinned.

But then the boy was screaming a warning as the forward viewscreen filled up with an asteroid.

Jango was already on it, turning the amazingly maneuverable *Slave I* up on its end and running up over the giant space rock.

"Stay calm, son," he assured Boba. "We'll be fine. That Jedi won't be able to follow us through this."

His declaration was accentuated by a sudden flash and a jarring buck as the sonic charge detonated far behind them.

"He got through it!" Boba cried a moment later, seeing the Jedi's ship reappear on the scan screen.

"This guy can't take a hint," said Jango, who remained unrattled. "Well, if we can't lose him, we'll have to finish him."

Boba cried out again, but his father was in complete control. He put the ship down a narrow tunnel creasing one of the larger asteroids. He had to slow a bit to maneuver, and when *Slave I* came out the other end, Jango and Boba saw the Jedi starfighter stream over and past them. The hunted had suddenly become the hunters.

"Get him, Dad!" Boba cried out. "Get him! Fire!"

Laser bolts burst out of *Slave I*, tracing lines all about the starfighter, which cut a snap-roll to the right and down.

Jango stayed with him, trying to line up another shot, but the Jedi was good, snap-rolling one after another, each time coming out near an asteroid and sliding behind it for cover.

Boba continued to urge his father on, but Jango kept his patience, figuring that sooner or later, the Jedi was going to run out of hiding places.

A fast dive, then a sudden turn back up, then a sudden roll and bank to the right had the Jedi moving behind yet another asteroid, but this time, instead of following, Jango cut in short of the rock and fired blindly past it.

Out came the Jedi's starfighter, right into the line of fire, and the ship bucked, pieces flying, as a laser bolt clipped it.

"You got him!" Boba yelled in victory.

"And now we just have to finish him," the ever-cool Jango explained. "There'll be no more dodging." He pushed a series of buttons, arming a torpedo and sliding open the tube, then moved to punch the red trigger. He paused, though, and smiled, and nodded for Boba to move closer.

Boba could hardly breathe as his father slid his hand onto the smooth trigger grip, then looked down at him and nodded.

The boy punched the trigger and *Slave I* jolted as the torpedo slid away, diving at the Jedi starfighter and taking up the chase as the starfighter bolted and tried to evade.

A few brief moments later, *Slave I*'s viewscreen lit up in the light of a tremendous explosion, forcing Boba and Jango to shield their eyes with their arms. When they recovered and looked back, they were greeted by pieces of wreckage and torn chunks of metal. The scan screen was clear.

"Got him!" Boba shouted. "Yeahhhh!"

"Nice shot, kid," Jango said, and he tousled Boba's hair again. "You earned that one. We won't see him again."

A few deft turns had *Slave I* out of the asteroids and speeding down toward Geonosis, and despite his earlier reasoning, Jango Fett allowed Boba to guide the craft down. Truly, this was no flight for a boy to pilot, but Boba Fett was so far above any ordinary boy.

Anakin traveled through great canyons of multicolored stone, across dunes of blowing and shifting sand, and along an ancient, long-dry riverbed. His only guide was the sensation of Shmi, of her pain. But it was not a definitive homing beacon, and though he suspected he was moving in the general direction, the landscape of Tatooine was vast and empty, and none knew how to hide among the sand and stones better than the Tusken Raiders.

On a high bluff, Anakin paused and scanned the horizon. Off to the south, he noted a huge vehicle, resembling a gigantic tilting box, plodding along on a single huge track. Nodding with recognition of the Jawas, and well aware that no one knew the movements of all creatures among the desert better than they, he kicked his speeder bike away.

He caught up to them soon after, riding into a group of the brown- and black-robed creatures, their inquisitive red eyes poking out at him from the shadows of huge cowls, their ceaseless chatter humming like strange music all about him.

It took him a long time to convince the Jawas that he wasn't interested in purchasing any droids, and a longer time to get them to understand that he was merely looking for information about any Tusken Raiders.

The Jawas talked excitedly among themselves, pointing this way and that, hopping all about. Jawas were no friends of Tuskens, who preyed on them as they preyed on anyone else they found vulnerable. Even worse to the Jawa salesman mentality, Tuskens never purchased any droids!

The group eventually came to agreement, and pointed as one to the east. With a nod, Anakin sped away. The lack of monetary compensation seemed to aggravate the Jawas, but Anakin had no time to care.

The asteroids rolled along their silent way, undisturbed, seemingly unshaken from the explosions and zigzagging vessels.

In a deep depression on the back side of one such rock huddled a small starfighter, its definitive outline and consistent colors showing stark contrast to the rough-edged and bleeding, broken mineral streaks of the asteroid.

"Blast. This is why I hate flying," Obi-Wan said to R4, and the droid's responding beeps showed that he was in complete agreement. Few things could rattle the Jedi Knight, but engaging in a space battle with a pilot as obviously skilled as Jango Fett was surely one of them. Unlike many of his Jedi associates, Obi-Wan Kenobi had never much enjoyed space travel, let alone piloting.

He winced as his asteroid came over and around, showing him again a glowing piece of torn metal that had taken up orbit within the belt. His ship was wounded from the laser blast— nothing substantial, just a thruster-angler—and he had understood that he could not hope to outmaneuver the clever torpedo. So he had ordered R4 to eject all the spare parts canisters, and fortunately, that had been enough to detonate the missile. Despite the success, between the shock of that blast and landing hard and fast on the asteroid to complete the ruse, Obi-Wan was relieved to see that his ship had remained intact.

He wanted no further space fights with Jango and his strange, and supremely efficient, ship, though, and so he had sat here as the minutes slipped past.

"Have you got their last trajectory logged?" he asked the droid, then nodded as R4 assured him that he did. "Well, I think we've waited long enough. Let's go." Obi-Wan paused for a moment, trying to digest all the amazing things he had seen on the trail of Jango Fett. "This mystery gets more wound up all the time, Arfour. Think maybe we'll finally get some answers?"

R4 gave a sound that Obi-Wan could only think of as a verbal shrug.

Following the path taken by *Slave I*, Obi-Wan was not surprised that it led straight for the red planet, Geonosis. What did surprise him, though, was that they were not alone up there. A series of beeps and whistles from R4 alerted him, and Obi-Wan adjusted his scan screen accordingly, locking on to a huge fleet of vessels, settled on the other side of the asteroid belt.

"Trade Federation ships," he mused aloud as he angled to get a better view. "So many?" He shook his head in confusion, noting several of the great battleships among the group; their unique design made them hard to miss—a sphere surrounded by a nearly enclosed ring. If the clone army was for the Republic, commissioned by a Jedi Master, and Jango Fett was the basis for the clones, then what ties would Jango have to the Trade Federation? And if Jango was indeed behind the assassination attempts on Senator Amidala, the leading voice of opposition to creating a Republic army, then why would the Trade Federation approve?

It occurred to Obi-Wan that he might have misjudged Jango, or misjudged his motivations, at least. Maybe Jango, like Obi-Wan and Anakin, had been chasing the bounty hunter who had tried to kill Amidala. Maybe the toxic dart had been fired not to silence the would-be assassin, but as punishment for the attempt on Amidala's life.

The Jedi couldn't convince himself of that, though. He still believed that Jango was the man behind the assassination attempt, and that he had killed the changeling so that she could not give him up. But why the clone army? And why the Trade Federation ties? There was no apparent logic to it.

He knew that he would get no answers up here, so he took his ship down toward Geonosis, keeping the asteroid belt between him and the Trade Federation fleet.

He went down low as soon as he broke Geonosis' atmosphere, ducking below any tracking systems that might be in place, skimming the red plains and broken stones, weaving around the buttes and mesas. The whole of the planet seemed a barren and arid red plain, but his scanners did pick up some activity in the distance. Obi-Wan skimmed that way, climbing one mesa and running low to its far end. He slid his ship under a rocky overhang and put her down, then climbed out and walked to the mesa edge.

The night air had a curious metallic taste to it, and the temperature was comfortable. A strong breeze blew in Obi-Wan's face, carrying that metallic taste and odor, and the occasional strange cry.

"I'll be back, Arfour."

The droid gave a long *"ooooo."*

"You'll be fine," Obi-Wan assured him. "And I won't be long." Glad to be back on the ground once again, Obi-Wan checked his bearings, measured against the area where he had noted the activity, and started off, moving along a rocky trail.

The hours were unbearable for Padmé. Owen and Beru were friendly enough, and Cliegg was obviously glad for the added company in his time of great concern and profound grief, but she could hardly speak to them, so worried was she for Anakin. She had never seen him in a mood like the one that had taken him from the moisture farm, his determination so palpable, so consuming, that it seemed almost destructive. She had felt Anakin's power in that parting, an inner strength beyond anything she had ever known.

If his mother was indeed alive, and she believed that Shmi was, since Anakin had said so, Padmé knew that no army would be strong enough to keep the young Jedi from her.

She didn't sleep that night, rising often from her bed and pacing all about the compound. She wandered into the garage area, alone with her thoughts—or so she believed.

"Hello, Miss Padmé," came a chipper voice, and as soon as Padmé got over the initial shock, she recognized the speaker.

"You can't sleep?" C-3PO asked.

"No, I have too many things on my mind, I guess."

"Are you worried about your work in the Senate?"

"No, I'm just concerned about Anakin. I said things . . . I'm afraid I might have hurt him. I don't know. Maybe I only hurt myself. For the first time in my life, I'm confused."

"I'm not sure it will make you feel any better, Miss Padmé, but I don't think there's been a time in my life when I haven't been confused."

"I want him to know that I care about him, Threepio," Padmé said quietly. "I do care about him. And now he's out there, and in danger—"

"Don't worry about Master Annie," the droid assured her,

moving over to pat her shoulder. "He can take care of himself. Even in this awful place."

"Awful?" Padmé asked. "You're not happy here?"

C-3PO stepped back and held his hands out wide, showing his battered coverings and the chipped insulation in those areas where some of his wiring showed. Padmé moved forward, bending to see, and noticed sand clinging in many of the droid's joints.

"Well, this is a very harsh environment, I'm afraid," the droid explained. "And when Master Annie made me, he never quite found the time to give me any outer coverings. Mistress Shmi did well in finishing me, but even with the coverings, the wind and the sand are quite harsh. It gets in under my coverings, and it's quite . . . itchy."

"Itchy?" Padmé echoed with a laugh—a much-needed laugh.

"I do not know how else to describe it, Miss Padmé. And I fear that the sand is doing damage to my wiring."

Padmé looked all around, her gaze settling on a chain hoist over an open tub of dark liquid. "You need an oil bath," she said.

"Oh, I would welcome a bath!"

Glad for the distraction, Padmé moved to the oil tub and began sorting out the hoist chain. In a short while she had C-3PO secured and everything in place, and she gently lowered the droid into the oil.

"Oooh!" the droid cried. "That tickles!"

"Tickles? You're sure it's not an itch?"

"I do know the difference between a tickle and an itch," C-3PO answered. Padmé giggled and forgot, for a while, all of her troubles.

As soon as he came upon the grisly scene, Anakin knew that it was the work of Tuskens. Three farmers, likely some of those whom Cliegg had been with before being forced to return home, lay dead about a campfire, their bodies battered and torn. A pair of eopies, long-legged dromedaries with big padded feet and equine faces that showed little intelligence, stood tethered nearby, lowing mournfully, and beyond them hung the smoking remains of a speeder.

Anakin ran his fingers through his short hair. "Calm down," he told himself. "Find her." He fell within himself then, within the Force, and sent his senses out far and wide, needing the confirmation that his mother had not yet met a similar fate.

A stab of pain assaulted him, and a cry that was both hopeful and helpless entered his mind.

"Mom," he mouthed breathlessly, and he knew that time was running out, that Shmi was in terrible pain and was barely holding on.

He didn't have the time to bury the poor farmers, but he did resolve to come back for them. He jumped astride the speeder bike and put it flat out, rushing across the dark desert landscape, following Shmi's call.

The trail was narrow and steep, but at least Obi-Wan was back on solid footing.

Or almost solid, he realized, as a shrill shriek split the air, startling him. His foot slipped. He nearly tumbled but caught his balance, as a bunch of stones fell loose, bouncing down the side of the mesa.

The Jedi drew out his lightsaber but did not ignite it. He moved along cautiously, down and around a bend in the rocky path.

He saw the large, lizardlike creature coming for him, its huge fangs dripping lines of drool. It stood on strong hind legs, its little forelegs twitching eagerly. The lightsaber hummed to life and Obi-Wan dived down to the side, slashing back as he fell, opening the creature's side from foreleg to hind. The creature landed and tried to turn, but as it spasmed in pain, it overbalanced and fell off the trail, plummeting hundreds of feet and shrieking all the way.

Obi-Wan had no time to watch the descent, though, for another of the beasts appeared, coming at him fast, its toothy maw open wide.

The Jedi filled that maw with lightsaber, shearing through teeth and gums, driving the blade right through the back of the creature's head. He pulled hard to the side, the energy blade tearing right through the beast's skull, and turned to face yet another leaping beast. Falling back and down, he let the lizard fly past, then he came up immediately and started to pursue. But abruptly he stopped, reversed his grip, and stabbed out behind him, impaling a fourth creature. He spun about, flipping the weapon from his right hand to his left, then slashed it out the side of the dying beast as he completed his circuit, coming right around to face the one that had leapt past.

The creature circled slowly, seemingly sizing him up, and Obi-Wan turned with it, but kept his eyes and ears scanning the area.

He tried to scare the creature off, and with two of its companions lying dead on the rocks and a third having gone over the cliff, he fully expected it to flee.

But not this fierce beast. It charged suddenly, jaws snapping.

A sidestep, forward step, and overhand slash had the creature's head rolling free on the ground.

"Fun place," the Jedi remarked after a while, when he was confident that no more of the creatures were about. He put his weapon away and moved along, and soon after rounded the corner of the mesa.

A great plain spread out wide before him with many tall shapes in the far distance, indistinguishable in the darkness. Obi-Wan took out his electrobinoculars and peered across the plain. He saw a cluster of great towers—not natural stalagmites like those he had seen dotting the landscape, but shaped structures. A roll of his finger increased the magnification, of both size and available light, and he scanned slowly to the side.

Trade Federation starships, scores of them, lined the region, settled on platforms. The Jedi watched in amazement as another platform rose beside one ship and thousands of Battle Droids stepped off it and into the vessel, which then lifted away.

And was quickly replaced by another starship, settling down on the platform.

Another platform rose to the side, and again, thousands of droids stepped off to board the waiting starship, and that one, now filled with droid soldiers, lifted away.

"Unbelievable," the Jedi muttered and he looked to the eastern horizon, trying to gauge the amount of time he had before dawn, wondering if he could make the run before the light found him.

Not if he had to slowly work his way down the mesa, he realized, and so he shrugged and stepped ahead, closing his eyes and finding his power in the Force. Then he leapt out, lifting himself with the Force to ease his descent. He hit a bluff many feet down, but sprang away and fell again, and again, half bouncing, half flying his way down to the dark plain.

The sun was still below the eastern rim, though the land was beginning to lighten around him, when he reached the grandest tower of the complex. The entryway was heavily guarded by battle droids, but Obi-Wan had no intention of going anywhere near that area. Using the Force and his own conditioning, the Jedi scaled the tower, until he came to a small window.

He slipped in silently and moved from shadow to shadow, then ducked behind a wind curtain as he heard the approach of a pair of strange-looking creatures—Geonosians, he supposed. They wore little clothing, and their skin was reddish, like the air about them, with flaps hanging in rolls in many places about their slender frames. Leathery wings showed behind their bony shoulders. Their heads were large and elongated, their skulls ridged top and side, and they had thick-lidded, bulbous eyes. Their expressions seemed to be locked in a perpetual scowl.

"Too many sentients," he heard one of them say.

"It is not your place to question Archduke Poggle the Lesser," the other scolded, and grumbling, the pair wandered away.

Obi-Wan moved out behind them, going the opposite way.

He slipped from shadow to shadow along a narrow corridor lined with pillars. He couldn't help but see the contrast between this place and Tipoca City. Where Tipoca City was a work of art, all rounded and smooth, all glass and light, this place was rough-edged, all sharp corners and utilitarian features.

The Jedi moved along, coming to an open vent, sharp noises and pounding echoing up from it. He dropped to the ground and looked all about, then crawled and peered over the edge.

A factory, a huge alignment of conveyor belts and pounding machines, lay below, in a wide-open area. Obi-Wan watched in blank amazement as many, many Geonosians—these without wings like the pair that had walked past him—worked at various stations assembling droids. At the far end of the conveyor, completed droids stepped off under their own power, walking away down a distant corridor.

To platforms that would lift them to waiting Trade Federation starships, the Jedi realized.

With a shake of his head, Obi-Wan ran along, and then he sensed something, fleeting but definite. He followed his instincts along the maze of corridors, at last coming to a vast underground chamber, with huge vaulted ceilings and rough-styled arches. He started across, moving pillar to pillar, sensing that something or someone was near.

He heard their voices before he saw them, and he fell flat against the stone.

A group of six figures walked past him, four in front and two behind. Two Geonosians were in that front row, along with a Neimoidian viceroy whom Obi-Wan knew all too well and a man whose features were also recognizable from busts the Jedi had seen in the Temple on Coruscant.

"Now we must persuade the Commerce Guild and the Corporate Alliance to sign the treaty," that former Jedi, Count Dooku, was saying. The man was tall and regal, with perfect posture and a graceful gait. His hair was silver and perfectly trimmed and his elegant features, strong jaw, and piercing eyes completed the look of a man who had once been among the greatest of the Jedi. He wore a black cape, clipped at his neck by a silver chain, and a black shirt and pants of the finest materials. In looking at him, in feeling his presence, Obi-Wan understood that nothing less would ever suit this one.

"What about the Senator from Naboo?" asked the Neimoidian, Nute Gunray, his beady eyes and thin features seeming smaller still beneath the tripronged headdress he always wore. "Is she dead yet? I'm not signing your treaty until I have her head on my desk."

Obi-Wan nodded, huge pieces of the puzzle starting to fall into place. It made sense to him that Nute Gunray would want Amidala dead, even if her voice of opposition to an army of the Republic was working in his favor. Amidala had embarrassed the Neimoidian badly in the Battle of Naboo, after all.

"I am a man of my word, Viceroy," one of the separatists answered.

"With these new battle droids we've built for you, Viceroy, you'll have the finest army in the galaxy," said the Geonosian whom Obi-Wan believed to be Poggle the Lesser. He didn't look much like the winged commoners and workers Obi-Wan had seen. His skin was lighter, more a grayish tan than red-tinted, and his head was huge, his large scowling mouth protruding just a bit, giving him a fierce appearance; an elongated chin that seemed more a long beard hung halfway down his torso.

They continued their banter, but had moved out of earshot by then, and Obi-Wan didn't dare step out to follow. They moved across the way, through an archway and up a flight of stairs.

After a short pause to make sure they were well along, Obi-Wan rushed out, peeking through to the stairs, then crept up them, coming to a narrow archway overlooking a smaller room. Inside, he saw the six who had passed, along with several others, notably three opposition Senators the Jedi recognized. First came Po Nudo of Ando, an Aqualish who looked as if he was wearing a helmet with great goggles, but was not, of course.

Beside him sat neckless Toonebuck Toora of Sy Myrth, with her rodentlike head and wide mouth, and the Quarren Senator Tessek, his face tentacles waggling anxiously. Obi-Wan had met this trio before, back on Coruscant.

Yes, he realized, it seemed he had walked into the center of the hive.

"You have met Shu Mai?" Count Dooku, seated at the head of the table, asked the three Senators. "Representing the Commerce Guild." Across the way, Shu Mai nodded deferentially. Her delicate and gray, wrinkled head was set on a long neck and her most striking feature, aside from long and pointy horizontal ears, was a hairstyle that looked much like a skin-covered horn, protruding out the back of her skull, rising up and curving forward.

"And this is San Hill, distinguished member of the Inter-Galactic Banking Clan," Dooku went on, indicating a creature with the longest and narrowest face Obi-Wan had ever seen.

Those gathered about the table murmured their greetings, nodded to each other, for many moments, and then they went silent, all eyes settling on Count Dooku, who seemed to Obi-Wan in complete control here, even above the Archduke of the planet.

"As I explained to you earlier, I'm quite convinced that ten thousand more systems will rally to our cause with your support," the Count said. "And let me remind you of our absolute commitment to capitalism . . . to the lower taxes, the reduced tariffs, and the eventual abolition of all trade barriers. Signing this treaty will bring you profits beyond your wildest imagination. What we are proposing is complete free trade." He looked to Nute Gunray, who nodded.

"Our friends in the Trade Federation have pledged their support," Count Dooku went on. "When their battle droids are combined with yours, we shall have an army greater than anything in the galaxy. The Republic will be overwhelmed."

"If I may, Count," said one of the others, one of the two who had trailed Dooku to the room.

"Yes, Passel Argente," Count Dooku said. "We are always interested in hearing from the Corporate Alliance."

The huddled and nervous man offered a slight bow to Dooku. "I am authorized by the Corporate Alliance to sign the treaty."

"We are most grateful for your cooperation, Magistrate," Dooku said.

Obi-Wan recognized that exchange for what it was, a play for the benefit of the other, less enthusiastic, people at the table. Count Dooku was trying to build some momentum.

That momentum hit a bit of a bump a moment later, though, when Shu Mai piped in. "The Commerce Guild at this time does not wish to become openly involved." However, she smoothed it over immediately. "But we shall support you in secret, and look forward to doing business with you."

Several chuckles erupted about the table, and Count Dooku only smiled. "That is all we ask," he assured Shu Mai. Then he looked to the distinguished member of the Banking Clan, and all the other gazes settled on San Hill, as well.

"The InterGalactic Banking Clan will support you wholeheartedly, Count Dooku," San Hill declared. "But only in a nonexclusive arrangement."

Obi-Wan settled back, trying to sort out the implications of it all. Count Dooku had it all falling together here, a threat beyond anything the Republic had expected. With the money of the bankers and the commercial and trade guilds behind him, and this factory—and likely many others like it—churning out armies of battle droids, the potential danger was staggering.

Was that why Sifo-Dyas had commissioned the clone army? Had the Master sensed this growing danger, perhaps? But if that was true, then what was the tie between Jango Fett and this group on Geonosis? Was it mere coincidence that the man chosen as source for the clone army to defend the Republic had been hired by the Trade Federation to kill Senator Amidala?

It seemed too much a coincidence to Obi-Wan, but he had little else to go on. He wanted to hang around and listen in some more, but he knew then that he had to get out of there, had to return to his ship and R4, and get a warning out across the galaxy to the Jedi Council.

Over the last hours, Obi-Wan had seen nothing but armies, clone and droid, and he knew that it would all be coming together very quickly in an explosion beyond anything the galaxy had seen in many, many centuries.

She wasn't seeing much with her eyes. Caked with blood and swollen from the beatings, they would hardly open. She wasn't hearing much with her ears, for the sounds around her were harsh and threatening, relentlessly so. And she wasn't feeling with her body, for there was nothing there but pain.

No, Shmi had fallen inside herself, reliving those moments long ago, when she and Anakin had lived their lives as Watto's slaves. It was not an easy life, but she had her Annie with her, and given that, Shmi could remember those times fondly. Only now, with the prospects for ever seeing her son again so distant, did she truly appreciate how much she had missed the boy over the last ten years. All those times staring up at the night sky, she had thought of him, had imagined him soaring across the galaxy, rescuing the downtrodden, saving planets from ravaging monsters and evil tyrants. But she had always expected to see her Annie again, had always expected him to walk onto the moisture farm one day, that impish smile of his, the one that could light up a room, greeting her as if they had never been apart.

Shmi had loved Cliegg and Owen. Truly she had. Cliegg was her rescuer, her dashing knight, and Owen had been like the son she had lost, always compassionate, always happy to listen to her endless stories of Anakin's exploits. And Shmi was growing to love Beru, too. Who could not? Beru was that special combination of compassion and quiet inner strength.

But despite the good fortune that had brought those three into her life, improving her lot a millionfold, Shmi Skywalker had always kept a special place in her heart reserved for her Annie, her son, her hero. And so now, as it seemed the end of her life was imminent, Shmi's thoughts focused on those memories she had of Anakin, while at the same time, she reached out to him with her heart. He was always different with such feelings, always so attuned to that mysterious Force. The Jedi who had come to Tatooine had seen it in him clearly.

Perhaps, then, Annie would feel her love for him now. She needed that, needed to complete the cycle, to let her son recognize that through it all, through the missing years and the great distances between them, she had loved him unconditionally and had thought of him constantly.

Annie was her comfort, her place to hide from the pain the Tuskens had, and were, exacting upon her battered body. Every day they came in and tortured her a bit more, prodding her with sharp spears or beating her with the blunt shafts and short whips. It was more than a desire to inflict pain, Shmi realized, though she didn't speak their croaking language. This was the Tusken way of measuring their enemies, and from the nods and the tone of their voices, she realized that her resilience had impressed them.

They didn't know that her resilience was wrought of a mother's love. Without the memories of Annie and the hope that he would feel her love for him, she would surely have given up long ago and allowed herself to die.

Under the pale light of a full moon, Anakin Skywalker pulled the speeder bike to the ridge of a high dune and peered across the desert wastes of Tatooine. Not too far below him, he saw an encampment spread about a small oasis, and he knew at once, even before spotting a figure, that it was a Tusken camp. He could sense his mother down there, could feel her pain.

He crept closer, studying the straw and skin huts for any anomalies that might clue him in to their respective purposes. One especially sturdy hut at the edge of the oasis caught and held his attention: It seemed less tended than the others, yet more solidly constructed. As he came around a bit more, he grew even more intrigued, noting that only one hut was guarded, by a pair of Tuskens flanking the entrance.

"Oh, Mom," Anakin whispered.

Silent as a shadow, the Padawan slipped through the encampment, moving hut to hut, flat against walls and belly-crawling across open spaces, working his way gradually toward the hut he felt held his mother. He came against its side at last, and put his hands against the soft skin wall, feeling the emotions and pain of the person within. A quick glance around the front showed him the two Tusken guards, sitting a short distance in front of the door.

Anakin drew and ignited his lightsaber, then crouched low, shielding the glow as much as he could. He slid the energy blade through the wall and easily cut the material away, then, without even pausing to see if any Tuskens were inside, he crawled through.

"Mom," he breathed again, and his legs weakened beneath him. The room was lit by dozens of candles, and by a shaft of pale moonlight, streaming through a hole in the roof, illuminating the figure of Shmi, tied facing against a rack to the side of the tent. Her arms were outstretched, bound at bloodied wrists, and her face, when she turned to the side, showed the weeks of beatings.

Anakin quickly cut her free and gently lowered her from the perch, into his arms and then down to the floor.

"Mom . . . Mom . . . Mom," he whispered softly. Anakin knew that she was alive, though she did not immediately respond and had come down so pitifully limp. He could feel her in the Force, though she was a thin, thin sensation.

He cradled her head and kept repeating her name softly, and finally, Shmi's eyelids fluttered open as much as she could manage through the swelling and the dried blood.

"Annie?" she whispered back. He could feel her wheezing as she tried to speak, and knew that many of her ribs had been crushed. "Annie? Is it you?"

Gradually her eyes began to focus upon him, and he could see a thin smile of recognition coming to her battered face.

"I'm here, Mom," he told her. "You're safe now. Hang on. I'm going to get you out of here."

"Annie? Annie?" Shmi replied, and she tilted her head, the way she often had when Anakin was a boy, seeming quite amused by him. "You look so handsome."

"Save your strength, Mom," he said, trying to calm her. "We've got to get away from here."

"My son," Shmi went on, and she seemed to be in a different place than Anakin, a safer place. "My grown-up son. I knew you'd come back to me. I knew it all along."

Anakin tried again to tell her to lie still and save her strength, but the words simply wouldn't come out of his mouth.

"I'm so proud of you, Annie. So proud. I missed you so much."

"I missed you, too, Mom, but we can talk later . . ."

"Now I am complete," Shmi announced then, and she looked straight up, past Anakin, past the hole in the ceiling, to the shining moon, it seemed.

Somewhere deep inside, Anakin understood. "Just stay with me, Mom," he pleaded, and he had to work very hard to keep the desperation out of his voice. "I'm going to make you well again. Everything's . . . going to be fine."

"I love . . ." Shmi started to say, but then she went very still, and Anakin saw the light leave her eyes.

Anakin could hardly draw his breath. Wide-eyed with disbelief, he lifted Shmi to his breast and rocked her there for a long time. She couldn't be gone! She just couldn't! He pulled her back again, staring into her eyes, silently pleading with her to answer him. But there was no light there, no flicker of life. He hugged her close, rocking her.

Then he laid her back to the floor and gently closed her eyes.

Anakin didn't know what to do. He sat motionless, staring at his dead mother, then looked up, his blue eyes blazing with hatred and rage. He replayed all of the recent events of his life in his head, wondering what he might have done differently, done better, to keep Shmi alive. He should never have left her here in the first place, he realized, should never have let Qui-Gon take him away from Tatooine without bringing his mother along, as well. She said she was proud of him, but how could he deserve her pride if he could not even save her?

He wanted Shmi to be proud of him, wanted to tell his mom all about the things that had come into his life, his Jedi training, all the good work he had already done, and most of all, about Padmé. Oh how he had wanted his mom to get to know Padmé! She would have loved her. How could she not? And Padmé would have loved her.

Now what was he going to do?

The minutes slipped past and Anakin just sat there, immobilized by his confusion, by a budding rage and the most profound sense of emptiness he had ever known. Only when the pale light began to grow around him, making the low-burning candles seem even thinner, did he even remember where he was.

He looked about, wondering how he might get his mother's body out of there—for he certainly wasn't going to leave it to the Tusken Raiders. He could hardly move, though. There seemed a profound pointlessness to it all, a series of motions without meaning.

At that time, the only meaning, the only purpose, that Anakin could fathom was that of the rage building within him, an anger at losing someone he did not wish to give up.

Some small part of him warned him not to give in to that anger, warned him that such emotions were of the dark side.

Then he looked at Shmi lying there, so still, seeming at peace but covered with the clear evidence of all the pain that had been inflicted upon her poor body these last days.

The Jedi Padawan climbed to his feet and took up his lightsaber, then boldly strode through the door.

The two Tusken guards gave a yelp and lifted their staves, rushing for him, but the blue-glowing blade ignited, and in a flash of killing light, Anakin took them down, left and right.

The rage was not sated.

Deep in his meditations, peering through the dark side, Master Yoda felt a sudden surge of anger, of outrage beyond control. The diminutive Master's eyes popped open wide at the overwhelming strength of that rage.

And then he heard a voice, a familiar voice, crying, "No, Anakin! No! Don't! No!"

It was Qui-Gon. Yoda knew that it was Qui-Gon. But Qui-Gon was dead, had become one with the Force! One could not retain consciousness and sense of self in that state; one could not speak from beyond the grave.

But Yoda had heard the ghostly call, and in his deep meditative state, his thoughts focused as precisely as they had ever been, the Jedi Master knew that he had not been mistaken.

He wanted to focus on that, then, perhaps to try to follow that call back to the ghostly source, but he could not, overwhelmed again by the surge of rage and pain and . . . power.

He made a noise and lurched forward, then came out of his trance as his door opened and Mace Windu rushed in.

"What is it?" Mace asked.

"Pain. Suffering. Death! I fear something terrible has happened. Young Skywalker is in pain. Terrible pain."

He didn't tell Mace the rest of it, that somehow Anakin's rush of agony manifesting in the Force had tapped into the spirit of the dead Jedi Master who had discovered him. Too much was happening here.

That disembodied familiar voice hung profoundly in Yoda's thoughts. For if it was true, if he had heard what he was sure he had heard . . .

Anakin, too, had heard the voice of Qui-Gon, imploring him to restrain himself, to deny the rage. He hadn't recognized it, though, for he was too full of pain and anger. He spotted a Tusken woman to the side, in front of another of the tents, carrying a pail of dirty water, and saw a Tusken child in the shadows of another nearby hut, staring at him with an incredulous expression.

Then he was moving, though he was hardly aware of his actions. His blade flashed and he ran on. The Tusken woman screamed, and was impaled.

Now all the camp seemed in motion, Tuskens rushing out of every hut, many with weapons in hand. But Anakin was into the dance of death then, into the energy of the Force. He leapt far and long, clearing one hut and coming down before another, his blade flashing even before he landed, even before the two Tuskens recognized that he had jumped between them.

A third came at him, thrusting forth a spear, but Anakin lifted an empty hand and set up a wall of Force energy as solid as stone. Then he shoved out with that hand, and the Tusken spearman flew away, fully thirty meters, smashing through the wall of yet another hut.

Anakin was off and running, off and leaping, his blade spinning left and right in a blur, every stab taking a Tusken down, writhing to the ground, every slash putting a piece of a Tusken on the ground.

Soon none were standing against him, all trying to flee, but Anakin would have none of that. He saw one group rush into a hut and reached out across the way, to a large boulder in the distance. It flew to his call, soaring across the sand, smashing one fleeing Tusken down and flying on.

Anakin dropped it on the hut full of Tuskens, crushing them all.

And then he was running, his strides enhanced by the Force, overcoming the fleeing creatures, slaughtering them, every one.

He didn't feel empty any longer. He felt a surge of energy and strength beyond anything he had ever known, felt full of the Force, full of power, full of life.

And then it was over, suddenly, it seemed, and Anakin stood

among the ruins of the encampment, dozens and dozens of dead Tusken Raiders all about him, and only a single hut still standing.

He put his lightsaber away and walked back to that hut, where he gently and reverently scooped his mother's body into his arms.

There!" Padmé announced, as she hoisted C-3PO back out of the oil bath. She had to fight hard to keep from giggling, for she had inadvertently lowered the droid too far, and now he was waving his arms about crazily, yelling that he was blind.

Padmé yanked him over to the side and found a cloth to wipe the excess oil off of his face. That done, she set the droid down on the floor and unhitched him.

"Better?" she asked.

"Oh, much better, Miss Padmé." C-3PO waved his arms about and seemed quite pleased.

"No itches?" Padmé asked, inspecting her work.

"No itches," C-3PO confirmed.

"Well, good," she said with a smile. But her smile faltered as she realized that she was done. She had used her work with the droid to shield her from her fears over the last hours—she had hardly even realized that the sun had risen—and now those fears for Anakin were already coming back to her.

She was running out of places to hide.

"Oh, Miss Padmé, thank you! Thank you!" said C-3PO. He came forward, his arms outstretched to hug her, but then he moved back suddenly, seeming to remember himself and his sudden lack of protocol.

"Thank you," he said again, with a little more dignity. "Thank you very much."

Owen Lars entered the garage area. "Well, there you are," he said to Padmé. "We've been looking all over for you."

"I was out here all the time, giving Threepio a much-needed bath."

"Well, Padmé," Owen said, and when she turned to regard him, Padmé saw that he was grinning widely. "I'm returning this droid to Anakin. I know that's what my mom would want."

Padmé smiled and nodded.

"He's back! He's back!" came Beru's call from outside the garage. Smiles gone, Padmé and Owen turned and rushed out.

They caught up with Beru outside, and Cliegg soon joined them, his hoverchair banging and clunking against furniture and doorways as he glided out of the house.

"Where?" Padmé asked.

Beru pointed across the desert.

Squinting and shielding her eyes from the glare of the suns, Padmé finally marked the black dot that was Anakin, rushing toward them. As the speck grew into a distinguishable form, she realized that he was not alone, that there was someone tied over the back of the speeder.

"Oh, Shmi," Cliegg Lars said breathlessly. He was trembling visibly.

Beru sniffled and struggled to keep from sobbing. Owen stood beside her, his hand draped across her shoulders, and when Padmé looked over at them, she noticed a tear sliding down Owen's cheek.

Anakin crossed into the compound a few moments later, pulling up short of the stunned group. Without a word, he dismounted and moved to unstrap his dead mother, lifting her and cradling her in his arms. He walked up to Cliegg and paused there for a bit, two men sharing a moment of grief.

Then, still without speaking, Anakin walked past the man and into the house.

All that time, the thing that struck Padmé the most was the look upon Anakin's face, an expression unlike anything she had ever seen on the Padawan: part rage, part grief, part guilt, and part resignation, even defeat. She knew that Anakin would need her, and soon.

But she had no idea of what she might do for him.

There wasn't much talking in the Lars homestead the rest of that day. Everyone just went about their chores, any chores, obviously trying to avoid the outpouring of grief that they all knew would inevitably come.

At work preparing a meal for Anakin, Padmé was surprised when Beru came up to help her, and even more surprised when the woman started some small talk with her.

"What's it like there?" Beru asked.

Padmé looked at her curiously. "I'm sorry?"

"On Naboo. What's it like?"

Padmé could hardly even register the question, for her thoughts remained with Anakin. It took her a long time to respond, but finally she managed to say, "Oh, it's very . . . very green. You know, with lots of water, and trees and plants everywhere. It's not like here at all." She turned away as soon as she finished, and knew she was being a bit rude. But all she wanted was to be with Anakin, and so she started loading the food tray.

"I think I like it here better," Beru remarked.

"Maybe you'll come and see it someday," Padmé said, more to be polite than anything else.

But Beru answered seriously. "I don't think so. I don't like to travel."

Padmé picked up the tray and turned to go. "Thanks, Beru," she said with as much of a smile as she could muster.

She found Anakin standing at a workbench in the garage, working on a part from the speeder bike.

"I brought you something to eat."

Anakin glanced at her, but immediately went back to his work. She noted that he was exaggerating every movement, obviously frustrated, obviously distracted from the task at hand. "The shifter broke," he explained, too intently. "Life seems so much simpler when you're fixing things. I'm good at fixing things. I always was. But I . . ."

Finally he slammed down the wrench he was using and just stood there, head bowed.

Padmé recognized that he was on the verge of collapse.

"Why did she have to die?" he mouthed quietly. Padmé slid the tray down on the workbench and moved behind him, putting her arms about his waist and resting her head comfortingly on his back.

"Why couldn't I save her?" Anakin asked. "I know I could have!"

"Annie, you tried." She squeezed him a bit tighter. "Sometimes there are things no one can fix. You're not all-powerful."

He stiffened at her words and pulled away from her suddenly—and angrily, she realized. "But I should be!" he growled, and then he looked at her, his face a mask of grim determination. "And someday I will be!"

"Anakin, don't say such things," Padmé replied fearfully, but he didn't even seem to hear her.

"I'll be the most powerful Jedi ever!" he railed on. "I promise you! I will even learn to stop people from dying!"

"Anakin—"

"It's all Obi-Wan's fault!" He stormed across the room and slammed his fist onto the workbench again, nearly dislodging the plate of food. "He put me out of the way."

"To guard me," she said quietly.

"I should have been out with him, hunting the assassins! I'd have had them a long time ago, and would've gotten here in time and my mother would still be alive!"

"You can't know—"

"He's jealous of me," Anakin rambled on, paying no attention to her at all. He wasn't talking to her, she realized, but was just playing it all out verbally for himself. She could hardly believe what she was hearing. "He put me out of the way because he knows that I'm already more powerful than he is. He's holding me back!"

He finished by picking up his wrench and throwing it across the garage, where it smashed against a far wall and clattered down among some spare parts.

"Anakin, what's wrong?" she cried at him.

Her volume and tone finally got his attention. "I just told you!"

"No!" Padmé yelled back at him. "No. What's *really* wrong?"

Anakin just stared at her, and she knew that she was on to something.

"I know it hurts, Anakin. But this is more than that. What's really wrong?"

He just stared at her.

"Annie?"

His body seemed to shrink then, and slump forward just a bit. "I . . . I killed them," he admitted, and if Padmé hadn't run to him and grabbed him close, he would have fallen over. "I killed them all," he admitted. "They're dead. Every single one of them."

He looked at her then, and it seemed to her as if he had suddenly returned to her from somewhere far, far away.

"You did battle . . ." she started to reason.

He ignored her. "Not just the men," he went on. "And the men are the only fighters among the Tuskens. No, not just them. The women and the children, too." His face contorted, as if he was teetering between anger and guilt. "They're like animals!" he said suddenly. "And I slaughtered them like animals! I hate them!"

Padmé sat back a bit, too stunned to respond. She knew that Anakin needed her to say something or do something, but she was paralyzed. He wasn't even looking at her—he was just staring off into the distance. But then he lowered his head and began to sob, his lean, strong shoulders shaking.

Padmé pulled him in and hugged him close, never wanting to let go. She still didn't know what to say.

"Why do I hate them?" Anakin asked her.

"Do you hate them, or do you hate what they did to your mother?"

"I hate them!" he insisted.

"And they earned your anger, Anakin."

He looked up at her, his eyes wet with tears. "But it was more than that," he started to say, and then he shook his head and buried his face against the softness of her breast.

A moment later, he looked back up, his expression showing that he was determined to explain. "I didn't . . . I couldn't . . ." He held one hand up outstretched, then clenched it into a fist. "I couldn't control myself," he admitted. "I . . . I don't want to hate them—I know that there is no place for hatred. But I just can't forgive them!"

"To be angry is to be human," Padmé assured him.

"To control your anger is to be a Jedi," Anakin was quick to reply, and he pulled away from her and stood up, turning to face the open door and the desert beyond.

Padmé was right there beside him, draping her arms about him. "Shhh," she said softly. She kissed him gently on the cheek. "You're human."

"No, I'm a Jedi. I know I'm better than this." He looked at her directly, shaking his head. "I'm sorry. I'm so sorry."

"You're like everybody else," Padmé said. She tried to draw closer, but Anakin held himself back from her.

He couldn't hold the pose of defiance for long, though, before he broke down again in sobs.

Padmé was there to hold him and rock him and tell him that everything would be all right.

Obi-Wan Kenobi slumped back in the seat of his starfighter, shaking his head in frustration. It had taken him a long while to extract himself safely from the factory city, and when he had at last found his starfighter, he had thought the adventure over. But not so.

"The transmitter is working," he told R4, who tootled his agreement. "But we're not receiving a return signal. Coruscant's too far." He spun to face the droid. "Can you boost the power?"

The beeps that came back at him were not comforting.

"Okay, then we'll have to try something else." Obi-Wan looked around for an answer. He didn't want to lift off from the planet and risk detection, but so far out and within the heavy and metallic Geonosian atmosphere, he had no chance of reaching distant Coruscant.

"Naboo is closer," he said suddenly, and R4 beeped. "Maybe we can contact Anakin and get the information relayed."

R4 replied with enthusiasm and Obi-Wan climbed back out of the cockpit to repeat the message with the changes for Anakin.

A few moments later, though, the droid signaled him that something was wrong.

With a frustrated growl, the Jedi climbed back up into the cockpit.

"How can he not be on Naboo?" he asked, and R4 gave an "*oooo.*" Rather than argue with a droid, Obi-Wan checked the instruments himself. Sure enough, Anakin's signal was not to be found coming from Naboo.

"Anakin? Anakin? Do you copy? This is Obi-Wan Kenobi?" he said, lifting his ship comm directly and shooting the call out toward the general area of Naboo.

After several minutes with no response, the Jedi put the comm back down and turned to R4. "He's not on Naboo, Arfour. I'm going to try to widen the search. I hope nothing's happened to him."

He sat back as the minutes slipped past. He knew that he was losing precious time, but his choices were limited. He couldn't head back to the city and risk capture, not with so much vital news to relay to the Jedi Council, nor did he want to blast away, for the same reasons. He still had so much to learn here.

So he waited, and finally, some time later, R4 tootled emphatically. Obi-Wan moved to the controls, his eyes widening as he got the confirmation. "That's Anakin's tracking signal all right, but it's coming from Tatooine! What in the blazes is he doing there? I told him to stay on Naboo!"

R4 gave another *"oooo."*

"All right, we're all set—we'll get these answers later." He climbed back out of the cockpit and jumped to the ground. "Transmit, Arfour. We haven't much time."

The droid locked on to him immediately.

"Anakin?" Obi-Wan asked. "Anakin, do you copy? This is Obi-Wan Kenobi."

R4 relayed the response, a series of beeps and whistles that the R4-P didn't normally use, but ones quite familiar to Obi-Wan.

"Artoo? Good, are you reading me clearly?"

The whistle came back affirmative.

"Record this message and take it to the Jedi Skywalker," Obi-Wan instructed the distant droid.

Another affirmative beep.

"Anakin, my long-range transmitter is knocked out. Retransmit this message to Coruscant."

The Jedi began to tell his tale then. He didn't know that the Geonosians had picked up his signal broadcasts and had triangulated those receptions to locate his starfighter. Wound up in his tale, he didn't notice the approach of the armed droidekas, rolling up near to him, then unrolling to their attack posture.

Even the two blazing Tatooine suns could not brighten the somber mood, the tangible grayness permeating the air, around the new grave outside the Lars compound. Two old headstones marked the ground next to the new one, a poignant reminder of the difficulties of life on the harsh world of Tatooine. The five of them—Cliegg, Anakin, Padmé, Owen, and Beru—had gathered, along with C-3PO, to bid farewell to Shmi.

"I know wherever you are, it's become a better place," Cliegg Lars said, and he took a handful of sand and tossed it on the new grave. "You were the most loving partner a man could ever have. Good-bye, my darling wife. And thank you."

He glanced briefly at Anakin, then lowered his head and fought back tears.

Anakin stepped forward and knelt before the marker. He picked up a handful of sand and let it slip through his fingers.

"I wasn't strong enough to save you, Mom," the young man said, suddenly feeling more like a boy. His shoulders bobbed once or twice, but he fought to regain control, and took a deep and determined breath. "I wasn't strong enough. But I promise I won't fail again." His breathing came in short rasps as another wave of grief nearly toppled him. But the young Padawan squared his shoulders and determinedly stood up. "I miss you so much."

Padmé came forward and put her hand on Anakin's shoulder, and all of them stood silent before the grave.

The moment held only briefly, though, broken by a series of urgent beeps and whistles. They turned as one to see R2-D2 rolling their way.

"Artoo, what are you doing here?" Padmé asked.

The droid whistled frantically.

"It seems that he is carrying a message from someone named Obi-Wan Kenobi," C-3PO quickly translated. "Does that mean anything to you, Master Anakin?"

Anakin squared his shoulders. "What is it?"

R2-D2 beeped and whistled.

"Retransmit?" Anakin asked. "Why, what's wrong?"

"He says it's quite important," C-3PO observed.

With a look to Cliegg and the other two, silently seeking their permission, Anakin, Padmé, and C-3PO followed the excited droid back to the Naboo ship. As soon as they got inside, R2 beeped and spun, and projected an image of Obi-Wan in front of them.

"Anakin, my long-range transmitter has been knocked out," the Jedi's hologram explained. "Retransmit this message to Coruscant." R2 stopped the message there, with Obi-Wan seeming to freeze in place.

Anakin looked at Padmé. "Patch it through to the Jedi Council chamber."

Padmé stepped over and flipped a button, then waited for confirmation that the signal was getting through. She nodded to Anakin, who turned back to R2.

"Go ahead, Artoo."

The droid gave a beep, and Obi-Wan's hologram began to move once more. "I have tracked the bounty hunter Jango Fett to the droid foundries of Geonosis. The Trade Federation is to take delivery of a droid army here and it is clear that Viceroy Gunray is behind the assassination attempts on Senator Amidala."

Anakin and Padmé exchanged knowing glances, neither of them very surprised by that information. Padmé thought back to her meeting with Typho and Panaka on Naboo, before she had left for Coruscant, secretly escorting the doomed starship.

"The Commerce Guild and Corporate Alliance have both pledged their armies to Count Dooku and are forming an—"

The hologram swung about. "Wait! Wait!"

Anakin and Padmé cringed as droidekas appeared in the hologram along with Obi-Wan, grabbing at him and restraining him. The hologram flickered, then broke apart.

Anakin jumped up and rushed at R2-D2, but pulled up short, realizing that there was nothing he could do.

Nothing at all.

On distant Coruscant, Yoda and Mace Windu and the other members of the Jedi Council watched the hologram transmission with trepidation and great sadness.

"He is alive," Yoda announced, after yet another viewing. "I feel him in the Force."

"But they have taken him," Mace put in. "And the wheels have begun to spin more dangerously."

"More happening on Geonosis, I feel, than has been revealed."

"I agree," Mace said. "We must not sit idly by." He looked at Yoda, as did everyone else in the room, and the little Jedi Master closed his eyes, seemingly very weary and very pained by it all.

"The dark side, I feel," he said. "And all is cloudy."

Mace nodded and turned a grim expression on the others. "Assemble," he ordered, a command that had not been given to the Jedi Council in many, many years.

"We will deal with Count Dooku," Mace said through the comlink to Anakin. "The most important thing for you, Anakin, is to stay where you are. Protect the Senator at all costs. That is your first priority."

"Understood, Master," Anakin replied.

His tone, so full of resignation and defeat, struck Padmé profoundly. It galled the fiery Senator to think that Anakin would be stuck here looking over her, when his Master was in obvious danger.

As the hologram switched off, she moved to the ship's console and began flicking switches and checking coordinates, confirming what she already knew. "They have to come halfway across the galaxy," she said, turning to Anakin, who seemed not to care. "They'll never get there in time to save him."

Still no response.

"Look, Geonosis is less than a parsec away!" Padmé announced, flipping a few more controls to show the flight line on the viewscreen. "Anakin?"

"You heard him."

"They can't get from Coruscant in time to save him!" Padmé reiterated, her voice rising. She started flicking the switches on the panel, preparing the engines for firing, but Anakin gently put his hand over hers, stopping her.

"If he's still alive," the young Jedi answered somberly.

Padmé stared at him hard, and he turned away and walked off.

"Anakin, are you just going to sit here and let him die?" she cried, chasing across the bridge to grab him roughly by the arm. "He's your friend! Your mentor!"

"He's like my father!" Anakin shot back at her. "But you heard Master Windu. He gave me strict orders to stay here."

Padmé understood what was happening. Anakin was doubting himself. He felt himself a failure because of his inability to save his mother, and, perhaps for the first time in his life, he was truly doubting his inner voice, his instincts. She had to find a way around that now, for Anakin's sake as much as for Obi-Wan's. If they stayed here and did nothing, Padmé believed that she would lose two friends: Obi-Wan to the Geonosians, and Anakin to his guilt.

"He gave you strict orders to stay here only so that you could protect me," Padmé corrected with a grin, hoping to remind him clearly that his previous orders, which he had ignored, had demanded that he stay on Naboo. She pulled back away from him, returning to the console, and flicked a few more switches. The engines roared to life.

"Padmé!"

"He gave you strict orders to protect me," she said again. "And I'm going to save Obi-Wan. So if you plan to protect me, you'll have to come along."

Anakin stared at her for a few moments, and she held his gaze, her head tilted, hair loose and cascading across half her face, but hardly dimming the brightness of her determination.

Anakin knew that they were acting outside the orders of Mace Windu, whatever Padmé's justification. He knew that this was not what was expected of him as a Jedi Padawan.

When had that ever stopped him?

Matching Padmé's determination, he went to the controls, and a few moments later, the Naboo starship roared up into the Tatooine sky.

The calm beauty of the Republic Executive Building on Coruscant, with its streaming fountains and reflecting pools, ridged columns and flowing statues, masked the turmoil within. The word had passed, from Obi-Wan to Yoda and the Jedi Council, and now from them to the Chancellor and leaders of the Senate, that the Republic was crumbling. The mood inside Chancellor Palpatine's office was both somber and frantic, everyone overwhelmed by a sense of despair and a need to act, frustrated by the apparent lack of options.

Yoda, Mace Windu, and Ki-Adi-Mundi represented the Jedi, lending an air of calm against the nervous energy of Senators Bail Organa and Ask Aak, and Representative Jar Jar Binks. Behind his great desk, Palpatine listened to it all with apparent despair, his aide, Mas Amedda, standing beside him, seeming on the verge of tears.

Silence hung in the room for several long moments after Mace Windu had finished his recounting of the message from Geonosis.

Yoda, leaning on his small cane, glanced at Bail Organa, always a reliable and competent man, and gave a slight nod. Catching the cue, the Senator from Alderaan began the discussion.

"The Commerce Guild is preparing for war," he said. "Given the report of Jedi Obi-Wan Kenobi, there can be no doubt of that."

"If the report is accurate," the fiery Ask Aak promptly responded.

"It is, Senator," Mace Windu assured him, and Ask Aak, a Senator of action, accepted that. Indeed, Yoda understood that Ask Aak had only made the remark because he had wanted the Jedi to openly support the report, to impress upon all the others that the situation was on the verge of catastrophe.

"Count Dooku must have made a treaty with them," Chancellor Palpatine reasoned.

"We must stop them before they're ready," Bail Organa said.

Jar Jar Binks moved front and center, trembling a bit but keeping his tongue in his mouth, at least. "Excueeze me, yousa honorable Supreme Chancellor, sir," the Gungan began. "Maybe dissen Jedi stoppen the rebel army."

"Thank you, Jar Jar," Palpatine politely replied, and turned to Yoda. "Master Yoda, how many Jedi are available to go to Geonosis?"

"Throughout the galaxy, thousands of Jedi there are," the diminutive Jedi Master replied. "To send on a special mission, only two hundred are available."

"With all due respect to the Jedi Order, that doesn't sound like enough," Bail Organa said.

"Through negotiation the Jedi maintain peace," Yoda replied. "To start a war, we do not intend."

His continued calm only seemed to push the frantic Ask Aak over the edge. "The debate is over!" he cried. "Now we need that clone army."

Yoda closed his eyes slowly, pained by the weight of reason behind the dreaded words.

"Unfortunately, the debate is not over," Bail Organa said. "The Senate will never approve the use of the army before the separatists attack. And by then, it will likely be too late."

"This is a crisis," Mas Amedda dared interject. "The Senate must vote the Chancellor emergency powers! He could then approve the use of the clones."

Palpatine rocked back at the suggestion, seeming profoundly shaken. "But what Senator would have the courage to propose such a radical amendment?" he asked hesitantly.

"I will!" Ask Aak declared.

Beside him, Bail Organa gave a helpless chuckle and shook his head. "They will not listen to you, I fear. Nor to me," he added quickly, when Ask Aak snapped a glare at him. "We have spent too much of our political capital debating the philosophies of the separatists and arguing for action. The Senate will not see our call as anything more than overly alarmist. We need a voice of reason, one willing to reverse position, even, given the gravity of the current situation."

"If only Senator Amidala was here," Mas Amedda reasoned.

Without hesitation, Jar Jar Binks stepped forward again. "Mesa mosto Supreme Chancellor," the Gungan said, squaring his sloping shoulders as much as possible. "Mesa gusto pallos," he said deferentially to all the others. "Mesa proud to proposing the motion to give Yousa Honor emergency powers."

Palpatine looked from the trembling Gungan to Bail Organa.

"He speaks for Amidala," the Senator from Alderaan said. "By all understanding within the Senate, Jar Jar Binks's words are a reflection of Senator Amidala's desires."

Palpatine nodded grimly, and Yoda sensed a strong fear from the man, as if he knew that he was about to be thrust forward in the most dangerous position he and the Republic had ever known.

Twisting slowly in the force field, restrained by crackling bolts of blue energy, Obi-Wan Kenobi could only watch helplessly as Count Dooku strode into the room. Wearing an expression that showed great sympathy, but one that Obi-Wan certainly did not trust, the regal man walked up right before the Jedi.

"Traitor," Obi-Wan said.

"Hello, my friend," Dooku replied. "This is a mistake. A terrible mistake. They've gone too far. This is madness!"

"I thought you were their leader here, Dooku," Obi-Wan replied, holding his voice as steady as possible.

"This had nothing to do with me, I assure you," the former Jedi insisted. He seemed almost hurt by the accusation. "I promise you that I will petition immediately to have you set free."

"Well, I hope it doesn't take too long. I have work to do." Obi-Wan noted a slight crack in Dooku's remorseful expression, a slight twinge of . . . anger?

"May I ask why a Jedi Knight is all the way out here on Geonosis?"

After a moment's reflection, Obi-Wan decided that he had little to lose here, and he wanted to continue to press Dooku, that he might gauge the truth. "I've been tracking a bounty hunter named Jango Fett. Do you know him?"

"There are no bounty hunters here that I'm aware of. Geonosians don't trust them."

Trust. There was a good word, Obi-Wan thought. "Well, who can blame them?" came his disarming reply. "But he is here, I assure you."

Count Dooku paused for a moment, then nodded, apparently conceding the point. "It's a great pity that our paths have never crossed before, Obi-Wan," he said, his voice warm and inviting. "Qui-Gon always spoke very highly of you. I wish he was still alive—I could use his help right now."

"Qui-Gon Jinn would never join you."

"Don't be so sure, my young Jedi," Count Dooku immediately replied, an offsetting smile on his face, one of confidence and calm. "You forget that Qui-Gon was once my apprentice just as you were once his."

"You believe that brings loyalty above his loyalty to the Jedi Council and the Republic?"

"He knew all about the corruption in the Senate," Dooku went on without missing a beat. "They all do, of course. Yoda and Mace Windu. But Qui-Gon would never have gone along with the status quo, with that corruption, if he had known the truth as I have." The pause was dramatic, demanding a prompt from Obi-Wan.

"The truth?"

"The truth," said a confident Dooku. "What if I told you that the Republic was now under the control of the Dark Lords of the Sith?"

That hit Obi-Wan as profoundly as any of the electric bolts holding him ever could. "No! That's not possible." His mind whirled, needing a denial. He alone among the living Jedi had battled a Sith Lord, and that contest had cost his beloved Master Qui-Gon his life. "The Jedi would be aware of it."

"The dark side of the Force has clouded their vision, my friend," Dooku calmly explained. "Hundreds of Senators are now under the influence of a Sith Lord called Darth Sidious."

"I don't believe you," Obi-Wan said flatly. He only wished he held that truth as solidly as he had just proclaimed.

"The viceroy of the Trade Federation was once in league with this Darth Sidious," Dooku explained, and given the events of a decade before, it seemed a reasonable claim. "But he was betrayed ten years ago by the Dark Lord. He came to me for help. He told me everything. The Jedi Council would not believe him. I tried many times to warn them, but they wouldn't listen to me. Once they sense the Dark Lord's presence and realize their error, it will be too late. You must join with me, Obi-Wan, and together we will destroy the Sith."

It all seemed so reasonable, so logical, so attuned to the legend of Count Dooku as Obi-Wan had learned it. But beneath the silken words and tone was a feeling Obi-Wan had that flew in the face of that logic.

"I will never join you, Dooku!"

The cultured and regal man gave a great and disappointed sigh, then turned to leave. "It may be difficult to secure your release," he tossed back at Obi-Wan as he exited the room.

* * *

Approaching Geonosis, Anakin employed the same techniques as Obi-Wan had, using the asteroid ring near Geonosis to hide the Naboo starship from the lurking Trade Federation fleet. And like his mentor, the Padawan recognized the unusual and threatening posture of the unexpected fleet.

Breaking atmosphere, Anakin brought the ship down low, skimming the surface, weaving through valleys and around towering rock formations, circling mesas. Padmé stood next to him, watching the skyline for some signs.

"See those columns of steam straight ahead?" she asked, pointing. "They're exhaust vents of some type."

"That'll do," agreed Anakin, and he banked the starship, zooming in at the distant lines of rising white steam. He brought the ship right into one steam cloud and slid her down, gently, through the vent.

When they had settled on firm ground, he and Padmé prepared to leave the ship.

"Look, whatever happens out there, follow my lead," Padmé told him. "I'm not interested in getting into a war here. As a member of the Senate, maybe I can find a diplomatic solution to this mess."

For Anakin, who had so recently used the diplomacy of the lightsaber, and to devastating effect, the words rang true—painfully so.

"Trust me on this?" Padmé added, and he knew that she had recognized the pain on his face.

"Don't worry," he said, and he made himself grin. "I've given up trying to argue with you."

Behind them as they headed for the landing ramp, R2 gave a plaintive wail.

"Stay with the ship," Padmé instructed both droids. Then she and Anakin went out into the underground complex, and recognized almost immediately that they had entered a huge droid factory.

* * *

Soon after the pair had departed, R2-D2's legs extended, lifting him off the securing platform, and he began rolling immediately for the ship exit.

"My sad little friend, if they had needed our help, they would have asked for it," C-3PO explained to him. "You have a lot to learn about humans."

R2 tootled back at him and continued to roll.

"For a mechanic, you seem to do an excessive amount of thinking," C3-PO countered. "I'm programmed to understand humans."

R2's responding question came as a burst of short and curt beeps.

"What does that mean?" C-3PO echoed. "That means, I'm in charge here!"

R2 didn't even respond. He just started rolling for the landing ramp, moving right out of the ship.

"Wait!" C-3PO cried. "Where are you going? Don't you have any sense at all?"

The replying beep was quite discordant.

"How rude!"

R2 just gained speed and rolled away.

"Please wait!" C-3PO cried. "Do you know where you're going?"

While the reply was far from confident, the last thing C-3PO wanted at that moment was to be left alone. He rushed to catch up to R2, and followed behind, fussing nervously.

Anakin and Padmé slipped along the vast, pillared corridors of the factory city, their footfalls dulled by the humming and banging noises of the many machines in use in the great halls below them. The place seemed deserted—too much so, Anakin believed.

"Where is everyone?" Padmé whispered, unconsciously echoing his thoughts.

Anakin held his hand up to silence her, and he tilted his head, sensing . . . something.

"Wait," he said.

Anakin moved his hand higher and continued to listen, not with his ears, but with his sensitivity to the Force. There was something here, something close. His instincts turned his eyes up toward the ceiling, and he watched in amazement and horror as the crossbeams above seemed to pulse, as if they were alive.

"Anakin!" Padmé cried, watching, too, as several winged forms seemed to grow right out of the pillars, detaching and dropping down. They were tall and lean, sinewy strong and not skinny, with orange-tinted skin.

Anakin's lightsaber flashed. Turning fast, on pure instinct and reflex, he slashed out, severing part of a wing from one creature swooping in at him. The creature tumbled past, bouncing along the ground, but another took its place, and then another, heading in boldly for the Padawan.

Anakin stabbed out to the right, retracted the blade immediately from the smoking flesh, then brought it spinning about above his head, slashing out to the left. Two more creatures went tumbling. "Run!" he shouted to Padmé, but she was already moving, along the corridor and toward a distant doorway. Waving his lightsaber to keep more of the stubborn creatures at bay, Anakin ran. He darted through the doorway behind her—and nearly fell over the end of a small walkway that extended out over a deep crevasse.

"Back," Padmé started to say, but even as she and Anakin began to turn, the door slammed closed behind them, leaving them trapped on the precarious perch. More of the winged creatures appeared above them, and even worse, the walkway began to retract.

Padmé didn't hesitate. She leapt out for the shortest fall, onto a conveyor belt below.

"Padmé!" Anakin cried frantically. He leapt down, too, landing behind her on the moving conveyor. And then the winged Geonosians were all about him, swarming and swooping, and he had to work his lightsaber desperately to keep them at bay.

* * *

"Oh my goodness," C-3PO said, turning all about as he scanned the immense factory. He and R2-D2 came onto a high ledge, overlooking the main area. "Machines creating machines. How perverse!"

R2 gave him an emphatic beep.

"Calm down," C-3PO said. "What are you talking about? I'm not in your way!"

R2 didn't bother to argue. He rolled forward, bumping 3PO off the ledge. The screaming droid bounced onto one unfortunate flying conveyor droid, then crashed down on a conveyor to the side. R2 went off the ledge next, willingly, his little jets igniting to carry him fast across the way to some distant consoles.

"Oh, blast you, Artoo!" C-3PO cried, trying hard to sort himself out. "You might have warned me, or told me of your plan." As he spoke, he finally managed to stand—just in time to rise before a horizontal slicer.

C-3PO gave a single scream for help before the spinning blade lopped his head from his shoulders, his body crumpling down onto the belt, his head bouncing away to land on yet another conveyor, this one bearing lines of other heads, those of battle droids.

One welder stop later, and C-3PO found his head grafted onto a battle droid body. "How ugly!" he exclaimed. "Why would one build such unattractive droids?" He managed to glance to the side, to see his still-standing body rolling into the line with the other droids, where a Battle Droid head got welded onto it.

"I'm so confused," the poor C-3PO wailed.

Above it all, R2-D2 wasn't watching his mechanical friend. He had spied his Mistress Padmé and went in fast pursuit.

Padmé flailed and rolled about the belt, scrambling to her feet, then diving back down low. She backpedaled, then rushed ahead suddenly to scramble under thumping pile drivers, machines slamming metal molds down hard enough to shape the parts of a heavy gauge droid. She dived under one stamper, then scrambled back to her feet right before another, backpedaling furiously, waiting for the precise moment as the heavy head went back up along the guide poles.

And then a winged Geonosian swooped upon her, grabbing at her and throwing her off balance. She used just enough of her attention to free herself momentarily, then hoped she had estimated right and burst forward suddenly, diving and crawling fast, and came out the other side just as the pile driver thundered down.

Right onto the head of the pursuing Geonosian, stamping it flat.

Padmé, facing yet another stamper, didn't even see it. She managed to roll through safely, but just as she emerged, a winged creature reared up right in front of her, wrapping her in its leathery wings and grabbing at her with strong arms.

Padmé wrestled valiantly, but the creature was too strong. It flew off to the side of the conveyor and then unceremoniously dropped her. Padmé landed hard inside a large empty vat. She recovered quickly and tried to scramble out, but the vat was deep and without handholds and she couldn't extract herself.

Anakin, battling furiously with a swarm of winged Geonosians, and all the while scrambling to avoid the deadly stamping machines, still managed somehow to see it all. "Padmé!" he cried as he came through a stamper to see disaster looming. There was no way he could get to her, he realized immediately, and the vat into which she had fallen was fast moving toward a pour of molten metal. "Padmé!"

And then he was fighting again, slashing aside yet another of the winged creatures, watching all the while in horror as his love neared her doom.

He fought wildly, beating the creatures away, scrambling desperately for Padmé and calling out to her. He crashed through another assembly line, sending droid parts everywhere, then leapt another belt, crossing the factory room toward Padmé, who was still struggling helplessly, as she moved ever closer to the pouring molten metal. He thought he might get to her, might leap with the Force, but then he passed too close to another machine and a vise closed over his arm, mechanically moving it into position before a programmed cutting machine.

Anakin kicked out, both feet slamming a winged creature that had pursued him in, knocking the Geonosian away. He struggled mightily against the unyielding grip of the machine and managed to turn enough, just in time, to avoid the cutting blade—with his arm, at least. He could only watch in horror as the machine sliced his lightsaber in half.

And then he looked back, realizing that in a moment, the lightsaber would be the least of his losses.

"Padmé!" he cried.

Across the way, R2-D2 had landed near Padmé's vat. He worked frantically, slipping his controller arm onto the computer access plug, then scrolling through the files.

R2-D2 coolly continued his work, trying to put aside his understanding that Padmé was about to become encased in molten metal.

At last he succeeded in shutting down the correct conveyor. It stopped short, Padmé less than a meter from the metal pour. She barely had time to register relief—a group of winged creatures swooped down upon her and gathered her up in strong grabbing arms.

Anakin, kicking away another of the creatures, continued to struggle with the machine gripping his arm. He could only watch in dismay as a group of deadly droidekas rolled up and unfolded into position around him.

And then an armored rocket-man dropped before him, with blaster leveled his way. "Don't move, Jedi!" the man ordered.

Senator Amidala sat on one side of the large conference table, with Anakin standing protectively behind her. Across the way sat Count Dooku, Jango Fett positioned behind him. It was hardly a balanced meeting, though, for Jango Fett was armed where Anakin was not, and the room was lined by Geonosian guards.

"You are holding a Jedi Knight, Obi-Wan Kenobi," Padmé said calmly, using the tone that had gotten her through so many Senatorial negotiations. "I am formally requesting you turn him over to me now."

"He has been convicted of espionage, Senator, and will be executed. In just a few hours, I believe."

"He is an officer of the Republic," she said, her voice rising a bit. "You can't do that."

"We don't recognize the Republic here," Dooku said. "However, if Naboo were to join our alliance, I could easily hear your plea for clemency."

"And if I don't join your rebellion, I assume this Jedi with me will also die."

"I don't wish to make you join our cause against your will, Senator, but you are a rational, honest representative of your people, and I assume you want to do what's in their best interest. Aren't they fed up with the corruption, the bureaucrats, the hypocrisy of it all? Aren't you? Be honest, Senator."

His words stung her, because she knew there was some truth in them. Just enough to give him a modicum of credibility, enough for Dooku to entice so many systems to join in his alliance. And of course, the reality of the situation around her stung her even more deeply. She knew that she was right, that her ideals meant something, but how did that measure up against the fact that she would be executed for holding them? And even more than that, how did her precious ideals hold up against the fact that Anakin would die for them, as well? She knew in that moment just how much she loved the Padawan, but knew, too, that she could not deny all that she had believed for all of her life, not even for his life and hers. "The ideals are still alive, Count, even if the institution is failing."

"You believe in the same ideals we believe in!" Dooku replied at once, seizing the apparent opening. "The same ideals we are striving to make prominent."

"If what you say is true, you should stay in the Republic and help Chancellor Palpatine put things right."

"The Chancellor means well, M'Lady, but he is incompetent," Dooku said. "He has promised to cut the bureaucracy, but the bureaucrats are stronger than ever. The Republic cannot be fixed, M'Lady. It is time to start over. The democratic process in the Republic is a sham. A game played on the voters. The time will come when that cult of greed called the Republic will lose even the pretext of democracy and freedom."

Padmé firmed her jaw against the assault, consciously reminding herself that he was exaggerating, playing things all in a light to give himself credibility. All she had to do to see through the lies, to see the fangs beneath the tempting sway of the serpent, was remind herself that he had taken Obi-Wan prisoner and meant to execute him. Would the Republic have taken such a prisoner and set him up for execution? Would she?

"I cannot believe that," she said with renewed determination. "I know of your treaties with the Trade Federation, the Commerce Guild, and the others, Count. What is happening here is not government that has been bought out by business, it's business becoming government! I will not forsake all that I have honored and worked for, and betray the Republic."

"Then you will betray your Jedi friends? Without your cooperation, I can do nothing to stop their execution."

"And in that statement lies the truth of your proposed improvement," she said flatly, her words holding firm against the turmoil and agony that was wracking her. In the silence that followed, Dooku's staring expression went from that of a polite dignitary to an angry enemy, for just a flash, before reverting to his usual calm and regal demeanor.

"And what about me?" Padmé continued. "Am I to be executed also?"

"I wouldn't think of such an offense," Dooku said. "But there are individuals who have a strong interest in your demise, M'Lady. It has nothing to do with politics, I'm afraid. It's purely personal, and they have already paid great sums to have you assassinated. I'm sure they will push hard to have you included in the executions. I'm sorry, but if you are not going to cooperate, I must turn you over to the Geonosians for justice. Without your cooperation, I've done all I can for you."

"Justice," Padmé echoed incredulously, with a shake of her head and a knowing smirk. And then there was silence.

Dooku waited patiently for a few moments, then turned and nodded to Jango Fett.

"Take them away!" the bounty hunter ordered.

Much to his dismay, C-3PO found out exactly what the Geonosian had meant when he had said, "Put him in the line!"

He was in group of drilling battle droids, a dozen lines of twenty in a rectangular formation, going through the extensive programming testing before being herded onto great landing pads to be scooped up by Trade Federation warships.

So flustered was the out-of-place protocol droid, and so unfamiliar with his new body, that when the Geonosian ordered, "Left face," he turned to the right, and when the drill leader then commanded, "March," the battle droid now facing him stomped right into him, bearing him backward, following its orders to a T without the ability to improvise.

"Oh, do stop!" C-3PO pleaded. "You are scratching me! Oh, I do beg you to stop!"

No response followed, because the droids had been programmed to respond only to the drill leader.

"Oh, do stop!" C-3PO begged again, fearful that he was going to be knocked over and trampled by the battle droid, and the four others marching behind it. His sensors, tied in to his new torso, showed him an effective solution to his problem. Without even realizing what he was doing, C-3PO fired his right-arm laser, point blank, into the pushing battle droid's chest, blasting the thing apart.

"Oh my!" C-3PO cried.

"Halt!" the Geonosian drill leader screamed, and all the droids immediately froze in place. Except for poor C-3PO, who stood there positively flummoxed, his torso rotating side to side as he tried to figure out what to do next. He heard the drill leader call out to "take four-dot-seven back for more training," and when he considered his position in the ranks, he knew the Geonosian was talking about him.

"Wait, no, it is a mistake," he cried as a pair of burly maintenance droids rolled over and scooped him up in their vise-grip arms. "Oh, but this is all wrong. I am programmed in over three million languages, not for marching!"

Even before he reached the end of the corridor, Mace Windu sensed Yoda's great sadness. The Master was sitting on a balcony overlooking the Galactic Senate. Below, chaos reigned. Uproar and screaming, loud opinions and counteropinions—the turmoil struck a profound chord in Mace Windu, who understood Yoda's sadness, and shared it. This was the government that he and his proud Order were sworn to protect, though right now many of the Senators hardly seemed worthy of that protection.

Right there and then, all the faults of the Republic were laid bare to Mace Windu, and to Master Yoda, all of the bureaucratic nonsense that seemed to inevitably get in the way of true progress. This was the chaos that had spawned Count Dooku and the separatist movement. This was the nonsense that gave credence to otherwise outlandish claims, and allowed the greedy special interests, like the Trade Federation, to exploit the galaxy.

The tall Jedi Master moved to the end of the corridor and sat down beside Yoda. He said nothing, because there was nothing to say. Their place was to observe and to fight in defense of the Republic.

However ridiculous many of the representatives of that body now appeared below them.

Mace and Yoda watched the Senators screaming furiously at each other, fists and other appendages waving in the air. At the podium across the way, Mas Amedda stood anxiously, glancing about and calling for order.

Finally, after many long minutes, the screaming died away.

"Order! Order!" Mas Amedda repeated many times, obviously trying to ensure that things did not spiral out of control once again.

Chancellor Palpatine moved front and center, and cast his gaze all about the amphitheater, meeting many eyes and trying hard to convey the gravity of the moment.

"In the regrettable absence of Senator Amidala," he said at length, speaking slowly and distinctly, "the chair recognizes the Senior Representative of Naboo, Jar Jar Binks."

Mace looked at Yoda, who closed his eyes against the ensuing onslaught of cheers and boos, seemingly equal in strength. Everyone in the Senate knew what was coming, and the weight of it threatened to rip the body politic apart.

Mace looked back at the floor and finally spotted Jar Jar, floating out before the podium on his platform, flanked by Gungan aides.

"Senators!" Jar Jar called. "Dellow felegates—"

The laughter was almost as deafening as the arguing, but the humor was lost quickly, as jeers erupted once more.

"Stay strong, Jar Jar," Mace quietly mouthed, looking down at the Gungan, whose face and ears were now bright red from embarrassment.

"Order!" Mas Amedda shouted from the podium. "The Senate will accord the Representative the courtesy of a hearing!"

The floor quieted, and Mas Amedda signaled to Jar Jar, who was by this time gripping the front of his platform tightly.

"In response to the direct threat to the Republic," the Gungan began, speaking clearly and directly, "mesa propose that the Senate give immediate emergency powers to the Supreme Chancellor."

There came a brief silence as everyone turned to look at everyone else. Gradually, a clapping began, and when the jeers erupted from opposing factions, the cheering grew even louder, soon drowning out the opposition. Though she wasn't even present, it was Amidala who had done this, Mace understood. All the years she had worked to win the trust of others had led to this crucial victory. If anyone other than a Representative of Naboo, a voice speaking for Amidala, had suggested such a drastic measure, then the debate would never have been so cleanly decided. But since she had apparently thrown in with the other side on the debate for the creation of an army, so, too, did many of those who had originally followed her lead in opposing that army.

The noise went on for many minutes, and while the jeering died away, the cheering only gained momentum. Finally, Chancellor Palpatine held up his hands, asking for quiet.

"It is with great reluctance that I have agreed to this calling," Palpatine began. "I love democracy—I love the Republic. I am mild by nature and do not desire to see the destruction of democracy. The power you give me I will lay down when this crisis has abated. I promise you. And as my first act with this new authority, I will create a grand army of the Republic to counter the increasing threats of the separatists."

"It is done, then," Mace said to Yoda, and the diminutive Jedi Master nodded grimly. "I will take what Jedi we have left and go to Geonosis to help Obi-Wan."

"And visit, I will, the cloners of Kamino and see this army they have created for the Republic," Yoda said.

Together, the two Jedi walked away from the Senate Hall.

It looked like many of the courtrooms scattered about the galaxy, a round room sectioned by curving railings and tall boxed-off areas, with rows of seats behind the main area for interested onlookers. But the makeup of the principals told Padmé that the resemblance to a hall of justice ended right there. Poggle the Lesser, the Archduke of Geonosis, presided over the gathering, helped by his Geonosian aide, Sun Fac, but clearly there would be no possibility of open-mindedness. Padmé recognized the others as separatist Senators, dignitaries of the various commercial guilds and the InterGalactic Banking Clan.

She watched them carefully, noting the visceral hatred in their eyes. This was no hearing, no trial. It was a proclamation of hatred, and nothing more.

And so Padmé was hardly surprised when Sun Fac stepped forward and announced, "You have been charged and found guilty of espionage."

So much for evidence, Padmé thought.

"Do you have anything to say before your sentence is carried out?" Archduke Poggle the Lesser asked.

Unshaken, the cool Senator stared the Geonosian straight in the eye. "You are committing an act of war, Archduke. I hope you are prepared for the consequences."

The Geonosian chuckled. "We build weapons, Senator. That is our business! Of course we're prepared!"

"Get on with it!" came the voice of Nute Gunray from the side. "Carry out the sentence. I want to see her suffer."

Padmé only shook her head. All this because she had foiled the Neimoidian's plans to exploit her planet when she was Queen. All this because she hadn't rolled over before the power of Gunray and his followers. And to think that she had agreed to mercy for the Neimoidians after their defeat on Naboo!

"Your other Jedi friend is waiting for you, Senator," Archduke Poggle the Lesser announced, and he waved to the guards. "Take them to the arena!"

At the back of the hall, the young boy soaked it all in and looked up at his father, a perfect older-version replica of himself. "Are they going to feed them to the beasts?" Boba Fett asked.

Jango Fett looked down at his eager son and chuckled. "Yes, Boba." He had many times told Boba stories of the Geonosian arena.

"Oh, I hope they use an acklay," said Boba matter-of-factly. "I want to see if it's as powerful as I've read."

Jango just smiled and nodded, amused that his son was already so interested in such things, and glad for the dispassion in his tone. Boba was being strictly pragmatic here, even in the face of the executions of three people. He was taking in the entire scenario with the cool and collected pragmatism that would allow him to survive in the harsh galaxy.

He was a good learner.

The jumble of information they were downloading into C-3PO would surely have overwhelmed the droid, conditioning him as intended, had his circuits not already been filled to near capacity with linguistic information. C-3PO engaged in multiple translations of each instruction pattern, and in doing so, managed to water them down enough so that they lost any real effect.

His subtlety seemed lost on the brutes programming him, and after a few short hours, they led him out of the room and across the large assembly hall.

It was there that C-3PO heard a plaintive and familiar whine.

"Artoo!" he called, swiveling his head. There was his dome-shaped companion, working at a console. R2-D2 swiveled his head and gave another *"oooo."*

"Oh, Artoo!" C-3PO wailed, and before he could even consider the action, he brought a laser sight up before his eyes, focusing on the restraining bolt set into his friend.

A single blast flew out, skimming the bolt from R2-D2, then ricocheting about the room.

"Hey!" cried one of the instructor droids, moving fast to C-3PO's side.

"Looks like this one needs more programming," another said.

The chief maintenance droid looked about the room and shook his dome. "Nah," he said. "No damage done. Get this one out to the yard and out of here!"

They led C-3PO away.

Soon after they were gone, R2-D2 rolled away from his console without notice. Since all of the relatively benign droids working in here were restrained by bolts, there were no real guards in the room.

The little droid was out and free soon after.

The tunnel was dark and fittingly gloomy, and quiet, except for the occasional echo of cheering from the huge crowd gathered in the arena stands beyond. A single cart was in there, an open oval with a sloping front end that somewhat resembled an insect's head with the top half cut away. Anakin and Padmé were unceremoniously thrown into it, then strapped in place against the framework, facing each other.

Both of them jerked as the cart started into motion, gliding along the dark tunnel.

"Don't be afraid," Anakin whispered.

Padmé smiled at him, her expression one of genuine calm. "I'm not afraid to die," she replied, her voice thick and soft. "I've been dying a little bit each day since you came back into my life."

"What are you talking about?"

Then she said it, and it was real and genuine and warm. "I love you."

"You love me?" he asked, overwhelmed. "You love me! I thought we decided not to fall in love. That we would be forced to live a lie. That it would destroy our lives." But her words had brought a wash of contentment over him.

"I think our lives are about to be destroyed anyway," Padmé replied. "My love for you is a puzzle, Annie, for which I have no answers. I can't control it—and now I don't care. I truly, deeply love you, and before we die, I want you to know."

Padmé leaned against her restraints and craned her head forward, and Anakin did likewise, the two coming close enough for their lips to meet in a soft and gentle kiss, one that lingered and deepened, one that said everything they both realized they should have spoken to each other before. One that, to them, mocked their false heroics in denying the feelings they'd had for each other all along.

The sweet moment was just that, though, a moment, for a crack of the driver's whip had the cart jerking out of the tunnel and into the blinding daylight, rolling onto the floor of a great stadium filled with Geonosian spectators.

Four sturdy posts, a meter in diameter, were centered on the arena floor, each set with chains, and one holding a familiar figure.

"Obi-Wan!" Anakin cried as he was pulled down from the cart, dragged over, and chained to the post beside his Master.

"I was beginning to wonder if you had gotten my message," Obi-Wan replied. Both he and Anakin winced as Padmé was similarly, roughly dragged over to the post next to Anakin, and roughly chained up. They saw her curl a bit, defensively, in what seemed a futile resistance. What they didn't see, though, was the resourceful Padmé managing to slip out a wire she had hidden in her belt.

"I retransmitted your message just as you requested, Master," Anakin explained. "Then we decided to come and rescue you."

"Good job!" came Obi-Wan's quick and sarcastic reply. He ended with a grunt as his arms were pulled up above his head, locking him helplessly in place. Anakin and Padmé were receiving similar treatment. They could turn a bit side to side, though, and so all three were able to watch the arrival of the dignitaries, the masters of ceremony—faces they had come to know all too well.

"The felons before you have been convicted of espionage against the Sovereign System of Geonosis," announced the lackey, Sun Fac. "Their sentence of death is to be carried out in this arena immediately!"

The wild cheering deafened the doomed trio.

"They like their executions," Obi-Wan said dryly.

At the dignitary box, Sun Fac gave way to Archduke Poggle the Lesser, who patted his hands in the air, calling for quiet. "I have decided on an especially entertaining contest this day," he announced, to more appreciative roaring. "Which of our pets would be most suited to carry out the executions of such distinguished criminals? I asked myself this over and over, and for many hours, could find no answer.

"And finally, I chose—" He paused dramatically and the crowd hushed. "—the reek!" At the side of the arena, a gate was lifted and out stepped a huge quadruped with massive shoulders, an elongated face, and three deadly horns, one sticking up from its snout and the other two protruding forward from either side of its wide mouth. The reek stood as tall as a Wookiee, as wide as a human male was tall, and more than four meters long. It was prodded forward into the arena by a line of picadors carrying long spears and riding creatures that were bovine in size, with elongated snouts.

After the cheering died away, Poggle surprised the crowd by announcing, "The nexu!" A second gate rose, revealing a large feline creature. Its head was an extraordinary thing, half the size of its body and with a fang-filled mouth that could open wide enough to bite a large human in half. A ridge of fur stood straight in a line from head to rump, ending right before its whipping, felinoid tail.

Before the surprised crowd could erupt again, Poggle shouted, "And the acklay!" and a third gate rose and the most hideous creature of all rushed in. It moved spiderlike on four legs, each ending in huge elongated claws. Other arms waved menacingly, similarly topped with claws that snapped in the air. Its head, crested by a long and wavy horn, was more than two meters above the ground, glancing about hungrily, and while the other two creatures seemed to need the prodding of the picadors, this one surely did not.

This last one, the acklay, seemed to be the true crowd-pleaser, especially to the young boy, Jango Fett's cloned son, sitting with the dignitaries. Boba grinned and began reciting all that he had read of the deadly beast's exploits.

"Well, this should be fun—for them, at least," lamented Obi-Wan, watching the frenzy mounting around him.

"What?" Anakin asked.

"Never mind," Obi-Wan replied. "You ready for the fight?"

"The fight?" Anakin asked skeptically, looking up at his chained wrists, then back at the three monsters, which had been milling about, and only now seemed to take note that lunch had been served.

"You want to give the crowd its money's worth, don't you?" Obi-Wan asked. "You take the one on the right. I'll take the one on the left."

"What about Padmé?" The two turned to discover that their clever companion had already used the concealed wire to pick the lock on one of her shackles, and had turned her body about, facing the post. She climbed right up the chain to the top of that post, then went to work on the other shackle.

"She seems to be on top of things," Obi-Wan commented wryly.

Anakin looked back just in time to react to the charge of the reek. Acting purely on reflex, the young Jedi leapt straight up, and the beast plowed into the pole beneath him. Seeing an opportunity, Anakin dropped upon the beast's back and wrapped his chain about its strong horn. The reek bucked and tugged, tearing the chain free of the post, and they were off, the reek bucking and Anakin holding on for dear life. He slapped the free end of the chain at the side of the reek's head, and the vicious beast bit it and held on, its stubbornness providing Anakin a makeshift bridle.

After downloading the schematics, R2-D2 had little trouble navigating the huge factory complex. The small droid rolled along, whistling casually to deflect any suspicion on the part of the many Geonosians milling about.

None of them seemed interested in him, anyway, though, and R2 thought he knew why. He had learned of a huge event taking place, a triple execution. He could easily enough guess the identities of the unfortunate prisoners.

He wandered along a meandering course through the complex, avoiding as many Geonosians as possible, passing those he could not with an air of detachment, trying not to look out of place.

He knew that it would get more crowded as he neared the arena, though, and could only hope that the Geonosians there would be too distracted by the thrilling events to bother with a little astromech droid.

Obi-Wan quickly came to learn why the acklay was such a crowd-pleaser. The creature reared up high and came straight in at him. When Obi-Wan rushed behind the pole, the acklay took a more direct route, crashing into the pole, its gigantic claws snapping the wood and the chain. Freed by the beast's fury, Obi-Wan turned and ran, sprinting right at the nearest picador, the acklay in fast pursuit. The Geonosian lowered his spear at the Jedi, but Obi-Wan dodged inside and grabbed it. A sudden tug pulled it free, and Obi-Wan snapped it against the picador's mount, causing the creature to rear. Hardly slowing, Obi-Wan planted the butt of the lance in the ground and leapt, pole-vaulting the picador and his mount.

Again the acklay took the more direct route, slamming into rider and mount, sending the Geonosian tumbling to the sand. Grabbing the picador up in the snap of a claw, the monster crunched the life from him.

Atop her post, Padmé worked frantically to free the chain. But already the felinelike nexu was leaping up to swipe at her with its deadly claws. She dodged, but the nexu came on again.

Padmé whipped it with the chain.

The beast didn't stop, its claws tearing into the pole as it climbed. Then, with a sudden burst, it leapt up to the top and reared before Padmé issuing a victorious roar.

The crowd hushed, sensing the first kill.

As the nexu slashed, Padmé turned in a circle the other way, and while the claws tore her shirt and superficially raked her back, she came around hard, delivering a solid blow across the beast's face with the free-flying end of the chain. The nexu fell back off the pole. Padmé leapt out and back, away from the creature and to the side, and let the chain tug her back, sending her in a spin about the pole. She tucked her legs as she spun, then double-kicked out, knocking the nexu to the ground.

Hardly pausing to consider her handiwork, she scrambled back up the pole, working furiously to free herself completely.

The crowd gasped as one.

"Foul!" cried Nute Gunray in the dignitary box. "She can't do that! Shoot her or something!"

"Wow!" Boba Fett yelled in obvious admiration. Jango put his hand on his son's shoulder, enjoying the show every bit as much as Boba.

"The nexu will have her, Viceroy," Poggle the Lesser assured the trembling Neimoidian.

Gunray remained standing, as did everyone else in the box, as did everyone else in the stadium. The crowd gasped again as Obi-Wan ran around behind the picador's fallen mount, then launched the stolen spear into the neck of the furious acklay. The beast screeched in pain and slapped the struggling orray mount aside.

Across the way, Padmé continued to work the chain as the nexu regained its balance and began to stalk back toward the pole. Finally, she was free.

But the nexu was right below her, looking up, drool spilling from its oversized maw, death in its eyes. It crouched, ready to spring.

And got trampled into the ground by Anakin and his reek mount.

"You okay?" he called.

"Sure."

"Jump on!" Anakin cried, and Padmé was already moving,

leaping down from the pole to fall into place right behind Anakin.

They passed the wounded and furious acklay next, and Obi-Wan was quick to take Padmé's hand and vault into place behind her.

Boba Fett yelped in glee again, as did many of the Geonosians.

Nute Gunray, though, wasn't quite so pleased. "This isn't how it's supposed to be!" he yelled at Count Dooku. "She's supposed to be dead by now!"

"Patience," the calm Count replied.

"No!" Nute Gunray shouted back at him. "Jango, finish her off!"

Jango turned an amused expression Nute Gunray's way, and nodded knowingly as Count Dooku motioned for him to stay put.

"Patience, Viceroy," Dooku said to the fuming Gunray. "She will die."

Even as he spoke, even as Gunray seemed about to explode with rage, the Count motioned back to the arena, and the Neimoidian turned to see a group of droidekas roll out from the side paddock. They surrounded the reek and the three prisoners and opened and unfolded into their battle position, giving Anakin no choice but to pull back hard on the makeshift rein and halt the creature.

"You see?" Dooku calmly asked.

The Count's expression changed, though, just for a moment, as a familiar hum began right behind him. He glanced to his right quickly, to see a purple lightsaber blade right beside Jango Fett's neck, then turned slowly to regard the wielder.

"Master Windu," he said with his typical charm. "How pleasant of you to join us! You're just in time for the moment of truth. I would think these two boys of yours could use a little more training."

"Sorry to disappoint you, Dooku," Mace coolly replied. "This party's over." With that, the Jedi Master gave a quick salute with his glowing lightsaber, the prearranged signal, and then brought the blade back in close to Jango Fett.

All about the stadium came a sudden and synchronized flash of lights as a hundred Jedi Knights ignited their lightsabers.

The crowd went perfectly silent.

After a moment's reflection, Count Dooku turned about just a bit, looking back at Mace Windu out of the corner of his eye. "Brave, but foolish, my old Jedi friend. You're impossibly outnumbered."

"I don't think so," Mace countered. "The Geonosians aren't warriors. One Jedi has to be worth a hundred Geonosians."

Count Dooku glanced about the stadium, his smile widening. "It wasn't the Geonosians I was thinking about. How well do you think one Jedi will match up against a thousand battle droids?"

He had timed it perfectly. Just as he finished, a line of battle droids came down the corridor behind Mace Windu, their lasers firing. The Jedi reacted at once, spinning about and flashing his lightsaber to deflect the many bolts, turning them back on his attackers. He knew that these few droids were the least of his troubles, though, for as he glanced around he saw the source of Dooku's confidence: thousands of battle droids rolling along every ramp, in the stands and out into the arena below.

The fight began immediately, the whole stadium filling with screaming laser bolts, Jedi leaping and spinning, trying to close into tight defensive groups, their lightsabers deflecting the bolts wildly. Geonosians scrambled all about, some trying to attack the Jedi—and dying for their trouble—others just scrambling to get out of the way of the wild fire.

Mace Windu spun about, recognizing that his most dangerous enemies were behind him. He faced Jango Fett—and found himself looking down the barrel of a stout flamethrower.

A burst of flames reached out for the Jedi Master, igniting his flowing robes. With both Dooku and the bounty hunter so close, and in such a vulnerable position, Mace just leapt away, lifting himself with the Force to fly out from the box and land in the arena. He pulled the burning robe from his back, throwing it aside.

All around him, the fight intensified, with Jedi battling scores of Geonosians in the stands, and many other Jedi rushing down to the arena floor to join the battle against the largest concentrations of Battle Droids. Mace winced when he spotted Obi-Wan, Anakin, and Padmé sent flying into the air by the terrified and bucking reek. He motioned to other Jedi, but needn't have, for those closest were already rushing toward their vulnerable companions, throwing lightsabers to Anakin and Obi-Wan.

When those two ignited their blades, Anakin's green and Obi-Wan's blue, and Padmé came up between them, a discarded blaster pistol in hand, Mace breathed a bit easier.

But only for a moment. Then the Jedi Master was a blur of motion once more, working his blade furiously to turn back the storm of laser bolts screaming at him from the multitude of battle droids. He joined Obi-Wan near the center of the arena soon after, and back-to-back, they went into action, moving into a crowd of droids, taking down several with deflected bolts, then slashing through, turning in unison as they went. Obi-Wan went at one droid with his lightsaber up high, but when that droid lifted its defenses appropriately, the two Jedi turned about, Mace coming around with his lightsaber down low, shearing the droid in half.

Behind Mace Windu and Obi-Wan, Anakin and Padmé fought in a similar back-to-back posture, with Anakin working in a mostly defensive manner, deflecting all the bolts coming at him and at Padmé, while she picked her shots carefully, taking down droid after droid after Geonosian.

But despite all the gallant efforts, despite the mounds of slaughtered enemies, Geonosian and droid alike, the outcome was beginning to show clearly, as the Jedi were being pushed back by sheer numbers. The general retreat flowed toward the arena, though that area would provide little respite. In addition to the droids and Jedi, the two monsters rushed about crazily, destroying everything in their path.

* * *

Into this maelstrom marched C-3PO, his body at least, with the head of a battle droid fixed firmly upon it. Shortly, however, this motley droid caught a blaster bolt in the neck. Down it went, the battle droid head bouncing free of the torso.

Across the arena, in a tunnel and marching toward daylight, 3PO's head, attached to a battle droid body, felt the sensation, but distantly.

"My legs aren't moving!" he cried, though of course his present legs certainly were. "I must need oil."

It was a time for improvisation, too wild a scene for coordinated and predetermined movements.

Just the kind of fight in which Padmé excelled. Firing a blaster with every step, she rushed to the same execution cart that had brought her and Anakin into the arena and scrambled atop the confused orray pulling it.

Right behind her came Anakin, his lightsaber a blur of motion, turning laser shots back at the battle droids. He leapt into the cart and Padmé kicked the orray away.

They charged the circuit, bouncing across the fallen droids and Geonosians, Padmé firing shot after shot and Anakin sending an even greater line of destruction out by turning aside all shots coming their way.

"You call this diplomacy?" said Anakin, deflecting blasts.

Padmé grinned and shouted back, "No, I call it 'aggressive negotiations'!"

C-3PO entered the maelstrom, and if his eye sockets would have allowed him to widen his eyes in surprise and terror, he surely would have.

"Where are we?" he cried. "A battle! Oh no! I'm just a protocol droid. I'm not made for this. I can't do it! I don't want to be destroyed!"

This mixed-up droid lasted about as long as his other half had, across the way. He came around to face the Jedi Master Kit

Fisto, who slammed him hard with a Force shove, knocking him to the ground. Next, the agile Jedi did a pirouette movement and with a vicious slice of his lightsaber, took down the battle droid that had been in line right beside C-3PO. It collapsed on top of C-3PO's prone form.

"Help! I'm trapped! I can't get up!" C-3PO wailed, a call that caught the attention of none.

Save one.

R2-D2 rolled into the arena and wove his way about the carnage and danger.

No number of battle droids could hope to separate Mace and Obi-Wan, so perfect were their movements, so attuned were they to each other. But the sheer bulk of the reek was too much even for a pair of lightsabers, and when the furious beast charged at the two Jedi, they had no choice but to dive apart.

The reek followed Mace, and he had to slash wildly to fend it off. He did manage to drive it back, but was butted and lost his lightsaber in the process. He came up facing the reek, and figured that he could outmaneuver it to get his weapon back easily enough, but then an armored rocket-man flew down in his path, blaster leveled.

Mace reached out with the Force and brought his lightsaber flying to his hand, moving like lightning to parry Jango's first shot. With the second shot, Mace was more in control, and his parry sent the bolt right back at the bounty hunter. But Jango was already in motion, diving sidelong and coming around ready to launch a series of shots the Jedi's way.

He was stopped by the reek. Unable to distinguish friend from foe, the reek bore down on Jango. He scored a couple of hits, but they hardly slowed the beast, and he was tossed away. The reek charged him, trying to stomp him as he rolled about desperately. Jango was fast, though. Every time he came around, he fired again, and again, his bolts burrowing into the furious reek's belly.

Finally, the huge bullish creature swayed, and Jango wisely rolled out the far side, opposite Mace, as the beast collapsed.

The Jedi was on him immediately, lightsaber weaving through the air. Jango dodged and lifted into the air with his rockets, trying to keep one step ahead of that deadly blade and to occasionally fire a bolt at Mace.

The man was good, Mace had to admit. Very good, and more than once the Jedi had to parry desperately to turn a bolt aside. He kept up his offensive flurry, though, keeping Jango on the defensive with sudden stabs and slashing cuts.

One misstep . . .

And then it happened, all of a sudden. Mace started to slash to the left, cut it short and stabbed straight out, then reversed his grip and sent the lightsaber slashing across, left to right. He spun a complete circuit, coming around to parry a blaster shot, but there was no shot forthcoming.

That left to right reversal had cleanly landed. Jango Fett's head flew free of his shoulders and fell out of his helmet, to settle in the dirt.

"Straight ahead," Obi-Wan told himself as the acklay came at him, its huge claws snapping in the air.

He went left, then right, then rolled forward at the beast, between the mighty arms and snapping claws, coming around and over with his borrowed lightsaber stabbing straight ahead, burning a hole in the creature's chest.

The acklay dived forward, trying to crush him under its bulk, and the Jedi leapt straight up as he connected. He came down on its back, landing lightly and stabbing repeatedly, before leaping away once more.

"Straight ahead," he told himself again as the enraged beast charged yet again.

Obi-Wan noted the blaster bolt coming at him from the side at the very last second, and turned his lightsaber down and under, deflecting the bolt right into the acklay's face.

The creature hardly slowed and the Jedi had to throw himself to the ground to dodge a swiping, snapping claw.

He rolled out to the side, to avoid a stomping leg, and managed to slash out again, cutting a deep gash.

The acklay howled and came on, and more blaster bolts came at the Jedi.

His lightsaber worked furiously, brilliantly, turning one bolt after another right into the charging beast, finally slowing it and stunning it.

Obi-Wan rushed in and leapt and stabbed, right in the face. He caught his foot on the creature's shoulder and ran right past it. He heard it fall behind him, thrashing in its death throes, but he knew that battle was done and went back to work on the battle droids.

That larger fight seemed far from won, and far from winnable. Mace Windu had finished with Jango Fett by then, and to the other side, Anakin and Padmé continued their perfect teamwork behind the overturned execution cart. Anakin turned all shots aimed at either of them, and Padmé picked off droid after droid. But even with that, even with all of the remaining Jedi fighting brilliantly in the arena, the droids continued to press in, herding them all together in a hopeless position.

"Artoo, what are you doing here?" C-3PO asked when his little friend rolled past his trapped body.

In response, R2-D2 fired a suction cup grapnel from a compartment, attaching it firmly to C-3PO's head.

"Wait!" C-3PO cried as R2-D2 began to tug. "No! How dare you? You're pulling too hard! Stop dragging me, you leadhead!" He felt the sparking as his head tore free of the Battle Droid body, and then R2-D2 pulled C-3PO's head over to its rightful body. R2-D2 extracted his welding arm and began reattaching the protocol droid's head.

"Artoo, be careful! You might burn my circuits. Are you sure my head's on straight?"

* * *

More Jedi went down under the sheer weight of the laser barrage. Less than half of them were still standing.

"Limited choices," Ki-Adi-Mundi said to the exhausted and bloody Mace Windu.

Soon they were down to just over twenty, all herded together, and in the stadium all about them stood rank after rank of battle droid, weapons leveled.

And then all movement stopped suddenly.

"Master Windu!" Count Dooku cried from the dignitary box. His expression showed that he had truly enjoyed the spectacle of the battle. "You have fought gallantly. Worthy of recognition in the Archives of the Jedi. Now it is finished." He paused and looked all about, leading the gazes of the trapped Jedi to the rows and rows of enemies still poised to destroy them.

"Surrender," Dooku ordered, "and your lives will be spared."

"We will not become hostages for you to use as barter, Dooku," Mace said without the slightest hesitation.

"Then I'm sorry, old friend," Count Dooku said, in a tone that didn't sound at all sorry. "You will have to be destroyed." He raised his hand and looked to his assembled army, prepared to give the signal.

But then Padmé, exhausted, dirty, and bloody, raised her head to the sky above and shouted, "Look!" All eyes turned up to see half a dozen gunships fast descending upon the arena, screaming down in a dusty cloud about the Jedi, clone troopers rushing out their open sides as they touched down.

A hailstorm of laserfire blasted the new arrivals, but the gunships had their shields up, covering the debarkation of their warriors.

Amid the sudden confusion and flashing laserfire, Master Yoda appeared in the dropdoor of one of the gunships, offering a salute to Mace and the others.

"Jedi, move!" Mace cried, and the survivors rushed to the nearest gunships, scrambling aboard. Mace climbed in right beside Yoda, and their ship lifted away immediately, cannons blaring, shattering and scattering battle droids as it soared up out of the arena.

Mace could hardly believe the incredible sight unfolding before him, as thousands of Republic ships rushed down on the assembled fleet of the Trade Federation, dropping tens of thousands of clone troopers to the surface of the planet. Behind him, Yoda continued to orchestrate the battle. "More battalions to the left," he instructed his signaler, who relayed it out to the field commanders. "Encircle them, we must, then divide."

After many minutes of a glow so bright that it hurt C-3PO's eyes, R2-D2 retracted his welding arm and tootled that the job was finished—C-3PO's head was back where it belonged.

"Oh, Artoo, you've put me back together!" C-3PO cried, and with some effort, he managed to stand upright. He realized then, from the hailstorm of fire outside the arena tunnel, and with many of those bolts ricocheting inside, that he was far from safe, and so he turned and began to amble away. Unfortunately for him, though, R2-D2 had not yet disengaged the sucker projectile from his forehead. The cord went taut, and C-3PO tumbled backward to the ground.

R2-D2 gave an apologetic whistle as he rolled by, disengaging and retracting the sucker as he went.

"I won't forget this!" C-3PO cried indignantly, and he scrambled up again and shuffled off after his infuriating friend.

With the gunships flying off and the battle droids in pursuit, Boba Fett finally found the opportunity to slip down onto the arena floor. He called for his father repeatedly, rushing from pile of carnage to pile of carnage. He passed the dead acklay, and then the reek, calling for Jango, but knowing what had happened, simply because his father, who was always there, wasn't there.

And then he saw the helmet.

"Dad," the boy breathed. His legs giving out beneath him, he fell to his knees beside Jango Fett's empty helmet.

Archduke Poggle the Lesser led Dooku and the others into the Geonosian command center, a huge room with a large circular viewscreen in its center and many other monitors about the walls, where Geonosian soldiers could monitor and direct the widening battle.

Poggle rushed to the side to confer with an army commander, then came back to Dooku and Nute Gunray, his expression fierce. "All of our communications have been jammed!" he informed them. "We are under attack, on land and from above!"

"The Jedi have amassed a huge army!" Nute Gunray cried.

"Where did they get them?" Dooku asked, sounding perplexed. "That doesn't seem possible. How did the Jedi come up with an army so quickly?"

"We must send all available droids into battle," Nute Gunray demanded.

But Dooku, staring at the myriad of scenes, at the many battles and explosions all about the region, was shaking his head before the Neimoidian could begin to argue his reasoning. "There are too many," the Count said, his voice full of resignation. "They will soon have us surrounded."

Even as he spoke, the three winced as the central screen

flashed, showing the explosive destruction of a major Geonosian defensive position.

"This is not going well at all," Nute Gunray admitted.

"Order a retreat," said Poggle, and he was trembling so forcefully that it seemed as if he might just fall over. "I am sending all my warriors deep into the catacombs to hide!" He nodded to several of his commanders as he finished, and they turned back to their comlinks, relaying the orders.

"We must get the cores of our ships back into space!" one of Nute Gunray's associates cried, and Gunray was nodding as he considered the words and the devastating scenes of battle flashing across the viewscreens.

"I'm going to Coruscant," Dooku announced. "My Master will not let the Republic get away with this treachery."

Poggle the Lesser rushed across the room to a console and punched in some codes, bringing up a holographic schematic of a planet-sized weapon. With a few keystrokes, he downloaded the schematic onto a cartridge and pulled it from the drive, turning to Dooku. "The Jedi must not find our designs," the Archduke insisted. "If they have any idea of what we are planning to create, we are doomed."

Dooku took the cartridge. "I will take the designs with me," he agreed. "The plans will be much safer with my Master."

With a curt bow, the Count swept from the room.

Obi-Wan, Anakin, and Padmé crouched in the open side of a gunship as it sped across the expanding battlefield outside the arena, its laser cannons blaring, its shields turning back the responding fire from the droids.

Below them, clone troopers rushed across the battlefield on speeder bikes, weaving their way and firing all the while.

"They're good," Obi-Wan remarked, and Anakin nodded.

Their attention went right back to their own situation, then, as the gunship approached a huge Techno Union starship and opened fire. Its laser cannons slammed away at the giant, but seemed to be having little effect.

"Aim right above the fuel cells!" Anakin cried to the gunner. With a slight adjustment, the gunner let fly his next burst.

Huge explosions rocked the starship and it began to tilt ominously to the side. The gunship, and others rushing in nearby, swerved aside as the great craft toppled.

"Good call!" Obi-Wan congratulated his Padawan, then he shouted to the crew, "Those Trade Federation starships are taking off! Target them quickly!"

"They're too big, Master," Anakin replied. "The ground-troopers will have to take them out."

The gunship roared across the widening battlefield, lasers blasting away, explosions erupting all about it, a scene of spectacular destruction and frenzy. Mace Windu shook his head and looked to Yoda.

"Capture Dooku, we must," Yoda said, his calm and steady voice as strong an anchor as Mace could have asked for in that momentous moment. "If escape he does, he will rally more systems to his cause."

Mace looked to the diminutive Master and nodded grimly. "Captain, land at that assembly point ahead," he ordered the clone driving his gunship, and the obedient pilot fast settled the craft. Mace, Ki-Adi-Mundi, and a host of clone troopers jumped out, but Yoda did not follow.

"To the forward command center, take me," he instructed, and the gunship lifted away.

As soon as they put down at the relative safety of the position that had been secured as the command center, the clone commander rushed to the open gunship dropdoor. "Master Yoda, all forward positions are advancing."

"Very good, very good," Yoda said. "Concentrate all your fire on the nearest starship."

"Yes, sir!"

The clone commander ran off, organizing his leaders as he went. Soon after, the forward groups began picking their targets in a more coordinated manner, and the concentrated fire suc-

ceeded where sporadic bursts could not, taking down one starship after another.

The gunship slowed and banked suddenly, circling a droid
gun emplacement, coming too fast around the back for the stationary system to swivel. A furious barrage destroyed the defensive position completely, but it did manage a single shot the
gunship's way, rocking the craft hard.

"Hold on!" Obi-Wan cried, grabbing the edge of the open
dropdoor.

"Can't think of a better choice!" Padmé yelled back at
him.

Obi-Wan turned a smirk her way, or started to, but then he
saw a Geonosian speeder soaring away, an unmistakable figure in
the open cockpit. Two fighters flanked the speeder, the trio
heading fast away from the main fighting. "Look! Over there!"

"It's Dooku!" Anakin cried. "Shoot him down!"

"We're out of ordnance, sir," the clone captain replied.

"Follow him!" Anakin ordered.

The pilot put the ship up on its side, banking fast to turn
into a straight run for the fleeing Count.

"We're going to need some help," Padmé remarked.

"No, there's no time," said Obi-Wan. "Anakin and I can
handle this."

As the gunship began to close, the fighters flanking Dooku
banked away suddenly, veering off left and right, turning to engage. The clone pilot of the gunship was up to the task, weaving
his way through their fire, but then another blast rocked the
ship, and with the vehicle up on edge, Obi-Wan and Anakin had
to hold on tight and scramble to stay in.

Padmé wasn't so fortunate.

One moment, she was beside Anakin, and then she was
gone, tumbling out the open dropdoor.

"Padmé!" Anakin screamed. Everything seemed to be happening in slow motion, and he couldn't catch her, couldn't
reach out fast enough.

She tumbled down and hit the ground hard, and lay very still.

"Padmé!" Anakin cried again, and then he yelled to the clone pilot, "Put the ship down!"

Obi-Wan stood before him, his hands on Anakin's shoulders, holding him steady and firm. "Don't let your personal feelings get in the way," he reminded his Padawan. He turned to the pilot. "Follow that speeder."

Anakin pushed to the side, peering over his Master's shoulder, and growled, "Lower the ship!"

Obi-Wan turned to face him again, and this time, his look was not so sympathetic. "Anakin," he said flatly, showing that there was no room for debate. "I can't take Dooku alone. If we catch him, we can end this war right now. We have a job to do."

"I don't care!" Anakin yelled at him. He pushed out to the side again and yelled at the pilot, "Put the ship down!"

"You'll be expelled from the Jedi Order," Obi-Wan said, his grim look showing no room for any argument.

The blunt statement hit Anakin hard. "I can't leave her," he said, his voice suddenly little more than a whisper.

"Come to your senses," said the uncompromising Obi-Wan. "What do you think Padmé would do if she were in your position?"

Anakin's shoulders slumped. "She would do her duty," he admitted. He turned and looked back toward where Padmé had fallen, but they were now too far off, and there was too much dust.

Gunships screamed left and right, trading fire with laser cannon emplacements. On the ground, thousands of clone troopers battled the droids, and it was already becoming apparent that these new soldiers were indeed superior. One against one, a battle droid was nearly a match for a clone trooper, and a super battle droid even more than a match. But in groups and formations, the improvisation of the clone troopers, reacting to the fast-changing battleground and following the relayed orders of their Jedi commander, was quickly giving them all of the best vantage points, all the high ground and the most defensible positions.

The battle soon extended far overhead, as well, as Republic warships engaged those Trade Federation ships that had managed to get offplanet, and those that had not yet landed. Most of those Trade Federation ships inside the asteroid belt and immediately within the perimeter of the battle were troop carriers rather than battleships, and so the Republic was fast gaining the upper hand there, as well.

Over at the command center, an exhausted and dirty Mace Windu joined Master Yoda, the two sharing looks that combined hope for the present and fear for the future.

"You decided to bring them," Mace stated.

"Troubling, it is," Yoda replied, his large eyes slowly blinking. "Two paths were there open, and this one alone offered the return of so many Jedi."

Mace Windu nodded his approval of that choice, but Yoda only looked at the turmoil and destruction raging about him and blinked his large eyes once more.

Obi-Wan pushed past Anakin, moving toward the pilot. "Follow that speeder!"

The gunship did just that, zooming low. They found the speeder soon enough, parked outside a large tower. The gunship skimmed to a stop, moving a bit lower, and Anakin and Obi-Wan leapt out, rushing to the tower door. Hardly pausing, Anakin burst through, lightsaber in hand, entering a huge hangar, with cranes and control panels, tug-ships and workbenches.

They found Count Dooku inside, standing at a control panel, working some instruments. A small interstellar sail ship sat nearby, a graceful, shining craft with a circular pod set on two lander legs, the retracted sails sweeping out to narrowing points behind it, like folded wings.

"You're going to pay for all the Jedi you killed today, Dooku!" Anakin yelled at him, moving in determinedly. Again he felt the tug of a determined Obi-Wan, holding him back.

"We move in together," Obi-Wan explained. "You slowly on the—"

"No! I'm taking him now!" And Anakin pulled away and charged ahead.

"Anakin, no!"

Like a charging reek, the young Jedi came on, his green lightsaber ready to cut Dooku in half. The Count looked at him out of the corner of his eye, smiling as if truly amused.

Anakin didn't catch the cue. His rage moved him along, as it had with the Tusken Raiders.

But this was no simple warrior enemy. Dooku's hand shot out toward the charging Jedi, sending forth a Force push as solid as any stone wall, and a burst of blue Force lightning, unknown to Jedi, charged all about the trapped and lifted Jedi Padawan.

Anakin managed to hold onto his lightsaber as he went up into the air, held there by the power of the Count. With a wave of his hand, Dooku sent Anakin flying across the room, to crash into a distant wall, where he slumped down, dazed.

"As you can see, my Jedi powers are far beyond yours," Dooku said with complete confidence and calm.

"I don't think so," Obi-Wan countered, moving toward him in a more measured and defensive manner, his borrowed blue lightsaber held across his body diagonally, up over one shoulder.

Dooku smiled and ignited a red-glowing blade.

Obi-Wan stepped slowly at first, then came on in a sudden rush, his blue blade coming in hard, right to left.

But with only a slight movement, the red blade stabbed under the blue, then lifted up, and Obi-Wan's blade went flying harmlessly high of the mark. With a slight reversal of his wrist, Dooku stabbed straight ahead, and Obi-Wan had to throw himself backward. He brought his lightsaber across as he did, trying to parry, but Dooku had already retracted his blade by then and had settled back into perfect defensive posture.

Against that posture, Obi-Wan's sudden flurry of attacks seemed exaggerated and inefficient, for Dooku defeated each, one after another, with a slight parry or dodge, seeming barely to move. For while Obi-Wan and most of the Jedi were sword fighters, Count Dooku was a fencer, following an older fighting style, one more effective against weapons like lightsabers than against projectile weapons like blasters. The Jedi on the whole had abandoned that old fighting style, considering it almost irrelevant against the enemies of the present galaxy, but Dooku had always held stubbornly to it, considering it among the highest of fighting disciplines.

Now, as the battle played out between the Count and Obi-Wan, the older way showed its brilliance. Obi-Wan leapt and spun, slashing side to side, chopping and thrusting, but all of Dooku's movements seemed far more efficient. He followed a single line, front and back, his feet shifting to keep him constantly in perfect balance as he retreated and came on suddenly with devastating thrusts that had Obi-Wan stumbling backward.

"Master Kenobi, you disappoint me," the Count taunted. "Yoda holds you in such high esteem."

His words spurred Obi-Wan forward with another series of slashes and chops, but Dooku's red blade angled left and then right, then up just enough to send Obi-Wan's descending blade slipping off to the side. Obi-Wan had to retreat soon after, gasping for breath.

"Come, come, Master Kenobi," Dooku said, his lips curled in a wicked smile. "Put me out of my misery."

Obi-Wan steadied himself and shifted his lightsaber from hand to hand, getting a better grip on it. Then he exploded into motion, coming on again fiercely, his blue lightsaber flashing all about. He kept a better measure of his cuts this time, though, reversing his angle often, turning a wide slash into a sudden thrust, and he soon had Dooku backing, the red blade working furiously to keep Obi-Wan at bay.

Obi-Wan pressed forward more forcefully, but Dooku continued to fend off the strikes, and then his momentum played out. He was too far forward, while Dooku remained in perfect balance, ready for a counterstrike.

And then it was Dooku suddenly pressing the attack, his red blade stabbing and retracting so quickly that most of Obi-Wan's cutting parries hit nothing but air. Obi-Wan had to jump back, and then back again, and again, as those thrusts moved ever closer to hitting home.

Dooku stepped forward suddenly, stabbing low for Obi-Wan's thigh. Down went the blue blade to intercept, but to Obi-Wan's horror, Dooku retracted his weapon and thrust it right back out, up high and across the other way. Obi-Wan couldn't get his weapon back to block, nor could he slide back fast enough.

Dooku's red blade stabbed hard into his left shoulder, and as he lurched back, Dooku retracted the blade and stabbed along its original course, digging into Obi-Wan's right thigh. The Jedi stumbled backward, tripping and crashing hard against the wall, but even as he fell, Dooku was there, his red blade rolling over and inside Obi-Wan's blade, and with a sudden jerk, he sent Obi-Wan's lightsaber bouncing across the floor.

"And so it ends," Dooku said to the helpless Obi-Wan. With a shrug, the elegant Count lifted his red blade up high, then brought it down hard at Obi-Wan's head.

A green blade cut in under it, stopping it with a shower of sparks.

The Count reacted immediately, backpedaling and turning to face Anakin. "That's brave of you, boy, but foolish. I would've thought you'd have learned your lesson."

"I'm a slow learner," Anakin replied coolly, and he came on then, so suddenly, so powerfully, his green blade whirling with such speed that he seemed almost encased in green light.

For the first time, Count Dooku lost his little confident smile. He had to work furiously to keep Anakin's blade at bay, dodging more than parrying. He tried to step out to the side, but stopped as if he had hit a wall, and his eyes widened a bit when he realized that this young Padawan, in the midst of that assault, had used the Force to block his exit.

"You have unusual powers, young Padawan," he sincerely congratulated. His little grin returned, and gradually Dooku put himself back on even footing with Anakin, trading thrust for slash and forcing Anakin to dodge and parry as often as he tried to strike.

"Unusual," Dooku said again. "But not enough to save you this time!" He came on hard, thinking to drive Anakin back and off balance as he had driven Obi-Wan back. But Anakin held his ground stubbornly, his green blade flashing left, right, and down so forcefully and precisely that none of Dooku's attacks got through.

Off to the side, Obi-Wan understood that it couldn't hold. Anakin was expending many times the energy of the efficient Dooku, and as soon as he tired . . .

Obi-Wan knew that he had to do something. He tried to come forward, but winced and fell back, in too much pain. As he collected his thoughts, he reached out with the Force instead, grabbing at his lightsaber and pulling it in to his grasp. "Anakin!" he called, and he tossed the young Padawan the blade. Anakin caught it without ever breaking the flow of his fighting, turning it under and igniting it immediately, putting it into the swirling flow.

Obi-Wan watched in admiration as Anakin worked the two blades in perfect harmony, spinning them over and about with blinding speed and precision.

And he watched with similar feelings the working of Count Dooku's red lightsaber, flashing ahead and back with equal precision, picking off attack after attack and even countering once or twice to interrupt the flow of Anakin's barrage.

Obi-Wan's heart leapt in hope as Anakin charged forward suddenly, bringing his green blade over his shoulder and across, down at the Count. Obi-Wan understood immediately, even before he noted Anakin's blue blade coming up and over the other way—the green blade would push the Count's lightsaber out of the way, clearing the path for the victorious strike!

But Dooku retracted impossibly fast, and Anakin's down-cutting green blade hit nothing but air.

Dooku stabbed straight ahead, intercepting the blue blade. The Count's hand worked up inside and over, then back around with a sudden twist, launching the blue lightsaber from Anakin's grasp. Dooku went on the offensive immediately, driving the surprised and off-balance Anakin back.

Anakin fought hard to regain his fighting posture, but Dooku was relentless, thrusting repeatedly, keeping the young Padawan stumbling backward.

And then he stopped, suddenly, and almost on reflex, Anakin turned back on him, roaring and slashing hard.

"No!" Obi-Wan cried.

Dooku stabbed ahead and slashed out suddenly, intercepting not Anakin's green blade, but the Padawan's arm, at the elbow. Half of Anakin's arm flew to the side, his hand still gripping the lightsaber.

Anakin dropped to the ground, grabbing his severed arm in agony.

Dooku gave another of his resigned shrugs. "And so it ends," he said for the second time.

Even as he spoke, though, the great hangar doors of the tower slid open, smoke from the battle outside pouring in. And through that smoke came a diminutive figure, but one seeming taller than all of them at that moment.

"Master Yoda," Dooku breathed.

"Count Dooku," said Yoda.

Dooku's eyes widened and he stepped back, turning to face Yoda directly. He brought his lightsaber up to his face, shut down the blade, then snapped it to the side in formal salute. "You have interfered with our plans for the last time."

A wave of Dooku's free hand sent a piece of machinery flying at the diminutive Jedi Master, seeming as if it would surely crush him.

But Yoda was ready, waving his own hand, Force-pushing the flying machinery harmlessly aside.

Dooku clutched up at the ceiling, breaking free great blocks that tumbled down at Yoda.

But small hands waved and the boulders dropped to the sides, bouncing across the floor all about the untouched Master Yoda.

Dooku gave a little growl and thrust forth his hand, loosing a line of blue lightning at the diminutive Master.

Yoda caught it in his own hand and turned it aside, but far from easily.

"Powerful you have become, Dooku," Yoda admitted, and the Count grinned—but Yoda promptly took that grin away by adding, "The dark side I sense in you."

"I have become more powerful than any Jedi," Dooku countered. "Even you, my old Master!"

More lightning poured forth from Dooku's hand, but Yoda continued to catch it and turn it, and seemed to become even more settled in his defensive posture.

"Much to learn you still have," Yoda remarked.

Dooku disengaged the futile lightning assault. "It is obvious this contest will not be decided by our knowledge of the Force, but by our skills with a lightsaber."

Yoda reverently drew out his lightsaber, its green blade humming to life.

Dooku gave a crisp salute, igniting his own red blade, but then, formalities over, he leapt at Yoda, a sudden and devastating thrust.

But one that never got close to hitting. With hardly a movement, Yoda turned the blade aside.

Dooku went into a wild flurry then, the likes of which he had not shown against Obi-Wan or Anakin, raining blows at the diminutive Master. But Yoda didn't even seem to move. He didn't step back or to the side, yet his subtle dodges and precision parries kept Dooku's blade slashing and stabbing harmlessly wide.

It went on and on for many moments, but eventually Dooku's flurry began to slow, and the Count, recognizing the futility of this attempt to overwhelm, stepped back fast.

Not fast enough.

With a sudden burst of sheer power, Master Yoda flew forward, his blade working so mightily that its residual glow outshone even those of both of Anakin's lightsabers when he was at the peak of his dance. Dooku held strong, though, his red blade parrying brilliantly, each block backed by the power of the Force, or else Yoda's strikes would have driven right through.

Just as he was about to launch a counter, though, Yoda was gone, leaping high and turning a somersault to land right behind Dooku, in perfect balance, striking hard.

Dooku reversed his grip and stabbed out behind him, intercepting the blow. He let go of his weapon altogether, tossing it just a bit, and spun about, catching it before it had even disengaged from Yoda's blade.

With a growl of rage, Dooku reached more deeply into the Force, letting it flow through him as if his physical form was a mere conduit for its power. His tempo increased suddenly and dramatically, three steps forward, two back, perfectly balanced all the while. His fighting style was one based on balance, on the back-and-forth charges, thrusts and sudden retreats, and now he came at Yoda with a series of cunning stabs, angled left and right.

Never could he strike low, though, for never did Yoda seem to be on the ground, leaping and spinning, flying all about, parrying each blow and offering cunning counters that had Dooku skipping backward desperately.

Dooku stabbed up high, turning the angle of his lightsaber in anticipation that Yoda would dodge left. But Yoda, as if in complete anticipation of the movement, veered neither left nor right, but rather, dropped to the ground. The Count had already retracted the missed thrust, and began a second stab, this time down low, but Yoda had anticipated that, too, and went right back up behind the stabbing blade.

A sudden stab by Yoda had Dooku quick-stepping back even more off-balance, for the first time, and then Yoda flew away, up and back.

The furious Dooku pursued, thrusting hard for Yoda's head. And in his rage when his stab missed yet again, he reverted to a slashing attack.

Yoda's green blade caught the blow, holding the red light-saber at bay, locking the two in a contest of strength, physical and of the Force.

"Fought well, you have, my old Padawan," Yoda congratu-lated, and his lightsaber began to move out, just a bit, forcing Dooku back.

"The battle is far from over!" Dooku stubbornly argued. "This is just the beginning!" Reaching into the Force, he took hold of one of the huge cranes within the hangar and threw it down at Obi-Wan and Anakin.

"Anakin!" Obi-Wan cried. He grabbed at the plummeting crane with the Force, and Anakin, startled awake, did so, as well. Even working together, they hadn't the strength left to stop its crushing descent.

But Yoda did.

Yoda grabbed the crane and held it fast, but in doing so, he had to release Dooku. The Count wasted no time, sprinting away, leaping up the ramp to his sail ship. As Yoda began to move the fallen crane harmlessly aside, the sail ship's engine roared to life, and all three Jedi watched helplessly as Count Dooku blasted away.

As Anakin and Obi-Wan walked over to the exhausted Yoda, Padmé rushed in, running to Anakin and wrapping the sorely wounded young man in a tight, desperate hug.

"A dark day, it is," Yoda said quietly.

EPILOGUE

In the gutters of lower Coruscant, a graceful sail ship glided down, its wings folding delicately as it went to its more conventional drives, settling easily inside the broken pavement of a seemingly abandoned building.

Count Dooku climbed out of his ship, walking to the shadows at the side of the secret landing ramp, where a hooded figure waited. He moved before the shadowy figure and bowed reverently.

"The Force is with us, Master Sidious."

"Welcome home, Lord Tyranus," the Sith Lord replied. "You have done well."

"I bring you good news, my lord. The war has begun."

"Excellent," Sidious said, his gravelly voice hinting at a hiss. From underneath the dark shadows of his huge cowl, the Dark Lord's smile widened. "Everything is going as planned."

Across the city, in the somber Jedi Temple, so many lamented the loss of friends and colleagues. Obi-Wan and Mace Windu stood staring out the window of Master Yoda's apartment while the diminutive Master sat in a chair across the way, contemplating the troubling events.

"Do you believe what Count Dooku said about Sidious

controlling the Senate?" Obi-Wan asked, breaking the contemplative silence. "It doesn't feel right."

Mace started to respond, but Yoda interjected, "Become unreliable, Dooku has. Joined the dark side. Lies, deceit, creating mistrust are his ways now."

"Nevertheless, I feel we should keep a closer eye on the Senate," Mace put in, and Yoda agreed.

After some more quiet contemplation, Mace turned a curious gaze upon Obi-Wan. "Where is your apprentice?"

"On his way to Naboo," Obi-Wan answered. "Escorting Senator Amidala home."

Mace nodded, and Obi-Wan caught a glimmer of concern in his dark eyes—concern that Obi-Wan shared about Anakin and Padmé. They let it go at that time, though, for there seemed greater problems at hand. Again, it was Obi-Wan who broke the silence.

"I have to admit, without the clones, it would not have been a victory."

"Victory?" Yoda echoed with great skepticism. "Victory, you say?"

Obi-Wan and Mace Windu turned as one to the great Jedi Master, catching clearly the profound sadness in his tone.

"Master Obi-Wan, not victory," Yoda went on. "The shroud of the dark side has fallen. Begun, this Clone War has!"

His words hung in the air about them, thick with emotion and concern, as dire a prediction as anyone in the Jedi Council had ever heard uttered.

Senator Bail Organa and Mas Amedda flanked Supreme Chancellor Palpatine as he stood on the balcony, overlooking the deployment of the Republic army. Below them, tens of thousands of clone troopers marched about in tight formations, an orderly procession that brought them in files ascending the landing ramps of the huge military assault ships.

A deep sadness marked the handsome features of Bail Organa, but when he looked over at the Supreme Chancellor, he saw there a grim determination.

On distant Naboo, in a rose-covered arbor overlooking the sparkling lake, Anakin and Padmé stood hand in hand, Anakin in his formal Jedi robes and Padmé in a beautiful white gown with flowered trim. Anakin's new mechanical arm hung at his side, the fingers clenching and opening in reflexive movements.

Before them stood a Naboo holy man, his hands raised above their heads as he recited the ancient texts of marriage.

And when the proclamation was made, R2-D2 and C-3PO, bearing witness to the union, whistled and clapped.

And Anakin Skywalker and Padmé Amidala shared their first kiss as husband and wife.

EPISODE III

REVENGE OF THE SITH™

MATTHEW STOVER

BASED ON THE STORY AND SCREENPLAY BY
GEORGE LUCAS

the author respectfully dedicates this adaptation

To George Lucas

with gratitude for the dreams of a generation,
and of generations to come,
for twenty-eight years, and counting . . .

thank you, sir.

This story happened a long time ago in a galaxy far, far away. It is already over. Nothing can be done to change it.

It is a story of love and loss, brotherhood and betrayal, courage and sacrifice and the death of dreams. It is a story of the blurred line between our best and our worst.

It is the story of the end of an age.

A strange thing about stories—

Though this all happened so long ago and so far away that words cannot describe the time or the distance, it is also happening right now. Right here.

It is happening as you read these words.

This is how twenty-five millennia come to a close. Corruption and treachery have crushed a thousand years of peace. This is not just the end of a republic; night is falling on civilization itself.

This is the twilight of the Jedi.

The end starts now.

INTRODUCTION

THE AGE OF HEROES

The skies of Coruscant blaze with war.

The artificial daylight spread by the capital's orbital mirrors is sliced by intersecting flames of ion drives and punctuated by starburst explosions; contrails of debris raining into the atmosphere become tangled ribbons of cloud. The nightside sky is an infinite lattice of shining hairlines that interlock planetoids and track erratic spirals of glowing gnats. Beings watching from rooftops of Coruscant's endless cityscape can find it beautiful.

From the inside, it's different.

The gnats are drive-glows of starfighters. The shining hairlines are light-scatter from turbolaser bolts powerful enough to vaporize a small town. The planetoids are capital ships.

The battle from the inside is a storm of confusion and panic, of galvened particle beams flashing past your starfighter so close that your cockpit rings like a broken annunciator, of the bootsole shock of concussion missiles that blast into your cruiser, killing beings you have trained with and eaten with and played and laughed and bickered with. From the inside, the battle is desperation and terror and the stomach-churning certainty that the whole galaxy is trying to kill you.

Across the remnants of the Republic, stunned beings watch in horror as the battle unfolds live on the HoloNet. Everyone knows the war has been going badly. Everyone knows that more Jedi are killed or captured every day, that the Grand Army of the Republic has been pushed out of system after system, but this—

A strike at the very heart of the Republic?

An *invasion* of *Coruscant itself*?

How can this *happen*?

It's a nightmare, and no one can wake up.

Live via HoloNet, beings watch the Separatist droid army flood the government district. The coverage is filled with images of overmatched clone troopers cut down by remorselessly powerful destroyer droids in the halls of the Galactic Senate itself.

A gasp of relief: the troopers seem to beat back the attack. There are hugs and even some quiet cheers in living rooms across the galaxy as the Separatist forces retreat to their landers and streak for orbit—

We won! beings tell each other. *We held them off!*

But then new reports trickle in—only rumors at first—that the attack wasn't an invasion at all. That the Separatists weren't trying to take the planet. That this was a lightning raid on the Senate itself.

The nightmare gets worse: the Supreme Chancellor is missing.

Palpatine of Naboo, the most admired man in the galaxy, whose unmatched political skills have held the Republic together. Whose personal integrity and courage prove that the Separatist propaganda of corruption in the Senate is nothing but lies. Whose charismatic leadership gives the whole Republic the will to fight on.

Palpatine is more than respected. He is loved.

Even the rumor of his disappearance strikes a dagger to the heart of every friend of the Republic. Every one of them knows it in her heart, in his gut, in its very bones—

Without Palpatine, the Republic will fall.

And now confirmation comes through, and the news is worse than anyone could have imagined. Supreme Chancellor

Palpatine has been captured by the Separatists—and not just the Separatists.

He's in the hands of General Grievous.

Grievous is not like other leaders of the Separatists. Nute Gunray is treacherous and venal, but he's Neimoidian: venality and treachery are expected, and in the Chancellor of the Trade Federation they're even virtues. Poggle the Lesser is Archduke of the weapon masters of Geonosis, where the war began: he is analytical and pitiless, but also pragmatic. Reasonable. The political heart of the Separatist Confederacy, Count Dooku, is known for his integrity, his principled stand against what he sees as corruption in the Senate. Though they believe he's wrong, many respect him for the courage of his mistaken convictions.

These are hard beings. Dangerous beings. Ruthless and aggressive.

General Grievous, though—

Grievous is a *monster.*

The Separatist Supreme Commander is an abomination of nature, a fusion of flesh and droid—and his droid parts have more compassion than what remains of his alien flesh. This half-living creature is a slaughterer of billions. Whole planets have burned at his command. He is the evil genius of the Confederacy. The architect of their victories.

The author of their atrocities.

And his durasteel grip has closed upon Palpatine. He confirms the capture personally in a wideband transmission from his command cruiser in the midst of the orbital battle. Beings across the galaxy watch, and shudder, and pray that they might wake up from this awful dream.

Because they know that what they're watching, live on the HoloNet, is the death of the Republic.

Many among these beings break into tears; many more reach out to comfort their husbands or wives, their crèche-mates or kin-triads, and their younglings of all descriptions, from children to cubs to spawn-fry.

But here is a strange thing: few of the younglings *need* comfort. It is instead the younglings who offer comfort to their elders. Across the Republic—in words or pheromones, in magnetic pulses, tentacle-braids, or mental telepathy—the message from the younglings is the same: *Don't worry. It'll be all right.*

Anakin and Obi-Wan will be there any minute.

They say this as though these names can conjure miracles.

Anakin and Obi-Wan. Kenobi and Skywalker. From the beginning of the Clone Wars, the phrase *Kenobi and Skywalker* has become a single word. They are everywhere. HoloNet features of their operations against the Separatist enemy have made them the most famous Jedi in the galaxy.

Younglings across the galaxy know their names, know everything about them, follow their exploits as though they are sports heroes instead of warriors in a desperate battle to save civilization. Even grown-ups are not immune; it's not uncommon for an exasperated parent to ask, when faced with offspring who have just tried to pull off one of the spectacularly dangerous bits of foolishness that are the stock-in-trade of high-spirited younglings everywhere, *So which were you supposed to be, Kenobi or Skywalker?*

Kenobi would rather talk than fight, but when there is fighting to be done, few can match him. Skywalker is the master of audacity; his intensity, boldness, and sheer jaw-dropping luck are the perfect complement to Kenobi's deliberate, balanced steadiness. Together, they are a Jedi hammer that has crushed Separatist infestations on scores of worlds.

All the younglings watching the battle in Coruscant's sky know it: when Anakin and Obi-Wan get there, those dirty Seppers are going to wish they'd stayed in bed today.

The adults know better, of course. That's part of what being a grown-up is: understanding that heroes are created by the HoloNet, and that the real-life Kenobi and Skywalker are only human beings, after all.

Even if they really are everything the legends say they are, who's to say they'll show up in time? Who knows where they are right now? They might be trapped on some Separatist backwater. They might be captured, or wounded. Even dead.

Some of the adults even whisper to themselves, *They might have fallen.*

Because the stories are out there. Not on the HoloNet, of course—the HoloNet news is under the control of the Office of the Supreme Chancellor, and not even Palpatine's renowned candor would allow tales like these to be told—but people hear whispers. Whispers of names that the Jedi would like to pretend never existed.

Sora Bulq. Depa Billaba. Jedi who have fallen to the dark. Who have joined the Separatists, or worse: who have massacred civilians, or even murdered their comrades. The adults have a sickening suspicion that Jedi cannot be trusted. Not anymore. That even the greatest of them can suddenly just . . . snap.

The adults know that legendary heroes are merely legends, and not heroes at all.

These adults can take no comfort from their younglings. Palpatine is captured. Grievous will escape. The Republic will fall. No mere human beings can turn this tide. No mere human beings would even try. Not even Kenobi and Skywalker.

And so it is that these adults across the galaxy watch the HoloNet with ashes where their hearts should be.

Ashes because they can't see two prismatic bursts of realspace reversion, far out beyond the planet's gravity well; because they can't see a pair of starfighters crisply jettison hyperdrive rings and streak into the storm of Separatist vulture fighters with all guns blazing.

A pair of starfighters. Jedi starfighters. Only two.

Two is enough.

Two is enough because the adults are wrong, and their younglings are right.

Though this is the end of the age of heroes, it has saved its best for last.

PART ONE

VICTORY

The dark is generous.

Its first gift is concealment: our true faces lie in the dark beneath our skins, our true hearts remain shadowed deeper still. But the greatest concealment lies not in protecting our secret truths, but in hiding from us the truths of others.

The dark protects us from what we dare not know.

Its second gift is comforting illusion: the ease of gentle dreams in night's embrace, the beauty that imagination brings to what would repel in day's harsh light. But the greatest of its comforts is the illusion that the dark is temporary: that every night brings a new day. Because it is day that is temporary.

Day is the illusion.

Its third gift is the light itself: as days are defined by the nights that divide them, as stars are defined by the infinite black through which they wheel, the dark embraces the light, and brings it forth from the center of its own self.

With each victory of the light, it is the dark that wins.

ANAKIN AND OBI-WAN

Antifighter flak flashed on all sides. Even louder than the clatter of shrapnel and the snarl of his sublight drives, his cockpit hummed and rang with near hits from the turbolaser fire of the capital ships crowding space around him. Sometimes his whirling spinning dive through the cloud of battle skimmed bursts so closely that the energy-scatter would slam his starfighter hard enough to bounce his head off the supports of his pilot's chair.

Right now Obi-Wan Kenobi envied the clones: at least they had helmets.

"Arfour," he said on internal comm, "can't you do something with the inertials?"

The droid ganged into the socket on his starfighter's left wing whistled something that sounded suspiciously like a human apology. Obi-Wan's frown deepened. R4-P17 had been spending too much time with Anakin's eccentric astromech; it was picking up R2-D2's bad habits.

New bursts of flak bracketed his path. He reached into the Force, feeling for a safe channel through the swarms of shrapnel and sizzling nets of particle beams.

There wasn't one.

He locked a snarl behind his teeth, twisting his starfighter around another explosion that could have peeled its armor like an overripe Ithorian starfruit. He hated this part. *Hated* it.

Flying's for droids.

His cockpit speakers crackled. *"There isn't a droid made that can outfly you, Master."*

He could still be surprised by the new depth of that voice. The calm confidence. The maturity. It seemed that only last week Anakin had been a ten-year-old who wouldn't stop pestering him about Form I lightsaber combat.

"Sorry," he muttered, kicking into a dive that slipped a turbo-laser burst by no more than a meter. "Was that out loud?"

"Wouldn't matter if it wasn't. I know what you're thinking."

"Do you?" He looked up through the cockpit canopy to find his onetime Padawan flying inverted, mirroring him so closely that but for the transparisteel between them, they might have shaken hands. Obi-Wan smiled up at him. "Some new gift of the Force?"

"Not the Force, Master. Experience. That's what you're always thinking."

Obi-Wan kept hoping to hear some of Anakin's old cocky grin in his tone, but he never did. Not since Jabiim. Perhaps not since Geonosis.

The war had burned it out of him.

Obi-Wan still tried, now and again, to spark a real smile in his former Padawan. And Anakin still tried to answer.

They both still tried to pretend the war hadn't changed them.

"Ah." Obi-Wan took a hand from the starfighter's control yoke to direct his upside-down friend's attention forward. Dead ahead, a blue-white point of light splintered into four laser-straight trails of ion drives. "And what does experience tell you we should do about those incoming tri-fighters?"

"That we should break—right!"

Obi-Wan was already making that exact move as Anakin spoke. But they were inverted to each other: breaking right shot him one way while Anakin whipped the other. The tri-fighters' cannons ripped space between them, tracking faster than their starfighters could slip.

His onboard threat display chimed a warning: two of the droids had remote sensor locks on him. The others must have lit up his partner. "Anakin! Slip-jaws!"

"My thought exactly."

They blew past the tri-fighters, looping in evasive spirals. The droid ships wrenched themselves into pursuit maneuvers that would have killed any living pilot.

The slip-jaws maneuver was named for the scissorlike mandibles of the Kashyyyk slash-spider. Droids closing rapidly on their tails, cannonfire stitching space on all sides, the two Jedi pulled their ships through perfectly mirrored rolls that sent them streaking head-on for each other from opposite ends of a vast Republic cruiser.

For merely human pilots, this would be suicide. By the time you can see your partner's starfighter streaking toward you at a respectable fraction of lightspeed, it's already too late for your merely human reflexes to react.

But these particular pilots were far from merely human.

The Force nudged hands on control yokes and the Jedi starfighters twisted and flashed past each other belly-to-belly, close enough to scorch each other's paint. Tri-fighters were the Trade Federation's latest space-superiority droid. But even the electronic reflexes of the tri-fighters' droid brains were too slow for this: one of his pursuers met one of Anakin's head-on. Both vanished in a blossom of flame.

The shock wave of debris and expanding gas rocked Obi-Wan; he fought the control yoke, barely keeping his starfighter out of a tumble that would have smeared him across the cruiser's ventral hull. Before he could straighten out, his threat display chimed again.

"Oh, marvelous," he muttered under his breath. Anakin's surviving pursuer had switched targets. "Why is it always me?"

"Perfect." Through the cockpit speakers, Anakin's voice carried grim satisfaction. *"Both of them are on your tail."*

"Perfect is *not* the word I'd use." Obi-Wan twisted his yoke, juking madly as space around him flared scarlet. "We have to split them up!"

"Break left." Anakin sounded calm as a stone. *"The turbolaser tower off your port bow: thread its guns. I'll take things from there."*

"Easy for you to say." Obi-Wan whipped sideways along the cruiser's superstructure. Fire from the pursuing tri-fighters blasted burning chunks from the cruiser's armor. "Why am I always the bait?"

"I'm right behind you. Artoo, lock on."

Obi-Wan spun his starfighter between the recoiling turbo-cannons close enough that energy-scatter made his cockpit clang like a gong, but still cannonfire flashed past him from the tri-fighters behind. "Anakin, they're all over me!"

"Dead ahead. Move right to clear my shot. Now!"

Obi-Wan flared his port jets and the starfighter kicked to the right. One of the tri-fighters behind him decided it couldn't follow and went for a ventral slip that took it directly into the blasts from Anakin's cannons.

It vanished in a boil of superheated gas.

"Good shooting, Artoo." Anakin's dry chuckle in the cockpit's speakers vanished behind the clang of lasers blasting ablative shielding off Obi-Wan's left wing.

"I'm running out of *tricks* here—"

Clearing the vast Republic cruiser put him on course for the curving hull of one of the Trade Federation's battleships; space between the two capital ships blazed with turbolaser exchanges. Some of those flashing energy blasts were as big around as his entire ship; the merest graze would blow him to atoms.

Obi-Wan dived right in.

He had the Force to guide him through, and the tri-fighter had only its electronic reflexes—but those electronic reflexes operated at roughly the speed of light. It stayed on his tail as if he were dragging it by a tow cable.

When Obi-Wan went left and Anakin right, the tri-fighter would swing halfway through the difference. The same with up and down. It was averaging his movements with Anakin's; some-how its droid brain had realized that as long as it stayed between the two Jedi, Anakin couldn't fire on it without hitting his part-ner. The tri-fighter was under no similiar restraint: Obi-Wan flew through a storm of scarlet needles.

"No wonder we're losing the war," he muttered. "They're getting *smarter.*"

"What was that, Master? I didn't copy."

Obi-Wan kicked his starfighter into a tight spiral toward the Federation cruiser. "I'm taking the deck!"

"Good idea. I need some room to maneuver."

Cannonfire tracked closer. Obi-Wan's cockpit speakers buzzed. *"Cut right, Obi-Wan! Hard right! Don't let him get a handle on you! Artoo, lock on!"*

Obi-Wan's starfighter streaked along the curve of the Sepa-ratist cruiser's dorsal hull. Antifighter flak burst on all sides as the cruiser's guns tried to pick him up. He rolled a right wingover into the service trench that stretched the length of the cruiser's hull. This low and close to the deck, the cruiser's antifighter guns couldn't depress their angle of fire enough to get a shot, but the tri-fighter stayed right on his tail.

At the far end of the service trench, the massive support but-tresses of the cruiser's towering bridge left no room for even Obi-Wan's small craft. He kicked his starfighter into a half roll that whipped him out of the trench and shot him straight up the tower's angled leading edge. One burst of his underjets jerked him past the forward viewports of the bridge with only meters to spare—and the tri-fighter followed his path exactly.

"Of course," he muttered. "That would have been too easy. Anakin, where *are* you?"

One of the control surfaces on his left wing shattered in a burst of plasma. It felt like being shot in the arm. He toggled switches, fighting the yoke. R4-P17 shrilled at him. Obi-Wan keyed internal comm. "Don't try to fix it, Arfour. I've shut it down."

"I have the lock!" Anakin said. *"Go! Firing—now!"*

Obi-Wan hit maximum drag on his intact wing, and his starfighter shot into a barely controlled arc high and right as Anakin's cannons vaporized the last tri-fighter.

Obi-Wan fired retros to stall his starfighter in the blind spot behind the Separatist cruiser's bridge. He hung there for a few seconds to get his breathing and heart under control. "Thanks, Anakin. That was—thanks. That's all."

"Don't thank me. It was Artoo's shooting."

"Yes. I suppose, if you like, you can thank your droid for me as well. And, Anakin—?"

"Yes, Master?"

"Next time, *you're* the bait."

This is Obi-Wan Kenobi:

A phenomenal pilot who doesn't like to fly. A devastating warrior who'd rather not fight. A negotiator without peer who frankly prefers to sit alone in a quiet cave and meditate.

Jedi Master. General in the Grand Army of the Republic. Member of the Jedi Council. And yet, inside, he feels like he's none of these things.

Inside, he still feels like a Padawan.

It is a truism of the Jedi Order that a Jedi Knight's education truly begins only when he becomes a Master: that everything important about being a Master is learned from one's student. Obi-Wan feels the truth of this every day.

He sometimes dreams of when he was a Padawan in fact as well as feeling; he dreams that his own Master, Qui-Gon Jinn, did not die at the plasma-fueled generator core in Theed. He dreams that his Master's wise guiding hand is still with him. But Qui-Gon's death is an old pain, one with which he long ago came to terms.

A Jedi does not cling to the past.

And Obi-Wan Kenobi knows, too, that to have lived his life

without being Master to Anakin Skywalker would have left him a different man. A lesser man.

Anakin has taught him so much.

Obi-Wan sees so much of Qui-Gon in Anakin that sometimes it hurts his heart; at the very least, Anakin mirrors Qui-Gon's flair for the dramatic, and his casual disregard for rules. Training Anakin—and fighting beside him, all these years—has unlocked something inside Obi-Wan. It's as though Anakin has rubbed off on him a bit, and has loosened that clenched-jaw insistence on absolute correctness that Qui-Gon always said was his greatest flaw.

Obi-Wan Kenobi has learned to relax.

He smiles now, and sometimes even jokes, and has become known for the wisdom gentle humor can provide. Though he does not know it, his relationship with Anakin has molded him into the great Jedi Qui-Gon always said he might someday be.

It is characteristic of Obi-Wan that he is entirely unaware of this.

Being named to the Council came as a complete surprise; even now, he is sometimes astonished by the faith the Jedi Council has in his abilities, and the credit they give to his wisdom. Greatness was never his ambition. He wants only to perform whatever task he is given to the best of his ability.

He is respected throughout the Jedi Order for his insight as well as his warrior skill. He has become the hero of the next generation of Padawans; he is the Jedi their Masters hold up as a model. He is the being that the Council assigns to their most important missions. He is modest, centered, and always kind.

He is the ultimate Jedi.

And he is proud to be Anakin Skywalker's best friend.

———————

"Artoo, where's that signal?"

From its socket beside the cockpit, R2-D2 whistled and

beeped. A translation spidered across Anakin's console readout: SCANNING. LOTS OF ECM SIGNAL JAMMING.

"Keep on it." He glanced at Obi-Wan's starfighter limping through the battle, a hundred meters off his left wing. "I can feel his jitters from all the way over here."

A tootle: A JEDI IS ALWAYS CALM.

"He won't think it's funny. Neither do I. Less joking, more scanning."

For Anakin Skywalker, starfighter battles were usually as close to fun as he ever came.

This one wasn't.

Not because of the overwhelming odds, or the danger he was in; he didn't care about odds, and he didn't think of himself as being in any particular danger. A few wings of droid fighters didn't much scare a man who'd been a Podracer since he was six, and had won the Boonta Cup at nine. Who was, in fact, the only human to ever *finish* a Podrace, let alone win one.

In those days he had used the Force without knowing it; he'd thought the Force was something inside him, just a feeling, an instinct, a string of lucky guesses that led him through maneuvers other pilots wouldn't dare attempt. Now, though . . .

Now—

Now he could reach into the Force and feel the engagement throughout Coruscant space as though the whole battle were happening inside his head.

His vehicle became his body. The pulses of its engines were the beat of his own heart. Flying, he could forget about his slavery, about his mother, about Geonosis and Jabiim, Aargonar and Muunilinst and all the catastrophes of this brutal war. About everything that had been done to him.

And everything he had done.

He could even put aside, for as long as the battle roared around him, the starfire of his love for the woman who waited for him on the world below. The woman whose breath was his only air, whose heartbeat was his only music, whose face was the only beauty his eyes would ever see.

He could put all this aside because he was a Jedi. Because it was time to do a Jedi's work.

But today was different.

Today wasn't about dodging lasers and blasting droids. Today was about the life of the man who might as well have been his father: a man who could die if the Jedi didn't reach him in time.

Anakin had been late once before.

Obi-Wan's voice came over the cockpit speakers, flat and tight. *"Does your droid have anything? Arfour's hopeless. I think that last cannon hit cooked his motivator."*

Anakin could see exactly the look on his former Master's face: a mask of calm belied by a jaw so tight that when he spoke his mouth barely moved. "Don't worry, Master. If his beacon's working, Artoo'll find it. Have you thought about how we'll find the Chancellor if—"

"No." Obi-Wan sounded absolutely certain. *"There's no need to consider it. Until the possible becomes actual, it is only a distraction. Be mindful of what is, not what might be."*

Anakin had to stop himself from reminding Obi-Wan that he wasn't a Padawan anymore. "I should have been here," he said through his teeth. "I *told* you. I should have *been* here."

"Anakin, he was defended by Stass Allie and Shaak Ti. If two Masters could not prevent this, do you think you could? Stass Allie is clever and valiant, and Shaak Ti is the most cunning Jedi I've ever met. She's even taught me *a few tricks."*

Anakin assumed he was supposed to be impressed. "But General Grievous—"

"Master Ti had faced him before, Anakin. After Muunilinst. She is not only subtle and experienced, but very capable indeed. Seats on the Jedi Council aren't handed out as party favors."

"I've noticed." He let it drop. The middle of a space battle was no place to get into this particular sore subject.

If only *he'd* been here, instead of Shaak Ti and Stass Allie, Council members or not. If he had been here, Chancellor Palpatine would be home and safe already. Instead, Anakin had been stuck running around the Outer Rim for months like some use-less Padawan, and all Palpatine had for protectors were Jedi who were *clever* and *subtle.*

Clever and subtle. He could whip any ten *clever and subtle* Jedi with his lightsaber tied behind his back.

But he knew better than to say so.

"Put yourself in the moment, Anakin. Focus."

"Copy that, Master," Anakin said dryly. "Focusing now."

R2-D2 twittered, and Anakin checked his console readout. "We've got him, Master. The cruiser dead ahead. That's Griev-ous's flagship—*Invisible Hand.*"

"Anakin, there are dozens *of cruisers dead ahead!"*

"It's the one crawling with vulture fighters."

The vulture fighters clinging to the long curves of the Trade Federation cruiser indicated by Palpatine's beacon gave it eerily life-like ripples, like some metallic marine predator bristling with Alderaanian walking barnacles.

"Oh. That one." He could practically hear Obi-Wan's stom-ach dropping. *"Oh,* this *should be easy . . ."*

Now some of them stripped themselves from the cruiser, ig-nited their drives, and came looping toward the two Jedi.

"Easy? No. But it might be fun." Sometimes a little teasing was the only way to get Obi-Wan to loosen up. "Lunch at Dex's says I'll blast two for each of yours. Artoo can keep score."

"Anakin—"

"All right, dinner. And I promise this time I won't let Artoo cheat."

"No games, Anakin. There's too much at stake." There, that was the tone Anakin had been looking for: a slightly scolding, schoolmasterish edge. Obi-Wan was back on form. *"Have your droid tight-beam a report to the Temple. And send out a call for any Jedi in starfighters. We'll come at it from all sides."*

"Way ahead of you." But when he checked his comm read-out, he shook his head. "There's still too much ECM. Artoo can't raise the Temple. I think the only reason we can even talk to each other is that we're practically side by side."

"And Jedi beacons?"

"No joy, Master." Anakin's stomach clenched, but he fought the tension out of his voice. "We may be the only two Jedi out here."

"Then we will have to be enough. Switching to clone fighter channel."

Anakin spun his comm dial to the new frequency in time to hear Obi-Wan say, *"Oddball, do you copy? We need help."*

The clone captain's helmet speaker flattened the humanity out of his voice. *"Copy, Red Leader."*

"Mark my position and form your squad behind me. We're going in."

"On our way."

The droid fighters had lost themselves against the background of the battle, but R2-D2 was tracking them on scan. Anakin shifted his grip on his starfighter's control yoke. "Ten vultures inbound, high and left to my orientation. More on the way."

"I have them. Anakin, wait—the cruiser's bay shields have dropped! I'm reading four, no, six ships incoming." Obi-Wan's voice rose. *"Tri-fighters! Coming in fast!"*

Anakin's smile tightened. This was about to get interesting.

"Tri-fighters first, Master. The vultures can wait."

"Agreed. Slip back and right, swing behind me. We'll take them on the slant."

Let Obi-Wan go first? With a blown left control surface and a half-crippled R-unit? With Palpatine's *life* at stake?

Not likely.

"Negative," Anakin said. "I'm going head-to-head. See you on the far side."

"Take it easy. Wait for Oddball and Squad Seven. Anakin—"

He could hear the frustration in Obi-Wan's voice as he kicked his starfighter's sublights and surged past; his former Master still hadn't gotten used to not being able to order Anakin around.

Not that Anakin had ever been much for following orders. Obi-Wan's, or anyone else's.

"Sorry we're late." The digitized voice of the clone whose call sign was Oddball sounded as calm as if he were ordering dinner. *"We're on your right, Red Leader. Where's Red Five?"*

"Anakin, form up!"

But Anakin was already streaking to meet the Trade Federation fighters. "Incoming!"

Obi-Wan's familiar sigh came clearly over the comm; Anakin knew exactly what the Jedi Master was thinking. The same thing he was *always* thinking.

He still has much to learn.

Anakin's smile thinned to a grim straight line as enemy starfighters swarmed around him. And he thought the same thing *he* always thought.

We'll see about that.

He gave himself to the battle, and his starfighter whirled and his cannons hammered, and droids on all sides began to burst into clouds of debris and superheated gas.

This was how *he* relaxed.

This is Anakin Skywalker:

The most powerful Jedi of his generation. Perhaps of any generation. The fastest. The strongest. An unbeatable pilot. An unstoppable warrior. On the ground, in the air or sea or space, there is no one even close. He has not just power, not just skill, but *dash:* that rare, invaluable combination of boldness and grace.

He is the best there is at what he does. The best there has ever been. And he knows it.

HoloNet features call him the Hero With No Fear. And why not? What should he be afraid of?

Except—

Fear lives inside him anyway, chewing away the firewalls around his heart.

Anakin sometimes thinks of the dread that eats at his heart as a dragon. Children on Tatooine tell each other of the dragons that live inside the suns; smaller cousins of the sun-dragons are supposed to live inside the fusion furnaces that power everything from starships to Podracers.

But Anakin's fear is another kind of dragon. A cold kind. A dead kind.

Not nearly dead enough.

Not long after he became Obi-Wan's Padawan, all those years ago, a minor mission had brought them to a dead system: one so immeasurably old that its star had long ago turned to a frigid dwarf of hypercompacted trace metals, hovering a quantum fraction of a degree above absolute zero. Anakin couldn't even remember what the mission might have been, but he'd never forgotten that dead star.

It had scared him.

"*Stars* can *die*—?"

"It is the way of the universe, which is another manner of saying that it is the will of the Force," Obi-Wan had told him. "Everything dies. In time, even stars burn out. This is why Jedi form no attachments: all things pass. To hold on to something— or someone—beyond its time is to set your selfish desires against the Force. That is a path of misery, Anakin; the Jedi do not walk it."

That is the kind of fear that lives inside Anakin Skywalker: the dragon of that dead star. It is an ancient, cold dead voice within his heart that whispers *all things die* . . .

In bright day he can't hear it; battle, a mission, even a report before the Jedi Council, can make him forget it's even there. But at night—

At night, the walls he has built sometimes start to frost over. Sometimes they start to crack.

At night, the dead-star dragon sometimes sneaks through the cracks and crawls up into his brain and chews at the inside of his skull. The dragon whispers of what Anakin has lost. And what he will lose.

The dragon reminds him, every night, of how he held his dying mother in his arms, of how she had spent her last strength to say *I knew you would come for me, Anakin . . .*

The dragon reminds him, every night, that someday he will lose Obi-Wan. He will lose Padmé. Or they will lose him.

All things die, Anakin Skywalker. Even stars burn out . . .

And the only answers he ever has for these dead cold whispers are his memories of Obi-Wan's voice, or Yoda's.

But sometimes he can't quite remember them.

all things die . . .

He can barely even think about it.

But right now he doesn't have a choice: the man he flies to rescue is a closer friend than he'd ever hoped to have. That's what puts the edge in his voice when he tries to make a joke; that's what flattens his mouth and tightens the burn-scar high on his right cheek.

The Supreme Chancellor has been family to Anakin: always there, always caring, always free with advice and unstinting aid. A sympathetic ear and a kindly, loving, unconditional acceptance of Anakin exactly as he is—the sort of acceptance Anakin could never get from another Jedi. Not even from Obi-Wan. He can tell Palpatine things he could never share with his Master.

He can tell Palpatine things he can't even tell Padmé.

Now the Supreme Chancellor is in the worst kind of danger. And Anakin is on his way despite the dread boiling through his blood. That's what makes him a real hero. Not the way the HoloNet labels him; not without fear, but *stronger* than fear.

He looks the dragon in the eye and doesn't even slow down.

If anyone can save Palpatine, Anakin will. Because he's already the best, and he's still getting better. But locked away behind the walls of his heart, the dragon that is his fear coils and squirms and hisses.

Because his real fear, in a universe where even stars can die, is that being the best will never be quite good enough.

Obi-Wan's starfighter jolted sideways. Anakin whipped by him and used his forward attitude jets to kick himself into a skew-flip: facing backward to blast the last of the tri-fighters on his tail. Now there were only vulture droids left.

A *lot* of vulture droids.

"Did you like that one, Master?"

"Very pretty." Obi-Wan's cannons stitched plasma across the hull of a swooping vulture fighter until the droid exploded. "But we're not through yet."

"Watch this." Anakin flipped his starfighter again and dived, spinning, directly through the flock of vulture droids. Their drives blazed as they came around. He led them streaking for the upper deck of a laser-scarred Separatist cruiser. *"I'm going to lead them through the needle."*

"Don't lead them anywhere." Obi-Wan's threat display tallied the vultures on Anakin's tail. Twelve of them. *Twelve.* "First Jedi principle of combat: survive."

"No choice." Anakin slipped his starfighter through the storm of cannonfire. *"Come down and thin them out a little."*

Obi-Wan slammed his control yoke forward as though jamming it against its impact-rest would push his battered fighter faster in pursuit. "Nothing fancy, Arfour." As though the damaged droid were even capable of anything fancy. "Just hold me steady."

He reached into the Force and felt for his shot. "On my mark, break left—*now!*" The shutdown control surface of his left wing turned the left break into a tight overhead spiral that traversed Obi-Wan's guns across the paths of four vultures—

flash flash flash flash

—and all four were gone.

He flew on through the clouds of glowing plasma. He couldn't waste time going around; Anakin still had eight of them on his tail.

And what was this? Obi-Wan frowned.

The cruiser looked familiar.

The needle? he thought. *Oh, please say you're kidding.*

* * *

Anakin's starfighter skimmed only meters above the cruiser's dorsal hull. Cannon misses from the vulture fighters swooping toward him blasted chunks out of the cruiser's armor.

"Okay, Artoo. Where's that trench?"

His forward screen lit with a topograph of the cruiser's hull. Just ahead lay the trench that Obi-Wan had led the tri-fighter into. Anakin flipped his starfighter through a razor-sharp wingover down past the rim. The walls of the service trench flashed past him as he streaked for the bridge tower at the far end. From here, he couldn't even see the minuscule slit between its support struts.

With eight vulture droids in pursuit, he'd never pull off a slant up the tower's leading edge as Obi-Wan had. But that was all right.

He wasn't planning to.

His cockpit comm buzzed. *"Don't try it, Anakin. It's too tight."*

Too tight for you, maybe. "I'll get through."

R2-D2 whistled nervous agreement with Obi-Wan.

"Easy, Artoo," Anakin said. "We've done this before."

Cannonfire blazed past him, impacting on the support struts ahead. Too late to change his mind now: he was committed. He would bring his ship through, or he would die.

Right now, strangely, he didn't actually care which.

"Use the Force." Obi-Wan sounded worried. *"Think* yourself *through, and the ship will follow."*

"What do you expect me to do? Close my eyes and whistle?" Anakin muttered under his breath, then said aloud, "Copy that. Thinking now."

R2-D2's squeal was as close to terrified as a droid can sound. Glowing letters spidered across Anakin's readout: ABORT! ABORT ABORT!

Anakin smiled. "Wrong thought."

Obi-Wan could only stare openmouthed as Anakin's starfighter snapped onto its side and scraped through the slit with centimeters to spare. He fully expected one of the struts to knock R2's dome off.

The vulture droids tried to follow . . . but they were just a hair too big.

When the first two impacted, Obi-Wan triggered his cannons in a downward sweep. The evasion maneuvers preprogrammed into the vulture fighters' droid brains sent them diving away from Obi-Wan's lasers—straight into the fireball expanding from the front of the struts.

Obi-Wan looked up to find Anakin soaring straight out from the cruiser with a quick snap-roll of victory. Obi-Wan matched his course—without the flourish.

"I'll give you the first four," Anakin said over the comm, *"but the other eight are mine."*

"Anakin—"

"All right, we'll split them."

As they left the cruiser behind, their sensors showed Squad Seven dead ahead. The clone pilots were fully engaged, looping through a dogfight so tight that their ion trails looked like a glowing ball of string.

"Oddball's in trouble. I'm going to help him out."

"Don't. He's doing his job. We need to do ours."

"Master, they're getting eaten alive over—"

"Every one of them would gladly trade his life for Palpatine's. Will you trade Palpatine's life for theirs?"

"No—no, of course not, but—"

"Anakin, I understand: you want to save everyone. You always do. But you *can't*."

Anakin's voice went tight. *"Don't remind me."*

"Head for the command ship." Without waiting for a reply, Obi-Wan targeted the command cruiser and shot away at maximum thrust.

The cross of burn-scar beside Anakin's eye went pale as he turned his starfighter in pursuit. Obi-Wan was right. He almost always was.

You can't save everyone

His mother's body, broken and bloody in his arms—

Her battered eyes struggling to open—

The touch of her smashed lips—

I knew you would come to me . . . I missed you so much . . .

That's what it was to be not quite good enough.

It could happen anytime. Anyplace. If he was a few minutes late. If he let his attention drift for a single second. If he was a whisker too weak.

Anyplace. Anytime.

But not here, and not now.

He forced his mother's face back down below the surface of his consciousness.

Time to get to work.

They flashed through the battle, dodging flak and turbolaser bolts, slipping around cruisers to eclipse themselves from the sensors of droid fighters. They were only a few dozen kilometers from the command cruiser when a pair of tri-fighters whipped across their path, firing on the deflection.

Anakin's sensor board lit up and R2-D2 shrilled a warning. "Missiles!"

He wasn't worried for himself: the two on his tail were coming at him in perfect tandem. Missiles lack the sophisticated brains of droid fighters; to keep them from colliding on their inbound vectors, one of them would lock onto his fighter's left drive, the other onto his right. A quick snap-roll would make those vectors intersect.

Which they did in a silent blossom of flame.

Obi-Wan wasn't so lucky. The pair of missiles locked onto his sublights weren't precisely side by side; a snap-roll would be worse than useless. Instead he fired retros and kicked his dorsal jets to halve his velocity and knock him a few meters planetward. The lead missile overshot and spiraled off into the orbital battle.

The trailing missile came close enough to trigger its proximity sensors, and detonated in a spray of glowing shrapnel. Obi-Wan's starfighter flew through the debris—and the shrapnel *tracked* him.

Little silver spheres flipped themselves into his path and latched onto the starfighter's skin, then split and sprouted spidery arrays of jointed arms that pried up hull plates, exposing the starfighter's internal works to multiple circular whirls of blade like ancient mechanical bone saws.

This was a problem.

"I'm hit." Obi-Wan sounded more irritated than concerned. *"I'm hit."*

"I have visual." Anakin swung his starfighter into closer pursuit. "Buzz droids. I count five."

"Get out of here, Anakin. There's nothing you can do."

"I'm not leaving you, Master."

Cascades of sparks fountained into space from the buzz droids' saws. *"Anakin, the mission! Get to the command ship! Get the Chancellor!"*

"Not without you," Anakin said through his teeth.

One of the buzz droids crouched beside the cockpit, silvery arms grappling with R4; another worked on the starfighter's nose, while a third skittered toward the ventral hydraulics. The last two of the aggressive little mechs had spidered to Obi-Wan's left wing, working on that damaged control surface.

"You can't help me." Obi-Wan still maintained his Jedi calm. *"They're shutting down the controls."*

"I can fix that . . ." Anakin brought his starfighter into line only a couple of meters off Obi-Wan's wing. "Steady . . . ," he muttered, "steady . . . ," and triggered a single burst of his right-side cannon that blasted the two buzz droids into gouts of molten metal.

Along with most of Obi-Wan's left wing.

Anakin said, "Whoops."

The starfighter bucked hard enough to knock Obi-Wan's skull against the transparisteel canopy. A gust of stinging smoke filled the cockpit. Obi-Wan fought the yoke to keep his starfighter out of an uncontrolled tumble. "Anakin, that's not *helping*."

"You're right, bad idea. Here, let's try this—move left and swing under—easy . . ."

"Anakin, you're too close! Wait—" Obi-Wan stared in disbelief as Anakin's starfighter edged closer and with a dip of its wing physically slammed a buzz droid into a smear of metal. The impact jolted Obi-Wan again, pounded a deep streak of dent into his starfighter's hull, and shattered the forward control surface of Anakin's wing.

Anakin had forgotten the first principle of combat. Again. As usual.

"You're going to get us both killed!"

His atmospheric scrubbers drained smoke from the cockpit, but now the droid on the forward control surface of Obi-Wan's starfighter's right wing had peeled away enough of the hull plates that its jointed saw arms could get deep inside. Sparks flared into space, along with an expanding fountain of gas that instantly crystallized in the hard vacuum. Velocity identical to Obi-Wan's, the shimmering gas hung on his starfighter's nose like a cloud of fog. "Blast," Obi-Wan muttered. "I can't see. My controls are going."

"You're doing fine. Stay on my wing."

Easier said than done. "I have to accelerate out of this."

"I'm with you. Go."

Obi-Wan eased power to his thrusters, and his starfighter parted the cloud, but new vapor boiled out to replace it as he went. "Is that last one still on my nose? Arfour, can you do anything?"

The only response he got came from Anakin. *"That's a negative on Arfour. Buzz droid got him."*

"It," Obi-Wan corrected automatically. "Wait—they attacked Arfour?"

"Not just Arfour. One of them jumped over when we hit."

Blast, Obi-Wan thought. *They* are *getting smarter.*

Through a gap torn in the cloud by the curve of his cockpit, Obi-Wan could see R2-D2 grappling with a buzz droid hand-to-hand. Well: saw-arm-to-saw-arm. Even flying blind and nearly out of control through the middle of a space battle, Obi-Wan could not avoid a second of disbelief at the bewildering variety of auxiliary tools and aftermarket behaviors Anakin had tinkered onto his starfighter's astromech, even beyond the sophisticated upgrades performed by the Royal Engineers of Naboo. The little device was virtually a partner in its own right.

R2's saw cut through one of the buzz droid's grapplers, sending the jointed arm flipping lazily off into space. Then it did the same to another. Then a panel opened in R2-D2's side and its datajack arm stabbed out and smacked the crippled buzz droid right off Anakin's hull. The buzz droid spun aft until it was caught in the blast wash of Anakin's sublights then blew away faster than even Obi-Wan's eye could follow.

Obi-Wan reflected that the Separatist droids weren't the only ones that were getting smarter.

The datajack retracted and a different panel opened, this time in R2-D2's dome. A claw-cable shot from it into the cloud of gas that still billowed from Obi-Wan's right forward wing, and pulled back out dragging a struggling buzz droid. The silver droid twisted and squirmed and its grapplers took hold of the cable, climbing back along it, saw arms waving, until Anakin popped the starfighter's underjets and R2 cut the cable and the buzz droid dropped away, tumbling helplessly through the battle.

"You know," Obi-Wan said, "I begin to understand why you speak of Artoo as though he's a living creature."

"Do you?" He could hear Anakin's smile. *"Don't you mean, it?"*

"Ah, yes." He frowned. "Yes, of course. It. Erm, thank it for me, will you?"

"Thank him yourself."

"Ah—yes. Thanks, Artoo."

The whistle that came back over the comm had a clear flavor of *you're welcome.*

Then the last of the fog finally dispersed, and the sky ahead was full of ship.

More than one kilometer from end to end, the vast command cruiser filled his visual field. At this range, all he could see were savannas of sand-colored hull studded with turbolaser mountains that lit up space with thunderbolts of disintegrating energy.

And that immense ship was getting bigger.

Fast.

"Anakin! We're going to collide!"

That's the plan. Head for the hangar.

"That's not—"

"I know: first Jedi principle of—"

"No. It's not going to *work*. Not for me."

"What?"

"My controls are gone. I can't head for *anything*."

"Oh. Well. All right, no problem."

"No *problem*?"

Then his starfighter clanged as if he'd crashed into a ship-sized gong.

Obi-Wan jerked and twisted his head around to find the other starfighter just above his tail. Literally just above: Anakin's left lead control surface was barely a hand span from Obi-Wan's sublight thrusters.

Anakin had *hit* him. On *purpose*.

Then he did it again.

CLANG

"What are you *doing*?"

"Just giving you . . ." Anakin's voice came slow, tight with concentration. *". . . a little help with your steering . . ."*

Obi-Wan shook his head. This was completely impossible. No other pilot would even attempt it. But for Anakin Skywalker, the completely impossible had an eerie way of being merely difficult.

He reflected that he should be used to it by now.

While these thoughts chased each other aimlessly through his mind, he had been staring bleakly at a blue shimmer of energy filling the yawning hangar bay ahead. Belatedly, he registered what he was looking at.

He thought, *Oh, this is bad.*

"Anakin—" Obi-Wan began. He tried rerouting control paths through his yoke. No luck.

Anakin drew up and tipped his forward surfaces down behind the sparking scrap that used to be Arfour.

"Anakin—!"

"Give me . . . just a second, Master." Anakin's voice had gone even tighter. A muffled thump, then another. Louder. And a scrape and a squeal of ripping metal. *"This isn't quite . . . as easy as it looks . . ."*

"Anakin!"

"What?"

"The hangar bay—"

"What about it?"

"Have you noticed that the *shield's still up*?"

"Really?"

"Really." Not to mention so close that Obi-Wan could practically *taste* it—

"Oh. Sorry. I've been busy."

Obi-Wan closed his eyes.

Reaching into the Force, his mind followed the starfighter's mangled circuitry to locate and activate the sublight engines' manual test board. With a slight push, he triggered a command normally used only in bench tests: full reverse.

The cometary tail of glowing debris shed by his disintegrating starfighter shot past him and evaporated in a cascade of miniature starbursts on contact with the hangar shield. Which was exactly what was about to happen to him.

The only effect of full reverse from his failing engines was to give him more time to see it coming.

Then Anakin's starfighter swooped in front of him, crossing left to right at a steep deflection. Energy flared from his cannons, and the shield emitters at the right side of the hangar door exploded into scrap. The blue shimmer of the bay shield flickered, faded, and vanished just as Obi-Wan came spinning across the threshold and slammed along the deck, trailing sparks and a scream of tortured metal.

His entire starfighter—what was left of it—vibrated with the roar of atmosphere howling out from the unshielded bay. Massive blast doors ground together like jaws. Another Force-touch on the manual test board cut power to his engines, but he couldn't trigger the explosive bolts on his cockpit canopy, and he had a bad feeling that those canopy bolts were the only thing on his craft that *weren't* about to explode.

His lightsaber found his hand and blue energy flared. One swipe and the canopy burst away, ripped into space by the hurricane of escaping air. Obi-Wan flipped himself up into the stunningly cold gale and let it blow him tumbling away as the remnants of his battered craft finally exploded.

He rode the shock wave while he let the Force right him in the air. He landed catfooted on the blackened streak—still hot enough to scorch his boots—that his landing had gouged into the deck.

The hangar was full of battle droids.

His shoulders dropped and his knees bent and his lightsaber came up to angle in front of his face. There were far too many for him to fight alone, but he didn't mind.

At least he was out of that blasted starfighter.

Anakin slipped his craft toward the hangar through a fountain of junk and flash-frozen gas. One last touch of the yoke twisted his starfighter through the closing teeth of the blast doors just as Obi-Wan's canopy went the other way.

Obi-Wan's ship was a hunk of glowing scrap punctuating a long smoking skid mark. Obi-Wan himself, beard rimed with frost, lightsaber out and flaming, stood in a tightening ring of battle droids.

Anakin slewed his starfighter into a landing that scattered droids with the particle blast from his sublight thrusters and for one second he was nine years old again, behind the controls of a starfighter in the Theed royal hangar, his first touch of a real ship's real cannons blasting battle droids—

He'd have done the same right here, except that Palpatine was somewhere on this ship. They just might need one of the light shuttles in this hangar to get the Chancellor safely to the surface; a few dozen cannon blasts bouncing around in here could wreck them all.

This he'd have to do by hand.

One touch blew his canopy and he sprang from the cockpit, flipping upward to stand on the wing. Battle droids opened fire instantly, and Anakin's lightsaber flashed. "Artoo, locate a computer link."

The little droid whistled at him, and Anakin allowed himself a tight smile. Sometimes he thought he could almost understand the droid's electrosonic code. "Don't worry about us. Find Palpatine. Go on, I'll cover you."

R2 popped out of its socket and bounced to the deck. Anakin jumped ahead of it into a cascade of blasterfire and let the Force direct his blade. Battle droids began to spark and collapse.

"Get to that link!" Anakin had to shout above the whine of blasters and the roar of exploding droids. "I'm going for Obi-Wan!"

"No need."

Anakin whirled to find Obi-Wan right behind him in the act of slicing neatly through the braincase of a battle droid.

"I appreciate the thought, Anakin," the Jedi Master said with a gentle smile. "But I've already come for you."

This, then, is Obi-Wan and Anakin:

They are closer than friends. Closer than brothers. Though Obi-Wan is sixteen standard years Anakin's elder, they have become men together. Neither can imagine life without the other. The war has forged their two lives into one.

The war that has done this is not the Clone Wars; Obi-Wan and Anakin's war began on Naboo, when Qui-Gon Jinn died at the hand of a Sith Lord. Master and Padawan and Jedi Knights together, they have fought this war for thirteen years. Their war is their life.

And their life is a weapon.

Say what you will about the wisdom of ancient Master Yoda, or the deadly skill of grim Mace Windu, the courage of Ki-Adi-Mundi, or the subtle wiles of Shaak Ti; the greatness of all these Jedi is unquestioned, but it pales next to the legend that has grown around Kenobi and Skywalker.

They stand alone.

Together, they are unstoppable. Unbeatable. They are the ultimate go-to guys of the Jedi Order. When the Good Guys absolutely, positively have to *win*, the call goes out.

Obi-Wan and Anakin always answer.

Whether Obi-Wan's legendary cleverness might beat Anakin's raw power, straight up, no rules, is the subject of schoolyard fist-fights, crèche-pool wriggle-matches, and pod-chamber stinkwars across the Republic. These struggles always end, somehow, with the combatants on both sides admitting that it doesn't matter.

Anakin and Obi-Wan would never fight each other.

They couldn't.

They're a team. They're *the* team.

And both of them are sure they always will be.

DOOKU

The storm of blasterfire ricocheting through the hangar bay suddenly ceased. Clusters of battle droids withdrew behind ships and slipped out hatchways.

Obi-Wan's familiar grimace showed past his blade as he let it shrink away. "I hate it when they do that."

Anakin's lightsaber was already back on his belt. "When they do what?"

"Disengage and fall back for no reason."

"There's always a reason, Master."

Obi-Wan nodded. "That's why I hate it."

Anakin looked at the litter of smoking droid parts scattered throughout the hangar bay, shrugged, and snugged his black glove. "Artoo, where's the Chancellor?"

The little droid's datajack rotated in the wall socket. Its holo-projector eye swiveled and the blue scanning laser built a ghostly image near Anakin's boot: Palpatine shackled into a large swivel chair. Even in the tiny translucent blur, he looked exhausted and in pain—but alive.

Anakin's heart thumped once, painfully, against his ribs. He wasn't too late. Not this time.

He dropped to one knee and squinted at the image. Palpatine looked as if he'd aged ten years since Anakin had last seen him. Muscle bulged along the young Jedi's jaw. If Grievous had hurt the Chancellor—had so much as *touched* him—

The hand of jointed durasteel inside his black glove clenched so hard that electronic feedback made his shoulder ache.

Obi-Wan spoke from over that shoulder. "Do you have a location?"

The image rippled and twisted into a schematic map of the cruiser. Far up at the top of the conning spire R2 showed a pulsar of brighter blue.

"In the General's Quarters." Obi-Wan scowled. "Any sign of Grievous himself?"

The pulsar shifted to the cruiser's bridge.

"Hmm. And guards?"

The holoimage rippled again, and transformed into an image of the cruiser's General's Quarters once more. Palpatine appeared to be alone: the chair sat in the center of an arc of empty floor, facing a huge curved viewing wall.

Anakin muttered, "That doesn't make *sense*."

"Of course it does. It's a trap."

Anakin barely heard him. He stared down at his black-gloved fist. He opened his fist, closed it, opened it again. The ache from his shoulder flowed down to the middle of his bicep—

And didn't stop.

His elbow sizzled, and his forearm; his wrist had been packed with red-hot gravel, and his hand—

His hand was on *fire*.

But it wasn't *his* hand. Or his wrist, or his forearm, or his elbow. It was a creation of jointed durasteel and electrodrivers.

"Anakin?"

Anakin's lips drew back from his teeth. "It hurts."

"What, your replacement arm? When did you have it equipped with pain sensors?"

"I *didn't*. That's the *point*."

"The pain is in your mind, Anakin—"

"No." Anakin's heart froze over. His voice went cold as space. "I can feel him."

"Him?"

"Dooku. He's here. Here on this ship."

"Ah." Obi-Wan nodded. "I'm sure he is."

"You *knew*?"

"I guessed. Do you think Grievous couldn't have found Palpatine's beacon? It can hardly be accident that through all the ECM, the Chancellor's homing signal was in the clear. This is a trap. A Jedi trap." Obi-Wan laid a warm hand upon Anakin's shoulder, and his face was as grim as Anakin had ever seen it. "Possibly a trap set for us. Personally."

Anakin's jaw tightened. "You're thinking of how he tried to recruit you on Geonosis. Before he sent you down for execution."

"It's not impossible that we will again face that choice."

"It's not a choice." Anakin rose. His durasteel hand clenched and stayed that way, a centimeter from his lightsaber. "Let him ask. My answer is right here on my belt."

"Be mindful, Anakin. The Chancellor's safety is our only priority."

"Yes—yes, of course." The ice in Anakin's chest thawed. "All right, it's a trap. Next move?"

Obi-Wan allowed himself a bit of a smile of his own as he headed for the nearest exit from the hangar bay. "Same as always, my young friend: we spring it."

"I can work with this plan." Anakin turned to his astromech. "You stay here, Artoo—"

The little droid interrupted him with a wheedling whirr.

"No arguments. Stay. I mean it."

R2-D2's whistling reply had a distinctly sulky tone.

"Listen, Artoo, someone has to maintain computer contact; do you see a datajack anywhere on *me*?"

The droid seemed to acquiesce, but not before wheeping what sounded like it might have been a suggestion where to look.

Waiting by the open hatchway, Obi-Wan shook his head. "Honestly, the way you talk to that thing."

Anakin started toward him. "Careful, Master, you'll hurt his feelings—" He stopped in his tracks, a curious look on his face as if he was trying to frown and to smile at the same time.

"Anakin?"

He didn't answer. He couldn't answer. He was looking at an image inside his head. Not an image. A reality.

A memory of something that hadn't happened yet.

He saw Count Dooku on his knees. He saw lightsabers crossed at the Count's throat.

Clouds lifted from his heart: clouds of Jabiim, of Aargonar, of Kamino, of even the Tusken camp. For the first time in too many years he felt young: as young as he really was.

Young, and free, and full of light.

"Master . . ." His voice seemed to be coming from someone else. Someone who hadn't seen what he'd seen. Hadn't done what he'd done. "Master, right here—right now—you and I . . ."

"Yes?"

He blinked. "I think we're about to win the war."

The vast semisphere of the view wall bloomed with battle. Sophisticated sensor algorithms compressed the combat that sprawled throughout the galactic capital's orbit to a view the naked eye could enjoy: cruisers hundreds of kilometers apart, exchanging fire at near lightspeed, appeared to be practically hull-to-hull, joined by pulsing cables of flame. Turbolaser blasts became swift shafts of light that shattered into prismatic splinters against shields, or bloomed into miniature supernovae that swallowed ships whole. The invisible gnat-clouds of starfighter dogfights became a gleaming dance of shadowmoths at the end of Coruscant's brief spring.

Within that immense curve of computer-filtered carnage, the only furnishing was one lone chair, centered in an expanse of empty floor. This was called the General's Chair, just as this apartment atop the flagship's conning spire was called the General's Quarters.

With his back to that chair and to the man shackled within it,

corrigibly untidy affairs of ordinary beings refuse to conform to the plainly obvious structure of How Society Ought To Be.

He is entirely incapable of caring what any given creature might feel for him. He cares only what that creature might do for him. Or to him.

Very possibly, he is what he is because other beings just aren't very . . . interesting.

Or even, in a sense, entirely real.

For Dooku, other beings are mostly abstractions, simple schematic sketches who fall into two essential categories. The first category is Assets: beings who can be used to serve his various interests. Such as—for most of his life, and to some extent even now—the Jedi, particularly Mace Windu and Yoda, both of whom had regarded him as their friend for so long that it had effectively blinded them to the truth of his activities. And of course—for now—the Trade Federation, and the InterGalactic Banking Clan, the Techno Union, the Corporate Alliance, and the weapon lords of Geonosis. And even the common rabble of the galaxy, who exist largely to provide an audience of sufficient size to do justice to his grandeur.

The other category is Threats. In this second set, he numbers every sentient being he cannot include in the first.

There is no third category.

Someday there may be not even a second; being considered a Threat by Count Dooku is a death sentence. A death sentence he plans to pronounce, for example, on his current allies: the heads of the aforementioned Trade Federation, InterGalactic Banking Clan, Techno Union, and Corporate Alliance, and Geonosian weaponeers.

Treachery is the way of the Sith.

Count Dooku watched with clinical distaste as the blue-scanned images of Kenobi and Skywalker engaged in a preposterous farce-chase, pursued by destroyer droids into and out of turbolift pods that shot upward and downward and even sideways.

"It will be," he said slowly, meditatively, as though he spoke only to himself, "an embarrassment to be captured by him."

The voice that answered him was so familiar that sometimes his very thoughts spoke in it, instead of in his own. "An embarrassment you can survive, Lord Tyranus. After all, he is the greatest Jedi alive, is he not? And have we not ensured that all the galaxy shares this opinion?"

"Quite so, my Master. Quite so." Again, Dooku sighed. Today he felt every hour of his eighty-three years. "It is . . . fatiguing, to play the villain for so long, Master. I find myself looking forward to an honorable captivity."

A captivity that would allow him to sit out the rest of the war in comfort; a captivity that would allow him to forswear his former allegiances—when he would conveniently appear to finally discover the true extent of the Separatists' crimes against civilization—and bind himself to the *new* government with his reputation for integrity and idealism fully intact.

The new government . . .

This had been their star of destiny for lo, these many years.

A government clean, pure, direct: none of the messy scramble for the favor of ignorant rabble and subhuman creatures that made up the Republic he so despised. The government he would serve would be Authority personified.

Human authority.

It was no accident that the primary powers of the Confederacy of Independent Systems were Neimoidian, Skakoan, Quarren and Aqualish, Muun and Gossam, Sy Myrthian and Koorivar and Geonosian. At war's end the aliens would be crushed, stripped of all they possessed, and their systems and their wealth would be given into the hands of the only beings who could be trusted with them.

Human beings.

Dooku would serve an Empire of Man.

And he would serve it as only he could. As he was *born* to. He would smash the Jedi Order to create it anew: not shackled by the corrupt, narcissistic, shabby little beings who called themselves politicians, but free to bring true authority and true peace to a galaxy that so badly needed both.

An Order that would not negotiate. Would not mediate.

An Order that would *enforce*.

The survivors of the Jedi Order would become the Sith Army.

The Fist of the Empire.

And that Fist would become a power beyond any Jedi's darkest dreams. The Jedi were not the only users of the Force in the galaxy; from Hapes to Haruun Kal, from Kiffu to Dathomir, powerful Force-capable humans and near-humans had long refused to surrender their children to lifelong bound servitude in the Jedi Order. They would not so refuse the Sith Army.

They would not have the choice.

Dooku frowned down at the holoimage. Kenobi and Skywalker were going through more low-comedy business with another balky turbolift—possibly Grievous having some fun with the shaft controls—while battle droids haplessly pursued.

Really, it was all so . . .

Undignified.

"May I suggest, Master, that we give Kenobi one last chance? The support of a Jedi of his integrity would be invaluable in establishing the political legitimacy of our Empire."

"Ah, yes. Kenobi." His Master's voice went silken. "You have long been interested in Kenobi, haven't you?"

"Of course. His Master was my Padawan; in a sense, he's practically my grandson—"

"He is too old. Too indoctrinated. Irretrievably poisoned by Jedi fables. We established that on Geonosis, did we not? In his mind, he serves the Force itself; reality is nothing in the face of such conviction."

Dooku sighed. He should, he supposed, have no difficulty

with this, having ordered the Jedi Master's death once already. "True enough, I suppose; how fortunate we are that I never labored under any such illusions."

"Kenobi must die. Today. At your hand. His death may be the code key of the final lock that will seal Skywalker to us forever."

Dooku understood: not only would the death of his mentor tip Skywalker's already unstable emotional balance down the darkest of slopes, but it would also remove the greatest obstacle to Skywalker's successful conversion. As long as Kenobi was alive, Skywalker would never be securely in the camp of the Sith; Kenobi's unshakable faith in the values of the Jedi would keep the Jedi blindfold on Skywalker's eyes and the Jedi shackles on the young man's true power.

Still, though, Dooku had some reservations. This had all come about too quickly; had Sidious thought through all the implications of this operation? "But I must ask, my Master: is Skywalker truly the man we want?"

"He is powerful. Potentially more powerful than even myself."

"Which is precisely," Dooku said meditatively, "why it might be best if I were to kill *him,* instead."

"Are you so certain that you can?"

"Please. Of what use is power unstructured by discipline? The boy is as much a danger to himself as he is to his enemies. And that mechanical arm—" Dooku's lip curled with cultivated distaste. "Revolting."

"Then perhaps you should have spared his real arm."

"Hmp. A gentleman would have learned to fight one-handed." Dooku flicked a dismissive wave. "He's no longer even entirely human. With Grievous, the use of these bio-droid devices is almost forgivable; he was such a disgusting creature already that his mechanical parts are clearly an improvement. But a blend of droid and *human?* Appalling. The depths of bad taste. How are we to justify associating with him?"

"How fortunate I am"—the silk in his Master's voice softened further—"to have an apprentice who feels it is appropriate to *lecture* me."

Dooku lifted an eyebrow. "I have overstepped, my Master," he said with his customary grace. "I am only observing, not arguing. Not at all."

"Skywalker's arm makes him, for our purposes, even better. It is the permanent symbol of the sacrifices he has made in the name of peace and justice. It is a badge of heroism that he must publicly wear for the rest of his life; no one can ever look at him and doubt his honor, his courage, his integrity. He is perfect, just as he is. *Perfect.* The only question that remains is whether he is capable of transcending the artificial limitations of his Jedi indoctrination. And that, my lord Count, is precisely what today's operation is designed to discover."

Dooku could not argue. Not only had the Dark Lord introduced Dooku to realms of power beyond his most spectacular fantasies, but Sidious was also a political manipulator so subtle that his abilities might be considered to dwarf even the power of the dark side itself. It was said that whenever the Force closes a hatch, it opens a viewport . . . and every viewport that had so much as cracked in this past thirteen standard years had found a Dark Lord of the Sith already at the rim, peering in, calculating how best to slip through.

Improving upon his Master's plan was near to impossible; his own idea, of substituting Kenobi for Skywalker, he had to admit was only the product of a certain misplaced sentimentality. Skywalker was almost certainly the man for the job.

He should be; Darth Sidious had spent a considerable number of years making him so.

Today's test would remove the *almost.*

He had no doubt that Skywalker would fall. Dooku understood that this was more than a test for Skywalker; though Sidious had never said so directly, Dooku was certain that he himself was being tested as well. Success today would show his Master that he was worthy of the mantle of Mastery himself: by the end of the coming battle, he would have initiated Skywalker into the manifold glories of the dark side, just as Sidious had initiated him.

He gave no thought to failure. Why should he?

"But—forgive me, Master. But Kenobi having fallen to my blade, are you certain Skywalker will ever accept my orders? You must admit that his biography offers little confidence that he is capable of obedience at all."

"Skywalker's power brings with it more than mere obedience. It brings creativity, and luck; we need never concern ourselves with the sort of instruction that Grievous, for example, requires. Even the blind fools on the Jedi Council see clearly enough to understand this; even they no longer try to tell him *how*, they merely tell him *what*. And he finds a way. He always has."

Dooku nodded. For the first time since Sidious had revealed the true subtlety of this masterpiece, Dooku allowed himself to relax enough to imagine the outcome.

With his heroic capture of Count Dooku, Anakin Skywalker will become the ultimate hero: the greatest hero in the history of the Republic, perhaps of the Jedi Order itself. The loss of his beloved partner will add just exactly the correct spice of tragedy to give melancholy weight to his every word, when he gives his HoloNet interviews denouncing the Senate's corruption as impeding the war effort, when he delicately—oh, so delicately, not to mention *reluctantly*—insinuates that corruption in the Jedi Order prolonged the war as well.

When he announces the creation of a new order of Force-using warriors.

He will be the perfect commanding general for the Sith Army.

Dooku could only shake his head in awe. And to think that only days earlier, the Jedi had seemed so close to uncovering, even destroying, all he and his Master had worked for. But he should never have feared. His Master never lost. He would never lose. He was the definition of unbeatable.

How can one defeat an enemy one thinks is a friend?

And now, with a single brilliant stroke, his Master would turn the Jedi Order back upon itself like an Ethrani ourobouros devouring its own tail.

This was the day. The hour.

The death of Obi-Wan Kenobi would be the death of the Republic.

Today would see the birth of the Empire.

"Tyranus? Are you well?"

"Am I . . ." Dooku realized that his eyes had misted. "Yes, my Master. I am beyond well. Today, the climax—the grand finale—the culmination of all your decades of work . . . I find myself somewhat overcome."

"Compose yourself, Tyranus. Kenobi and Skywalker are nearly at the door. Play your part, my apprentice, and the galaxy is ours."

Dooku straightened and for the first time looked his Master in the eyes.

Darth Sidious, Dark Lord of the Sith, sat in the General's Chair, shackled to it at the wrist and ankle.

Dooku bowed to him. "Thank you, Chancellor."

Palpatine of Naboo, Supreme Chancellor of the Republic, replied, "Withdraw. They are here."

THE WAY OF THE SITH

The turbolift's door whished open. Anakin pressed himself against the wall, a litter of saber-sliced droid parts around his feet. Beyond appeared to be a perfectly ordinary lift lobby: pale and bare and empty.

Made it. At last.

Anakin's whole body hummed to the tune of his blue-hot blade.

"Anakin."

Obi-Wan stood against the opposite wall. He looked calm in a way Anakin could barely understand. He gave a significant stare down at the lightsaber in Anakin's hand. "Anakin, rescue," he said softly. "Not mayhem."

Anakin kept his weapon right where it was. "And Dooku?"

"Once the Chancellor is safe," Obi-Wan said with a ghost of a smile, "we can blow up the ship."

Anakin's mechanical fingers tightened until the grip of his lightsaber creaked. "I'd rather do it by hand."

Obi-Wan slipped cautiously through the turbolift's door. Nothing shot at him. He beckoned. "I know this is difficult, Anakin. I know it's personal for you on many levels. You must take extra care to be mindful of your training here—and not only your *combat* training."

Heat rose in Anakin's cheeks. "I am *not—*" *your Padawan anymore* snarled inside his head, but that was adrenaline talking; he bit back the words and said instead, "—going to let you down, Master. Or Chancellor Palpatine."

"I have no doubt of that. Just remember that Dooku is no mere Dark Jedi like that Ventress woman; he is a Lord of the Sith. The jaws of this trap are about to snap shut, and there may be danger here beyond the merely physical."

"Yes." Anakin let his blade shrink away and moved past Obi-Wan into the turbolift lobby. Distant concussions boomed throughout the ship, and the floor rocked like a raft on a river in flood; he barely noticed. "I just—there has been so much—what he's *done*—not just to the Jedi, but to the *galaxy*—"

"Anakin . . . ," Obi-Wan began warningly.

"Don't worry. I'm not angry, and I'm not looking for revenge. I'm just—" He lifted his lightsaber. "I'm just looking forward to ending it."

"Anticipation—"

"Is distraction. I know. And I know that hope is as hollow as fear." Anakin let himself smile, just a bit. "And I know everything else you're dying to tell me right now."

Obi-Wan's slightly rueful bow of acknowledgment was as affectionate as a hug. "I suppose at some point I will eventually have to stop trying to train you."

Anakin's smile broadened toward a soft chuckle. "I think that's the first time you've ever admitted it."

They stopped at the door to the General's Quarters: a huge oval of opalescent iridiite chased with gold. Anakin stared at his ghostly almost-reflection while he reached into the room beyond with the Force, and let the Force reach into him. "I'm ready, Master."

"I know you are."

They stood a moment, side by side.

Anakin didn't look at him; he stared into the door, through the door, searching in its shimmering depths for a hint of an unguessable future.

He couldn't imagine not being at war.

"Anakin." Obi-Wan's voice had gone soft, and his hand was warm on Anakin's arm. "There is no other Jedi I would rather have at my side right now. No other man."

Anakin turned, and found within Obi-Wan's eyes a depth of feeling he had only rarely glimpsed in all their years together; and the pure uncomplicated love that rose up within him then felt like a promise from the Force itself.

"I . . . wouldn't have it any other way, Master."

"I believe," his onetime Master said with a gently humorous look of astonishment at the words coming out of his mouth, "that you should get used to calling me Obi-Wan."

"Obi-Wan," Anakin said, "let's go get the Chancellor."

"Yes," Obi-Wan said. "Let's."

Inside a turbolift pod, Dooku watched hologrammic images of Kenobi and Skywalker cautiously pick their way down the curving stairs from the entrance balcony to the main level of the General's Quarters, moving slowly to stay braced against the pitching of the cruiser. The ship shuddered and bucked with multiple torpedo bursts, and the lights went out again; lighting was always the first to fail as power was diverted from life support to damage control.

"My lord." On the intraship comm, Grievous sounded actively concerned. *"Damage to this ship is becoming severe. Thirty percent of automated weapons systems are down, and we may soon lose hyperspace capability."*

Dooku nodded judiciously to himself, frowning down at the translucent blue ghosts slinking toward Palpatine. "Sound the retreat for the entire strike force, General, and prepare the ship for jump. Once the Jedi are dead, I will join you on the bridge."

"As my lord commands. Grievous out."

"Indeed you are, you vile creature," Dooku muttered to the dead comlink. "Out of luck, and out of time."

He cast the comlink aside and ignored its clatter across the deck. He had no further use for it. Let it be destroyed along with Grievous, those repulsive bodyguards of his, and the rest of the cruiser, once he was safely captured and away.

He nodded to the two hulking super battle droids that flanked him. One opened the lift door and they marched through, pivoting to take positions on either side.

Dooku straightened his cloak of shimmering armorweave and strode grandly into the half-dark lift lobby. In the pale emergency lighting, the door to the General's Quarters still smoldered where those two idiotic peasants had lightsabered it; to pick his way through the hole would risk getting his trousers scorched. Dooku sighed and gestured, and the opalescent wreckage of the door silently slid itself out of his way.

He certainly did not intend to fight two Jedi with his pants on fire.

Anakin slid along the bank of chairs on one side of the immense situation table that dominated the center of the General's Quarters' main room; Obi-Wan mirrored him on the opposite side. Silent lightning flashed and flared: the room's sole illumination came from the huge curving view wall at its far end, a storm of turbolaser blasts and flak bursts and the miniature supernovae that were the deaths of entire ships.

A stark shadow against that backdrop of carnage: the silhouette of one tall chair.

Anakin caught Obi-Wan's eye across the table and nodded toward the dark shape ahead. Obi-Wan replied with the Jedi hand signal for *approach with caution*, and added the signal for *be ready for action*.

Anakin's mouth compressed. Like he needed to be told. After all the trouble they'd had with the turbolifts, anything could be up here by now. The place could be full of droidekas, for all they knew.

The lights came back on.

Anakin froze.

The dark figure in the chair—it *was* Chancellor Palpatine, it was, and there were no droids to be seen, and his heart should have leapt within his chest, but—

Palpatine looked bad.

The Chancellor looked beyond old, looked ancient like Yoda was ancient: possessed of incomprehensible age. And exhausted, and in pain. And worse—

Anakin saw in the Chancellor's face something he'd never dreamed he'd find there, and it squeezed breath from his lungs and wiped words from his brain.

Palpatine looked *frightened*.

Anakin didn't know what to say. He couldn't *imagine* what to say. All he could imagine was what Grievous and Dooku must have done to put fear on the face of this brave good man—

And that imagining ignited a sizzle in his blood that drew his face tight and clouded his heart and started again the low roll of thunder in his ears: thunder from Aargonar. From Jabiim.

Thunder from the Tusken camp.

If Obi-Wan was struck by any similar distress, it was invisible. With his customary grave courtesy, the Jedi Master inclined his head. "Chancellor," he said, a calmly respectful greeting as though they had met by chance on the Grand Concourse of the Galactic Senate.

Palpatine's only response was a tight murmur. "Anakin, *behind* you—!"

Anakin didn't turn. He didn't have to. It wasn't just the clack of boot heels and clank of magnapeds crossing the threshold of the entrance balcony; the Force gathered within him and around him in a sudden clench like the fists of a startled man.

In the Force, he could feel the focus of Palpatine's eyes: the source of the fear that rolled off him in billows like vapor down a block of frozen air. And he could feel the even colder wave of power, colder than the frost on a mynock's mouth, that slid into the room behind him like an ice dagger into his back.

Funny, he thought. *After Ventress, somehow I always expect the dark side to be hot . . .*

Something unlocked in his chest. The thunder in his ears dissolved into red smoke that coiled at the base of his spine. His lightsaber found his hand, and his lips peeled off his teeth in a smile that a krayt dragon would have recognized.

That trouble he was having with talking went away.

"This," he murmured to Palpatine, and to himself, "is not a problem."

The voice that spoke from the entrance balcony was an elegant basso with undernotes of oily resonance like a kriin-oak cavernhorn.

Count Dooku's voice.

"General Kenobi. Anakin Skywalker. Gentlemen—a term I use in its loosest possible sense—you are my prisoners."

Now Anakin didn't have any troubles at all.

The entrance balcony provided an appropriate angle—far above the Jedi, looking down upon them—for Dooku to make final assessments before beginning the farce.

Like all true farce, the coming denouement would proceed with remorseless logic from its ridiculous premise: that Dooku could ever be overcome by mere Jedi. Any Jedi. What a pity his old friend Mace couldn't have joined them today; he had no doubt the Korun Master would have enjoyed the coming show.

Dooku had always preferred an educated audience.

At least Palpatine was here, shackled within the great chair at the far end of the room, the space battle whirling upon the view wall behind him as though his stark silhouette spread great wings of war. But Palpatine was less audience than he was author.

Not at all the same thing.

Skywalker gave Dooku only his back, but his blade was already out and his tall, lean frame stood frozen with anticipation: so motionless he almost seemed to shiver. Pathetic. It was an insult to call this boy a Jedi at all.

Kenobi, now—he was something else entirely: a classic of his obsolete kind. He simply stood gazing calmly up at Dooku and the super battle droids that flanked him, hands open, utterly relaxed, on his face only an expression of mild interest.

Dooku derived a certain melancholy satisfaction—a pleasurably lonely contemplation of his own unrecognized greatness—from a brief reflection that Skywalker would never understand how much thought and planning, how much *work,* Lord Sidious had invested in so hastily orchestrating his sham victory. Nor would he ever understand the artistry, the true mastery, that Dooku would wield in his own defeat.

But thus was life. Sacrifices must be made, for the greater good.

There was a war on, after all.

He called upon the Force, gathering it to himself and wrapping himself within it. He breathed it in and held it whirling inside his heart, clenching down upon it until he could feel the spin of the galaxy around him.

Until he became the axis of the Universe.

This was the real power of the dark side, the power he had suspected even as a boy, had sought through his long life until Darth Sidious had shown him that it had been his all along. The dark side didn't bring him to the center of the universe. It *made* him the center.

He drew power into his innermost being until the Force itself existed only to serve his will.

Now the scene below subtly altered, though to the physical eye there was no change. Powered by the dark side, Dooku's perception took the measure of those below him with exhilarating precision.

Kenobi was luminous, a transparent being, a window onto a sunlit meadow of the Force.

Skywalker was a storm cloud, flickering with dangerous lightning, building the rotation that threatens a tornado.

And then there was Palpatine, of course: he was beyond power. He showed nothing of what might be within. Though seen with the eyes of the dark side itself, Palpatine was an event horizon. Beneath his entirely ordinary surface was absolute, perfect nothingness. Darkness beyond darkness.

A black hole of the Force.

And he played his helpless-hostage role perfectly.

"Get help!" The edge of panic in his hoarse half whisper sounded real even to Dooku. "You *must* get help. Neither of you is any match for a Sith Lord!"

Now Skywalker turned, meeting Dooku's direct gaze for the first time since the abandoned hangar on Geonosis. His reply was clearly intended as much for Dooku as for Palpatine. "Tell that to the one Obi-Wan left in pieces on Naboo."

Hmp. Empty bravado. Maul had been an animal. A skilled animal, but a beast nonetheless.

"Anakin—" In the Force, Dooku could feel Kenobi's disapproval of Skywalker's boasting; and he could also feel Kenobi's effortless self-restraint in focusing on the matter at hand. "This time, we do it *together.*"

Dooku's sharp eye picked up the tightening of Skywalker's droid hand on his lightsaber's grip. "I was about to say exactly that."

Fine, then. Time to move this little comedy along.

Dooku leaned forward, and his cloak of armorweave spread like wings; he lifted gently into the air and descended to the main level in a slow, dignified Force-glide. Touching down at the head of the situation table, he regarded the two Jedi from under a lifted brow.

"Your weapons, please, gentlemen. Let's not make a mess of this in front of the Chancellor."

Obi-Wan lifted his lightsaber into the balanced two-handed guard of Ataro: Qui-Gon's style, and Yoda's. His blade crackled into existence, and the air smelled of lightning. "You won't escape us this time, Dooku."

"Escape you? Please." Dooku allowed his customary mild smile to spread. "Do you think I orchestrated this entire operation with the intent to *escape*? I could have taken the Chancellor outsystem hours ago. But I have better things to do with my life than to babysit him while I wait for the pair of you to attempt a rescue."

Skywalker brought his lightsaber to a Shien ready: hand of black-gloved durasteel cocked high at his shoulder, blade angling upward and away. "This is a little more than an attempt."

"And a little less than a rescue."

With a flourish, Dooku cast his cloak back from his right shoulder, clearing his sword arm—which he used to gesture idly at the pair of super battle droids still on the entrance balcony above. "Now please, gentlemen. Must I order the droids to open fire? That becomes so untidy, what with blaster bolts bouncing about at random. Little danger to the three of us, of course, but I should certainly hate for any harm to come to the Chancellor."

Kenobi moved toward him with a slow, hypnotic grace, as though he floated on an invisible repulsor plate. "Why do I find that difficult to believe?"

Skywalker mirrored him, swinging wide toward Dooku's flank. "You weren't so particular about bloodshed on Geonosis."

"Ah." Dooku's smile spread even farther. "And how *is* Senator Amidala?"

"Don't—" The thunderstorm that was Skywalker in the Force boiled with sudden power. "Don't even speak her name."

Dooku waved this aside. The lad's personal issues were too tiresome to pursue; he knew far too much already about Skywalker's messy private life. "I bear Chancellor Palpatine no ill will, foolish boy. He is neither soldier nor spy, whereas you and your friend here are both. It is only an unfortunate accident of history that he has chosen to defend a corrupt Republic against my endeavor to reform it."

"You mean *destroy* it."

"The Chancellor is a civilian. You and General Kenobi, on the other hand, are legitimate military targets. It is up to you whether you will accompany me as captives—" A twitch of the Force brought his lightsaber to his hand with invisible speed, its brilliant scarlet blade angled downward at his side. "—or as *corpses.*"

"Now, there's a coincidence," Kenobi replied dryly as he swung around Dooku to place the Count precisely between Skywalker and himself. "You face the identical choice."

Dooku regarded each of them in turn with impregnable calm. He lifted his blade in the Makashi salute and swept it again to a low guard. "Just because there are two of you, do not presume you have the advantage."

"Oh, we know," Skywalker said. "Because there are two of *you.*"

Dooku barely managed to restrain a jolt of surprise.

"Or maybe I should say, *were* two of you," the young Jedi went on. "We're on to your partner *Sidious;* we tracked him all over the galaxy. He's probably in Jedi custody right now."

"Is he?" Dooku relaxed. He was terribly, terribly tempted to wink at Palpatine, but of course that would never do. "How fortunate for you."

Quite simple, in the end, he thought. *Isolate Skywalker, slaughter Kenobi.* Beyond that, it would be merely a matter of spinning Skywalker up into enough of a frenzy to break through his Jedi restraint and reveal the infinite vista of Sith power.

Lord Sidious would take it from there.

"Surrender." Kenobi's voice deepened into finality. "You will be given no further chance."

Dooku lifted an eyebrow. "Unless one of you happens to be carrying Yoda in his pocket, I hardly think I shall need one."

The Force crackled between them, and the ship pitched and bucked under a new turbolaser barrage, and Dooku decided that the time had come. He flicked a false glance over his shoulder— a hint of distraction to draw the attack—

And all three of them moved at once.

The ship shuddered and the red smoke surged from Anakin's spine into his arms and legs and head and when Dooku gave the slightest glance of concern over his shoulder, distracted for half an instant, Anakin just couldn't wait anymore.

He sprang, lightsaber angled for the kill.

Obi-Wan leapt from Dooku's far side in perfect coordination—and they met in midair, for the Sith Lord was no longer between them.

Anakin looked up just in time to glimpse the bottom of Dooku's rancor-leather boot as it came down on his face and smacked him tumbling toward the floor; he reached into the Force to effortlessly right himself and touched down in perfect balance to spring again toward the lightning flares, scarlet against sky blue, that sprayed from clashing lightsabers as Dooku pressed Obi-Wan away with a succession of weaving, flourishing thrusts that drove the Jedi's blade out of line while they reached for his heart.

Anakin launched himself at Dooku's back—and the Count half turned, gesturing casually while holding Obi-Wan at bay with an elegant one-handed bind. Chairs leapt up from the situation table and whirled toward Anakin's head. He slashed the first one in half contemptuously, but the second caught him across the knees and the third battered his shoulder and knocked him down.

He snarled to himself and reached through the Force to pick up some chairs of his own—and the situation table itself slammed into him and drove him back to crush him against the wall. His lightsaber came loose from his slackening fingers and clattered across the tabletop to drop to the floor on the far side.

And Dooku barely even seemed to be paying attention to him.

Pinned, breathless, half stunned, Anakin thought, *If this keeps up, I am going to get mad.*

While effortlessly deflecting a rain of blue-streaking cuts from Kenobi, Dooku felt the Force shove the situation table away from the wall and send it hurtling toward his back with astonishing speed; he barely managed to lift himself enough that he could backroll over it instead of having it shatter his spine.

"My my," he said, chuckling. "The boy has some power after all."

His backroll brought him to his feet directly in front of the lad, who was charging, headlong and unarmed, after the table he had tossed, and was already thoroughly red in the face.

"I'm *twice* the Jedi I was last time!"

Ah, Dooku thought. *Such a fragile little ego. Sidious will have to help him with that. But until then—*

The grip of Skywalker's blade whistled through the air to meet his hand in perfect synchrony with a sweeping slash. "My powers have *doubled* since we last met—"

"How lovely for you." Dooku neatly sidestepped, cutting at the boy's leg, yet Skywalker's blade met the cut as he passed and he managed to sweep his blade behind his head to slap aside the casual thrust Dooku aimed at the back of his neck—but his clumsy charge had put him in Kenobi's path, so that the Jedi Master had to Force-roll over his partner's head.

Directly at Dooku's upraised blade.

Kenobi drove a slash at the scarlet blade while he pivoted in the air, and again Dooku sidestepped so that now it was Kenobi in Skywalker's way.

"Really," Dooku said, "this is pathetic."

Oh, they were certainly energetic enough, leaping and whirling, raining blows almost at random, cutting chairs to pieces and Force-hurling them in every conceivable direction, while Dooku continued, in his gracefully methodical way, to out-maneuver them so thoroughly it was all he could do to keep from laughing out loud.

It was a simple matter of countering their tactics, which were depressingly straightforward; Skywalker was the swift one, whooshing here and there like a spastic hawk-bat—attempting a Jedi variant of neek-in-the-middle so they could come at him from both sides—while Kenobi came on in a measured Shii-Cho cadence, deliberate as a lumberdroid, moving step by step, cutting off the angles, clumsy but relentlessly dogged as he tried to chivvy Dooku into a corner.

Whereas all Dooku need do was to slip from one side to another—and occasionally flip over a head here and there—so that he could fight each of them in turn, rather than both of them at the same time. He supposed that in their own milieu, they might actually prove reasonably effective; it was clear that their style had been developed by fighting as a team against large numbers of opponents. They were not prepared to fight together against a single Force-user, certainly not one of Dooku's power; he, on the other hand, had always fought alone. It was laughably easy to keep the Jedi tripping and stumbling and getting in each other's way.

They didn't even comprehend how utterly he dominated the combat. Because they fought as they had been trained, by releasing all desire and allowing the Force to flow through them, they had no hope of countering Dooku's mastery of Sith techniques. They had learned nothing since he had bested them on Geonosis.

They allowed the Force to direct them; Dooku directed the Force.

He drew their strikes to his parries, and drove his own ripostes with thrusts of dark power that subtly altered the Jedi's balance and disrupted their timing. He could have slaughtered both of them as casually as that creature Maul had destroyed the vigos of the Black Sun.

However, only one death was in his plan, and this dumbshow was becoming tiresome. Not to mention tiring. The dark power that served him went only so far, and he was, after all, not a young man.

He leaned into a thrust at Kenobi's gut that the Jedi Master deflected with a rising parry, bringing them chest-to-chest, blades flaring, locked together a handbreadth from each other's throats. "Your moves are too slow, Kenobi. Too predictable. You'll have to do better."

Kenobi's response to this friendly word was to regard him with a twinkle of gentle amusement in his eye.

"Very well, then," the Jedi said, and shot straight upward over Dooku's head so fast it seemed he'd vanished.

And in the space where Kenobi's chest had been was now only the blue lightning of Skywalker's blade driving straight for Dooku's heart.

Only a desperate whirl to one side made what would have been a smoking hole in his chest into a line of scorch through his armorweave cloak.

Dooku thought, *What?*

He threw himself spinning up and away from the two Jedi to land on the situation table, disengaging for a moment to recover his composure—that had been *entirely* too close—but by the time his boots touched down Kenobi was there to meet him, blade weaving through a defensive velocity so bewilderingly fast that Dooku dared not even try a strike; he threw a feint toward Kenobi's face, then dropped and spun in a reverse ankle-sweep—

But not only did Kenobi easily overleap this attack, Dooku nearly lost his *own* foot to a slash from *Skywalker* who had again come out of *nowhere* and now carved through the table so that it collapsed under Dooku's weight and dumped the Sith Lord unceremoniously to the floor.

This was *not* in the plan.

Skywalker slammed his following strike down so hard that the shock of deflecting it buckled Dooku's elbows. Dooku threw himself into a backroll that brought him to his feet—and Kenobi's blade was there to meet his neck. Only a desperate whirling slash-block, coupled with a wheel kick that caught Kenobi on the thigh, bought him enough time to leap away again, and when he touched down—

Skywalker was already there.

The first overhand chop of Skywalker's blade slid off Dooku's instinctive guard. The second bent Dooku's wrist. The third flash of blue forced Dooku's scarlet blade so far to the inside that his own lightsaber scorched his shoulder, and Dooku was forced to give ground.

Dooku felt himself blanch. Where had *this* come from?

Skywalker came on, mechanically inexorable, impossibly powerful, a destroyer droid with a lightsaber: each step a blow and each blow a step. Dooku backed away as fast as he dared; Skywalker stayed right on top of him. Dooku's breath went short and hard. He no longer tried to block Skywalker's strikes but only to guide them slanting away; he could not meet Skywalker strength-to-strength—not only did the boy wield tremendous reserves of Force energy, but his sheer physical power was astonishing—

And only then did Dooku understand that he'd been suckered.

Skywalker's Shien ready-stance had been a ruse, as had his Ataro gymmnastics; the boy was a Djem So stylist, and as fine a one as Dooku had ever seen. His own elegant Makashi simply did not generate the kinetic power to meet Djem So head-to-head. Especially not while also defending against a second attacker.

It was time to alter his own tactics.

He dropped low and spun into another reverse ankle-sweep—the weakness of Djem So was its lack of mobility—that slapped Skywalker's boot sharply enough to throw the young Jedi off balance, giving Dooku the opportunity to leap away—

Only to find himself again facing the wheel of blue lightning that was Kenobi's blade.

Dooku decided that the comedy had ended.

Now it was time to kill.

Kenobi's Master had been Qui-Gon Jinn, Dooku's own Padawan; Dooku had fenced Qui-Gon thousands of times, and he knew every weakness of the Ataro form, with its ridiculous acrobatics. He drove a series of flashing thrusts toward Kenobi's legs to draw the Jedi Master into a flipping overhead leap so that Dooku could burn through his spine from kidneys to shoulder blades—and this image, this plan, was so clear in Dooku's mind that he almost failed to notice that Kenobi met every one of his thrusts without so much as moving his feet, staying perfectly centered, perfectly balanced, blade never moving a millimeter more than was necessary, deflecting without effort, riposting with flickering strikes and stabs swifter than the tongue of a Garollian ghost viper, and when Dooku felt Skywalker regain his feet and stride once more toward his back, he finally registered the source of that blinding defensive velocity Kenobi had used a moment ago, and only then, belatedly, did he understand that Kenobi's Ataro and Shii-Cho had been ploys, as well.

Kenobi had become a master of Soresu.

Dooku found himself having a sudden, unexpected, overpowering, and entirely distressing *bad feeling* about this . . .

His farce had suddenly, inexplicably, spun from humorous to deadly serious and was tumbling rapidly toward terrifying. Realization burst through Dooku's consciousness like the blossoming fireballs of dying ships outside: this pair of Jedi fools had somehow managed to become entirely dangerous.

These clowns might—just possibly—actually be able to *beat* him.

No sense taking chances; even his Master would agree with that. Lord Sidious could come up with a new plan more easily than a new apprentice.

He gathered the Force once more in a single indrawn breath that summoned power from throughout the universe; the slightest whipcrack of that power, negligent as a flick of his wrist, sent Kenobi flying backward to crash hard against the wall, but Dooku didn't have time to enjoy it.

Skywalker was all over him.

The shining blue lightsaber whirled and spat and every overhand chop crashed against Dooku's defense with the unstoppable power of a meteor strike; the Sith Lord spent lavishly of his reserve of the Force merely to meet these attacks without being cut in half, and Skywalker—

Skywalker was getting *stronger*.

Each parry cost Dooku more power than he'd used to throw Kenobi across the room; each block aged him a decade.

He decided he'd best revise his strategy once again.

He no longer even tried to strike back. Force exhaustion began to close down his perceptions, drawing his consciousness back down to his physical form, trapping him within his own skull until he could barely even feel the contours of the room around him; he dimly sensed stairs at his back, stairs that led up to the entrance balcony. He retreated up them, using the higher ground for leverage, but Skywalker just kept on coming, tirelessly ferocious.

That blue blade was everywhere, flashing and whirling faster and faster until Dooku saw the room through an electric haze, and now *Kenobi* was back in the picture: with a shout of the Force, he shot like a torpedo up the stairs behind Skywalker, and Dooku decided that under these rather extreme circumstances, it was at least arguably permissible for a gentleman to cheat.

"Guards!" he said to the pair of super battle droids that still stood at attention to either side of the entrance. "Open fire!"

Instantly the two droids sprang forward and lifted their hands. Energy hammered out from the heavy blasters built into their arms; Skywalker whirled and his blade batted every blast back at the droids, whose mirror-polished carapace armor deflected the bolts again. Galvened particle beams screeched through the room in blinding ricochets.

Kenobi reached the top of the stairs and a single slash of his lightsaber dismantled both droids. Before their pieces could even hit the floor Dooku was in motion, landing a spinning side-stamp that folded Skywalker in half; he used his last burst of dark power to continue his spin into a blindingly fast wheel-kick that brought his heel against the point of Kenobi's chin with a *crack* like the report of a huge-bore slugthrower, knocking the Jedi Master back down the stairs. Sounded like he'd broken his neck.

Wouldn't that be lovely?

There was no sense in taking chances, however.

While Kenobi's bonelessly limp body was still tumbling toward the floor far below, Dooku sent a surge of energy through the Force. Kenobi's fall suddenly accelerated like a missile burning the last of its drives before impact. The Jedi Master struck the floor at a steep angle, skidded along it, and slammed into the wall so hard the hydrofoamed permacrete buckled and collapsed onto him.

This Dooku found exceedingly gratifying.

Now, as for Skywalker—

Which was as far as Dooku got, because by the time his attention returned to the younger Jedi, his vision was rather completely obstructed by the sole of a boot approaching his face with something resembling terminal velocity.

The impact was a blast of white fire, and there was a second impact against his back that was the balcony rail, and then the room turned upside down and he fell toward the ceiling, but not really, of course: it only felt that way because he had flipped over the rail and he was falling headfirst toward the floor, and neither his arms nor his legs were paying any attention to what he was trying to make them do. The Force seemed to be busy elsewhere, and really, the whole process was entirely mortifying.

He was barely able to summon a last surge of dark power before what would have been a disabling impact. The Force cradled him, cushioning his fall and setting him on his feet.

He dusted himself off and fixed a supercilious gaze on Skywalker, who now stood upon the balcony looking down at him— and Dooku couldn't hold the stare; he found this reversal of their original positions oddly unsettling.

There was something troublingly *appropriate* about it.

Seeing Skywalker standing where Dooku himself had stood only moments ago . . . it was as though he was trying to remember a dream he'd never actually had . . .

He pushed this aside, drawing once more upon the certain knowledge of his personal invincibility to open a channel to the Force. Power flowed into him, and the weight of his years dropped away.

He lifted his blade, and beckoned.

Skywalker leapt from the balcony. Even as the boy hurtled downward, Dooku felt a new twist in the currents of the Force between them, and he finally understood.

He understood how Skywalker was getting stronger. Why he no longer spoke. How he had become a machine of battle. He understood why Sidious had been so interested in him for so long.

Skywalker was a natural.

There was a thermonuclear furnace where his heart should be, and it was burning through the firewalls of his Jedi training. He held the Force in the clench of a white-hot fist. He was half Sith already, and he didn't even know it.

This boy had the gift of fury.

And even now, he was holding himself back; even now, as he landed at Dooku's flank and rained blows upon the Sith Lord's defenses, even as he drove Dooku backward step after step, Dooku could feel how Skywalker kept his fury banked behind walls of will: walls that were hardened by some uncontrollable dread.

Dread, Dooku surmised, of himself. Of what might happen if he should ever allow that furnace he used for a heart to go su-percritical.

Dooku slipped aside from an overhand chop and sprang backward. "I sense great fear in you. You are consumed by it. Hero With No Fear, indeed. You're a *fraud,* Skywalker. You are nothing but a posturing child."

He pointed his lightsaber at the young Jedi like an accusing finger. "Aren't you a little old to be afraid of the dark?"

Skywalker leapt for him again, and this time Dooku met the boy's charge easily. They stood nearly toe-to-toe, blades flashing faster than the eye could see, but Skywalker had lost his edge: a simple taunt was all that had been required to shift the focus of his attention from winning the fight to controlling his own emo-tions. The angrier he got, the more afraid he became, and the fear fed his anger in turn; like the proverbial Corellian multipede, now that he had started *thinking* about what he was doing, he could no longer walk.

Dooku allowed himself to relax; he felt that spirit of playfulness coming over him again as he and Skywalker spun 'round each other in their lethal dance. Whatever fun was to be had, he should enjoy while he could.

Then Sidious, for some reason, decided to intervene.

"Don't fear what you're feeling, Anakin, *use* it!" he barked in Palpatine's voice. "Call upon your fury. Focus it, and he cannot stand against you. *Rage* is your weapon. Strike now! *Strike! Kill* him!"

Dooku thought blankly, *Kill me?*

He and Skywalker paused for one single, final instant, blades locked together, staring at each other past a sizzling cross of scarlet against blue, and in that instant Dooku found himself wondering in bewildered astonishment if Sidious had suddenly lost his mind. Didn't he understand the advice he'd just given?

Whose side was he on, anyway?

And through the cross of their blades he saw in Skywalker's eyes the promise of hell, and he felt a sickening presentiment that he already knew the answer to that question.

Treachery is the way of the Sith.

JEDI TRAP

This is the death of Count Dooku:

A starburst of clarity blossoms within Anakin Skywalker's mind, when he says to himself *Oh. I get it, now* and discovers that the fear within his heart can be a weapon, too.

It is that simple, and that complex.

And it is final.

Dooku is dead already. The rest is mere detail.

The play is still on; the comedy of lightsabers flashes and snaps and hisses. Dooku & Skywalker, a one-time-only command performance, for an audience of one. Jedi and Sith and Sith and Jedi, spinning, whirling, crashing together, slashing and chopping, parrying, binding, slipping and whipping and ripping the air around them with snarls of power.

And all for nothing, because a nuclear flame has consumed Anakin Skywalker's Jedi restraint, and fear becomes fury without effort, and fury is a blade that makes his lightsaber into a toy.

The play goes on, but the suspense is over. It has become mere pantomime, as intricate and as meaningless as the space–time curves that guide galactic clusters through a measureless cosmos.

Dooku's decades of combat experience are irrelevant. His mastery of swordplay is useless. His vast wealth, his political influence, impeccable breeding, immaculate manners, exquisite taste—all the pursuits and points of pride to which he has devoted so much of his time and attention over the long, long years of his life—are now chains hung upon his spirit, bending his neck before the ax.

Even his knowledge of the Force has become a joke.

It is this knowledge that shows him his death, makes him handle it, turn it this way and that in his mind, examine it in detail like a black gemstone so cold it burns. Dooku's elegant farce has degenerated into bathetic melodrama, and not one shed tear will mark the passing of its hero.

But for Anakin, in the fight there is only terror, and rage.

Only he stands between death and the two men he loves best in all the world, and he can no longer afford to hold anything back. That imaginary dead-star dragon tries its best to freeze away his strength, to whisper him that Dooku has beaten him before, that Dooku has all the power of the darkness, to remind him how Dooku took his hand, how Dooku could strike down even Obi-Wan himself seemingly without effort and now Anakin is all alone and he will never be a match for any Lord of the Sith—

But Palpatine's words *rage is your weapon* have given Anakin permission to unseal the shielding around his furnace heart, and all his fears and all his doubts shrivel in its flame.

When Count Dooku flies at him, blade flashing, Watto's fist cracks out from Anakin's childhood to knock the Sith Lord tumbling back.

When with all the power that the dark side can draw from throughout the universe, Dooku hurls a jagged fragment of the durasteel table, Shmi Skywalker's gentle murmur *I knew you would come for me, Anakin* smashes it aside.

His head has been filled with the smoke from his smothered heart for far too long; it has been the thunder that darkens his mind. On Aargonar, on Jabiim, in the Tusken camp on Tatooine, that smoke had clouded his mind, had blinded him and left him flailing in the dark, a mindless machine of slaughter; but here, now, within this ship, this microscopic cell of life in the infinite sterile desert of space, his firewalls have opened so that the terror and the rage are *out there,* in the fight instead of in his head, and Anakin's mind is clear as a crystal bell.

In that pristine clarity, there is only one thing he must do.

Decide.

So he does.

He decides to *win.*

He decides that Dooku should lose the same hand he took. Decision is reality, here: his blade moves simultaneously with his will and blue fire vaporizes black Corellian nanosilk and disintegrates flesh and shears bone, and away falls a Sith Lord's lightsaber hand, trailing smoke that tastes of charred meat and burned hair. The hand falls with a bar of scarlet blaze still extending from its spastic death grip, and Anakin's heart sings for the fall of that red blade.

He reaches out and the Force catches it for him.

And then Anakin takes Dooku's other hand as well.

Dooku crumples to his knees, face blank, mouth slack, and his weapon whirs through the air to the victor's hand, and Anakin finds his vision of the future happening before his eyes: two blades at Count Dooku's throat.

But here, now, the truth belies the dream. Both lightsabers are in *his* hands, and the one in his hand of flesh flares with the synthetic bloodshine of a Sith blade.

Dooku, cringing, shrinking with dread, still finds some hope in his heart that he is wrong, that Palpatine has not betrayed him, that this has all been proceeding according to plan—

Until he hears "Good, Anakin! Good! I *knew* you could do it!" and registers this is Palpatine's voice and feels within the darkest depths of all he is the approach of the words that are to come next.

"Kill him," Palpatine says. "Kill him now."

In Skywalker's eyes he sees only flames.

"Chancellor, please!" he gasps, desperate and helpless, his

aristocratic demeanor invisible, his courage only a bitter memory. He is reduced to begging for his life, as so many of his victims have. "Please, you promised me *immunity*! We had a *deal*! *Help* me!"

And his begging gains him a share of mercy equal to that which he has dispensed.

"A deal only if you released me," Palpatine replies, cold as intergalactic space. "Not if you used me as bait to kill my friends."

And he knows, then, that all has indeed been going according to plan. Sidious's plan, not his own. This had been a Jedi trap indeed, but Jedi were not the quarry.

They were the bait.

"Anakin," Palpatine says quietly. "Finish him."

Years of Jedi training make Anakin hesitate; he looks down upon Dooku and sees not a Lord of the Sith but a beaten, broken, cringing old man.

"I shouldn't—"

But when Palpatine barks, "Do it! Now!" Anakin realizes that this isn't actually an order. That it is, in fact, nothing more than what he's been waiting for his whole life.

Permission.

And Dooku—

As he looks up into the eyes of Anakin Skywalker for the final time, Count Dooku knows that he has been deceived not just today, but for many, many years. That he has never been the true apprentice. That he has never been the heir to the power of the Sith. He has been only a tool.

His whole life—all his victories, all his struggles, all his heritage, all his principles and his sacrifices, everything he's done, everything he owns, everything he's been, all his dreams and grand vision for the future Empire and the Army of Sith—have been only a pathetic sham, because all of them, all of *him*, add up only to this.

He has existed only for this.

This.

To be the victim of Anakin Skywalker's first cold-blooded murder.

First but not, he knows, the last.

Then the blades crossed at his throat uncross like scissors.

Snip.

And all of him becomes nothing at all.

═══════

Murderer and murdered each stared blindly.

But only the murderer blinked.

I did that.

The severed head's stare was fixed on something beyond living sight. The desperate plea frozen in place on its lips echoed silence. The headless torso collapsed with a slowly fading sigh from the cauterized gape of its trachea, folding forward at the waist as though making obeisance before the power that had ripped away its life.

The murderer blinked again.

Who am *I*?

Was he the slave boy on a desert planet, valued for his astonishing gift with machines? Was he the legendary Podracer, the only human to survive that deadly sport? Was he the unruly, high-spirited, trouble-prone student of a great Jedi Master? The star pilot? The hero? The lover? The Jedi?

Could he be all these things—could he be *any* of them—and still have done what he has done?

He was already discovering the answer at the same time that he finally realized that he needed to ask the question.

The deck bucked as the cruiser absorbed a new barrage of torpedoes and turbolaser fire. Dooku's severed staring head bounced along the deck and rolled away, and Anakin woke up.

"What—?"

He'd been having a dream. He'd been flying, and fighting,

and fighting again, and somehow, in the dream, he could do whatever he wanted. In the dream, whatever he did was the right thing to do simply because he wanted to do it. In the dream there were no rules, there was only power.

And the power was his.

Now he stood over a headless corpse that he couldn't bear to see but he couldn't make himself look away, and he knew it hadn't been a dream at all, that he'd really *done* this, the blades were still in his hands and the ocean of wrong he'd dived into had closed over his head.

And he was drowning.

The dead man's lightsaber tumbled from his loosening fingers. "I—I couldn't stop myself . . ."

And before the words left his lips he heard how hollow and obvious was the lie.

"You did well, Anakin." Palpatine's voice was warm as an arm around Anakin's shoulders. "You did not only well, but *right*. He was too dangerous to leave alive."

From the Chancellor this sounded true, but when Anakin repeated it inside his head he knew that Palpatine's truth would be one he could never make himself believe. A tremor that began between his shoulder blades threatened to expand into a full case of the shakes. "He was an unarmed *prisoner* . . ."

That, now—that simple unbearable fact—*that* was truth. Though it burned him like his own lightsaber, truth was something he could hang on to. And somehow it made him feel a little better. A little stronger. He tried another truth: not that he couldn't have stopped himself, but—

"I shouldn't have done that," he said, and now his voice came out solid, and simple, and final. Now he could look down at the corpse at his feet. He could look at the severed head.

He could see them for what they were.

A crime.

He'd become a war criminal.

Guilt hit him like a fist. He *felt* it—a punch to his heart that smacked breath from his lungs and buckled his knees. It hung on his shoulders like a yoke of collapsium: an invisible weight beyond his mortal strength, crushing his life.

There were no words in him for this. All he could say was, "It was wrong."

And that was the sum of it, right there.

It was wrong.

"Nonsense. Disarming him was nothing; he had powers beyond your imagination."

Anakin shook his head. "That doesn't matter. It's not the Jedi way."

The ship shuddered again, and the lights went out.

"Have you never noticed that the Jedi way," Palpatine said, invisible now within the stark shadow of the General's Chair, "is not always the *right* way?"

Anakin looked toward the shadow. "You don't understand. You're not a Jedi. You *can't* understand."

"Anakin, listen to me. How many lives have you just saved with this stroke of a lightsaber? Can you count them?"

"But—"

"It wasn't wrong, Anakin. It may be *not the Jedi way,* but it was *right.* Perfectly natural—he took your hand; you wanted revenge. And your revenge was *justice.*"

"Revenge is never just. It *can't* be—"

"Don't be childish, Anakin. Revenge is the *foundation* of justice. Justice began with revenge, and revenge is still the only justice some beings can ever hope for. After all, this is hardly your first time, is it? Did Dooku deserve mercy more than did the Sand People who tortured your mother to death?"

"That was *different.*"

In the Tusken camp he had lost his mind; he had become a force of nature, indiscriminate, killing with no more thought or intention than a sand gale. The Tuskens had been killed, slaughtered, massacred—but that had been beyond his control, and now it seemed to him as if it had been done by someone else: like a story he had heard that had little to do with him at all.

But Dooku—

Dooku had been murdered.

By him.

On purpose.

Here in the General's Quarters, he had looked into the eyes of a living being and coldly decided to end that life. He could have chosen the right way. He could have chosen the Jedi way.

But instead—

He stared down at Dooku's severed head.

He could never unchoose this choice. He could never take it back. As Master Windu liked to say, there is no such thing as a second chance.

And he wasn't even sure he wanted one.

He couldn't let himself think about this. Just as he didn't let himself think about the dead on Tatooine. He put his hand to his eyes, trying to rub away the memory. "You promised we would never talk about that again."

"And we won't. Just as we need never speak of what has happened here today." It was as though the shadow itself spoke kindly. "I have always kept your secrets, have I not?"

"Yes—yes, of course, Chancellor, but—" Anakin wanted to crawl away into a corner somewhere; he felt sure that if things would just *stop* for a while—an hour, a minute—he could pull himself together and find some way to keep moving forward. He had to keep moving forward. Moving forward was all he could do.

Especially when he couldn't stand to look back.

The view wall behind the General's Chair blossomed with looping ion spirals of inbound missiles. The shuddering of the ship built itself into a continuous quake, gathering magnitude with each hit.

"Anakin, my restraints, please," the shadow said. "I'm afraid this ship is breaking up. I don't think we should be aboard when it does."

In the Force, the field-signatures of the magnetic locks on the Chancellor's shackles were as clear as text saying UNLOCK ME LIKE THIS; a simple twist of Anakin's mind popped them open.

The shadow grew a head, then shoulders, then underwent a sudden mitosis that left the General's Chair standing behind and turned its other half into the Supreme Chancellor.

Palpatine picked his way through the debris that littered the gloom-shrouded room, moving surprisingly quickly toward the stairs. "Come along, Anakin. There is very little time."

The view wall flared white with the missiles' impacts, and one of them must have damaged the gravity generators: the ship seemed to heel over, forcing Palpatine to clutch desperately at the banister and sending Anakin skidding down a floor that had suddenly become a forty-five-degree ramp.

He rolled hard into a pile of rubble: shattered permacrete, hydrofoamed to reduce weight. "Obi-Wan—!"

He sprang to his feet and waved away the debris that had buried the body of his friend. Obi-Wan lay entirely still, eyes closed, dust-caked blood matting his hair where his scalp had split.

Bad as Obi-Wan looked, Anakin had stood over the bodies of too many friends on too many battlefields to be panicked by a little blood. One touch to Obi-Wan's throat confirmed the strength of his pulse, and that touch also let Anakin's Force perception flow through the whole body of his friend. His breathing was strong and regular, and no bones were broken: this was a concussion, no more.

Apparently Obi-Wan's head was somewhat harder than the cruiser's interior walls.

"Leave him, Anakin. There is no time." Palpatine was half hanging from the banister, both arms wrapped around a stanchion. "This whole spire may be about to break free—"

"Then we'll all be adrift together." Anakin glanced up at the Supreme Chancellor and for that instant he didn't like the man at all—but then he reminded himself that brave as Palpatine was, his was the courage of conviction; the man was no soldier. He had no way of truly comprehending what he was asking Anakin to do.

"His fate," he said in case Palpatine had not understood, "will be the same as ours."

With Obi-Wan unconscious and Palpatine waiting above, with responsibility for the lives of his two closest friends squarely upon him, Anakin found that he had recovered his inner balance. Under pressure, in crisis, with no one to call upon for help, he could focus again. He had to.

This was what he'd been born for: saving people.

The Force brought Obi-Wan's lightsaber to his hand and he clipped it to his friend's belt, then hoisted the limp body over his shoulder and let the Force help him run lightly up the steeply canted floor to Palpatine's side.

"Impressive," Palpatine said, but then he cast a significant gaze up the staircase, which the vector of the artificial gravity had made into a vertical cliff. "But what now?"

Before Anakin could answer, the erratic gravity swung like a pendulum; while they both clung to the railing, the room seemed to roll around them. All the broken chairs and table fragments and hunks of rubble slid toward the opposite side, and now instead of a cliff the staircase had become merely a corrugated stretch of floor.

"People say"—Anakin nodded toward the door to the turbo-lift lobby—"when the Force closes a hatch, it opens a viewport. After you?"

GRIEVOUS

The ARC-170s of Squad Seven had joined the V-wings of Squad Four in swarming the remaining vulture fighters that had screened the immense Trade Federation flagship, *Invisible Hand*. Clone pilots destroyed droid after droid with machine-like precision of their own. When the last of the vultures had been converted to an expanding globe of superheated gas, the clone fighters peeled away, leaving *Invisible Hand* exposed to the full fire of Home Fleet Strike Group Five: three *Carrack*-class light cruisers—*Integrity, Indomitable,* and *Perseverance*—in support of the Dreadnaught *Mas Ramdar*.

Strike Group Five had deployed in a triangle around *Mas Ramdar*, maintaining a higher orbit to pin *Invisible Hand* deep in Coruscant's gravity well. Turbolasers blasted against *Invisible Hand*'s faltering shields, but the flagship was giving as good as it got: *Mas Ramdar* had sustained so much damage already that it was little more than a target to absorb the *Hand*'s return fire, and *Indomitable* was only a shell, most of its crew dead or evacuated, being run remotely by its commander and bridge crew; it swung unsteadily through the *Hand*'s vector cone of escape routes to block any attempt to run up toward jump.

As its shields finally failed, *Invisible Hand* began to roll, whirling like a bullet from a rifled slugthrower, trailing spiral jets of crystallizing gas that gushed from multiple hull ruptures. The rolling picked up speed, breaking the targeting locks of the ship's Republic adversaries. Unable to pound the same point again and again, their turbolasers weren't powerful enough to breach the *Hand*'s heavy armor directly; their tracking points became rings that circled the ship, chewing gradually into the hull in tightening garrotes of fire.

On the *Hand*'s bridge, overheated Neimoidians were strapped into their battle stations in full crash webbing. The air reeked of burning metal and the funk of reptilian stress hormones, and the erratically shifting gravity threatened to add a sharper stench: the faces of several of the bridge officers had already paled from healthy gray-green to nauseated pink.

The sole being on the bridge who was not strapped into a chair stalked from one side to the other, floor-length cape draped over shoulders angular as exposed bone. He ignored the jolts of impact and was unaffected by the swirl of unpredictable gravity as he paced the deck with metal-on-metal clanks; he walked on taloned creations of magnetized duranium, jointed to grab and crush like the feet of a Vratixan blood eagle.

His expression could not be read—his face was a mask of bleached ceramic armorplast stylized to evoke a humanoid skull—but the pure venom in the voice that hissed through the mask's electrosonic vocabulator made up for it.

"Either get the gravity generators calibrated or disable them altogether," he snarled at a blue-scanned image of a cringing Neimoidian engineer. "If this continues, you won't live long enough to be killed by the Republic."

"But, but, but sir—it's really up to the repair droids—"

"And because they *are* droids, it's useless to threaten them. So I am threatening *you*. Understand?"

He turned away before the stammering engineer could summon a reply. The hand he extended toward the forward viewscreen wore a jointed gauntlet of armorplast fused to its bones of duranium alloy. "Concentrate fire on *Indomitable*," he told the senior gunnery officer. "All batteries at maximum. Fire for effect. Blast that hulk out of space, and we'll make a hyperspace jump through its wreckage."

"But—the forward towers are already *overloading,* sir." The officer's voice trembled on the edge of panic. "They'll be at critical failure in less than a *minute*—"

"Burn them out."

"But sir, once they're gone—"

The rest of the senior gunnery officer's objection was lost in the wetly final crunching sound his face made under the impact of an armorplast fist. That same fist opened, seized the collar of the officer's uniform, and yanked his corpse out of the chair, ripping the crash webbing free along with it.

An expressionless skull-face turned toward the junior gunnery officer. "Congratulations on your promotion. Take your post."

"Y-y-yes, sir." The newly promoted senior gunnery officer's hands shook so badly he could barely unbuckle his crash web, and his face had gone deathly pink.

"Do you understand your orders?"

"Y-y-y—"

"Do you have any objections?"

"N-n-n—"

"Very well, then," General Grievous said with flat, impenetrable calm. "Carry on."

───────────

This is General Grievous:

Durasteel. Ceramic armorplast-plated duranium. Electrodrivers and crystal circuitry.

Within them: the remnants of a living being.

He doesn't breathe. He doesn't eat. He cannot laugh, and he does not cry.

A lifetime ago he was an organic sentient being. A lifetime

ago he had friends, a family, an occupation; a lifetime ago he had things to love, and things to fear. Now he has none of these.

Instead, he has *purpose*.

It's built into him.

He is built to intimidate. The resemblance to a human skeleton melded with limbs styled after the legendary Krath war droids is entirely intentional. It is a face and form born of childhood's infinite nightmares.

He is built to dominate. The ceramic armorplast plates protecting limbs and torso and face can stop a burst from a starfighter's laser cannon. Those indestructible arms are ten times stronger than human, and move with the blurring speed of electronic reflexes.

He is built to eradicate. Those human-sized hands have human-sized fingers for exactly one reason: to hold a lightsaber.

Four of them hang inside his cloak.

He has never constructed a lightsaber. He has never bought one, nor has he recovered one that was lost. Each and all, he has taken from the dead hands of Jedi he has killed.

Personally.

He has many, many such trophies; the four he carries with him are his particular favorites. One belonged to the interminable K'Kruhk, whom he had bested at Hypori; another to the Viraanntesse Jedi Jmmaar, who'd fallen at Vandos; the other two had been created by Puroth and Nystammall, whom Grievous had slaughtered together on the flame-grass plains of Tovarskl so that each would know the other's death, as well as their own; these are murders he recalls with so much pleasure that touching these souvenirs with his hands of armorplast and durasteel brings him something resembling joy.

But only resembling.

He remembers joy. He remembers anger, and frustration. He remembers grief and sorrow.

He doesn't actually feel any of them. Not anymore.

He's not designed for it.

White-hot sparks zipped and crackled through the smoke that billowed across the turbolift lobby. Over Anakin's shoulder, the unconscious Jedi Master wheezed faintly. Beside his other shoulder, Palpatine coughed harshly into the sleeve of his robe, held over his face for protection from caustic combustion products of the overloading circuitry.

"Artoo?" Anakin shook his comlink sharply. The blasted thing had been on the blink ever since Obi-Wan had stepped on it during one of the turbolift fights.

"Artoo, do you copy? I need you to activate—" The smoke was so thick he could barely make out the numerals on the code plate. "—elevator three-two-two-four. *Three-two-two-four,* do you copy?"

The comlink emitted a fading *fwheep* that might have been an acknowledgment, and the doors slid apart, but before Anakin could carry Obi-Wan through, the turbolift pod shot upward and the artificial gravity vector shifted again, throwing him and his partner into a heap next to Palpatine in the lobby's opposite corner.

Palpatine was struggling to rise, still coughing, sounding weak. Anakin let the Force lift Obi-Wan back to his shoulder, then picked himself up. "Perhaps you should stay down, sir," he said to the Chancellor. "The gravity swings are getting worse."

Palpatine nodded. "But, Anakin—"

Anakin looked up. The turbolift doors still stood open. "Wait here, sir."

He opened himself more fully to the Force and in his mind placed himself and Obi-Wan balanced on the edge of the open doorway above. Holding this image, he leapt, and the Force made his intention into reality: his leap carried him and the unconscious Jedi Master precisely to the rim.

The altered gravitic vector had made the turbolift shaft into a horizontal hallway of unlit durasteel, laser-straight, shrinking into darkness. Anakin was familiar with the specs for Trade Federation command cruisers; the angled conning spire was some three hundred meters long. As it stood, they could walk it in two or three minutes. But if the wrong gravity shift were to catch them inside the shaft . . .

He shook his head, grimly calculating the odds. "We'll have to be fast."

He glanced back over his shoulder, down at Palpatine, who still huddled below. "Are you all right, Chancellor? Are you well enough to run?"

The Supreme Chancellor finally rose, patting his robes in a futile attempt to dust them off. "I haven't run since I was a boy on Naboo."

"It's never too late to start getting into shape." Anakin reached through the Force to give Palpatine a little help in clambering up to the open doorway. "There are light shuttles on the hangar deck. We can be there in five minutes."

Once Palpatine was safely within the shaft-hall, Anakin said, "Follow me," and turned to go, but the Chancellor stopped him with a hand on his arm.

"Anakin, wait. We need to get to the bridge."

Through an entire shipful of combat droids? Not likely. "The hangar deck's right below—well, *beside* us, now. It's our best chance."

"But the bridge—*Grievous* is there."

Now Anakin did stop. Grievous. The most prolific slaughterer of Jedi since Durge. In all the excitement, Anakin had entirely forgotten that the bio-droid general was aboard.

"You've defeated Dooku," Palpatine said. "Capture Grievous, and you will have dealt a wound from which the Separatists may never recover."

Anakin thought blankly: *I could do it.*

He had dreamed of capturing Grievous ever since Muunilinst—and now the general was close. So close Anakin could practically *smell* him . . . and Anakin had never felt so powerful. The Force was with him today in ways more potent than he had ever experienced.

"Think of it, Anakin." Palpatine stood close by his shoulder, opposite to Obi-Wan, so close he needed only to whisper. "You have destroyed their political head. Take their military commander, and you will have practically won the war. *Single-handed*. Who else could do that, Anakin? Yoda? Mace Windu? They couldn't even capture Dooku. Who would have a chance against Grievous, if not Anakin Skywalker? The Jedi have never faced a crisis like the Clone Wars—but also they have never had a hero like *you*. You can save them. You can save *everyone*."

Anakin jerked, startled. He turned a sharp glance toward Palpatine. The way he had said that . . .

Like a voice out of his dreams.

"That's—" Anakin tried to laugh; it came out a little shaky. "That's not what Obi-Wan keeps telling me."

"Forget Obi-Wan," Palpatine said. "He has no idea how powerful you truly are. *Use* your power, Anakin. Save the Republic."

Anakin could see it, vivid as a HoloNet feature: arriving at the Senate with Grievous in electrobonds, standing modestly aside as Palpatine announced the end of the war, returning to the Temple, to the Council Chamber, where finally, after all this time, there would be a chair waiting, just for him.

They could hardly refuse him Mastership now, after he had won the war for them . . .

But then Obi-Wan shifted on his shoulder, moaning faintly, and Anakin snapped back to reality.

"No," he said. "Sorry, Chancellor. My orders are clear. This is a rescue mission; your safety is my only priority."

"I will never be safe while Grievous lives," Palpatine countered. "Master Kenobi will recover at any moment. Leave him here with me; he can see me safely to the hangar deck. Go for the general."

"I—I *would* like to, sir, but—"

"I can make it an order, Anakin."

"With respect, sir: no. You can't. My orders come from the Jedi Council, and the Council's orders come from the Senate. You have no direct authority."

The Chancellor's face darkened. "That may change."

Anakin nodded. "And perhaps it should, sir. But until it does, we'll do things my way. Let's go."

"Sir?" The thin voice of the comm officer interrupted Grievous's pacing. "We are being hailed by *Integrity*, sir. They propose a cease-fire."

Dark yellow eyes squinted through the skull-mask at the tactical displays. A pause in the combat would allow *Invisible Hand*'s turbolaser batteries to cool, and give the engineers a chance to get the gravity generators under control. "Acknowledge receipt of transmission. Stand by to cease fire."

"Standing by, sir." The gunnery officer was still shaking.

"Cease fire."

The lances of energy that had joined the *Hand* to the Home Fleet Strike Force melted away.

"Further transmission, sir. It's *Integrity*'s commander."

Grievous nodded. "Initiate."

A ghostly image built itself above the bridge's ship-to-ship hologenerator: a young human male of distinctly average height and build, wearing the uniform of a lieutenant commander. The only thing distinctive about his otherwise rather bland features was the calm confidence in his eyes.

"*General Grievous,*" the young man said briskly, "*I am Lieutenant Commander Lorth Needa of RSS* Integrity. *At my request, my superiors have consented to offer you the chance to surrender your ship, sir.*"

"Surrender?" Grievous's vocabulator produced a very creditable reproduction of a snort. "Preposterous."

"*Please give this offer careful deliberation, General, as it will not be repeated. Consider the lives of your crew.*"

Grievous cast an icy glance around his bridge full of craven Neimoidians. "Why should I?"

The young man did not look surprised, though he did show a trace of sadness. "*Is this your reply, then?*"

"Not at all." Grievous drew himself up; by straightening the angles of his levered joints, he could add half a meter to his already imposing height. "I have a counteroffer. Maintain your cease-fire, move that hulk *Indomitable* out of my way, and withdraw to a minimum range of fifty kilometers until this ship achieves hyperspace jump."

"If I may use your word, sir: preposterous."

"Tell these superiors of yours that if my demands are not met within ten minutes, I will personally disembowel Supreme Chancellor Palpatine, live on the HoloNet. Am I understood?"

The young officer took this without a blink. *"Ah. The Chancellor is aboard your ship, then."*

"He is. Your pathetic Jedi so-called heroes have failed. They are dead, and Palpatine remains in my hands."

"Ah," the young officer repeated. *"So you will, of course, allow me to speak with him. To, ah, reassure my superiors that you are not simply—well, to put it charitably—bluffing?"*

"I would not lower myself to lie to the likes of you." Grievous turned to the comm officer. "Patch in Count Dooku."

The comm officer stroked his screen, then shook his head. "He's not responding, sir."

Grievous shook his head disgustedly. "Just *show* the Chancellor, then. Bring up my quarters on the security screen."

The security officer stroked his own screen, and made a choking sound. "Hrm, sir?"

"What are you *waiting* for? Bring it up!"

He'd gone as pink as the gunner. "Perhaps you should have a look *first,* sir?"

The plain urgency in his tone brought Grievous to his side without another word. The general bent over the screen that showed the view inside his quarters and found himself looking at jumbled piles of energy-sheared wreckage surrounding the empty shape of the General's Chair.

And that—that there—that looked like it could have been a body . . .

Draped in a cape of armorweave.

Grievous turned back toward the intership holocomm. "The Chancellor is—indisposed."

"*Ah. I see.*"

Grievous suspected that the young officer saw entirely too well. "I *assure* you—"

"*I do not require your assurance, General. You have the same amount of time you offered us. Ten minutes from now, I will have either your surrender, or confirmation that Supreme Chancellor Palpatine is alive, unharmed—and present—or* Invisible Hand *will be destroyed.*"

"Wait—you can't simply—"

"*Ten minutes, General. Needa out.*"

When Grievous turned to the bridge security officer, his mask was blankly expressionless as ever, but he made up for it with the open murder in his voice.

"Dooku is dead and the Jedi are loose. They have the Chancellor. Find them and bring them to me."

His armorplast fingers curled into a fist that crashed down on the security console so hard the entire thing collapsed into a sparking, smoking ruin.

"*Find* them!"

RESCUE

Anakin counted paces as he trotted along the turbolift shaft, Obi-Wan over his shoulder and Palpatine at his side. He'd reached 102—only a third of the way along the conning spire—when he felt the gravity begin to shift.

Exactly the wrong way: changing the rest of the long, long shaft from *ahead* to *down*.

He put out his free arm to stop the Chancellor. "This is a problem. Find something to hang on to while I get us out of here."

One of the turbolift doors was nearby, seemingly lying on its side. Anakin's lightsaber found his hand and its sizzling blade burned open the door controls, but before he could even move aside the sparking wires, the gravitic vector lurched toward vertical and he fell, skidding along the wall, free hand grabbing desperately at a loop of cable, catching it, hanging from it—

And the turbolift doors opened.

Inviting. Safe. And mockingly out of reach: a meter above his outstretched arm—

And his other arm was the only thing holding Obi-Wan above a two-hundred-meter drop down which his lightsaber's handgrip now clanked and clattered, fading toward infinity. For half a second Anakin was actually glad Obi-Wan was unconscious, because he wasn't in the mood for another lecture about hanging on to his lightsaber right now, and that thought blew away and vanished because something *had grabbed on to his leg*—

He looked down.

It was Palpatine.

The Chancellor hugged Anakin's ankle with improbable strength, peering fearfully into the darkness below. "Anakin, do something! You have to *do* something!"

I'm open to suggestions, he thought, but he said, "Don't panic. Just hang on."

"I don't think I can . . ." The Chancellor turned his anguished face upward imploringly. "Anakin, I'm slipping. Give me your hand—you have to *give* me your *hand*!"

And drop Obi-Wan? Not in this millennium.

"Don't *panic*," Anakin repeated. The Chancellor had clearly lost his head. "I can get us out of this."

He wished he were as confident as he sounded. He had been counting on the artificial gravity to continue to swing until the shaft turned back into a hallway, but instead it seemed to have stopped where it was.

This would be an especially lousy time for the generators to start working right.

He fixed a measuring glance on the open lift doorway above; perhaps the Force could give him enough of a boost to carry all three of them to safety.

But that was an exceedingly large *perhaps.*

Obi-Wan, old buddy old pal, he thought, *this would be a really good time to wake up.*

Obi-Wan Kenobi opened his eyes to find himself staring at what he strongly suspected was Anakin's butt.

It *looked* like Anakin's butt—well, his pants, anyway—though it was thoroughly impossible for Obi-Wan to be certain, since he had never before had occasion to examine Anakin's butt upside down, which it currently appeared to be, nor from this rather uncomfortably close range.

And how he might have arrived at this angle and this range was entirely baffling.

He said, "Um, have I missed something?"

"Hang on," he heard Anakin say. "We're in a bit of a situation here."

So it *was* Anakin's butt after all. He supposed he might take a modicum of comfort from that. Looking up, he discovered Anakin's legs, and his boots—and a somewhat astonishing close-up view of the Supreme Chancellor, as Palpatine seemingly balanced overhead, supported only by a white-knuckled death-grip on Anakin's ankle.

"Oh, hello, Chancellor," he said mildly. "Are you well?"

The Chancellor cast a distressed glance over his shoulder. "I *hope* so . . ."

Obi-Wan followed the Chancellor's gaze; above Palpatine rose a long, long vertical shaft—

Which was when he finally realized that he wasn't looking *up* at all.

This must be what Anakin had meant by *a bit of a situation*.

"Ah," Obi-Wan said. At least he was finally coming to understand where he stood.

Well, lay. Hung. Whatever.

"And Count Dooku?"

Anakin said, "Dead."

"Pity." Obi-Wan sighed. "Alive, he might have been a help to us."

"Obi-Wan—"

"Not in this particular situation, granted, but nonetheless—"

"Can we discuss this *later*? The ship's breaking apart."

"Ah."

A familiar electrosonic *feroo-wheep* came thinly through someone's comlink. "Was that Artoo? What does he want?"

"I asked him to activate the elevator," Anakin said.

From the distant darkness above came a *clank*, and a *shirr*, and a *clonk*, all of which evoked in Obi-Wan's still-somewhat-addled brain the image of turbolift brakes unlocking. The accuracy of his imagination was swiftly confirmed by a sudden downdraft that smelled strongly of burning oil, followed closely by the bottom of a turbolift pod hurtling down the shaft like a meteorite down a well.

Obi-Wan said, "Oh."

"It seemed like a good idea at the time—"

"No need to get defensive."

"Artoo!" Anakin shouted. "Shut it down!"

"No time for that," Obi-Wan said. "Jump."

"Jump?" Palpatine asked with a shaky laugh. "Don't you mean, *fall*?"

"Um, actually, yes. Anakin—?"

Anakin let go.

They fell.

And fell. The sides of the turboshaft blurred.

And fell some more, until the gravitic vector finally eased a couple of degrees and they found themselves sliding along the side of the shaft, which was quickly turning into the bottom of the shaft, and the lift pod was still shrieking toward them faster than they could possibly run until Anakin finally got the comlink working and shouted, "Artoo, open the doors! All of them! All floors!"

One door opened just as they skidded onto it and all three of them tumbled through. They landed in a heap on a turbolift lobby's opposite wall as the pod shot past overhead.

They gradually managed to untangle themselves. "Are . . . all of your rescues so . . ." Palpatine gasped breathlessly. ". . . *entertaining*?"

Obi-Wan gave Anakin a thoughtful frown.

Anakin returned it with a shrug.

"Actually, now that you mention it," Obi-Wan said, "yes."

Anakin stared into the tangled masses of wreckage that littered the hangar bay, trying to pick out anything that still even resembled a ship. This place looked as if it had taken a direct hit;

wind howled against his back through the open hatchway where Obi-Wan stood with Chancellor Palpatine, and scraps of debris whirled into the air, blown toward space through gaps in the scorched and buckled blast doors.

"None of those ships will get us anywhere!" Palpatine shouted above the wind, and Anakin had to agree. "What are we going to do?"

Anakin shook his head. He didn't know, and the Force wasn't offering any clues. "Obi-Wan?"

"How should I know?" Obi-Wan said, bracing himself in the doorway, robe whipping in the wind. "You're the hero, I'm just a Master!"

Past Obi-Wan's shoulder Anakin saw a cadre of super battle droids marching around a corner into the corridor. "Master! Behind you!"

Obi-Wan whirled, lightsaber flaring to meet a barrage of blaster bolts. "Protect the Chancellor!"

And let you have all the fun? Anakin pulled the Chancellor into the hangar bay and pressed him against the wall beside the hatch. "Stay under cover until we handle the droids!"

He was about to jump out beside Obi-Wan when he remembered that he had dropped his lightsaber down the turboshaft; fighting super battle droids without it would be a bit tricky. Not to mention that Obi-Wan would never let him hear the end of it.

"Droids are not our only problem!" Palpatine pointed across the hangar bay. "Look!"

On the far side of the bay, masses of wreckage were shifting, sliding toward the wall against which Anakin and Palpatine stood. Then debris closer to them began to slide, followed by piles closer still. An invisible wave-front was passing through the hangar bay; behind it, the gravitic vector was rotated a full ninety degrees.

Gravity shear.

Anakin's jaw clenched. This just kept getting better and better.

He unspooled a length of his utility belt's safety cable and passed the end to Palpatine. The wind made it sing. "Cinch this around your waist. Things are about to get a little wild!"

"What's *happening*?"

"The gravity generators have desynchronized—they'll tear the ship apart!" Anakin grabbed one of the zero-g handles beside the hatchway, then leaned out into the firestorm of blaster bolts and saber flares and touched Obi-Wan's shoulder. "Time to go!"

"What?"

Explanation was obviated as the shear-front moved past them and the wall became the floor. Anakin grabbed the back of Obi-Wan's collar, but not to save him from falling; the torque of the gravity shear had buckled the blast doors—which were now overhead—and the hurricane of escaping air blasting from the corridor shaft blew the Jedi Master up through the hatch. Anakin dragged him out of the gale just as pieces of super battle droids began hurtling upward into the hangar bay like misfiring torpedoes.

Some of the super battle droids were still intact enough to open fire as they flew past. "Hang on to my belt!" Obi-Wan shouted and spun his lightsaber through an intricate flurry to deflect bolt after bolt. Anakin could do nothing but hold him braced against the gale; his grip on the zero-g handle was the only thing keeping him and Obi-Wan from being blown out into space and taking Palpatine with them.

"This is not the best plan we've ever had!" he shouted.

"This was a *plan*?" Palpatine sounded appalled.

"We'll make our way forward!" Obi-Wan shouted. "There are only droids back here! Once we hit live-crew areas, there will be escape pods!"

Only droids back here echoed inside Anakin's head. "Obi-Wan, *wait*!" he cried. "Artoo's still here somewhere! We can't leave him!"

"He's probably been destroyed, or blown into space!" Obi-Wan deflected blaster bursts from the last two gale-blown droids. They tumbled up to the gap in the blast doors and vanished into the infinite void. Obi-Wan put away his lightsaber and fought his way back to a grip beside Anakin's. "We can't afford the time to search for him. I'm sorry, Anakin. I know how much he meant to you."

Anakin desperately fished out his comlink. "Artoo! Artoo, come in!" He shook it, and shook it again. Artoo couldn't have been destroyed. He just *couldn't.* "Artoo, do you copy? Where are you?"

"Anakin—" Obi-Wan's hand was on his arm, and the Jedi Master leaned so close that his low tone could be heard over the rising gale. "We must go. Being a Jedi means allowing things— even things we love—to pass out of our lives."

Anakin shook the comlink again. "Artoo!" He couldn't just leave him. He couldn't. And he didn't exactly have an explanation.

Not one he could ever give Obi-Wan, anyway.

There are so few things a Jedi ever owns; even his lightsaber is less a possession than an expression of his identity. To be a Jedi is to renounce possessions. And Anakin had tried so hard, tried for so long, to do just that.

Even on their wedding day, Anakin had had no devotion-gift for his new wife; he didn't actually *own* anything.

But love will find a way.

He had brought something like a gift to her apartments in Theed, still a little shy with her, still overwhelmed by finding the feelings in her he'd felt so long himself, not knowing quite how to give her a gift which wasn't really a gift. Nor was it his to give.

Without anything of his own to give except his love, all he could bring her was a friend.

"I didn't have many friends when I was a kid," he'd told her, "so I built one."

And C-3PO had shuffled in behind him, gleaming as though he'd been plated with solid gold.

Padmé had lit up, her eyes gleaming, but she had at first tried to protest. "I can't accept him," she'd said. "I know how much he means to you."

Anakin had only laughed. What use is a protocol droid to a Jedi? Even one as upgraded as 3PO—Anakin had packed his creation with so many extra circuits and subprograms and heuristic algorithms that the droid was practically human.

"I'm not giving him to you," he'd told her. "He's not even really mine to give; when I built him, I was a slave, and everything I did belonged to Watto. Cliegg Lars bought him along with my mother; Owen gave him back to me, but I'm a Jedi. I have renounced possessions. I guess that means he's free now. What I'm really doing is asking you to look after him for me."

"Look after him?"

"Yes. Maybe even give him a job. He's a little fussy," he'd admitted, "and maybe I shouldn't have given him quite so much self-consciousness—he's a worrier—but he's very smart, and he might be a real help to a big-time diplomat . . . like, say, a Senator from Naboo?"

Padmé then had extended her hand and graciously invited C-3PO to join her staff, because on Naboo, high-functioning droids were respected as thinking beings, and 3PO had been so flustered at being treated like a sentient creature that he'd been barely able to speak, beyond muttering something about hoping he might make himself useful, because after all he was "fluent in over six million forms of communication." Then she had turned to Anakin and laid her soft, soft hand along his jawline to draw him down to kiss her, and that was all he had needed, all he had hoped for; he would give her everything he had, everything he was—

And there had come another day, two years later, a day that had meant nearly as much to him as the day they had wed: the day he had finally passed his trials.

The day he had become a Jedi Knight.

As soon as circumstances allowed he had slipped away, on his own now, no Master over his shoulder, no one to monitor his comings and his goings and so he could take himself to the vast Coruscant complex at 500 Republica where Naboo's senior Senator kept her spacious apartments.

And he had then, finally, two years late, a devotion-gift for her.

He had then one thing that he truly owned, that he had earned, that he was not required to renounce. One gift he could give her to celebrate their love.

The culmination of the Ceremony of Jedi Knighthood is the severing of the new Jedi Knight's Padawan braid. And it was this that he laid into Padmé's trembling hand.

One long, thin braid of his glossy hair: such a little thing, of no value at all.

Such a little thing, that meant the galaxy to him.

And she had kissed him then, and laid her soft cheek against his jaw, and she had whispered in his ear that she had something for him as well.

Out from her closet had whirred R2-D2.

Of course Anakin knew him; he had known him for years—the little droid was a decorated war hero himself, having saved Padmé's life back when she had been Queen of Naboo, not to mention helping the nine-year-old Anakin destroy the Trade Federation's Droid Control Ship, breaking the blockade and saving the planet. The Royal Engineers of Naboo's aftermarket wizardry made their modified R-units the most sought after in the galaxy; he'd tried to protest, but she had silenced him with a soft finger against his lips and a gentle smile and a whisper of "After all, what does a politician need with an astromech?"

"But I'm a Jedi—"

"That's why I'm not giving him to you," she'd said with a smile. "I'm asking you to look after him. He's not really a gift. He's a friend."

All this flashed through Anakin's mind in the stretching second before his comlink finally crackled to life with a familiar *fwee-wheoo*, and his heart unclenched.

"Artoo, where are you? Come on, we have to get out of here!"

High above, on the wall that was supposed to be the floor, the lid of a battered durasteel storage locker shifted, pushed aside by a dome of silver and blue. The lid swung fully open and R2-D2 righted itself, deployed its booster rockets, and floated out from the locker, heading for the far exit.

Anakin gave Obi-Wan a fierce grin. Let someone he loves pass out of his life? Not likely. "What are we waiting for?" he said. "Let's go!"

From *Invisible Hand*'s bridge, the ship's spin made the vast curve of Coruscant's horizon appear to orbit the ship in a dizzying whirl. Each rotation also brought a view of the lazily tumbling wreckage of the conning spire, ripped from the ship and cast out of orbit by centripetal force, as it made the long burning fall toward the planetary city's surface.

General Grievous watched them both while his droid circuitry ticked off the seconds remaining in the life of his ship.

He had no fear for his own life; his specially designed escape module was preprogrammed to take him directly to a ship already primed for jump. Mere seconds after he sealed himself and the Chancellor within the module's heavily armored hull, they would be taken aboard the fleeing ship, which would then make a series of randomized microjumps to prevent being tracked before entering the final jump to the secret base on Utapau.

But he was not willing to go without the Chancellor. This operation had cost the Confederacy dearly in ships and personnel; to leave empty-handed would be an even graver cost in prestige. Winning this war was more than half a matter of propaganda: much of the weakness of the Republic grew from its citizens' superstitious dread of the Separatists' seemingly inevitable victory—a dread cultivated and nourished by the CIS shadowfeed that poisoned government propaganda on the HoloNet. The common masses of the Republic believed that the Republic was losing; to see the legendary Grievous himself beaten back and fleeing a battle would give them hope that the war might be won.

And hope was simply not to be allowed.

His built-in comlink buzzed in his left ear. He touched the sensor implant in the jaw of his mask. "Yes."

"The Jedi almost certainly escaped the conning spire, sir." The voice was that of one of his precious, custom-built IG 100-series MagnaGuards: prototype self-motivating humaniform combat droids designed, programmed, and armed specifically to fight Jedi. *"We recovered a lightsaber from the base of the turbolift shaft before the spire tore free."*

"Copy that. Stand by for instructions." One long stride put Grievous next to the Neimoidian security officer. "Have you located them, or are you about to die?"

"I, ah, I ah—" The security officer's trembling finger pointed to a schematic of *Invisible Hand*'s hangar deck, where a bright blip slid slowly through Bay One.

"What is that?"

"It's, it's, it's the Chancellor's *beacon,* sir."

"What? The Jedi never deactivated it? Why not?"

"I, well, I can't actually—"

"Idiots." He looked down at the cringing security officer, considering killing the fool just for taking so long to figure this out.

The Neimoidian might as well have read Grievous's thought spelled out across his bone-colored mask. "If, if, if you hadn't—er, I mean, please recall my security console has been destroyed, and so I have been forced to reroute—"

"Silence." Grievous gave a mental shrug. The fool would be dead or captured soon enough regardless. "Order all combat droids to terminate their search algorithms and converge on the bridge. Wait, strike that: leave the battle droids. Useless things," he muttered into his mask. "A greater danger to us than to Jedi. Super battle droids and droidekas *only*, do you understand? We will take no chances."

As the security officer turned to his screens, Grievous again touched the sensor implant along the jaw of his mask. "IG-One-oh-one."

"Sir."

"Assemble a team of super battle droids and droidekas—as many as you can gather—and report to the hangar deck. I'll give you the exact coordinates as soon as they are available."

"Yes, sir."

"You will find at least one Jedi, possibly two, in the company of Chancellor Palpatine, imprisoned in a ray shield. They are to be considered extremely dangerous. Disarm them and deliver them to the bridge."

"If they are so dangerous, perhaps we should execute them on the spot."

"No. My orders are clear that the Chancellor is not to be harmed. And the Jedi—"

The general's right hand slipped beneath his cape to stroke the array of lightsabers clipped there.

"The Jedi, I will execute *personally*."

A sheet of shimmering energy suddenly flared in front of them, blocking the corridor on the far side of the intersection they were trotting across, and Obi-Wan stopped so short that Anakin almost slammed into his back. He reached over and caught Palpatine by the arm. "Careful, sir," he said, low. "Better not touch it till we know what it is."

Obi-Wan unclipped his lightsaber, activated it, and cautiously extended its tip to touch the energy field; an explosive burst of power flared sparks and streaks in all directions, nearly knocking the weapon from his hands. "Ray shield," he said, more to himself than to the others. "We'll have to find a way around—"

But even as he spoke another sheet shimmered into existence

across the mouth of the corridor they'd just left, and two more sizzled into place to seal the corridors to either side.

They were boxed in.

Caught.

Obi-Wan stood there for a second or two, blinking, then looked at Anakin and shook his head in disbelief. "I thought we were smarter than this."

"Apparently not. The oldest trap in the book, and we walked right into it." Anakin felt as embarrassed as Obi-Wan looked. "Well, *you* walked right into it. I was just trying to keep up."

"Oh, so now this is *my* fault?"

Anakin gave him a slightly wicked smile. "Hey, you're the Master. I'm just a hero."

"Joke some other time," Obi-Wan muttered. "It's the dark side—the shadow on the Force. Our instincts still can't be trusted. Don't you feel it?"

The dark side was the last thing Anakin wanted to think about right now. "Or, you know, it could be that knock on the head," he offered.

Obi-Wan didn't even smile. "No. All our choices keep going awry. How could they even locate us so precisely? Something is definitely wrong, here. Dooku's death should have lifted the shadow—"

"If you've a taste for mysteries, Master Kenobi," Palpatine interrupted pointedly, "perhaps you could solve the mystery of how we're going to *escape*."

Obi-Wan nodded, scowling darkly at the ray shield box as though seeing it for the first time; after a moment, he took out his lightsaber again, ignited it, and sank its tip into the deck at his feet. The blade burned through the durasteel plate almost without resistance—and then flared and bucked and spat lightning as it hit a shield in place in a gap below the plate, and almost threw Obi-Wan into the annihilating energy of the ray shield behind him.

"No doubt in the ceiling as well." He looked at the others and sighed. "Ideas?"

"Perhaps," Palpatine said thoughtfully, as though the idea had only just occurred to him, "we should simply surrender to General Grievous. With the death of Count Dooku, I'm sure that the two of you can . . ." He cast a significant sidelong glance at Anakin. ". . . *negotiate* our release."

He's persistent, I'll give him that, Anakin thought. He caught himself smiling as he recalled discussing "negotiation" with Padmé, on Naboo before the war; he came back to the present when he realized that undertaking "aggressive negotiations" could prove embarrassing under his current lightsaber-challenged circumstances.

"*I* say . . . ," he put in slowly, "patience."

"Patience?" Obi-Wan lifted an eyebrow. "That's a plan?"

"You know what Master Yoda says: *Patience you must have, until the mud settles and the water becomes clear.* So let's wait."

Obi-Wan looked skeptical. "Wait."

"For the security patrol. A couple of droids will be along in a moment or two; they'll have to drop the ray shield to take us into custody."

"And then?"

Anakin shrugged cheerfully. "And then we'll wipe them out."

"Brilliant as usual," Obi-Wan said dryly. "What if they turn out to be destroyer droids? Or something worse?"

"Oh, come on, Master. Worse than destroyers? Besides, security patrols are always those skinny useless little battle droids."

At that moment, four of those skinny useless battle droids came marching toward them, one along each corridor, clanking along with blaster rifles leveled. One of them triggered one of its preprogrammed security commands: *"Hand over your weapons!"* The other three chimed in with enthusiastic barks of *"Roger, roger!"* and a round of spastic head-bobbing.

"See?" Anakin said. "No problem."

Before Obi-Wan could reply, concealed doors in the corridor walls zipped suddenly aside. Through them rolled the massive bronzium wheels of destroyer droids, two into each corridor.

The eight destroyers unrolled themselves behind the battle droids, haloed by sparkling energy shields, twin blaster cannons targeting the two Jedi's chests.

Obi-Wan sighed. "You were saying?"

"Okay, fine. It's the dark side. Or something." Anakin rolled his eyes. "I guess you're off the hook for the ray shield trap."

Through those same doorways marched sixteen super battle droids to back up the destroyers, their arm cannons raised to fire over the destroyers' shields.

Behind the super battle droids came two droids of a type Anakin had never seen. He had an idea what they were, though.

And he was not happy about it.

Obi-Wan scowled at them as they approached. "You're the expert, Anakin. What are those things?"

"Remember what you were saying about *worse than destroyers?*" Anakin said grimly. "I think we're looking at them."

They walked side by side, their gait easy and straightforward, almost as smooth as a human's. In fact, they could have *been* human—humans who were two meters tall and made out of metal. They wore long swirling cloaks that had once been white, but now were stained with smoke and what Anakin strongly suspected was blood. They walked with the cloaks thrown back over one shoulder, to clear their left arms, where they held some unfamiliar staff-like weapon about two meters long—something like the force-pike of a Senate Guard, but shorter, and with an odd-looking discharge blade at each end.

They walked like they were made to fight, and they had clearly seen some battle. The chest plate of one bore a round shallow crater surrounded by a corona of scorch, a direct blaster hit that hadn't come close to penetrating; the other bore a scar from its cranial dome down through one dead photoreceptor—a scar that looked like it might have come from a lightsaber.

This droid looked like it had fought a Jedi, and survived.

The Jedi, he guessed, hadn't.

These two droids threaded between the super battle droids and destroyers and casually shoved aside one battle droid hard enough that it slammed into the wall and collapsed into a sparking heap of metal.

The one with the damaged photoreceptor pointed its staff at them, and the ray shields around them dropped. "He *said,* hand over your *weapons,* Jedi!"

This definitely wasn't a preprogrammed security command.

Anakin said softly, "I saw an Intel report on this; I think those are Grievous's personal bodyguard droids. Prototypes built to his specifications." He looked from Obi-Wan to Palpatine and back again. "To fight Jedi."

"Ah," Obi-Wan said. "Then under the circumstances, I suppose we need a Plan B."

Anakin nodded at Palpatine. "The Chancellor's idea is sounding pretty good right now."

Obi-Wan nodded thoughtfully.

When the Jedi Master turned away to offer his lightsaber to the bodyguard droid, Anakin leaned close to the Supreme Chancellor and murmured, "So you get your way, after all."

Palpatine answered with a slight, unreadable smile. "I frequently do."

As super battle droids came forward with electrobinders for their wrists and a restraining bolt for R2-D2, Obi-Wan cast one frowning look back over his shoulder.

"Oh, Anakin," he said, with the sort of quiet, pained resignation that would be recognized instantly by any parent exhausted by a trouble-prone child. *"Where* is your *lightsaber?"*

Anakin couldn't look at him. "It's not lost, if that's what you're thinking." This was the truth: Anakin could feel it in the Force, and he knew exactly where it was.

"No?"

"No."

"Where is it, then?"

"Can we talk about this later?"

"Without your lightsaber, you may not *have* a 'later.'"

"I don't need a lecture, okay? How many times have we had this talk?"

"Apparently, one time less than we needed to."

Anakin sighed. Obi-Wan could still make him feel about nine years old. He gave a sullen nod toward one of the droid body-guards. "He's got it."

"He does? And how did this happen?"

"I don't want to talk about it."

"Anakin—"

"Hey, he's got yours, too!"

"That's different—"

"This weapon is your *life*, Obi-Wan!" He did a credible-enough Kenobi impression that Palpatine had to smother a snort. "You must take *care* of it!"

"Perhaps," Obi-Wan said, as the droids clicked the binders onto their wrists and led them all away, "we should talk about this later."

Anakin intoned severely, "Without your *lightsaber*, you may not *have* a—"

"All right, all right." The Jedi Master surrendered with a rue-ful smile. "You win."

Anakin grinned at him. "I'm sorry? What was that?" He couldn't remember the last time he'd won an argument with Obi-Wan. "Could you speak up a little?"

"It's not very Jedi to gloat, Anakin."

"I'm not gloating, Master," he said with a sidelong glance at Palpatine. "I'm just . . . savoring the moment."

───────

This is how it feels to be Anakin Skywalker, for now:

The Supreme Chancellor returns your look with a hint of smile and a sliver of an approving nod, and for you, this tiny, triv-ial, comradely victory sparks a warmth and ease that relaxes the dragon-grip of dread on your heart.

Forget that you are captured; you and Obi-Wan have been captured before. Forget the deteriorating ship, forget the Jedi-killing droids; you've faced worse. Forget General Grievous. What is he compared with Dooku? He can't even use the Force.

So now, here, for you, the situation comes down to this: you are walking between the two best friends you have ever had, with your precious droid friend faithfully whirring after your heels—

On your way to win the Clone Wars.

What you have done—what happened in the General's Quarters and, more important, *why* it happened—is all burning away in Coruscant's atmosphere along with Dooku's decapitated corpse. Already it seems as if it happened to somebody else, as if *you* were somebody else when you did it, and it seems as if that man—the dragon-haunted man with a furnace for a heart and a mind as cold as the surface of that dead star—had really only been an image reflected in Dooku's open staring eyes.

And by the time what's left of the conning spire crashes into the kilometers-thick crust of city that is the surface of Coruscant, those dead eyes will have burned away, and the dragon will burn with them.

And you, for the first time in your life, will truly be free.

This is how it feels to be Anakin Skywalker.

For now.

OBI-WAN AND ANAKIN 2

This is Obi-Wan Kenobi in the light:

As he is prodded onto the bridge along with Anakin and Chancellor Palpatine, he has no need to look around to see the banks of control consoles tended by terrified Neimoidians. He doesn't have to turn his head to count the droidekas and super battle droids, or to gauge the positions of the brutal droid body-guards. He doesn't bother to raise his eyes to meet the cold yellow stare fixed on him through a skull-mask of armorplast.

He doesn't even need to reach into the Force.

He has already let the Force reach into him.

The Force flows over him and around him as though he has stepped into a crystal-pure waterfall lost in the green coils of a forgotten rain forest; when he opens himself to that sparkling stream it flows into him and through him and out again without the slightest interference from his conscious will. The part of him that calls itself Obi-Wan Kenobi is no more than a ripple, an eddy in the pool into which he endlessly pours.

There are other parts of him here, as well; there is nothing here that is *not* a part of him, from the scuff mark on R2-D2's dome to the tattered hem of Palpatine's robe, from the spidering crack in one transparisteel panel of the curving view wall above to the great starships that still battle beyond it.

Because this is all part of the Force.

Somehow, mysteriously, the cloud that has darkened the Force for near to a decade and a half has lightened around him now, and he finds within himself the limpid clarity he recalls from his schooldays at the Jedi Temple, when the Force was pure, and clean, and perfect. It is as though the darkness has withdrawn, has coiled back upon itself, to allow him this moment of clarity, to return to him the full power of the light, if only for the moment; he does not know why, but he is incapable of even wondering. In the Force, he is beyond questions.

Why is meaningless; it is an echo of the past, or a whisper from the future. All that matters, for this infinite now, is *what,* and *where,* and *who.*

He is all sixteen of the super battle droids, gleaming in laser-reflective chrome, arms loaded with heavy blasters. He is those blasters and he is their targets. He is all eight destroyer droids waiting with electronic patience within their energy shields, and both bodyguards, and every single one of the shivering Neimoidians. He is their clothes, their boots, even each drop of reptile-scented moisture that rolls off them from the misting sprays they use to keep their internal temperatures down. He is the binders that cuff his hands, and he is the electrostaff in the hands of the bodyguard at his back.

He is both of the lightsabers that the other droid bodyguard marches forward to offer to General Grievous.

And he is the general himself.

He is the general's duranium ribs. He is the beating of Grievous's alien heart, and is the silent pulse of oxygen pumped through his alien veins. He is the weight of four lightsabers at the general's belt, and is the greedy anticipation the captured weapons sparked behind the general's eyes. He is even the plan for his own execution simmering within the general's brain.

He is all these things, but most importantly, he is still Obi-Wan Kenobi.

This is why he can simply stand. Why he can simply wait. He has no need to attack, or to defend. There will be battle here, but he is perfectly at ease, perfectly content to let the battle start when it will start, and let it end when it will end.

Just as he will let himself live, or let himself die.

This is how a great Jedi makes war.

─────────

General Grievous lifted the two lightsabers, one in each dura-nium hand, to admire them by the light of turbolaser blasts out-side, and said, "Rare trophies, these: the weapon of Anakin Skywalker, and the weapon of General Kenobi. I look forward to adding them to my collection."

"That will not happen. I am in control here."

The reply came through Obi-Wan's lips, but it was not truly Obi-Wan who spoke. Obi-Wan was not in control; he had no need for control. He had the Force.

It was the Force that spoke through him.

Grievous stalked forward. Obi-Wan saw death in the cold yellow stare through the skull-mask's eyeholes, and it meant nothing to him at all.

There was no death. There was only the Force.

He didn't have to tell Anakin to subtly nudge Chancellor Palpatine out of the line of fire; part of him *was* Anakin, and was doing this already. He didn't have to tell R2-D2 to access its combat subprograms and divert power to its booster rockets, claw-arm, and cable-gun; the part of him that was the little as-tromech had seen to all these things before they had even en-tered the bridge.

Grievous towered over him. "So confident you are, Kenobi."

"Not confident, merely calm." From so close, Obi-Wan could see the hairline cracks and pitting in the bone-pale mask, and could feel the resonance of the general's electrosonic voice humming in his chest. He remembered the Question of Master Jrul: *What is the good, if not the teacher of the bad? What is the bad, if not the task of the good?*

He said, "We can resolve this situation without further violence. I am willing to accept your surrender."

"I'm sure you are." The skull-mask tilted inquisitively. "Does this preposterous *I-will-accept-your-surrender* line of yours ever actually *work*?"

"Sometimes. When it doesn't, people get hurt. Sometimes they die." Obi-Wan's blue-gray eyes met squarely those of yellow behind the mask. "By *people,* in this case, you should understand that I mean *you*."

"I understand enough. I understand that I will kill you." Grievous threw back his cloak and ignited both lightsabers. "Here. Now. With your own blade."

The Force replied through Obi-Wan's lips, "I don't think so."

The electrodrivers that powered Grievous's limbs could move them faster than the human eye can see; when he swung his arm, it and his fist and the lightsaber within it would literally vanish: wiped from existence by sheer mind-numbing speed, an imitation quantum event. No human being could move remotely as fast as Grievous, not even Obi-Wan—but he didn't have to.

In the Force, part of him was Grievous's intent to slaughter, and the surge from intent to action translated to Obi-Wan's response without thought. He had no need for a plan, no use for tactics.

He had the Force.

That sparkling waterfall coursed through him, washing away any thought of danger, or safety, of winning or losing. The Force, like water, takes on the shape of its container without effort, without thought. The water that was Obi-Wan poured itself into the container that was Grievous's attack, and while some materials might be water-tight, Obi-Wan had yet to encounter any that were entirely, as it were, *Force*-tight . . .

While the intent to swing was still forming in Grievous's mind, the part of the Force that was Obi-Wan was also the part of the Force that was R2-D2, as well as an internal fusion-welder

Anakin had retrofitted into R2-D2's primary grappling arm, and so there was no need for actual communication between them; it was only Obi-Wan's personal sense of style that brought his customary gentle smile to his face and his customary gentle murmur to his lips.

"Artoo?"

Even as he opened his mouth, a panel was sliding aside in the little droid's fuselage; by the time the droid's nickname had left his lips, the fusion-welder had deployed and fired a blinding spray of sparks hot enough to melt duranium, and in the quarter of a second while even Grievous's electronically enhanced reflexes had him startled and distracted, the part of the Force that was Obi-Wan tried a little trick, a secret one that it had been saving up for just such an occasion as this.

Because all there on the bridge was one in the Force, from the gross structure of the ship itself to the quantum dance of the electron shells of individual atoms—and because, after all, the nerves and muscles of the bio-droid general were creations of electronics and duranium, not living tissue with will of its own—it was just barely possible that with exactly the right twist of his mind, in that one vulnerable quarter of a second while Grievous was distracted, flinching backward from a spray of flame hot enough to burn even his armored body, Obi-Wan might be able to temporarily reverse the polarity of the electrodrivers in the general's mechanical hands.

Which is exactly what he did.

Durasteel fingers sprang open, and two lightsabers fell free.

He reached through the Force and the Force reached through him; his blade flared to life while still in the air; it flipped toward him, and as he lifted his hands to meet it, its blue flame flashed between his wrists and severed the binders before the handgrip smacked solidly into his palm.

Obi-Wan was so deep in the Force that he wasn't even suprised it had worked.

He made a quarter turn to face Anakin, who was already in the air, having leapt simultaneously with Obi-Wan's gentle murmur because Obi-Wan and Anakin were, after all, two parts of the same thing; Anakin's flip carried him over Obi-Wan's head at the perfect range for Obi-Wan's blade to flick out and burn through his partner's binders, and while Grievous was still flinching away from the fountain of fusion fire, Anakin landed with his own hand extended; Obi-Wan felt a liquid surge in the waterfall that he was, and Anakin's lightsaber sang through the air and Anakin caught it, and so, one single second after Grievous had begun to summon the intent to swing, Obi-Wan Kenobi and Anakin Skywalker stood back-to-back in the center of the bridge, expressionlessly staring past the snarling blue energy of their lightsabers.

Obi-Wan regarded the general without emotion. "Perhaps you should reconsider my offer."

Grievous braced himself against a control console, its dura-steel housing buckling under his grip. "This is my answer!"

He ripped the console wholly into the air, right out from under the hands of the astonished Neimoidian operator, raised it over his head, and hurled it at the Jedi. They split, rolling out of the console's way as it crashed to the deck, spitting smoke and sparks.

"Open *fire!*" Grievous shook his fists as though each held a Jedi's neck. "Kill them! *Kill them all!*"

For one more second there was only the scuttle of priming levers on dozens of blasters.

One second after that, the bridge exploded into a firestorm.

Grievous hung back, crouching, watching for a moment as his two MagnaGuards waded into the Jedi, electrostaffs whirling through the blinding hail of blasterfire that ricocheted around the bridge. Grievous had fought Jedi before, sometimes even in open battle, and he had found that fighting any one Jedi was much like fighting any other.

Kenobi, though—

The ease with which Kenobi had taken command of the situation was frightening. More frightening was the fact that of the two, Skywalker was reportedly the greater warrior. And even their *R2* unit could fight: the little astromech had some kind of aftermarket cable-gun it had used to entangle the legs of a super droid and yank it off its feet, and now was jerking the droid this way and that so that its arm cannons were blasting chunks off its squadmates instead of the Jedi.

Grievous was starting to think less about winning this particular encounter than about surviving it.

Let his MagnaGuards fight the Jedi; that's what they were designed for—and they were doing their jobs well. IG-101 had pressed Kenobi back against a console, lightning blazing from his electrostaff's energy shield where it pushed on Kenobi's blade; the Jedi general might have died then and there, except that one of the simple-minded super battle droids turned both arm cannons on his back, giving Kenobi the chance to duck and allow the hammering blaster bolts to slam 101 stumbling backward. Skywalker had stashed the Chancellor somewhere—that sniveling coward Palpatine was probably trembling under one of the control consoles—and had managed to sever both of 102's legs below the knee, which for some reason he apparently expected to end the fight; he seemed completely astonished when 102 whirled nimbly on one end of his electrostaff and used the stumps of his legs to thump Skywalker so soundly the Jedi went down skidding.

On the other hand, Grievous thought, *this might be salvageable after all.*

He tapped his internal comlink's jaw sensor to the general droid command frequency. "The Chancellor is hiding under one of the consoles. Squad Sixteen, find him, and deliver him to my escape pod immediately. Squad Eight, stay on mission. Kill the Jedi."

Then the ship bucked, sharper than it ever had, and the view wall panels whited out as radiation-scatter sleeted through the bridge. Alarm klaxons blared. The nav console flared sparks into the face of a Neimoidian pilot, setting his uniform on fire and adding his screams to the din, and another console exploded, ripping the newly promoted senior gunnery officer into a pile of shredded meat.

Ah, Grievous thought. In all the excitement, he had entirely forgotten about Lieutenant Commander Needa and *Integrity.*

The other pilot—the one who wasn't shrieking and slapping at the flames on his uniform until his own hands caught fire— leaned as far away from his screaming partner as his crash webbing would allow and shouted, "General, that shot destroyed the last of the aft control cells! The ship is *deorbiting!* We're going to burn!"

"Very well," Grievous said calmly. "Stay on course." Now it no longer mattered whether his bodyguards could overpower the Jedi or not: they would all burn together.

He tapped his jaw sensor to the control frequency for the escape pods; one coded order ensured that his personal pod would be waiting for him with engines hot and systems checks complete.

When he looked back to the fight, all he could see of IG-102 was one arm, the saber-cut joint still white hot. Skywalker was pursuing two super battle droids that had Palpatine by the arms. While Skywalker dismantled the droids with swift cuts, Kenobi was in the process of doing the same to IG-101—the MagnaGuard was hopping on its one remaining leg, whirling its electrostaff with its one remaining arm, and screeching some improbable threat regarding its staff and Kenobi's body cavities—and after Kenobi cut off the arm, 101 went hopping after him, still screeching. The droid actually managed to land one glancing kick before the Jedi casually severed its other leg, after which 101's limbless torso continued to writhe on the deck, howling.

With both MagnaGuards down, all eight destroyers opened up, dual cannons erupting gouts of galvened particle beams. The two Jedi leapt together to screen the Chancellor, and before Grievous could command the destroyers to cease fire, the Jedi had deflected enough of the bolts to blow apart three-quarters of the remaining super battle droids and send the survivors scurrying for cover beside what was left of the cringing Neimoidians.

The destroyers began to close in, hosing down the Jedi with heavy fire, advancing step by step, cannons against lightsabers; the Jedi caught every blast and sent them back against the destroyers' shields that flared in spherical haloes as they absorbed the reflected bolts. The destroyers might very well have prevailed over the Jedi, except for one unexpected difficulty—

Gravity shear.

All eight of them suddenly seemed, inexplicably, to leap into the air, followed by Skywalker, and Palpatine, and chairs and pieces of MagnaGuards and everything else on the bridge that was not bolted to the deck, except for Kenobi, who managed to grab a control console and now was hanging by one hand, upside down, still effortlessly deflecting blaster bolts.

The surviving Neimoidian pilot was screaming orders for the droids to magnetize, then started howling that the ship was breaking up, and managed to make so much annoying noise that Grievous smashed his skull out of simple irritation. Then he looked around and realized he'd just killed the last of his crew: all the bridge crew he hadn't slain personally had sucked up the bulk of the random blaster ricochets.

Grievous shook the pilot's brains off his fist. Disgusting creatures, Neimoidians.

The invisible plane of altered gravity passed over the biodroid general without effect—his talons of magnetized duranium kept him right where he was—and as one of the MagnaGuards' electrostaffs fell past him, his invisibly fast hand snatched it from the air. When another plane of gravity shear swept through the bridge, droids, Chancellor, and Jedi all fell back to the floor.

Though the droideka, also known as the destroyer droid, was the most powerful infantry combat droid in general production, it had one major design flaw. The energy shield that was so effective in stopping blasters, slugs, shrapnel, and even lightsabers was precisely tuned to englobe the droid in a standing position; if the droid was no longer standing—say, if it was knocked down, or thrown into a wall—the shield generator could not distinguish a floor or a wall from a weapon, and would keep ramping up power to disintegrate this perceived threat until the generator shorted itself out.

Between falling to the ceiling, bouncing off it, and falling back to the floor, the sum total output of all the shield generators of Squad Eight was, currently, one large cloud of black smoke.

It was impossible to say which one of them opened fire on the Jedi, and it didn't matter; inside of two seconds, eight droidekas had become eight piles of smoking scrap, and two Jedi, entirely unscathed, walked out of the smoke side by side.

Without a word, they parted to bracket the general.

Grievous clicked the electrostaff's power setting to overload; it spat lightning around him as he lifted it to combat ready. "I am sorry I don't have time to fight you—it would have been an interesting match—but I have an appointment with an escape pod. And you . . ."

He pointed at the transparisteel view wall and triggered his own concealed cable-gun, not unlike the one that fancy astromech of theirs had; the cable shot out and its grappling claw buried itself in one of the panel supports.

"You," he said, "have appointments with death."

The Jedi leapt, and Grievous hurled the overloading electrostaff—but not at the Jedi.

He threw it at a window.

One of the transparisteel panels of the view wall had cracked under a glancing hit from a starfighter's cannon; when the sparking electrostaff hit it squarely and exploded like a proton grenade, the whole panel blew out into space.

A hurricane roared to life, raging through the bridge, seizing Neimoidian corpses and pieces of droids and wreckage and hurling them out through the gap along with a white fountain of flash-frozen air. Grievous sprang straight up into the instant hurricane, narrowly avoiding the two Jedi, whose leaps had become frantic tumbles as they tried to avoid being sucked through along with him. Grievous, though, had no need to breathe, nor had he any fear of his body fluids boiling in the vacuum—the pressurized synthflesh that enclosed the living parts within his droid exoskeleton saw to that—so he simply rode the storm right out into space until he reached the end of the cable and it snapped tight and swung him whipping back toward *Invisible Hand*'s hull.

He cast off the cable. His hands and feet of magnetized duranium let him scramble along the hull without difficulty, the light-spidered curve of Coruscant's nightside whirling around him. He clambered over to the external locks of the bridge escape pods and punched in a command code. Looking back over his shoulder, he experienced a certain chilly satisfaction as he watched empty escape pods blast free of the *Hand*'s bridge and streak away.

All of them.

Well: all but one.

No trick of the Force would spring Kenobi and Skywalker out of this one. It was a shame he didn't have a spy probe handy to leave on the bridge; he would have enjoyed watching the Republic's greatest heroes burn.

The ion streaks of the escape pods spiraled through the battle that still flashed and flared silently in the void, pursued by starfighters and armed retrieval ships. Grievous nodded to himself; that should occupy them long enough for his command pod to make the run to his escape ship.

As he entered his customized pod, he reflected that he was, for the first time in his career, violating orders: though he was under strict orders to leave the Chancellor unharmed, Palpatine was about to die alongside his precious Jedi.

Then Grievous shrugged, and sighed. What more could he have done? There was a war on, after all.

He was sure Lord Sidious would forgive him.

On the bridge, a blast shield had closed over the destroyed transparisteel window, and every last surviving combat-model droid had been cut to pieces even before the atmosphere had had a chance to stabilize.

But there was a more serious problem.

The bucking of the ship had become continuous. White-hot sparks outside streamed backward past the view wall windows. Those sparks, according to the three different kinds of alarms that were all screaming through the bridge at once, were what was left of the ablative shielding on the nose of the disabled cruiser.

Anakin stared grimly down at a console readout. "All the escape pods are gone. Not one left on the whole ship." He looked up at Obi-Wan. "We're trapped."

Obi-Wan appeared more interested than actually concerned. "Well. Here's a chance to display your legendary piloting skills, my young friend. You can fly this cruiser, can't you?"

"Flying's no problem. The trick is *landing*, which, ah . . ." Anakin gave a slightly shaky laugh. "Which, you know, this cruiser is not exactly designed to do. Even when it's in *one* piece."

Obi-Wan looked unimpressed. "And so?"

Anakin unsnapped the crash webbing that held the pilot's corpse and pulled the body from its chair. "And so you'd better strap in," he said, settling into the chair, his fingers sliding over the unfamiliar controls.

The cruiser bounced even harder, and its attitude began to skew as a new klaxon joined the blare of the other alarms. "That wasn't me!" Anakin jerked his hands away from the board. "I haven't even *done* anything yet!"

"It certainly wasn't." Palpatine's voice was unnaturally calm. "It seems someone is shooting at us."

"Wonderful," Anakin muttered. "Could this day get any better?"

"Perhaps we can talk with them." Obi-Wan moved over to the comm station and began working the screen. "Let them know we've captured the ship."

"All right, take the comm," Anakin said. He pointed at the copilot's station. "Artoo: second chair. Chancellor?"

"Yes?"

"Strap in. Now. We're going in hot." Anakin grimaced at the

scraps of burning hull flashing past the view wall. "In more ways than one."

The vast space battle that had ripped and battered Coruscant space all this long, long day, finally began to flicker out.

The shimmering canopy of ion trails and turbolaser bursts was fading into streaks of ships achieving jump as the Separatist strike force fled in full retreat. The light of Coruscant's distant star splintered through iridescent clouds of gas crystals that were the remains of starfighters, and of pilots. Damaged cruisers limped toward spaceyards, passing shattered hulks that hung dead in the infinite day that is interplanetary space. Prize crews took command of surrendered ships, imprisoning the living among their crews and affixing restraining bolts to the droids.

The dayside surface of the capital planet was shrouded in smoke from a million fires touched off by meteorite impacts of ship fragments; far too many had fallen to be tracked and destroyed by the planet's surface-defense umbrella. The nightside's sheet of artificial lights faded behind the red-white glow from craters of burning steel; each impact left a caldera of unimaginable death. In the skies of Coruscant now, the important vessels were no longer warships, but were instead the fire-suppression and rescue craft that crisscrossed the planet.

Now one last fragmentary ship screamed into the atmosphere, coming in too fast, too steep, pieces breaking off to spread apart and stream their own contrails of superheated vapor; banks of turbolasers on the surface-defense towers isolated their signature, and starfighters whipped onto interception courses to thin out whatever fragments the SD towers might miss, and far above, beyond the atmosphere, on the bridge of RSS *Integrity,* Lieutenant Commander Lorth Needa spoke urgently to a knee-high blue ghost scanned into existence by the phased-array lasers in a holocomm: an alien in Jedi robes, with bulging eyes set in a wrinkled face and long, pointed, oddly flexible ears.

"You have to stand down the surface-defense system, sir! It's

General Kenobi!" Needa insisted. "His code verifies, Skywalker is with him—and *they have Chancellor Palpatine!*"

"Heard and understood this is," the Jedi responded calmly. *"Tell me what they require."*

Needa glanced down at the boil of hull plating that was burning off the falling cruiser, and even as he looked, the ship broke in half at the hangar deck; the rear half tumbled, exploding in sections, but whoever was flying the front half must have been one of the greatest pilots Needa had ever even *heard* of: the front half wobbled and slewed but somehow righted itself using nothing but a bank of thrusters and its atmospheric drag fins.

"First, a flight of fireships," Needa said, more calmly now. "If they don't get the burnoff under control, there won't be enough hull left to make the surface. And a hardened docking platform, the strongest available; they won't be able to set it down. This won't be a landing, it will be a controlled crash. Repeat: a controlled crash."

"Heard and understood this is," the hologrammic Jedi repeated. *"Crossload their transponder signature."* When this was done, the Jedi nodded grave approval. *"Thank you, Lieutenant Commander. Valiant service for the Republic you have done today—and the gratitude of the Jedi Order you have earned. Yoda out."*

On the bridge of *Integrity,* Lorth Needa now could only stand, and watch, hands clasped behind his back. Military discipline kept him expressionless, but pale bands began at his knuckles and spread whiteness nearly to his wrists.

Every bone in his body ached with helplessness.

Because he knew: that fragment of a ship was a death trap. No one could land such a hulk, not even Skywalker. Each second that passed before its final breakup and burn was a miracle in itself, a testament to the gifts of a pilot who was justly legendary—but when each second is a miracle, how many of them can be strung together in a row?

Lorth Needa was not religious, nor was he a philosopher or

metaphysician; he knew of the Force only by reputation, but nonetheless now he found himself asking the Force, in his heart, that when the fiery end came for the men in that scrap of a ship, it might as least come quickly.

His eyes stung. The irony of it burned the back of his throat. The Home Fleet had fought brilliantly, and the Jedi had done their superhuman part; against all odds, the Republic had won the day.

Yet this battle had been fought to save Supreme Chancellor Palpatine.

They had won the battle, but now, as Needa stood watching helplessly, he couldn't help feeling that they were about to lose the war.

———

This is Anakin Skywalker's masterpiece:

Many people say he is the best star pilot in the galaxy, but that's merely talk, born of the constant HoloNet references to his unmatched string of kills in starfighter combat. Blowing up vulture droids and tri-fighters is simply a matter of superior reflexes and trust in the Force; he has spent so many hours in the cockpit that he wears a Jedi starfighter like clothes. It's his own body, with thrusters for legs and cannons for fists.

What he is doing right now transcends mere flying the way Jedi combat transcends a schoolyard scuffle.

He sits in a blood-spattered, blaster-chopped chair behind a console he's never seen before, a console with controls designed for alien fingers. The ship he's in is not only bucking like a maddened dewback through brutal coils of clear-air turbulence, it's on fire and breaking up like a comet ripping apart as it crashes into a gas giant. He has only seconds to learn how to maneuver an alien craft that not only has no aft control cells, but has no *aft* at all.

This is, put simply, impossible. It can't be done.

He's going to do it anyway.

Because he is Anakin Skywalker, and he doesn't believe in *impossible*.

He extends his hands and for one long, long moment he merely strokes controls, feeling their shape under his fingers, listening to the shivers his soft touch brings to each remaining control surface of the disintegrating ship, allowing their resonances to join inside his head until they resolve into harmony like a Ferroan joy-harp virtuoso checking the tuning of his instrument.

And at the same time, he draws power from the Force. He gathers perception, and luck, and sucks into himself the instinctive, preconscious *what-will-happen-in-the-next-ten-seconds* intuition that has always been the core of his talent.

And then he begins.

On the downbeat, atmospheric drag fins deploy; as he tweaks their angles and cycles them in and out to slow the ship's descent without burning them off altogether, their contrabass roar takes on a punctuated rhythm like a heart that skips an occasional beat. The forward attitude thrusters, damaged in the ship-to-ship battle, now fire in random directions, but he can feel where they're taking him and he strokes them in sequence, making their song the theme of his impromptu concerto.

And the true inspiration, the sparkling grace note of genius that brings his masterpiece to life, is the soprano counterpoint: a syncopated sequence of exterior hatches in the outer hull sliding open and closed and open again, subtly altering the aerodynamics of the ship to give it just exactly the amount of sideslip or lift or yaw to bring the huge half cruiser into the approach cone of a pinpoint target an eighth of the planet away.

It is the Force that makes this possible, and more than the Force. Anakin has no interest in serene acceptance of what the Force will bring. Not here. Not now. Not with the lives of Palpatine and Obi-Wan at stake. It's just the opposite: he seizes upon the Force with a stark refusal to fail.

He *will* land this ship.

He *will* save his friends.

Between his will and the will of the Force, there is no contest.

PART TWO

SEDUCTION

The dark is generous, and it is patient.

It is the dark that seeds cruelty into justice, that drips contempt into compassion, that poisons love with grains of doubt.

The dark can be patient, because the slightest drop of rain will cause those seeds to sprout.

The rain will come, and the seeds will sprout, for the dark is the soil in which they grow, and it is the clouds above them, and it waits behind the star that gives them light.

The dark's patience is infinite.

Eventually, even stars burn out.

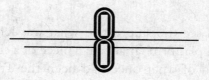

FAULT LINES

Mace Windu hung on to the corrugated hatch grip beside the gunship's open troop bay with one hand, squinting into the wind that whipped his overcloak behind him. His other hand shaded his eyes against the glare from one of the orbital mirrors that concentrated the capital planet's daylight. The mirror was slowly turning aside now, allowing a band of twilight to approach the gunship's destination.

That destination, a kilometer-thick landing platform in the planet's vast industrial zone, was marked with a steeply slanting tower of smoke and vapor that stretched from the planet's surface to the uppermost reaches of the atmosphere, a tower that only now was beginning to spread and coil from its tiny source point to a horizon-spanning smear across the stratospheric winds.

The gunship roared over the bottomless canyons of durasteel and permacrete that formed the landscape of Coruscant, arrowing straight for the industrial zone without regard for the rigid traffic laws that governed flight on the galactic planet; until martial law was officially lifted by the Senate, the darkening skies would be traveled only by Republic military craft, Jedi transports, and emergency vehicles.

The gunship qualified as all three.

Mace could see the ship now—what was left of it—resting on the scorched platform far ahead: a piece of a ship, a fragment, less than a third of what once had been the Trade Federation flagship, still burning despite the gouts of fire-suppression foam raining down on it from five different ships and the emergency-support clone troops who surrounded it on the platform.

Mace shook his head. Skywalker again. The chosen one.

Who else could have brought in this hulk? Who else could have even come close?

The gunship swung into a hot landing, repulsors howling; Mace hopped out before it could settle, and gave the pilot an open-palm gesture to signal him to wait. The pilot, faceless within his helmet, responded with a closed fist.

Though, of course, the pilot wasn't faceless at all. Under his armored helmet, that clone pilot had a face that Mace Windu remembered all too well.

That face would always remind him that he had once held Dooku within his grasp, and had let him slip away.

Across the platform, an escape pod hatch cycled open. Emergency crews scrambled with an escape slide, and a moment later the Supreme Chancellor, Obi-Wan Kenobi, and Anakin Skywalker were all on the deck beside the burning ship, closely followed by a somewhat battered R2 unit that lifted itself down on customized maneuvering rockets.

Mace strode swiftly out to meet them.

Palpatine's robes were scorched and tattered at the hem, and he seemed weak; he leaned a bit on Skywalker's shoulder as they moved away from the ship. On Skywalker's other side, Master Kenobi seemed a touch the worse for wear himself: caked with dust and leaking a trickle of blood from a scalp wound.

Skywalker, by contrast, looked every bit the HoloNet hero he was supposed to be. He seemed to tower over his companions, as though he had somehow gotten even taller in the months since Mace had seen him last. His hair was tousled, his color was high, and his walk still had the grounded grace of a natural fighter, but there was something new in his physicality: in the way he moved his head, perhaps, or the way the weight of Palpatine's arm on his shoulder seemed somehow to belong there . . . or something less definable. Some new ease, new confidence. An aura of inner power.

Presence.

Skywalker was not the same young man the Council had sent off to the Outer Rim five standard months ago.

"Chancellor," Mace said as he met them. "Are you well? Do you need medical attention?" He gestured over his shoulder at the waiting gunship. "I have a fully equipped field surgery—"

"No, no, no need," Palpatine said, rather faintly. "Thank you, Master Windu, but I am well. Quite well, thanks to these two."

Mace nodded. "Master Kenobi? Anakin?"

"Never better," Skywalker replied, looking as if he meant it, and Kenobi only shrugged, with a slight wince as he touched his scalp wound.

"Only a bump on the head. That field surgery must be needed elsewhere."

"It is." Mace looked grim. "We don't have even a preliminary estimate of civilian casualties."

He waved off the gunship, and it roared away toward the countless fires that painted red the approach of night.

"A shuttle is on its way. Chancellor, we'll have you on the Senate floor within the hour. The HoloNet has already been notified that you will want to make a statement."

"I will. I will, indeed." Palpatine touched Mace on the arm. "You have always been of great value to me, Master Windu. Thank you."

"The Jedi are honored to serve the Senate, sir." There might have been the slightest emphasis on the word *Senate*. Mace remained expressionless as he subtly moved his arm away from the Chancellor's hand. He looked at Obi-Wan. "Is there anything else to report, Master Kenobi? What of General Grievous?"

"Count Dooku was there," Skywalker interjected. He had a look on his face that Mace couldn't decipher, proud yet wary—even unhappy. "He's dead now."

"Dead?" He looked from Anakin to Obi-Wan and back again. "Is this true? You killed Count *Dooku?*"

"My young friend is too modest; *he* killed Count Dooku." Smiling, Kenobi touched the lump on his head. "I was . . . taking a nap."

"But . . ." Mace blinked. Dooku was to the Separatists what Palpatine was to the Republic: the center of gravity binding together a spiral galaxy of special interests. With Dooku gone, the Confederacy of Independent Systems would no longer really be a confederacy at all. They'd fly to pieces within weeks.

Within *days.*

Mace said again, "But . . ."

And, in the end, he couldn't think of a *but.*

This was all so astonishing that he very nearly—almost, but not quite—cracked a smile.

"That is," he said, "the best news I've heard since . . ." He shook his head. "Since I can't remember. Anakin—how did you *do* it?"

Inexplicably, young Skywalker looked distinctly uncomfortable; that newly confident presence of his collapsed as suddenly as an overloaded deflector, and instead of meeting Mace's eyes, his gaze flicked to Palpatine. Somehow Mace didn't think this was modesty. He looked to the Chancellor as well, his elation sinking, becoming puzzlement tinged with suspicion.

"It was . . . entirely extraordinary," Palpatine said blandly, oblivious to Mace's narrowing stare. "I know next to nothing of swordplay, of course; to my amateur's eye, it seemed that Count Dooku may have been . . . a trace overconfident. Especially after having disposed of Master Kenobi so neatly."

Obi-Wan flushed, just a bit—and Anakin flushed considerably more deeply.

"Perhaps young Anakin was simply more . . . highly *motivated,*" Palpatine said, turning a fond smile upon him. "After all,

Dooku was fighting only to slay an enemy; Anakin was fighting to save—if I may presume the honor—a friend."

Mace's scowl darkened. Fine words. Perhaps even true words, but he still didn't like them.

No one on the Jedi Council had ever been comfortable with Skywalker's close relationship with the Chancellor—they'd had more than one conversation about it with Obi-Wan while Skywalker had still been his Padawan—and Mace was less than happy to hear Palpatine speaking for a young Jedi who seemed unprepared to speak for himself. He said, "I'm sure the Council will be very interested in your full report, Anakin," with just enough emphasis on *full* to get his point across.

Skywalker swallowed, and then, just as suddenly as it had collapsed, that aura of calm, centered confidence rebuilt itself around him. "Yes. Yes of course, Master Windu."

"And we must report that Grievous escaped," Obi-Wan said. "He is as cowardly as ever."

Mace accepted this news with a nod. "But he is only a military commander. Without Dooku to hold the coalition together, these so-called independent systems will splinter, and they know it." He looked straight into the Supreme Chancellor's eyes. "This is our best chance to sue for peace. We can end this war right now."

And while Palpatine answered, Mace Windu reached into the Force.

To Mace's Force perception, the world crystallized around them, becoming a gem of reality shot through with flaws and fault lines of possibility. This was Mace's particular gift: to see how people and situations fit together in the Force, to find the shear planes that can cause them to break in useful ways, and to intuit what sort of strike would best make the cut. Though he could not consistently determine the significance of the structures he perceived—the darkening cloud upon the Force that had risen with the rebirth of the Sith made that harder and harder with each passing day—the presence of shatterpoints was always clear.

Mace had supported the training of Anakin Skywalker, though it ran counter to millennia of Jedi tradition, because from the structure of fault lines in the Force around him, he had been able to intuit the truth of Qui-Gon Jinn's guess: that the young slave boy from Tatooine was in fact the prophesied chosen one, born to bring balance to the Force. He had argued for the elevation of Obi-Wan Kenobi to Mastership, and to give the training of the chosen one into the hands of this new, untested Master, because his unique perception had shown him powerful lines of destiny that bound their lives together, for good or ill. On the day of Palpatine's election to the Chancellorship, he had seen that Palpatine was himself a shatterpoint of unimaginable significance: a man upon whom might depend the fate of the Republic itself.

Now he saw the three men together, and the intricate lattice of fault lines and stress fractures that bound them each to the other was so staggeringly powerful that its structure was beyond calculation.

Anakin was somehow a pivot point, the fulcrum of a lever with Obi-Wan on one side, Palpatine on the other, and the galaxy in the balance, but the dark cloud on the Force prevented his perception from reaching into the future for so much as a hint of where this might lead. The balance was already so delicate that he could not guess the outcome of any given shift: the slightest tip in any direction would generate chaotic oscillation. Anything could happen.

Anything at all.

And the lattice of fault lines that bound all three of them to each other stank of the dark side.

He lifted his head and looked to the sky, picking out the dropping star of the Jedi shuttle as it swung toward them through the darkening afternoon.

"I'm afraid peace is out of the question while Grievous is at large," the Chancellor was saying sadly. "Dooku was the only check on Grievous's monstrous lust for slaughter; with Dooku gone, the general has been unleashed to rampage across the galaxy. I'm afraid that, far from being over, this war is about to get a very great deal *worse*."

"And what of the Sith?" Obi-Wan said. "Dooku's death should have at least begun the weakening of the darkness, but instead it feels stronger than ever. I fear Master Yoda's intuition is correct: that Dooku was merely the apprentice to the Sith Lord, not the Master."

Mace started walking toward the small-craft dock where the Jedi shuttle would land, and the others fell in with him.

"The Sith Lord, if one still exists, will reveal himself in time. They always do." He hoped Obi-Wan would take the hint and shut up about it; Mace had no desire to speak openly of the investigation in front of the Supreme Chancellor.

The less Palpatine knew, the better.

"A more interesting puzzle is Grievous," he said. "He had you at his mercy, Chancellor, and mercy is not numbered among his virtues. Though we all rejoice that he spared you, I cannot help but wonder why."

Palpatine spread his hands. "I can only assume the Separatists preferred to have me as a hostage rather than as a martyr. Though it is of course impossible to say; it may merely have been a whim of the general. He is notoriously erratic."

"Perhaps the Separatist leadership can restrain him, in exchange for certain . . ." Mace let his gaze drift casually to a point somewhere above the Chancellor's head. ". . . considerations."

"Absolutely not." Palpatine drew himself up, straightening his robes. "A negotiated peace would be a recognition of the CIS as the legitimate government of the rebellious systems— tantamount to losing the war! No, Master Windu, this war can end only one way. Unconditional surrender. And while Grievous lives, that will never happen."

"Very well," Mace said. "Then the Jedi will make the capture of General Grievous our particular task." He glanced at Anakin and Obi-Wan, then back to Palpatine. He leaned close to the Chancellor and his voice went low and final, with a buried intensity that hinted—just the slightest bit—of suspicion, and warning. "This war has gone on far too long already. We will find him, and this war *will* end."

"I have no doubt of it." Palpatine strolled along, seemingly oblivious. "But we should never underestimate the deviousness of the Separatists. It is possible that even the war itself has been only one further move," he said with elegant, understated precision, "in some greater game."

As the Jedi shuttle swung toward the Chancellor's private landing platform at the Senate Offices, Obi-Wan watched Anakin pretending not to stare out the window. On the platform was a small welcome-contingent of Senators, and Anakin was trying desperately to look as if he wasn't searching that little crowd hungrily for a particular face. The pretense was a waste of time; Anakin radiated excitement so powerfully in the Force that Obi-Wan could practically hear the thunder of his heartbeat.

Obi-Wan gave a silent sigh. He had entirely too good an idea whose face his former Padawan was so hoping to see.

When the shuttle touched down, Master Windu caught his eye from beyond Anakin's shoulder. The Korun Master made a nearly invisible gesture, to which Obi-Wan did not visibly respond; but when Palpatine and Anakin and R2 all debarked toward the crowd of well-wishers, Obi-Wan stayed behind.

Anakin stopped on the landing deck, looking back at Obi-Wan. "You coming?"

"I haven't the courage for politics," Obi-Wan said, showing his usual trace of a smile. "I'll brief the Council."

"Shouldn't I be there, too?"

"No need. This isn't the formal report. Besides—" Obi-Wan nodded toward the clot of HoloNet crews clogging the pedestrian gangway. "—someone has to be the poster boy."

Anakin looked pained. "Poster *man*."

"Quite right, quite right," Obi-Wan said with a gentle chuckle. "Go meet your public, Poster Man."

"Wait a minute—this whole operation was *your* idea. You planned it. You led the rescue. It's your turn to take the bows."

"You won't get out of it that easily, my young friend. Without you, I wouldn't even have made it to the flagship. You killed Count Dooku, and single-handedly rescued the Chancellor . . . all while, I might be forgiven for adding, carrying some old broken-down Jedi Master unconscious on your back. Not to mention making a landing that will be the standard of Impossible in every flight manual for the next thousand years."

"Only because of your training, Master—"

"That's just an excuse. You're the hero. Go spend your glorious day surrounded by—" Obi-Wan allowed himself a slightly disparaging cough. "—politicians."

"Come on, Master—you *owe* me. And not just for saving your skin for the tenth time—"

"*Ninth* time. Cato Neimoidia doesn't count; it was your fault in the first place." Obi-Wan waved him off. "See you at the Outer Rim briefing in the morning."

"Well . . . all right. Just this once." Anakin laughed and waved, and then headed briskly off to catch up with Palpatine as the Chancellor waded into the Senators with the smooth-as-oiled-transparisteel ease of the lifelong politician.

The hatch cycled shut, the shuttle lifted off, and Obi-Wan's smile faded as he turned to Mace Windu. "You wanted to speak with me."

Windu moved close to Obi-Wan's position by the window, nodding out at the scene on the landing platform. "It's Anakin. I don't like his relationship with Palpatine."

"We've had this conversation before."

"There is something between them. Something new. I could see it in the Force." Mace's voice was flat and grim. "It felt powerful. And incredibly dangerous."

Obi-Wan spread his hands. "I trust Anakin with my life."

"I know you do. I only wish we could trust the Chancellor with Anakin's."

"Yes," Obi-Wan said, frowning. "Palpatine's policies are . . . sometimes questionable. But he dotes on Anakin like a kindly old uncle on his favorite nephew."

Mace stared out the window. "The Chancellor loves power. If he has any other passion, I have not seen it."

Obi-Wan shook his head with a trace of disbelief. "I recall that not so long ago, you were something of an admirer of his."

"Things," Mace Windu said grimly, "change."

Flying over a landscape pocked with smoldering wreckage where once tall buildings filled with living beings had gleamed in the sun, toward a Temple filled with memories of so many, many Jedi who would never return from this war, Obi-Wan could not disagree.

After a moment, he said, "What would you have me do?"

"I am not certain. You know my power; I cannot always interpret what I've seen. Be alert. Be mindful of Anakin, and be careful of Palpatine. He is not to be trusted, and his influence on Anakin is dangerous."

"But Anakin is the chosen one—"

"All the more reason to fear an outsider's influence. We have circumstantial evidence that traces Sidious to Palpatine's inner circle."

Suddenly Obi-Wan had difficulty breathing. "Are you certain?"

Mace shook his head. "Nothing is certain. But this raid—the capture of Palpatine had to be an inside job. And the timing . . . we were closing *in* on him, Master Kenobi! The information you and Anakin discovered—we had traced the Sith Lord to an abandoned factory in The Works, not far from where Anakin landed the cruiser. When the attack began, we were tracking him through the downlevel tunnels." Mace stared out the viewport at a vast residential complex that dominated the skyline to the west. "The trail led to the sub-basement of Five Hundred Republica."

Five Hundred Republica was the most exclusive address on the planet. Its inhabitants included only the incredibly wealthy or the incredibly powerful, from Raith Sienar of the Sienar Systems conglomerate to Palpatine himself. Obi-Wan could only say, "Oh."

"We have to face the possibility—the probability—that what

Dooku told you on Geonosis was actually *true*. That the Senate is under the influence—under the control—of Darth Sidious. That it has been for *years*."

"Do you—" Obi-Wan had to swallow before he could go on. "Do you have any suspects?"

"Too many. All we know of Sidious is that he's bipedal, of roughly human conformation. Sate Pestage springs to mind. I wouldn't rule out Mas Amedda, either. The Sith Lord might even be hiding among the Red Guards. There's no way to know."

"Who's handling the questioning?" Obi-Wan asked. "I'd be happy to sit in; my perceptions are not so refined as some, but—" .

Mace shook his head. "Interrogate the Supreme Chancellor's personal aides and advisors? Impossible."

"But—"

"Palpatine will never allow it. Though he hasn't said so . . ." Mace stared out the window. ". . . I'm not sure he even believes the Sith exist."

Obi-Wan blinked. "But—how can he—"

"Look at it from his point of view: the only real evidence we have is Dooku's word. And he's dead now."

"The Sith Lord on Naboo—the Zabrak who killed Qui-Gon—"

Mace shrugged. "Destroyed. As you know." He shook his head. "Relations with the Chancellor's Office are . . . difficult. I feel he has lost his trust in the Jedi; I have certainly lost my trust in him."

"But he doesn't have the authority to interfere with a Jedi investigation . . ." Obi-Wan frowned, suddenly uncertain. "Does he?"

"The Senate has surrendered so much power, it's hard to say where his authority stops."

"It's that bad?"

Mace's jaw locked. "The only reason Palpatine's not a suspect is because he *already* rules the galaxy."

"But we are closer than we have ever been to rooting out the

Sith," Obi-Wan said slowly. "That can only be good news. I would think that Anakin's friendship with Palpatine could be of use to us in this—he has the kind of access to Palpatine that other Jedi might only dream of. Their friendship is an asset, not a danger."

"You can't tell him."

"I beg your pardon?"

"Of the whole Council, only Yoda and myself know how deep this actually goes. And now you. I have decided to share this with you because you are in the best situation to watch Anakin. Watch him. Nothing more."

"We—" Obi-Wan shook his head helplessly. "We don't keep secrets from each other."

"You must keep this one." Mace laced his fingers together and squeezed until his knuckles crackled like blasterfire. "Skywalker is arguably the most powerful Jedi alive, and he is still getting stronger. But he is not *stable*. You know it. We all do. It is why he cannot be given Mastership. We must keep him off the Council, despite his extraordinary gifts. And Jedi prophecy . . . is not absolute. The less he has to do with Palpatine, the better."

"But surely—" Obi-Wan stopped himself. He thought of how many times Anakin had violated orders. He thought of how unflinchingly loyal Anakin was to anyone he considered a friend. He thought of the danger Palpatine faced unknowingly, with a Sith Lord among his advisers . . .

Master Windu was right. This was a secret Anakin could not be trusted to keep.

"What *can* I tell him?"

"Tell him nothing. I sense the dark side around him. Around them both."

"As it is around us all," Obi-Wan reminded him. "The dark side touches all of us, Master Windu. Even you."

"I know that too well, Obi-Wan." For one second Obi-Wan saw something raw and haunted in the Korun Master's eyes. Mace turned away. "It is possible that we may have to . . . move against Palpatine."

"Move *against*—?"

"If he is truly under the control of a Sith Lord, it may be the only way."

Obi-Wan's whole body had gone numb. This didn't seem real. It was not possible that he was actually having this conversation.

"You haven't *been* here, Obi-Wan." Mace stared bleakly down at his hands. "You've been off fighting the war in the Outer Rim. You don't know what it's been like, dealing with all the petty squabbles and special interests and greedy, grasping fools in the Senate, and Palpatine's constant, cynical, ruthless maneuvering for power—he carves away chunks of our freedom and bandages the wounds with tiny scraps of security. And for what? Look at this planet, Obi-Wan! We have given up so much freedom—how secure do we *look*?"

Obi-Wan's heart clenched. This was not the Mace Windu he knew and admired; it was as though the darkness in the Force was so much thicker here on Coruscant that it had breathed poison into Mace's spirit—and perhaps was even breeding suspicion and dissension among the members of the Jedi Council.

The greatest danger from the darkness outside came when Jedi fed it with the darkness within.

He had feared he might find matters had deteriorated when he returned to Coruscant and the Temple; not even in his darkest dreams had he thought it would get this bad.

"Master Windu—Mace. We'll go to Yoda together," he said firmly. "And among the three of us we'll work something out. We will. You'll see."

"It may be too late already."

"It may be. And it may not be. We can only do what we can do, Mace. A very, very wise Jedi once said to me, *We don't have to win. All we have to do is fight.*"

Some of the lines erased themselves from the Korun Master's face then, and when he met Obi-Wan's eye there was a quirk at the corner of his mouth that might someday develop into a smile—a tired, sad smile, but a smile nonetheless. "I seem," he said slowly, "to have forgotten that particular Jedi. Thank you for reminding me."

"It was the least I could do," Obi-Wan said lightly, but a sad weight had gathered on his chest.

Things change, indeed.

Anakin's heart pounded in his throat, but he kept smiling, and nodding, and shaking hands—and trying desperately to work his way toward a familiar golden-domed protocol droid who hung back beyond the crowd of Senators, right arm lifted in a small, tentative wave at R2-D2.

She wasn't here. Why wasn't she here?

Something must have happened.

He *knew*, deep in his guts, that something had happened to her. An accident, or she was sick, or she'd been caught in one of the vast number of buildings hit by debris from the battle today . . . She might be trapped somewhere *right now*, might be wounded, might be *smothering*, calling out his name, might be feeling the approach of *flames*—

Stop it, he told himself. *She's not hurt.* If anything had happened to her, he would know. Even from the far side of the Outer Rim, he would know.

So why wasn't she here?

Had something . . .

He could barely breathe. He couldn't make himself even think it. He couldn't stop himself from thinking it.

Had something *changed*? For her?

In how she felt?

He managed to disengage himself from Tundra Dowmeia's clammy grip and insistent invitations to visit his family's deepwater estate on Mon Calamari; he slid past the Malastarian Senator Ask Aak with an apologetic shrug.

He had a different Senator on his mind.

R2 was wheeping and beeping and whistling intensely when Anakin finally struggled free of the mass of sweaty, grasping politicians; C-3PO had turned away dismissively. "It couldn't have been that bad. Don't exaggerate! You're hardly even dented."

R2's answering *feroo* sounded a little defensive. C-3PO sent a wisp of static through his vocabulator that sounded distinctly like a disapproving sniff. "On that point I agree; you're long overdue for a tune-up. And, if I may say so, a *bath*."

"Threepio—"

Anakin came up close beside the droid he had built in the back room of his mother's slave hovel on Tatooine: the droid who had been both project and friend through his painful child-hood: the droid who now served the woman he loved . . .

Threepio had been with her all these months, had seen her every day, had *touched* her, perhaps even *today*—he could feel echoes of her resonating outward from his electroplated shell, and they left him breathless.

"Oh, Master Anakin!" Threepio exclaimed. "I am *very* glad to find you well! One does worry, when friends fall out of touch! Why, I was saying to the Senator, just the other day—or was it last week? Time seems to run together so; do you think you might have the opportunity to adjust my internal calendar set-tings while you're—"

"Threepio, have you *seen* her?" Anakin was trying so hard not to shout that his voice came out a strangled croak. "Where *is* she? Why isn't she *here*?"

"Oh, well, certainly, certainly. Officially, Senator Amidala is *extremely* busy," C-3PO said imperturbably. "She has been se-questered all day in the Naboo embassy, reviewing the new Se-curity Act, preparing for tomorrow's debate—"

Anakin couldn't breathe. She wasn't *here,* hadn't come to meet him, over some *debate*?

The Senate. He *hated* the Senate. Hated everything about it.

A red haze gathered inside his head. Those self-righteous, narrow-minded, grubby little *squabblers* . . . He'd be doing the galaxy a *favor* if he were to go over there right *now* and just—

"Wait," he murmured, blinking. "Did you say, *officially*?"

"Oh, yes, Master Anakin." Threepio sounded entirely virtuous. "That is my *official* answer to all queries regarding the Senator's whereabouts. All afternoon."

The red haze evaporated, leaving only sunlight and dizzyingly fresh air.

Anakin smiled.

"And *un*officially?"

The protocol droid leaned close with an exaggeratedly conspiratorial whisper: "Unofficially, she's waiting in the hallway."

It felt like being struck by lightning. But in a good way. In the best way any man has ever felt since, roughly, the birth of the universe.

Threepio gave a slight nod at the other Senators and the HoloNet crews on the gangway. "She thought it best to avoid a, ah, *public* scene. And she wished for me to relate to you that she believes the *both* of you might . . . *avoid* a public *scene* . . . all *afternoon*. And perhaps all night, as well."

"Threepio!" Anakin blinked at him. He felt an irrational desire to giggle. "What exactly are you suggesting?"

"I'm sure I couldn't say, sir. I am only performing as per the Senator's instructions."

"You—" Anakin shook his head in wonder while his smile grew to a grin he thought might split open his cheeks. "You are amazing."

"Thank you, Master Anakin, though credit for that is due largely—" C-3PO made an elegantly gracious bow. "—to my creator."

Anakin could only go on grinning.

With that, the golden protocol droid laid an affectionate hand on R2's dome. "Come along, Artoo. I have found the most delightful body shop down in the Lipartian Way."

They moved away, whirring and clanking after the Senators who were already off among the HoloNet crews. Anakin's smile faded as he watched them go.

He felt a presence at his shoulder and turned to find Palpatine beside him with a warm smile and a soft word, as he always seemed to be when Anakin was troubled.

"What is it, Anakin?" the Chancellor asked kindly. "Something is disturbing you. I can tell."

Anakin shrugged and gave his head a dismissive shake, embarrassed. "It's nothing."

"Anakin, anything that might upset a man such as yourself is certainly *some*thing. Let me help."

"There's nothing you can do. It's just—" Anakin nodded after 3PO and R2. "I was just thinking that even after all I've done, See-Threepio is still the only person I know who calls me *Master.*"

"Ah. The Jedi Council." Palpatine slid an arm around Anakin's shoulders and gave him a comradely squeeze. "I believe I can be of some use to you in this problem after all."

"You can?"

"I should be very much surprised if I couldn't."

Palpatine's smile was still warm, but his eyes had gone distant.

"You may have noticed that I have a certain gift," he murmured, "for getting my way."

PADMÉ

From the shadow of a great pillar stretching up into the reddening afternoon that leaked through the vaulted roof of transparisteel over the Atrium of the Senate Office Building, she watched Senators clustering in through the archway from the Chancellor's landing platform, and then she saw the Chancellor himself and C-3PO and yes, that was *R2-D2!*—and so *he* could not be far behind . . . and only then did she finally find him among them, tall and straight, his hair radiation-bleached to golden streaks and on his lips a lively smile that opened her chest and unlocked her heart.

And she could breathe again.

Through the swirl of HoloNet reporters and the chatter of Senators and the gently comforting tones of Palpatine's most polished, reassuringly paternal voice, she did not move, not so much as to lift a hand or turn her head. She was silent, and still, only letting herself breathe, feeling the beat of her heart, and she could have stood there forever, in the shadows, and had her fondest dreams all fulfilled, simply by watching him be alive . . .

But when he moved away from the group, pacing in soft conversation with Bail Organa of Alderaan, and she heard Bail saying something about *the end of Count Dooku* and *the end of the war* and *finally an end to Palpatine's police-state tactics,* her breath caught again and she held it, because she knew the next thing she heard would be *his* voice.

"I wish that were so," he said, "but the fighting will continue until General Grievous is spare parts. The Chancellor is very clear on this, and I believe the Senate and the Jedi Council will both agree."

And beyond that, there was no hope she could be happier—until his eye found her silent, still shadow, and he straightened, and a new light broke over his golden face and he said, "Excuse me," to the Senator from Alderaan, and a moment later he came to her in the shadows and they were in each other's arms.

Their lips met, and the universe became, one last time, perfect.

———

This is Padmé Amidala:

She is an astonishingly accomplished young woman, who in her short life has been already the youngest-ever elected Queen of her planet, a daring partisan guerrilla, and a measured, articulate, and persuasive voice of reason in the Republic Senate.

But she is, at this moment, none of these things.

She can still play at them—she pretends to be a Senator, she still wields the moral authority of a former Queen, and she is not shy about using her reputation for fierce physical courage to her advantage in political debate—but her inmost reality, the most fundamental, unbreakable core of her being, is something entirely different.

She is Anakin Skywalker's wife.

Yet *wife* is a word too weak to carry the truth of her; *wife* is such a small word, such a common word, a word that can come from a downturned mouth with so many petty, unpleasant echoes. For Padmé Amidala, saying *I am Anakin Skywalker's wife* is saying neither more nor less than *I am alive.*

Her life before Anakin belonged to someone else, some

lesser being to be pitied, some poor impoverished spirit who could never suspect how profoundly life should be lived.

Her real life began the first time she looked into Anakin Skywalker's eyes and found in there not the uncritical worship of little Annie from Tatooine, but the direct, unashamed, smoldering passion of a powerful Jedi: a *young* man, to be sure, but every centimeter a *man*—a man whose legend was already growing within the Jedi Order and beyond. A man who knew exactly what he wanted and was honest enough to simply *ask* for it; a man strong enough to unroll his deepest feelings before her without fear and without shame. A man who had loved her for a decade, with faithful and patient heart, while he waited for the act of destiny he was sure would someday open her own heart to the fire in his.

But though she loves her husband without reservation, love does not blind her to his faults. She is older than he, and wise enough to understand him better than he does himself. He is not a perfect man: he is prideful, and moody, and quick to anger— but these faults only make her love him the more, for his every flaw is more than balanced by the greatness within him, his capacity for joy and cleansing laughter, his extraordinary generosity of spirit, his passionate devotion not only to her but also in the service of every living being.

He is a wild creature who has come gently to her hand, a vine tiger purring against her cheek. Every softness of his touch, every kind glance or loving word is a small miracle in itself. How can she not be grateful for such gifts?

This is why she will not allow their marriage to become public knowledge. Her husband *needs* to be a Jedi. Saving people is what he was born for; to take that away from him would cripple every good thing in his troubled heart.

Now she holds him in their infinite kiss with both arms tight around his neck, because there is a cold dread in the center of her heart that whispers this kiss is not infinite at all, that it's only a pause in the headlong rush of the universe, and when it ends, she will have to face the future.

And she is terrified.

Because while he has been away, everything has changed.

Today, here in the hallway of the Senate Office Building, she brings him news of a gift they have given each other—a gift of joy, and of terror. This gift is the edge of a knife that has already cut their past from their future.

For these long years they have held each other only in secret, only in moments stolen from the business of the Republic and the war; their love has been the perfect refuge, a long quiet afternoon, warm and sunny, sealed away from fear and doubt, from duty and from danger. But now she carries within her a planetary terminator that will end their warm afternoon forever and leave them blind in the oncoming night.

She is more, now, than Anakin Skywalker's wife.

She is the mother of Anakin Skywalker's unborn child.

After an all-too-brief eternity, the kiss finally ended.

She clung to him, just breathing in the presence of him after so long, murmuring love against his broad strong chest while he murmured love into the coils of her softly scented hair.

Some time later, she found words again. "Anakin, Anakin, oh my Anakin, I—I can't believe you're *home*. They told me . . ." She almost choked on the memory. "There were whispers . . . that you'd been *killed*. I couldn't—every day—"

"Never believe stories like that," he whispered. "Never. I will always come back to you, Padmé."

"I've lived a year for every hour you were away—"

"It's been a lifetime. Two."

She reached up to the burn-scar high on his cheek. "You were hurt . . ."

"Nothing serious," he said with half a smile. "Just an unfriendly reminder to keep up with my lightsaber practice."

"Five *months*." It was almost a moan. "Five months—how could they *do* that to us?"

He rested his cheek lightly on the crown of her head. "If the Chancellor hadn't been kidnapped, I'd still be out there. I'm almost—it's terrible to say it, but I'm *grateful*. I'm glad he was kidnapped. It's like it was all arranged just to bring me home again . . ."

His arms were so strong, and so warm, and his hand touched her hair in the softest caress, as though he was afraid she were as fragile as a dream, and he bent down for another kiss, a new kiss, a kiss that would wipe away every dark dream and all the days and hours and minutes of unbearable dread—

But only steps away, the main vault of the Atrium still held Senators and HoloNet crews, and the knowledge of the price Anakin would pay when their love became known made her turn her face aside, and put her hands on his chest to hold him away. "Anakin, not here. It's too risky."

"No, *here*! *Exactly* here." He drew her against him again, effortlessly overpowering her halfhearted resistance. "I'm tired of the deception. Of the sneaking and the lying. We have *nothing* to be ashamed of! We love each other, and we are married. Just like trillions of beings across the galaxy. This is something we should *shout*, not whisper—"

"No, Anakin. *Not* like all those others. They are not Jedi. We can't let our love force you out of the Order—"

"Force me out of the Order?" He smiled down at her fondly. "Was that a pun?"

"Anakin—" He could still make her angry without even trying. "*Listen* to me. We have a duty to the Republic. Both of us—but yours is now so much more important. You are the face of the Jedi, Anakin. Even after these years of war, many people still love the Jedi, and it's mostly because they love *you*, do you understand that? They love the *story* of you. You're like something out of a bedtime tale, the secret prince, hidden among the peasants, growing up without ever a clue of his special destiny—except for you it's all *true*. Sometimes I think that the only reason the people of the Republic still believe we can win the war is because *you're* fighting it for them—"

"And it always comes back to politics for you," Anakin said. His smile had gone now. "I'm barely even home, and you're already trying to talk me into going back to the war—"

"This isn't about politics, Anakin, it's about *you*."

"Something has changed, hasn't it?" Thunder gathered in his voice. "I felt it, even outside. Something has changed."

She lowered her head. "Everything has changed."

"What is it? What?" He took her by the shoulders now, his hands hard and irresistibly powerful. "There's someone else. I can *feel* it in the Force! There is someone coming *between* us—"

"Not the way you think," she said. "Anakin, listen—"

"Who is it? *Who?*"

"*Stop* it. Anakin, *stop*. You'll hurt us."

His hands sprang open as though she had burned them. He took an unsteady step backward, his face suddenly ashen. "Padmé—I would never—I'm so sorry, I just—"

He leaned on the pillar and brought a hand weakly to his eyes. "The Hero With No Fear. What a joke . . . Padmé, I can't *lose* you. I *can't*. You're all I *live* for. Wait . . ." He lifted his head, frowning quizzically. "Did you say, *us?*"

She reached for him, and he came to meet her hand. Rising tears burned her eyes, and her lip trembled. "I'm . . . Annie, I'm *pregnant* . . ."

She watched him as everything their child would mean cycled through his mind, and her heart caught when she saw first of all the wild, almost explosive joy that dawned over his face, because that meant that whatever he had gone through on the Outer Rim, he was still her Annie.

It meant that the war that had scarred his face had not scarred his spirit.

And she watched that joy fade as he began to understand that their marriage could not stay hidden much longer; that even the voluminous robes she wore could not conceal a pregnancy forever. That he would be cast out in disgrace from the Jedi Order. That she would be relieved of her post and recalled to Naboo. That the very celebrity that had made him so important to the war would turn against them both, making them the freshest possible meat for an entire galaxy full of scandalmongers.

And she watched him decide that he didn't care.

"That is," he said slowly, that wild spark returning to his eyes, ". . . *wonderful* . . . Padmé—that's *wonderful*. How long have you known?"

She shook her head. "What are we going to *do*?"

"We're going to be happy, that's what we're going to do. And we're going to be *together*. All *three* of us."

"But—"

"No." He laid a gentle finger on her lips, smiling down at her. "No buts. No worries. You worry too much as it is."

"I have to," she said, smiling through the tears in her eyes. "Because you never worry at all."

Anakin lurched upright in bed, gasping, staring blindly into alien darkness.

How she had *screamed* for him—how she had begged for him, how her strength had failed on that alien table, how at the last she could only whimper, *Anakin, I'm sorry. I love you. I love you*—thundered inside his head, blinding him to the contours of the night-shrouded room, deafening him to every sound save the turbohammer of his heart.

His hand of flesh found unfamiliar coils of sweat-damp silken sheets around his waist. Finally he remembered where he was.

He half turned, and she was with him, lying on her side, her glorious fall of hair fanned across her pillow, eyes closed, half a smile on her precious lips, and when he saw the long, slow rise and fall of her chest with the cycle of her breathing, he turned away and buried his face in his hands and sobbed.

The tears that ran between his fingers then were tears of gratitude.

She was alive, and she was with him.

In silence so deep he could hear the whirring of the electro-drivers in his mechanical hand, he disentangled himself from the sheets and got up.

Through the closet, a long curving sweep of stairs led to the veranda that overlooked Padmé's private landing deck. Leaning on the night-chilled rail, Anakin stared out upon the endless nightscape of Coruscant.

It was still burning.

Coruscant at night had always been an endless galaxy of light, shining from trillions of windows in billions of buildings that reached kilometers into the sky, with navigation lights and advertising and the infinite streams of speeders' running lights coursing the rivers of traffic lanes overhead. But tonight, local power outages had swallowed ragged swaths of the city into vast nebulae of darkness, broken only by the malignant red-dwarf glares of innumerable fires.

Anakin didn't know how long he stood there, staring. The city looked like he felt. Damaged. Broken in battle.

Stained with darkness.

And he'd rather look at the city than think about why he was out here looking at it in the first place.

She moved more quietly than the smoky breeze, but he felt her approach.

She took a place beside him at the railing and laid her soft human hand along the back of his hard mechanical one. And she simply stood with him, staring silently out across the city that had become her second home. Waiting patiently for him to tell her what was wrong. Trusting that he would.

He could feel her patience, and her trust, and he was so grateful for both that tears welled once more. He had to blink out at the burning night, and blink again, to keep those fresh tears from spilling over onto his cheeks. He put his flesh hand on top of hers and held it gently until he could let himself speak.

"It was a dream," he said finally.

She accepted this with a slow, serious nod. "Bad?"

"It was—like the ones I used to have." He couldn't look at her. "About my mother."

Again, a nod, but even slower, and more serious. "And?"

"And—" He looked down at her small, slim fingers, and he

slipped his between them, clasping their two hands into a knot of prayer. "It was about you."

Now she turned aside, leaning once more upon the rail, staring out into the night, and in the slowly pulsing rose-glow of the distant fires she was more beautiful than he had ever seen her. "All right," she said softly. "It was about me."

Then she simply waited, still trusting.

When Anakin could finally make himself tell her, his voice was raw and hoarse as though he'd been shouting all day. "It was . . . about you *dying*," he said. "I couldn't stand it. I can't stand it."

He couldn't look at her. He looked at the city, at the deck, at the stars, and he found no place he could bear to see.

All he could do was close his eyes.

"You're going to die in childbirth."

"Oh," she said.

That was all.

She had only a few months left to live. They had only a few months left to love each other. She would never see their child. And all she said was, "Oh."

After a moment, the touch of her hand to his cheek brought his eyes open again, and he found her gazing up at him calmly. "And the baby?"

He shook his head. "I don't know."

She nodded and pulled away, drifting toward one of the veranda chairs. She lowered herself into it and stared down at her hands, clasped together in her lap.

He couldn't take it. He couldn't watch her be calm and accepting about her own death. He came to her side and knelt.

"It won't happen, Padmé. I won't let it. I could have saved my mother—a day earlier, an hour—I . . ." He bit down on the rising pain inside him, and spoke through clenched teeth. "This dream will *not* become real."

She nodded. "I didn't think it would."

He blinked. "You didn't?"

"This is Coruscant, Annie, not Tatooine. Women don't die in childbirth on *Coruscant*—not even the twilighters in the downlevels. And I have a top-flight medical droid, who assures me I am in perfect health. Your dream must have been . . . some kind of metaphor, or something."

"I—my dreams are *literal*, Padmé. I wouldn't know a metaphor if it *bit* me. And I couldn't see the place you were in— you might not even *be* on Coruscant . . ."

She looked away. "I had been thinking—about going somewhere . . . somewhere else. Having the baby in secret, to protect you. So you can stay in the Order."

"I don't *want* to stay in the Order!" He took her face between his palms so that she had to look into his eyes, so that she had to see how much he meant every word he said. "Don't protect me. I don't need it. We have to start thinking, right now, about how we can protect *you*. Because all I want is for us to be together."

"And we will be," she said. "But there must be more to your dream than death in childbirth. That doesn't make any sense."

"I know. But I can't begin to guess what it might be. It's too—I can't even think about it, Padmé. I'll go crazy. What are we going to do?"

She kissed the palm of his hand of flesh. "We're going to do what you told me, when I asked you the same question this afternoon. We're going to be happy together."

"But we—we can't just . . . *wait*. *I* can't. I have to *do* something."

"Of course you do." She smiled fondly. "That's who you are. That's what being a hero is. What about Obi-Wan?"

He frowned. "What about him?"

"You told me once that he is as wise as Yoda and as powerful as Mace Windu. Couldn't he help us?"

"No." Anakin's chest clenched like a fist squeezing his heart. "I can't—I'd have to *tell* him . . ."

"He's your best friend, Annie. He must suspect already."

"It's one thing to have him suspect. It's something else to shove it in his face. He's still on the Council. He'd *have* to report me. And . . ."

"And what? Is there something you haven't told me?"

He turned away. "I'm not sure he's on my side."

"*Your* side? Anakin, what are you saying?"

"He's on the Jedi Council, Padmé. I *know* my name has come up for Mastery—I'm more powerful than any Jedi Master alive. But someone is blocking me. Obi-Wan could tell me who, and why . . . but he *doesn't*. I'm not sure he even stands up for me with them."

"I can't believe that."

"It has nothing to do with believing," he murmured, softly bitter. "It's the truth."

"There must be some *reason,* then. Anakin, he's your best friend. He loves you."

"Maybe he does. But I don't think he trusts me." His eyes went as bleak as the empty night. "And I'm not sure we can trust him."

"Anakin!" She clutched at his arm. "What would make you *say* that?"

"*None* of them trust me, Padmé. None of them. You know what I feel, when they look at me?"

"Anakin—"

He turned to her, and everything in him ached. He wanted to cry and he wanted to rage and he wanted to make his rage a weapon that would cut himself free forever. "Fear," he said. "I feel their *fear*. And for *nothing*."

He could show them something, though. He could show them a *reason* for their fear.

He could show them what he'd discovered within himself in the General's Quarters on *Invisible Hand*.

Something of it must have risen on his face, because he saw a flicker of doubt shadow her eyes, just for a second, just a flash, but still it burned into him like a lightsaber and he shuddered, and his shudder turned into a shiver that became shaking, and he gathered her to his chest and buried his face in her hair, and the strong sweet warmth of her cooled him, just enough.

"Padmé," he murmured, "oh, Padmé, I'm so sorry. Forget I said anything. None of that matters now. I'll be gone from the Order soon—because I will not let you go away to have our baby in some alien place. I will not let you face my dream alone. I *will* be there for you, Padmé. Always. No matter what."

"I know it, Annie. I know." She pulled gently away and looked up at him. Tears sparkled like red gems in the firelight.

Red as the synthetic bloodshine of Dooku's lightsaber.

He closed his eyes.

She said, "Come upstairs, Anakin. The night's getting cold. Come up to our bed."

"All right. All right." He found that he could breathe again, and his shaking had stilled. "Just—"

He put his arm around her shoulders so that he didn't have to meet her eyes. "Just don't say anything to Obi-Wan, all right?"

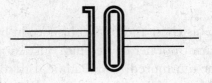

MASTERS

Obi-Wan sat beside Mace Windu while they watched Yoda scan the report. Here in Yoda's simple living space within the Jedi Temple, every softly curving pod chair and knurled organiform table hummed with gentle, comforting power: the same warm strength that Obi-Wan remembered enfolding him even as an infant. These chambers had been Yoda's home for more than eight hundred years. Everything within them echoed with the harmonic resonance of Yoda's calm wisdom, tuned through centuries of his touch. To sit within Yoda's chambers was to inhale serenity; to Obi-Wan, this was a great gift in these troubled times.

But when Yoda looked at them through the translucent shimmer of the holoprojected report on the contents of the latest amendment to the Security Act, his eyes were anything but calm: they had gone narrow and cold, and his ears had flattened back along his skull.

"This report—from where does it come?"

"The Jedi still have friends in the Senate," Mace Windu replied in his grim monotone, "for now."

"When presented this amendment is, passed it will be?"

Mace nodded. "My source expects passage by acclamation. Overwhelming passage. Perhaps as early as this afternoon."

"The Chancellor's goal in this—unclear to me it is," Yoda

said slowly. "Though nominally in command of the Council, the Senate may place him, the Jedi he cannot control. Moral, our authority has always been; much more than merely *legal*. Simply follow orders, Jedi do not!"

"I don't think he intends to control the Jedi," Mace said. "By placing the Jedi Council under the control of the Office of the Supreme Chancellor, this amendment will give him the constitutional authority to disband the Order itself."

"Surely you cannot believe this is his intention."

"*His* intention?" Mace said darkly. "Perhaps not. But *his* intentions are irrelevant; all that matters now is the intent of the Sith Lord who has our government in his grip. And the Jedi Order may be all that stands between him and galactic domination. What do you *think* he will do?"

"Authority to disband the Jedi, the Senate would never grant."

"The Senate will vote to grant exactly that. This afternoon."

"The implications of this, they must not comprehend!"

"It no longer matters what they comprehend," Mace said. "They know where the power is."

"But even disbanded, even without legal authority, still Jedi we would be. Jedi Knights served the Force long before there was a Galactic Republic, and serve it we will when this Republic is but dust."

"Master Yoda, that day may be coming sooner than any of us think. That day may be *today*." Mace shot a frustrated look at Obi-Wan, who picked up his cue smoothly.

"We don't know what the Sith Lord's plans may be," Obi-Wan said, "but we can be certain that Palpatine is not to be trusted. Not anymore. This draft resolution is not the product of some overzealous Senator; we may be sure Palpatine wrote it himself and passed it along to someone he controls—to make it look like the Senate is once more 'forcing him to reluctantly accept extra powers in the name of security.' We are afraid that they will continue to do so until one day he's 'forced to reluctantly accept' dictatorship for *life*."

"I am convinced this is the next step in a plot aimed directly at the heart of the Jedi," Mace said. "This is a move toward our destruction. The dark side of the Force surrounds the Chancellor."

Obi-Wan added, "As it has surrounded and cloaked the Separatists since even before the war began. If the Chancellor is being influenced through the dark side, this whole war may have been, from the beginning, a plot by the Sith to destroy the Jedi Order."

"Speculation!" Yoda thumped the floor with his gimer stick, making his hoverchair bob gently. "On theories such as these we cannot rely. *Proof* we need. Proof!"

"Proof may be a luxury we cannot afford." A dangerous light had entered Mace Windu's eyes. "We must be ready to *act*."

"Act?" Obi-Wan asked mildly.

"He cannot be allowed to move against the Order. He cannot be allowed to prolong the war needlessly. Too many Jedi have died already. He is dismantling the Republic itself! I have *seen* life outside the Republic; so have you, Obi-Wan. Slavery. Torture. Endless war."

Mace's face darkened with the same distant, haunted shadow Obi-Wan had seen him wear the day before. "I have seen it in Nar Shaddaa, and I saw it on Haruun Kal. I saw what it did to Depa, and to Sora Bulq. Whatever its flaws, the Republic is our sole hope for justice, and for peace. It is our only defense against the dark. Palpatine may be about to do what the Separatists cannot: bring down the Republic. If he tries, he must be removed from office."

"Removed?" Obi-Wan said. "You mean, *arrested*?"

Yoda shook his head. "To a dark place, this line of thought will lead us. Great care, we must take."

"The Republic *is* civilization. It's the only one we have." Mace looked deeply into Yoda's eyes, and into Obi-Wan's, and Obi-Wan could feel the heat in the Korun Master's gaze. "We must be prepared for radical action. It is our duty."

"But," Obi-Wan protested numbly, "you're talking about *treason* . . ."

"I'm not afraid of words, Obi-Wan! If it's treason, then so be it. I would do this right now, if I had the Council's support. The *real* treason," Mace said, "would be failure to *act*."

"Such an act, destroy the Jedi Order it could," Yoda said. "Lost the trust of the public, we have already—"

"No disrespect, Master Yoda," Mace interrupted, "but that's a politician's argument. We can't let public opinion stop us from doing what's *right*."

"*Convinced* it is right, I am *not*," Yoda said severely. "Working behind the scenes we should be, to uncover Lord Sidious! To move against Palpatine while the Sith still exist—this may be part of the Sith plan *itself*, to turn the Senate and the public against the Jedi! So that we are not only disbanded, but *outlawed*."

Mace was half out of his pod. "To *wait* gives the Sith the advantage—"

"Have the advantage *already*, they do!" Yoda jabbed at him with his gimer stick. "*Increase* their advantage we will, if in haste we act!"

"Masters, Masters, please," Obi-Wan said. He looked from one to the other and inclined his head respectfully. "Perhaps there is a middle way."

"Ah, of course: Kenobi the Negotiator." Mace Windu settled back into his seating pod. "I should have guessed. That is why you asked for this meeting, isn't it? To mediate our differences. If you can."

"So sure of your skills you are?" Yoda folded his fists around the head of his stick. "Easy to negotiate, this matter is not!"

Obi-Wan kept his head down. "It seems to me," he said carefully, "that Palpatine himself has given us an opening. He has said—both to you, Master Windu, and in the HoloNet address he gave following his rescue—that General Grievous is the true obstacle to peace. Let us forget about the rest of the Separatist leadership, for now. Let Nute Gunray and San Hill and the rest run wherever they like, while we put every available Jedi and all of our agents—the whole of Republic Intelligence, if we can—to work on locating Grievous himself. This will force the hand of the Sith Lord; he will know that Grievous cannot elude our full efforts for long, once we devote ourselves exclusively to his capture. It will draw Sidious out; he will have to make some sort of move, if he wishes the war to continue."

"If?" Mace said. "The war has been a Sith operation from the beginning, with Dooku on one side and Sidious on the other—it has always been a plot aimed at *us*. At the Jedi. To bleed us dry of our youngest and best. To make us into something we were never intended to be."

He shook his head bitterly. "I had the truth in my hands years ago—back on Haruun Kal, in the first months of the war. I had it, but I did not understand how right I was."

"Seen glimpses of this truth, we all have," Yoda said sadly. "Our arrogance it is, which has stopped us from fully opening our eyes."

"Until now," Obi-Wan put in gently. "We understand now the goal of the Sith Lord, we know his tactics, and we know where to look for him. His actions will reveal him. He cannot escape us. He *will* not escape us."

Yoda and Mace frowned at each other for one long moment, then both of them turned to Obi-Wan and inclined their heads in mirrors of his respectful bow.

"Seen to the heart of the matter, young Kenobi has."

Mace nodded. "Yoda and I will remain on Coruscant, monitoring Palpatine's advisers and lackeys; we'll move against Sidious the instant he is revealed. But who will capture Grievous? I have fought him blade-to-blade. He is more than a match for most Jedi."

"We'll worry about that once we find him," Obi-Wan said. A slight, wistful smile crept over his face. "If I listen hard enough, I can almost hear Qui-Gon reminding me that *until the possible becomes actual, it is only a distraction*."

General Grievous stood wide-legged, hands folded behind him, as he stared out through the reinforced viewport at the towering sphere of the Geonosian Dreadnaught. The immense ship looked small, though, against the scale of the vast sinkhole that rose around it.

This was Utapau, a remote backworld on the fringe of the Outer Rim. At ground level—far above where Grievous stood now—the planet appeared to be a featureless ball of barren rock, scoured flat by endless hyperwinds. From orbit, though, its cities and factories and spaceports could be seen as the planet's rotation brought its cavernous sinkholes one at a time into view. These sinkholes were the size of inverted mountains, and every available square meter of their interior walls was packed with city. And every square meter of every city was under the guns of Separatist war droids, making sure that the Utapauns behaved themselves.

Utapau had no interest in the Clone Wars; it had never been a member of the Republic, and had carefully maintained a stance of quiet neutrality.

Right up until Grievous had conquered it.

Neutrality, in these times, was a joke; a planet was neutral only so long as neither the Republic nor the Confederacy wanted it. If Grievous could laugh, he would have.

The members of the Separatist leadership scurried across the permacrete landing platform like the alley rats they were— scampering for the ship that would take them to the safety of the newly constructed base on Mustafar.

But one alley rat was missing from the scuttle.

Grievous shifted his gaze fractionally and found the reflection of Nute Gunray in the transparisteel. The Neimoidian viceroy stood dithering in the control center's doorway. Grievous regarded the reflection of the bulbous, cold-blooded eyes below the tall peaked miter.

"Gunray." He made no other motion. "Why are you still here?"

"Some things should be said privately, General." The viceroy's reflection cast glances either way along the hallway beyond the door. "I am disturbed by this new move. You told us that Utapau would be safe for us. Why is the Leadership Council being moved now to Mustafar?"

Grievous sighed. He had no time for lengthy explanations; he was expecting a secret transmission from Sidious himself. He could not take the transmission with Gunray in the room, nor could he follow his natural inclinations and boot the Neimoidian viceroy so high he'd burn up on reentry. Grievous still hoped, every day, that Lord Sidious would give him leave to smash the skulls of Gunray and his toady, Rune Haako. Repulsive sniveling grub-greedy scum, both of them. And the rest of the Separatist leadership was every bit as vile.

But for now, a pretense of cordiality had to be maintained.

"Utapau," Grievous said slowly, as though explaining to a child, "is a hostile planet under military occupation. It was never intended to be more than a stopgap, while the defenses of the base on Mustafar were completed. Now that they are, Mustafar is the most secure planet in the galaxy. The stronghold prepared for you can withstand the entire Republic Navy."

"It should," Gunray muttered. "Construction nearly bankrupted the Trade Federation!"

"Don't whine to me about money, Viceroy. I have no interest in it."

"You had better, General. It's my *money* that finances this entire war! It's my money that pays for that *body* you wear, and for those insanely expensive MagnaGuards of yours! It's my *money*—"

Grievous moved so swiftly that he seemed to teleport from the window to half a meter in front of Gunray. "How much use is your money," he said, flexing his hand of jointed duranium in the Neimoidian's face, "against *this*?"

Gunray flinched and backed away. "I was only—I have some concerns about your ability to keep us *safe*, General, that's all. I—we—the Trade Federation cannot work in a climate of fear. What about the *Jedi*?"

"Forget the Jedi. They do not enter into this equation."

"They will be entering into that *base* soon enough!"

"The base is secure. It can stand against a thousand Jedi. *Ten* thousand."

"Do you *hear* yourself? Are you *mad*?"

"What I am," Grievous replied evenly, "is unaccustomed to having my orders challenged."

"We are the Leadership Council! You cannot give *us* orders! *We* give the orders here!"

"Are you certain of that? Would you care to wager?" Grievous leaned close enough that he could see the reflection of his mask in Gunray's rose-colored eyes. "Shall we, say, bet your life on it?"

Gunray kept on backing away. "You tell us we'll be safe on Mustafar—but you *also* told us you would deliver Palpatine as a *hostage,* and *he* managed to escape your grip!"

"Be thankful, Viceroy," Grievous said, admiring the smooth flexion of his finger joints as though his hand were some species of exotic predator, "that you have not found *yourself* in my grip."

He went back to the viewport and reassumed his original position, legs wide, hands clasped behind his back. To look on the sickly pink in Gunray's pale green cheeks for one second longer was to risk forgetting his orders and splattering the viceroy's brains from here to Ord Mantell.

"Your ship is waiting."

His auditory sensors clearly picked up the slither of Gunray's sandals retreating along the corridor, and not a second too soon: his sensors were also registering the whine of the control center's holocomm warming up. He turned to face the disk, and when the enunciator chimed to indicate the incoming transmission, he pressed the ACCEPT key and knelt.

Head down, he could see only the scanned image of the hem of the great Lord's robes, but that was all he needed to see.

"Yes, Lord Sidious."

"Have you moved the Separatist Council to Mustafar?"

"Yes, Master." He risked a glance out the viewport. Most of the council had reached the starship. Gunray should be joining them any second; Grievous had seen firsthand how fast the viceroy could run, given proper motivation. "The ship will lift off within moments."

"Well done, my general. Now you must turn your hand to preparing our trap there on Utapau. The Jedi hunt you personally at last; you must be ready for their attack."

"Yes, Master."

"I am arranging matters to give you a second chance to do my bidding, Grievous. Expect that the Jedi sent to capture you will be Obi-Wan Kenobi."

"Kenobi?" Grievous's fists clenched hard enough that his carpal electrodrivers whined in protest. "And Skywalker?"

"I believe Skywalker will be . . . otherwise engaged."

Grievous dropped his head even lower. "I will not fail you again, my Master. Kenobi will die."

"See to it."

"Master? If I may trouble you with boldness—why did you not let me kill Chancellor Palpatine? We may never get a better chance."

"The time was not yet ripe. Patience, my general. The end of the war is near, and victory is certain."

"Even with the loss of Count Dooku?"

"Dooku was not lost, he was sacrificed—a strategic sacrifice, as one offers up a piece in dejarik: to draw the opponent into a fatal blunder."

"I was never much the dejarik player, my Master. I prefer *real* war."

"And you shall have your fill, I promise you."

"This fatal blunder you speak of—if I may once again trouble you with boldness . . ."

"You will come to understand soon enough."

Grievous could hear the smile in his Master's voice.

"All will be clear, once you meet my new apprentice."

Anakin finger-combed his hair as he trotted out across the re-stricted landing deck atop the Temple ziggurat near the base of the High Council Tower. Far across the expanse of deck stood the Supreme Chancellor's shuttle. Anakin squinted at it, and at the two tall red-robed guards that stood flanking its open access ramp.

And coming toward him from the direction of the shuttle, shielding his eyes and leaning against the morning wind that whipped across the unprotected field—was that Obi-Wan?

"Finally," Anakin muttered. He'd scoured the Temple for his former Master; he'd nearly giving up hope of finding him when a passing Padawan had mentioned that he'd seen Obi-Wan on his way out to the landing deck to meet Palpatine's shuttle. He hoped Obi-Wan wouldn't notice he hadn't changed his clothes.

It wasn't like he could explain.

Though his secret couldn't last, he wasn't ready for it to come out just yet. He and Padmé had agreed last night that they would keep it as long as they could. He wasn't ready to leave the Jedi Order. Not while she was still in danger.

Padmé had said that his nightmare must be only a metaphor, but he knew better. He knew that Force prophecy was not absolute—but his had never been wrong. Not in the slightest detail. He had known as a boy that he would be chosen by the Jedi. He had known his adventures would span the galaxy. As a mere nine-year-old, long before he even understood what love was, he had looked upon Padmé Amidala's flawless face and seen there that she would love him, and that they would someday marry.

There had been no metaphor in his dreams of his mother. Screaming in pain. Tortured to death.

I knew you would come to me, Annie . . . I missed you so much.

He could have saved her.

Maybe.

It had always seemed so obvious to him—that if he had only returned to Tatooine a day earlier, an hour, he could have found his mother and she would still be alive. And yet—

And yet the great prophets of the Jedi had always taught that the gravest danger in trying to prevent a vision of the future from coming to pass is that in doing so, a Jedi can actually *bring* it to pass—as though if he'd run away in time to save his mother, he might have made himself somehow responsible for her death.

As though if he tried to save Padmé, he could end up—blankly impossible though it was—killing her *himself* . . .

But to do nothing . . . to simply wait for Padmé to die . . .

Could something be *more* than impossible?

When a Jedi had a question about the deepest subtleties of the Force, there was one source to whom he could always turn; and so, first thing that morning, without even taking time to stop by his own quarters for a change of clothing, Anakin had gone to Yoda for advice.

He'd been surprised by how graciously the ancient Jedi Master had invited him into his quarters, and by how patiently Yoda had listened to his stumbling attempts to explain his question without giving away his secret; Yoda had never made any attempt to conceal what had always seemed to Anakin to be a gruff disapproval of Anakin's very existence.

But this morning, despite clearly having other things on his mind—even Anakin's Force perceptions, far from the most subtle, had detected echoes of conflict and worry within the Master's chamber—Yoda had simply offered Anakin a place on one of the softly rounded pod seats and suggested that they meditate together.

He hadn't even asked for details.

Anakin had been so grateful—and so relieved, and so unexpectedly hopeful—that he'd found tears welling into his eyes, and some few minutes had been required for him to compose himself into proper Jedi serenity.

After a time, Yoda's eyes had slowly opened and the deep furrows on his ancient brow had deepened further. "Premonitions . . . premonitions . . . deep questions they are. Sense the future, once all Jedi could; now few alone have this skill. Visions . . . gifts from the Force, and curses. Signposts and snares. These visions of yours . . ."

"They are of pain," Anakin had said. "Of suffering."

He had barely been able to make himself add: "And death."

"In these troubled times, no surprise this is. Yourself you see, or someone you know?"

Anakin had not trusted himself to answer.

"Someone close to you?" Yoda had prompted gently.

"Yes," Anakin had replied, eyes turned away from Yoda's too-wise stare. Let him think he was talking about Obi-Wan. It was close enough.

Yoda's voice was still gentle, and understanding. "The fear of loss is a path to the dark side, young one."

"I won't let my visions come true, Master. I *won't*."

"Rejoice for those who transform into the Force. Mourn them not. Miss them not."

"Then why do we fight at all, Master? Why save *anybody*?"

"Speaking of *anybody*, we are not," Yoda had said sternly. "Speaking of you, and your vision, and your *fear*, we are. The shadow of greed, attachment is. What you fear to lose, train yourself to release. Let go of fear, and loss cannot harm you."

Which was when Anakin had realized Yoda wasn't going to be any help at all. The greatest sage of the Jedi Order had nothing better to offer him than more pious babble about Letting Things Pass Out Of His Life.

Like he hadn't heard that a million times already.

Easy for *him*—who had *Yoda* ever cared about? *Really* cared about? Of one thing Anakin was certain: the ancient Master had never been in love.

Or he would have known better than to expect Anakin to just fold his hands and close his eyes and settle in to *meditate* while what was left of Padmé's life evaporated like the ghost-mist of dew in a Tatooine winter dawn . . .

So all that had been left for him was to find some way to re-spectfully extricate himself.

And then go find Obi-Wan.

Because he wasn't about to give up. Not in this millennium.

The Jedi Temple was the greatest nexus of Force energy in

the Republic; its ziggurat design focused the Force the way a lightsaber's gemstone focused its energy stream. With the thousands of Jedi and Padawans within it every day contemplating peace, seeking knowledge, and meditating on justice and surrender to the will of the Force, the Temple was a fountain of the light.

Just being on its rooftop landing deck sent a surge of power through Anakin's whole body; if the Force was ever to show him a way to change the dark future of his nightmares, it would do so here.

The Jedi Temple also contained the archives, the vast library that encompassed the Order's entire twenty-five millennia of existence: everything from the widest-ranging cosmographical surveys to the intimate journals of a billion Jedi Knights. It was there Anakin hoped to find everything that was known about prophetic dreams—and everything that was known about preventing these prophecies from coming to pass.

His only problem was that the deepest secrets of the greatest Masters of the Force were stored in restricted holocrons; since the Lorian Nod affair, some seventy standard years before, access to these holocrons was denied to all but Jedi Masters.

And he couldn't exactly explain to the archives Master why he wanted them.

But now here was Obi-Wan—Obi-Wan would help him, Anakin *knew* he would—if only Anakin could figure out the right way to ask . . .

While he was still hunting for words, Obi-Wan reached him. "You missed the report on the Outer Rim sieges."

"I—was held up," Anakin said. "I have no excuse."

That, at least, was true.

"Is Palpatine here?" Anakin asked. It was a convenient-enough way to change the subject. "Has something happened?"

"Quite the opposite," Obi-Wan said. "That shuttle did not bring the Chancellor. It is waiting to bring *you* to *him*."

"Waiting? For *me*?" Anakin frowned. Worries and lack of sleep had his head full of fog; he couldn't make this make sense.

He patted his robes vacantly. "But—my beacon hasn't gone off. If the Council wanted me, why didn't they—"

"The Council," Obi-Wan said, "has not been consulted."

"I don't understand."

"Nor do I." Obi-Wan stepped close, nodding minutely back toward the shuttle. "They simply arrived, some time ago. When the deck-duty Padawans questioned them, they said the Chancellor has requested your presence."

"Why wouldn't he go through the Council?"

"Perhaps he has some reason to believe," Obi-Wan said carefully, "that the Council might have resisted sending you. Perhaps he did not wish to reveal his reason for this summons. Relations between the Council and the Chancellor are . . . stressed."

A queasy knot began to tie itself behind Anakin's ribs. "Obi-Wan, what's going on? Something's wrong, isn't it? You know something, I can tell."

"Know? No: only suspect. Which is not at all the same thing."

Anakin remembered what he'd said to Padmé about exactly that last night. The queasy knot tightened. "And?"

"And that's why I am out here, Anakin. So I can talk to you. Privately. *Not* as a member of the Jedi Council—in fact, if the Council were to find out about this conversation . . . well, let's say, I'd rather they didn't."

"*What* conversation? I still don't know what's going on!"

"None of us does. Not really." Obi-Wan put a hand on Anakin's shoulder and frowned deeply into his eyes. "Anakin, you know I am your friend."

"Of course you are—"

"No. No *of courses*, Anakin. Nothing is *of course* anymore. I am your friend, and *as* your friend, I am asking you: be wary of Palpatine."

"What do you mean?"

"I know you are *his* friend. I am concerned that he may not be yours. Be careful of him, Anakin. And be careful of your own feelings."

"Careful? Don't you mean, *mindful*?"

Obi-Wan's frown deepened. "No. I don't. The Force grows ever darker around us, and we are all affected by it, even as we affect it. This is a dangerous time to be a Jedi. Please, Anakin—please be *careful*."

Anakin tried for his old rakish smile. "You worry too much."

"I *have* to—"

"—because I don't worry at all, right?" Anakin finished for him.

Obi-Wan's frown softened toward a smile. "How did you know I was going to say that?"

"You're wrong, you know." Anakin stared off through the morning haze toward the shuttle, past the shuttle—

Toward 500 Republica, and Padmé's apartment.

He said, "I worry plenty."

The ride to Palpatine's office was quietly tense. Anakin had tried making conversation with the two tall helmet-masked figures in the red robes, but they weren't exactly chatty.

Anakin's discomfort only increased when he arrived at Palpatine's office. He had been here so often that he didn't even really see it, most times: the deep red runner that matched the softly curving walls, the long comfortable couches, the huge arc of window behind Palpatine's desk—these were all so familiar that they were usually almost invisible, but today—

Today, with Obi-Wan's voice whispering *be wary of Palpatine* in the back of his head, everything looked different. New. And not in a good way.

Some indefinable gloom shrouded everything, as though the orbital mirrors that focused the light of Coruscant's distant sun into bright daylight had somehow been damaged, or smudged with the brown haze of smoke that still shrouded the cityscape. The light of the Chancellor's lampdisks seemed brighter than usual, almost harsh, but somehow that only deepened the gloom. He discovered now an odd, accidental echo of memory, a new harmonic resonance inside his head, when he looked at the curving view wall that threw into silhouette the Chancellor's single large chair.

Palpatine's office reminded him of the General's Quarters on *Invisible Hand.*

And it struck him as unaccountably sinister that the robes worn by the Chancellor's cadre of bodyguards were the exact color of Palpatine's carpet.

Palpatine himself stood at the view wall, hands clasped behind him, gazing out upon the smoke-hazed morning.

"Anakin." He must have seen Anakin's reflection in the curve of transparisteel; he had not moved. "Join me."

Anakin came up beside him, mirroring his stance. Endless cityscape stretched away before them. Here and there, the remains of shattered buildings still smoldered. Space lane traffic was beginning to return to normal, and rivers of gnat-like speeders and air taxis and repulsor buses crisscrossed the city. In the near distance, the vast dome of the Galactic Senate squatted like a gigantic gray mushroom sprung from the duracrete plain that was Republic Plaza. Farther, dim in the brown haze, he could pick out the quintuple spires that topped the ziggurat of the Jedi Temple.

"Do you see, Anakin?" Palpatine's voice was soft, hoarse with emotion. "Do you see what they have done to our magnificent city? This war *must* end. We cannot allow such . . . such . . ."

His voice trailed away, and he shook his head. Gently, Anakin laid a hand on Palpatine's shoulder, and a hint of frown fleeted over his face at how frail seemed the flesh and bone beneath the robe. "You know you have my best efforts, and those of every Jedi," he said.

Palpatine nodded, lowering his head. "I know I have yours, Anakin. The rest of the Jedi . . ." He sighed. He looked even more exhausted than he had yesterday. Perhaps he had passed a sleepless night as well.

"I have asked you here," he said slowly, "because I need your help on a matter of extreme delicacy. I hope I can depend upon your discretion, Anakin."

Anakin went still for a moment, then he very slowly lifted his hand from the Chancellor's shoulder.

Be wary of Palpatine

"As a Jedi, there are . . . limits . . . to my discretion, Chancellor."

"Oh, of course. Don't worry, my boy." A flash of his familiar fatherly smile forced its way into his eyes. "Anakin, in all the years we have been friends, have I ever asked you to do anything even the slightest bit against your conscience?"

"Well—"

"And I never will. I am very proud of your accomplishments as a Jedi, Anakin. You have won many battles the Jedi Council insisted to me were already lost—and you saved my *life*. It's frankly appalling that they still keep you off the Council yourself."

"My time will come . . . when I am older. And, I suppose, wiser." He didn't want to get into this with Palpatine; talking with the Chancellor like this—seriously, man-to-man—made him feel good, feel strong, despite Obi-Wan's warning. He certainly didn't want to start whining about being passed over for Mastery like some preadolescent Padawan who hadn't been chosen for a scramball team.

"Nonsense. Age is no measure of wisdom. They keep you off the Council because it is the last hold they have on you, Anakin; it is how they control you. Once you're a Master, as you deserve, how will they make you do their bidding?"

"Well . . ." Anakin gave him a half-sheepish smile. "They can't exactly *make* me, even now."

"I know, my boy. I know. That is precisely the point. You are not like them. You are younger. Stronger. *Better.* If they cannot control you now, what will happen once you are a Master in your own right? How will they keep your toes on their political line? You may become more powerful than all of them together. That is why they keep you down. They fear your power. They fear *you.*"

Anakin looked down. This had struck a little close to the bone. "I have sensed . . . something like that."

"I have asked you here today, Anakin, because I have fears of my own." He turned, waiting, until Anakin met his eye, and on Palpatine's face was something approaching bleak despair. "I am coming to fear the Jedi themselves."

"Oh, Chancellor—" Anakin broke into a smile of disbelief. "There is no one more loyal than the Jedi, sir—surely, after all this time—"

But Palpatine had already turned away. He lowered himself into the chair behind his desk and kept his head down as though he was ashamed to say this directly to Anakin's face. "The Council keeps pushing for more control. More autonomy. They have lost all respect for the rule of law. They have become more concerned with avoiding the oversight of the Senate than with winning the war."

"With respect, sir, many on the Council would say the same of *you*." He thought of Obi-Wan, and he had to stop himself from wincing. Had he betrayed a confidence just now?

Or had Obi-Wan been doing the Council's bidding after all? . . . *Be wary of Palpatine,* he'd said, and *be careful of your feelings* . . .

Were these honest warnings, out of concern for him? Or had they been *calculated:* seeds of doubt planted to hedge Anakin away from the one man who really understood him?

The one man he could really trust . . .

"Oh, I have no doubt of it," Palpatine was saying. "Many of the Jedi on your Council would prefer I was out of office altogether—because they know I'm on to them, now. They're shrouded in secrecy, obsessed with covert action against mysteriously faceless enemies—"

"Well, the Sith are hardly faceless, are they? I mean, Dooku himself—"

"Was he truly a Lord of the Sith? Or was he just another in your string of fallen Jedi, posturing with a red lightsaber to intimidate you?"

"I . . ." Anakin frowned. How could he be sure? "But *Sidious* . . ."

"Ah, yes, the mysterious Lord Sidious. 'The *Sith infiltrator* in the *highest* levels of *government*.' Doesn't that sound a little overly familiar to you, Anakin? A little overly *convenient*? How do you know this Sidious even exists? How do you know he is not a *fiction,* a fiction created by the Jedi Council, to give them an excuse to harass their political enemies?"

"The Jedi are not political—"

"In a democracy, *everything* is political, Anakin. And everyone. This imaginary Sith Lord of theirs—even if he does exist, is he anyone to be feared? To be hunted down and exterminated without trial?"

"The Sith are the definition of evil—"

"Or so you have been trained to believe. I have been reading about the history of the Sith for some years now, Anakin. Ever since the Council saw fit to finally reveal to me their . . . *assertion* . . . that these millennium-dead sorcerers had supposedly sprung back to life. Not every tale about them is sequestered in your conveniently secret Temple archives. From what I have read, they were not so different from Jedi; seeking power, to be sure, but so does your Council."

"The dark side—"

"Oh, yes, yes, certainly, the dark side. Listen to me: if this 'Darth Sidious' of yours were to walk through *that* door right *now*—and I could somehow stop you from killing him on the spot—do you know what I would do?"

Palpatine rose, and his voice rose with him. "I would ask him to *sit down,* and I would ask him if he has any power he could use to *end this war!*"

"You would—you would—" Anakin couldn't quite make himself believe what he was hearing. The blood-red rug beneath his feet seemed to shift under him, and his head was starting to spin.

"And if he said he *did,* I'd bloody well offer him a *brandy* and *talk it out!*"

"You—Chancellor, you can't be *serious*—"

"Well, not entirely." Palpatine sighed, and shrugged, and

lowered himself once more into his chair. "It's only an example, Anakin. I would do anything to return peace to the galaxy, do you understand? That's all I mean. After all—" He offered a tired, sadly ironic smile. "—what are the chances of an actual Sith Lord ever walking through that door?"

"I wouldn't know," Anakin said feelingly, "but I do know that you probably shouldn't use that . . . *example* . . . in front of the Jedi Council."

"Oh, yes." Palpatine chuckled. "Yes, quite right. They might take it as an excuse to accuse *me*."

"I'm sure they'd never do *that*—"

"I am not. I am no longer sure they'll stop at anything, Anakin. That's actually the reason I asked you here today." He leaned forward intently, resting his elbows on the desk. "You may have heard that this afternoon, the Senate will call upon this office to assume direct control of the Jedi Council."

Anakin's frown deepened. "The Jedi will no longer report to the Senate?"

"They will report to me. Personally. The Senate is too unfocused to conduct this war; we've seen this for years. Now that this office will be the single authority to direct the prosecution of the war, we'll bring a quick end to things."

Anakin nodded. "I can see how that will help, sir, but the Council probably won't. I can tell you that they are in no mood for further constitutional amendments."

"Yes, thank you, my friend. But in this case, I have no choice. This war must be won."

"Everyone agrees on that."

"I hope they do, my boy. I hope they do."

Inside his head, he heard the echo of Obi-Wan, murmuring *relations between the Council and the Chancellor are . . . stressed.* What had been going on, here in the capital?

Weren't they all on the same side?

"I can assure you," he said firmly, "that the Jedi are absolutely dedicated to the core values of the Republic."

One of Palpatine's eyebrows arched. "Their actions will

speak more loudly than their words—as long as someone keeps an eye on them. And that, my boy, is exactly the favor I must ask of you."

"I don't understand."

"Anakin, I am asking you—as a personal favor to me, in respect for our long friendship—to accept a post as my personal representative on the Jedi Council."

Anakin blinked.

He blinked again.

He said, "Me?"

"Who else?" Palpatine spread his hands in a melancholy shrug. "You are the only Jedi I know, truly *know*, that I can trust. I *need* you, my boy. There is no one else who can do this job: to be the eyes and ears—and the voice—of the Republic on the Jedi Council."

"On the Council . . . ," Anakin murmured.

He could see himself seated in one of the low, curving chairs, opposite Mace Windu. Opposite *Yoda*. He might sit next to Ki-Adi-Mundi, or Plo Koon—or even beside Obi-Wan! And he could not quite ignore the quiet whisper, from down within the furnace doors that sealed his heart, that he was about to become the youngest Master in the twenty-five-thousand-year history of the Jedi Order . . .

But none of that really mattered.

Palpatine had somehow seen into his secret heart, and had chosen to offer him the one thing he most desired in all the galaxy. He didn't care about the Council, not really—that was a childish dream. He didn't need the Council. He didn't need recognition, and he didn't need respect. What he needed was the rank itself.

All that mattered was Mastery.

All that mattered was Padmé.

This was a gift beyond gifts: as a Master, he could access those forbidden holocrons in the restricted vault.

He could find a way to save her from his dream . . .

He shook himself back to the present. "I . . . am overwhelmed, sir. But the Council elects its own members. They will never accept this."

"I promise you they will," Palpatine murmured imperturbably. He swung his chair around to gaze out the window toward the distant spires of the Temple. "They need you more than they realize. All it will take is for someone to properly . . ."

He waved a hand expressively.

". . . *explain* it to them."

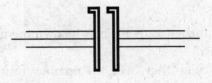

POLITICS

Orbital mirrors rotated, resolving the faint light of Coruscant's sun to erase the stars; fireships crosshatched the sky with contrails of chemical air scrubber, bleaching away the last reminders of the fires of days past; chill remnants of night slid down the High Council Tower of the Jedi Temple; and within the cloistered chamber itself, Obi-Wan was still trying to talk them out of it.

"Yes, of course I trust him," he said patiently. "We can always trust Anakin to do what he thinks is right. But we *can't* trust him to do what he's *told*. He can't be made to simply *obey*. Believe me: I've been trying for many years."

Conflicting currents of energy swirled and clashed in the Council Chamber. Traditionally, decisions of the Council were reached by quiet, mutual contemplation of the flow of the Force, until all the Council was of a single mind on the matter. But Obi-Wan knew of this tradition only by reputation, from tales in the archives and stories told by Masters whose tenure on the Council predated the return of the Sith. In the all-too-short years since Obi-Wan's own elevation, argument in this Chamber was more the rule than the exception.

"An unintentional opportunity, the Chancellor has given

us," Yoda said gravely. "A window he has opened into the operations of his office. Fools we would be, to close our eyes."

"Then we should use someone else's eyes," Obi-Wan said. "Forgive me, Master Yoda, but you just don't know him the way I do. None of you does. He is *fiercely* loyal, and there is not a gram of deception in him. You've all seen it; it's one of the arguments that some of you, here in this room, have used against elevating him to Master: he *lacks true Jedi reserve,* that's what you've said. And by that we all mean that he wears his emotions like a HoloNet banner. How can you ask him to lie to a friend—to *spy* upon him?"

"That is why we must call upon a friend to ask him," said Agen Kolar in his gentle Zabrak baritone.

"You don't understand. Don't make him choose between me and Palpatine—"

"*Why not?*" asked the holopresence of Plo Koon from the bridge of *Courageous,* where he directed the Republic Navy strike force against the Separatist choke point in the Ywllandr system. "*Do you fear you would lose such a contest?*"

"You don't know how much Palpatine's friendship has meant to him over the years. You're asking him to use that friendship as a weapon! To stab his friend in the back. Don't you understand what this will cost him, even if Palpatine is entirely innocent? *Especially* if he's innocent. Their relationship will never be the same—"

"And that," Mace Windu said, "may be the best argument in favor of this plan. I have told you all what I have seen of the energy between Skywalker and the Supreme Chancellor. Anything that might distance young Skywalker from Palpatine's influence is worth the attempt."

Obi-Wan didn't need to reach into the Force to know that he would lose this argument. He inclined his head. "I will, of course, abide by the ruling of this Council."

"Doubt of that, none of us has." Yoda turned his green gaze on the other councilors. "But if to be done this is, decide we must how best to use him."

The holopresence of Ki-Adi-Mundi flickered in and out of focus as the Cerean Master leaned forward, folding his hands. *"I, too, have reservations on this matter, but it seems that in these desperate times, only desperate plans have hope of success. We have seen that young Skywalker has the power to battle a Sith Lord alone, if need be; he has proven that with Dooku. If he is indeed the chosen one, we must keep him in play against the Sith—keep him in a position to fulfill his destiny."*

"And even if the prophecy has been misread," Agen Kolar added, "Anakin is the one Jedi we can best hope would survive an encounter with a Sith Lord. So let us also use him to help us set our trap. In Council, let us emphasize that we are intensifying our search for Grievous. Anakin will certainly report this to the Chancellor's Office. Perhaps, as you say, that will draw Sidious into action."

"It may not be enough," Mace Windu said. "Let us take this one step farther—we should appear shorthanded, and weak, giving Sidious an opening to make a move he thinks will go unobserved. I'm thinking that perhaps we should let the Chancellor's Office know that Yoda and I have both been forced to take the field—"

"Too risky that is," Yoda said. "And too convenient. One of us only should go."

"Then it should be you, Master Yoda," Agen Kolar said. "It is your sensitivity to the broader currents of the Force that a Sith Lord has most reason to fear."

Obi-Wan felt the ripple of agreement flow through the Chamber, and Yoda nodded solemnly. "The Separatist attack on Kashyyyk, a compelling excuse will make. And good relations with the Wookiees I have; destroy the droid armies I can, and still be available to Coruscant, should Sidious take our bait."

"Agreed." Mace Windu looked around the half-empty Council Chamber with a deepening frown. "And one last touch. Let's let the Chancellor know, through Anakin, that our most cunning and insightful Master—and our most tenacious—is to lead the hunt for Grievous."

"So Sidious will need to act, and act fast, if the war is to be maintained," Plo Koon added approvingly.

Yoda nodded judiciously. "Agreed." Agen Kolar assented as well, and Ki-Adi-Mundi.

"This sounds like a good plan," Obi-Wan said. "But what Master do you have in mind?"

For a moment no one spoke, as though astonished he would ask such a question.

Only after a few seconds in which Obi-Wan looked from the faces of one Master to the next, puzzled by the expressions of gentle amusement each and every one of them wore, did it finally register that all of them were looking at *him*.

Bail Organa stopped cold in the middle of the Grand Concourse that ringed the Senate's Convocation Chamber. The torrent of multispecies foot traffic that streamed along the huge curving hall broke around him like a river around a boulder. He stared up in disbelief at one of the huge holoprojected Proclamation Boards; these had recently been installed above the concourse to keep the thousands of Senators up to the moment on news of the war, and on the Chancellor's latest executive orders.

His heart tripped, and he couldn't seem to make his eyes focus. He pushed his way through the press to a hardcopy stand and punched a quick code. When he had the flimsies in his hands, they still said the same thing.

He'd been expecting this day. Since yesterday, when the Senate had voted to give Palpatine control of the Jedi, he'd known it would come soon. He'd even started planning for it.

But that didn't make it any easier to bear.

He found his way to a public comm booth and keyed a privacy code. The transparisteel booth went opaque as stone, and a moment later a hand-sized image shimmered into existence above the small holodisk: a slender woman in floor-length white, with short, neatly clipped auburn hair and a clear, steadily intelligent gaze from her aquamarine eyes. *"Bail,"* she said. *"What's happened?"*

Bail's elegantly thin goatee pulled downward around his mouth. "Have you seen this morning's decree?"

"The Sector Governance Decree? Yes, I have—"

"It's time, Mon," he said grimly. "It's time to stop talking, and start *doing*. We have to bring in the Senate."

"I agree, but we must tread carefully. Have you thought about whom we should consult? Whom we can trust?"

"Not in detail. Giddean Danu springs to mind. I'm sure we can trust Fang Zar, too."

"Agreed. What about Iridik'k-stallu? Her hearts are in the right place. Or Chi Eekway."

Bail shook his head. "Maybe later. It'll take a few hours at least to figure out exactly where they stand. We need to start with Senators we *know* we can trust."

"All right. Then Terr Taneel would be my next choice. And, I think, Amidala of Naboo."

"Padmé?" Bail frowned. "I'm not sure."

"You know her better than I do, Bail, but to my mind she is exactly the type of Senator we need. She is intelligent, principled, extremely articulate, and she has the heart of a warrior."

"She is also a longtime associate of Palpatine," he reminded her. "He was her ambassador during her term as Queen of Naboo. How sure can you be that she will stand with us, and not with him?"

Senator Mon Mothma replied serenely, *"There's only one way to find out."*

By the time the doors to the Jedi Council Chamber finally swung open, Anakin was already angry.

If asked, he would have denied it, and would have thought he was telling the truth . . . but they had left him out here for so *long,* with nothing to do but stare through the soot-smudged curve of the High Council Tower's window ring at the scarred skyline of Galactic City—damaged in a battle *he* had won, by the way, *personally*. Almost *single-handedly*—and with nothing to think about except why it was taking them so long to reach such a simple decision . . .

Angry? Not at all. He was sure he wasn't angry. He kept telling himself he wasn't angry, and he made himself believe it.

Anakin walked into the Council Chamber, head lowered in a show of humility and respect. But down inside him, down around the nuclear shielding that banked his heart, he was hiding.

It wasn't anger he was hiding. His anger was only camouflage.

Behind his anger hid the dragon.

He remembered too well the first time he had entered this Chamber, the first time he had stood within a ring of Jedi Masters gathered to sit in judgment upon his fate. He remembered how Yoda's green stare had seen into his heart, had seen the cold worm of dread eating away at him, no matter how hard he'd tried to deny it: the awful fear he'd felt that he might never see his mother again.

He couldn't let them see what that worm had grown into.

He moved slowly into the center of the circle of brown-toned carpet, and turned toward the Senior Members.

Yoda was unreadable as always, his rumpled features composed in a mask of serene contemplation.

Mace Windu could have been carved from stone.

Ghost-images of Ki-Adi-Mundi and Plo Koon hovered a centimeter above their Council seats, maintained by the seats' internal holoprojectors. Agen Kolar sat alone, between the empty chairs belonging to Shaak Ti and Stass Allie.

Obi-Wan sat in the chair that once had belonged to Oppo Rancisis, looking pensive. Even worried.

"Anakin Skywalker." Master Windu's tone was so severe that the dragon inside Anakin coiled instinctively. "The Council has decided to comply with Chancellor Palpatine's directive, and with the instructions of the Senate that give him the unprecedented authority to command this Council. You are hereby granted a seat at the High Council of the Jedi, as the Chancellor's personal representative."

Anakin stood very still for a long moment, until he could be absolutely sure he had heard what he thought he'd heard.

Palpatine had been right. He seemed to be right about a lot of things, these days. In fact—now that Anakin came to think of it—he couldn't remember a single instance when the Supreme Chancellor had been wrong.

Finally, as it began to sink in upon him, as he gradually allowed himself to understand that the Council had finally decided to grant him his heart's desire, that they finally had recognized his accomplishments, his dedication, his *power*, he took a slow, deep breath.

"Thank you, Masters. You have my pledge that I will uphold the highest principles of the Jedi Order."

"Allow this appointment lightly, the Council does not." Yoda's ears curled forward at Anakin like accusing fingers. "Disturbing is this move by Chancellor Palpatine. On many levels."

They have become more concerned with avoiding the oversight of the Senate than they are with winning the war . . .

Anakin inclined his head. "I understand."

"I'm not sure you do." Mace Windu leaned forward, staring into Anakin's eyes with a measuring squint.

Anakin was barely paying attention; in his mind, he was already leaving the Council Chamber, riding the turbolift to the archives, demanding access to the restricted vault by authority of his new rank—

"You will attend the meetings of this Council," the Korun Master said, "but you will not be granted the rank and privileges of a Jedi Master."

"What?"

It was a small word, a simple word, an instinctive recoil from words that felt like punches, like stun blasts exploding inside his brain that left his head ringing and the room spinning around him—but even to his own ears, the voice that came from his lips didn't sound like his own. It was deeper, darker, clipped and oiled, resonating from the depths of his heart.

It didn't sound like him at all, and it smoked with fury.

"How dare you? How *dare* you?"

Anakin stood welded to the floor, motionless. He wasn't even truly aware of speaking. It was as if someone else were using his mouth—and now, finally, he recognized the voice.

It sounded like Dooku. But it was not Dooku's voice.

It was the voice of Dooku's destroyer.

"No Jedi in this room can match my power—no Jedi in the *galaxy*! You think you can deny Mastery to *me*?"

"The Chancellor's representative you are," Yoda said. "And it is as his representative you shall attend the Council. Sit in this Chamber you will, but no vote will you have. The Chancellor's views you shall present. His wishes. His ideas and directives. Not your own."

Up from the depths of his furnace heart came an answer so far transcending fury that it sounded cold as interstellar space. "This is an insult to me, and to the Chancellor. Do not imagine that it will be tolerated."

Mace Windu's eyes were as cold as the voice from Anakin's mouth. "Take your seat, young Skywalker."

Anakin matched his stare. *Perhaps I'll take yours.* His own voice, inside his head, had a hot black fire that smoked from the depths of his furnace heart. *You think you can stop me from saving my love? You think you can make me watch her die? Go ahead and Vaapad this, you*—

"Anakin," Obi-Wan said softly. He gestured to an empty seat beside him. "Please."

And something in Obi-Wan's gentle voice, in his simple, straightforward request, sent his anger slinking off ashamed, and Anakin found himself alone on the carpet in the middle of the Jedi Council, blinking.

He suddenly felt very young, and very foolish.

"Forgive me, Masters." His bow of contrition couldn't hide the blaze of embarrassment that climbed his cheeks.

The rest of the session passed in a haze; Ki-Adi-Mundi said something about no Republic world reporting any sign of Grievous, and Anakin felt a dull shock when the Council assigned the task of coordinating the search to Obi-Wan *alone*.

On top of everything else, now they were splitting up the *team?*

He was so numbly astonished by it all that he barely registered what they were saying about a droid landing on Kashyyyk—but he had to say *something,* he couldn't just *sit* here for his whole first meeting of the Council, Master or not—and he knew the Kashyyyk system almost as well as he knew the back alleys of Mos Espa. "I can handle it," he offered, suddenly brightening. "I could clear that planet in a day or two—"

"Skywalker, your assignment is *here*." Mace Windu's stare was hard as durasteel, and only a scrape short of openly hostile.

Then Yoda volunteered, and for some reason, the Council didn't even bother to vote.

"It is settled then," Mace said. "May the Force be with us all."

And as the holopresences of Plo Koon and Ki-Adi-Mundi winked out, as Obi-Wan and Agen Kolar rose and spoke together in tones softly grave, as Yoda and Mace Windu walked from the room, Anakin could only sit, sick at heart, stunned with helplessness.

Padmé—oh, Padmé, what are we going to do?

He didn't know. He didn't have a clue. But he knew one thing he *wasn't* going to do.

He wasn't going to give up.

Even with the Council against him—even with the whole *Order* against him—he would find a way.

He would save her.

Somehow.

"I am no happier than the rest of you about this," Padmé said, gesturing at the flimsiplast of the Sector Governance Decree on Bail Organa's desk. "But I've known Palpatine for years; he was my most trusted adviser. I'm not prepared to believe his intent is to dismantle the Senate."

"Why should he bother?" Mon Mothma countered. "As a practical matter—as of this morning—the Senate no longer exists."

Padmé looked from one grim face to another. Giddean Danu nodded his agreement. Terr Taneel kept her eyes down, pretending to be adjusting her robes. Fang Zar ran a hand over his unruly gray-streaked topknot.

Bail leaned forward. His eyes were hard as chips of stone. "Palpatine no longer has to worry about controlling the Senate. By placing his own lackeys as governors over every planet in the Republic, he controls our systems *directly*." He folded his hands, and squeezed them together until his knuckles hurt. "He's become a dictator. We *made* him a dictator."

And he's my husband's friend, and mentor, Padmé thought. *I shouldn't even be listening to this.*

"But what can we *do* about it?" Terr Taneel asked, still gazing down at her robe with a worried frown.

"That's what we asked you here to discuss," Mon Mothma told her calmly. "What we're going to do about it."

Fang Zar shifted uncomfortably. "I'm not sure I like where this is going."

"None of us likes where *anything* is going," Bail said, half rising. "That's exactly the point. We can't let a thousand years of democracy disappear without a fight!"

"A *fight*?" Padmé said. "I can't believe what I'm hearing— Bail, you sound like a Separatist!"

"I—" Bail sank back into his seat. "I apologize. That was not my intent. I asked you all here because of all the Senators in the galaxy, you four have been the most consistent—and *influential*— voices of reason and restraint, doing all you could to preserve our poor, tattered Constitution. We don't want to hurt the Republic. With your help, we hope to *save* it."

"It has become increasingly clear," Mon Mothma said, "that Palpatine has become an enemy of democracy. He must be stopped."

"The Senate gave him these powers," Padmé said. "The Senate can rein him in."

Giddean Danu sat forward. "I fear you underestimate just how deeply the Senate's corruption has taken hold. Who will vote against Palpatine now?"

"*I* will," Padmé said. She discovered that she meant it. "And I'll find others, too."

She'd have to. No matter how much it hurt Anakin. *Oh, my love, will you ever find a way to forgive me?*

"You do that," Bail said. "Make as much noise as you can—keep Palpatine watching what you're doing in the Senate. That should provide some cover while Mon Mothma and I begin building our organization—"

"Stop." Padmé rose. "It's better to leave some things unsaid. Right now, it's better I don't know anything about . . . anything."

Don't make me lie to my husband was her unspoken plea. She tried to convey it with her eyes. *Please, Bail. Don't make me lie to him. It will break his heart.*

Perhaps he saw something there; after a moment's indecision, he nodded. "Very well. Other matters can be left for other times. Until then, this meeting must remain absolutely secret. Even hinting at an effective opposition to Palpatine can be, as we've all seen, very dangerous. We must agree never to speak of these matters except among the people who are now in this room. We must bring no one into this secret without the agreement of each and every one of us."

"That includes even those closest to you," Mon Mothma added. "Even your families—to share anything of this will expose them to the same danger we all face. No one can be told. No one."

Padmé watched them all nod, and what could she do? What

could she say? *You can keep your own secrets, but I'll have to tell my Jedi husband, who is Palpatine's beloved protégé . . .*

She sighed. "Yes. Yes: agreed."

And all she could think as the little group dispersed to their own offices was *Oh, Anakin—Anakin, I'm sorry . . .*

I'm so sorry.

Anakin was glad the vast vaulted Temple hallway was deserted save for him and Obi-Wan; he didn't have to keep his voice down.

"This is *outrageous.* How can they *do* this?"

"How can they not?" Obi-Wan countered. "It's your friendship with the Chancellor—the same friendship that got you a seat at the Council—that makes it impossible to grant you Mastery. In the Council's eyes, that would be the same as giving a vote to Palpatine himself!"

He waved this off. He didn't have time for the Council's political maneuvering—*Padmé* didn't have time. "I didn't ask for this. I don't *need* this. So if I wasn't friends with Palpatine I'd be a Master already, is that what you're saying?"

Obi-Wan looked pained. "I don't know."

"I have the power of any five Masters. Any *ten.* You know it, and so do they."

"Power alone is no credit to you—"

Anakin flung an arm back toward the Council Tower. "*They're* the ones who call me the chosen one! Chosen for what? To be a dupe in some slimy political game?"

Obi-Wan winced as if he'd been stung. "Didn't I warn you, Anakin? I told you of the . . . tension . . . between the Council and the Chancellor. I was very clear. Why didn't you *listen*? You walked right into it!"

"Like that ray shield trap." Anakin snorted. "Should I blame *this* on the dark side, too?"

"However it happened," Obi-Wan said, "you are in a very . . . delicate situation."

"*What* situation? Who cares about *me*? I'm no Master, I'm just a *kid*, right? Is that what it's about? Is Master Windu turning everyone against me because until I came along, he was the youngest Jedi ever named to the Council?"

"No one cares about that—"

"Sure they don't. Let me tell you something a smart *old* man said to me not so long ago: *Age is no measure of wisdom.* If it were, Yoda would be twenty times as wise as *you* are—"

"This has nothing to do with Master Yoda."

"That's right. It has to do with *me*. It has to do with them all being *against* me. They always *have* been—most of them didn't even want me to *be* a Jedi. And if they'd won out, where would they be right now? Who would have done the things I've done? Who would have saved Naboo? Who would have saved Kamino? Who would have killed Dooku, and rescued the Chancellor? Who would have come for you and Alpha after Ventress—"

"Yes, Anakin, yes. Of course. No one questions your accomplishments. It's your relationship to Palpatine that is the problem. And it is a very *serious* problem."

"I'm too close to him? Maybe I am. Maybe I should alienate a man who's been nothing but kind and generous to me ever since I first *came* to this planet! Maybe I should reject the only man who gives me the respect I *deserve*—"

"Anakin, stop. *Listen* to yourself. Your thoughts are of jealousy, and pride. These are dark thoughts, Anakin. Dangerous thoughts, in these dark times—you are focused on yourself when you need to focus on your service. Your outburst in the Council was an eloquent argument *against* granting you Mastery. How can you be a Jedi Master when you have not mastered yourself?"

Anakin passed his flesh hand over his eyes and drew a long, heavy breath. In a much lower, calmer, quieter tone, he said, "What do I have to do?"

Obi-Wan frowned. "I'm sorry?"

"They want something from me, don't they? That's what

this is really about. That's what it's been about from the beginning. They won't give me my rank until I give them what they want."

"The Council does not operate that way, Anakin, and you know it."

Once you're a Master, as you deserve, how will they make you do their bidding?

"Yes, I know it. Sure I do," Anakin said. Suddenly he was tired. So incredibly tired. It hurt to talk. It hurt even to stand here. He was sick of the whole business. Why couldn't it just be *over*? "Tell me what they want."

Obi-Wan's eyes shifted, and the sick fatigue in Anakin's guts turned darker. How bad did it have to be to make Obi-Wan unable to look him in the eye?

"Anakin, look, I'm on your side," Obi-Wan said softly. He looked tired, too: he looked as tired and sick as Anakin felt. "I never wanted to see you put in this situation."

"What situation?"

Still Obi-Wan hesitated.

Anakin said, "Look, whatever it is, it's not getting any better while you're standing here working up the nerve to tell me. Come on, Obi-Wan. Let's have it."

Obi-Wan glanced around the empty hall as if he wanted to make sure they were still alone; Anakin had a feeling it was just an excuse to avoid facing him when he spoke.

"The Council," Obi-Wan said slowly, "approved your appointment because Palpatine trusts you. They want you to report on all his dealings. They have to know what he's up to."

"They want me to *spy* on the *Supreme Chancellor of the Republic?*" Anakin blinked numbly. No wonder Obi-Wan couldn't look him in the face. "Obi-Wan, that's *treason!*"

"We are at war, Anakin." Obi-Wan looked thoroughly miserable. "The Council is sworn to uphold the principles of the Republic through any means necessary. We *have* to. Especially when the greatest enemy of those principles seems to be the Chancellor himself!"

Anakin's eyes narrowed and turned hard. "Why didn't the Council give me this assignment while we were in session?"

"Because it's not for the record, Anakin. You must be able to understand why."

"What I understand," Anakin said grimly, "is that you are trying to turn me against Palpatine. You're trying to make me keep *secrets* from him—you want to make me *lie* to him. That's what this is *really* about."

"It *isn't*," Obi-Wan insisted. He looked wounded. "It's about keeping an eye on who he deals with, and who deals with him."

"He's not a bad man, Obi-Wan—he's a *great* man, who's holding this Republic together with his bare *hands*—"

"By staying in office long after his term has expired. By gathering dictatorial powers—"

"The Senate *demanded* that he stay! They *pushed* those powers on him—"

"Don't be naïve. The Senate is so intimidated they give him anything he wants!"

"Then it's *their* fault, not his! They should have the guts to stand up to him!"

"That is what we're asking *you* to do, Anakin."

Anakin had no answer. Silence fell between them like a hammer.

He shook his head and looked down at the fist he had made of his mechanical hand.

Finally, he said, "He's my *friend*, Obi-Wan."

"Yes," Obi-Wan said softly. Sadly. "I know."

"If *he* asked me to spy on *you*, do you think I would do it?"

Now it was Obi-Wan's turn to fall silent.

"You know how kind he has been to me." Anakin's voice was hushed. "You know how he's looked after me, how he's done everything he could to help me. He's like *family*."

"The *Jedi* are your family—"

"No." Anakin turned on his former Master. "No, the Jedi are *your* family. The only one you've ever known. But I'm not *like* you—I had a mother who *loved* me—"

And a wife who loves me, he thought. *And soon a child who will love me, too.*

"Do you *remember* my mother? Do you remember what *happened* to her—?"

—because you didn't let me go to save her? he finished silently. *And the same will happen to Padmé, and the same will happen to our child.*

Within him, the dragon's cold whisper chewed at his strength. *All things die, Anakin Skywalker. Even stars burn out.*

"Anakin, yes. Of course. You know how sorry I am for your mother. Listen: we're not asking you to act against Palpatine. We're only asking you to . . . monitor his activities. You must believe me."

Obi-Wan stepped closer and put a hand on Anakin's arm. With a long, slowly indrawn breath, he seemed to reach some difficult decision. "Palpatine himself may be in danger," he said. "This may be the only way you can help him."

"What are you talking about?"

"I am not supposed to be telling you this. Please do not reveal we have had this conversation. To *anyone,* do you understand?"

Anakin said, "I can keep a secret."

"All right." Obi-Wan took another deep breath. "Master Windu traced Darth Sidious to Five Hundred Republica before Grievous's attack—we think that the Sith Lord is someone within Palpatine's closest circle of advisers. *That* is who we want you to spy on, do you understand?"

A fiction created by the Jedi Council . . . . an excuse to harass their political enemies . . .

"If Palpatine is under the influence of a Sith Lord, he may be in the gravest danger. The only way we can help him is to find Sidious, and to stop him. What we are asking of you is *not* treason, Anakin—it may be the only way to save the Republic!"

If this Darth Sidious of yours were to walk through that door right now . . . I would ask him to sit down, and I would ask him if he has any power he could use to end this war

"So all you're really asking," Anakin said slowly, "is for me to help the Council find Darth Sidious."

"Yes." Obi-Wan looked relieved, incredibly relieved, as though some horrible chronic pain had suddenly and inexplicably eased. "Yes, that's it exactly."

Locked within the furnace of his heart, Anakin whispered an echo—not quite an echo—slightly altered, just at the end: *I would ask him to sit down, and I would ask him if he has any power he could use—*

—to save Padmé.

The gunship streaked through the capital's sky.

Obi-Wan stared past Yoda and Mace Windu, out through the gunship's window at the vast deployment platform and the swarm of clones who were loading the assault cruiser at the far end.

"You weren't there," he said. "You didn't see his face. I think we have done a terrible thing."

"We don't always have the right answer," Mace Windu said. "Sometimes there *isn't* a right answer."

"Know how important your friendship with young Anakin is to you, I do." Yoda, too, stared out toward the stark angles of the assault cruiser being loaded for the counterinvasion of Kashyyyk; he stood leaning on his gimer stick as though he did not trust his legs. "Allow such attachments to pass out of one's life, a Jedi must."

Another man—even another Jedi—might have resented the rebuke, but Obi-Wan only sighed. "I suppose—he is the chosen one, after all. The prophecy says he was born to bring balance to the Force, but . . ."

The words trailed off. He couldn't remember what he'd been about to say. All he could remember was the look on Anakin's face.

"Yes. Always in motion, the future is." Yoda lifted his head and his eyes narrowed to thoughtful slits. "And the prophecy, misread it could have been."

Mace looked even grimmer than usual. "Since the fall of

Darth Bane more than a millennium ago, there have been hundreds of thousands of Jedi—hundreds of thousands of Jedi feeding the light with each work of their hands, with each breath, with every beat of their hearts, bringing justice, building civil society, radiating peace, acting out of selfless love for all living things—and in all these thousand years, there have been only two Sith at any time. Only two. Jedi create light, but the Sith do not create darkness. They merely use the darkness that is always there. That has always been there. Greed and jealousy, aggression and lust and fear—these are all natural to sentient beings. The legacy of the jungle. Our inheritance from the dark."

"I'm sorry, Master Windu, but I'm not sure I follow you. Are you saying—to follow your metaphor—that the Jedi have cast too much light? From what I have seen these past years, the galaxy has not become all that bright a place."

"All I am saying is that we don't *know*. We don't even truly understand what it *means* to *bring balance to the Force*. We have no way of anticipating what this may involve."

"An infinite mystery is the Force," Yoda said softly. "The more we learn, the more we discover how much we do not know."

"So you both feel it, too," Obi-Wan said. The words hurt him. "You both can feel that we have turned some invisible corner."

"In motion, are the events of our time. Approach, the crisis does."

"Yes." Mace interlaced his fingers and squeezed until his knuckles popped. "But we're in a spice mine without a glow rod. If we stop walking, we'll never reach the light."

"And what if the light just isn't there?" Obi-Wan asked. "What if we get to the end of this tunnel and find only night?"

"Faith must we have. Trust in the will of the Force. What other choice is there?"

Obi-Wan accepted this with a nod, but still when he thought of Anakin, dread began to curdle below his heart. "I should have argued more strongly in Council today."

"You think Skywalker won't be able to handle this?" Mace Windu said. "I thought you had more confidence in his abilities."

"I trust him with my life," Obi-Wan said simply. "And that is precisely the problem."

The other two Jedi Masters watched him silently while he tried to summon the proper words.

"For Anakin," Obi-Wan said at length, "there is nothing more important than friendship. He is the most loyal man I have ever met—loyal beyond reason, in fact. Despite all I have tried to teach him about the sacrifices that are the heart of being a Jedi, he—he will never, I think, truly understand."

He looked over at Yoda. "Master Yoda, you and I have been close since I was a boy. An infant. Yet if ending this war one week sooner—one *day* sooner—were to require that I sacrifice your life, you know I would."

"As you should," Yoda said. "As I would yours, young Obi-Wan. As any Jedi would any other, in the cause of peace."

"Any Jedi," Obi-Wan said, "except Anakin."

Yoda and Mace exchanged glances, both thoughtfully grim. Obi-Wan guessed they were remembering the times Anakin had violated orders—the times he had put at risk entire operations, the lives of thousands, the control of whole planetary systems—to save a friend.

More than once, in fact, to save Obi-Wan.

"I think," Obi-Wan said carefully, "that abstractions like *peace* don't mean much to him. He's loyal to *people,* not to principles. And he expects loyalty in return. He will stop at nothing to save me, for example, because he thinks I would do the same for him."

Mace and Yoda gazed at him steadily, and Obi-Wan had to lower his head.

"Because," he admitted reluctantly, "he *knows* I would do the same for him."

"Understand exactly where your concern lies, I do not." Yoda's green eyes had gone softly sympathetic. "*Named* must your fear be, before banish it you can. Do you fear that perform his task, he cannot?"

"Oh, no. That's not it at all. I am firmly convinced that Anakin can do anything. Except betray a friend. What we have done to him today . . ."

"But that is what Jedi *are*," Mace Windu said. "That is what we have pledged ourselves to: selfless service—"

Obi-Wan turned to stare once more toward the assault ship that would carry Yoda and the clone battalions to Kashyyyk, but he could see only Anakin's face.

If he *asked me to spy on* you, *do you think I would do it?*

"Yes," he said slowly. "That's why I don't think he will ever trust us again."

He found his eyes turning unaccountably hot, and his vision swam with unshed tears.

"And I'm not entirely sure he should."

NOT FROM A JEDI

The sunset over Galactic City was stunning tonight: enough particulates from the fires remained in the capital planet's atmosphere to splinter the light of its distant blue-white sun into a prismatic smear across multilayered clouds.

Anakin barely noticed.

On the broad curving veranda that doubled as the landing deck for Padmé's apartment, he watched from the shadows as Padmé stepped out of her speeder and graciously accepted Captain Typho's good night. As Typho flew the vehicle off toward the immense residential tower's speeder park, she dismissed her two handmaidens and sent C-3PO on some busywork errand, then turned to lean on the veranda's balcony right where Anakin had leaned last night.

She gazed out on the sunset, but he gazed only at her.

This was all he needed. To be here, to be with her. To watch the sunset bring a blush to her ivory skin.

If not for his dreams, he'd withdraw from the Order today. Now. The Lost Twenty would be the Lost Twenty-One. Let the scandal come; it wouldn't destroy their lives. Not their real lives. It would destroy only the lives they'd had before each other: those separate years that now meant nothing at all.

He said softly, "Beautiful, isn't it?"

She jumped as if he'd pricked her with a needle. "Anakin!"

"I'm sorry." He smiled fondly as he moved out from the shadows. "I didn't mean to startle you."

She held one hand pressed to her chest as though to keep her heart from leaping out. "No—no, it's all right. I just—Anakin, you shouldn't be out here. It's still *daylight*—"

"I couldn't wait, Padmé. I had to see you." He took her in his arms. "Tonight is *forever* from now—how am I supposed to live that long without you?"

Her hand went from her chest to his. "But we're in full view of a million people, and you're a very famous man. Let's go inside."

He drew her back from the edge of the veranda, but made no move to enter the apartment. "How are you feeling?"

Her smile was radiant as Tatooine's primary as she took his flesh hand and pressed it to the soft fullness of her belly. "He keeps kicking."

"He?" Anakin asked mildly. "I thought you'd ordered your medical droid not to spoil the surprise."

"Oh, I didn't get this from the Emdee. It's my . . ." Her smile went softly sly. ". . . motherly intuition."

He felt a sudden pulse against his palm and laughed. "Motherly intuition, huh? With a kick that hard? Definitely a girl."

She laid her head against his chest. "Anakin, let's go inside."

He nuzzled her gleaming coils of hair. "I can't stay. I'm on my way to meet with the Chancellor."

"Yes, I heard about your appointment to the Council. Anakin, I'm so proud of you."

He lifted his head, an instant scowl gathering on his forehead. Why did she have to bring that up?

"There's nothing to be proud of," he said. "This is just political maneuvering between the Council and the Chancellor. I got caught in the middle, that's all."

"But to be on the Council, at your age—"

"They put me on the Council because they *had* to. Because he told them to, once the Senate gave him control of the Jedi."

His voice lowered toward a growl. "And because they think they can use me against him."

Padmé's eyes went oddly remote, and thoughtful. "*Against* him," she echoed. "The Jedi don't trust him?"

"That doesn't mean much. They don't trust me, either." Anakin's mouth compressed to a thin bitter line. "They'll give me a chair in the Council Chamber, but that's as far as it will go. They won't accept me as a Master."

Her gaze returned from that thoughtful distance, and she smiled up at him. "Patience, my love. In time, they will recognize your ability."

"They already recognize my abilities. They *fear* my abilities," he said bitterly. "But this isn't even about that. Like I said: it's a political game."

"Anakin—"

"I don't know what's happening to the Order, but whatever it is, I don't like it." He shook his head. "This war is destroying everything the Republic is supposed to stand for. I mean, what are we fighting for, anyway? What about all this is worth saving?"

Padmé nodded sadly, disengaging from Anakin's arms and drifting away. "Sometimes I wonder if we're on the wrong side."

"The wrong side?"

You think everything I've accomplished has been for nothing—?

He frowned at her. "You can't mean that."

She turned from him, speaking to the vast airway beyond the veranda's edge. "What if the democracy we're fighting for no longer *exists*? What if the Republic itself has become the very evil we've been fighting to destroy?"

"Oh, this again." Anakin irritably waved off her words. "I've been hearing that garbage ever since Geonosis. I never thought I'd hear it from you."

"A few seconds ago you were saying almost the same thing!"

"Where would the Republic be without Palpatine?"

"I don't know," she said. "But I'm not sure it would be worse than where we are."

All the danger, all the suffering, all the killing, all my friends who gave their lives—?

All for nothing—?

He bit down on his temper. "Everybody complains about Palpatine having too much power, but nobody offers a better alternative. Who *should* be running the war? The *Senate*? You're in the Senate, you know those people—how many of them do *you* trust?"

"All I know is that things are going wrong here. Our government is headed in exactly the wrong direction. You know it, too—you just *said* so!"

"I didn't mean that. I just—I'm tired of this, that's all. This political garbage. Sometimes I'd rather just be back out on the front lines. At least out there, I know who the bad guys are."

"I'm becoming afraid," she replied in a bitter undertone, "that I might know who the bad guys are *here*, too."

His eyes narrowed. "You're starting to sound like a Separatist."

"Anakin, the whole galaxy knows now that Count Dooku is dead. This is the time we should be pursing a *diplomatic* resolution to the war—but instead the fighting is intensifying! Palpatine's your friend, he might listen to you. When you see him tonight, ask him, in the name of simple *decency,* to offer a ceasefire—"

His face went hard. "Is that an order?"

She blinked. "What?"

"Do *I* get any say in this?" He stalked toward her. "Does *my* opinion matter? What if I don't agree with you? What if I think Palpatine's way is the *right* way?"

"Anakin, hundreds of thousands of beings are dying every day!"

"It's a *war,* Padmé. We didn't *ask* for it, remember? You were *there*—maybe we should have 'pursued a diplomatic resolution' in that *beast* arena!"

"I was—" She shrank away from what she saw on his face, blinking harder, brows drawn together. "I was only *asking* . . ."

"Everyone is *only asking*. Everyone *wants* something from me. And *I'm* the bad guy if they don't *get* it!" He spun away from her, cloak whirling, and found himself at the veranda's edge, leaning on the rail. The durasteel piping groaned in his mechanical grip.

"I'm sick of this," he muttered. "I'm sick of all of it."

He didn't hear her come to him; the rush of aircars through the lanes below the veranda drowned her footsteps. He didn't see the hurt on her face, or the hint of tears in her eyes, but he could feel them, in the tentative softness of her touch when she stroked his arm, and he could hear them in her hesitant voice. "Anakin, what is it? What is it really?"

He shook his head. He couldn't look at her.

"Nothing that's your fault," he said. "Nothing you can help."

"Don't shut me out, Anakin. Let me try."

"You can't help me." He stared down through dozens of crisscross lanes of traffic, down toward the invisible bedrock of the planet. "I'm trying to help *you*."

He'd seen something in her eyes, when he'd mentioned the Council and Palpatine.

He'd seen it.

"What aren't you telling me?"

Her hand went still, and she did not answer.

"I can feel it, Padmé. I sense you're keeping a secret."

"Oh?" she said softly. Lightly. "That's funny, I was thinking the same about *you*."

He just kept staring down over the rail into the invisible distance below. She moved close to him, moved against him, her arm sliding around his shoulders, her cheek leaning lightly on his arm. "Why does it have to be like this? Why does there have to even be such a thing as war? Can't we just . . . go *back*? Even just to pretend. Let's pretend we're back at the lake on Naboo, just the two of us. When there was no war, no politics. No plotting. Just us. You and me, and love. That's all we need. You and me, and love."

Right now Anakin couldn't remember what that had been like.

"I have to go," he said. "The Chancellor is waiting."

Two masked, robed, silent Red Guards flanked the door to the Chancellor's private box at the Galaxies Opera. Anakin didn't need to speak; as he approached, one of them said, "You are expected," and opened the door.

The small round box had only a handful of seats, overlooking the spread of overdressed beings who filled every seat in the orchestra; on this opening night, it seemed everyone had forgotten there was a war on. Anakin barely gave a glance toward the immense sphere of shimmering water that rippled gently in the stage's artificial zero-g; he had no interest in ballet, Mon Calamari or otherwise.

In the dim semi-gloom, Palpatine sat with the speaker of the Senate, Mas Amedda, and his administrative aide, Sly Moore. Anakin stopped at the back of the box.

If I were the spy the Council wants me to be, I suppose I should be creeping up behind them so that I can listen in.

A spasm of distaste passed over his face; he took care to wipe it off before he spoke. "Chancellor. Sorry I'm late."

Palpatine turned toward him, and his face lit up. "Yes, Anakin! Don't worry. Come in, my boy, come in. Thank you for your report on the Council meeting this afternoon—it made most interesting reading. And now I have good news for you— Clone Intelligence has located General Grievous!"

"That's tremendous!" Anakin shook his head, wondering if Obi-Wan would be embarrassed to have been scooped by the clones. "He won't escape us again."

"I'm going to—Moore, take a note—I will direct the Council to give *you* this assignment, Anakin. Your gifts are wasted on Coruscant—you should be out in the field. You can attend Council meetings by holoconference."

Anakin frowned. "Thank you, sir, but the Council coordinates Jedi assignments."

"Of course, of course. Mustn't step on any Jedi toes, must we? They are so jealous of their political prerogatives. Still, I shall wonder at their collective wisdom if they choose someone else."

"As I said in my report, they've already assigned Obi-Wan to find Grievous." *Because they want to keep me here, where I am supposed to spy on you.*

"To find him, yes. But you are the best man to *apprehend* him—though of course the Jedi Council cannot always be trusted to do the right thing."

"They try. I—believe they try, sir."

"Do you still? Sit down." Palpatine looked at the other two beings in the box. "Leave us."

They rose and withdrew. Anakin took Mas Amedda's seat.

Palpatine gazed distractedly down at the graceful undulations of the Mon Calamari principal soloist for a long moment, frowning as though there was so much he wanted to say, he was unsure where to begin. Finally he sighed heavily and leaned close to Anakin.

"Anakin, I think you know by now that I cannot rely upon the Jedi Council. That is why I put you on it. If they have not yet tried to use you in their plot, they soon will."

Anakin kept his face carefully blank. "I'm not sure I understand."

"You must sense what I have come to suspect," Palpatine said grimly. "The Jedi Council is after more than independence from Senate oversight; I believe they intend to control the Republic itself."

"Chancellor—"

"I believe they are planning treason. They hope to overthrow my government, and replace me with someone weak enough that Jedi mind tricks can control his every word."

"I can't believe the Council—"

"Anakin, search your feelings. You do know, don't you?"

Anakin looked away. "I know they don't trust you . . ."

"Or the Senate. Or the Republic. Or democracy itself, for that matter. The Jedi Council is not *elected*. It selects its own members according to its own rules—a less generous man than I might say *whim*—and gives them authority backed by power. They rule the Jedi as they hope to rule the Republic: by fiat."

"I admit . . ." Anakin looked down at his hands. ". . . my faith in them has been . . . shaken."

"How? Have they approached you already? Have they ordered you to do something dishonest?" Palpatine's frown cleared into a gently wise smile that was oddly reminiscent of Yoda's. "They want you to spy on me, don't they?"

"I—"

"It's all right, Anakin. I have nothing to hide."

"I—don't know what to say . . ."

"Do you remember," Palpatine said, drawing away from Anakin so that he could lean back comfortably in his seat, "how as a young boy, when you first came to this planet, I tried to teach you the ins and outs of politics?"

Anakin smiled faintly. "I remember that I didn't much care for the lessons."

"For *any* lessons, as I recall. But it's a pity; you should have paid more attention. To understand politics is to understand the fundamental nature of thinking beings. Right now, you should remember one of my first teachings: all those who gain power are afraid to lose it."

"The Jedi use their power for *good*," Anakin said, a little too firmly.

"Good is a point of view, Anakin. And the Jedi concept of *good* is not the only valid one. Take your Dark Lords of the Sith, for example. From my reading, I have gathered that the Sith believed in justice and security every bit as much as the Jedi—"

"Jedi believe in justice and *peace*."

"In these troubled times, is there a difference?" Palpatine asked mildly. "The Jedi have not done a stellar job of bringing peace to the galaxy, you must agree. Who's to say the Sith might not have done better?"

"This is another of those arguments you probably shouldn't

bring up in front of the Council, if you know what I mean," Anakin replied with a disbelieving smile.

"Oh, yes. Because the Sith would be a threat to the Jedi Order's *power*. Lesson one."

Anakin shook his head. "Because the Sith are *evil*."

"From a Jedi's point of view," Palpatine allowed. "*Evil* is a label we all put on those who threaten us, isn't it? Yet the Sith and the Jedi are similar in almost every way, including their quest for greater power."

"The Jedi's quest is for greater *understanding*," Anakin countered. "For greater knowledge of the Force—"

"Which brings with it greater power, does it not?"

"Well . . . yes." Anakin had to laugh. "I should know better than to argue with a politician."

"We're not arguing, Anakin. We're just talking." Palpatine shifted his weight, settling in comfortably. "Perhaps the real difference between the Jedi and the Sith lies only in their orientation; a Jedi gains power through understanding, and a Sith gains understanding through power. This is the true reason the Sith have always been more powerful than the Jedi. The Jedi fear the dark side so much they cut themselves off from the most important aspect of life: passion. Of any kind. They don't even allow themselves to love."

Except for me, Anakin thought. *But then, I've never been exactly the perfect Jedi.*

"The Sith do not fear the dark side. The Sith *have* no fear. They embrace the whole spectrum of experience, from the heights of transcendent joy to the depths of hatred and despair. Beings have these emotions for a reason, Anakin. That is why the Sith are more powerful: they are not afraid to *feel*."

"The Sith rely on passion for strength," Anakin said, "but when that passion runs dry, what's left?"

"Perhaps nothing. Perhaps a great deal. Perhaps it never runs dry at all. Who can say?"

"They think inward, only about themselves."

"And the Jedi don't?"

"The Jedi are selfless—we *erase* the self, to join with the flow of the Force. We care only about *others* . . ."

Palpatine again gave him that smile of gentle wisdom. "Or so you've been trained to believe. I hear the voice of Obi-Wan Kenobi in your answers, Anakin. What do you *really* think?"

Anakin suddenly found the ballet a great deal more interesting than Palpatine's face. "I . . . don't know anymore."

"It is said that if one could ever entirely comprehend a single grain of sand—really, truly understand *everything* about it—one would, at the same time, entirely comprehend the universe. Who's to say that a Sith, by looking inward, sees less than a Jedi does by looking out?"

"The Jedi—Jedi are *good*. That's the difference. I don't care *who* sees *what*."

"What the Jedi are," Palpatine said gently, "is a group of very powerful beings you consider to be your comrades. And you are loyal to your friends; I have known that for as long as I have known you, and I admire you for it. But are your friends loyal to *you*?"

Anakin shot him a sudden frown. "What do you mean?"

"Would a true friend ask you to do something that's wrong?"

"I'm not sure it's wrong," Anakin said. Obi-Wan might have been telling the truth. It was possible. They might only want to catch Sidious. They might really be trying to protect Palpatine.

They might.

Maybe.

"Have they asked you to break the Jedi Code? To violate the Constitution? To betray a friendship? To betray your own *values*?"

"Chancellor—"

"*Think,* Anakin! I have always tried to teach you to think—yes, yes, Jedi do not think, they *know*, but those stale answers aren't good enough now, in these changing times. Consider their motives. Keep your mind clear of assumptions. The fear of losing power is a weakness of both the Jedi and the Sith."

Anakin sank lower in his seat. Too much had happened in too short a time. Everything jumbled together in his head, and none of it seemed to make complete sense.

Except for what Palpatine said.

That made too *much* sense.

"This puts me in mind of an old legend," Palpatine murmured idly. "Anakin—are you familiar with *The Tragedy of Darth Plagueis the Wise?*"

Anakin shook his head.

"Ah, I thought not. It is not a story the Jedi would tell you. It's a Sith legend, of a Dark Lord who had turned his sight inward so deeply that he had come to comprehend, and master, life itself. And—because the two are one, when seen clearly enough—death itself."

Anakin sat up. Was he actually hearing this? "He could keep someone safe from death?"

"According to the legend," Palpatine said, "he could directly influence the midi-chlorians to create life; with such knowledge, to maintain life in someone already living would seem a small matter, don't you agree?"

A universe of possibility blossomed inside Anakin's head. He murmured, "Stronger than *death* . . ."

"The dark side seems to be—from my reading—the pathway to many abilities some would consider unnatural."

Anakin couldn't seem to get his breath. "What happened to him?"

"Oh, well, it *is* a tragedy, after all, you know. Once he has gained this ultimate power, he has nothing to fear save losing it— that's why the Jedi Council brought him to mind, you know."

"But what *happened?*"

"Well, to safeguard his power's existence, he teaches the path toward it to his apprentice."

"And?"

"And his apprentice kills him in his sleep," Palpatine said with a careless shrug. "Plageuis never sees it coming. That's the tragic irony, you see: he can save anyone in the galaxy from death—except himself."

"What about the apprentice? What happens to *him*?"

"Oh, him. *He* goes on to become the greatest Dark Lord the Sith have ever known . . ."

"So," Anakin murmured, "it's only a tragedy for *Plagueis*—for the apprentice, the legend has a *happy* ending . . ."

"Oh, well, yes. Quite right. I'd never really thought of it that way—rather like what we were talking about earlier, isn't it?"

"What if," Anakin said slowly, almost not daring to speak the words, "it's not just a legend?"

"I'm sorry?"

"What if Darth Plagueis really *lived*—what if someone really *had* this power?"

"Oh, I am . . . rather certain . . . that Plagueis did indeed exist. And if someone actually had this power—well, he would indeed be one of the most powerful men in the galaxy, not to mention virtually immortal . . ."

"How would I *find* him?"

"I'm sure I couldn't say. You could ask your friends on the Jedi Council, I suppose—but of course, if they ever found him they'd kill him on the spot. Not as punishment for any crime, you understand. Innocence is irrelevant to the Jedi. They would kill him simply for being Sith, and his knowledge would die with him."

"I just—I have to—" Anakin found himself half out of his seat, fists clenched and trembling. He forced himself to relax and sit back down, and he took a deep breath. "You seem to know so much about this, I need you to tell me: would it be possible, possible at all, to learn this power?"

Palpatine shrugged, regarding him with that smile of gentle wisdom.

"Well, clearly," he said, "not from a Jedi."

*　*　*

For a long, long time after leaving the opera house, Anakin sat motionless in his idling speeder, eyes closed, resting his head against the edge of his mechanical hand. The speeder bobbed gently in the air-wakes of the passing traffic; he didn't feel it. Klaxons blared, rising and fading as angry pilots swerved around him; he didn't hear them.

Finally he sighed and lifted his head. He stroked a private code into the speeder's comm screen. After a moment the screen lit up with an image of Padmé's half-asleep face.

"Anakin—?" She rubbed her eyes, blinking. *"Where are you? What time is it?"*

"Padmé, I can't—" He stopped himself, huffing a sigh out through his nose. "Listen, Padmé, something's come up. I have to spend the night at the Temple."

"Oh . . . well, all right, Anakin. I'll miss you."

"I'll miss you, too." He swallowed. "I miss you already."

"We'll be together tomorrow?"

"Yes. And soon, for the rest of our lives. We'll never have to be apart again."

She nodded sleepily. *"Rest well, my love."*

"I'll do my best. You, too."

She blew him a kiss, and the screen went blank.

Anakin fired thrusters and slid the speeder expertly into traffic, angling toward the Jedi Temple, because that part—the part about spending the night at the Temple—was the part that wasn't a lie.

The lie was that he was going to rest. That he was going to even try. How could he rest when every time he closed his eyes he could see her screaming on the birthing table?

Now the Council's insult burned hotter than ever; he even had a name, a story, a place to start—but how could he explain to the archives Master why he needed to research a Sith legend of immortality?

Yet maybe he didn't need the archives after all.

The Temple was still the greatest nexus of Force energy on

the planet, perhaps even the galaxy, and it was unquestionably the best place in the galaxy for intense, focused meditation. He had much he needed the Force to teach him, and a very short time to learn.

He would start by thinking inward.

Thinking about *himself* . . .

THE WILL OF THE FORCE

When her handmaiden Moteé awakened her with the word that C-3PO had announced a Jedi was waiting to see her, Padmé flew out of bed, threw on a robe, and hurried out to her living room, a smile breaking through her sleepiness like the dawn outside—

But it was Obi-Wan.

The Jedi Master had his back to her, hands clasped behind him as he drifted restlessly about the room, gazing with abstracted lack of interest at her collection of rare sculpture.

"Obi-Wan," she said breathlessly, "has—" She bit off the following *something happened to Anakin?* How would she explain why this was the first thing out of her mouth?

"—has See-Threepio offered you anything to drink?"

He turned to her, a frown clearing from his brow. "Senator," he said warmly. "So good to see you again. I apologize for the early hour, and yes, your protocol droid has been quite insistent on offering me refreshment." His frown began to regather. "But as you may guess, this is not a social call. I've come to speak with you about Anakin."

Her years in politics had trained her well; even as her heart lurched and a shrill *How much does he* know? echoed inside her head, her face remained only attentively blank.

A primary rule of Republic politics: tell as much truth as you can. Especially to a Jedi. "I was very happy to learn of his appointment to the Council."

"Yes. It is perhaps less than he deserves—though I'm afraid it may be more than he can handle. Has he been to see you?"

"Several times," she said evenly. "Something is wrong, isn't it?"

Obi-Wan tilted his head, and a hint of rueful smile showed through his beard. "You should have been a Jedi."

She managed a light laugh. "And you should never go into politics. You're not very good at hiding your feelings. What is it?"

"It's Anakin." With his pretense of cheer fading away, he seemed to age before her eyes. He looked very tired, and profoundly troubled. "May I sit?"

"Please." She waved him to the couch and lowered herself onto its edge beside him. "Is he in trouble again?"

"I certainly hope not. This is more . . . a personal matter." He shifted his weight uncomfortably. "He's been put in a difficult position as the Chancellor's representative, but I think there's more to it than that. We—had words, yesterday, and we parted badly."

Her heart shrank; he *must* know, and he'd come to confront her—to bring their whole lives crashing down around their ears. She ached for Anakin, but her face showed only polite curiosity.

"What were these words about?" she asked delicately.

"I'm afraid I can't tell you," he said with a vaguely apologetic frown. "Jedi business. You understand."

She inclined her head. "Of course."

"It's only that—well, I've been a bit worried about him. I was hoping he may have talked to you."

"Why would he talk to *me* about—" She favored him with her best friendly-but-skeptical smile. "—Jedi business?"

"Senator—Padmé. Please." He gazed into her eyes with nothing on his face but compassion and fatigued anxiety. "I am not blind, Padmé. Though I have tried to be, for Anakin's sake. And for yours."

"What do you mean?"

"Neither of you is very good at hiding feelings, either."

"Obi-Wan—"

"Anakin has loved you since the day you met, in that horrible junk shop on Tatooine. He's never even tried to hide it, though we do not speak of it. We . . . pretend that I don't know. And I was happy to, because it made him happy. *You* made him happy, when nothing else ever truly could." He sighed, his brows drawing together. "And you, Padmé, skilled as you are on the Senate floor, cannot hide the light that comes to your eyes when anyone so much as mentions his name."

"I—" She lurched to her feet. "I can't—Obi-Wan, don't make me talk about this . . ."

"I don't mean to hurt you, Padmé. Nor even to make you uncomfortable. I'm not here to interrogate you; I have no interest in the details of your relationship."

She turned away, walking just to be moving, barely conscious of passing through the door out onto the dawn-painted veranda. "Then why *are* you here?"

He followed her respectfully. "Anakin is under a great deal of pressure. He carries tremendous responsibilities for a man so young; when I was his age I still had some years to go as a Padawan. He is—changing. Quickly. And I have some anxiety about what he is changing into. It would be a . . . very great mistake . . . were he to leave the Jedi Order."

She blinked as though he'd slapped her. "Why—that seems . . . *unlikely,* doesn't it? What about this prophecy the Jedi put so much faith in? Isn't he the chosen one?"

"Very probably. But I have scanned this prophecy; it says only that a chosen one will be born and bring balance to the Force; nowhere does it say he has to be a Jedi."

She blinked harder, fighting down a surge of desperate hope that left her breathless. "He doesn't *have* to—?"

"My Master, Qui-Gon Jinn, believed that it was the will of the Force that Anakin should be trained as a Jedi—and we all have a certain, oh, I suppose you could call it a Jedi-centric bias. It is a Jedi prophecy, after all."

"But the will of the Force—isn't that what Jedi follow?"

"Well, yes. But you must understand that not even the Jedi know all there is to be known about the Force; no mortal mind can. We speak of the *will of the Force* as someone ignorant of gravity might say it is the will of a river to flow to the ocean: it is a metaphor that describes our ignorance. The simple truth—if any truth is ever simple—is that we do not truly know what the will of the Force may be. We can *never* know. It is so far beyond our limited understanding that we can only surrender to its mystery."

"What does this have to do with Anakin?" She swallowed, but her voice stayed tight and thin. "And with me?"

"I fear that some of his current . . . difficulty . . . has to do with your relationship."

If you only knew how much, she thought. "What do you want me to do?"

He looked down. "I cannot tell you what to do, Padmé. I can only ask you to consider Anakin's best interests. You know the two of you can never be together while he remains in the Order."

A bleak chill settled into her chest. "Obi-Wan, I can't talk about this."

"Very well. But remember that the Jedi are his family. The Order gives his life *structure*. It gives him a direction. You know how . . . undisciplined he can be."

And that's why he is the only Jedi I could ever love . . . "Yes. Yes, of course."

"If his true path leads him away from the Jedi, so be it. But please, for both of your sakes, tread carefully. Be sure. Some decisions can never be reversed."

"Yes," she said slowly. Feelingly. "I know that too well."

He nodded as though he understood, though of course he did not understand at all. "We all do, these days."

A soft chiming came from within his robe. "Excuse me," he said, and turned aside, producing a comlink from an inner pocket. "Yes . . . ?"

A man's voice came thinly through the comlink, deep and clipped: *"We are calling the Council into special session. We've located General Grievous!"*

"Thank you, Master Windu," Obi-Wan said. "I'm on my way."

General Grievous? Her eyes went hot, and stung with sudden tears. And so they would take her Anakin away from her again.

She felt a stirring below her ribs. Away from *us,* she amended, and there was so much love and fear and joy and loss all swirling and clashing within her that she dared not speak. She only stared blindly out across the smog-shrouded cityscape as Obi-Wan came close to her shoulder.

"Padmé," he said softly. Gently. Almost regretfully. "I will not tell the Council of this. Any of it. I'm very sorry to burden you with this, and I—I hope I haven't upset you too much. We have all been friends for so long . . . and I hope we always will be."

"Thank you, Obi-Wan," she said faintly. She couldn't look at him. From the corner of her eye she saw him incline his head respectfully and turn to go.

For a moment she said nothing, but as his footsteps receded she said, "Obi-Wan?"

She heard him stop.

"You love him, too, don't you?"

When he didn't answer, she turned to look. He stood motionless, frowning, in the middle of the expanse of buff carpeting.

"You do. You love him."

He lowered his head. He looked very alone.

"Please do what you can to help him," he said, and left.

* * *

The holoscan of Utapau rotated silently in the center of the Jedi Council Chamber. Anakin had brought the holoprojector from the Chancellor's office; Obi-Wan wondered idly if the projector had been scanned for recording devices planted by the Chancellor to spy on their meeting, then dismissed the thought. In a sense, Anakin *was* the Chancellor's recording device.

And that's our fault, he thought.

The only Council members physically present, other than Obi-Wan and Anakin, were Mace Windu and Agen Kolar. The Council reached a quorum by the projected holopresences of Ki-Adi-Mundi, en route to Mygeeto, Plo Koon on Cato Neimoidia, and Yoda, who was about to make planetfall on Kashyyyk.

"Why Utapau?" Mace Windu was saying. "A neutral system, of little strategic significance, and virtually no planetary defense force—"

"Perhaps that is itself the reason," Agen Kolar offered. "Easily taken, and their sinkhole-based culture can hide a tremendous number of droids from long-range scans."

Ki-Adi-Mundi's frown wrinkled the whole length of his forehead. *"Our agents on Utapau have made no report of this."*

"They may be detained, or dead," Obi-Wan said.

Mace Windu leaned toward Anakin, scowling. "How could the Chancellor have come by this information when we know nothing about it?"

"Clone Intelligence intercepted a partial message in a diplomatic packet from the Chairman of Utapau," Anakin told him. "We've only managed to verify its authenticity within the past hour."

Obi-Wan felt a frown crawl onto his forehead at the way Anakin now referred to the Chancellor's Office as *we . . .*

"Clone Intelligence," Mace said heavily, "reports to *us.*"

"I beg your pardon, Master Windu, but that is no longer the case." Though Anakin's expression was perfectly solemn, Obi-Wan thought he could detect a hint of satisfaction in his young friend's voice. "I thought it had been already made clear. The constitutional amendment bringing the Jedi under the Chancellor's Office naturally includes troops commanded by Jedi. Palpatine is now Supreme Commander of the Grand Army of the Republic."

"Pointless it is, to squabble over jurisdiction," the image of Yoda said. *"Act on this, we must."*

"I believe we all agree on that," Anakin said briskly. "Let's move to the operational planning. The Chancellor has requested that I lead this mission, and so I—"

"The *Council* will decide this," Mace said sternly. "Not the Chancellor."

"Dangerous, Grievous is. To face him, steady minds are needed. Masters, we should send."

Perhaps of all the Council, only Obi-Wan could detect the shadow of disappointment and hurt that crept into Anakin's eyes. Obi-Wan understood perfectly, and could even sympathize: to take the field would have slipped Anakin out from under the pressures of what he saw as his conflicting duties.

"Given the strain on our current resources," Mace Windu said, "I recommend we send only one Jedi—Master Kenobi."

Which would leave Mace and Agen Kolar—both among the greatest bladesbeings the Jedi Order had ever produced—here on Coruscant in case Sidious did indeed take this opportunity to make a dramatic move. Not to mention Anakin, who was a brigade's worth of firepower in his own right.

Obi-Wan nodded. Perfectly logical. Everyone would agree.

Except Anakin. He leaned forward, red climbing his cheeks. "He wasn't so successful the *last* time he met Grievous!"

"Anakin—" Obi-Wan began.

"No offense, my Master. I am only stating a fact."

"Oh no, not at all. You're quite right. But I have a feel for how he fights now—and for how he runs away. I am certain I can catch him."

"Master—"

"And you, my young friend, have duties here on Coruscant.

Extremely *important* duties, that require your *full attention*," Obi-Wan reminded him. "Am I being clear?"

Anakin didn't answer. He sank back into his chair and turned away.

"Obi-Wan, my choice is," Yoda said.

Ki-Adi-Mundi's image nodded. *"I concur. Let's put it to a vote."*

Mace Windu counted nods. "Six in favor."

He waited, looking at Anakin. "Further comment?"

Anakin only stared at the wall.

After a moment, Mace shrugged.

"It is unanimous."

Senator Chi Eekway accepted a tube of Aqualish hoi-broth from C-3PO's refeshment tray. "I am very grateful to be included here," she said, her dewlaps jiggling as she tilted her blue head in a gesture around Padmé's living room at the gathering of Senators. "I speak directly only for my own sector, of course, but I can tell you that many Senators are becoming very nervous indeed. You may not know that the new governors are arriving with full regiments of clone troops—what they call *security forces*. We all have begun to wonder if these regiments are intended to protect us from the Separatists . . . or to protect the governors from *us*."

Padmé looked up from the document reader in her hand. "I have . . . reliable information . . . that General Grievous has been located, and that the Jedi are already moving against his position. The war may be over in a matter of days."

"But what then?" Bail Organa leaned forward, elbows to knees, fingers laced together. "How do we make Palpatine withdraw his governors? How do we stop him from garrisoning troops in *all* our systems?"

"We don't have to *make* him do anything," Padmé said reasonably. "The Senate granted him executive powers only for the duration of the emergency—"

"Yet it is only Palpatine himself who has the authority to declare when the emergency is over," Bail countered. "How do we make him surrender power back to the Senate?"

Chi Eekway shifted backward. "There are many who are willing to do just that," she said. "Not just my own people. Many Senators. We are ready to *make* him surrender power."

Padmé snapped the document reader closed. She looked from Senator to Senator expressionlessly. "Would anyone care for further refreshment?"

"Senator Amidala," Eekway said, "I fear you don't understand—"

"Senator Eekway. Another hoi-broth?"

"No, that's—"

"Very well, then." She looked up at C-3PO. "Threepio, that will be all. Please tell Moteé and Ellé that they are dismissed for the day, then you are free to power down for a while."

"Thank you, Mistress," Threepio replied. "Though I must say, this discussion has been *most* stimu—"

"Threepio." Padmé's tone went a trace extra firm. "That will be *all*."

"Yes, Mistress. Of course. I quite understand." The droid turned stiffly and shuffled out of the room.

As soon as 3PO was safely out of earshot, Padmé brandished the document reader as though it were a weapon. "This is a very dangerous step. We cannot let this turn into another war."

"That's the last thing any of us wants," Bail said with a disapproving look at Senator Eekway. "Alderaan has no armed forces; we don't even have a planetary defense system. A political solution is our only option."

"Which is the purpose of this petition," Mon Mothma said, laying her soft hand over Padmé's. "We're hoping that a show of solidarity within the Senate might stop Palpatine from further subverting the Constitution, that's all. With the signatures of a full two thousand Senators—"

"—we still have less than we need to stop his supermajority

from amending the Constitution any way he happens to want," Padmé finished for her. She weighed the reader in her hand. "I am willing to present this to Palpatine, but I am losing faith in the Senate's readiness, or even ability, to rein him in. I think we should consult the Jedi."

Because I really think they can help, or because I just can't stand to lie to my husband? She couldn't say. She hoped that both were true, though she was sure only of the second.

Bana Breemu examined her long, elegantly manicured fingertips. "That," she said remotely, "would be dangerous."

Mon Mothma nodded. "We don't know where the Jedi stand in all this."

Padmé sat forward. "The Jedi aren't any happier with the situation than we are."

Senator Breemu's high-arched cheekbones made the look she gave Padmé appear even more distant and skeptical. "You seem . . . remarkably well informed about Jedi business, Senator Amidala."

Padmé felt herself flush, and she didn't trust herself to answer.

Giddean Danu shook his head, doubt plainly written across his dark face. "If we are to openly oppose the Chancellor, we need the support of the Jedi. We need their moral authority. Otherwise, what do we have?"

"The *moral authority* of the Jedi, such as it is," Bana Breemu said, "has been spent lavishly upon war; I fear they have none left for politics."

"*One* Jedi, then," Padmé offered to the others. *At least let me speak the truth to my love. At least. Please,* she pleaded with them silently. "There is one Jedi—one whom I truly know all of us can trust absolutely . . ."

Her voice trailed off into appalled silence when she realized that she wasn't talking about Anakin.

This had been all about him when she'd started—all about her love, her need to be open with him, the pain that keeping this secret stabbed her heart at each and every beat—but when the

thought had turned to *trust*, when it became a question of someone she knew, truly and abolutely *knew*, she could trust—

She discovered that she was talking about Obi-Wan.

Anakin . . . Something was breaking inside her. *Oh, my love,
what are they doing to us?*

Chi Eekway shook her head. "Patience, Senator."

Fang Zar unknotted his fingers from his raggedly bushy
beard and shrugged. "Yes, we cannot block the Chancellor's
supermajority—but we can show him that opposition to his
methods is growing. Perhaps that alone might persuade him to
moderate his tactics."

Bana Breemu went back to examining her fingertips. "When
you present the Petition of the Two Thousand, many things may
change."

"But," Giddean Danu said, "will they change for the better?"

Bail Organa and Mon Mothma exchanged glances that whispered of some shared secret. Bail said slowly, "Let us see what we
can accomplish in the Senate before we involve the Jedi."

And as one after another of the Senators agreed, Padmé
could only sit in silence. In mourning.

Grieving for the sudden death of an illusion.

Anakin—Anakin, I love you. If only—

But that *if only* would take her to a place she could not bear
to go. In the end, she could only return to the thought she
feared would echo within her for the rest of her life.

Anakin, I'm sorry.

The last of the hovertanks whirred up the ramp into the sky-
shrouding wedge of the assault cruiser. It was followed by rank
upon immaculately regimented rank of clone troopers, mar-
shaled by battalions, marching in perfect synchrony.

Standing alongside Obi-Wan on the landing deck, Anakin
watched them go.

He couldn't quite make himself believe he wasn't going
along.

It wasn't that he really *wanted* to go with Obi-Wan to

Utapau—even though it'd be a relief to pull out of the political quagmire that was sucking him down. But how could he leave Padmé now? He didn't even care anymore about being the Jedi to capture Grievous, though such a feat would almost certainly bring him his Mastery. He was no longer certain he needed to be a Master at all.

Through the long, black hours of meditation last night—meditation that was often indistinguishable from brooding—he had begun to sense a deeper truth within the Force: a submerged reality, lurking like a Sarlacc beneath the sunlit sands of Jedi training.

Somewhere down there was all the power he would ever need.

So no, it wasn't that he wanted to go. It was more, inexplicably, that he wanted Obi-Wan to *stay*.

There was a cold void in his chest that he was afraid would soon fill with regret, and grief.

Of course there was no chance at all that Obi-Wan wouldn't go; he'd be the last Jedi in the galaxy to defy an order of the Council. Not for the first time, Anakin found himself wishing that Obi-Wan could be a little more like the late Qui-Gon. Though he'd known Qui-Gon for mere days, Anakin could almost see him right now, brow furrowing as he gently inclined his head over his shorter Padawan; he could almost hear his gentle baritone instructing Obi-Wan to *be mindful of the currents of the living Force: to do one's duty is not always to do right. Concern yourself with right action. Let duty take care of itself.*

But he couldn't say that. Though he'd passed his trials many months ago, to Obi-Wan he was still the learner, not the Master.

All he could say was, "I have a bad feeling about this."

Obi-Wan was frowning as he watched a clone deck crew load his blue-and-white starfighter onto the assault cruiser's flight deck. "I'm sorry, Anakin. Did you say something?"

"You're going to need me on this one, Master." And he could feel an unexpected truth there, too—if he *were* to go along, if he could somehow bring himself to forget about Padmé for a few days, if he could somehow get himself away from Palpatine and the Council and his meditations and politics and everything here on Coruscant that was dragging him this way and that way and sucking him under, if he could just tag along and play the *Kenobi and Skywalker* game for a few days, everything might still be all right.

If only.

"It may be nothing but a wild bantha chase," Obi-Wan said. "Your job here is much more important, Anakin."

"I know: the Sith." The word left a bitter taste in Anakin's mouth. The Council's manipulation had a rank stench of politics on it. "I just—" Anakin shrugged helplessly, looking away. "I don't like you going off without me like this. It's a bad idea to split up the team. I mean, look what happened *last* time."

"Don't remind me."

"You want to go spend another few months with somebody like Ventress? Or worse?"

"Anakin." Anakin could hear a gentle smile in Obi-Wan's voice. "Don't worry. I have enough clones to take three systems the size of Utapau's. I believe I should be able to handle the situation, even without your help."

Anakin had to answer his smile. "Well, there's always a first time."

Obi-Wan said, "We're not really splitting up, Anakin. We've worked on our own many times—like when you took Padmé to Naboo while I went to Kamino and Geonosis."

"And look how *that* turned out."

"All right, bad example," Obi-Wan admitted, his smile shading toward rueful. "Yet years later, here we all are: still alive, and still friends. My point, Anakin, is that even when we work separately, we work together. We have the same goals: end the war, and save the Republic from the Sith. As long as we're on the same side, everything will come out well in the end. I'm certain of it."

"Well . . ." Anakin sighed. "I suppose you could be right. You are, once in a while. Occasionally."

Obi-Wan chuckled and clapped him on the shoulder. "Farewell, old friend."

"Master, wait." Anakin turned to face him fully. He couldn't just stand here and let him walk away. Not now. He had to say *something* . . .

He had a sinking feeling he might not get another chance.

"Master . . . ," he said hesitantly, "I know I've . . . disappointed you in these past few days. I have been arrogant. I have . . . not been very appreciative of your training, and what's worse, of your friendship. I offer no excuse, Master. My frustration with the Council . . . I know that none of it is your fault, and I apologize. For all of it. Your friendship means everything to me."

Obi-Wan gripped Anakin's mechanical hand, and with his other he squeezed Anakin's arm above the joining of flesh and metal. "You are wise and strong, Anakin. You are a credit to the Jedi Order, and you have far surpassed my humble efforts at instruction."

Anakin felt his own smile turn melancholy. "Just the other day, you were saying that my power is no credit to me."

"I'm not speaking of your power, Anakin, but of your heart. The greatness in you is a greatness of spirit. Courage and generosity, compassion and commitment. These are your virtues," Obi-Wan said gently. "You have done great things, and I am very proud of you."

Anakin found he had nothing to say.

"Well." Obi-Wan looked down, chuckling, releasing Anakin's hand and arm. "I believe I hear General Grievous calling my name. Good-bye, old friend. May the Force be with you."

All Anakin could offer in return was a reflexive echo.

"May the Force be with you."

He stood, still and silent, and watched Obi-Wan walk away. Then he turned and slowly, head hanging, moved toward his speeder.

The Chancellor was waiting.

14

FREE FALL IN THE DARK

A chill wind scoured the Chancellor's private landing deck at the Senate Office Building. Anakin stood wrapped in his cloak, chin to his chest, staring down at the deck below his feet. He didn't feel the chill, or the wind. He didn't hear the whine of the Chancellor's private shuttle angling in for a landing, or smell the swirls of brown smog coiling along the wind.

What he saw were the faces of Senators who had stood on this deck to cheer for him; what he heard were exclamations of joy and congratulations when he returned their Supreme Chancellor to them unharmed. What he felt was a memory of hot pride at being the focus of so many eager HoloNet crews, anxious to get even the slightest glimpse of the man who had conquered Count Dooku.

How many days ago had that been? He couldn't remember. Not many. When you don't sleep, days smear together into a haze of fatigue so deep it becomes a physical pain. The Force could keep him upright, keep him moving, keep him thinking, but it could not give him rest. Not that he wanted rest. Rest might bring sleep.

What sleep might bring, he could not bear to know.

He remembered Obi-Wan telling him about some poet he'd

once read—he couldn't remember the name, or the exact quote, but it was something about how there is no greater misery than to remember, with bitter regret, a day when you were happy . . .

How had everything gone so fast from so right to so wrong?

He couldn't even imagine.

Greasy dust swirled under the shuttle's repulsors as it settled to the deck. The hatch cycled open, and four of Palpatine's personal guards glided out, long robes catching the breeze in silken blood-colored ripples. They split into two pairs to flank the doors as the Chancellor emerged beside the tall, bulky form of Mas Amedda, the Speaker of the Senate. The Chagrian's horns tilted over Palpatine as they walked together, seemingly deep in conversation.

Anakin moved forward to meet them. "Chancellor," he said, bowing a greeting. "Lord Speaker."

Mas Amedda looked at Anakin with a curl to his blue lips that, on a human, would have signaled disgust; it was a Chagrian smile. "Greetings, Your Grace. I trust the day finds you well?"

Anakin's eyes felt as if they'd been dusted with sand. "Very well, Lord Speaker, thank you for asking."

Amedda turned back to Palpatine, and Anakin's polite smile faded to a twist of contempt. Maybe he was just overtired, but somehow, looking at the curlings of the Chagrian's naked head-tentacles as they twisted across his chest, he found himself hoping that Obi-Wan hadn't been lying to him about Sidious. He rather hoped that Mas Amedda might be a secret Sith, because something about the Speaker of the Senate was so revolting that Anakin could easily imagine just slicing his head in half . . .

It gradually dawned on Anakin that Palpatine was giving Mas Amedda the brush-off, and was sending the Redrobes with him.

Good. He wasn't in the mood to play games. By themselves, they could talk straight with each other. A little straight talk might be just what he needed. A little straight talk might burn through the fog of half-truths and subtle confusions that the Jedi Council had poured into his head.

"So, Anakin," Palpatine said as the others moved away, "did you see your friend off?"

Anakin nodded. "If I didn't hate Grievous so much, I'd almost feel sorry for him."

"Oh?" Palpatine appeared mildly interested. "Are Jedi allowed to hate?"

"Figure of speech," Anakin said, waving this off. "It doesn't matter how I feel about Grievous. Obi-Wan will soon have his head."

"Provided, of course," Palpatine murmured as he took Anakin's arm to guide him toward the entryway, "that the Council didn't make a mistake. I still believe Master Kenobi is not the Jedi for this job."

Anakin shrugged irritably. Why did everyone keep bringing up things he didn't want to talk about? "The Council was . . . very sure in its decision."

"Certainty is a fine thing," the Chancellor allowed. "Though it too often happens that those who are the most entirely certain are also the most entirely wrong. What will the Council do if Kenobi proves unable to apprehend Grievous without your help?"

"I'm sure I cannot say, sir. I imagine they will deal with that if and when it happens. The Jedi teach that anticipation is distraction."

"I am no philosopher, Anakin; in my work, anticipation is often my sole hope of success. I must anticipate the actions of my adversaries—and even those of my allies. Even—" He opened a hand toward Anakin, smiling. "—my friends. It is the only way I can be prepared to take advantage of opportunity . . . and conversely, to avoid disaster."

"But if a disaster comes about by the will of the Force—"

"I'm afraid I don't believe in the will of the Force," Palpatine said, his smile turning apologetic. "I believe it is *our* will that matters. I believe that everything good in our civilization has come about not by the blind action of some mystical field of energy, but by the focused will of *people:* lawmakers and warriors, inventors and engineers, struggling with every breath of their bodies to shape galactic culture. To improve the lives of all."

They stood now before the vaulted door to Palpatine's office. "Please come in, Anakin. Much as I enjoy a philosophical chat, that was not the reason I asked you to meet me. We have business to discuss, and I fear it may be very serious business indeed."

Anakin followed him through the outer chambers to Palpatine's intimate private office. He took up a respectful standing position opposite Palpatine's desk, but the Chancellor waved him to a chair. "Please, Anakin, make yourself comfortable. Some of this may be difficult for you to hear."

"Everything is, these days," Anakin muttered as he took a seat.

Palpatine didn't seem to hear. "It concerns Master Kenobi. My friends among the Senators have picked up some . . . disturbing rumors about him. Many in the Senate believe that Kenobi is not fit for this assignment."

Anakin frowned. "Are you serious?"

"I'm most serious, I'm afraid. It is a . . . complicated situation, Anakin. It seems there are some in the Senate who now regret having granted me emergency powers."

"There have been dissenters and naysayers since before Geonosis, sir. Why should it be cause for concern now? And how does it affect Obi-Wan?"

"I'm getting to that." Palpatine took a deep breath and swung his chair around so that he could gaze through his window of armored transparisteel onto the cityscape beyond. "The difference is that now, some of these Senators—actually a large number of them—seem to have given up on democracy. Unable to achieve their ends in the Senate, they are organizing into a cabal, preparing to remove me by . . . other means."

"You mean treason?" Anakin had enough Jedi discipline to force away his memory of using that word with Obi-Wan.

"I'm afraid so. The rumor is that the ringleaders of this group may have fallen victim to the . . . persuasive powers . . . of the Jedi Council, and are on their way to becoming accomplices in the Council's plot against the Republic."

"Sir, I—" Anakin shook his head. "This just seems . . . ridiculous."

"And it may be entirely false. Remember that these are only rumors. Entirely unconfirmed. Senate gossip is rarely accurate, but if this *is* true . . . we must be *prepared*, Anakin. I still have friends enough in the Senate to catch the scent of whatever this disloyal cabal is cooking up. And I have a very good idea of who the leaders are; in fact, my final meeting this afternoon is with a delegation representing the cabal. I would like you to be present for that as well."

"Me?" Couldn't everyone leave him alone for day? For even a few *hours*? "What for?"

"Your Jedi senses, Anakin. Your ability to read evil intent. I have no doubt these Senators will put some virtuous façade on their plotting; with your help, we will pierce that veil and discover the truth."

Anakin sighed, rubbing his stinging eyes. How could he let Palaptine down? "I'm willing to try, sir."

"We won't try, Anakin. We will *do*. After all, they are only Senators. Most of them couldn't hide what they're thinking from a brain-damaged blindworm, let alone the most powerful Jedi in the galaxy."

He leaned back in his chair and steepled his fingers pensively. "The Jedi Council, however, is another matter entirely. A secret society of antidemocratic beings who wield tremendous power, individually as well as collectively—how am I to trace the labyrinth of *their* plots? That's why I put you on the Council. If these rumors are true, you may be democracy's last hope."

Anakin let his chin sink once more to his chest, and his eyelids scraped shut. It seemed like he was always *somebody's* last hope.

Why did everyone always have to make their problems into *his* problems? Why couldn't people just let him be?

How was he supposed to deal with all this when Padmé could *die?*

He said slowly, eyes still closed, "You still haven't told me what this has to do with Obi-Wan."

"Ah, that—well, that is the difficult part. The *disturbing* part. It seems that Master Kenobi has been in contact with a certain Senator who is known to be among the leaders of this cabal. Apparently, very *close* contact. The rumor is that he was seen leaving this Senator's residence this very morning, at an . . . unseemly hour."

"Who?" Anakin opened his eyes and sat forward. "Who is this Senator? Let's go question *him.*"

"I'm sorry, Anakin. But the Senator in question is, in fact, a *her.* A woman you know quite well, in fact."

"You—" He wasn't hearing this. He couldn't be. "You mean—"

Anakin choked on her name.

Palpatine gave him a look of melancholy sympathy. "I'm afraid so."

Anakin coughed his voice back to life. "That's *impossible!* I would *know*—she doesn't . . . she couldn't—"

"Sometimes the closest," Palpatine said sadly, "are those who cannot see."

Anakin sat back, stunned. He felt like he'd been punched in the chest by a Gamorrean. By a *rancor.* His ears rang, and the room whirled around him.

"I would know," he repeated numbly. "I would know . . ."

"Don't take it too hard," Palpatine said. "It may be only idle gossip. All this may be only a figment of my overheated imagination; after all these years of war, I find myself inspecting every shadow that might hide an enemy. That is what I need from *you,* Anakin: I need you to find the truth. To set my mind at rest."

A distant smolder kindled under Anakin's breastbone, so faint as to be barely there at all, but even a hint of that fire gave Anakin the strength to throw himself to his feet.

"I can do that," he said.

The flame grew stronger now. Hotter. The numb fatigue that had dragged at his limbs began to burn away.

"Good, Anakin. I knew I could count on you."

"Always, sir. Always."

He turned to go. He would go to her. He would see her. He would get the truth. He would do it *now*. Right now. In the middle of the day. It didn't matter who might see him.

This was business.

"I know who my friends are," he said, and left.

He moved through Padmé's apartment like a shadow, like a ghost at a banquet. He touched nothing. He looked at everything.

He felt as if he'd never seen it before.

How could she do this to him?

Sometimes the closest are those who cannot see.

How *could* she?

How could *he*?

In the Force, the whole apartment stank of Obi-Wan.

His finger traced the curving back of her couch.

Here. Obi-Wan had sat here.

Anakin rounded the couch and settled into that same spot. His hand fell naturally to the seat beside him . . . and there he felt an echo of Padmé.

The dragon whispered, *That's a little close for casual conversation.*

This was a different kind of fear. Even colder. Even uglier.

Fear that Palpatine might be *right* . . .

The apartment's air still hummed with discord and worry, and there was a smell of oxidized spices and boiled seaweed— hoi-broth, that was it. Someone in the past few hours had been drinking hoi-broth in this room.

Padmé hated hoi-broth.

And Obi-Wan was allergic to it—once on a diplomatic mission to Ando, his violent reaction to a ceremonial toast had nearly triggered an intersystem incident.

So Padmé had been entertaining other visitors, too.

From a pocket on his equipment belt he pulled a flimsi of Palpatine's list of suspect Senators. He scanned down the list, looking for names of Senators he knew well enough that he might recognize the Force-echoes of their presence here. Many he'd never heard of; there were thousands of Senators, after all. But those he knew by reputation were the cream of the Senate: people like Terr Taneel, Fang Zar, Bail Organa, Garm Bel Iblis—

He began to think Palpatine *was* just imagining things after all. These beings were known to be incorruptible.

He frowned down at the flimsi. It was *possible* . . .

A Senator might carefully construct a reputation, appearing to all the galaxy as honest and upright and honorable, all the while holding the rotten truth of himself so absolutely secret that no one would sense his evil until he had so much power that it was too late to stop him . . .

It *was* possible.

But so many? Could they *all* have accomplished that?

Could Padmé?

Suspicion leaked back into his mind and gathered itself into so thick a cloud that he didn't sense her approach until she was already in the room.

"Anakin? What are you doing here? It's still the middle of the afternoon . . ."

He looked up to find her standing in the archway in full Senatorial regalia: heavy folds of burgundy robes and a coif like a starfighter's hyperdrive ring. Instead of a smile, instead of sunlight in her eyes, instead of the bell-clear joy with which she had always greeted him, her face was nearly expressionless: attentively blank.

Anakin called it her Politician Look, and he hated it.

"Waiting for you," he replied, a little unsteadily. "What are *you* doing here in the middle of the afternoon?"

"I have a very important meeting in two hours," she said stiffly. "I left a document reader here this morning—"

"This meeting—is it with the *Chancellor*?" Anakin's voice came out low and harsh. "Is it his *last meeting of the afternoon*?"

"Y-yes, yes it is." She frowned, blinking. "Anakin, what's—"

"I have to be there, too." He crumpled the flimsi and stuffed it back into his equipment belt. "I'm starting to look forward to it."

"Anakin, what is it?" She came toward him, one hand reaching for him. "What's wrong?"

He lurched to his feet. "Obi-Wan's been here, hasn't he?"

"He came by this morning." She stopped. Her hand slowly lowered back to her side. "Why?"

"What did you talk about?"

"Anakin, why are you acting like this?"

One long stride brought him to her. He towered over her. For one stretching second she looked very small, very insignificant, very much like some kind of bug that he could crush beneath his heel and just keep on walking.

"What did you *talk* about?"

She gazed steadily up at him, and on her face was only concern, shaded with growing hurt. "We talked about you."

"What *about* me?"

"He's worried about you, Anakin. He says you're under a lot of stress."

"And he's *not*?"

"The way you've been acting, since you got back—"

"*I'm* not the one doing the *acting*. I'm not the one doing the pretending! I'm not the one sneaking *in* here in the *morning*!"

"No," she said with a smile. She reached up to lay the palm of her hand along the line of his jaw. "That's usually when you're sneaking *out*."

Her touch unclenched his heart.

He half fell into a chair and pressed the edge of his flesh hand against his eyes.

When he could overcome his embarrassment enough to speak, he said softly, "I'm sorry, Padmé. I'm sorry. I know I've been . . . difficult to deal with. I just—I feel like I'm in free fall. Free fall in the dark. I don't know which way is up. I don't know where I'll be when I land. Or crash."

He frowned against his fingers, squeezing his eyes more tightly shut to make sure no tears leaked out. "I think it's going to be a crash."

She sat on the wide-rolled arm of his chair and laid her slim arm along his shoulders. "What has happened, my love? You've always been so sure of yourself. What's changed?"

"Nothing," he said. "Everything. I don't know. It's all so screwed up, I can't even tell you. The Council doesn't trust me, Palpatine doesn't trust the Council. They're plotting against each other and both sides are pressuring *me*, and—"

"Surely that's only your imagination, Anakin. The Jedi Council is the bedrock of the Republic."

"The bedrock of the Republic is *democracy*, Padmé— something the Council doesn't much like when votes don't go their way. *All those who gain power are afraid to lose it*—that's something you should remember." He looked up at her. "You and your *friends* in the *Senate*."

She took this without a blink. "But Obi-Wan is on the Council; *he'd* never participate in anything the least bit underhanded—"

"You think so?"

Because it's not for the record, Anakin. You must be able to understand why.

He shook the memory away. "It doesn't matter. Obi-Wan's on his way to Utapau."

"What is this really about?"

"I don't *know*," he said helplessly. "I don't know *anything* anymore. All I know is, I'm not the Jedi I should be. I'm not the *man* I should be."

"You're the man for me," she said, leaning toward him to kiss his cheek, but he pulled away.

"You don't understand. *Nobody* understands. I'm one of the

most powerful Jedi alive, but it's not enough. It'll *never* be enough, not until—"

His voice trailed away, and his eyes went distant, and his memory burned with an alien birthing table, and blood, and screams.

"Until what, my love?"

"Until I can *save* you," he murmured.

"Save me?"

"From my nightmares."

She smiled sadly. "Is that what's bothering you?"

"I won't lose you, Padmé. I can't." He sat forward and twisted to take both of her hands, small and soft and deceptively strong and beyond precious, between his own. "I am still learning, Padmé—I have found a key to truths deeper than the Jedi could ever teach me. I will become so powerful that I will keep you *safe*. Forever. I *will*."

"You don't need more power, Anakin." She gently extricated one of her hands and used it to draw him close. "I believe you can save me from anything, just as you are."

She pulled him to her and their lips met, and Anakin gave himself to the kiss, and while it lasted, he believed it, too.

A shroud of twilight lowered upon Galactic City.

Anakin stood at what a clone trooper would have called parade rest—a wide, balanced stance, feet parallel, hands clasped behind his back. He stood one pace behind and to the left of the chair where Palpatine sat, behind his broad desk in the small private office attached to his large public one.

On the other side of the desk stood the Senate delegation.

The way they had looked at him, when they had entered the office—the way their eyes still, even now, flicked to his, then away again before he could fully meet their gaze—the way none of them, not even Padmé, dared to ask why the Supreme Chancellor had a Jedi at his shoulder during what was supposed to be a private meeting . . . it seemed to him that they already guessed why he was here.

They were simply afraid to bring it up.

Now they couldn't be sure where the Jedi stood. The only thing that was clear was where Anakin stood—

Respectfully in attendance upon Supreme Chancellor Palpatine.

Anakin studied the Senators.

Fang Zar: face creased with old laugh lines, dressed in robes so simple they might almost be homespun, unruly brush of hair gathered into a tight topknot, and an even more unruly brush of beard that sprayed uncontrolled around his jaw. He had a gentle, almost simplistic way of speaking that could easily lead one to forget that he was one of the sharpest political minds in the Senate. Also, he was such a close friend of Garm Bel Iblis that the powerful Corellian Senator might as well have been present in person.

Anakin had watched him closely throughout the meeting. Fang Zar had something on his mind, that was certain—something that he did not seem willing to say.

Nee Alavar and Malé-Dee he could dismiss as threats; the two stood together—perhaps needing each other for moral support—and neither had said anything at all. And then, of course, there was Padmé.

Glowing in her Senatorial regalia, the painted perfection of her face luminous as all four of Coruscant's moons together, not a single hair out of place in her elaborate coif—

Speaking in her Politician Voice, and wearing her Politician Look.

Padmé did the talking. Anakin had a sickening suspicion that this was all her idea.

"We are not attempting to delegitimize your government," she was saying. "That's why we're here. If we were trying to organize an opposition—if we sought to impose our requests as demands—we would hardly bring them before you in this fashion. This petition has been signed by two thousand Senators, Chancellor. We ask only that you instruct your governors not to interfere with the legitimate business of the Senate, and that you open peace talks with the Separatists. We seek only to end the war, and bring peace and stability back to our homeworlds. Surely you can understand this."

"I understand a great many things," Palpatine said.

"This system of governors you have created is very troubling—it seems that you are imposing military controls even on loyalist systems."

"Your reservations are noted, Senator Amidala. I assure you that the Republic governors are intended only to make your systems safer—by coordinating planetary defense forces, and ensuring that neighboring systems mesh into cooperative units, and bringing production facilities up to speed in service to the war effort. That's all. They will in no way compete with the duties and prerogatives—with the power—of the Senate."

Something in the odd emphasis he put on the word *power* made Anakin think Palpatine was speaking more for Anakin's benefit than for Padmé's.

All those who gain power are afraid to lose it

"May I take it, then," Padmé said, "that there will be no further amendments to the Constitution?"

"My dear Senator, what has the Constitution to do with this? I thought we were discussing ending the war. Once the Separatists have been defeated, then we can start talking about the Constitution again. Must I remind you that the extraordinary powers granted to my office by the Senate are only in force for the duration of the emergency? Once the war ends, they expire automatically."

"And your governors? Will they 'expire,' too?"

"They are not *my* governors, my lady, they are the Republic's," Palpatine replied imperturbably. "The fate of their positions will be in the hands of the Senate, where it belongs."

Padmé did not seem reassured. "And peace talks? Will you offer a cease-fire? Have you even *tried* a diplomatic resolution to the war?"

"You must trust me to do the right thing," he said. "That is, after all, why I am here."

Fang Zar roused himself. "But surely—"

"I have said I will do what is *right*," Palpatine said, a testy edge sharpening his voice. He rose, drawing himself up to his full height, then inclining his head with an air of finality. "And that should be enough for your . . . committee."

His tone said: *Don't let the door crunch you on the way out.*

Padmé's mouth compressed into a thin, grim line. "On behalf of the Delegation of the Two Thousand," she said with tight-drawn formality, "I thank you, Chancellor."

"And I thank you, Senator Amidala, and your friends—" Palpatine lifted the document reader containing the petition. "—for bringing this to my attention."

The Senators turned reluctantly and began to file out. Padmé paused, just for a second, to meet Anakin's eyes with a gaze as clear as a slap on the mouth.

He stayed expressionless. Because in the end, no matter how much he wanted to, no matter how much it hurt . . . he couldn't quite make himself believe he was on her side.

DEATH ON UTAPAU

When constructing an effective Jedi trap—as opposed to the sort that results in nothing more than an embarrassingly brief entry in the Temple archives—there are several design features that one should include for best results.

The first is an irresistible bait. The commanding general of an outlaw nation, personally responsible for billions of deaths across the galaxy, is ideal.

The second is a remote, nearly inaccessible location, one that is easily taken and easily fortified, with a sharply restricted field of action. It should also, ideally, belong to someone else, preferably an enemy; the locations used for Jedi traps never survive the operation unscathed, and many don't survive it at all. An excellent choice would be an impoverished desert planet in the Outer Rim, with unwarlike natives, whose few cities are built in a cluster of sinkholes on a vast arid plateau. A city in a sinkhole is virtually a giant kill-jar; once a Jedi flies in, all one need do is seal the lid.

Third, since it is always a good idea to remain well out of reach when plotting against a Jedi's life—on the far side of the galaxy is considered best—one should have a reliable proxy to do the actual murder. The exemplar of a reliable proxy would be, for example, the most prolific living Jedi killer, backed up by a squad of advanced combat droids designed, built, and armed specifically to fight Jedi. Making one's proxy double as the bait is an impressively elegant stroke, if it can be managed, since it ensures that the Jedi victim will voluntarily place himself in contact with the Jedi killer—and will continue to do so even *after* he realizes the extent of the trap, out of a combination of devotion to duty and a not-entirely-unjustified arrogance.

The fourth element of an effective Jedi trap is a massively overwhelming force of combat troops who are willing to burn the whole planet, including themselves if necessary, to ensure that the Jedi in question does not escape.

A textbook example of the ideal Jedi trap is the one that waited on Utapau for Obi-Wan Kenobi.

As Obi-Wan sent his starfighter spiraling in toward a landing deck that protruded from the sheer sandstone wall of the biggest of Utapau's sinkhole-cities, he reviewed what he knew of the planet and its inhabitants.

There wasn't much.

He knew that despite its outward appearance, Utapau was not a true desert planet; there was water aplenty in an underground ocean that circled its globe. The erosive action of this buried ocean had undermined vast areas of its surface, and frequent groundquakes collapsed them into sinkholes large enough to land a *Victory*-class Star Destroyer, where civilization could thrive below reach of the relentless scouring hyperwinds on the surface. He knew that the planet had little in the way of high technology, and that their energy economy was based on wind power; the planet's limited interstellar trade had begun only a few decades before, when offworld water-mining companies had discovered that the waters of the world-ocean were rich in dissolved trace elements. He knew that the inhabitants were near-human, divided into two distinct species, the tall, lordly, slow-moving Utapauns, nicknamed Ancients for their astonishing longevity, and the stubby Utai, called Shorts, both for their stature and for their brief busy lives.

And he knew that Grievous was here.

How he knew, he could not say; so far as he could tell, his conviction had nothing to do with the Force. But within seconds of the *Vigilance*'s realspace reversion, he was sure. This was it. One way or another, this was the place his hunt for General Grievous would come to a close.

He felt it in his bones: Utapau was a planet for endings.

He was going in alone; Commander Cody and three battalions of troopers waited in rapid-deployment vehicles—LAAT/i's and *Jadthu*-class landers—just over the horizon. Obi-Wan's plan was to pinpoint Grievous's location, then keep the bio-droid general busy until the clones could attack; he would be a one-man diversionary force, holding the attention of what was sure to be thousands or tens of thousands of combat droids directed inward toward him and Grievous, to cover the approach of the clones. Two battalions would strike full-force, with the third in reserve, both to provide reinforcements and to cover possible escape routes.

"I can keep them distracted for quite some time," Obi-Wan had told Cody on the flight deck of *Vigilance*. "Just don't take too long."

"Come on, boss," Cody had said, smiling out of Jango Fett's face, "have I ever let you down?"

"Well—" Obi-Wan had said with a slim answering smile, "Cato Neimoidia, for starters . . ."

"That was Anakin's fault; *he* was the one who was late . . ."

"Oh? And who will you blame it on *this* time?" Obi-Wan had chuckled as he climbed into his starfighter's cockpit and strapped himself in. "Very well, then. I'll try not to destroy all the droids before you get there."

"I'm counting on you, boss. Don't let me down."

"Have I ever?"

"Well," Cody had said with a broad grin, "there *was* Cato Neimoidia . . ."

Obi-Wan's fighter bucked through coils of turbulence; the rim of the sinkhole caught enough of the hyperwinds above that the first few levels of city resided in a semipermanent hurricane.

Whirling blades of wind-power turbines stuck out from the sink-hole's sides on generator pods so scoured by the fierce winds that they might themselves have been molded of liquid sandstone. He fought the fighter's controls to bring it down level after level until the wind had become a mere gale; even after reaching the landing deck in the depths of the sinkhole, R4-G9 had to extend the starfighter's docking claws to keep it from being blown, skidding, right off the deck.

A ribbed semitransparent canopy swung out to enfold the landing deck; once it had settled into place around him, the howl of winds dropped to silence and Obi-Wan popped the cockpit.

A pack of Utai was already scampering toward the starfighter, which stood alone on the deck; they carried a variety of tools and dragged equipment behind them, and Obi-Wan assumed they were some sort of ground crew. Behind them glided the stately form of an Utapaun in a heavy deck-length robe of deep scarlet that had a lapel collar so tall it concealed his vestigial ear-disks. The Utapaun's glabrous scalp glistened with a sheen of moisture, and he walked with a staff that reminded Obi-Wan vaguely of Yoda's beloved gimer stick.

That was quick, Obi-Wan thought. *Almost like they've been expecting me.*

"Greetings, young Jedi," the Utapaun said gravely in accented Basic. "I am Tion Medon, master of port administration for this place of peace. What business could bring a Jedi to our remote sanctuary?"

Obi-Wan sensed no malice in this being, and the Utapaun radiated a palpable aura of fear; Obi-Wan decided to tell the truth. "My business is the war," he said.

"There is no war here, unless you have brought it with you," Medon replied, a mask of serenity concealing what the Force told Obi-Wan was anxiety verging on panic.

"Very well, then," Obi-Wan said, playing along. "Please permit me to refuel here, and to use your city as a base to search the surrounding systems."

"For what do you search?"

"Even in the Outer Rim, you must have heard of General Grievous. It is he I seek, and his army of droids."

Tion Medon took another step closer and leaned down to bring his face near Obi-Wan's ear. "He is here!" Medon whispered urgently. "We are hostages—we are being watched!"

Obi-Wan nodded matter-of-factly. "Thank you, Master Medon," he said in a thoroughly ordinary voice. "I am grateful for your hospitality, and will depart as soon as your crew refuels my starfighter."

"Listen to me, young Jedi!" Medon's whisper became even more intense. "You must depart in *truth!* I was *ordered* to reveal their presence—this is a trap!"

"Of course it is," Obi-Wan said equably.

"The tenth level—thousands of war droids—*tens* of thousands!"

"Have your people seek shelter." Obi-Wan turned casually and scanned upward, counting levels. On the tenth, his eye found a spiny spheroid of metal: a Dreadnaught-sized structure that clearly had not been there for long—its gleaming surface had not yet been scoured to matte by the sand in the constant winds. He nodded absently and spoke softly, as though to himself. "Geenine, take my starfighter back to the *Vigilance*. Instruct Commander Cody to inform Jedi Command on Coruscant that I have made contact with General Grievous. I am engaging now. Cody is to attack in full force, as planned."

The astromech beeped acknowledgment from its forward socket, and Obi-Wan turned once more to Tion Medon. "Tell them I promised to file a report with Republic Intelligence. Tell them I really only wanted fuel enough to leave immediately."

"But—but what will you *do?*"

"If you have warriors," Obi-Wan said gravely, "now is the time."

In the holocomm center of Jedi Command, within the heart of the Temple on Coruscant, Anakin watched a life-sized holoscan of Clone Commander Cody report that Obi-Wan had made contact with General Grievous.

"We are beginning our supporting attack as ordered. And—if I may say so, sirs—from my experience working with General Kenobi, I have a suspicion that Grievous does not have long to live."

If I were there with *him,* Anakin thought, *it'd be more than a suspicion. Obi-Wan, be* careful—

"Thank you, Commander." Mace Windu's face did not betray the slightest hint of the mingled dread and anticipation Anakin was sure he must be feeling; while Anakin himself felt ready to burst, Windu looked calm as a stone. "Keep us apprised of your progress. May the Force be with you, and with Master Kenobi."

"I'm sure it will be, sir. Cody out."

The holoscan flickered to nothingness. Mace Windu turned brief but seemingly significant glances upon the other two Masters in attendance, both holoscans themselves: Ki-Adi-Mundi from the fortified command center on Mygeeto, and from a guerrilla outpost on Kashyyyk, Yoda.

Then he turned to Anakin. "Take this report to the Chancellor."

"Of course I will, Master."

"And take careful note of his reaction. We will need a full account."

"Master?"

"What he says, Anakin. Who he calls. What he does. Everything. Even his facial expressions. It's very important."

"I don't understand—"

"You don't have to. Just do it."

"Master—"

"Anakin, do I have to remind you that you are still a Jedi? You are still subject to the orders of this Council."

"Yes, Master Windu. Yes, I am," he said, and left.

Once Skywalker was gone, Mace Windu found himself in a chair, staring at the doorway through which the young Jedi

Knight had left. "Now we shall see," he murmured. "At last. The waters will begin to clear."

Though he shared the command center with the holoscans of two other Jedi Masters, Mace wasn't talking to them. He spoke to the grim, clouded future inside his head.

"Have you considered," Ki-Adi-Mundi said carefully, from far-away Mygeeto, *"that if Palpatine refuses to surrender power, removing him is only a first step?"*

Mace looked at the blue ghost of the Cerean Master. "I am not a politician. Removing a tyrant is enough for me."

"But it will not be enough for the Republic," Ki-Adi-Mundi countered sadly. *"Palpatine's dictatorship has been legitimized—and can be legalized, even enshrined in a revised Constitution—by the supermajority he controls in the Senate."*

The grim future inside Mace's head turned even darker. The Cerean was right.

"Filled with corruption, the Senate is," Yoda agreed from Kashyyyk. *"Controlled, they must be, until replaced the corrupted Senators can be, with Senators honest and—"*

"Do you *hear* us?" Mace lowered his head into his hands. "How have we come to this? Arresting a Chancellor. Taking over the *Senate*—! It's as though Dooku was *right*—to save the Republic, we'll have to destroy it . . . ."

Yoda lifted his head, and his eyes slitted as though he struggled with some inner pain. *"Hold on to hope we must; our true enemy, Palpatine is not, nor the Senate; the true enemy is instead the Sith Lord Sidious, who controls them both. Once destroyed Sidious is . . . all these other concerns, less dire they will instantly become."*

"Yes." Mace Windu rose, and moved to the window, hands folded behind his back. "Yes, that is true."

Indigo gloom gathered among the towers outside.

"And we have put the chosen one in play against the last Lord of the Sith," he said. "In that, we must place our faith, and our hopes for the future of the Republic."

* * *

The landing deck canopy parted, and the blue-and-white Jedi starfighter blasted upward into the gale. From deep shadows at the rear of the deck, Obi-Wan watched it go.

"I suppose I am committed, now," he murmured.

Through electrobinoculars produced from his equipment belt, he examined that suspiciously shiny spheroid high above on the tenth level. The spray of spines had to be droid-control antennas. That's where Grievous would be: at the nerve center of his army.

"Then that's where I should be, too." He looked around, frowning. "Never an air taxi when you need one . . ."

The reclosing of the deck canopy quieted the howl of the wind outside, and now from deeper within the city Obi-Wan could hear a ragged choir of hoarsely bellowing cries that had the resonance of large animals—they reminded him of something . . .

Suubatars, that was it—they sounded vaguely like the calls of the suubatars he and Anakin had ridden on one of their last missions before the war, back when the biggest worry Obi-Wan had was how to keep his promise to Qui-Gon . . .

But he had no time for nostalgia. He could practically hear Qui-Gon reminding him to focus on the now, and give himself over to the living Force.

So he did.

Mere moments of following the cries through the shadows of deserted hallways carved into the sandstone brought Obi-Wan in sight of an immense, circular arena-like area, where a ring of balcony was joined to a flat lower level by spokes of broad, corrugated ramps; the ceiling above was hung with yellowish lamprods that cast a light the same color as the sunbeams striking through an arc of wide oval archways open to the interior of the sinkhole outside. The winds that whistled through those wide archways also went a long way toward cutting the eye-watering

reptile-den stench down from overpowering to merely nause-
ating.

Squatting, lying, and milling aimlessly about the lower level
were a dozen or so large lizard-like beasts that looked like the
product of some mad geneticist's cross of Tatooine krayt dragons
with Haruun Kal ankkoxen: four meters tall at the shoulder, long
crooked legs that ended in five-clawed feet clearly designed for
scaling rocky cliffs, ten meters of powerful tail ridged with spines
and tipped with a horn-bladed mace, a flexible neck leading up to
an armor-plated head that sported an impressive cowl of spines of
its own—they looked fearsome enough that Obi-Wan might
have thought them some sort of dangerous wild predators or vicious watchbeasts, were it not for the docile way they tolerated
the team of Utai wranglers who walked among them, hosing
them down, scraping muck from their scales, and letting them
take bundles of greens from their hands.

Not far from where Obi-Wan stood, several large racks were
hung with an array of high-backed saddles in various styles and
degrees of ornamentation, very much indeed like those the Al-
wari of Ansion had strapped to their suubatars.

Now he *really* missed Anakin . . .

Anakin disliked living mounts almost as much as Obi-
Wan hated to fly. Obi-Wan had long suspected that it was
Anakin's gift with machines that worked against him with suu-
batar or dewback or bantha; he could never get entirely comfortable riding anything with a mind of its own. He could vividly
imagine Anakin's complaints as he climbed into one of these
saddles.

It seemed an awfully long time since Obi-Wan had had an
opportunity to tease Anakin a bit.

With a sigh, he brought himself back to business. Moving
out of the shadows, he walked down one of the corrugated
ramps and made a slight, almost imperceptible hand gesture in
the direction of the nearest of the Utai dragonmount wranglers.
"I need transportation."

The Short's bulging eyes went distant and a bit glassy, and

he responded with a string of burbling glottal hoots that had a decidedly affirmative tone.

Obi-Wan made another gesture. "Get me a saddle."

With another string of affirmative burbles, the Short waddled off.

While he waited for his saddle, Obi-Wan examined the dragonmounts. He passed up the largest, and the one most heavily muscled; he skipped over the leanest built-for-speed beast, and didn't even approach the one with the fiercest gleam in its eye. He didn't actually pay attention to outward signs of strength or health or personality; he was using his hands and eyes and ears purely as focusing channels for the Force. He didn't know what he was looking for, but he trusted that he would recognize it when he found it.

Qui-Gon, he reflected with an inward smile, would approve.

Finally he came to a dragonmount with a clear, steady gleam in its round yellow eyes, and small, close-set scales that felt warm and dry. It neither shied back from his hand nor bent submissively to his touch, but only returned his searching gaze with calm, thoughtful intelligence. Through the Force, he felt in the beast an unshakable commitment to obedience and care for its rider: an almost Jedi-like devotion to service as the ultimate duty.

This was why Obi-Wan would always prefer a living mount. A speeder is incapable of caring if it crashes.

"This one," he said. "I'll take this one."

The Short had returned with a plain, sturdily functional saddle; as he and the other wranglers undertook the complicated task of tacking up the dragonmount, he nodded at the beast and said, "Boga."

"Ah," Obi-Wan said. "Thank you."

He took a sheaf of greens from a nearby bin and offered them to the dragonmount. The great beast bent its head, its wickedly hooked beak delicately withdrew the greens from Obi-Wan's hand, and it chewed them with fastidious thoroughness.

"Good girl, Boga. Erm—" Obi-Wan frowned at the Short. "—she *is* a *she,* isn't she?"

The wrangler frowned back. "Warool noggagllo?" he said, shrugging, which Obi-Wan took to mean *I have no idea what you're saying to me*.

"Very well, then," Obi-Wan said with an answering shrug. "*She* you will have to be, then, Boga. Unless you care to tell me otherwise."

Boga made no objection.

He swung himself up into the saddle and the dragonmount rose, arching her powerful back in a feline stretch that lifted Obi-Wan more than four meters off the floor. Obi-Wan looked down at the Utai wranglers. "I cannot pay you. As compensation, I can only offer the freedom of your planet; I hope that will suffice."

Without waiting for a reply that he would not have understood anyway, Obi-Wan touched Boga on the neck. Boga reared straight up and raked the air with her hooked foreclaws as though she were shredding an imaginary hailfire droid, then gathered herself and leapt to the ring-balcony in a single bound. Obi-Wan didn't need to use the long, hook-tipped goad strapped in a holster alongside the saddle; nor did he do more than lightly hold the reins in one hand. Boga seemed to understand exactly where he wanted to go.

The dragonmount slipped sinuously through one of the wide oval apertures into the open air of the sinkhole, then turned and seized the sandstone with those hooked claws to carry Obi-Wan straight up the sheer wall.

Level after level they climbed. The city looked and felt deserted. Nothing moved save the shadows of clouds crossing the sinkhole's mouth far, far above; even the wind-power turbines had been locked down.

The first sign of life he saw came on the tenth level itself; a handful of other dragonmounts lay basking in the midday sun, not far from the durasteel barnacle of the droid-control center. Obi-Wan rode Boga right up to the control center's open archway, then jumped down from the saddle.

The archway led into a towering vaulted hall, its durasteel decking bare of furnishing. Deep within the shadows that gathered in the hall stood a cluster of five figures. Their faces were the color of bleached bone. Or ivory armorplast.

They looked like they might, just possibly, be waiting for him.

Obi-Wan nodded to himself.

"You'd best find your way home, girl," he said, patting Boga's scaled neck. "One way or another, I doubt I'll have further need of your assistance."

Boga gave a soft, almost regretful honk of acknowledgment, then bent a sharper curve into her long flexible neck to place her beak gently against Obi-Wan's chest.

"It's all right, Boga. I thank you for your help, but to stay here will be dangerous. This area is about to become a free-fire zone. Please. Go home."

The dragonmount honked again and moved back, and Obi-Wan stepped from the sun into the shadow.

A wave-front of cool passed over him with the shade's embrace. He walked without haste, without urgency. The Force layered connections upon connections, and brought them all to life within him: the chill deck plates beneath his boots, and the stone beneath those, and far below that the smooth lightless currents of the world-ocean. He became the turbulent swirl of wind whistling through the towering vaulted hall; he became the sunlight outside and the shadow within. His human heart in its cage of bone echoed the beat of an alien one in a casket of armorplast, and his mind whirred with the electronic signal cascades that passed for thought in Jedi-killer droids.

And when the Force layered into his consciousness the awareness of the structure of the great hall itself, he became aware, without surprise and without distress, that the entire expanse of vaulted ceiling above his head was actually a storage hive.

Filled with combat droids.

Which made him also aware, again without surprise and without distress, that he would very likely die here.

Contemplation of death brought only one slight sting of regret, and more than a bit of puzzlement. Until this very moment, he had never realized he'd always expected, for no discernible reason—

That when he died, Anakin would be with him.

How curious, he thought, and then he turned his mind to business.

Anakin had a feeling Master Windu was going to be disappointed.

Palpatine had hardly reacted at all.

The Supreme Chancellor of the Republic sat at the small desk in his private office, staring distractedly at an abstract twist of neuranium that Anakin had always assumed was supposed to be some kind of sculpture, and merely sighed, as though he had matters of much greater importance on his mind.

"I'm sorry, sir," Anakin said, shifting his weight in front of Palpatine's desk. "Perhaps you didn't hear me. Obi-Wan has made contact with General Grievous. His attack is already under way—they're fighting *right now,* sir!"

"Yes, yes, of course, Anakin. Yes, quite." Palpatine still looked as if he was barely paying attention. "I entirely understand your concern for your friend. Let us hope he is up to the task."

"It's not just concern for Obi-Wan, sir; taking General Grievous will be the final victory for the Republic—!"

"Will it?" He turned to Anakin, and a distinctly troubled frown chased the distraction from his face. "I'm afraid, my boy, that our situation is a great deal more grave than even I had feared. Perhaps you should sit down."

Anakin didn't move. "What do you mean?"

"Grievous is no longer the real enemy. Even the Clone Wars themselves are now only . . . a distraction."

"What?"

"The Council is about to make its move," Palpatine said, grim and certain. "If we don't stop them, by this time tomorrow the Jedi may very well have taken over the Republic."

Anakin burst into astonished laughter. "But sir—please, you can't possibly *believe* that—"

"Anakin, I *know.* I will be the first to be arrested—the first to be *executed*—but I will be far from the last."

Anakin could only shake his head in disbelief. "Sir, I know that the Council and you have . . . disagreements, but—"

"This is far beyond any personal dispute between me and the members of the Council. This is a plot *generations* in the making—a plot to take over the Republic itself. Anakin, *think*—you know they don't trust you. They never have. You know they have been keeping things from you. You know they have made plans behind your back—you know that even your great friend *Obi-Wan* has not told you what their true intentions are . . . It's because you're not *like* them, Anakin—you're a *man,* not just a Jedi."

Anakin's head drew down toward his shoulders as though he found himself under enemy fire. "I don't—they wouldn't—"

"Ask yourself: why did they send you to me with this news? *Why?* Why not simply notify me through normal channels?"

And take careful note of his reaction. We will need a full account

"Sir, I—ah—"

"No need to fumble for an explanation," he said gently. "You've already as much as admitted they've ordered you to spy upon me. Don't you understand that anything you tell them tonight—whatever it may be—will be used as an excuse to order my execution?"

"That's impossible—" Anakin sought desperately for an argument. "The Senate—the Senate would never allow it—"

"The Senate will be powerless to stop it. I told you this is bigger than any personal dislike between the Council and myself. I am only one man, Anakin. My authority is granted by the Senate; it is the Senate that is the true government of the Republic. Killing me is nothing; to control the Republic, the Jedi will have to take over the Senate *first.*"

"But the Jedi—the Jedi *serve* the Senate—!"

"Do they?" Palpatine asked mildly. "Or do they serve certain *Senators*?"

"This is all—I'm sorry, Chancellor, please, you have to understand how this *sounds* . . ."

"Here—" The Chancellor rummaged around within his desk for a moment, then brought forth a document reader. "Do you know what this is?"

Anakin recognized the seal Padmé had placed on it. "Yes, sir—that's the Petition of the Two Thousand—"

"*No*, Anakin! No!" Palpatine slammed the document reader on his desktop hard enough to make Anakin jump. "It is a roll of *traitors*."

Anakin went absolutely still. "What?"

"There are, now, only two kinds of Senators in our government, Anakin. Those whose names are on this so-called *petition*," Palpatine said, "and those whom the Jedi are about to *arrest*."

Anakin could only stare.

He couldn't argue. He couldn't even make himself disbelieve.

He had only one thought.

Padmé . . . ?

How much trouble was she in?

"Didn't I *warn* you, Anakin? Didn't I tell you what Obi-Wan was up to? Why do you think he was meeting with the leaders of this . . . delegation . . . behind your *back*?"

"But—but, sir, please, surely, all they asked for is an end to the war. It's what the Jedi want, too. I mean, it's what we *all* want, isn't it? Isn't it?"

"Perhaps. Though *how* that end comes about may be the single most important thing about the war. More important, even, than who wins."

Oh, Padmé, Anakin moaned inside his head. *Padmé, what have you gotten yourself into?*

"Their . . . sincerity . . . may be much to be admired," Palpatine said. "Or it would be, were it not that there was much more to that meeting than met the eye."

Anakin frowned. "What do you mean?"

"Their . . . petition . . . was nothing of the sort. It was, in fact, a not-so-veiled *threat*." Palpatine sighed regretfully. "It was a show of force, Anakin. A demonstration of the political power the Jedi will be able to muster in support of their rebellion."

Anakin blinked. "But—but surely—" he stammered, rounding Palpatine's desk, "surely Senator *Amidala,* at least, can be trusted . . ."

"I understand how badly you need to believe that," the Chancellor said. "But Senator Amidala is hiding something. Surely you sensed it."

"If she is—" Anakin swayed; the floor seemed to be tilting under his feet like the deck of *Invisible Hand.* "Even if she *is,*" he said, his voice flat, overcontrolled, "it doesn't mean that what she is hiding is treason."

Palpatine's brows drew together. "I'm surprised your Jedi insights are not more sensitive to such things."

"I simply don't sense betrayal in Senator Amidala," Anakin insisted.

Palpatine leaned back in his chair, steepling his fingers, studying Anakin skeptically. "Yes, you do," he said after a moment. "Though you don't want to admit it. Perhaps it is because neither you nor she yet understands that by betraying me, she is also betraying *you.*"

"She couldn't—" Anakin pressed a hand to his forehead; his dizziness was getting worse. When had he last eaten? He couldn't remember. It might have been before the last time he'd slept. "She could *never . . .*"

"Of course she could," Palpatine said. "That is the nature of politics, my boy. Don't take it too personally. It doesn't mean the two of you can't be happy together."

"What—?" The room seemed to darken around him. "What do you mean?"

"Please, Anakin. Are we not past the point of playing childish games with one another? I *know,* do you understand? I have *always* known. I have pretended ignorance only to spare you discomfort."

Anakin had to lean on the desk. "What—what do you know?"

"Anakin, Padmé was my Queen; I was her ambassador to the Senate. Naboo is my *home.* You of all people know how I value loyalty and friendship; do you think I have no friends among the civil clergy in Theed? Your secret ceremony has never *been* secret. Not from me, at any rate. I have always been very happy for you both."

"You—" Words whirled through Anakin's mind, and none of them made sense. "But if she's going to *betray* us—"

"*That,* my boy," Palpatine said, "is entirely up to *you.*"

The fog inside Anakin's head seemed to solidify into a long, dark tunnel. The point of light at the end was Palpatine's face. "I don't—I don't understand . . ."

"Oh yes, that's very clear." The Chancellor's voice seemed to be coming from very far away. "Please sit, my boy. You're looking rather unwell. May I offer you something to drink?"

"I—no. No, I'm all right." Anakin sank gratefully into a dangerously comfortable chair. "I'm just—a little tired, that's all."

"Not sleeping well?"

"No." Anakin offered an exhausted chuckle. "I haven't been sleeping well for a few years, now."

"I quite understand, my boy. Quite." Palpatine rose and rounded his desk, sitting casually on its front edge. "Anakin, we must stop pretending. The final crisis is approaching, and our only hope to survive it is to be completely, absolutely, ruthlessly honest with each other. And with ourselves. You must understand that what is at stake here is nothing less than the fate of the galaxy."

"I don't know—"

"Don't be afraid, Anakin. What is said between us here need never pass beyond these walls. Anakin, *think:* think how hard it has been to hold all your secrets inside. Have you ever needed to keep a secret from *me*?"

He ticked his fingers one by one. "I have kept the secret of your marriage all these years. The slaughter at the Tusken camp, you shared with me. I was there when you executed Count Dooku. And I know where you got the power to defeat him. You see? You have never needed to *pretend* with me, the way you must with your Jedi comrades. Do you understand that you need never hide *anything* from me? That I accept you exactly as you are?"

He spread his hands as though offering a hug. "Share with me the truth. Your absolute truth. Let yourself *out*, Anakin."

"I—" Anakin shook his head. How many times had he dreamed of not having to pretend to be the perfect Jedi? But what else could he be? "I wouldn't even know how to begin."

"It's quite simple, in the end: tell me what you want."

Anakin squinted up at him. "I don't understand."

"Of course you don't." The last of the sunset haloed his ice-white hair and threw his face into shadow. "You've been trained to never think about that. The Jedi never ask what *you* want. They simply *tell* you what you're *supposed* to want. They never give you a choice at all. That's why they take their students—their *victims*—at an age so young that choice is meaningless. By the time a Padawan is old enough to *choose*, he has been so indoctrinated—so *brainwashed*—that he is incapable of even considering the question. But you're different, Anakin. You had a real life, outside the Jedi Temple. You can break through the fog of lies the Jedi have pumped into your brain. I ask you again: what do you want?"

"I still don't understand."

"I am offering you . . . anything," Palpatine said. "Ask, and it is yours. A glass of water? It's yours. A bag full of Corusca gems? Yours. Look out the window behind me, Anakin. Pick something, and it's yours."

"Is this some kind of joke?"

"The time for jokes is past, Anakin. I have never been more

serious." Within the shadow that cloaked Palpatine's face, Anakin could only just see the twin gleams of the Chancellor's eyes. "Pick something. Anything."

"All right . . ." Shrugging, frowning, still not understanding, Anakin looked out the window, looking for the most ridiculously expensive thing he could spot. "How about one of those new SoroSuub custom speeders—"

"Done."

"Are you serious? You know how much one of those costs? You could practically outfit a *battle* cruiser—"

"Would you prefer a battle cruiser?"

Anakin went still. A cold void opened in his chest. In a small, cautious voice, he said, "How about the Senatorial Apartments?"

"A private apartment?"

Anakin shook his head, staring up at the twin gleams in the darkness on Palpatine's face. "The whole building."

Palpatine did not so much as blink. "Done."

"It's privately owned—"

"Not anymore."

"You can't just—"

"Yes, I can. It's yours. Is there anything else? Name it."

Anakin gazed blankly out into the gathering darkness. Stars began to shimmer through the haze of twilight. A constellation he recognized hung above the spires of the Jedi Temple.

"All right," Anakin said softly. "Corellia. I'll take Corellia."

"The planet, or the whole system?"

Anakin stared.

"Anakin?"

"I just—" He shook his head blankly. "I can't figure out if you're kidding, or completely insane."

"I am neither, Anakin. I am trying to impress upon you a fundamental truth of our relationship. A fundamental truth of *yourself.*"

"What if I really *wanted* the Corellian system? The whole Five Brothers—*all* of it?"

"Then it would be yours. You can have the whole sector, if you like." The twin gleams within the shadow sharpened. "Do you understand, now? I will give you *anything you want.*"

The concept left him dizzy. "What if I wanted—what if I went along with Padmé and her friends? What if I want the *war* to *end*?"

"Would tomorrow be too soon?"

"How—" Anakin couldn't seem to get his breath. "How can you do that?"

"Right now, we are only discussing *what. How* is a different issue; we'll come to that presently."

Anakin sank deeper into the chair while he let everything sink deeper into his brain. If only his head would stop spinning—why did Palpatine have to start all this *now*?

This would all be easier to comprehend if the nightmares of Padmé didn't keep screaming inside his head.

"And in exchange?" he asked, finally. "What do *I* have to do?"

"You have to do what you *want.*"

"What I want?"

"Yes, Anakin. Yes. Exactly that. Only that. Do the one thing that the Jedi fear most: make up your *own* mind. Follow your own *conscience*. Do what *you* think is right. I know that you have been longing for a life greater than that of an ordinary Jedi. *Commit* to that life. I know you burn for greater power than any Jedi can wield; give yourself *permission* to *gain* that power, and allow yourself license to *use* it. You have dreamed of leaving the Jedi Order, having a family of your own—one that is based on *love*, not on enforced rules of self-denial."

"I—can't . . . I can't just . . . *leave* . . ."

"But you can."

Anakin couldn't breathe.

He couldn't blink.

He sat frozen. Even thought was impossible.

"You can have every one of your dreams. Turn aside from the

lies of the Jedi, and follow the truth of yourself. Leave them. Join me on the path of true power. Be my friend, Anakin. Be my student. My apprentice."

Anakin's vision tunneled again, but this time there was no light at the far end. He pulled back his hand, and it was shaking as he brought it up to support his face.

"I'm sorry," he said. "I'm sorry, but—but as much as I want those things—as much as I care for you, sir—I can't. I just can't. Not yet. Because there's only one thing I *really* want, right now. Everything else will just have to wait."

"I know what you truly want," the shadow said. "I have only been waiting for you to admit it to yourself." A hand—a human hand, warm with compassion—settled onto his shoulder. "Listen to me: *I can help you save her.*"

"You—"

Anakin blinked blindly.

"How can *you* help?"

"Do you remember that myth I told you of, *The Tragedy of Darth Plagueis the Wise?*" the shadow whispered.

The myth—

. . . directly influence the midi-chlorians to create life; with such knowledge, to maintain life in someone already living would seem a small matter . . .

"Yes," Anakin said. "Yes, I remember."

The shadow leaned so close that it seemed to fill the world.

"Anakin, it's no mere myth."

Anakin swallowed.

"Darth Plagueis was real."

Anakin could force out only a strangled whisper. "*Real . . . ?*"

"Darth Plagueis was my Master. He taught me the key to his power," the shadow said, dryly matter-of-fact, "before I killed him."

Without understanding how he had moved, without even intending to move, without any transition of realization or dawning understanding, Anakin found himself on his feet. A blue bar of sizzling energy terminated a centimeter from Palpatine's chin, its glow casting red-edged shadows up his face and across the ceiling.

Only gradually did Anakin come to understand that this was his lightsaber, and that it was in his hand.

"You," he said. Suddenly he was neither dizzy nor tired.

Suddenly everything made sense.

"It's *you*. It's *been* you all *along*!"

In the clean blue light of his blade he stared into the face of a man whose features were as familiar to him as his own, but now seemed as alien as an extragalactic comet—because now he finally understood that those familiar features were only a mask.

He had never seen this man's real face.

"I should *kill* you," he said. "I *will* kill you!"

Palpatine gave him that wise, kindly-uncle smile Anakin had been seeing since the age of nine. "For what?"

"You're a *Sith Lord*!"

"I am," he said simply. "I am also your friend."

The blue bar of energy wavered, just a bit.

"I am also the man who has always been here for you. I am the man you have never needed to lie to. I am the man who wants nothing from you but that you follow your conscience. If that conscience requires you to commit murder, simply over a . . . philosophical difference . . . I will not resist."

His hands opened, still at his sides. "Anakin, when I told you that you can have anything you want, did you think I was excluding my life?"

The floor seemed to soften beneath Anakin's feet, and the room started to swirl darkness and ooze confusion. "You—you won't even *fight*—?"

"Fight you?" In the blue glow that cast shadows up from Palpatine's chin, the Chancellor looked astonished that he would suggest such a thing. "But what will happen when you kill me? What will happen to the Republic?" His tone was gently reasonable. "What will happen to Padmé?"

"*Padmé . . .*"

Her name was a gasp of anguish.

"When I die," Palpatine said with the air of a man reminding a child of something he ought to already know, "my knowledge dies with me."

The sizzling blade trembled.

"Unless, that is, I have the opportunity to teach it . . . to my apprentice . . ."

His vision swam.

"I . . ." A whisper of naked pain, and despair. "I don't know what to *do* . . ."

Palpatine gazed upon him, loving and gentle as he had ever been, though only a whisker shy of a lightsaber's terminal curve.

And what if this face was *not* a mask? What if the true face of the Sith was exactly what he saw before him: a man who had cared for him, had helped him, had been his loyal friend when he'd thought he had no other?

What *then*?

"Anakin," Palpatine said kindly, "let's talk."

The four bodyguard droids spread out in a shallow arc between Obi-Wan and Grievous, raising their electrostaffs. Obi-Wan stopped a respectful distance away; he still carried bruises from one of those electrostaffs, and he felt no particular urge to add to his collection.

"General Grievous," he said, "you're under arrest."

The bio-droid general stalked toward him, passing through his screen of bodyguards without the slightest hint of reluctance. "Kenobi. Don't tell me, let me guess: this is the part where you give me the chance to surrender."

"It can be," Obi-Wan allowed equably. "Or, if you like, it can be the part where I dismantle your exoskeleton and ship you back to Coruscant in a cargo hopper."

"I'll take option three." Grievous lifted his hand, and the bodyguards moved to box Obi-Wan between them. "That's the one where I watch you die."

Another gesture, and the droids in the ceiling hive came to life.

They uncoiled from their sockets heads-downward, with a rising chorus of whirring and buzzing and clicking that thickened until Obi-Wan might as well have stumbled into a colony of Corellian raptor-wasps. They began to drop free of the ceiling, first only a few, then many, like the opening drops of a summer cloudburst; finally they fell in a downpour that shook the stone-mounted durasteel of the deck and left Obi-Wan's ears ringing. Hundreds of them landed and rolled to standing; as many more stayed attached to the overhead hive, hanging upside down by their magnapeds, weapons trained so that Obi-Wan now stood at the focus of a dome of blasters.

Through it all, Obi-Wan never moved.

"I'm sorry, was I not clear?" he said. "There is no *option three*."

Grievous shook his head. "Do you never tire of this pathetic banter?"

"I rarely tire at all," Obi-Wan said mildly, "and I have no better way to pass the time while I wait for you to either decide to surrender, or choose to die."

"That choice was made long before I ever met *you*." Grievous turned away. "Kill him."

Instantly the box of bodyguards around Obi-Wan filled with crackling electrostaffs whipping faster than the human eye could see—which was less troublesome than it might have been, for that box was already empty of Jedi.

The Force had let him collapse as though he'd suddenly fainted, then it brought his lightsaber from his belt to his hand and ignited it while he turned his fall into a roll; that roll carried his lightsaber through a crisp arc that severed the leg of one of the bodyguards, and as the Force brought Obi-Wan back to his feet, the Force also nudged the crippled bodyguard to topple sideways into the path of the blade and sent it clanging to the floor in two smoking, sparking pieces.

One down.

The remaining three pressed the attack, but more cautiously; their weapons were longer than his, and they struck from beyond the reach of his blade. He gave way before them, his defensive velocities barely keeping their crackling discharge blades at bay.

Three MagnaGuards, each with a double-ended weapon that generated an energy field impervious to lightsabers, each with reflexes that operated near lightspeed, each with hypersophisticated heuristic combat algorithms that enabled it to learn from experience and adapt its tactics instantly to any situation, were certainly beyond Obi-Wan's ability to defeat, but it was not Obi-Wan who would defeat them; Obi-Wan wasn't even fighting. He was only a vessel, emptied of self. The Force, shaped by his skill and guided by his clarity of mind, fought through him.

In the Force, he felt their destruction: it was somewhere above and behind him, and only seconds away.

He went to meet it with a backflipping leap that the Force used to lift him neatly to an empty droid socket in the ceiling hive. The MagnaGuards sprang after him but he was gone by the time they arrived, leaping higher into the maze of girders and cables and room-sized cargo containers that was the control center's superstructure.

Here, said the Force within him, and Obi-Wan stopped, balancing on a girder, frowning back at the oncoming killer droids that leapt from beam to beam below him like malevolent durasteel primates. Though he could feel its close approach, he had no idea from where their destruction might come . . . until the Force showed him a support beam within reach of his blade and whispered, *Now.*

His blade flicked out and the durasteel beam parted, freshcut edges glowing white hot, and a great hulk of ship-sized cargo container that the beam had been supporting tore free of its other supports with shrieks of anguished metal and crashed down upon all three MagnaGuards with the finality of a meteor strike.

Two, three, and four.

Oh, thought Obi-Wan with detached approval. *That worked out rather well.*

Only ten thousand to go. Give or take.

An instant later the Force had him hurtling through a storm of blasterfire as every combat droid in the control center opened up on him at once.

Letting go of intention, letting go of desire, letting go of life, Obi-Wan fixed his entire attention on a thread of the Force that pulled him toward Grievous: not where Grievous was, but where Grievous would be when Obi-Wan got there . . .

Leaping girder to girder, slashing cables on which to swing through swarms of ricocheting particle beams, blade flickering so fast it became a deflector shield that splattered blaster bolts in all directions, his presence alone became a weapon: as he spun and whirled through the control center's superstructure, the blasts of particle cannons from power droids destroyed equipment and shattered girders and unleashed a torrent of red-hot debris that crashed to the deck, crushing droids on all sides. By the time he flipped down through the air to land catfooted on the deck once more, nearly half the droids between him and Grievous had been destroyed by their own not-so-friendly fire.

He cut his way into the mob of remaining troops as smoothly as if it were no more than a canebrake near some sunlit beach; his steady pace left behind a trail of smoking slices of droid.

"Keep *firing*!" Grievous roared to the spider droids that flanked him. *"Blast him!"*

Obi-Wan felt the massive shoulder cannon of a spider droid track him, and he felt it fire a bolt as powerful as a proton grenade, and he let the Force nudge him into a leap that carried him just far enough toward the fringe of the bolt's blast radius so that instead of shattering his bones it merely gave him a very strong, very hot *push*—

—that sent him whirling over the rest of the droids to land directly in front of Grievous.

A single slash of his lightsaber amputated the shoulder cannon of one power droid and continued into a spinning Force-assisted kick that brought his boot heel to the point of the other power droid's duranium chin, snapping the droid's head back hard enough to sever its cervical sensor cables. Blind and deaf, the power droid could only continue to obey its last order; it staggered in a wild circle, its convulsively firing cannon blasting random holes in droids and walls alike, until Obi-Wan deactivated it with a precise thrust that burned a thumb-sized hole through its thoracic braincase.

"General," Obi-Wan said with a blandly polite smile as though unexpectedly greeting, on the street, someone he privately disliked. "My offer is still open."

Droid guns throughout the control center fell silent; Obi-Wan stood so close to Grievous that the general was in the line of fire.

Grievous threw back his cloak imperiously. "Do you believe that I would surrender to you *now*?"

"I am still willing to take you alive." Obi-Wan's nod took in the smoking, sparking wreckage that filled the control center. "So far, no one has been hurt."

Grievous tilted his head so that he could squint down into Obi-Wan's face. "I have *thousands* of troops. You cannot defeat them all."

"I don't have to."

"This is *your* chance to surrender, General Kenobi." Grievous swept a duranium hand toward the sinkhole-city behind him. "Pau City is in my grip; lay down your blade, or I will *squeeze* . . . until this entire sinkhole brims over with innocent blood."

"That's not what it's about to brim with," Obi-Wan said. "You should pay more attention to the weather."

Yellow eyes narrowed behind a mask of armorplast. "What?"

"Have a look outside." He pointed his lightsaber toward the archway. "It's about to start raining clones."

Grievous said again, turning to look, "What?"

A shadow had passed over the sun as though one of the towering thunderheads on the horizon had caught a stray current in the hyperwinds and settled above Pau City. But it wasn't a cloud.

It was the *Vigilance*.

While twilight enfolded the sinkhole, over the bright desert above assault craft skimmed the dunes in a tightening ring centered on the city. Hailfire droids rolled out from caves in the wind-scoured mesas, unleashing firestorms of missiles toward the oncoming craft for exactly 2.5 seconds apiece, which was how long it took for the *Vigilance*'s sensor operators to transfer data to its turbolaser batteries.

Thunderbolts roared down through the atmosphere, and hailfire droids disintegrated. Pinpoint counterfire from the bubble turrets of LAAT/i's met missiles in blossoming fireballs that were ripped to shreds of smoke as the oncoming craft blasted through them.

LAAT/i's streaked over the rim of the sinkhole and spiraled downward with all guns blazing, crabbing outward to keep their forward batteries raking on the sinkhole's wall, while at the rim above, *Jadthu*-class armored landers hovered with bay doors wide, trailing sprays of polyplast cables like immense ice-white tassels that looped all the way to the ocean mouths that gaped at the lowest level of the city. Down those tassels, rappelling so fast they seemed to be simply falling, came endless streams of armored troopers, already firing on the combat droids that marched out to meet them.

Streamers of cables brushed the outer balcony of the control center, and down them slid white-armored troopers, each with one hand on his mechanized line-brake and the other full of DC-15 blaster rifle on full auto, spraying continuous chains of packeted particle beams. Droids wheeled and dropped and leapt into the air and burst to fragments. Surviving droids opened up on the clones as though grateful for something to shoot at, blasting holes in armor, cooking flesh with superheated steam from deep-tissue hits, blowing some troopers entirely off their cables to tumble toward a messy final landing ten levels below.

When the survivors of the first wave of clones hit the deck, the next wave was right behind them.

Grievous turned back to Obi-Wan. He lowered his head like an angry bantha, yellow glare fixed on the Jedi Master. "To the death, then."

Obi-Wan sighed. "If you insist."

The bio-droid general cast back his cloak, revealing the four lightsabers pocketed there. He stepped back, spreading wide his duranium arms. "You will not be the first Jedi I have killed, nor will you be the last."

Obi-Wan's only reply was to subtly shift the angle of his lightsaber up and forward.

The general's wide-spread arms now *split* along their lengths, dividing in half—even his *hands* split in half—

Now he had *four* arms. And four hands.

And each hand took a lightsaber as his cloak dropped to the floor.

They snarled to life and Grievous spun all four of them in a flourishing velocity so fast and so seamlessly integrated that he seemed to stand within a pulsing sphere of blue and green energy.

"Come on, then, Kenobi! Come for me!" he said. "I have been trained in your Jedi arts by Lord Tyranus himself!"

"Do you mean Count Dooku? What a curious coincidence," Obi-Wan said with a deceptively pleasant smile. "I trained the man who killed him."

With a convulsive snarl, Grievous lunged.

The sphere of blue lightsaber energy around him bulged toward Obi-Wan and opened like a mouth to bite him in half. Obi-Wan stood his ground, his blade still.

Chain-lightning teeth closed upon him.

This is how it feels to be Anakin Skywalker, right now:

You don't remember putting away your lightsaber.

You don't remember moving from Palpatine's private office to his larger public one; you don't remember collapsing in the chair where you now sit, nor do you remember drinking water from the half-empty glass that you find in your mechanical hand.

You remember only that the last man in the galaxy you still

thought you could trust has been lying to you since the day you met.

And you're not even angry about it.

Only stunned.

"After all, Anakin, you are the last man who has a right to be angry at someone for keeping a secret. What else was I to do?"

Palpatine sits in his familiar tall oval chair behind his familiar desk; the lampdisks are full on, the office eerily bright.

Ordinary.

As though this is merely another one of your friendly conversations, the casual evening chats you've enjoyed together for so many years.

As though nothing has happened.

As though nothing has changed.

"Corruption had made the Republic a cancer in the body of the galaxy, and no one could burn it out; not the judicials, not the Senate, not even the Jedi Order itself. I was the only man strong and skilled enough for this task; I was the only man who dared even *attempt* it. Without my small deception, how should I have cured the Republic? Had I revealed myself to you, or to anyone else, the Jedi would have hunted me down and murdered me without trial—very much as you nearly did, only a moment ago."

You can't argue. Words are beyond you.

He rises, moving around his desk, taking one of the small chairs and drawing it close to yours.

"If only you could know how I have longed to tell you, Anakin. All these years—since the very day we met, my boy. I have watched over you, waiting as you grew in strength and wisdom, biding my time until now, today, when you are finally ready to understand who you truly are, and your true place in the history of the galaxy."

Numb words blur from your numb lips. "The chosen one . . ."

"Exactly, my boy. *Exactly.* You *are* the chosen one." He leans toward you, eyes clear. Steady. Utterly honest. "Chosen by *me.*"

He turns a hand toward the panorama of light-sprayed cityscape through the window behind his desk. "Look out there, Anakin. A trillion beings on this planet alone—in the galaxy as a whole, uncounted quadrillions—and of them all, I have chosen *you,* Anakin Skywalker, to be the heir to my power. To all that I am."

"But that's not . . . that's not the prophecy. That's not the prophecy of the chosen one . . ."

"Is this such a problem for you? Is not your quest to find a way to *overturn* prophecy?" Palpatine leaned close, smiling, warm and kindly. "Anakin, do you think the Sith did not know of this prophecy? Do you think we would simply sleep while it came to *pass?*"

"You mean—"

"This is what you must understand. This Jedi submission to fate . . . this is not the way of the Sith, Anakin. This is not my way. This is not your way. It has never been. It need never be."

You're drowning.

"I am not . . . ," you hear yourself say, ". . . on your side. I am not *evil.*"

"Who said anything about evil? I am bringing peace to the galaxy. Is that evil? I am offering you the power to save Padmé. Is that evil? Have I attacked you? Drugged you? Are you being tortured? My boy, I am *asking* you. I am asking you to *do the right thing.* Turn your back on treason. On all those who would harm the Republic. I'm asking you to do exactly what you have sworn to do: bring peace and justice to the galaxy. And save Padmé, of course—haven't you sworn to protect *her,* too . . . ?"

"I—but—I—" Words will not fit themselves into the answers you need. If only Obi-Wan were here—Obi-Wan would know what to say. What to do.

Obi-Wan could handle this.

Rght now, you know you can't.

"I—I'll turn you over to the Jedi Council—*they'll* know what to do—"

"I'm sure they will. They are already planning to overthrow the Republic; you'll give them exactly the excuse they're looking for. And when they come to execute me, will that be justice? Will they be bringing *peace*?"

"They won't—they *wouldn't*—!"

"Well, of course I hope you're correct, Anakin. You'll forgive me if I don't share your blind loyalty to your comrades. I suppose it does indeed come down, in the end, to a question of loyalty," he said thoughtfully. "That's what you must ask yourself, my boy. Whether your loyalty is to the Jedi, or to the Republic."

"It's not—it's not *like* that—"

Palpatine lifted his shoulders. "Perhaps not. Perhaps it's simply a question of whether you love Obi-Wan Kenobi more than you love your wife."

There is no more searching for words.

There are no longer words at all.

"Take your time. Meditate on it. I will still be here when you decide."

Inside your head, there is only fire. Around your heart, the dragon whispers that all things die.

This is how it feels to be Anakin Skywalker, right now.

———

There is an understated elegance in Obi-Wan Kenobi's lightsaber technique, one that is quite unlike the feel one might get from the other great swordsbeings of the Jedi Order. He lacks entirely the flash, the pure bold *élan* of an Anakin Skywalker; there is nowhere in him the penumbral ferocity of a Mace Windu or a Depa Billaba nor the stylish grace of a Shaak Ti or a Dooku, and he is nothing resembling the whirlwind of destruction that Yoda can become.

He is simplicity itself.

That is his power.

Before Obi-Wan had left Coruscant, Mace Windu had told him of facing Grievous in single combat atop a mag-lev train during the general's daring raid to capture Palpatine. Mace had told him how the computers slaved to Grievous's brain had apparently analyzed even Mace's unconventionally lethal Vaapad and had been able to respond in kind after a single exchange.

"He must have been trained by Count Dooku," Mace had said, "so you can expect Makashi as well; given the number of Jedi he has fought and slain, you must expect that he can attack in any style, or all of them. In fact, Obi-Wan, I believe that of all living Jedi, you have the best chance to defeat him."

This pronouncement had startled Obi-Wan, and he had protested. After all, the only form in which he was truly even proficient was Soresu, which was the most common lightsaber form in the Jedi Order. Founded upon the basic deflection principles all Padawans were taught—to enable them to protect themselves from blaster bolts—Soresu was very simple, and so restrained and defense-oriented that it was very nearly downright passive.

"But surely, Master Windu," Obi-Wan had said, "you, with the power of Vaapad—or Yoda's mastery of Ataro—"

Mace Windu had almost smiled. "I created Vaapad to answer my weakness: it channels my own darkness into a weapon of the light. Master Yoda's Ataro is also an answer to weakness: the limitations of reach and mobility imposed by his stature and his age. But for you? What weakness does Soresu answer?"

Blinking, Obi-Wan had been forced to admit he'd never actually thought of it that way.

"That is so like you, Master Kenobi," the Korun Master had said, shaking his head. "I am called a great swordsman because I invented a lethal style; but who is greater, the creator of a killing form—or the master of the classic form?"

"I'm very flattered that you would consider me a master, but really—"

"Not a master. *The* master," Mace had said. "Be who you are, and Grievous will never defeat you."

So now, facing the tornado of annihilating energy that is Grievous's attack, Obi-Wan simply is who he is.

———

The electrodrivers powering Grievous's mechanical arms let each of the four attack thrice in a single second; integrated by combat algorithms in the bio-droid's electronic network of peripheral processors, each of the twelve strikes per second came from a different angle with different speed and intensity, an unpredictably broken rhythm of slashes, chops, and stabs of which every single one could take Obi-Wan's life.

Not one touched him.

After all, he had often walked unscathed through hornet-swarms of blasterfire, defended only by the Force's direction of his blade; countering twelve blows per second was only difficult, not impossible. His blade wove an intricate web of angles and curves, never truly fast but always just fast enough, each motion of his lightsaber subtly interfering with three or four or eight of the general's strikes, the rest sizzling past him, his precise, minimal shifts of weight and stance slipping them by centimeters.

Grievous, snarling fury, ramped up the intensity and velocity of his attacks—sixteen per second, eighteen—until finally, at twenty strikes per second, he overloaded Obi-Wan's defense.

So Obi-Wan used his defense to attack.

A subtle shift in the angle of a single parry brought Obi-Wan's blade in contact not with the blade of the oncoming lightsaber, but with the handgrip.

—*slice*—

The blade winked out of existence a hairbreadth before it would have burned through Obi-Wan's forehead. Half the severed lightsaber skittered away, along with the duranium thumb and first finger of the hand that had held it.

Grievous paused, eyes pulsing wide, then drawing narrow. He lifted his maimed hand and stared at the white-hot stumps that held now only half a useless lightsaber.

Obi-Wan smiled at him.

Grievous lunged.

Obi-Wan parried.

Pieces of lightsabers bounced on the durasteel deck.

Grievous looked down at the blade-sliced hunks of metal that were all he had left in his hands, then up at Obi-Wan's shining sky-colored blade, then down at his hands again, and then he seemed to suddenly remember that he had an urgent appointment somewhere else.

Anywhere else.

Obi-Wan stepped toward him, but a shock from the Force made him leap back just as a scarlet HE bolt struck the floor right where he'd been about to place his foot. Obi-Wan rode the explosion, flipping in the air to land upright between a pair of super battle droids that were busily firing upon the flank of a squad of clone troopers, which they continued to do until they found themselves falling in pieces to the deck.

Obi-Wan spun.

In the chaos of exploding droids and dying men, Grievous was nowhere to be seen.

Obi-Wan waved his lightsaber at the clones. "The general!" he shouted. "Which way?"

One trooper circled his arm as though throwing a proton grenade back toward the archway where Obi-Wan had first entered. He followed the gesture and saw, for an instant in the sunshadow of the *Vigilance* outside, the back curves of twin bladed rings—ganged together to make a wheel the size of a starfighter—rolling swiftly off along the sinkhole rim.

General Grievous was very good at running away.

"Not this time," Obi-Wan muttered, and cut a path through the tangled mob of droids all the way to the arch in a single sustained surge, reaching the open air just in time to see the bladewheeler turn; it was an open ring with a pilot's chair inside, and in the pilot's chair sat Grievous, who lifted one of his body-guards' electrostaffs in a sardonic wave as he took the scooter straight out over the edge. Four claw-footed arms deployed, digging into the rock to carry him down the side of the sinkhole, angling away at a steep slant.

"Blast." Obi-Wan looked around. Still no air taxis. Not that he had any real interest in flying through the storm of battle that raged throughout the interior of the sinkhole, but there was certainly no way he could catch Grievous on foot . . .

From around the corner of an interior tunnel, he heard a resonant *honnnnk!* as though a nearby bantha had swallowed an air horn.

He said, "Boga?"

The beaked face of the dragonmount slowly extended around the interior angle of the tunnel.

"Boga! Come here, girl! We have a general to catch."

Boga fixed him with a reproachful glare. *"Honnnnnk."*

"Oh, very well." Obi-Wan rolled his eyes. "I was wrong; you were right. Can we please *go* now?"

The remaining fifteen meters of dragonmount hove into view and came trotting out to meet him. Obi-Wan sprang to the saddle, and Boga leapt to the sinkhole's rim in a single bound. Her huge head swung low, searching, until Obi-Wan spotted Grievous's blade-wheeler racing away toward the landing decks below.

"*There*, girl—that's him! Go!"

Boga gathered herself and sprang to the rim of the next level down, poised for an instant to get her bearings, then leapt again down into the firestorm that Pau City had become. Obi-Wan spun his blade in a continuous whirl to either side of the dragonmount's back, disintegrating shrapnel and slapping away stray blasterfire. They plummeted through the sinkhole-city, gaining tens of meters on Grievous with every leap.

On one of the landing decks, the canopy was lifting and parting to show a small, ultrafast armored shuttle of the type favored by the famously nervous Neimoidian executives of the Trade

Federation. Grievous's wheeler sprayed a fan of white-hot sparks as it tore across the landing deck; the bio-droid whipped the wheeler sideways, laying it down for a skidding halt that showered the shuttle with molten durasteel.

But before he could clamber out of the pilot's chair, several metric tons of Jedi-bearing dragonmount landed on the shuttle's roof, crouched and threatening and hissing venomously down at him.

"I hope you have another vehicle, General!" Obi-Wan waved his lightsaber toward the shuttle's twin rear thrusters. "I believe there's some damage to your sublights!"

"You're insane! There's no—"

Obi-Wan shrugged. "Show him, Boga."

The dragonmount dutifully pointed out the damage with two whistling strikes of her massive tail-mace—*wham* and *wham* again—which crumpled the shuttle's thruster tubes into crimped-shut knots of metal.

Obi-Wan beckoned. "Let's settle this, shall we?"

Grievous's answer was a shriek of tortured gyros that wrenched the wheeler upright, and a metal-on-metal scream of blades ripping into deck plates that sent it shooting straight toward the sinkhole wall—and, with the claw-arms to help, straight *up* it.

Obi-Wan sighed. "Didn't we just *come* from there?"

Boga coiled herself and sprang for the wall, and the chase was on once more.

They raced through the battle, clawing up walls, shooting through tunnels, skidding and leaping, sprinting where the way was clear and screeching into high-powered serpentines where it was not, whipping around knots of droids and bounding over troopers. Boga ran straight up the side of a clone hovertank and sprang from its turret directly between the high-slanting ringwheels of a hailfire, and a swipe of Obi-Wan's blade left the droid crippled behind them. Native troops had taken the field: Utapaun dragonriders armed with sparking power lances charged along causeways, spearing droids on every side. Grievous ran right over anything in his path, the blades of his wheeler shredding droid and trooper and dragon alike; behind him, Obi-Wan's lightsaber caught and returned blaster bolts in a spray that shattered any droid unwise enough to fire on him. A few stray bolts he batted into the speeding wheeler ahead, but without visible effect.

"Fine," he muttered. "Let's try this from a little *closer*."

Boga gained steadily. Grievous's vehicle had the edge in raw speed, but Boga could out-turn it and could make instant leaps at astonishing angles; the dragonmount also had an uncanny instinct for where the general might be heading, as well as a seemingly infinite knowledge of useful shortcuts through side tunnels, along sheer walls, and over chasms studded with locked-down wind turbines. Grievous tried once to block Obi-Wan's pursuit by screeching out onto a huge pod that held a whole bank of wind turbines and knocking the blade-brakes off them with quick blows of the electrostaff, letting the razor-edged blades spin freely in the constant gale, but Obi-Wan merely brought Boga alongside the turbines and stuck his lightsaber into their whirl. Sliced-free chunks of carboceramic blade shrieked through the air and shattered on the stone on all sides, and with a curse Grievous kicked his vehicle into motion again.

The wheeler roared into a tunnel that seemed to lead straight into the rock of the plateau. The tunnel was jammed with groundcars and dragonmounts and wheelers and jetsters and all manner of other vehicles and every kind of beast that might bear or draw the vast numbers of Utapauns and Utai fleeing the battle. Grievous blasted right into them, blade-wheel chewing through groundcars and splashing the tunnel walls with chunks of shredded lizard; Boga raced along the walls above the traffic, sometimes even galloping on the ceiling with claws gouging chunks from the rock.

With a burst of sustained effort that strangled her *honnnk*ing to thin gasps for air, Boga finally pulled alongside Grievous. Obi-Wan leaned forward, stretching out with his lightsaber, barely able to reach the wheeler's back curve, and carved away an arc of the wheeler's blade-tread, making the vehicle buck and skid; Grievous answered with a thrust of his electrostaff that crackled lightning against Boga's extended neck. The great beast jerked sideways, honking fearfully and whipping her head as though the burn was a biting creature she could shake off her flank.

"One more leap, Boga!" Obi-Wan shouted, pressing himself along the dragonmount's shoulder. "Bring me even with him!"

The dragonmount complied without hesitation, and when Grievous thrust again, Obi-Wan's free hand flashed out and seized the staff below its discharge blade, holding it clear of Boga's vulnerable flesh. Grievous yanked on the staff, nearly pulling Obi-Wan out of the saddle, then jabbed it back at him, discharge blade sparking in his face—

With a sigh, Obi-Wan realized he needed both hands.

He dropped his lightsaber.

As his deactivated handgrip skittered and bounced along the tunnel behind him, he reflected that it was just as well Anakin wasn't there after all; he'd have never heard the end of it.

He got his other hand on the staff just as Grievous jerked the wheeler sideways, half laying it down to angle for a small side tunnel just ahead. Obi-Wan hung on grimly. Through the Force he could feel Boga's exhaustion, the buildup of anaerobic breakdown products turning the dragonmount's mighty legs to cloth. An open archway showed daylight ahead. Boga barely made the turn, and they raced side by side along the empty darkened way, joined by the spark-spitting rod of the electrostaff.

As they cleared the archway to a small, concealed landing deck deep in a private sinkhole, Obi-Wan leapt from the saddle, yanking on the staff to swing both his boots hard into the side of Grievous's duranium skull. The wheeler's internal gyros screamed at the sudden impact and shift of balance. Their shrieks cycled up to bursts of smoke and fragments of metal as their catastrophic failure sent the wheeler tumbling in a white-hot cascade of sparks.

Dropping the staff, Obi-Wan leapt again, the Force lifting him free of the crash.

Grievous's electronic reflexes sent him out of the pilot's chair in the opposite direction.

The wheeler flipped over the edge of the landing deck and into the shadowy abyss of the sinkhole. It trailed smoke all the way down to a distant, delayed, and very final crash.

The electrostaff had rolled away, coming to rest against the landing jack of a small Techno Union starfighter that stood on the deck a few meters behind Obi-Wan. Behind Grievous, the archway back into the tunnel system was filled with a panting, exhausted, but still dangerously angry dragonmount.

Obi-Wan looked at Grievous.

Grievous looked at Obi-Wan.

There was no longer any need for words between them.

Obi-Wan simply stood, centered in the Force, waiting for Grievous to make his move.

A concealed compartment in the general's right thigh sprang open, and a mechanical arm delivered a slim hold-out blaster to his hand. He brought it up and fired so fast that his arm blurred to invisiblity.

Obi-Wan . . . reached.

The electrostaff flipped into the air between them, one discharge blade catching the bolt. The impact sent the staff whirling—

Right into Obi-Wan's hand.

There came one instant's pause, while they looked into each other's eyes and shared an intimate understanding that their relationship had reached its end.

Obi-Wan charged.

Grievous backed away, unleashing a stream of blaster bolts as fast as his half a forefinger could pull the trigger.

Obi-Wan spun the staff, catching every bolt, not even slowing down, and when he reached Grievous he slapped the blaster out of his hand with a crack of the staff that sent blue lightning scaling up the general's arm.

His following strike was a stiff stab into Grievous's jointed

stomach armor that sent the general staggering back. Obi-Wan
hit him again in the same place, denting the armorplast plate,
cracking the joint where it met the larger, thicker plates of his
chest as Grievous flailed for balance, but when he spun the staff
for his next strike the general's flailing arm flailed itself against
the middle of the staff and his other hand found it as well and he
seized it, yanking himself upright against Obi-Wan's grip, his
metal skull-face coming within a centimeter of the Jedi Master's
nose.

He snarled, "Do you think I am foolish enough to arm my
bodyguards with weapons that can actually *hurt* me?"

Instead of waiting for an answer he spun, heaving Obi-Wan
right off the deck with effortless strength, whipping up him over
his head to slam him to the deck with killing power; Obi-Wan
could only let go of the staff and allow the Force to angle his fall
into a stumbling roll. Grievous sprang after him, swinging the
electrostaff and slamming it across Obi-Wan's flank before the
Jedi Master could recover his balance. The impact sent Obi-Wan
tumbling sideways and the electroburst discharge set his robe on
fire. Grievous stayed right with him, attacking before Obi-Wan
could even realize exactly what was happening, attacking faster
than thought—

But Obi-Wan didn't need to think. The Force was with him,
and he *knew.*

When Grievous spun the staff overhand, discharge blade sizzling down at Obi-Wan's head for the killing blow, Obi-Wan
went to the inside.

He met Grievous chest-to-chest, his upraised hand blocking
the general's wrist; Grievous snarled something incoherent and
bore down on the Jedi Master's block with all his weight, driving
the blade closer and closer to Obi-Wan's face—

But Obi-Wan's arm had the Force to give it strength, and the
general's arm only had the innate crystalline intermolecular
structure of duranium alloy.

Grievous's forearm bent like a cheap spoon.

While the general stared in disbelief at his mangled arm, Obi-Wan had been working the fingers of his free hand around the lower edge of Grievous's dented, joint-loose stomach plate.

Grievous looked down. "What?"

Obi-Wan slammed the elbow of his blocking arm into the general's clavicle while he yanked as hard as he could on the stomach plate, and it ripped free in his hand. Behind it hung a translucent sac of synthskin containing a tangle of green and gray organs.

The true body of the alien inside the droid.

Grievous howled and dropped the staff to seize Obi-Wan with his three remaining arms. He lifted the Jedi Master over his head again and hurled him tumbling over the landing deck toward the precipice above the gloom-shrouded drop. Reaching into the Force, Obi-Wan was able to connect with the stone itself as if he were anchored to it with a cable tether; instead of hurtling over the edge he slammed down onto the rock hard enough to crush all breath from his lungs.

Grievous picked up the staff again and charged.

Obi-Wan still couldn't breathe. He had no hope of rising to meet the general's attack.

All he could do was extend a hand.

As the bio-droid loomed over him, electrostaff raised for the kill, the hold-out blaster flipped from the deck into Obi-Wan's palm, and with no hesitation, no second thoughts, not even the faintest pause to savor his victory, he pulled the trigger.

The bolt ripped into the synthskin sac.

Grievous's guts exploded in a foul-smelling shower the color of a dead swamp. Energy chained up his spine and a mist of vaporized brain burst out both sides of his skull and sent his face spinning off the precipice.

The electrostaff hit the deck, followed shortly by the general's knees.

Then by what was left of his head.

Obi-Wan lay on his back, staring at the circle of cloudless sky

above the sinkhole while he gasped air back into into his spas-
ming lungs. He barely managed to roll over far enough to
smother the flames on his robe, then fell back.

And simply enjoyed being alive.

Much too short a time later—long before he was actually
ready to get up—a shadow fell across him, accompanied by the
smell of overheated lizard and an admonitory *honnnk*.

"Yes, Boga, you're right," Obi-Wan agreed reluctantly.
Slowly, painfully, he pushed himself to his feet.

He picked up the electrostaff, and paused for one last glance
at the remains of the bio-droid general.

"So . . ." He summoned a condemnation among the most
offensive in his vocabulary. ". . . *uncivilized.*"

He triggered his comlink, and directed Cody to report to
Jedi Command on Coruscant that Grievous had been destroyed.

"Will do, General," said the tiny holoscan of the clone commander. *"And congratulations. I knew you could do it."*

Apparently everyone did, Obi-Wan thought, *except Grievous,
and me . . .*

*"General? We do still have a little problem out here. About ten
thousand heavily armed little problems, actually."*

"On my way. Kenobi out."

Obi-Wan sighed and clambered painfully onto the dragonmount's saddle.

"All right, girl," he said. "Let's go win *that* battle, too."

As has been said, the textbook example of a Jedi trap is the
one that was set on Utapau, for Obi-Wan Kenobi.

It worked perfectly.

The final element essential to the creation of a truly effective
Jedi trap is a certain coldness of mind—a detachment, if you will,
from any desire for a particular outcome.

The best way to arrange matters is to create a win–win situation.

For example, one might use as one's proxy a creature that
not only is expendable, but would eventually have to be killed

anyway. Thus, if one's proxy fails and is destroyed, it's no loss—
in fact, the targeted Jedi has actually done one a favor, by taking
care of a bit of dirty work one would otherwise have to do one-
self.

And the final stroke of perfection is to organize the Jedi trap
so that by walking into it at all, the Jedi has already lost.

That is to say, a Jedi trap works best when one's true goal is
merely to make sure that the Jedi in question spends some hours
or days off somewhere on the far side of the galaxy. So that he
won't be around to interfere with one's *real* plans.

So that by the time he can return, it will be already too late.

REVELATION

Mace Windu stood in the darkened comm center of Jedi Command, facing a life-sized holoscan of Yoda, projected from a concealed Wookiee comm center in the heart of a wroshyr tree on Kashyyyk.

"Minutes ago," Mace said, "we received confirmation from Utapau: Kenobi was successful. Grievous is dead."

"Time it is to execute our plan."

"I will personally deliver the news of Grievous's death." Mace flexed his hands. "It will be up to the Chancellor to cede his emergency powers back over to the Senate."

"Forget not the existence of Sidious. Anticipate your action, he may. Masters will be necessary, if the Lord of the Sith you must face."

"I have chosen four of our best. Master Tiin, Master Kolar, and Master Fisto are all here, in the Temple. They are preparing already."

"What about Skywalker? The chosen one."

"Too much of a risk," Mace replied. "I am the fourth."

With a slow purse of the lips and an even slower nod, Yoda said, *"On watch you have been too long, my Padawan. Rest you must."*

"I will, Master. When the Republic is safe once more." Mace straightened. "We are waiting only for your vote."

"Very well, then. Have my vote, you do. May the Force be with you."

"And with you, Master."

But he spoke to empty air; the holoscan had already flickered to nonexistence.

Mace lowered his head and stood in the darkness and the silence.

The door of the comm center shot open, spilling yellow glare into the gloom and limning the silhouette of a man half collapsed against the frame.

"Master . . ." The voice was a hoarse half whisper. "Master Windu . . . ?"

"Skywalker?" Mace was at his side in an instant. "What's wrong? Are you hurt?"

Anakin took Mace's arm in a grip of desperate strength, and used it like a crutch to haul himself upright.

"Obi-Wan . . . ," he said faintly. "I need to talk to *Obi-Wan*—!"

"Obi-Wan is operational on Utapau; he has destroyed General Grievous. We are leaving now to tell the Chancellor, and to see to it that he steps down as he has promised—"

"Steps—steps *down*—" Anakin's voice had a sharply bitter edge. "You have no *idea* . . ."

"Anakin—? What's wrong?"

"Listen to me—*you have to listen to me*—" Anakin sagged against him, shaking; Mace wrapped his arms around the young Jedi and guided him into the nearest chair. "You can't—please, Master Windu, give me your word, promise me it'll be an *arrest*, promise you're not going to *hurt* him—"

"Skywalker—Anakin. You must try to answer. Have you been attacked? Are you injured? You have to tell me what's wrong!"

Anakin collapsed forward, face into his hands.

Mace reached into the Force, opening the eye of his special gift of perception—

What he found there froze his blood.

The tangled web of fault lines in the Force he had seen connecting Anakin to Obi-Wan and to Palpatine was no more; in their place was a single spider-knot that sang with power enough to crack the planet. Anakin Skywalker no longer had shatterpoints. He *was* a shatterpoint.

The shatterpoint.

Everything depended on him.

Everything.

Mace said slowly, with the same sort of deliberate care he would use in examining an unknown type of bomb that might have the power to destroy the universe itself, "Anakin, look at me."

Skywalker raised his head.

"Are you hurt? Do you need—"

Mace frowned. Anakin's eyes were raw, and red, and his face looked swollen. For a long time he didn't know if Anakin would answer, if he *could* answer, if he could even speak at all; the young Jedi seemed to be struggling with something inside himself, as though he fought desperately against the birth of a monster hatching within his chest.

But in the Force, there was no *as though;* there was no *seemed to be.* In the Force, Mace could feel the monster inside Anakin Skywalker, a *real* monster, *too* real, one that was eating him alive from the inside out.

Fear.

This was the wound Anakin had taken. This was the hurt that had him shaking and stammering and too weak to stand. Some black fear had hatched like fever wasps inside the young Knight's brain, and it was killing him.

Finally, after what seemed forever, Anakin opened his blood-raw eyes.

"Master Windu . . ." He spoke slowly, painfully, as though

each word ripped away a raw hunk of his own flesh. "I have . . . bad news."

Mace stared at him.

"Bad news?" he repeated blankly.

What news could be bad enough to make a Jedi like Anakin Skywalker collapse? What *news* could make Anakin Skywalker look like the stars had gone out?

Then, in nine simple words, Anakin told him.

This is the moment that defines Mace Windu.

Not his countless victories in battle, nor the numberless battles his diplomacy has avoided. Not his penetrating intellect, or his talents with the Force, or his unmatched skills with the lightsaber. Not his dedication to the Jedi Order, or his devotion to the Republic that he serves.

But this.

Right here.

Right now.

Because Mace, too, has an *attachment*. Mace has a secret love.

Mace Windu loves the Republic.

Many of his students quote him to students of their own: *"Jedi do not fight for peace. That's only a slogan, and is as misleading as slogans always are. Jedi fight for* civilization, *because only* civilization *creates* peace.*"*

For Mace Windu, for all his life, for all the lives of a thousand years of Jedi before him, true civilization has had only one true name: the Republic.

He has given his life in the service of his love. He has taken lives in its service, and lost the lives of innocents. He has seen beings that he cares for maimed, and killed, and sometimes worse: sometimes so broken by the horror of the struggle that their only answer was to commit horrors greater still.

And because of that love now, here, in this instant, Anakin Skywalker has nine words for him that shred his heart, burn its pieces, and feed him its smoking ashes.

Palpatine is Sidious. The Chancellor is the Sith Lord.

He doesn't even hear the words, not really; their true meaning is too large for his mind to gather in all at once.

They mean that all he's done, and all that has been done to him—

That all the Order has accomplished, all it has suffered—

All the Galaxy *itself* has gone through, all the years of suffering and slaughter, the death of entire *planets*—

Has all been for nothing.

Because it was all done to save the Republic.

Which was already gone.

Which had already fallen.

The corpse of which had been defended only by a Jedi Order that was now under the command of a Dark Lord of the Sith.

Mace Windu's entire existence has become crystal so shot-through with flaws that the hammer of those nine words has crushed him to sand.

But because he is Mace Windu, he takes this blow without a change of expression.

Because he is Mace Windu, within a second the man of sand is stone once more: pure Jedi Master, weighing coldly the risk of facing the last Dark Lord of the Sith without the chosen one—

Against the risk of facing the last Dark Lord of the Sith with a chosen one eaten alive by fear.

And because he is Mace Windu, the choice is no choice at all.

"Anakin, wait in the Council Chamber until we get back."

"Wh—what? Master—"

"That's an *order*, Anakin."

"But—but—but the *Chancellor*—" Anakin says desperately, clutching at the Jedi Master's hand. "What are you going to *do*?"

And it is the true measure of Mace Windu that, even now, he still is telling the truth when he says, "Only as much as I have to."

In the virtual nonspace of the HoloNet, two Jedi Masters meet.

One is ancient, tiny, with skin of green leather and old wisdom in his eyes, standing in a Kashyyyk cave hollowed from the trunk of a vast wroshyr tree; the other is tall and fierce, seated before a holodisk in Coruscant's Jedi Temple.

To each other, they are blue ghosts, given existence by scanning lasers. Though they are light-years apart, they are of one mind; it hardly matters who says what.

Now they know the truth.

For more than a decade, the Republic has been in the hands of the Sith.

Now, together, blue ghost to blue ghost, they decide to take it back.

PART THREE

APOCALYPSE

The dark is generous, and it is patient, and it always wins.

It always wins because it is everywhere.

It is in the wood that burns in your hearth, and in the kettle on the fire; it is under your chair and under your table and under the sheets on your bed. Walk in the midday sun and the dark is with you, attached to the soles of your feet.

The brightest light casts the darkest shadow.

THE FACE OF THE DARK

Depowered lampdisks were rings of ghostly gray floating in the gloom. The shimmering jewelscape of Coruscant haloed the knife-edged shadow of the chair.

This was the office of the Chancellor.

Within the chair's shadow sat another shadow: deeper, darker, formless and impenetrable, an abyssal umbra so profound that it drained light from the room around it.

And from the city. And the planet.

And the galaxy.

The shadow waited. It had told the boy it would. It was looking forward to keeping its word.

For a change.

Night held the Jedi Temple.

On its rooftop landing deck, thin yellow light spilled in a stretching rectangle through a shuttle's hatchway, reflecting upward onto the faces of three Jedi Masters.

"I'd feel better if Yoda were here." This Master was a Nautiloid, tall and broad-shouldered, his glabrous scalp-tentacles restrained by loops of embossed leather. "Or even Kenobi. On Ord Cestus, Obi-Wan and I—"

"Yoda is pinned down on Kashyyyk, and Kenobi is out of contact on Utapau. The Dark Lord has revealed himself, and we dare not hesitate. Think not of *if*, Master Fisto; this duty has fallen to us. We will suffice." This Master was an Iktotchi, shorter and slimmer than the first. Two long horns curved downward from his forehead to below his chin. One had been amputated after being shattered in battle a few months before. Bacta had accelereated its regrowth, and the once maimed horn was now a match to the other. "We will suffice," he repeated. "We will have to."

"Peace," said the third Master, a Zabrak. Dew had gathered on his array of blunt vestigial skull-spines, glistening very like sweat. He gestured toward a Temple door that had cycled open. "Windu is coming."

Clouds had swept in with the twilight, and now a thin drizzling rain began to fall. The approaching Master walked with his shaven head lowered, his hands tucked within his sleeves.

"Master Ti and Gate Master Jurokk will direct the Temple's defense," he said as he reached the others. "We are shutting down all nav beacons and signal lights, we have armed the older Padawans, and all blast doors are sealed and code-locked." His gaze swept the Masters. "It's time to go."

"And Skywalker?" The Zabrak Master cocked his head as though he felt a distant disturbance in the Force. "What of the chosen one?"

"I have sent him to the Council Chamber until our return." Mace Windu turned a grim stare upon the High Council Tower, squinting against the thickening rain. His hands withdrew from his sleeves. One of them held his lightsaber.

"He has done his duty, Masters. Now we shall do ours."

He walked between them into the shuttle.

The other three Masters shared a significant silence, then Agen Kolar nodded to himself and entered; Saesee Tiin stroked his regrown horn, and followed.

"I'd *still* feel better if Yoda were here . . . ," Kit Fisto muttered, and then went in as well.

Once the hatch had sealed behind him, the Jedi Temple belonged entirely to the night.

Alone in the Chamber of the Jedi Council, Anakin Skywalker wrestled with his dragon.

He was losing.

He paced the Chamber in blind arcs, stumbling among the chairs. He could not feel currents of the Force around him; he could not feel echoes of Jedi Masters in these ancient seats.

He had never dreamed there was this much pain in the universe.

Physical pain he could have handled even without his Jedi mental skills; he'd always been tough. At four years old he'd been able to take the worst beating Watto would deliver without so much as making a sound.

Nothing had prepared him for this.

He wanted to rip open his chest with his bare hands and claw out his heart.

"What have I *done?*" The question started as a low moan but grew to a howl he could no longer lock behind his teeth. *"What have I done?"*

He knew the answer: he had done his duty.

And now he couldn't imagine why.

When I die, Palpatine had said, so calmly, so warmly, so reasonably, *my knowledge dies with me . . .*

Everywhere he looked, he saw only the face of the woman he loved beyond love: the woman for whom he channeled through his body all the love that had ever existed in the galaxy. In the universe.

He didn't care what she had done. He didn't care about conspiracies or cabals or secret pacts. Treason meant nothing to him now. She was everything that had ever been loved by anyone, and he was watching her die.

His agony somehow became an invisible hand, stretching out through the Force, a hand that found her, far away, alone in her apartment in the dark, a hand that felt the silken softness of her skin and the sleek coils of her hair, a hand that dissolved into a field of pure energy, of pure *feeling* that reached *inside* her—

And now he felt her, really *felt* her in the Force, as though she could have been some kind of Jedi, too, but more than that: he felt a bond, a connection, deeper and more intimate than he'd ever had before with anyone, even Obi-Wan; for a precious eternal instant he *was* her . . . he was the beat of her heart and he was the motion of her lips and he was her soft words as though she spoke a prayer to the stars—

I love you, Anakin. I am yours, in life, and in death, wherever you go, whatever you do, we will always be one. Never doubt me, my love. I am yours.

—and her purity and her passion and the truth of her love flowed into him and through him and every atom of him screamed to the Force *how can I let her die?*

The Force had no answer for him.

The dragon, on the other hand, did.

All things die, Anakin Skywalker. Even stars burn out.

And no matter how hard he tried to summon it, no wisdom of Yoda's, no teaching of Obi-Wan's, not one scrap of Jedi lore came to him that could choke the dragon down.

But there *was* an answer; he'd heard it just the other night.

With such knowledge, to maintain life in someone already living would seem a small matter, don't you agree?

Anakin stopped. His agony evaporated.

Palpatine was right.

It *was* simple.

All he had to do was decide what he wanted.

The Coruscant nightfall was spreading through the galaxy.

The darkness in the Force was no hindrance to the shadow in the Chancellor's office; it *was* the darkness. Wherever darkness dwelled, the shadow could send perception.

In the night, the shadow felt the boy's anguish, and it was

good. The shadow felt the grim determination of four Jedi Masters approaching by air.

This, too, was good.

As a Jedi shuttle settled to the landing deck outside, the shadow sent its mind into the far deeper night within one of the several pieces of sculpture that graced the office: an abstract twist of solid neuranium, so heavy that the office floor had been specially reinforced to bear its weight, so dense that more sensitive species might, from very close range, actually percieve the tiny warping of the fabric of space–time that was its gravitation.

Neuranium of more than roughly a millimeter thick is impervious to sensors; the standard security scans undergone by all equipment and furniture to enter the Senate Office Building had shown nothing at all. If anyone had thought to use an advanced gravimetric detector, however, they might have discovered that one smallish section of the sculpture massed slightly less than it should have, given that the manifest that had accompanied it, when it was brought from Naboo among the then-ambassador's personal effects, clearly stated that it was a single piece of solid-forged neuranium.

The manifest was a lie. The sculpture was not entirely solid, and not all of it was neuranium.

Within a long, slim, rod-shaped cavity around which the sculpture had been forged rested a device that had lain, waiting, in absolute darkness—darkness beyond darkness—for decades.

Waiting for night to fall on the Republic.

The shadow felt Jedi Masters stride the vast echoic emptiness of the vaulted halls outside. It could practically hear the cadence of their boot heels on the Alderaanian marble.

The darkness within the sculpture whispered of the shape and the feel and every intimate resonance of the device it cradled. With a twist of its will, the shadow triggered the device.

The neuranium got warm.

A small round spot, smaller than the circle a human child might make of thumb and forefinger, turned the color of old blood.

Then fresh blood.

Then open flame.

Finally a spear of scarlet energy lanced free, painting the office with the color of stars seen through the smoke of burning planets.

The spear of energy lengthened, drawing with it out from the darkness the device, then the scarlet blade shrank away and the device slid itself within the softer darkness of a sleeve.

As shouts of the Force scattered Redrobes beyond the office's outer doors, the shadow gestured and lampdisks ignited. Another shout of the Force burst open the inner door to the private office. As Jedi stormed in, a final flick of the shadow's will triggered a recording device concealed within the desk.

Audio only.

"Why, Master Windu," said the shadow. "What a pleasant surprise."

Shaak Ti felt him coming before she could see him. The infra- and ultrasound-sensitive cavities in the tall, curving montrals to either side of her head gave her a sense analogous to touch: the texture of his approaching footsteps was ragged as old sacking. As he rounded the corner to the landing deck door, his breathing felt like a pile of gravel and his heartbeat was spiking like a Zabrak's head.

He didn't look good, either; he was deathly pale, even for a human, and his eyes were raw.

"Anakin," she said warmly. Perhaps a friendly word was what he needed; she doubted he'd gotten many from Mace Windu. "Thank you for what you have done. The Jedi Order is in your debt—the whole galaxy, as well."

"Shaak Ti. Get out of my way."

Shaky as he looked, there was nothing unsteady in his voice: it was deeper than she remembered, more mature, and it carried undertones of authority that she had never heard before.

And she was not blind to the fact he had neglected to call her *Master*.

She put forth a hand, offering calming energies through the Force. "The Temple is sealed, Anakin. The door is code-locked."

"And you're in the way of the pad."

She stepped aside, allowing him to the pad; she had no reason to keep him here against his will. He punched the code hungrily. "If Palpatine retaliates," she said reasonably, "is not your place here, to help with our defense?"

"I'm the *chosen one*. My place is *there*." His breathing roughened, and he looked as if he was getting even sicker. "I have to be there. That's the prophecy, isn't it? *I have to be there*—"

"Anakin, why? The Masters are the best of the Order. What can you possibly do?"

The door slid open.

"I'm the chosen one," he repeated. "Prophecy can't be changed. I'll do—"

He looked at her with eyes that were dying, and a spasm of unendurable pain passed over his face. Shaak Ti reached for him— he should be in the infirmary, not heading toward what might be a savage battle—but he lurched away from her hand.

"I'll do what I'm *supposed* to do," he said, and sprinted into the night and the rain.

[*the following is a transcript of an audio recording presented before the Galactic Senate on the afternoon of the first Empire Day; identities of all speakers verified and confirmed by voiceprint analysis*]

PALPATINE: Why, Master Windu. What a pleasant surprise.

MACE WINDU: Hardly a surprise, Chancellor. And it will be pleasant for neither of us.

PALPATINE: I'm sorry? Master Fisto, hello. Master Kolar, greetings. I trust you are well. Master Tiin—I see your horn has regrown; I'm very glad. What brings four Jedi Masters to my office at this hour?

MACE WINDU: We know who you are. What you are. We are here to take you into custody.

PALPATINE: I beg your pardon? What I am? When last I checked, I was Supreme Chancellor of the Republic you are sworn to serve. I hope I misunderstand what you mean by *custody,* Master Windu. It smacks of treason.

MACE WINDU: You're under arrest.

PALPATINE: Really, Master Windu, you cannot be serious. On what charge?

MACE WINDU: You're a Sith Lord!

PALPATINE: Am I? Even if true, that's hardly a crime. My philosophical outlook is a personal matter. In fact— the last time I read the Constitution, anyway—we have very strict laws against this type of persecution. So I ask you again: what is my alleged crime? How do you expect to justify your mutiny before the Senate? Or do you intend to arrest the Senate as well?

MACE WINDU: We're not here to argue with you.

PALPATINE: No, you're here to imprison me without trial. Without even the pretense of legality. So this is the plan, at last: the Jedi are taking over the Republic.

MACE WINDU: Come with us. Now.

PALPATINE: I shall do no such thing. If you intend to murder me, you can do so right here.

MACE WINDU: Don't try to resist.

[*sounds that have been identified by frequency resonances to be the ignition of several lightsabers*]

PALPATINE: Resist? How could I possibly resist? This is *murder,* you Jedi traitors! How can *I* be any threat to you? Master Tiin—you're the telepath. What am I think-ing right now?

[*sounds of scuffle*]

KIT FISTO: Saesee—

AGEN KOLAR: [*garbled; possibly "It doesn't hurt"(?)*]

[*sounds of scuffle*]

PALPATINE: Help! Help! Security—*someone*! Help me! *Murder! Treason!*

[*recording ends*]

A fountain of amethyst energy burst from Mace Windu's fist. "Don't try to resist."

The song of his blade was echoed by green fire from the hands of Kit Fisto, Agen Kolar, and Saesee Tiin. Kolar and Tiin closed on Palpatine, blocking the path to the door. Shadows dripped and oozed color, weaving and coiling up office walls, slipping over chairs, spreading along the floor.

"Resist? How could I possibly resist?" Still seated at the desk, Palpatine shook an empty fist helplessly, the perfect image of a tired, frightened old man. "This is *murder*, you Jedi traitors! How can *I* be any threat to you?"

He turned desperately to Saesee Tiin. "Master Tiin—you're the telepath. What am I thinking right now?"

Tiin frowned and cocked his head. His blade dipped. A smear of red-flashing darkness hurtled from behind the desk.

Saesee Tiin's head bounced when it hit the floor.

Smoke curled from the neck, and from the twin stumps of the horns, severed just below the chin.

Kit Fisto gasped, "Saesee!"

The headless corpse, still standing, twisted as its knees buck-led, and a thin sigh escaped from its trachea as it folded to the floor.

"It doesn't . . ." Agen Kolar swayed.

His emerald blade shrank away, and the handgrip tumbled from his opening fingers. A small, neat hole in the middle of his forehead leaked smoke, showing light from the back of his head.

". . . hurt . . ."

He pitched forward onto his face, and lay still.

Palpatine stood at the doorway, but the door stayed shut. From his right hand extended a blade the color of fire.

The door locked itself at his back.

"Help! Help!" Palpatine cried like a man in desperate fear for his life. "Security—*someone*! Help me! *Murder! Treason!*"

Then he smiled.

He held one finger to his lips, and, astonishingly, he winked.

In the blank second that followed, while Mace Windu and Kit Fisto could do no more than angle their lightsabers to guard, Palpatine swiftly stepped over the bodies back toward his desk, reversed his blade, and drove it in a swift, surgically precise stab down through his desktop.

"That's enough of *that*."

He let it burn its way free through the front, then he turned, lifting his weapon, appearing to study it as one might study the face of a beloved friend one has long thought dead. Power gathered around him until the Force shimmered with darkness.

"If you only knew," he said softly, perhaps speaking to the Jedi Masters, or perhaps to himself, or perhaps even to the scarlet blade lifted now as though in mocking salute, "how long I have been waiting for this . . ."

Anakin's speeder shrieked through the rain, dodging forked bolts of lightning that shot up from towers into the clouds, slicing across traffic lanes, screaming past spacescrapers so fast that his shock-wake cracked windows as he passed.

He didn't understand why people didn't just get out of his way. He didn't understand how the trillion beings who jammed Galactic City could go about their trivial business as though the universe hadn't changed. How could they think they counted for anything, compared with him?

How could they think they still mattered?

Their blind lives meant nothing now. None of them. Because ahead, on the vast cliff face of the Senate Office Building, one window spat lightning into the rain to echo the lightning of the storm outside—but this lightning was the color of clashing lightsabers.

Green fans, sheets of purple—

And crimson flame.

He was too late.

The green fire faded and winked out; now the lightning was only purple and red.

His repulsorlifts howled as he heeled the speeder up onto its side, skidding through wind-shear turbulence to bring it to a bobbing halt outside the window of Palpatine's private office. A blast of lightning hit the spire of 500 Republica, only a kilometer away, and its white burst flared off the window, flash-blinding him; he blinked furiously, slapping at his eyes in frustration.

The colorless glare inside his eyes faded slowly, bringing into focus a jumble of bodies on the floor of Palpatine's private office.

Bodies in Jedi robes.

On Palpatine's desk lay the head of Kit Fisto, faceup, scalp-tentacles unbound in a squid-tangle across the ebonite. His lid-less eyes stared blindly at the ceiling. Anakin remembered him in the arena at Geonosis, effortlessly carving his way through wave after wave of combat droids, on his lips a gently humorous smile as though the horrific battle were only some friendly jest. His severed head wore that same smile.

Maybe he thought death was funny, too.

Anakin's own blade sang blue as it slashed through the window and he dived through the gap. He rolled to his feet among a litter of bodies and sprinted through a shattered door along the small private corridor and through a doorway that flashed and flared with energy-scatter.

Anakin skidded to a stop.

Within the public office of the Supreme Chancellor of the Galactic Republic, a last Jedi Master battled alone, blade-to-blade, against a living shadow.

Sinking into Vaapad, Mace Windu fought for his life.

More than his life: each whirl of blade and whipcrack of lightning was a strike in defense of democracy, of justice and peace, of the rights of ordinary beings to live their own lives in their own ways.

He was fighting for the Republic that he loved.

Vaapad, the seventh form of lightsaber combat, takes its name from a notoriously dangerous predator native to the moons of Sarapin: a vaapad attacks its prey with whipping strikes of its blindingly fast tentacles. Most have at least seven. It is not uncommon for them to have as many as twelve; the largest ever killed had twenty-three. With a vaapad, one never knew how many tentacles it had until it was dead: they move too fast to count. Almost too fast to see.

So did Mace's blade.

Vaapad is as aggressive and powerful as its namesake, but its power comes at great risk: immersion in Vaapad opens the gates that restrain one's inner darkness. To use Vaapad, a Jedi must allow himself to *enjoy* the fight; he must give himself over to the thrill of battle. The rush of *winning*. Vaapad is a path that leads through the penumbra of the dark side.

Mace Windu created this style, and he was its only living master.

This was Vaapad's ultimate test.

Anakin blinked and rubbed his eyes again. Maybe he was still a bit flash-blind—the Korun Master seemed to be fading in and out of existence, half swallowed by a thickening black haze in which danced a meter-long bar of sunfire. Mace pressed back the darkness with a relentless straight-ahead march; his own blade, that distinctive amethyst blaze that had been the final sight of so many evil beings across the galaxy, made a haze of its own: an oblate sphere of purple fire within which there seemed to be dozens of swords slashing in all directions at once.

The shadow he fought, that blur of speed—could that be *Palpatine*?

Their blades flared and flashed, crashing together with bursts of fire, weaving nets of killing energy in exchanges so fast that Anakin could not truly see them—

But he could feel them in the Force.

The Force itself roiled and burst and crashed around them, boiling with power and lightspeed ricochets of lethal intent.

And it was darkening.

Anakin could feel how the Force fed upon the shadow's murderous exaltation; he could feel fury spray into the Force though some poisonous abscess had crested in both their hearts.

There was no Jedi restraint here.

Mace Windu was cutting loose.

Mace was deep in it now: submerged in Vaapad, swallowed by it, he no longer truly existed as an independent being.

Vaapad is a channel for darkness, and that darkness flowed both ways. He accepted the furious speed of the Sith Lord, drew the shadow's rage and power into his inmost center—

And let it fountain out again.

He reflected the fury upon its source as a lightsaber redirects a blaster bolt.

There was a time when Mace Windu had feared the power of the dark; there was a time when he had feared the darkness in himself. But the Clone Wars had given him a gift of understanding: on a world called Haruun Kal, he had faced his darkness and had learned that the power of darkness is not to be feared.

He had learned that it is fear that gives the darkness power.

He was not afraid. The darkness had no power over him. But—

Neither did he have power over it.

Vaapad made him an open channel, half of a superconducting loop completed by the shadow; they became a standing wave of battle that expanded into every cubic centimeter of the Chancellor's office. There was no scrap of carpet nor shred of chair that might not at any second disintegrate in flares of red or purple; lampstands became brief shields, sliced into segments that whirled through the air; couches became terrain to be climbed for advantage or overleapt in retreat. But there was still only the cycle of power, the endless loop, no wound taken on either side, not even the possibility of fatigue.

Impasse.

Which might have gone on forever, if Vaapad were Mace's only gift.

The fighting was effortless for him now; he let his body handle it without the intervention of his mind. While his blade spun and crackled, while his feet slid and his weight shifted and his shoulders turned in precise curves of their own direction, his mind slid along the circuit of dark power, tracing it back to its limitless source.

Feeling for its shatterpoint.

He found a knot of fault lines in the shadow's future; he chose the largest fracture and followed it back to the here and the now—

And it led him, astonishingly, to a man standing frozen in the slashed-open doorway. Mace had no need to look; the presence in the Force was familiar, and was as uplifting as sunlight breaking through a thunderhead.

The chosen one was here.

Mace disengaged from the shadow's blade and leapt for the window; he slashed away the transparisteel with a single flourish.

His instant's distraction cost him: a dark surge of the Force nearly blew him right out of the gap he had just cut. Only a desperate Force-push of his own altered his path enough that he slammed into a stanchion instead of plunging half a kilometer from the ledge outside. He bounced off and the Force cleared his head and once again he gave himself to Vaapad.

He could feel the end of this battle approaching, and so

could the blur of Sith he faced; in the Force, the shadow had become a pulsar of fear. Easily, almost effortlessly, he turned the shadow's fear into a weapon: he angled the battle to bring them both out onto the window ledge.

Out in the wind. Out with the lightning. Out on a rain-slicked ledge above a half-kilometer drop.

Out where the shadow's fear made it hesitate. Out where the shadow's fear turned some of its Force-powered speed into a Force-powered grip on the slippery permacrete.

Out where Mace could flick his blade in one precise arc and slash the shadow's lightsaber in half.

One piece flipped back in through the cut-open window. The other tumbled from opening fingers, bounced on the ledge, and fell through the rain toward the distant alleys below.

Now the shadow was only Palpatine: old and shrunken, thinning hair bleached white by time and care, face lined with exhaustion.

"For all your power, you are no Jedi. All you are, my lord," Mace said evenly, staring past his blade, "is under arrest."

"Do you see, Anakin? Do you?" Palpatine's voice once again had the broken cadence of a frightened old man's. "Didn't I warn you of the Jedi and their treason?"

"Save your twisted words, my lord. There are no politicians here. The Sith will never regain control of the Republic. It's over. You've lost." Mace leveled his blade. "You lost for the same reason the Sith always lose: defeated by your own fear."

Palpatine lifted his head.

His eyes smoked with hate.

"Fool," he said.

He lifted his arms, his robes of office spreading wide into raptor's wings, his hands hooking into talons.

"Fool!" His voice was a shout of thunder. "Do you think the fear you feel is *mine?*"

Lighting blasted the clouds above, and lightning blasted from Palpatine's hands, and Mace didn't have time to comprehend what Palpatine was talking about; he had time only to slip back into Vaapad and angle his blade to catch the forking arcs of pure, dazzling hatred that clawed toward him.

Because Vaapad is more than a fighting style. It is a state of mind: a channel for darkness. Power passed into him and out again without touching him.

And the circuit completed itself: the lightning reflected back to its source.

Palpatine staggered, snarling, but the blistering energy that poured from his hands only intensified.

He fed the power with his pain.

"Anakin!" Mace called. His voice sounded distant, blurred, as if it came from the bottom of a well. "Anakin, help me! This is your chance!"

He felt Anakin's leap from the office floor to the ledge, felt his approach behind—

And Palpatine was not afraid.

Mace could feel it: he wasn't worried at all.

"Destroy this traitor," the Chancellor said, his voice raised over the howl of writhing energy that joined his hands to Mace's blade. "This was never an arrest. It's an *assassination!*"

That was when Mace finally understood. He had it. The key to final victory. Palpatine's shatterpoint. The absolute shatterpoint of the Sith.

The shatterpoint of the dark side itself.

Mace thought, blankly astonished, *Palpatine trusts Anakin Skywalker* . . .

Now Anakin was at Mace's shoulder. Palpatine still made no move to defend himself from Skywalker; instead he ramped up the lightning bursting from his hands, bending the fountain of Mace's blade back toward the Korun Master's face.

Palpatine's eyes glowed with power, casting a yellow glare that burned back the rain from around them. "He is a traitor, Anakin. Destroy him."

"You're the chosen one, Anakin," Mace said, his voice going thin with strain. This was beyond Vaapad; he had no strength left to fight against his own blade. "Take him. It's your *destiny.*"

Skywalker echoed him faintly. "Destiny . . ."

"Help me! I can't hold on any longer!" The yellow glare from Palpatine's eyes spread outward through his flesh. His skin flowed like oil, as though the muscle beneath was burning away, as though even the bones of his skull were softening, were bending and bulging, deforming from the heat and pressure of his electric hatred. "He is *killing* me, Anakin—! Please, Ana*aahhh*—"

Mace's blade bent so close to his face that he was choking on ozone. "Anakin, he's too *strong* for me—"

"*Ahhh*—" Palpatine's roar above the endless blast of lightning became a fading moan of despair.

The lightning swallowed itself, leaving only the night and the rain, and an old man crumpled to his knees on a slippery ledge.

"I . . . can't. I give up. I . . . I am too weak, in the end. Too old, and too weak. Don't kill me, Master Jedi. Please. I surrender."

Victory flooded through Mace's aching body. He lifted his blade. "You Sith *disease*—"

"*Wait*—" Skywalker seized his lightsaber arm with desperate strength. "Don't kill him—you can't just *kill* him, Master—"

"Yes, I can," Mace said, grim and certain. "I have to."

"You came to *arrest* him. He has to stand *trial*—"

"A trial would be a joke. He controls the courts. He controls the Senate—"

"So are you going to kill all *them,* too? Like he *said* you would?"

Mace yanked his arm free. "He's too dangerous to be left alive. If you could have taken *Dooku* alive, would you have?"

Skywalker's face swept itself clean of emotion. "That was *different*—"

Mace turned toward the cringing, beaten Sith Lord. "You can explain the difference after he's dead."

He raised his lightsaber.

"*I* need him *alive!*" Skywalker shouted. "I need him to save *Padmé!*"

Mace thought blankly, *Why?* And moved his lightsaber toward the fallen Chancellor.

Before he could follow through on his stroke, a sudden arc of blue plasma sheared through his wrist and his hand tumbled away with his lightsaber still in it and Palpatine roared back to his feet and lightning speared from the Sith Lord's hands and without his blade to catch it, the power of Palpatine's hate struck him full-on.

He had been so intent on Palpatine's shatterpoint that he'd never thought to look for Anakin's.

Dark lightning blasted away his universe.

He fell forever.

Anakin Skywalker knelt in the rain.

He was looking at a hand. The hand had brown skin. The hand held a lightsaber. The hand had a charred oval of tissue where it should have been attached to an arm.

"What have I done?"

Was it his voice? It must have been. Because it was his question.

"What have I done?"

Another hand, a warm and human hand, laid itself softly on his shoulder.

"You're following your destiny, Anakin," said a familiar gentle voice. "The Jedi are traitors. You saved the Republic from their treachery. You can see that, can't you?"

"You were right," Anakin heard himself saying. "Why didn't I know?"

"You couldn't have. They cloaked themselves in deception, my boy. Because they feared your power, they could never trust you."

Anakin stared at the hand, but he no longer saw it. "Obi-Wan—Obi-Wan trusts me . . ."

"Not enough to tell you of their plot."

Treason echoed in his memory.

. . . *this is not an assignment for the record* . . .

That warm and human hand gave his shoulder a warm and human squeeze. "I do not fear your power, Anakin, I *embrace* it.

You are the greatest of the Jedi. You can be the greatest of the Sith. I believe that, Anakin. I believe in *you*. *I* trust you. I *trust* you. I trust *you*."

Anakin looked from the dead hand on the ledge to the living one on his shoulder, then up to the face of the man who stood above him, and what he saw there choked him like an invisible fist crushing his throat.

The hand on his shoulder was human.

The face . . . wasn't.

The eyes were a cold and feral yellow, and they gleamed like those of a predator lurking beyond a fringe of firelight; the bone around those feral eyes had swollen and melted and flowed like durasteel spilled from a fusion smelter, and the flesh that blanketed it had gone corpse-gray and coarse as rotten synthplast.

Stunned with horror, stunned with revulsion, Anakin could only stare at the creature. At the shadow.

Looking into the face of the darkness, he saw his future.

"Now come inside," the darkness said.

After a moment, he did.

Anakin stood just within the office. Motionless.

Palpatine examined the damage to his face in a broad expanse of wall mirror. Anakin couldn't tell if his expression might be revulsion, or if this were merely the new shape of his features. Palpatine lifted one tentative hand to the misshapen horror that he now saw in the mirror, then simply shrugged.

"And so the mask becomes the man," he sighed with a hint of philosophical melancholy. "I shall miss the face of Palpatine, I think; but for our purpose, the face of Sidious will serve. Yes, it will serve."

He gestured, and a hidden compartment opened in the office's ceiling above his desk. A voluminous robe of heavy black-on-black brocade floated downward from it; Anakin felt the current in the Force that carried the robe to Palpatine's hand.

He remembered playing a Force game with a shuura fruit, sitting across a long table from Padmé in the retreat by the lake on Naboo. He remembered telling her how grumpy Obi-Wan would be to see him use the Force so casually.

Palaptine seemed to catch his thought; he gave a yellow sidelong glance as the robe settled onto his shoulders.

"You must learn to cast off the petty restraints that the Jedi have tried to place upon your power," he said. "Anakin, it's time. I need you to help me restore order to the galaxy."

Anakin didn't respond.

Sidious said, "Join me. Pledge yourself to the Sith. Become my apprentice."

A wave of tingling started at the base of Anakin's skull and spread over his whole body in a slow-motion shockwave.

"I—I can't."

"Of course you can."

Anakin shook his head and found that the rest of him threatened to begin shaking as well. "I—came to save your life, sir. Not to betray my friends—"

Sidious snorted. "*What* friends?"

Anakin could find no answer.

"And do you think that task is finished, my boy?" Sidious seated himself on the corner of the desk, hands folded in his lap, the way he always had when offering Anakin fatherly advice; the misshapen mask of his face made the familiarity of his posture into something horrible. "Do you think that killing one traitor will end treason? Do you think the Jedi will ever stop until I am dead?"

Anakin stared at his hands. The left one was shaking. He hid it behind him.

"It's them or me, Anakin. Or perhaps I should put it more plainly: It's them or *Padmé*."

Anakin made his right hand—his black-gloved hand of durasteel and electrodrivers—into a fist.

"It's just—it's not . . . easy, that's all. I have—I've been a Jedi for so long—"

Sidious offered an appalling smile. "There is a place within you, my boy, a place as briskly clean as ice on a mountaintop, cool and remote. Find that high place, and look down within yourself; breathe that clean, icy air as you regard your guilt and shame. Do not deny them; observe them. Take your horror in your hands and look at it. Examine it as a phenomenon. Smell it. Taste it. Come to know it as only you can, for it is yours, and it is precious."

As the shadow beside him spoke, its words became true. From a remote, frozen distance that was at the same time more extravagantly, hotly intimate than he could have ever dreamed, Anakin handled his emotions. He dissected them. He reassembled them and pulled them apart again. He still felt them—if anything, they burned hotter than before—but they no longer had the power to cloud his mind.

"You have found it, my boy: I can feel you there. That cold distance—that mountaintop within yourself—that is the first key to the power of the Sith."

Anakin opened his eyes and turned his gaze fully upon the grotesque features of Darth Sidious.

He didn't even blink.

As he looked upon that mask of corruption, the revulsion he felt was real, and it was powerful, and it was—

Interesting.

Anakin lifted his hand of durasteel and electrodrivers and cupped it, staring into its palm as though he held there the fear that had haunted his dreams for his whole life, and it was no larger than the piece of shuura he'd once stolen from Padmé's plate.

On the mountain peak within himself, he weighed Padmé's life against the Jedi Order.

It was no contest.

He said, "Yes."

"Yes to what, my boy?"

"Yes, I want your knowledge."

"Good. Good!"

"I want your power. I want the power to stop death."

"That power only my Master truly achieved, but together we will find it. The Force is strong with you, my boy. You can do *anything*."

"The Jedi betrayed you," Anakin said. "The Jedi betrayed both of us."

"As you say. Are you ready?"

"I am," he said, and meant it. "I give myself to you. I pledge myself to the ways of the Sith. Take me as your apprentice. Teach me. Lead me. Be my Master."

Sidious raised the hood of his robe and draped it to shadow the ruin of his face.

"Kneel before me, Anakin Skywalker."

Anakin dropped to one knee. He lowered his head.

"It is your will to join your destiny forever with the Order of the Sith Lords?"

There was no hesitation. "Yes."

Darth Sidious laid a pale hand on Anakin's brow. "Then it is done. You are now one with the Order of the Dark Lords of the Sith. From this day forward, the truth of you, my apprentice, now and forevermore, will be Darth . . ."

A pause; a questioning in the Force—

An answer, dark as the gap between galaxies—

He heard Sidious say it: his new name.

Vader.

A pair of syllables that meant *him*.

Vader, he said to himself. *Vader.*

"Thank you, my Master."

"Every single Jedi, including your friend Obi-Wan Kenobi, have been revealed as enemies of the Republic now. You understand that, don't you?"

"Yes, my Master."

"The Jedi are relentless. If they are not destroyed to the last being, there will be civil war without end. To sterilize the Jedi Temple will be your first task. Do what must be done, Lord Vader."

"I always have, my Master."

"Do not hesitate. Show no mercy. Leave no living creature behind. Only then will you be strong enough with the dark side to save Padmé."

"What of the other Jedi?"

"Leave them to me. After you have finished at the Temple, your second task will be the Separatist leadership, in their 'secret bunker' on Mustafar. When you have killed them all, the Sith will rule the galaxy once more, and we shall have peace. Forever.

"Rise, Darth Vader."

The Sith Lord who once had been a Jedi hero called Anakin Skywalker stood, drawing himself up to his full height, but he looked not outward upon his new Master, nor upon the planet-city beyond, nor out into the galaxy that they would soon rule. He instead turned his gaze inward: he unlocked the furnace gate within his heart and stepped forth to regard with new eyes the cold freezing dread of the dead-star dragon that had haunted his life.

I am Darth Vader, he said within himself.

The dragon tried again to whisper of failure, and weakness, and inevitable death, but with one hand the Sith Lord caught it, crushed away its voice; it tried to rise then, to coil and rear and strike, but the Sith Lord laid his other hand upon it and broke its power with a single effortless twist.

I am Darth Vader, he repeated as he ground the dragon's corpse to dust beneath his mental heel, as he watched the dragon's dust and ashes scatter before the blast from his furnace heart, *and you—*

You are nothing at all.

He had become, finally, what they all called him.

The Hero With No Fear.

Gate Master Jurokk sprinted through the empty vaulted hallway, clattering echoes of his footsteps making him sound like a platoon. The main doors of the Temple were slowly swinging inward in answer to the code key punched into the outside lockpad.

The Gate Master had seen him on the monitor.

Anakin Skywalker.

Alone.

The huge doors creaked inward; as soon as they were wide enough for the Gate Master to pass, he slipped through.

Anakin stood in the night outside, shoulders hunched, head down against the rain.

"Anakin!" he gasped, running up to the young man. "Anakin, what happened? Where are the Masters?"

Anakin looked at him as though he wasn't sure who the Gate Master was. "Where is Shaak Ti?"

"In the meditation chambers—we felt something happen in the Force, something awful. She's searching the Force in deep meditation, trying to get some feel for what's going on . . ."

His words trailed away. Anakin didn't seem to be listening.

"Something *has* happened, hasn't it?"

Jurokk looked past him now. The night beyond the Temple was full of clones. Battalions of them. Brigades.

Thousands.

"Anakin," he said slowly, "what's going on? Something's happened. Something horrible. How bad *is* it—?"

The last thing Jurokk felt was the emitter of a lightsaber against the soft flesh beneath his jaw; the last thing he heard, as blue plasma chewed upward through his head and burst from the top of his skull and burned away his life, was Anakin Skywalker's melancholy reply.

"You have no idea . . ."

ORDER SIXTY-SIX

Pau City was a cauldron of battle.

From his observation post just off the landing ramp of the command lander on the tenth level, Clone Commander Cody swept the sinkhole with his electrobinoculars. The droid-control center lay in ruins only a few meters away, but the Separatists had learned the lesson of Naboo; their next-generation combat droids were equipped with sophisticated self-motivators that kicked in automatically when control signals were cut off, delivering a program of standing orders.

Standing Order Number One was, apparently, Kill Everything That Moves.

And they were doing a good job of it, too.

Half the city was rubble, and the rest was a firestorm of droids and clones and Utapaun dragon cavalry, and just when Commander Cody was thinking how he really wished they had a Jedi or two around right now, several metric tons of dragon-mount hurtled from the sky and hit the roof of the command lander hard enough to buckle the deck beneath it.

Not that it did the ship any harm; *Jadthu*-class landers are basically flying bunkers, and this particular one was triple-armored and equipped with internal shock buffers and inertial dampeners powerful enough for a fleet corvette, to protect the sophisticated command-and-control equipment inside.

Cody looked up at the dragonmount, and at its rider. "General Kenobi," he said. "Glad you could join us."

"Commander Cody," the Jedi Master said with a nod. He was still scanning the battle around them. "Did you contact Coruscant with the news of the general's death?"

The clone commander snapped to attention and delivered a crisp salute. "As ordered, sir. Erm, sir?"

Kenobi looked down at him.

"Are you all right, sir? You're a bit of a mess."

The Jedi Master wiped away some of the dust and gore that smeared his face with the sleeve of his robe—which was charred, and only left a blacker smear across his cheek. "Ah. Well, yes. It has been a . . . stressful day." He waved out at Pau City. "But we still have a battle to win."

"Then I suppose you'll be wanting this," Cody said, holding up the lightsaber his men had recovered from a traffic tunnel. "I believe you dropped it, sir."

"Ah. Ah, yes."

The weapon floated gently up to Kenobi's hand, and when he smiled down at the clone commander again, Cody could swear the Jedi Master was blushing, just a bit. "No, ah, need to mention this to, erm, Anakin, is there, Cody?"

Cody grinned. "Is that an order, sir?"

Kenobi shook his head, chuckling tiredly. "Let's go. You'll have noticed I *did* manage to leave a few droids for you . . ."

"Yes, sir." A silent buzzing vibration came from a compartment concealed within his armor. Cody frowned. "Go on ahead, General. We'll be right behind you."

That concealed compartment held a secure comlink, which was frequency-locked to a channel reserved for the commander in chief.

Kenobi nodded and spoke to his mount, and the great beast overleapt the clone commander on its way down into the battle.

Cody withdrew the comlink from his armor and triggered it.

A holoscan appeared on the palm of his gauntlet: a hooded man.

"It is time," the holoscan said. *"Execute Order Sixty-Six."*

Cody responded as he had been trained since before he'd even awakened in his crèche-school. "It will be done, my lord."

The holoscan vanished. Cody stuck the comlink back into its concealed recess and frowned down toward where Kenobi rode his dragonmount into selflessly heroic battle.

Cody was a clone. He would execute the order faithfully, without hesitation or regret. But he was also human enough to mutter glumly, "Would it have been too much to ask for the order to have come through *before* I gave him back the bloody *lightsaber* . . . ?"

The order is given once. Its wave-front spreads to clone commanders on Kashyyyk and Felucia, Mygeeto and Tellanroaeg and every battlefront, every military installation, every hospital and rehab center and spaceport cantina in the galaxy.

Except for Coruscant.

On Coruscant, Order Sixty-Six is already being executed.

Dawn crept across Galactic City. Fingers of morning brought a rose-colored glow to the wind-smeared upper reach of a vast twisting cone of smoke.

Bail Organa was a man not given to profanity, but when he caught a glimpse of the source of that smoke from the pilot's chair of his speeder, the curse it brought to his lips would have made a Corellian dockhand blush.

He stabbed a code that canceled his speeder's programmed

route toward the Senate Office Building, then grabbed the yoke and kicked the craft into a twisting dive that shot him through half a dozen crisscrossing streams of air traffic.

He triggered his speeder's comm. "Antilles!"

The answer from the captain of his personal crew was instant. *"Yes, my lord?"*

"Route an alert to SER," he ordered. "The Jedi Temple is on fire!"

"Yes, sir. We know. Senate Emergency Response has announced a state of martial law, and the Temple is under lockdown. There's been some kind of Jedi rebellion."

"What are you talking about? That's impossible. Why aren't there fireships onstation?"

"I don't have any details, my lord; we only know what SER is telling us."

"Look, I'm right on top of it. I'm going down there to find out what's happening."

"My lord, I wouldn't recommend it—"

"I won't take any chances." Bail hauled the control yoke to slew the speeder toward the broad landing deck on the roof of the Temple ziggurat. "Speaking of not taking chances, Captain: order the duty crew onto the *Tantive* and get her engines warm. I've got a bad feeling about this."

"Sir?"

"Just do it."

Bail set the speeder down only a few meters from the deck entrance and hopped out. A squad of clone troopers stood in the open doorway. Smoke billowed out from the hallway behind them.

One of the troopers lifted a hand as Bail approached. "Don't worry, sir, everything is under control here."

"Under control? Where are the SER teams? What is the *army* doing here?"

"I'm sorry, I can't talk about that, sir."

"Has there been some kind of attack on the Temple?"

"I'm sorry, I can't talk about that, sir."

"Listen to me, Sergeant, I am a Senator of the Galactic Republic," Bail said, improvising, "and I am late for a meeting with the Jedi Council—"

"The Jedi Council is not in session, sir."

"Maybe you should let me see for myself."

The four clones moved together to block his path. "I'm sorry, sir. Entry is forbidden."

"I am a *Senator*—"

"Yes, sir." The clone sergeant snapped his DC-15 to his shoulder, and Bail, blinking, found himself staring into its blackened muzzle from close enough to kiss it. "And it is time for you to leave, sir."

"When you put it that way . . ." Bail backed off, lifting his hands. "Yes, all right, I'm going."

A burst of blasterfire ripped through the smoke and scattered into the dawn outside. Bail stared with an open mouth as a Jedi flashed out of nowhere and started cutting down clones. No: not a Jedi.

A boy.

A child, no more than ten years old, swinging a lightsaber whose blade was almost as long as he was tall. More blasterfire came from inside, and a whole platoon of clones came pelting toward the landing deck, and the ten-year-old was hit, and hit again, and then just shot to rags among the bodies of the troopers he'd killed, and Bail started backing away, faster now, and in the middle of it all, a clone wearing the colors of a commander came out of the smoke and pointed at Bail Organa.

"No witnesses," the commmander said. "Kill him."

Bail ran.

He dived through a hail of blasterfire, hit the deck, and rolled under his speeder to the opposite side. He grabbed on to its pilot's-side door and swung his leg onto a tail fin, using the vehicle's body as cover while he stabbed the keys to reinitialize its autorouter. Clones charged toward him, firing as they came.

His speeder heeled over and blasted away.

Bail pulled himself inside as the speeder curved up into the congested traffic lanes. He was white as flimsiplast, and his hands were shaking so badly he could barely activate his comm.

"Antilles! Organa to Antilles. Come in, Captain!"

"Antilles here, my lord."

"It's worse than I thought. Far worse than you've heard. Send someone to Chance Palp—no, strike that. Go yourself. Take five men and go to the spaceport. I know at least one Jedi ship is on the ground there; Saesee Tiin brought in *Sharp Spiral* late last night. I need you to steal his homing beacon."

"What? His beacon? Why?"

"No time to explain. Get the beacon and meet me at the *Tantive*. We're leaving the planet."

He stared back at the vast column of smoke that boiled from the Jedi Temple.

"While we still can."

———

Order Sixty-Six is the climax of the Clone Wars.

Not the end—the Clone Wars will end some few hours from now, when a coded signal, sent by Nute Gunray from the secret Separatist bunker on Mustafar, deactivates every combat droid in the galaxy at once—but the climax.

It's not a thrilling climax; it's not the culmination of an epic struggle. Just the opposite, in fact. The Clone Wars were never an epic struggle. They were never intended to be.

What is happening right now is why the Clone Wars were fought in the first place. It is their reason for existence. The Clone Wars have always been, in and of themselves, from their very inception, the revenge of the Sith.

They were irresistible bait. They took place in remote locations, on planets that belonged, primarily, to "somebody else." They were fought by expendable proxies. And they were constructed as a win–win situation.

The Clone Wars were the perfect Jedi trap.

By fighting at all, the Jedi lost.

With the Jedi Order overextended, spread thin across the galaxy, each Jedi is alone, surrounded only by whatever clone troops he, she, or it commands. War itself pours darkness into the Force, deepening the cloud that limits Jedi perception. And the clones have no malice, no hatred, not the slightest ill intent that might give warning. They are only following orders.

In this case, Order Sixty-Six.

Hold-out blasters appear in clone hands. ARC-170s drop back onto the tails of Jedi starfighters. AT-STs swivel their guns. Turrets on hovertanks swung silently.

Clones open fire, and Jedi die.

All across the galaxy. All at once.

Jedi die.

Kenobi never saw it coming.

Cody had coordinated the heavy-weapons operators from five different companies spread over an arc of three different levels of the sinkhole-city. He'd served under Kenobi in more than a dozen operations since the beginning of the Outer Rim sieges, and he had a very clear and unsentimental estimate of just how hard to kill the unassuming Jedi Master was. He wasn't taking any chances.

He raised his comlink. "Execute."

On that order, T-21 muzzles swung, shoulder-fired torps locked on, and proton grenade launchers angled to precisely calibrated elevations.

"Fire."

They did.

Kenobi, his dragonmount, and all five of the destroyer droids he'd been fighting vanished in a fireball that for an instant outshone Utapau's sun.

Visual polarizers in Cody's helmet cut the glare by 78 percent; his vision cleared in plenty of time to see shreds of dragonmount and twisted hunks of droid raining into the ocean mouth at the bottom of the sinkhole.

Cody scowled and keyed his comlink. "Looks like the lizard took the worst of it. Deploy the seekers. All of them."

He stared down into the boil of the ocean mouth.

"I want to see the body."

C-3PO paused in the midst of dusting the Tarka-Null original on its display pedestal near his mistress's bedroom view wall, and used the electrostatic tissue to briefly polish his own photoreceptors. The astromech in the green Jedi starfighter docking with the veranda below—could that be R2-D2?

Well, this should be interesting.

Senator Amidala had spent the better part of these predawn hours simply staring over the city, toward the plume of smoke that rose from the Jedi Temple; now, at last, she might get some answers.

He might, too. R2-D2 was far from the sort of sparkling conversationalist with whom C-3PO preferred to associate, but the little astromech had a positive gift for jacking himself into the motherboards of the most volatile situations . . .

The cockpit popped open, and inevitably the Jedi within was revealed to be Anakin Skywalker. In watching Master Anakin climb down from the starfighter's cockpit, 3PO's photoreceptors captured data that unexpectedly activated his threat-aversion subroutines. "Oh," he said faintly, clutching at his power core. "Oh, I don't like the looks of *this* at all . . ."

He dropped the electrostatic tissue and shuffled as quickly as he could to the bedroom door. "My lady," he called to Senator Amidala, where she stood by the broad window. "On the veranda. A Jedi starfighter," he forced out. "Has docked, my lady."

She blinked, then rushed toward the bedroom door.

C-3PO shuffled along behind her and slipped out through the open door, making a wide circle around the humans, who were engaged in one of those inexplicable embraces they seemed so fond of.

Reaching the starfighter, he said, "Artoo, are you all right? What is going on?"

The astromech squeaked and beeped; C-3PO's autotranslator interpreted: NOBODY TELLS ME ANYTHING.

"Of course not. You don't keep up your end of the conversation."

A whirring squeal: SOMETHING'S WRONG. THE FACTORS DON'T BALANCE.

"You can't possibly be more confused than I am."

YOU'RE RIGHT. NOBODY CAN BE MORE CONFUSED THAN YOU ARE.

"Oh, very funny. Hush now—what was that?"

The Senator was sitting now, leaning distractedly on one of the tasteful, elegant bistro tables that dotted the veranda, while Master Anakin stood above her. "I think—he's saying something about a *rebellion*—that the Jedi have tried to overthrow the Republic! And—oh, my goodness. Mace Windu has tried to assassinate Chancellor Palpatine! Can he be *serious*?"

I DON'T KNOW. ANAKIN DOESN'T TALK TO ME ANYMORE.

C-3PO shook his cranial assembly helplessly. "How can Master Windu be an assassin? He has such impeccable manners."

LIKE I TOLD YOU: THE FACTORS DON'T ADD UP.

"I've been hearing the most awful rumors—they're saying the government is going to *banish* us—banish *droids,* can you imagine?"

DON'T BELIEVE EVERYTHING YOU HEAR.

"Shh. Not so loud!"

I'M ONLY SAYING THAT WE DON'T KNOW THE TRUTH.

"Of course we don't." C-3PO sighed. "And we likely never will."

"What about Obi-Wan?"

She looked stricken. Pale and terrified.

It made him love her more.

He shook his head. "Many of the Jedi have been killed."

"But . . ." She stared out at the rivers of traffic crosshatching the sky. "Are you *sure*? It seems so . . . *unbelievable* . . ."

"I was there, Padmé. It's all true."

"But . . . but how could *Obi-Wan* be involved in something like that?"

He said, "We may never know."

"Outlawed . . . ," she murmured. "What happens now?"

"All Jedi are required to surrender themselves immediately," he said. "Those who resist . . . are being dealt with."

"Anakin—they're your *family*—"

"They're traitors. *You're* my family. You and the baby."

"How can *all* of them be traitors—?"

"They're not the only ones. There were Senators in this as well."

Now, finally, she looked at him, and fear shone from her eyes.

He smiled.

"Don't worry. I won't let anything happen to you."

"To *me*?"

"You need to distance yourself from your . . . friends . . . in the Senate, Padmé. It's very important to avoid even the appearance of disloyalty."

"Anakin—you sound like you're *threatening* me . . ."

"This is a dangerous time," he said. "We are all judged by the company we keep."

"But—I've opposed the war, I opposed Palpatine's emergency powers—I publicly called him a *threat to democracy*!"

"That's all behind us now."

"*What* is? What I've done? Or democracy?"

"Padmé—"

Her chin came up, and her eyes hardened. "Am I under suspicion?"

"Palpatine and I have discussed you already. You're in the clear, so long as you avoid . . . inappropriate associations."

"How am I *in the clear*?"

"Because you're with *me*. Because I *say* you are."

She stared at him as if she'd never seen him before. "You told him."

"He knew."

"Anakin—"

"There's no more need for secrets, Padmé. Don't you see? *I'm not a Jedi anymore*. There *aren't* any Jedi. There's just *me*."

He reached for her hand. She let him take it. "And you, and our child."

"Then we can *go*, can't we?" Her hard stare melted to naked appeal. "We can leave this planet. Go somewhere we can be *together*—somewhere *safe*."

"We'll be together *here*," he said. "You *are* safe. I have *made* you safe."

"Safe," she echoed bitterly, pulling her hand away. "As long as Palpatine doesn't change his mind."

The hand she had pulled from his grasp was trembling.

"The Separatist leadership is in hiding on Mustafar. I'm on my way to deal with them right now."

"*Deal* with them?" The corners of her mouth drew down. "Like the Jedi are being *dealt with*?"

"This is an important mission. I'm going to end the war."

She looked away. "You're going alone?"

"Have faith, my love," he said.

She shook her head helplessly, and a pair of tears spilled from her eyes. He touched them with his mechanical hand; the fingertips of his black glove glistened in the dawn.

Two liquid gems, indescribably precious—because they were *his*. He had earned them. As he had earned *her*; as he had earned the child she bore.

He had paid for them with innocent blood.

"I love you," he said. "This won't take long. Wait for me."

Fresh tears streamed onto her ivory cheeks, and she threw herself into his arms. "Always, Anakin. Forever. Come back to me, my love—my *life*. Come back to me."

He smiled down on her. "You say that like I'm already gone."

═══════

Icy salt water shocked Obi-Wan back to full consciousness. He hung in absolute blackness; there was no telling how far underwater he might be, nor even which direction might be up. His lungs were choked, half full of water, but he didn't panic or even particularly worry; mostly, he was vaguely pleased to discover that even in his semiconscious fall, he'd managed to hang on to his lightsaber.

He clipped it back to his belt by feel, and—using only a minor exercise of Jedi discipline to suppress convulsive coughing—he contracted his diaphragm, forcing as much water from his lungs as he could. He took from his equipment belt his rebreather, and a small compressed-air canister intended for use in an emergency, when the breathable environment was not adequate to sustain his life.

Obi-Wan was fairly certain that his current situation qualified as an emergency.

He remembered . . .

Boga's wrenching leap, twisting in the air, the shock of impacts, multiple detonations blasting both of them farther and farther out from the sinkhole wall . . .

Using her massive body to shield Obi-Wan from his own troops.

Boga had *known*, somehow . . . the dragonmount had known what Obi-Wan had been incapable of even suspecting, and without hesitation she'd given her life to save her rider.

I suppose that makes me more than her rider, Obi-Wan thought as he discarded the canister and got his rebreather snugged into place. *I suppose that makes me her friend.*

It certainly made her mine.

He let grief take him for a moment; grief not for the death of a noble beast, but for how little time Obi-Wan had had to appreciate the gift of his friend's service.

But even grief is an attachment, and Obi-Wan let it flow out of his life.

Good-bye, my friend.

He didn't try to swim; he seemed to be hanging motionless, suspended in infinite night. He relaxed, regulated his breathing, and let the water take him whither it would.

C-3PO barely had time to wish his little friend good luck and remind him to stay alert as Master Anakin brushed past him and climbed into the starfighter's cockpit, then fired the engine and blasted off, taking R2-D2 goodness knows where—probably to some preposterously horrible alien planet and into a perfectly ridiculous amount of danger—with never a thought how his loyal *droid* might feel about being *dragged* across the galaxy without so much as a by-your-leave . . .

Really, what *had* happened to that young man's manners?

He turned to Senator Amidala and saw that she was crying.

"Is there anything I can do, my lady?"

She didn't even turn his way. "No, thank you, Threepio."

"A snack, perhaps?"

She shook her head.

"A glass of water?"

"No."

All he could do was stand there. "I feel so *helpless* . . ."

She nodded, looking away again, up at the fading spark of her husband's starfighter.

"I know, Threepio," she said. "We all do."

* * *

In the underground shiplift beneath the Senate Office Building, Bail Organa was scowling as he boarded *Tantive IV.* When Captain Antilles met him at the top of the landing ramp, Bail nodded backward at the scarlet-clad figures posted around the accessways. "Since when do Redrobes guard Senate ships?"

Antilles shook his head. "I don't know, sir. I have a feeling there are some Senators whom Palpatine doesn't want leaving the planet."

Bail nodded. "Thank the Force I'm not one of them. Yet. Did you get the beacon?"

"Yes, sir. No one even tried to stop us. The clones at Chance Palp seemed confused—like they're not quite sure who's in charge."

"That'll change soon. Too soon. We'll *all* know who's in charge," Bail said grimly. "Prepare to raise ship."

"Back to Alderaan, sir?"

Bail shook his head. "Kashyyyk. There's no way to know if any Jedi have lived through this—but if I had to bet on one, my money'd be on Yoda."

Some undefinable time later, Obi-Wan felt his head and shoulders breach the surface of the lightless ocean. He unclipped his lightsaber and raised it over his head. In its blue glow he could see that he had come up in a large grotto; holding the lightsaber high, he tucked away his rebreather and sidestroked across the current to a rock outcropping that was rugged enough to offer handholds. He pulled himself out of the water.

The walls of the grotto above the waterline were pocked with openings; after inspecting the mouths of several caves, Obi-Wan came upon one where he felt a faint breath of moving air. It had a distinctly unpleasant smell—it reminded him more than a bit of the dragonmount pen—but when he doused his lightsaber for a moment and listened very closely, he could hear a faint rumble that might have been distant wheels and repulsorlifts passing over sandstone—and what was that? An air horn? Or possibly a very disturbed dragon . . . at any rate, this seemed to be the appropriate path.

He had walked only a few hundred meters before the gloom ahead of him was pierced by the white glare of high-intensity searchlights. He let his blade shrink away and pressed himself into a deep, narrow crack as a pair of seeker droids floated past.

Apparently Cody hadn't given up yet.

Their searchlights illuminated—and, apparently, awakened— some sort of immense amphibian cousin of a dragonmount; it blinked sleepily at them as it lifted its slickly glistening starfighter-sized head.

Oh, Obi-Wan thought. *That explains the smell.*

He breathed into the Force a suggestion that these small bobbing spheroids of circuitry and durasteel were actually, contrary to smell and appearance, some unexpected variety of immortally delicious confection sent down from the heavens by the kindly gods of Huge Slimy Cave-Monsters.

The Huge Slimy Cave-Monster in question promptly opened jaws that could engulf a bantha and snapped one of the seekers from the air, chewing it to slivers with every evidence of satisfaction. The second seeker emitted a startled and thoroughly alarmed *wheeepwheepwheep* and shot away into the darkness, with the creature in hot pursuit.

Reigniting his lightsaber and moving cautiously back out into the cavern, Obi-Wan came upon a nest of what must have been infant Huge Slimy Cave-Monsters; picking his way around it as they lunged and snapped and squalled at him, he reflected absently that people who thought all babies were cute should really get out more.

Obi-Wan walked, and occasionally climbed or slid or had to leap, and walked some more.

Soon the darkness in the cavern gave way to the pale glow of Utapaun traffic lighting, and Obi-Wan found himself standing in a smallish side tunnel off a major thoroughfare. This was clearly little traveled, though; the sandy dust on its floor was so thick it was practically a beach. In fact, he could clearly see the tracks of the last vehicle to pass this way.

Broad parallel tracks pocked with divots: a blade-wheeler.

And beside them stretched long splay-clawed prints of a running dragon.

Obi-Wan blinked in mild astonishment. He had never entirely grown accustomed to the way the Force always came through for him—but neither was he reluctant to accept its gifts. Frowning thoughtfully, he followed the tracks a short distance around a curve, until the tunnel gave way to the small landing platform.

Grievous's starfighter was still there. As were the remains of Grievous.

Apparently not even the local rock-vultures could stomach him.

───

Tantive IV swept through the Kashyyyk system on silent running; this was still a combat zone. Captain Antilles wouldn't even risk standard scans, because they could so easily be detected and backtraced by Separatist forces.

And the Separatists weren't the only ones Antilles was worried about.

"There's the signal again, sir. Whoops. Wait, I'll get it back." Antilles fiddled some more with the controls on the beacon. "Blasted thing," he muttered. "What, you can't calibrate it without using the Force?"

Bail stared through the forward view wall. Kashyyyk was only a tiny green disk two hundred thousand kilometers away. "Do you have a vector?"

"Roughly, sir. It seems to be on an orbital tangent, headed outsystem."

"I think we can risk a scan. Tight beam."

"Very well, sir."

Antilles gave the necessary orders, and moments later the

scan tech reported that the object they'd picked up seemed to be some sort of escape pod. "It's not a Republic model, sir—wait, here comes the database—"

The scan tech frowned at his screen. "It's . . . Wookiee, sir. That doesn't make any sense. Why would a Wookiee escape pod be *outbound* from *Kashyyyk*?"

"Interesting." Bail didn't yet allow himself to hope. "Lifesigns?"

"Yes—well, maybe . . . this reading doesn't make any . . ." The scan tech could only shrug. "I'm not sure, sir. Whatever it is, it's no Wookiee, that's for sure . . ."

For the first time all day, Bail Organa allowed himself to smile. "Captain Antilles?"

The captain saluted crisply. "On our way, sir."

Obi-Wan took General Grievous's starfighter screaming out of the atmosphere so fast he popped the gravity well and made jump before the *Vigilance* could even scramble its fighters. He reverted to realspace well beyond the system, kicked the starfighter to a new vector, and jumped again. A few more jumps of random direction and duration left him deep in interstellar space.

"You know," he said to himself, "integral hyperspace capability is rather useful in a starfighter; why don't *we* have it yet?"

While the starfighter's nav system whirred and chunked its way through recalculating his position, he punched codes to gang his Jedi comlink into the starfighter's system.

Instead of a holoscan, the comlink generated an audio signal—an accelerating series of beeps.

Obi-Wan knew that signal. Every Jedi did. It was the recall code.

It was being broadcast on every channel by every HoloNet repeater. It was supposed to mean that the war was over. It was supposed to mean that the Council had ordered all Jedi to return to the Temple immediately.

Obi-Wan suspected it actually meant what had happened on Utapau was far from an isolated incident.

He keyed the comlink for audio. He took a deep breath.

"Emergency Code Nine Thirteen," he said, and waited.

The starfighter's comm system cycled through every response frequency.

He waited some more.

"Emergency Code Nine Thirteen. This is Obi-Wan Kenobi. Repeat: Emergency Code Nine Thirteen. Are there any Jedi out there?"

He waited. His heart thumped heavily.

"Any Jedi, please respond. This is Obi-Wan Kenobi declaring a Nine Thirteen Emergency."

He tried to ignore the small, still voice inside his head that whispered he might just be the only one out here.

He might just be the only one, period.

He started punching coordinates for a single jump that would bring him close enough to pick up a signal directly from Coruscant when a burst of fuzz came over his comlink. A quick glance confirmed the frequency: a Jedi channel.

"Please repeat," Obi-Wan said. "I'm locking onto your signal. Please repeat."

The fuzz became a spray of blue laser, which gradually resolved into a fuzzy figure of a tall, slim human with dark hair and an elegant goatee. *"Master Kenobi? Are you all right? Have you been wounded?"*

"Senator Organa!" Obi-Wan exclaimed with profound relief. "No, I'm not wounded—but I'm certainly *not* all right. I need help. My clones turned on me. I barely escaped with my life!"

"There have been ambushes all over the galaxy."

Obi-Wan lowered his head, offering a silent wish to the Force that the victims might find peace within it.

"Have you had contact with any other survivors?"

"Only one," the Alderaanian Senator said grimly. *"Lock onto my coordinates. He's waiting for you."*

* * *

A curve of knuckle, skinned, black scab corrugated with dirt and leaking red—

The fringe of fray at the cuff of a beige sleeve, dark, crusted with splatter from the death of a general—

The tawny swirl of grain in wine-dark tabletop of polished Alderaanian kriin—

These were what Obi-Wan Kenobi could look at without starting to shake.

The walls of the small conference room on *Tantive IV* were too featureless to hold his attention; to look at a wall allowed his mind to wander . . .

And the shaking began.

The shaking got worse when he met the ancient green stare of the tiny alien seated across the table from him, for that wrinkled leather skin and those tufts of withered hair were his earliest memory, and they reminded Obi-Wan of the friends who had died today.

The shaking got worse still when he turned to the other being in the room, because he wore politician's robes that reminded Obi-Wan of the enemy who yet lived.

The deception. The death of Jedi Masters he had admired, of Jedi Knights who had been his friends. The death of his oath to Qui-Gon.

The death of Anakin.

Anakin must have fallen along with Mace and Agen, Saesee and Kit; fallen along with the Temple.

Along with the Order itself.

Ashes.

Ashes and dust.

Twenty-five thousand years wiped from existence in a single day.

All the dreams. All the promises.

All the *children* . . .

"We took them from their *homes.*" Obi-Wan fought to stay in his chair; the pain inside him demanded motion. It became wave after wave of tremors. "We *promised* their *families*—"

"Control yourself, you must; still Jedi, you are!"

"Yes, Master Yoda." That scab on his knuckle—focused on that, he could suppress the shaking. "Yes, we are Jedi. But what if we're the *last*?"

"If the last we are, unchanged our duty is." Yoda settled his chin onto hands folded over the head of his gimer stick. He looked every day of his nearly nine hundred years. "While one Jedi lives, survive the Order does. Resist the darkness with every breath, we must."

He lifted his head and the stick angled to poke Obi-Wan in the shin. "Especially the darkness in *ourselves,* young one. Of the dark side, despair is."

The simple truth of this called to him. Even despair is attachment: it is a grip clenched upon pain.

Slowly, very slowly, Obi-Wan Kenobi remembered what it was to be a Jedi.

He leaned back in his chair and covered his face with both hands, inhaling a thin stream of air between his palms; into himself with the air he brought pain and guilt and remorse, and as he exhaled, they trailed away and vanished in the air.

He breathed out his whole life.

Everything he had done, everything he had been, friends and enemies, dreams and hopes and fears.

Empty, he found clarity. Scrubbed clean, the Force shone through him. He sat up and nodded to Yoda.

"Yes," he said. "We may be the last. But what if we're *not*?"

Green leather brows drew together over lambent eyes. "The Temple beacon."

"Yes. Any surviving Jedi might still obey the recall, and be killed."

Bail Organa looked from one Jedi to the other, frowning. "What are you saying?"

"I'm saying," Obi-Wan replied, "that we have to go back to Coruscant."

"It's too dangerous," the Senator said instantly. "The whole planet is a *trap*—"

"Yes. We have a—ah . . ."

The loss of Anakin stabbed him.

Then he let that go, too.

"*I* have," he corrected himself, "a policy on traps . . ."

THE FACE OF THE SITH

Mustafar burned with lava streaming from volcanoes of glittering obsidian.

At the fringe of its gravity well, a spray of prismatic starlight warped a starfighter into existence. Declamping from its hyperdrive ring, the starfighter streaked into an atmosphere choked with dense smoke and cinders.

The starfighter followed a preprogrammed course toward the planet's lone installation, an automated lava mine built originally by the Techno Union to draw precious metals from the continuous rivers of burning stone. Upgraded with the finest mechanized defenses that money could buy, the settlement had become the final redoubt of the leaders of the Confederacy of Independent Systems. It was absolutely impenetrable.

Unless one had its deactivation codes.

Which was how the starfighter could land without causing the installation's defenses to so much as stir.

The habitable areas of the settlement were spread among towers that looked like poisonous toadstools sprung from the bank of a river of fire. The main control center squatted atop the largest, beside the small landing deck where the starfighter had alit. It was from this control center, less than an hour before, that a coded command had been transmitted over every HoloNet repeater in the galaxy.

At that signal, every combat droid in every army on every planet marched back to its transport, resocketed itself, and turned itself off. The Clone Wars were over.

Almost.

There was a final detail.

A dark-cloaked figure swung down from the cockpit of the starfighter.

Bail Organa strode onto the *Tantive*'s shuttle deck to find Obi-Wan and Yoda gazing dubiously at the tiny cockpit of Obi-Wan's starfighter. "I suppose," Obi-Wan was saying reluctantly, "if you don't mind riding on my lap . . ."

"That may not be necessary," Bail said. "I've just been summoned back to Coruscant by Mas Amedda; Palpatine has called the Senate into Extraordinary Session. Attendance is required."

"Ah." Obi-Wan's mouth turned downward. "It's clear what this will be about."

"I am," Bail said slowly, "concerned it might be a trap."

"Unlikely this is." Yoda hobbled toward him. "Unknown, is the purpose of your sudden departure from the capital; dead, young Obi-Wan and I are both presumed to be."

"And Palpatine won't be moving against the Senate as a whole," Obi-Wan added. "At least, not yet; he'll need the illusion of democracy to keep the individual star systems in line. He won't risk a general uprising."

Bail nodded. "In that case—" He took a deep breath. "—perhaps I can offer Your Graces a lift?"

Inside the control center of the Separatist bunker on Mustafar . . .

Wat Tambor was adjusting the gas mix inside his armor—

Poggle the Lesser was massaging his fleshy lip-tendrils—

Shu Mai was fiddling with the brass binding that restrained her hair into the stylish curving horn that rose behind her head—

San Hill was stretching his bodystocking, which had begun to ride up in the crotch—

Rune Haako was shifting his weight nervously from foot to foot—

While Nute Gunray spoke to the holopresence of Darth Sidious.

"The plan has gone exactly as you promised, my lord," Gunray said. "This is a glorious day for the galaxy!"

"Yes, indeed. Thanks, in great part, to you, Viceroy, and to your associates of the Techno Union and the IBC. And, of course, Archduke Poggle. You have all performed magnificently. Have your droid armies completed shutdown?"

"Yes, my lord. Nearly an hour ago."

"Excellent! You will be handsomely rewarded. Has my new apprentice, Darth Vader, arrived?"

"His ship touched down only a moment ago."

"Good, good," the holoscan of the cloaked man said pleasantly. *"I have left your reward in his hands. He will take care of you."*

The door cycled open.

A tall cloaked figure, slim but broad-shouldered, face shadowed by a heavy hood, stood in the doorway.

San Hill beat the others to the greeting. "Welcome, Lord Vader!" His elongated legs almost tangled with each other in his rush to shake the hand of the Sith Lord. "On behalf of the leadership of the Confederacy of Independent Systems, let me be the first to—"

"Very well. You will be the first."

The cloaked figure stepped inside and made a gesture with a black-gloved hand. Blast doors slammed across every exit. The control panel exploded in a shower of sparking wires.

The cloaked figure threw back its hood.

San Hill recoiled, hands flapping like panicked birds sewn to his wrists.

He had time to gasp, "You're—you're *Anakin Skywalker!*" before a fountain of blue-white plasma burned into his chest, curving through a loop that charred all three of his hearts.

The Separatist leadership watched in frozen horror as the corpse of the head of the InterGalactic Banking Clan collapsed like a depowered protocol droid.

"The resemblance," Darth Vader said, "is deceptive."

The Senate Guard blinked, then straightened and smoothed the drape of his robe. He risked a glance at his partner, who flanked the opposite side of the door.

Had they really just gotten as lucky as he thought they had?

Were this Senator and his aides really walking right out of the turbolift with a couple of as-yet-uncaptured *Jedi*?

Wow. Promotions all around.

The guard tried not to stare at the two Jedi, and did his best to sound professional. "Welcome back, Senator. May I see your clearance?"

An identichip was produced without hesitation: Bail Organa, senior Senator from Alderaan.

"Thank you. You may proceed." The guard handed back the identichip. He was rather pleased with how steady and business-like he sounded. "We will take custody of the Jedi."

Then the taller of the two Jedi murmured gently that it would be better if he and his counterpart were to stay with the Senator, and really, he seemed like such a reasonable fellow, and it was such a good idea—after all, the Grand Convocation Chamber of the Galactic Senate was so secure there was really no way for a Jedi to cause any trouble for anyone and they could just as easily be apprehended on their way out, and the guard didn't want to seem like an unreasonable fellow himself, and so he found himself nodding and agreeing that yes, indeed, it would be better if the Jedi stayed with the Senator.

And everyone was so reasonable and agreeable that it seemed perfectly reasonable and agreeable to the guard that the Jedi and the Senator, instead of staying together as they'd said, made low-voiced *Force-be-with-you* farewells; it never occurred to the guard to object even when the Senator entered the Convocation Chamber and the two Jedi headed off for . . . well, apparently, somewhere else.

All eight members of Decoy Squad Five were deployed at a downlevel loading dock, where supplies that Jedi could not grow in their own Temple gardens had been delivered daily.

Not anymore.

This deep in Coruscant's downlevels, the sun never shone; the only illumination came from antiquated glow globes, their faded light yellow as ancient parchment, that only darkened the shadows around. In those shadows lived the dregs of the galaxy, squatters and scavengers, madmen and fugitives from the justice above. Parts of Coruscant's downlevels could be worse than Nar Shaddaa.

The men of Decoy Squad Five would have been alert on any post. They were bred to be. Here, though, they were in a combat zone, where their lives and their missions depended on their perceptions, and on how fast their blasters could come out from inside those Jedi-style robes.

So when a ragged, drooling hunchback lurched out of the gloom nearby, a bundle cradled in his arms, Decoy Squad Five took it for granted that he was a threat. Blasters appeared with miraculous speed. "Halt. Identify yourself."

"No, no, no, Yer Graces, oh, no, I'm bein' here to *help*, y'see, I'm on *yerr* side!" The hunchback slurped drool back into his slack lips as he lurched toward them. "Lookit I got here, I mean, *lookit*—'sa Jedi *babby*, ennit?"

The sergeant of the squad squinted at the bundle in the hunchback's arms. "A Jedi baby?"

"Oooh, sher. Sher, Yer Grace. Jedi babby, sher azzell iddiz! Come from outcher Temple, dinnit? Lookit!"

The hunchback was now close enough that the sergeant could see what he carried in his filthy bundle. It *was* a baby. Sort of. It was the ugliest baby the sergeant had ever seen, alien or not, wizened and shriveled like a worn-out purse of moldly leather, with great pop eyes and a toothless idiot's grin.

The sergeant frowned skeptically. "Anyone could grab some deformed kid and claim it's anything they want. How do you know it's a Jedi?"

The baby said, "My lightsaber, the first clue would be, hmm?"

A burning blade of green slanted across the sergeant's face so close he could smell the ozone, and the hunchback wasn't a hunchback anymore: he now held a lightsaber the color of a summer sky, and he said in a clipped, educated Coruscanti accent, "Please don't try to resist. No one has to get hurt."

The men of Decoy Squad Five disagreed.

Six seconds later, all eight of them were dead.

Yoda looked up at Obi-Wan. "To hide the bodies, no point there is."

Obi-Wan nodded agreement. "These are clones; an abandoned post is as much a giveaway as a pile of corpses. Let's get to that beacon."

Bail slipped into the rear of the Naboo delegation's Senate pod as Palpatine thundered from the podium, "These Jedi murderers left me *scarred*, left me *deformed*, but they could not scar my *integrity*! They could not deform my *resolve*! The remaining traitors will be hunted down, rooted out wherever they may hide, and brought to justice, dead or alive! All collaborators will suffer the same fate. Those who protect the enemy *are* the enemy! Now is the time! Now we will strike back! Now we will *destroy* the *destroyers*! *Death to the enemies of democracy!*"

The Senate roared.

Amidala didn't even glance at Bail as he slid into a seat beside her. On the opposite side, Representative Binks nodded at him, but said nothing, blinking solemnly. Bail frowned; if even the irrepressible Jar Jar was worried, this looked to be even worse than he'd expected. And he had expected it to be very, very bad.

He touched Amidala's arm softly. "It's all a lie. You know that, don't you?"

She stared frozenly toward the podium. Her eyes glistened with unshed tears. "I don't know *what* I know. Not anymore. Where have you been?"

"I was . . . held up." As she once had told him, some things were better left unsaid.

"He's been presenting evidence all afternoon," she said in a flat, affectless monotone. "Not just the assassination attempt. The Jedi were about to overthrow the Senate."

"It's a lie," he said again.

In the center of the Grand Convocation Chamber, Palpatine leaned upon the Chancellor's Podium as though he drew strength from the Great Seal on its front. "This has been the most trying of times, but we have passed the test. The war is *over*!"

The Senate roared.

"The Separatists have been utterly defeated, and the *Republic will stand*! United! United and *free*!"

The Senate roared.

"The Jedi Rebellion was our final test—it was the last gasp of the forces of darkness! Now we have left that darkness behind us forever, and a new day has begun! It is *morning* in the Republic!"

The Senate roared.

Padmé stared without blinking. "Here it comes," she said numbly.

Bail shook his head. "Here what comes?"

"You'll see."

"Never again will we be divided! Never again will sector turn against sector, planet turn against planet, *sibling* turn against *sibling*! We are one nation, *indivisible*!"

The Senate roared.

"To ensure that we will always stand together, that we will

always speak with a single voice and act with a single hand, the Republic must change. We must *evolve*. We must *grow*. We have become an empire in fact; let us become an Empire in name as well! We *are* the first *Galactic Empire*!"

The Senate went wild.

"What are they doing?" Bail said. "Do they understand what they're *cheering* for?"

Padmé shook her head.

"We are an Empire," Palpatine went on, "that will continue to be ruled by this august body! We are an Empire that will never return to the political maneuvering and corruption that have wounded us so deeply; we are an Empire that will be directed by a *single* sovereign, chosen for *life*!"

The Senate went wilder.

"We are an Empire ruled by the *majority*! An Empire ruled by a new Constitution! An Empire of *laws,* not of politicians! An Empire devoted to the preservation of a just society. Of a *safe* and *secure* society! We are an Empire that will *stand ten thousand years*!"

The roar of the Senate took on a continuous boiling roll like the inside of a permanent thunderstorm.

"We will celebrate the anniversary of this day as *Empire Day.* For the sake of our *children*. For our children's children! For the next ten thousand years! Safety! Security! Justice and peace!"

The Senate went berserk.

"Say it with me! Safety, Security, Justice, and Peace! Safety, Security, Justice, and Peace!"

The Senate took up the chant, louder and louder until it seemed the whole galaxy roared along.

Bail couldn't hear Padmé over the din, but he could read her lips.

So this is how liberty dies, she was saying to herself. *With cheering, and applause.*

"We can't let this happen!" Bail lurched to his feet. "I have to get to my pod—we can still enter a motion—"

"No." Her hand seized his arm with astonishing strength, and for the first time since he'd arrived, she looked straight into his eyes. "No, Bail, you can't enter a motion. You *can't*. Fang Zar has already been arrested, and Tundra Dowmeia, and it won't be long until the entire Delegation of the Two Thousand are declared enemies of the state. You stayed off that list for good reason; don't add your name by what you do today."

"But I can't just stand by and *watch*—"

"You're right. You can't just watch. You have to vote *for* him."

"What?"

"Bail, it's the only way. It's the only hope you have of remaining in a position to do *anyone* any good. Vote for Palpatine. Vote for the Empire. Make Mon Mothma vote for him, too. Be good little Senators. Mind your manners and keep your heads down. And keep doing . . . all those things we can't talk about. All those things I can't know. *Promise* me, Bail."

"Padmé, what you're talking about—what we're *not* talking about—it could take *twenty years*! Are you under suspicion? What are you going to do?"

"Don't worry about me," she said distantly. "I don't know I'll live that long."

———

Within the Separatist leadership bunker's control center were dozens of combat droids. There were armed and armored guards. There were automated defense systems.

There were screams, and tears, and pleas for mercy.

None of them mattered.

The Sith had come to Mustafar.

Poggle the Lesser, Archduke of Geonosis, scrambled like an animal through a litter of severed arms and legs and heads, both metal and flesh, whimpering, fluttering his ancient gauzy wings until a bar of lightning flash-burned his own head free of his neck.

Shu Mai, president and CEO of the Commerce Guild, looked up from her knees, hands clasped before her, tears streaming down her shriveled cheeks. "We were promised a *reward*," she gasped. "A h—h—*handsome* reward—"

"I am your reward," the Sith Lord said. "You don't find me handsome?"

"Please!" she screeched through her sobbing. *"Pleee—"*

The blue-white blade cut into and out from her skull, and her corpse swayed. A negligent flip of the wrist slashed through her column of neck rings. Her brain-burned head tumbled to the floor.

The only sound, then, was a panicky stutter of footfalls as Wat Tambor and the two Neimoidians scampered along a hallway toward a nearby conference room.

The Sith Lord was in no hurry to pursue. All the exits from the control center were blast-shielded, and they were sealed, and he had destroyed the controls.

The conference room was, as the expression goes, a dead end.

Thousands of clone troops swarmed the Jedi Temple.

Multiple battalions on each level were not just an occupying force, but engaged in the long, painstaking process of preparing dead bodies for positive identification. The Jedi dead were to be tallied against the rolls maintained in the Temple archives; the clone dead would be cross-checked with regimental rosters. All the dead had to be accounted for.

This was turning out to be somewhat more complicated than the clone officers had expected. Though the fighting had ended hours ago, troopers kept turning up missing. Usually small patrolling squads—five troopers or less—that still made random sweeps through the Temple hallways, checking every door and window, every desk and every closet.

Sometimes when those closets were opened, what was found inside was five dead clones.

And there were disturbing reports as well; officers coordinating the sweeps recorded a string of sightings of movement—usually a flash of robe disappearing around a corner, caught in a trooper's peripheral vision—that on investigation seemed to have been only imagination, or hallucination. There were also multiple reports of inexplicable sounds coming from out-of-the-way areas that turned out to be deserted.

Though clone troopers were schooled from even before awakening in their Kaminoan crèche-schools to be ruthlessly pragmatic, materialistic, and completely impervious to superstition, some of them began to suspect that the Temple might be haunted.

In the vast misty gloom of the Room of a Thousand Fountains, one of the clones on the cleanup squad caught a glimpse of someone moving beyond a stand of Hylaian marsh bamboo. "Halt!" he shouted. "You there! Don't move!"

The shadowy figure darted off into the gloom, and the clone turned to his squad brothers. "Come on! Whatever that was, we can't let it get away!"

Clones pelted off into the mist. Behind them, at the spill of bodies they'd been working on, fog and gloom gave birth to a pair of Jedi Masters.

Obi-Wan stepped over white-armored bodies to kneel beside blaster-burned corpses of children. Tears flowed freely down tracks that hadn't had a chance to dry since he'd first entered the Temple. "Not even the younglings survived. It looks like they made a stand here."

Yoda's face creased with ancient sadness. "Or trying to flee they were, with some turning back to slow the pursuit."

Obi-Wan turned to another body, an older one, a Jedi fully mature and beyond. Grief punched a gasp from his chest. "Master Yoda—it's the *Troll* . . ."

Yoda looked over and nodded bleakly. "Abandon his young students, Cin Drallig would not."

Obi-Wan sank to his knees beside the fallen Jedi. "He was my lightsaber instructor . . ."

"And his, was I," Yoda said. "Cripple us, grief will, if let it we do."

"I know. But . . . it's one thing to know a friend is dead, Master Yoda. It's another to find his *body* . . ."

"Yes." Yoda moved closer. With his gimer stick, he pointed at a bloodless gash in Drallig's shoulder that had cloven deep into his chest. "Yes, it is. See this, do you? This wound, no blaster could make."

An icy void opened in Obi-Wan's heart. It swallowed his pain and his grief, leaving behind a precariously empty calm.

He whispered, "A *lightsaber*?"

"Business with the recall beacon, have we still." Yoda pointed with his stick at figures winding toward them among the trees and pools. "Returning, the clones are."

Obi-Wan rose. "I will learn who did this."

"Learn?"

Yoda shook his head sadly.

"Know already, you do," he said, and hobbled off into the gloom.

Darth Vader left nothing living behind when he walked from the main room of the control center.

Casually, carelessly, he strolled along the hallway, scoring the durasteel wall with the tip of his blade, enjoying the sizzle of disintegrating metal as he had savored the smoke of charred alien flesh.

The conference room door was closed. A barrier so paltry would be an insult to the blade; a black-gloved hand made a fist. The door crumpled and fell.

The Sith Lord stepped over it.

The conference room was walled with transparisteel. Beyond, obsidian mountains rained fire upon the land. Rivers of lava embraced the settlement.

Rune Haako, aide and confidential secretary to the viceroy of the Trade Federation, tripped over a chair as he stumbled back.

He fell to the floor, shaking like a grub in a frying pan, trying to scrabble beneath the table.

"Stop!" he cried. "Enough! We *surrender,* do you understand? You can't just *kill* us—"

The Sith Lord smiled. "Can't I?"

"We're unarmed! We surrender! Please—please, you're a *Jedi*!"

"You fought a war to destroy the Jedi." Vader stood above the shivering Neimoidian, smiling down upon him, then fed him half a meter of plasma. "Congratulations on your success."

The Sith Lord stepped over Haako's corpse to where Wat Tambor clawed uselessly at the transparisteel wall with his armored gauntlets. The head of the Techno Union turned at his approach, cringing, arms lifted to shield his faceplate from the flames in the dragon's eyes. "Please, I'll give you *anything. Anything you want!*"

The blade flashed twice; Tambor's arms fell to the floor, followed by his head.

"Thank you."

Darth Vader turned to the last living leader of the Confederacy of Independent Systems.

Nute Gunray, viceroy of the Trade Federation, stood trembling in an alcove, blood-tinged tears streaming down his green-mottled cheeks. "The war . . . ," he whimpered. "The war is *over*—Lord Sidious *promised*—he promised we would be left in *peace* . . ."

"His transmission was garbled." The blade came up. "He promised you would be left in *pieces.*"

In the main holocomm center of the Jedi Temple, high atop the central spire, Obi-Wan used the Force to reach deep within the shell of the recall beacon's mechanism, subtly altering the pulse calibration to flip the signal from *come home* to *run and hide*. Done without any visible alteration, it would take the troopers quite a while to detect the recalibration, and longer still to reset it. This was all that could be done for any surviving Jedi: a warning, to give them a fighting chance.

Obi-Wan turned from the recall beacon to the internal security scans. He had to find out exactly what he was warning them against.

"Do this not," Yoda said. "Leave we must, before discovered we are."

"I have to *see* it," Obi-Wan said grimly. "Like I said downstairs: knowing is one thing. Seeing is another."

"Seeing will only cause you pain."

"Then it is pain that I have earned. I won't hide from it." He keyed a code that brought up a holoscan of the Room of a Thousand Fountains. "I am not afraid."

Yoda's eyes narrowed to green-gold slits. "You should be."

Stone-faced, Obi-Wan watched younglings run into the room, fleeing a storm of blasterfire; he watched Cin Drallig and a pair of teenage Padawans—was that Whie, the boy Yoda had brought to Vjun?—backing into the scene, blades whirling, cutting down the advancing clone troopers with deflected bolts.

He watched a lightsaber blade flick into the shot, cutting down first one Padawan, then the other. He watched the brisk stride of a caped figure who hacked through Drallig's shoulder, then stood aside as the old Troll fell dying to let the rest of the clones blast the children to shreds.

Obi-Wan's expression never flickered.

He opened himself to what he was about to see; he was prepared, and centered, and trusting in the Force, and yet . . .

Then the caped man turned to meet a cloaked figure behind him, and he was—

He was—

Obi-Wan, staring, wished that he had the strength to rip his eyes out of his head.

But even blind, he would see this forever.

He would see his friend, his student, his brother, turn and kneel in front of a black-cloaked Lord of the Sith.

His head rang with a silent scream.

"The traitors have been destroyed, Lord Sidious. And the archives are secured. Our ancient holocrons are again in the hands of the Sith."

"Good . . . good . . . Together, we shall master every secret of the Force." The Sith Lord purred like a contented rancor. *"You have done well, my new apprentice. Do you feel your power growing?"*

"Yes, my Master."

"Lord Vader, your skills are unmatched by any Sith before you. Go forth, my boy. Go forth, and bring peace to our Empire."

Fumbling nervelessly, Obi-Wan somehow managed to shut down the holoscan. He leaned on the console, but his arms would not support him; they buckled and he twisted to the floor.

He huddled against the console, blind with pain.

Yoda was as sympathetic as the root of a wroshyr tree. "Warned, you were."

Obi-Wan said, "I should have let them *shoot* me . . ."

"What?"

"No. That was already too late—it was already too late at Geonosis. The Zabrak, on Naboo—I should have died *there* . . . before I ever *brought* him here—"

"*Stop* this, you will!" Yoda gave him a stick-jab in the ribs sharp enough to straighten him up. "*Make* a Jedi fall, one cannot; beyond even Lord Sidious, this is. *Chose* this, Skywalker did."

Obi-Wan lowered his head. "And I'm afraid I might know why."

"Why? *Why* matters not. There is no *why*. There is only a Lord of the Sith, and his apprentice. Two Sith." Yoda leaned close. "And two Jedi."

Obi-Wan nodded, but he still couldn't meet the gaze of the ancient Master. "I'll take Palpatine."

"Strong enough to face Lord Sidious, you will never be. Die you will, and painfully."

"Don't make me kill Anakin," he said. "He's like my *brother*, Master."

"The boy you trained, gone he is—twisted by the dark side.

Consumed by Darth Vader. Out of this misery, you must put him. To visit our new Emperor, *my* job will be."

Now Obi-Wan did face him. "Palpatine faced Mace and Agen and Kit and Saesee—four of the greatest swordsmen our Order has ever produced. By *himself.* Even both of us together wouldn't have a chance."

"True," Yoda said. "But both of us apart, a chance we might *create . . .*"

CHIAROSCURO

C-3PO identified the craft docking on the veranda as a DC0052 Intergalactic Speeder; to be on the safe side, he left the security curtain engaged.

In these troubled times, safety outweighed courtesy, even for him.

A cloaked and hooded human male emerged from the DC0052 and approached the veil of energy. C-3PO moved to meet him. "Hello, may I help you?"

The human lifted his hands to his hood; instead of taking it down, he folded it back far enough that C-3PO could register the distinctive relationship of eyes, nose, mouth, and beard.

"Master Kenobi!" C-3PO had long ago been given detailed and quite specific instructions on the procedure for dealing with the unexpected arrival of furtive Jedi.

He instantly deactivated the security curtain and beckoned. "Come inside, quickly. You may be seen."

As C-3PO swiftly ushered him into the sitting room, Master Kenobi asked, "Has Anakin been here?"

"Yes," C-3PO said reluctantly. "He arrived shortly after he and the army saved the Republic from the Jedi Rebellion—"

He cut himself off when he noticed that Master Kenobi suddenly looked fully prepared to dismantle him bolt by bolt. Perhaps he should not have been so quick to let the Jedi in.

Wasn't he some sort of outlaw, now?

"I, ah, I should—" C-3PO stammered, backing away. "I'll just go get the Senator, shall I? She's been lying down—after the Grand Convocation this morning, she didn't feel entirely well, and so—"

The Senator appeared at the top of the curving stairway, belting a soft robe over her dressing gown, and C-3PO decided his most appropriate course of action would be to discreetly withdraw.

But not too far; if Master Kenobi was up to mischief, C-3PO had to be in a position to alert Captain Typho and the security staff on the spot.

Senator Amidala certainly didn't seem inclined to *treat* Master Kenobi as a dangerous outlaw . . .

Quite the contrary, in fact: she seemed to have fallen into his arms, and her voice was thoroughly choked with emotion as she expressed a possibly inappropriate level of joy at finding the Jedi still alive.

There followed some discussion that C-3PO didn't entirely understand; it was political information entirely outside his programming, having to do with Master Anakin, and the Republic having fallen, whatever that meant, and with something called a Sith Lord, and Chancellor Palpatine, and the dark side of the Force, and really, he couldn't make sense of any of it. The only parts he clearly understood had to do with the Jedi Order being outlawed and all but wiped out (that news had been all over the Lipartian Way this morning) and the not-altogether-unexpected revelation that Master Kenobi had come here seeking Master Anakin. They *were* partners, after all (though despite all their years together, Master Anakin's recent behavior made it sadly clear that Master Kenobi's lovely manners had entirely failed to rub off).

"When was the last time you saw him? Do you know where he is?"

C-3PO's photoreceptors registered the Senator's flush as she lowered her eyes and said, "No."

Three years running the household of a career politician stopped C-3PO from popping back out and reminding the Senator that Master Anakin had told her just yesterday he was on his way to Mustafar; he knew very well that the Senator's memory failed only when she decided it should.

"Padmé, you must help me," Master Kenobi said. "Anakin must be found. He must be stopped."

"How can you *say* that?" She pulled back from him and turned away, folding her arms over the curve of her belly. "He's just won the war!"

"The war was never the Republic against the Separatists. It was Palpatine against the Jedi. We lost. The rest of it was just play-acting."

"It was real enough for everyone who *died*!"

"Yes." Now it was Master Kenobi's turn to lower his eyes. "Including the children at the Temple."

"What?"

"They were *murdered*, Padmé. I saw it." He took her shoulders and turned her back to face him. "They were murdered by *Anakin*."

"It's a *lie*—" She pushed him away forcefully enough that C-3PO nearly triggered the security alert then and there, but Master Kenobi only regarded her with an expression that matched C-3PO's internal recognition files of sadness and pity. "He could *never* . . . he could never . . . not my Anakin . . ."

Master Kenobi's voice was soft and slow. "He must be found."

Her reply was even softer; C-3PO's aural sensor barely recorded it at all.

"You've decided to kill him."

Master Kenobi said gravely, "He has become a very great threat."

At this, the Senator's medical condition seemed to finally overcome her; her knees buckled, and Master Kenobi was forced to catch her and help her onto the sofa. Apparently Master Kenobi knew somewhat more about human physiology than did C-3PO; though his photoreceptors hadn't been dark to the ongoing changes in Senator Amidala's contour, C-3PO had no idea what they might signify.

At any rate, Master Kenobi seemed to comprehend the situation instantly. He settled her comfortably onto the sofa and stood frowning down at her.

"Anakin is the father, isn't he?"

The Senator looked away. Her eyes were leaking again.

The Jedi Master said, hushed, "I'm very sorry, Padmé. If it could be different . . ."

"Go away, Obi-Wan. I won't help you. I can't." She turned her face away. "I won't help you kill him."

Master Kenobi said again, "I'm very sorry," and left.

C-3PO tentatively returned to the sitting room, intending to inquire after the Senator's health, but before he could access a sufficiently delicate phrase to open the discussion, the Senator said softly, "Threepio? Do you know what this is?"

She lifted toward him the pendant that hung from the cord of jerba leather she always wore around her neck.

"Why, yes, my lady," the protocol droid replied, bemused but happy, as always, to be of service. "It's a snippet of japor. Younglings on Tatooine carve tribal runes into them to make amulets; they are supposed by superstitious folk to bring good fortune and protect one from harm, and sometimes are thought to be love charms. I must say, my lady, I'm quite surprised you've forgotten, seeing as how you've worn that one ever since it was given to you so many years ago by Master An—"

"I hadn't forgotten what it was, Threepio," she said distantly. "Thank you. I was . . . reminding myself of the boy who gave it to me."

"My lady?" If she hadn't forgotten, why would she ask? Before C-3PO could phrase a properly courteous interrogative, she said, "Contact Captain Typho. Have him ready my skiff."

"My lady? Are you going somewhere?"

"*We* are," she said. "We're going to Mustafar."

From the shadows beneath the mirror-polished skiff's landing ramp, Obi-Wan Kenobi watched Captain Typho try to talk her out of it.

"My lady," the Naboo security chief protested, "at least let me come *with* you—"

"Thank you, Captain, but there's no need," Padmé said distantly. "The war's over, and . . . this is a *personal* errand. And, Captain? It must *remain* personal, do you understand? You know nothing of my leaving, nor where I am bound, nor when I can be expected to return."

"As you wish, my lady," Typho said with a reluctant bow. "But I *strongly* disagree with this decision."

"I'll be fine, Captain. After all, I have Threepio to look after me."

Obi-Wan could clearly hear the droid's murmured "Oh, dear."

After Typho finally climbed into his speeder and took off, Padmé and her droid boarded the skiff. She wasted no time at all; the skiff's repulsorlifts engaged before the landing ramp had even retracted.

Obi-Wan had to jump for it.

He swung inside just as the hatch sealed itself and the gleaming starship leapt for the sky.

Darth Vader stood on the command bridge of the Mustafar control center, hand of durasteel clasping hand of flesh behind him, and gazed up through the transparisteel view wall at the galaxy he would one day rule.

He paid no attention to the litter of corpses around his feet.

He could feel his power growing, indeed. He had the measure of his "Master" already; not long after Palpatine shared the secret of Darth Plagueis's discovery, their relationship would undergo a sudden . . . transformation.

A fatal transformation.

Everything was proceeding according to plan.

And yet . . .

He couldn't shake a certain creeping sensation . . . a kind of cold, slimy ooze that slithered up the veins of his legs and spread clammy tendrils through his guts . . .

Almost as though he was still *afraid* . . .

She will die, you know, the dragon whispered.

He shook himself, scowling. Impossible. He was Darth Vader. Fear had no power over him. He had destroyed his fear.

All things die.

Yet it was as though when he had crushed the dragon under his boot, the dragon had sunk venomed fangs into his heel.

Now its poison chilled him to the bone.

Even stars burn out.

He shook himself again and strode toward the holocomm. He would talk to his Master.

Palpatine had always helped him keep the dragon down.

A comlink chimed.

Yoda opened his eyes in the darkness.

"Yes, Master Kenobi?"

"We're landing now. Are you in position?"

"I am."

A moment of silence.

"Master Yoda . . . if we don't see each other again—"

"Think not of *after,* Obi-Wan. Always now, even eternity will be."

Another moment of silence.

Longer.

"May the Force be with you."

"It is. And may the Force be with you, young Obi-Wan."

The transmission ended.

Yoda rose.

A gesture opened the grating of the vent shaft where he had waited in meditation, revealing the vast conic well that was the

Grand Convocation Chamber of the Galactic Senate. It was sometimes called the Senate Arena.

Today, this nickname would be particularly apt.

Yoda stretched blood back into his green flesh.

This was his time.

Nine hundred years of study and training, of teaching and of meditation, all now focused, and refined, and resolved into this single moment; the sole purpose of his vast span of existence had been to prepare him to enter the heart of night and bring his light against the darkness.

He adjusted the angle of his blade against his belt.

He draped his robe across his shoulders.

With reverence, with gratitude, without fear, and without anger, Yoda went forth to war.

A silvery flash outside caught Darth Vader's eye, as though an elegantly curved mirror swung through the smoke and cinders, picking up the shine of white-hot lava. From one knee, he could look right through the holoscan of his Master while he continued his report.

He was no longer afraid; he was too busy pretending to be respectful.

"The Separatist leadership is no more, my Master."

"It is finished, then." The image offered a translucent mockery of a smile. *"You have restored peace and justice to the galaxy, Lord Vader."*

"That is my sole ambition. Master."

The image tilted its head, its smile twisting without transition to a scowl. *"Lord Vader—I sense a disturbance in the Force. You may be in danger."*

He glanced at the mirror flash outside; he knew that ship. *In danger of being kissed to death, perhaps . . .*

"How should I be in danger, Master?"

"I cannot say. But the danger is real; be mindful."

Be mindful, be mindful, he thought with a mental sneer. *Is that the best you can do? I could get that much from Obi-Wan . . .*

"I will, my Master. Thank you."

The image faded.

He got to his feet, and now the sneer was on his lips and in his eyes. "You're the one who should be *mindful,* my 'Master.' I *am* a disturbance in the Force."

Outside, the sleek skiff settled to the deck. He spent a moment reassembling his Anakin Skywalker face: he let Anakin Skywalker's love flow through him, let Anakin Skywalker's glad smile come to his lips, let Anakin Skywalker's youthful energy bring a joyous bounce to his step as he trotted to the entrance over the mess of corpses and severed body parts.

He'd meet her outside, and he'd keep her outside. He had a feeling she wouldn't approve of the way he had . . . redecorated . . . the control center.

And after all, he thought with a mental shrug, *there's no arguing taste . . .*

The holding office of the Supreme Chancellor of the Republic comprised the nether vertex of the Senate Arena; it was little more than a circular preparations area, a green room, where guests of the Chancellor might be entertained before entering the Senate Podium—the circular pod on its immense hydraulic pillar, which contained controls that coordinated the movement of floating Senate delegation pods—and rising into the focal point of the chamber above.

Above that podium, the vast holopresence of a kneeling Sith bowed before a shadow that stood below. Guards in scarlet flanked the shadow; a Chagrian toady cringed nearby.

"But the danger is real; be mindful."

"I will, my Master. Thank you."

The holopresence faded, and where its huge translucency had knelt was now revealed another presence, a physical presence, tiny and aged, clad in robes and leaning on a twist of wood. But his physical presence was an illusion; the truth of him could be seen only in the Force.

In the Force, he was a fountain of light.

"Pity your new disciple I do; so lately an apprentice, so soon without a Master."

"Why, Master Yoda, what a delightful surprise! Welcome!" The voice of the shadow hummed with anticipation. "Let me be the first to wish you Happy Empire Day!"

"Find it happy, you will not. Nor will the murderer you call Vader."

"Ah." The shadow stepped closer to the light. "So *that* is the threat I felt. Who is it, if I may ask? Who have you sent to kill him?"

"Enough it is that you know your *own* destroyer."

"Oh, pish, Master Yoda. It wouldn't be Kenobi, would it? *Please* say it's Kenobi—Lord Vader gets such a thrill from killing people who care for him . . ."

Behind the shadow, some meters away, Mas Amedda—the Chagrian toady who was Speaker of the Galactic Senate—heard a whisper in Palpatine's voice. *Flee.*

He did.

Neither light nor shadow gave his exit a glance.

"So easily slain, Obi-Wan is not."

"Neither are you, apparently; but that is about to change." The shadow took another step, and another.

A lightsaber appeared, green as sunlight in a forest. "The test of that, today will be."

"Even a fraction of the dark side is more power than your Jedi arrogance can conceive; living in the light, you have never seen the depth of the darkness."

The shadow spread arms that made its sleeves into black wings.

"Until now."

Lightning speared from outstretched hands, and the battle was on.

Padmé stumbled down the landing ramp into Anakin's arms. Her eyes were raw and numb; once inside the ship, her emotional control had finally shattered and she had sobbed the whole way there, crying from relentless mind-shredding dread, and so her lips were swollen and her whole body shook and she was just so *grateful,* so incredibly grateful, that again she flooded with fresh tears: grateful that he was alive, grateful that he'd come bounding across the landing deck to meet her, that he was still strong and beautiful, that his arms still were warm around her and his lips were soft against her hair.

"Anakin, my *Anakin* . . ." She shivered against his chest. "I've been so *frightened* . . ."

"Shh. Shh, it's all right." He stroked her hair until her trembling began to fade, then he cupped her chin and gently raised her face to look into his eyes. "You never need to worry about me. Didn't you understand? No one can hurt me. No one will ever hurt either of us."

"It wasn't that, my love, it was—oh, Anakin, he said such terrible things about you!"

He smiled down at her. "About me? Who would want to say bad things about me?" He chuckled. "Who would dare?"

"Obi-Wan." She smeared tears from her cheeks. "He said— he told me you turned to the dark side, that you murdered Jedi . . . even *younglings* . . ."

Just having gotten the words out made her feel better; now all she had to do was rest in his arms while he held her and hugged her and promised her he would never do anything like any of that, and she started half a smile aimed up toward his eyes—

But instead of the light of love in his eyes, she saw only reflections of lava.

He didn't say, *I could never turn to the dark side.*

He didn't say, *Murder younglings? Me? That's just crazy.*

He said, "Obi-Wan's *alive?*"

His voice had dropped an octave, and had gone colder than the chills that were spreading from the base of her spine.

"Y-yes—he, he said he was looking for you . . ."

"Did you tell him where I am?"

"*No*, Anakin! He wants to *kill* you. I didn't tell him *anything*—I wouldn't!"

"Too bad."

"Anakin, what—"

"He's a traitor, Padmé. He's an enemy of the state. He has to die."

"Stop it," she said. "Stop *talking* like that . . . you're frightening me!"

"You're not the one who needs to be afraid."

"It's like—it's like—" Tears brimmed again. "I don't even know who you *are* anymore . . ."

"I'm the man who *loves* you," he said, but he said it through clenched teeth. "I'm the man who would do *anything* to protect you. *Everything* I have done, I have done for *you*."

"Anakin . . ." Horror squeezed her voice down to a whisper: small, and fragile, and very young. ". . . what *have* you done?"

And she prayed that he wouldn't actually answer.

"What I have done is bring *peace* to the Republic."

"The Republic is *dead*," she whispered. "You killed it. You and Palpatine."

"It needed to die."

New tears started, but they didn't matter; she'd never have enough tears for this. "Anakin, can't we just . . . *go*? Please. Let's leave. Together. Today. Now. Before you—before something happens—"

"Nothing will happen. Nothing *can* happen. *Let* Palpatine call himself Emperor. Let him. He can do the dirty work, all the messy, brutal oppression it'll take to unite the galaxy forever— unite it *against* him. He'll make himself into the most hated man in history. And when the time is right, we'll throw him *down*—"

"Anakin, stop—"

"Don't you see? We'll be *heroes*. The whole galaxy will *love* us, and we will *rule*. *Together*."

"Please stop—Anakin, please, stop, I can't *stand* it . . ."

He wasn't listening to her. He wasn't looking at her. He was looking past her shoulder.

Feral joy burned from his eyes, and his face was no longer human.

"You . . ."

From behind her, calmly precise, with that clipped Coruscanti accent: "Padmé. Move away from him."

"Obi-Wan?" She whirled, and he was on the landing ramp, still and sad. *"No!"*

"You," growled a voice that should have been her love's. "You *brought* him here . . ."

She turned back, and now he *was* looking at her.

His eyes were full of flame.

"Anakin?"

"Padmé, move *away.*" There was an urgency in Obi-Wan's voice that sounded closer to fear than Padmé had ever heard from him. "He's not who you think he is. He *will* harm you."

Anakin's lips peeled off his teeth. "I would thank you for this, if it were a gift of love."

Trembling, shaking her head, she began to back away. "No, Anakin—no . . ."

"Palpatine was right. Sometimes it is the closest who cannot see. I loved you too much, Padmé."

He made a fist, and she couldn't breathe.

"I loved you too much to *see* you! To see what you *are!*"

A veil of red descended on the world. She clawed at her throat, but there was nothing there her hands could touch.

"Let her go, Anakin."

His answer was a predator's snarl, over the body of its prey. "You will not take her from me!"

She wanted to scream, to beg, to howl, *No, Anakin, I'm sorry! I'm sorry . . . I love you . . . ,* but her locked throat strangled the truth inside her head, and the world-veil of red smoked toward black.

"Let her go!"

"Never!"

The ground fell away beneath her, and then a white flash of impact blasted her into night.

In the Senate Arena, lightning forked from the hands of a Sith, and bent away from the gesture of a Jedi to shock Redrobes into unconsciousness.

Then there were only the two of them.

Their clash transcended the personal; when new lightning blazed, it was not Palpatine burning Yoda with his hate, it was the Lord of all Sith scorching the Master of all Jedi into a smoldering huddle of clothing and green flesh.

A thousand years of hidden Sith exulted in their victory.

"Your time is *over*! The *Sith* rule the galaxy! Now and *forever*!"

And it was the whole of the Jedi Order that rocketed from its huddle, making of its own body a weapon to blast the Sith to the ground.

"At an end your rule is, and not short enough it was, I must say."

There appeared a blade the color of life.

From the shadow of a black wing, a small weapon—a hold-out, an easily concealed backup, a tiny bit of treachery expressing the core of Sith mastery—slid into a withered hand and spat a flame-colored blade of its own.

When those blades met, it was more than Yoda against Palpatine, more the millennia of Sith against the legions of Jedi; this was the expression of the fundamental conflict of the universe itself.

Light against dark.

Winner take all.

Obi-Wan knelt beside Padmé's unconscious body, where she lay limp and broken in the smoky dusk. He felt for a pulse. It was thin, and erratic. "Anakin—Anakin, what have you *done*?"

In the Force, Anakin burned like a fusion torch. "You turned her against me."

Obi-Wan looked at the best friend he had ever had. "You did that yourself," he said sadly.

"I'll give you a chance, Obi-Wan. For old times' sake. Walk away."

"If only I could."

"Go some place out of the way. Retire. Meditate. That's what you like, isn't it? You don't have to fight for peace anymore. Peace is *here*. My Empire *is* peace."

"*Your* Empire? It will *never* have peace. It was founded on treachery and innocent blood."

"Don't make me kill you, Obi-Wan. If you are not with me, you are against me."

"Only Sith deal in absolutes, Anakin. The truth is never black and white." He rose, spreading empty hands. "Let me take Padmé to a medcenter. She's hurt, Anakin. She needs medical attention."

"She stays."

"Anakin—"

"*You* don't get to take her *anywhere*. You don't get to *touch* her. She's *mine*, do you understand? It's *your* fault, *all* of it—you made her *betray me!*"

"Anakin—"

Anakin's hand sprouted a bar of blue plasma.

Obi-Wan sighed.

He brought out his own lighstaber and angled it before him. "Then I will do what I must."

"You'll try," Anakin said, and leapt.

Obi-Wan met him in the air.

Blue blades crossed, and the volcano above echoed their lightning with a shout of fire.

C-3PO cautiously poked his head around the rim of the skiff's hatch.

Though his threat-avoidance subroutines were in full screaming overload, and all he really wanted to be doing was finding some nice dark closet in which to fold himself and power down until this was all over—preferably an *armored* closet, with a door that locked from the inside, or could be welded shut (he wasn't particular on that point)—he found himself nonetheless creeping down the skiff's landing ramp into what appeared to be a perfectly appalling rain of molten *lava* and burning *cinders* . . .

Which was an entirely ridiculous thing for any sensible droid to be doing, but he kept going because he hadn't liked the sound of those conversations at all.

Not one little bit.

He couldn't be entirely certain what the disagreement among the humans was concerned with, but one element had been entirely clear.

She's hurt, Anakin . . . she needs medical attention . . .

He shuffled out into the swirling smoke. Burning rocks clattered around him. The Senator was nowhere to be seen, and even if he could find her, he had no idea how he could get her back to her ship—he certainly had not been designed for transporting anything heavier than a tray of cocktails; after all, weight-bearing capability was what *cargo* droids were for—but through the volcano's roar and the gusts of wind, his sonoreceptors picked up a familiar *ferooo-wheep peroo,* which his auto-translation protocol converted to DON'T WORRY. YOU'LL BE ALL RIGHT.

"Artoo?" C-3PO called. "Artoo, are you out here?"

A few steps more and C-3PO could see the little astromech: he'd tangled his manipulator arm in the Senator's clothing and was dragging her across the landing deck. "Artoo! Stop that this instant! You'll damage her!"

R2-D2's dome swiveled to bring his photoreceptor to bear on the nervous protocol droid. WHAT EXACTLY DO YOU SUGGEST? it whistled.

"Well . . . oh, all right. We'll do it together."

* * *

There came a turning point in the clash of the light against the dark.

It did not come from a flash of lightning or slash of energy blade, though there were these in plenty; it did not come from a flying kick or a surgically precise punch, though these were traded, too.

It came as the battle shifted from the holding office to the great Chancellor's Podium; it came as the hydraulic lift beneath the Podium raised it on its tower of durasteel a hundred meters and more, so that it became a laserpoint of battle flaring at the focus of the vast emptiness of the Senate Arena; it came as the Force and the podium's controls ripped delegation pods free of the curving walls and made of them hammers, battering rams, catapult stones crashing and crushing against each other in a rolling thunder-roar that echoed the Senate's cheers for the galaxy's new Emperor.

It came when the avatar of light resolved into the lineage of the Jedi; when the lineage of the Jedi refined into one single Jedi.

It came when Yoda found himself alone against the dark.

In that lightning-speared tornado of feet and fists and blades and bashing machines, his vision finally pierced the darkness that had clouded the Force.

Finally, he saw the truth.

This truth: that he, the avatar of light, Supreme Master of the Jedi Order, the fiercest, most implacable, most devastatingly powerful foe the darkness had ever known . . .

just—

didn't—

have it.

He'd never had it. He had lost before he started.

He had lost before he was born.

The Sith had changed. The Sith had grown, had adapted, had invested a thousand years' intensive study into every aspect of not only the Force but Jedi lore itself, in preparation for exactly this day. The Sith had remade themselves.

They had become *new.*

While the Jedi—

The Jedi had spent that same millennium training to refight the *last* war.

The new Sith could not be destroyed with a lightsaber; they could not be burned away by any torch of the Force. The brighter his light, the darker their shadow. How could one win a war against the dark, when war itself had become the dark's own weapon?

He knew, at that instant, that this insight held the hope of the galaxy. But if he fell here, that hope would die with him.

Hmmm, Yoda thought. *A problem this is . . .*

Blade-to-blade, they were identical. After thousands of hours in lightsaber sparring, they knew each other better than brothers, more intimately than lovers; they were complementary halves of a single warrior.

In every exchange, Obi-Wan gave ground. It was his way. And he knew that to strike Anakin down would burn his own heart to ash.

Exchanges flashed. Leaps were sideslipped or met with flying kicks; ankle sweeps skipped over and punches parried. The door of the control center fell in pieces, and then they were inside among the bodies. Consoles exploded in fountains of white-hot sparks as they ripped free of their moorings and hurtled through the air. Dead hands spasmed on triggers and blaster bolts sizzled through impossibly intricate lattices of ricochet.

Obi-Wan barely caught some and flipped them at Anakin: a desperation move. Anything to distract him; anything to slow him down. Easily, contemptuously, Anakin sent them back, and the bolts flared between their blades until their galvening faded and the particles of the packeted beams dispersed into radioactive fog.

"Don't make me destroy you, Obi-Wan." Anakin's voice had

gone deeper than a well and bleak as the obsidian cliffs. "You're no match for the power of the dark side."

"I've heard that before," Obi-Wan said through his teeth, parrying madly, "but I never thought I'd hear it from *you*."

A roar of the Force blasted Obi-Wan back into a wall, smashing breath from his lungs, leaving him swaying, half stunned. Anakin stepped over bodies and lifted his blade for the kill.

Obi-Wan had only one trick left, one that wouldn't work twice—

But it was a very good trick.

It had, after all, worked rather splendidly on Grievous . . .

He twitched one finger, reaching through the Force to reverse the polarity of the electrodrivers in Anakin's mechanical hand.

Durasteel fingers sprang open, and a lightsaber tumbled free.

Obi-Wan reached. Anakin's lightsaber twisted in the air and flipped into his hand. He poised both blades in a cross before him. "The flaw of power is arrogance."

"You hesitate," Anakin said. "The flaw of *compassion*—"

"It's not compassion," Obi-Wan said sadly. "It's reverence for life. Even yours. It's respect for the man you were."

He sighed. "It's regret for the man you should have been."

Anakin roared and flew at him, using both the Force and his body to crash Obi-Wan back into the wall once more. His hands seized Obi-Wan's wrists with impossible strength, forcing his arms wide. "I am so *sick* of your *lectures!*"

Dark power bore down with his grip.

Obi-Wan felt the bones of his forearms bending, beginning to feather toward the greenstick fractures that would come before the final breaks.

Oh, he thought. *Oh, this is bad.*

The end came with astonishing suddenness.

The shadow could feel how much it cost the little green freak to bend back his lightnings into the cage of energy that enclosed them both; the creature had reached the limits of his strength. The shadow released its power for an instant, long enough only to whirl away through the air and alight upon one of the delegation pods as it flew past, and the creature leapt to follow—

Half a second too slow.

The shadow unleashed its lightning while the creature was still in the air, and the little green freak took its full power. The shock blasted him backward to crash against the podium, and he fell.

He fell a long way.

The base of the Arena was a hundred meters below, littered with twisted scraps and jags of metal from the pods destroyed in the battle, and as the little green freak fell, finally, above, the victorious shadow became once again only Palpatine: a very old, very tired man, gasping for air as he leaned on the pod's rail.

Old he might have been, but there was nothing wrong with his eyesight; he scanned the wreckage below, and he did not see a body.

He flicked a finger, and in the Chancellor's Podium a dozen meters away, a switch tripped and sirens sounded throughout the enormous building; another surge of the Force sent his pod streaking in a downward spiral to the holding office at the base of the Podium tower. Clone troops were already swarming into it.

"It was Yoda," he said as he swung out of the pod. "Another assassination attempt. Find him and kill him. If you have to, blow up the building."

He didn't have time to direct the search personally. The Force hummed a warning in his bones: Lord Vader was in danger.

Mortal danger.

Clones scattered. He stopped one officer. "You. Call the shuttle dock and tell them I'm on my way. Have my ship warmed and ready."

The officer saluted, and Palpatine, with vigor that surprised even himself, ran.

* * *

With the help of the Force, Yoda sprinted along the service accessway below the Arena faster than a human being could run; he sliced conduits as he passed, filling the accessway behind him with coils of high-voltage cables, twisting and spitting lightning. Every few dozen meters, he paused just long enough to slash a hole in the accessway's wall; once his pursuers got past the cables, they would have to divide their forces to search each of his possible exits.

But he knew they could afford to; there were thousands of them.

He pulled his comlink from inside his robe without slowing down; the Force whispered a set of coordinates and he spoke them into the link. "Delay not," he added. "Swiftly closing is the pursuit. Failed I have, and kill me they will."

The Convocation Center of the Galactic Senate was a drum-mounted dome more than a kilometer in diameter; even with the aid of the Force, Yoda was breathing hard by the time he reached its edge. He cut through the floor beneath him and dropped down into another accessway, this one used for maintenance on the huge lighting system that shone downward onto Republic Plaza through transparisteel panels that floored the underside of the huge dome's rim. He cut into the lightwell; the reflected wattage nearly blinded him to the vertiginous drop below the transparisteel on which he stood.

Without hesitation he cut through that as well and dived headlong into the night.

Catching the nether edges of his long cloak to use as an improvised airfoil, he let the Force guide him in a soaring free fall away from the Convocation Center; he was too small to trigger its automated defense perimeter, but the open-cockpit speeder toward which he fell would get blasted from the sky if it deviated one meter inward from its curving course.

He released his robe so that it flapped upward, making a sort of drogue that righted him in the air so that he fell feetfirst into the speeder's passenger seat beside Bail Organa.

While Yoda strapped himself in, the Senator from Alderaan pulled the rented speeder through a turn that would have impressed Anakin Skywalker, and shot away toward the nearest intersection of Coruscant's congested skyways.

Yoda's eyes squeezed closed.

"Master Yoda? Are you wounded?"

"Only my pride," Yoda said, and meant it, though Bail could not possibly understand how deep that wound went, nor how it bled. "Only my pride."

With Anakin's grip on his wrists bending his arms near to breaking, forcing both their lightsabers down in a slow but unstoppable arc, Obi-Wan let go.

Of everything.

His hopes. His fears. His obligation to the Jedi, his promise to Qui-Gon, his failure with Anakin.

And their lightsabers.

Startled, Anakin instinctively shifted his Force grip, releasing one wrist to reach for his blade; in that instant Obi-Wan twisted free of his other hand and with the Force caught up his own blade, reversing it along his forearm so that his swift parry of Anakin's thundering overhand not only blocked the strike but directed both blades to slice through the wall against which he stood. He slid Anakin's following thrust through the wall on the opposite side, guiding both blades again up and over his head in a circular sweep so that he could use the power of Anakin's next chop to drive himself backward through the wall, outside into the smoke and the falling cinders.

Anakin followed, constantly attacking; Obi-Wan again gave ground, retreating along a narrow balcony high above the black-sand shoreline of a lake of fire.

Mustafar hummed with death behind his back, only a moment away, somewhere out there among the rivers of molten rock. Obi-Wan let Anakin drive him toward it.

It was a place, he decided, they should reach together.

Anakin forced him back and back, slamming his blade down with strength that seemed to flow from the volcano overhead. He spun and whirled and sliced razor-sharp shards of steel from the wall and shot them at Obi-Wan with the full heat of his fury. He slashed through a control panel along the walkway, and the ray shield that had held back the lava storm vanished.

Fire rained around them.

Obi-Wan backed to the end of the balcony; behind him was only a power conduit no thicker than his arm, connecting it to the main collection plant of the old lava mine, over a riverbed that flowed with white-hot molten stone. Obi-Wan stepped backward onto the conduit without hesitation, his balance flawless as he parried chop after chop.

Anakin came on.

Out on the tightrope of power conduit, their blades blurred even faster than before. They chopped and slashed and parried and blocked. Lava bombs thundered to the ground below, shedding drops of burning stone that scorched their robes. Smoke shrouded the planet's star, and now the only light came from the hell-glow of the lava below them and from their blades themselves. Flares of energy crackled and spat.

This was not Sith against Jedi. This was not light against dark or good against evil; it had nothing to do with duty or philosophy, religion or morals.

It was Anakin against Obi-Wan.

Personally.

Just the two of them, and the damage they had done to each other.

Obi-Wan backflipped from the conduit to a coupling nexus of the main collection plant; when Anakin flew in pursuit, Obi-Wan leapt again. They spun and whirled throughout its levels, up its stairs, and across its platforms; they battled out onto the collection panels over which the cascades of lava poured, and Obi-Wan, out on the edge of the collection panel, hunching under a curve of durasteel that splashed aside gouts of lava, deflecting

Force blasts and countering strikes from this creature of rage that had been his best friend, suddenly comprehended an unexpectedly profound truth.

The man he faced was everything Obi-Wan had devoted his life to destroying: Murderer. Traitor. Fallen Jedi. Lord of the Sith. And here, and now, despite it all . . .

Obi-Wan still loved him.

Yoda had said it, flat-out: *Allow such attachments to pass out of one's life, a Jedi must,* but Obi-Wan had never let himself understand. He had argued for Anakin, made excuses, covered for him again and again and again; all the while this attachment he denied even feeling had blinded him to the dark path his best friend walked.

Obi-Wan knew there was, in the end, only one answer for attachment . . .

He let it go.

The lake of fire, no longer held back by the ray shield, chewed away the shore on which the plant stood, and the whole massive structure broke loose, sending both warriors skidding, scrabbling desperately for handholds down tilting durasteel slopes that were rapidly becoming cliffs; they hung from scraps of cable as the plant's superstructure floated out into the lava, sinking slowly as its lower levels melted and burned away.

Anakin kicked off from the toppling superstructure, swinging through a wide arc over the lava's boil. Obi-Wan shoved out and met him there, holding the cable with one hand and the Force, angling his blade high. Anakin flicked a Shien whipcrack at his knees. Obi-Wan yanked his legs high and slashed through the cable above Anakin's hand, and Anakin fell.

Pockets of gas boiled to the surface of the lava, gouting flame like arms reaching to gather him in.

But Anakin's momentum had already swung back toward the dissolving wreck of the collection plant, and the Force carried him within reach of another cable. Obi-Wan whipped his legs around his cable, altering its arc to bring him within reach of the one from which Anakin now dangled, but Anakin was on to this game now, and he swung cable-to-cable ahead of Obi-Wan's advance, using the Force to carry himself higher and higher, forcing Obi-Wan to counter by doing the same; on this terrain, altitude was everything.

Simultaneous surges of the Force carried them both spinning up off the cables to the slant of the toppling superstructure's crane deck. Obi-Wan barely got his feet on the metal before Anakin pounced on him and they stood almost toe-to-toe, blades whirling and crashing on all sides, while around them the collection plant's maintenance droids still tinkered mindlessly away at the doomed machinery, as they would continue to do until lava closed over them and they melted to their constituent molecules and dissolved into the flow.

A roar louder even than the volcano's eruption came from the river ahead; metal began to shriek and stretch. The river dropped away in a vertical sheet of fire that vanished into boiling clouds of smoke and gases.

The whole collection plant was being carried, inexorably, out over a vast lava-fall.

Obi-Wan decided he didn't really want to see what was at the bottom.

He turned Anakin's blade aside with a two-handed block and landed a solid kick that knocked the two apart. Before Anakin could recover his balance, Obi-Wan took a running leap that became a graceful dive headlong off the crane deck. He hurtled down past level after level, and only a few tens of meters above the lava itself the Force called a dangling cable to his hand, turning his dive into a swing that carried him high and far, to the very limit of the cable.

And he let it go.

As though jumping from a swing in the Temple playrooms, his velocity sent him flying up and out over a catenary arc that shot him toward the river's shore.

Toward. Not quite *to*.

But the Force had led him here, and again it had not betrayed him: below, humming along a few meters above the lava river, came a big, slow old repulsorlift platform, carrying droids and equipment out toward a collection plant that its programming was not sophisticated enough to realize was about to be destroyed.

Obi-Wan flipped in the air and let the Force bring him to a catfooted landing. An adder-quick stab of his lightsaber disabled the platform's guidance system, and Obi-Wan was able to direct it back toward the shore with a simple shift of his weight.

He turned to watch as the collection plant shrieked like the damned in a Corellian hell, crumbling over the brink of the falls until it vanished into invisible destruction.

Obi-Wan lowered his head. "Good-bye, old friend."

But the Force whispered a warning, and Obi-Wan lifted his head in time to see Anakin come hurtling toward him out from the boil of smoke above the falls, perched on a tiny repulsorlift droid. The little droid was vastly swifter than Obi-Wan's logy old cargo platform, and Anakin was easily able to swing around Obi-Wan and cut him off from the shore. Obi-Wan shifted weight one way, then another, but Anakin's droid was nimble as a sand panther; there was no way around, and this close to the lava, the heat was intense enough to crisp Obi-Wan's hair.

"This is the end for you, Master," he said. "I wish it were otherwise."

"Yes, Anakin, so do I," Obi-Wan said as he sprinted into a leaping dive, making a spear of his blade.

Anakin leaned aside and deflected the thrust almost contemptuously; he missed a cut at Obi-Wan's legs as the Jedi Master flew past him.

Obi-Wan turned his dive into a forward roll that left him barely teetering on the rim of a low cliff, just above the soft black sand of the riverbank. Anakin snarled a curse as he realized he'd been suckered, and leapt off his droid at Obi-Wan's back—

Half a second too slow.

Obi-Wan's whirl to parry didn't meet Anakin's blade. It met his knee. Then his other knee.

And while Anakin was still in the air, burned-off lower legs only starting their topple down the cliff, Obi-Wan's recovery to guard brought his blade through Anakin's left arm above the elbow. He stepped back as Anakin fell.

Anakin dropped his lightsaber, clawing at the edge of the cliff with his mechanical hand, but his grip was too powerful for the lava bank and it crumbled, and he slid down onto the black sand. His severed legs and his severed arm rolled into the lava below him and burned to ash in sudden bursts of scarlet flame.

The same color, Obi-Wan observed distantly, as a Sith blade.

Anakin scrabbled at the soft black sand, but struggling only made him slip farther. The sand itself was hot enough that digging his durasteel fingers into it burned off his glove, and his robes began to smolder.

Obi-Wan picked up Anakin's lightsaber. He lifted his own as well, weighing them in his hands. Anakin had based his design upon Obi-Wan's. So similar they were.

So differently they had been used.

"Obi-Wan . . . ?"

He looked down. Flame licked the fringes of Anakin's robe, and his long hair had blackened, and was beginning to char.

"You were the chosen one! It was said you would destroy the Sith, not join them. It was you who would bring balance to the Force, not leave it in darkness. You were my brother, Anakin," said Obi-Wan Kenobi. "I loved you, but I could not save you."

A flash of metal through the sky, and Obi-Wan felt the darkness closing in around them both. He knew that ship: the Chancellor's shuttle. Now, he supposed, the *Emperor*'s shuttle.

Yoda had failed. He might have died.

He might have left Obi-Wan alone: the last Jedi.

Below his feet, Darth Vader burst into flame.

"I *hate* you," he screamed.

Obi-Wan looked down. It would be a mercy to kill him.

He was not feeling merciful.

He was feeling calm, and clear, and he knew that to climb down to that black beach might cost him more time than he had.

Another Sith Lord approached.

In the end, there was only one choice. It was a choice he had made many years before, when he had passed his trials of Jedi Knighthood, and sworn himself to the Jedi forever. In the end, he was still Obi-Wan Kenobi, and he was still a Jedi, and he would not murder a helpless man.

He would leave it to the will of the Force.

He turned and walked away.

After a moment, he began to run.

He began to run because he realized, if he was fast enough, there was one thing he still could do for Anakin. He still could do honor to the memory of the man he had loved, and to the vanished Order they both had served.

At the landing deck, C-3PO stood on the skiff's landing ramp, waving frantically. "Master Kenobi! Please hurry!"

"Where's Padmé?"

"Already inside, sir, but she is badly hurt."

Obi-Wan ran up the ramp to the skiff's cockpit and fired the engines. As the Chancellor's shuttle curved in toward the landing deck, the sleek mirror-finished skiff streaked for the stars.

Obi-Wan never looked back.

A NEW JEDI ORDER

A Naboo skiff reverted to realspace and flashed toward an alien medical installation in the asteroid belt of Polis Massa.

Tantive IV reentered reality only moments behind.

And on Mustafar, below the red thunder of a volcano, a Sith Lord had already snatched from sand of black glass the charred torso and head of what once had been a man, and had already leapt for the cliffbank above with effortless strength, and had already roared to his clones to *bring the medical capsule immediately!*

The Sith Lord lowered the limbless man tenderly to the cool ground above, and laid his hand across the cracked and blackened mess that once had been his brow, and he set his will upon him.

Live, Lord Vader. Live, my apprentice.

Live.

Beyond the transparent crystal of the observation dome on the airless crags of Polis Massa, the galaxy wheeled in a spray of hard, cold pinpricks through the veil of infinite night.

Beneath that dome sat Yoda. He did not look at the stars.

He sat a very long time.

Even after nearly nine hundred years, the road to self-knowledge was rugged enough to leave him bruised and bleeding.

He spoke softly, but not to himself.

Though no one was with him, he was not alone.

"My failure, this was. Failed the Jedi, I did."

He spoke to the Force.

And the Force answered him. *Do not blame yourself, my old friend.*

As it sometimes had these past thirteen years, when the Force spoke to him, it spoke in the voice of Qui-Gon Jinn.

"Too old I was," Yoda said. "Too rigid. Too arrogant to see that the old way is not the *only* way. These Jedi, I trained to become the Jedi who had trained me, long centuries ago—but those ancient Jedi, of a different time they were. Changed, has the galaxy. Changed, the Order did not—because *let* it change, *I* did not."

More easily said than done, my friend.

"An infinite mystery is the Force." Yoda lifted his head and turned his gaze out into the wheel of stars. "Much to learn, there still is."

And you will have time to learn it.

"Infinite knowledge . . ." Yoda shook his head. "Infinite time, does that require."

With my help, you can learn to join with the Force, yet retain consciousness. You can join your light to it forever. Perhaps, in time, even your physical self.

Yoda did not move. "Eternal life . . ."

The ultimate goal of the Sith, yet they can never achieve it; it comes only by the release of self, not the exaltation of self. It comes through compassion, not greed. Love is the answer to the darkness.

"Become one with the Force, yet influence still to have . . ." Yoda mused. "A power greater than all, it is."

It cannot be granted; it can only be taught. It is yours to learn, if you wish it.

Slowly, Yoda nodded. "A very great Jedi Master you have become, Qui-Gon Jinn. A very great Jedi Master you always were, but too blind I was to see it."

He rose, and folded his hands before him, and inclined his head in the Jedi bow of respect.

The bow of the student, in the presence of the Master.

"Your apprentice, I gratefully become."

He was well into his first lesson when the hatch cycled open behind him. He turned.

In the corridor beyond stood Bail Organa. He looked stricken.

"Obi-Wan is asking for you at the surgical theater," he said. "It's Padmé. She's dying."

Obi-Wan sat beside her, holding one cold, still hand in both of his. "Don't give up, Padmé."

"Is it . . ." Her eyes rolled blindly. "It's a girl. Anakin thinks it's a girl."

"We don't know yet. In a minute . . . you have to stay *with* us."

Below the opaque tent that shrouded her from chest down, a pair of surgical droids assisted with her labor. A general medical droid fussed and tinkered among the clutter of scanners and equipment.

"If it's . . . a girl—oh, oh, oh *no* . . ."

Obi-Wan cast an appeal toward the medical droid. "Can't you do something?"

"All organic damage has been repaired." The droid checked another readout. "This systemic failure cannot be explained."

Not physically, Obi-Wan thought. He squeezed her hand as though he could keep life within her body by simple pressure. "Padmé, you *have* to hold on."

"If it's a girl . . . ," she gasped, "name her Leia . . ."

One of the surgical droids circled out from behind the tent, cradling in its padded arms a tiny infant, already swabbed clean and breathing, but without even the hint of tears.

The droid announced softly, "It's a boy."

Padmé reached for him with her trembling free hand, but she had no strength to take him; she could only touch her fingers to the baby's forehead.

She smiled weakly. *"Luke . . ."*

The other droid now rounded the tent as well, with another clean, quietly solemn infant. ". . . and a girl."

But she had already fallen back against her pillow.

"Padmé, you have twins," Obi-Wan said desperately. "They *need* you—please hang on . . ."

"Anakin . . ."

"Anakin . . . isn't here, Padmé," he said, though he didn't think she could hear.

"Anakin, I'm sorry. I'm so sorry . . . Anakin, please, I *love* you . . ."

In the Force, Obi-Wan felt Yoda's approach, and he looked up to see the ancient Master beside Bail Organa, both staring the same grave question down through the surgical theater's observation panel.

The only answer Obi-Wan had was a helpless shake of his head.

Padmé reached across with her free hand, with the hand she had laid upon the brow of her firstborn son, and pressed something into Obi-Wan's palm.

For a moment, her eyes cleared, and she knew him.

"Obi-Wan . . . there . . . is still good in him. I know there is . . . still . . ."

Her voice faded to an empty sigh, and she sagged back against the pillow. Half a dozen different scanners buzzed with conflicting alarm tones, and the medical droids shooed him from the room.

He stood in the hall outside, looking down at what she had pressed into his hand. It was a pendant of some kind, an amulet, unfamiliar sigils carved into some sort of organic material, strung on a loop of leather. In the Force, he could feel traces of the touch of her skin.

When Yoda and Bail came for him, he was still standing there, staring at it.

"She put this in my hand—" For what seemed the dozenth

time this day, he found himself blinking back tears. "—and I don't even know what it is."

"Precious to her, it must have been," Yoda said slowly. "Buried with her, perhaps it should be."

Obi-Wan looked down at the simple, child-like symbols carved into it, and felt from it in the Force soaring echoes of transcendent love, and the bleak, black despair of unendurable heartbreak.

"Yes," he said. "Yes. Perhaps that would be best."

Around a conference table on *Tantive IV,* Bail Organa, Obi-Wan Kenobi, and Yoda met to decide the fate of the galaxy.

"To Naboo, send her body . . ." Yoda stretched his head high, as though tasting a current in the Force. "Pregnant, she must still appear. Hidden, safe, the children must be kept. Foundation of the new Jedi Order, they will be."

"We should split them up," Obi-Wan said. "Even if the Sith find one, the other may survive. I can take the boy, Master Yoda, and you take the girl. We can hide them away, keep them safe— train them as Anakin *should* have been trained—"

"No." The ancient Master lowered his head again, closing his eyes, resting his chin on his hands that were folded over the head of his stick.

Obi-Wan looked uncertain. "But how are they to learn the self-discipline a Jedi needs? How are they to master skills of the Force?"

"Jedi training, the sole source of self-discipline is not. When right is the time for skills to be taught, to us the living Force will bring them. Until then, wait we will, and watch, and learn."

"I can . . ." Bail Organa stopped, flushing slightly. "I'm sorry to interrupt, Masters; I know little about the Force, but I do know something of love. The Queen and I—well, we've always talked of adopting a girl. If you have no objection, I would like to take Leia to Alderaan, and raise her as our daughter. She would be loved with us."

Yoda and Obi-Wan exchanged a look. Yoda tilted his head. "No happier fate could any child ask for. With our blessing, and that of the Force, let Leia be your child."

Bail stood, a little jerkily, as though he simply could no longer keep his seat. His flush had turned from embarrassment to pure uncomplicated joy. "Thank you, Masters—I don't know what else to say. Thank you, that's all. What of the boy?"

"Cliegg Lars still lives on Tatooine, I think—and Anakin's stepbrother . . . Owen, that's it, and his wife, Beru, still work the moisture farm outside Mos Eisley . . ."

"As close to kinfolk as the boy can come," Yoda said approvingly. "But Tatooine, not like Alderaan it is—deep in the Outer Rim, a wild and dangerous planet."

"Anakin survived it," Obi-Wan said. "Luke can, too. And I can—well, I could take him there, and watch over him. Protect him from the worst of the planet's dangers, until he can learn to protect himself."

"Like a father you wish to be, young Obi-Wan?"

"More an . . . eccentric old uncle, I think. It is a part I can play very well. To keep watch over Anakin's son—" Obi-Wan sighed, finally allowing his face to register a suggestion of his old gentle smile. "I can't imagine a better way to spend the rest of my life."

"Settled it is, then. To Tatooine, you will take him."

Bail moved toward the door. "If you'll excuse me, Masters, I have to call the Queen . . ." He stopped in the doorway, looking back. "Master Yoda, do you think Padmé's twins will be able to defeat Palpatine?"

"Strong the Force runs, in the Skywalker line. Only hope, we can. Until the time is right, disappear we will."

Bail nodded. "And I must do the same—metaphorically, at least. You may hear . . . disturbing things . . . about what I do in the Senate. I must appear to support the new Empire, and my comrades with me. It was . . . Padmé's wish, and she was a shrewder political mind than I'll ever be. Please trust that what we do is only a cover for our true task. We will never betray the legacy of the Jedi. I will never surrender the Republic to the Sith."

"Trust in this, we always will. Go now; for happy news, your Queen is waiting."

Bail Organa bowed, and vanished into the corridor.

When Obi-Wan moved to follow, Yoda's gimer stick barred his way. "A moment, Master Kenobi. In your solitude on Tatooine, training I have for you. I and my new Master."

Obi-Wan blinked. "Your new Master?"

"Yes." Yoda smiled up at him. "And your *old* one . . ."

C-3PO shuffled along the starship's hallway beside R2-D2, following Senator Organa who had, by all accounts, inherited them both. "I'm certain I can't say why she malfunctioned," he was telling the little astromech. "Organics are so terribly complicated, you know."

Ahead, the Senator was met by a man whose uniform, C-3PO's conformation-recognition algorithm informed him, indicated he was a captain in the Royal Alderaan Civil Fleet.

"I'm placing these droids in your care," the Senator said. "Have them cleaned, polished, and refitted with the best of everything; they will belong to my new daughter."

"How lovely!" C-3PO exclaimed. "His daughter is the child of Master Anakin and Senator Amidala," he explained to R2-D2. "I can hardly wait to tell her all about her parents! I'm sure she will be *very* proud—"

"Oh, and the protocol droid?" Senator Organa said thoughtfully. "Have its mind wiped."

The captain saluted.

"Oh," said C-3PO. "Oh, dear."

In the newly renamed Emperor Palpatine Surgical Reconstruction Center on Coruscant, a hypersophisticated prototype Ubrikkian DD-13 surgical droid moved away from the project that it and an enhanced FX-6 medical droid had spent many days rebuilding.

It beckoned to a dark-robed shadow that stood at the edge of the pool of high-intensity light. "My lord, the construction is finished. He lives."

"Good. Good."

The shadow flowed into the pool of light as though the overhead illuminators had malfunctioned.

Droids stepped back as it came to the rim of the surgical table.

On the table was strapped the very first patient of the EmPal SuRecon Center.

To some eyes, it might have been a pieced-together hybrid of droid and human, encased in a life-support shell of gleaming black, managed by a thoracic processor that winked pale color against the shadow's cloak. To some eyes, its jointed limbs might have looked ungainly, clumsy, even monstrous; the featureless curves of black that served it for eyes might have appeared inhuman, and the underthrust grillwork of its vocabulator might have suggested the jaws of a saurian predator built of polished blast armor, but to the shadow—

It was *glorious*.

A magnificent jewel box, created both to protect and to exhibit the greatest treasure of the Sith.

Terrifying.

Mesmerizing.

Perfect.

The table slowly rotated to vertical, and the shadow leaned close.

"Lord Vader? Lord Vader, can you hear me?"

This is how it feels to be Anakin Skywalker, forever:

The first dawn of light in your universe brings pain.

The light burns you. It will always burn you. Part of you will always lie upon black glass sand beside a lake of fire while flames chew upon your flesh.

You can hear yourself breathing. It comes hard, and harsh, and it scrapes nerves already raw, but you cannot stop it. You can never stop it. You cannot even slow it down.

You don't even have lungs anymore.

Mechanisms hardwired into your chest breathe for you. They will pump oxygen into your bloodstream forever.

Lord Vader? Lord Vader, can you hear me?

And you can't, not in the way you once did. Sensors in the shell that prisons your head trickle meaning directly into your brain.

You open your scorched-pale eyes; optical sensors integrate light and shadow into a hideous simulacrum of the world around you.

Or perhaps the simulacrum is perfect, and it is the world that is hideous.

Padmé? Are you here? Are you all right? you try to say, but another voice speaks for you, out from the vocabulator that serves you for burned-away lips and tongue and throat.

"Padmé? Are you here? Are you all right?"

I'm very sorry, Lord Vader. I'm afraid she died. It seems in your anger, you killed her.

This burns hotter than the lava had.

"No . . . no, it is not *possible!*"

You loved her. You will always love her. You could never will her death.

Never.

But you remember . . .

You remember *all* of it.

You remember the dragon that you brought Vader forth from your heart to slay. You remember the cold venom in Vader's blood. You remember the furnace of Vader's fury, and the black hatred of seizing her throat to silence her lying mouth—

And there is one blazing moment in which you finally understand that there was no dragon. That there was no Vader. That there was only you. Only Anakin Skywalker.

That it was all you. Is you.

Only you.

You did it.

You killed her.

You killed her because, finally, when you *could* have saved her, when you could have gone *away* with her, when you could have been thinking about *her*, you were thinking about *yourself* . . .

It is in this blazing moment that you finally understand the trap of the dark side, the final cruelty of the Sith—

Because now your *self* is all you will ever have.

And you rage and scream and reach through the Force to crush the shadow who has destroyed you, but you are so far less now than what you were, you are more than half machine, you are like a painter gone blind, a composer gone deaf, you can remember where the power was but the power you can touch is only a memory, and so with all your world-destroying fury it is only droids around you that implode, and equipment, and the table on which you were strapped shatters, and in the end, you cannot touch the shadow.

In the end, you do not even want to.

In the end, the shadow is all you have left.

Because the shadow understands you, the shadow forgives you, the shadow gathers you unto itself—

And within your furnace heart, you burn in your own flame.

This is how it feels to be Anakin Skywalker.

Forever . . .

The long night has begun.

Huge solemn crowds line Palace Plaza in Theed, the capital of Naboo, as six beautiful white gualaars draw a flower-draped open casket bearing the remains of a beloved Senator through the Triumphal Arch, her fingers finally and forever clasping a snippet of japor, one that had been carved long ago by the hand of a nine-year-old boy from an obscure desert planet in the far Outer Rim . . .

On the jungle planet of Dagobah, a Jedi Master inspects the unfamiliar swamp of his exile . . .

From the bridge of a Star Destroyer, two Sith Lords stand with a sector governor named Tarkin, and survey the growing skeleton of a spherical battle station the size of a moon . . .

But even in the deepest night, there are some who dream of dawn.

On Alderaan, the Prince Consort delivers a baby girl into the loving arms of his Queen.

And on Tatooine, a Jedi Master brings an infant boy to the homestead of Owen and Beru Lars—

Then he rides his eopie off into the Jundland Wastes, toward the setting suns.

The dark is generous, and it is patient, and it always wins—but in the heart of its strength lies weakness: one lone candle is enough to hold it back.

Love is more than a candle.
Love can ignite the stars.

ABOUT THE AUTHORS

TERRY BROOKS is the *New York Times* bestselling author of more than twenty-five books. His novels *Running with the Demon* and *A Knight of the Word* were selected by the *Rocky Mountain News* as two of the best science fiction/fantasy novels of the twentieth century. He lives with his wife, Judine, in the Pacific Northwest and Hawaii. Visit the world of Shannara online at www.shannara.com and at www.Terrybrooks.net.

R. A. SALVATORE was born in Massachusetts in 1959. He is the acclaimed author of the DemonWars trilogy: *The Demon Awakens, The Demon Spirit,* and *The Demon Apostle,* as well as *Mortalis, Bastion of Darkness,* and the *New York Times* bestseller *Star Wars: The New Jedi Order: Vector Prime.* He lives in Massachusetts with his wife, Diane, and their three children. Visit the author's website at www.rasalvatore.com.

MATTHEW STOVER is the *New York Times* bestselling author of five previous novels, including *Star Wars: Shatterpoint; Star Wars: The New Jedi Order: Traitor; Heroes Die;* and *The Blade of Tyshalle.* He is an expert in several varieties of martial arts. Stover lives outside Chicago.

STAR WARS
THE OLD REPUBLIC

IN A GALAXY DIVIDED

YOU MUST CHOOSE A SIDE

CREATE YOUR OWN EPIC STORY

IN THIS HIGHLY ANTICIPATED

MULTI-PLAYER ONLINE VIDEOGAME

YOUR SAGA BEGINS AT
WWW.STARWARSTHEOLDREPUBLIC.COM